Van Buren D̶ ̶̶̶ ̶̶r̶a̶r̶y̶
Decatur, MI

P9-DFD-003

DISCARDED

CRACK
IN THE
SKY

OTHER BOOKS BY TERRY C. JOHNSTON

Dance on the Wind
Buffalo Palace

Carry the Wind
BorderLords
One-Eyed Dream

Cry of the Hawk
Winter Rain
Dream Catcher

SON OF THE PLAINS NOVELS
Long Winter Gone
Seize the Sky
Whisper of the Wolf

THE PLAINSMEN NOVELS
Sioux Dawn
Red Cloud's Revenge
The Stalkers
Black Sun
Devil's Backbone
Shadow Riders
Dying Thunder
Blood Song
Reap the Whirlwind
Trumpet on the Land
A Cold Day in Hell
Wolf Mountain Moon

BANTAM BOOKS

New York
Toronto
London
Sydney
Auckland

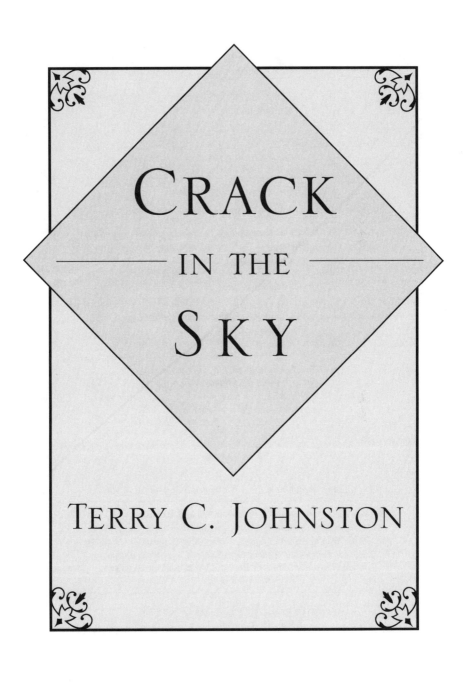

CRACK

IN THE

SKY

TERRY C. JOHNSTON

Joh

CRACK IN THE SKY
A Bantam Book / October 1997

All rights reserved.
Copyright © 1997 by Terry C. Johnston

Book design by Ellen Cipriano

Map by Jeffrey L. Ward

No part of this book may be reproduced or transmitted in any form or
by any means, electronic or mechanical, including photocopying,
recording, or by any information storage and retrieval system,
without permission in writing from the publisher.
For information address: Bantam Books.

Library of Congress Cataloging-in-Publication Data
Johnston, Terry C., 1947–
Crack in the sky : a novel / by Terry C. Johnston.
p.   cm.
"Titus Bass trilogy prequel, volume three."
ISBN 0-553-09078-X
1. Bass, Titus (Fictitious character)—Fiction.   2. Frontier and
pioneer life—West (U.S.)—Fiction.   I. Title.
PS3560.O392C7   1997
813'.54—dc21   *97-18896*
CIP

Published simultaneously in the United States and Canada

Bantam Books are published by Bantam Books, a division of Bantam
Doubleday Dell Publishing Group, Inc. Its trademark, consisting of
the words "Bantam Books" and the portrayal of a rooster, is Registered
in U.S. Patent and Trademark Office and in other countries.
Marca Registrada. Bantam Books, 1540 Broadway, New York,
New York 10036.

PRINTED IN THE UNITED STATES OF AMERICA
BVG 10 9 8 7 6 5 4 3 2 1

2/99
mcn

For all that he has
done to boost my career over the years—
for all that his friendship has come to mean to me
while we've ridden this wild frontier
of the publishing world together,
this tale of Titus Bass is
dedicated with deep admiration to
my editor,

TOM DUPREE

Well, I knocked about
Among the mountains, hunting beaver streams,
Alone—no, not alone, for there were dreams
And memories that grew. And more and more
I knew, whatever I was hunting for,
It wasn't beaver.

—John G. Neihardt
Song of Jed Smith

Crack in the Sky

TOBACCO PLAINS

Columbia R.

Clark's Fork

Flathead's Lake

BITTERROOT RANGE

Snake River

NEZ PERCE

Astoria •

Clearwater

River

Fort Vancouver •

Columbia River

Tillamook Bay

Grande Ronde

Salmon

River

John Day

River

SALMON RIVER MOUNTAINS

Western Limits of Buffalo Range 1830

Salmon R.

CAYUSE

Jedediah Smith Brigade
Umpqua Massacre, 1828 ✕

Umpqua River

SHOSHONE

CAMAS PRAIRIE

Pumice Stone Valley

Snake River

Rogue River

Bridger's Fork

UPPER CALIFORNIA

BANNOCKS

Ogden's or Unknown River

GREAT SANDY DESERT

Unknown Lake

Pyramid Lake

THE GREAT BASIN:

11 degrees of latitude, 10 degrees of longitude,
elevation above sea between 1 and 5000 feet,
surrounded by lofty mountains, contents almost
unknown but believed to be filled with rivers,
and lakes which have no communication with the sea,
deserts and oases which have never been explored
and savage tribes which no traveler
has seen or described.

Pacific Ocean

SIERRA NEVADA OF CALIFORNIA

San Francisco •

• San Jose

PAH-UTAH INDIANS

Monterey •

Colorado River

LOWER CALIFORNIA

MOHAVE INDIANS

San Bernardino •

SALT PLAIN

• San Gabriel

San Pedro •

San Diego •

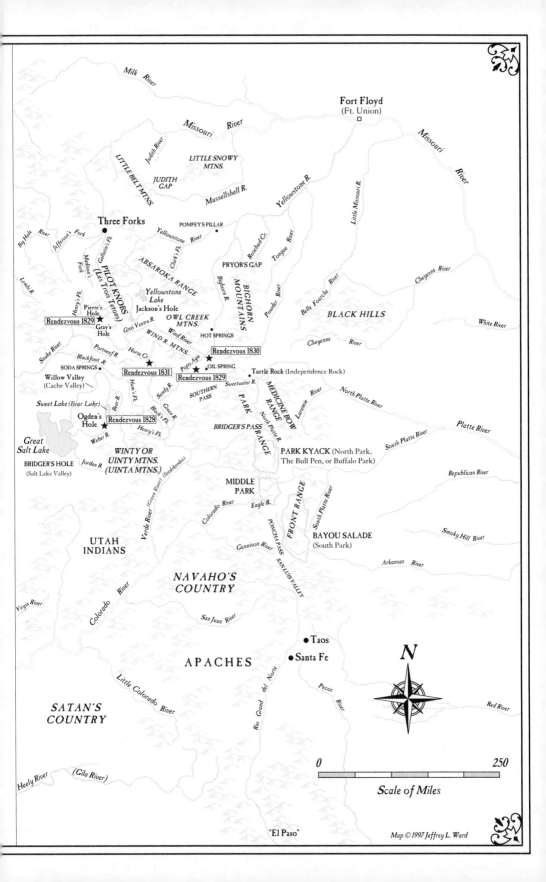

Milk River

Missouri River

Fort Floyd
(Ft. Union) □

Missouri River

Judith River

LITTLE BELT MTNS.

LITTLE SNOWY MTNS.

JUDITH GAP

Mussellshell R.

Yellowstone R.

Little Missouri R.

Missouri River

Big Hole River

Jefferson's Fork

Three Forks

Gallatin's Fk.

PILOT KNOBS
(Les Trois Tetons)

ABSAROKA RANGE

POMPEY'S PILLAR

Clark's Fk.

Yellowstone River

Rosebud Cr.

Tongue River

Cheyenne River

Madison's Fork

Lembi R.

Henry's Fk.

Pierre's Hole

Yellowstone Lake

Jackson's Hole

PRYOR'S GAP

BIGHORN MOUNTAINS

Bighorn R.

Powder River

Belle Fourche River

BLACK HILLS

White River

Rendezvous 1829 ★

Gray's Hole

Gros Ventre R.

OWL CREEK MTNS.

Wind River

WIND R. MTNS.

HOT SPRINGS

Cheyenne River

Snake River

Portneuf R.

Blackfoot R.

Horse Cr.

Rendezvous 1830

SODA SPRINGS •

Willow Valley
(Cache Valley)

Ham's Fk.

Rendezvous 1831 ★

Sandy R.

Popo Agie

OIL SPRING

Rendezvous 1829 ★

Turtle Rock (Independence Rock)

Sweetwater R.

MEDICINE BOW RANGE

Laramie River

North Platte River

Sweet Lake (Bear Lake)

Bear R.

Ogden's Hole ★

Rendezvous 1828 ★

Green R.

Black's Fk.

SOUTHERN PASS

PARK RANGE

North Platte R.

BRIDGER'S PASS

Great Salt Lake

BRIDGER'S HOLE
(Salt Lake Valley)

Weber R.

WINTY OR UINTY MTNS.
(UINTA MTNS.)

Henry's Fk.

Jordan R.

Verde River (Green River) (Seedskeeder)

PARK KYACK (North Park,
The Bull Pen, or Buffalo Park)

South Platte River

Platte River

Republican River

UTAH INDIANS

MIDDLE PARK

Colorado River

Eagle R.

FRONT RANGE

South Platte River

Smoky Hill River

NAVAHO'S COUNTRY

Colorado River

Gunnison River

PONCHA PASS

SAN LUIS VALLEY

BAYOU SALADE
(South Park)

Arkansas River

Virgin River

San Juan River

APACHES

Little Colorado River

Rio Grand del Norte

• Taos

• Santa Fe

Pecos River

Red River

N

SATAN'S COUNTRY

Heely River

(Gila River)

"El Paso"

0   250

Scale of Miles

Map © 1997 Jeffrey L. Ward

CRACK
IN THE
SKY

ONE

Just like the bone-numbing scream of the enemy, the wind tormented those branches of the towering spruce overhead.

Titus Bass jolted awake, coming up even before his eyes were open.

He sat there, sweaty palm clutching his rifle, heart thundering in his ears so loudly that it drowned out near everything but that next faint, thready scream emanating from somewhere above.

The frightening cry faded into no more than a gentle sough as the gust of wind wound its way on down the canyon, sailing past their camp, farther still into the river valley fed by the numberless streams and creeks they were trapping that spring.

As his breathing slowed, Titus swiped the dew of sweat from his face with a broad hand—remembering where he was. Remembering why he was here. Then peered around at the other dark forms sprawled on the ground, all of them radiating from the ember heap of last night's fire like the hardwood spokes on a wagon wheel. Downright eerie, quiet as death itself were those eight other men. Not one of them snoring, sputtering, or talking in his sleep. Almost as if the eight shapeless cocoons of buffalo robes and thick wool blankets weren't alive at all.

Only he—finding himself suddenly alone in this suddenly

still wilderness. Alone with this clap of dark gathered here beneath the utter black of sky just beyond the tops of the tall pines. Alone with the remembrance of those cries and screams and death-calls from the Blackfoot warriors as the enemy charged forward, scrambling up the boulders toward the handful of American trappers who had taken refuge there in the rocks, preparing to sell their no-account lives just as dearly as any men ever would dare in that high and terrible country where the most hated band of red-skinned thieves and brigands roamed, and plundered, and murdered.

It had been that way for far longer than he had been in the mountains. And sitting right then and there in the dark, Titus Bass had no reason to doubt that the Blackfoot would still be raiding and killing long after his own bones were bleaching beneath the sun that rose every morning to burn away the mists tucked back in every wrinkle in the cloud-tall Rocky Mountains.

Rising in a slow crescendo, the cry began again above him, like a long fingernail dragged up a man's spine. Looking up against the tarry darkness of that sky pricked only with tiny, cold dots of light, he watched the blacker branches sway and bob with the growing insistence of the wind, blotting out the stars here and there as they weaved back and forth. Groaning, whining— those branches tossed against one another, rubbing and creaking with the frightening cry that had brought him suddenly awake.

With the next swirling gust of breeze, Titus discovered he was damp, sweating beneath the robe and thick woolen blanket. After kicking both off his legs he sat listening to that noisy rustle of wind as it muscled its way through the tops of the trees overhead and hurtled on down into the valley, descending from the slopes of that granite and scree and bone-colored talus above their camp. A wind given its birth far higher in the places where the snow never departed, above him across that barren ground where even trees failed to grow. Those high and terrible places where if a man had the grit or were fool enough, he could climb and climb and climb until he reached the very top of the tallest gray spire, there to stand and talk eye to eye with whatever fearsome god ruled from on high.

Such a feat was for other men. Not the likes of Titus Bass. The spooky nearness of that god and the sky he ruled was close enough from right here. It had been ever since he had first come to these mountains, running from all that was, racing headlong to seize all that could be.

This coming summer it would be three years since he first laid eyes on that jagged purple rip stretched across the far horizon—three years since Titus Bass had journeyed eagerly into these high places. That would make this . . . spring of twenty-eight.

In many ways, that was a lifetime spent out here already.

Twice now he had been spared. First with those Arapaho who'd hacked off his topknot and left him for dead. Had it not been for the young mule carrying him out of enemy country, Bass was certain his bones would be bleaching beneath the sun of uncounted days yet to come. Then a second time—only a matter of weeks ago—that Blackfoot raiding party had tightened their red noose around a last-stand where Titus and the others had prepared to sell their lives dearly. Nine men who saw no real chance of coming out on the winning side of the bad hand dealt them.

There in the dark now, Titus wondered just how many times a man might be given another chance, another go at his life. How often could a reasonable person expect to have the odds tipped in his favor? Once? Maybe. Twice? If a man were near that lucky, then Bass figured he might well be inching closer to that day when his luck had just plain run out . . . gone like the tiny grains of sand that slipped through the narrow neck of an hourglass, one by one by one in a tumble of seemingly insignificant moments lost to the ebb of time.

The days of a man's life eventually reaching the end of his ledger. Come the call for him to pay the fiddler.

As he turned to glance at the heap of ash in the fire pit, Bass heard one of the animals snuffle out there in the darkness. He strained his eyes to peer into the inky gloom. After listening intently, he finally stared at the faint, glowing embers—wondering if he should throw some more wood on, or just curl down within his bedding and try falling back to sleep.

Absently digging at an itch nagging the back of his neck, he decided he would forget the fire. This was high season for ticks, tiny troublesome creatures who only weeks ago had killed one of the men already with the fever they carried. But his fingers reassured him that this itch was no tick, not even the lice he had played host to when he had first reached these Shining Mountains—digging so often and voraciously at his hide that the trio who happened upon Titus came to call him Scratch.

The name stuck, through all the seasons. With the coming and going of all those faces. Scratch—

Another snuffle from the horses.

They're restless with the wind, he thought, shoving the blanket down off his legs and reaching for his moccasins. Horse be the kind of critter gets itself spooked easy enough in the wind, unable to smell danger. What with all this night moving around them, rustling—

One of them snorted loudly, in just that way the Shoshone cayuses did when all was not well.

He rose without knotting the moccasins around his ankles and snatched the pistol from beneath the wool blanket capote he had rolled for a pillow, then swept up the long, full-stocked flintlock rifle he curled up with between his legs every night. After that deadly battle with the Blackfeet, Scratch had even given the weapon its own name, calling it Ol' Make-'Em-Come.

One of the other men stirred, mumbling as he turned over within his blankets, and fell quiet again.

Bass stepped from the ring of bodies, around the far side of their camp rather than heading directly for that patch of ground where they had driven their animals and confined them within a rope corral before turning in for the night.

"Better for a man to count ribs than to count tracks," explained Jack Hatcher.

Far more preferable that a careful man's animals should go without the finest grazing possible than to discover those animals were run off by skulking brownskins. Putting a feller afoot in a hostile wilderness. Forced to cache most all his plunder, then follow those horses' tracks with only what a man could carry on his own back.

Was that hiss more of the wind soughing through the trees up ahead? Or . . . could it have been a whisper?

In the darkness, and this cold, Scratch knew a man's ears might well play tricks on him.

Scratch stopped, held his breath, listened.

Behind him in camp he thought he heard one of them stir, throwing back his bedding, muttering now in a low voice that alerted the others. They were coming out of their deep sleep as quiet as men in a dangerous land could.

From beyond the trees the wind's whisper grew insistent now. Then a second whisper—and the gorge suddenly rose in Bass's throat. Whoever was out there realized the camp was awakening. He brought up the long rifle and stepped into the gloom between the tall trees, cautiously.

With a shriek the uneasy quiet was instantly shattered. A boom rocked the trees around him, the dark grove streaked with a muzzle flash.

The bastards had guns!

One of the trappers in camp grunted as the rest shouted and cried to the others, all hell breaking loose at once as shrill voices screeched battle calls from the dark timber.

In a crouch, he lunged forward. Not back to camp as more guns began to boom. But making for the horses.

The red niggers were after the remuda!

Behind him the voices of his friends grew loud as they met the assault—an instant before the dark shapes of the animals took form, congealing out of the darkness. Milling four-leggeds . . . then a two-legged took shape, and a second, he saw among the stock: slapping, yelling, driving some of the horses out of the rope corral. More of the huge shadows hopped within their sideline hobbles, attempting to break to freedom, straining to join those captured animals the raiders goaded into the darkness.

He recognized Hannah's bawl. That high, brassy cry the mule gave when frightened—like that day Silas Cooper was about to kill the mare, or that day Bass lost his scalp and was left for dead.

Stepping to the edge of that copse of trees, he recognized her big, peaked ears on a nearby shadow. One of the raiders struggled to keep his hold on the mule's horsehair halter. Scratch stepped sideways, close enough to make out the warrior's body, seeing how young he was.

"Let go of 'er!"

Whirling around in a crouch, the youngster reached for the tomahawk at his belt, the metal head glinting with starshine as it flashed out at the end of the arm he swung back over his shoulder.

At Scratch's hip the rifle boomed, its flash bright as midday—temporarily blinding Titus as he shoved the rifle into his left hand, snatching the pistol from his belt with his right. Ahead of him the raider crumpled in half, hit low in the gut with a ball of lead more than a half-inch round. Flopping to his side, the wounded man struggled to reach for the tomahawk that landed inches from his fingertips, the other arm clutched across his abdomen.

Bass leaped out of the trees, landing with a foot on the raider's wrist. Instantly the Indian took the free hand and struggled to reach the knife scabbard flopping at his hip. Hannah snorted, bobbing her head, yanking back at her picket rope with that recognition of blood.

Not about to waste another shot on the thief, Scratch stuffed the pistol into his belt, raised the rifle above his head in both hands, then savagely drove the metal butt plate straight down into the warrior's face. And a second time as the Indian twisted and thrashed, his last ragged breaths spewing from the crushed hole in his head like frosty streamers. After a third and harder blow, he no longer moved.

Stepping over his victim, Bass pulled the pistol free, crouched slightly, and slipped forward again into the darkness. To this side and that he shoved the frightened, chivvied animals, forcing a path through their midst. A hobbled horse clumsily lunged out of his way, and into that gap suddenly leaped another warrior, a long dagger clutched in one hand, a tomahawk held in the other. From side to side he rocked, gazing wickedly at the white man with a crooked smile.

Bass squeezed the trigger as he brought the pistol up. When the ball struck the warrior high in the chest, it drove him backward off his feet to land among the legs and hooves of the hobbled animals.

"Simms!"

It was Hatcher's voice somewhere behind his right shoulder.

"Here, goddammit!"

"Ye see Bass?"

"He ain't with me," explained the voice coming from a different side of camp.

How he wished he had picked up his powder horn and shooting pouch before he'd left his bedding. Unable to reload, Titus instead leaned down and pulled the knife and tomahawk free from the warrior's hands, then straightened and yelled, "Jack! I'm over here!"

"Bass?" Hatcher cried. "Was that Scratch's voice?"

"Sounded like him—"

The voice had to be Kinkead's, nearly muffled with the gunshot.

"Goddammit!" that booming voice screamed.

"Matt!"

A new voice asked, "You see Bass over by you, Rufus?"

While the trappers called to one another back in camp, no more than fifteen feet in front of him, Titus watched a warrior appear out of the night and those shadows clinging among the trees. The Indian crouched, stopping long enough to study the small clearing where the trappers had made their camp. From there it was plain to see that the horse thief had John Rowland's narrow back all to himself. Raising his short horn bow, the warrior drew back on the string.

On instinct Bass flung his arm back, hurling the knife at the target. Too quickly. Off its mark, the weapon clattered against a nearby tree. The enemy jerked to the side, wheeling to find the white man behind him. Drawing back on his bow string once more, he now aimed the arrow at Scratch.

Startled at the noise, Rowland turned. "Shit!"

As he leaped to the side, Titus grumbled, "Never was any good with stickers—"

And with that he flung the tomahawk at the raider, striking the horse thief low in the chest.

"Scratch is over here!" Rowland sang out as the warrior crumpled forward onto his face.

Behind them on the far side of their camp, four of the trappers squatted behind some baggage. Among them Hatcher rose. He intently watched the night shadows as Bass emerged from the trees, his eyes raking the meadow for more of the enemy.

"That the last of 'em?" Hatcher asked.

"Dunno," Elbridge Gray admitted below him, squatting there as he shoved the ramrod down the muzzle of his rifle.

"Keep yer goddamned eyes peeled on that line of trees," Hatcher commanded, slapping Solomon Fish on the shoulder as he turned. "Kinkead? Where the hell're you?"

"I don't see him nowhere," Caleb Wood cried with fear in his voice.

From across camp Rufus Graham shouted, "He go out with them horses?"

"Horses," Bass muttered angrily at himself, whirling around. Then he turned back suddenly to yell at Rowland. "Your gun loaded, Johnny?"

"Yeah, why?"

"Come with me," Bass growled, growing more angry with himself as he dashed away. "The goddamned horses."

As the two white men drew close, the animals neighed and whinnied—some recognizing their smell, others still frightened. They milled nervously in what was left of their rope corral strung in a wide circle, looped tree to tree to tree. That one section cut by the raiders was not enough for the horses to dare snatch at their freedom: with a hand still clutching the end of the rope he had cut, one of the warriors lay dead. The foreign smell of the Indian, perhaps that faint hint of his blood on the wind, kept the rest of their nervous animals from bolting past the body sprawled on the forest floor.

"How many you figger the niggers got?" Rowland asked as he moved among the horses, quieting them—patting necks, stroking withers and flanks.

"Likely a handful," Bass replied, worried. For he still hadn't seen her among the others.

Simms was suddenly at the far side of the corral, ducking under the rope. "Mule's over here, Scratch!"

"Damn," he croaked thickly, shoving his way through the rangy Indian cayuses, fighting his way to the mule. He stopped, finding he could breathe again just at the sight of her.

Reaching Hannah's side, Titus laid an arm affectionately over her neck, hugging the animal.

"Kinkead's hurt," the stocky Simms said as he came to a halt beside Bass. "Hurt bad."

"He gonna make it?"

"Hatcher don't know yet," Simms admitted, his pale, whitish-blond hair aglow in the night.

"Damn." Scratch turned toward the far side of the corral. His eyes found Rowland. "Me and Johnny stay here while you get some more rope."

"They cut through more'n one place?"

"No," he answered Simms. "We're lucky. Who was they anyway?"

Isaac shrugged. "From the quick look-see I got of the two of 'em we dropped . . . likely they was Blackfoots."

He swallowed hard. Blackfoot again. "G'won—get the rope, Isaac."

Simms turned and moved away without a word.

Blackfoot.

What were the chances this had been a different raiding party from the one that had struck Hatcher's outfit weeks ago as they were trapping their way northwest from Shoshone country? Slim chance, if any. When Goat Horn had brought his warriors across those days and nights of hard riding to pull the trappers' fat out of the fire, reaching the white men as the Blackfoot raiders were circling in tighter and tighter to make the kill . . . what were the chances that those angry, defeated Blackfoot had been driven on north, back to their own country?

And what were the chances they had doubled back to try again?

"They was Bug's Boys awright," the rail-thin Rowland said behind him.

Turning, Bass saw John standing over one of the bodies.

"You get this'un, Scratch?"

Titus stepped over to the Indian lying sprawled on the ground. "The first'un," Bass admitted. "Didn't kill him right off with a ball. Not much more'n a boy."

"Ain't much left of the young'un's face."

Swallowing, Titus declared, "He come on a man's errand."

"Damn if he didn't. Looks of it—this here boy was ready to chop you into boudin meat."

Shaking his head, Bass turned away, watching Simms approaching. "It don't make the killing any easier, Johnny."

"By jam—these niggers're wuss'n animals," Isaac declared as he came to a halt. "Blackfeets is like painters and wolves, Scratch. No better. A little smarter mayhaps. But they ain't wuth no more'n a critter."

"Isaac's right," Rowland said, bobbing his head of unkempt hair. "And your hand put two of 'em outta their misery this night."

"Two?" Simms echoed with interest, stroking at his long, pale beard.

Jabbing a bony thumb over his shoulder, Rowland explained, " 'Nother'un's back there—nigger was fixin' to lay me out when Bass finished him."

"Damn. If that don't take the circle!" the overly solemn Simms said with uncharacteristic enthusiasm. "Two of 'em. C'mon, let's get this here rope up quick. Jack wants us back in camp so we can figger what's to do about them horses the others got off with."

In minutes Bass was kneeling at Kinkead's feet with some of the others. Titus asked Hatcher, "How he be?"

"I'm fit as any the rest of you sonsabitches," Kinkead grumbled as he pulled out the thick twig he had been clenching between his teeth. For the moment this stocky man was sitting propped back against a pack of beaver, Caleb Wood behind one shoulder for support. Matthew turned his chin toward the other shoulder and growled, "Leave me be, Mad Jack! You never was any good with a knife—"

"Shuddup, child," Hatcher ordered. "An' quit yer hitchin'! Ye're making this wuss'n it has to be."

Kinkead gasped in pain, flung his head back with a groan, and shoved the twig back between his teeth as Hatcher proceeded to dig into the dark, moist wound on the big man's muscular chest. From it fluttered the long shaft of a Blackfoot arrow—buried deep in the right breast.

"Hold him still, goddammit!" Hatcher ordered, exasperated. "Help me, Bass. Hold him down!"

Now there were three restraining that bull of a man almost as wide as he was tall.

"You gonna finish it sometime afore the damn sun comes up?" Bass eventually asked in a grunt as he tried to stay atop Kinkead's strong legs.

"I can feel the goddamned arrow point," Hatcher admitted, shifting the knife blade this way, then that, with one hand, his other gently tugging now and then on the shaft. "I don't wanna pull the goddamned thing free 'thout the arrow point. Hold him down, or I ain't gonna get this done afore a month of sunrises!"

Kinkead growled like a wounded bear, hissing around his twig at Hatcher as Jack rose to his knees above the man, brought back his arm, and suddenly slammed a fist against Kinkead's jaw.

Spitting the twig free, the wild-eyed Kinkead almost succeeded in getting up despite the other three. Unfazed by the blow, he angrily spat, "What the hell you go and do that for—"

Jack swung his fist again, harder this time, connecting with a crack like a cottonwood popping in the dead of winter. Kinkead's eyes rolled back, and his head sagged to the side, all that dead weight propped back against Caleb Wood.

"Now I can get done what needs doing 'thout him jabberin'," Hatcher said as he resituated himself over Kinkead. "You boys can't keep him still . . . by bloody damn I'll put him to sleep my own self."

In a matter of moments Hatcher's deft touch had extracted the arrow. All that probing and digging left a mess of Kinkead's chest, but both shaft and arrow point were free. "Get yer medeecins, Isaac," he ordered. "Patch him up and get him covered quick."

Simms turned away toward his bedroll.

Jack rose, wiped his skinning knife across his legging, and shoved it back into the scabbard at his hip. "The rest of ye, gather round." He looked among them until he spotted Rowland. "How many they get away with, Johnny?"

Rowland shrugged and nodded to Bass.

Titus answered. "Maybe half a dozen, Jack."

"Damn." Hatcher was deep in thought a few moments. "Every man make sure yer loaded. Leave behind any extra guns ye got with Rufus and Isaac."

"Me?" Simms asked as he returned with his parfleche of herbs.

"You and Rufus gonna stay behind here with Matt," Hatcher ordered. "Drag up some cover, case they double back to make another go at us."

"Where you going?" Graham asked with that slight lisp of his as he started to drag a bundle of pelts over.

"Me and the others," the tall, angular Hatcher said, "we're going after them horses."

Domesticated four-legged critters were worth their weight in beaver plews in this country. Horses or mules, it made little difference to this small band of American fur trappers.

Yet this was more than a matter of having a few of their animals stolen from them. The thieves had been Blackfoot—likely some of the same bunch who had struck them earlier that spring. Had that whole raiding party come at them this time, they could have run right over the white men like a herd of elk trampling across a meadow of wildflowers.

This had become a matter of honor. A matter of a warrior's pride. It didn't take very many seasons surviving in these mountains before a trapper came to understand that blood was the only language the Blackfoot understood. Force, and might, and blood.

If they let a small band of the enemy get away with a handful of horses . . .

Hell, there was never the slightest debate. The six saddled up and rode north toward the far-off spine of the distant mountains, feeling their way in the darkness, hoping that their guess was right. They could wait until first light to circle around camp and locate the enemy's trail. Or they could push out now in the dark, gambling that they would pick up the trail a few hours from now when dawn finally overtook them—without wasting that time and miles in sitting on their hands.

As the first ballooning of light emerged out of the east, they reached the foothills on the southern slopes of the range, Hatcher riding at the head of the others, who were strung back from him in a vee like the long-necked honkers that had been winging their way north overhead for weeks now, returning to summer haunts.

"There!" Hatcher hurled his voice over his shoulder, throwing up an arm to stop the others as he reined up.

Clattering to a halt, the rest gazed down the open, grassy slopes broken by stands of timber, cut here and there with narrow freshets flowing bank-to-bank with spring runoff fed from the snowfields far above them.

"They're covering ground," Bass declared as he studied the distant figures.

"Damn if they ain't," the beefy Fish agreed.

Hatcher turned his horse around, his half-feral eyes moving from man to man to man accusingly. "Ye boys figger us to go on? Or do we cut our losses and turn back now?"

"It's a long shot," Rowland said almost apologetically.

"Yeah," Wood stated. "Ain't no guarantee we'll ever catch up after all this riding—"

"They can't run forever," Bass grumbled, exasperated at their second-guessing. "I'm fixin' to go, even if the rest of you don't."

"Just you?" Rowland squeaked. "You'd be teched—"

With a shrug Titus interrupted, "If'n it's just me, I'll wait till dark one night soon and crawl in, cut them horses loose. Ride back this way . . . ride back like hell itself."

"Eegod, boys! Just like a Injun would do it his own self!" Hatcher said, a grin of admiration beginning to crease his face.

"Damn straight," Bass said, grinning too, determination bright in his eyes.

A half-wild look in his eyes, Hatcher glanced over the others, the grin fading from his mouth as he said, "Bass is right. Those sumbitches can't run forever. They'll have to stop one day soon—for graze, or water, or just to climb down from the bony backs of our god-blessed ponies."

"And then we'll have 'em," Gray said with sudden enthusiasm. He wore a cap he had stitched together himself from a scrap of old wool blanket, sewn with a peak on either side to crudely resemble wolf ears.

Rowland shook his head. "If'n we ain't dead in the saddle afore then our own selves."

Hatcher nudged his horse up close to Rowland. "Ye comin', Johnny?"

"Ain't a thing wrong in you turning back to help Isaac and Rufus see to Kinkead," Bass declared protectively. "No man can fault you there."

For a moment Rowland appeared to consider that option. Then he sighed, "I come this far awready."

Titus quickly slapped Rowland on the back and turned to Hatcher. "C'mon, Jack—let's go see this through."

Dawn came and went, then midday with it. In the early afternoon they crossed a wide, shallow creek, tarrying only long enough to water their horses a little, not enough to make the animals loggy. No more than a few moments for man and beast to gulp down the cold, clear mountain runoff, enough to give the saddle horses a burst of newfound energy. They pushed on into the afternoon and watched as the sun began to tumble toward the horizon behind their left shoulders.

"How many more you figger?" Solomon Fish asked the others who were stretched on their bellies with him, all six having left their animals tied in a copse of trees far below them before they scrambled up the slope to the top of the rimrock that color of old, sun-dried blood.

Eyeing the warriors below, Elbridge Gray replied, "Baker's dozen, at least."

The lean-faced Rowland stared down at the two hands he held up, flipping up fingers slowly, then folding them back down as he mouthed his numbers. "That makes more'n . . . oh, shit! We ain't got us—"

"Hush yer face, Johnny!" Hatcher snapped.

"Way I see it," Bass declared, "with that other bunch what just come in to join up with them horse thieves, looks to be they evened up the odds now."

Rowland gulped, "Even . . . evened up the odds?"

"Yepper," Titus replied. "I figger things is about a draw now."

Mad Jack cackled low, wagging his head, eyes merry in the deepening twilight. "Eegod—if'n ye don't take the circle, Titus Bass! With us having even-up odds, just what ye got in mind for to get our horses back from that camp they're making down there?"

"Wh-what *I* got in mind?" Scratch asked with a snort. "You're the one with all the notions, Jack. I'm just here to help out. I ain't no smart nigger now."

"I was hoping ye was gonna show us ye was a lot more dad-blamed smarter'n me, coon," Hatcher said. " 'Cause I ain't got no plan neither. No way. Nothing 'cept my hankering to sashay in there quiet as can be come slap-dark, cut loose what's ours, an' run the rest off so's they can't trail us."

"Gotta be quick and brassy 'bout it," Titus added.

"Pick yourself a strong one to ride out with," Solomon advised gravely.

Caleb Wood finally spoke up, "Chances are good these red niggers gonna come fair boiling after us, on horse or foot."

"No two ways about it, boys," Jack reminded the rest, "we gotta drive off all their ponies."

"Don't know about you," Bass said as he started scooting back down the slope, a bone-deep weariness penetrating to his core, "but this here's one child gonna grab him a few hours shut-eye till it's time to go crawling in there and kill us some Blackfoots."

"Dead on my feet, my own self," Hatcher agreed, flinging his arms back and stretching like a skinny, long-legged cat. "C'mon, boys. It's been a long day awready. And from the looks of things, we're fixin' to lose some more sleep tonight."

Bass lay curled up in the frosty, fireless dark with the others, listening to the men snort and clear their throats, turn about and flop over, doing their best to root around and get themselves comfortable on the cold, cheerless ground. He wondered if the others were thinking on the Blackfoot and their fire. Likely the rest were all thinking on the same thing he had on his mind. Women.

He brought his hand up and gently touched the long braid tied in what hair hung in front of his right ear. Thinking about Pretty Water—how she had braided it for him the first time, then taught him to do it for himself.

For some reason tonight, he couldn't get her out of his thoughts. That Shoshone gal who had taken on the boldest share of his nursing after buffalo hunters had discovered Bass near the spot where they had killed the sacred white medicine calf. According to that band of wandering Snake Indians, Scratch was responsible for bringing them that calf—a powerful, mystical symbol of the Creator's blessing, a promise of plenty after so many, many weeks of want.

A damned lucky thing it had been for Titus Bass too. A hole in his chest from an Arapaho bullet, the scalp ripped from the crown of his head, grown weak as a newborn beaver kit after days of wandering half-conscious clinging to the back of his steadfast Hannah . . . never before had Scratch been so close to death's door as he was that day last summer when Hatcher's bunch and the Shoshone hunters happed onto him.

Suddenly become hero to the tribe if not their savior—Bass was treated like a chief, picked from the ground by the hunters and laid upon downy soft buffalo robes. Dragged on a travois back to the huge camp where Titus was descended upon by the women of the tribe, every last one of them clucking and chattering at once as they hoisted him into a huge buffalo-hide lodge where he would stay for the next two weeks while he was knitting up.

As he began to put back on the weight he had lost in his ordeal, the Shoshone women started out to care for him in relays, coming and going to change the noxious, slimy poultices they compressed into his bullet wounds, supporting him gently against their fragrant softness as they poured rich, greasy soup past his lips, or bathed him with scraps of cloth dipped in cool water. There had been nothing remarkable about any of those hovering faces, or the healing hands, or the gentle chatter he did not understand in the least . . . until one morning he awoke to the soft, lyric humming of a new woman he found sitting by the low flames warming the fire pit.

With her back turned toward him, for the longest time Bass contented himself to watch her sway gently back and forth in time to her half-whispered song as she repeatedly poked her bone awl through a piece of smoked leather, then drove the end of some sinew through the hole, down and through over and over again, tightening each stitch with a tug of her deft fingers.

He so surprised her the moment he asked for water that she stabbed herself with the awl.

But as soon as she whirled on him with a startled jerk, placing that bleeding fingertip to her lips where she licked at the blood—Bass's mouth went dry. Finding himself pasty-tongued as he looked into those eyes that reminded him so much of Marissa Guthrie's, that settler's daughter back along the river south of St. Louis.

"What's her name?" he had asked Hatcher later.

"Like that'un, eh?" Jack had said, his merry green eyes twinkling with devilment. "Some punkins, I'll say."

Now he was growing testy. "Her name, dammit."

"Pretty Water," Hatcher answered with a grin forming. "Got stabbed, did ye?"

"Stabbed?"

"Yer heart, nigger. Got stabbed in yer heart!"

As Titus lay there now in the cold and the dark, listening to the discomfort of the others on the ground, to the night sounds of their horses and the closeness of wild critters who owned this forest, Bass had to admit she had stabbed him in the heart.

Women. They had long been his weakness. How they preyed upon his heart, pierced him to his soul. Time and again hadn't they loved holding a mirror up to his life, showing him just how weak he truly was. Not strong at all . . . oh, no. Women—like Amy, and Abigail, and Marissa. Then Fawn had renewed his faith in himself and the gentler sex—the sort of woman who unconditionally gave more than she got. Strange how she hadn't expected any more from him than what he was prepared to give during their brief time together that first winter with the Ute.

A sudden lick of shame flushed through him.

What right had she to expect that he would stay on when spring freed the mountain passes and softened the ice clogging the high country streams where the flat-tails were awaiting the beaver men and their iron traps? A man simply didn't pack along a woman, not a beaver man like Titus Bass. Come winter, was the time for bedding down with a woman, lying back in a lodge . . . maybeso a quick tangle or two with some likely gals come rendezvous when the sun was summer-high. A fella just had no business, no real need, to pack along a full-time night-woman. Looking after himself and his animals, his weapons and his traps, was truly more than enough to keep a man's attention. That, and constantly watching over his shoulder, or the skyline ahead, for brownskins.

Man didn't need no woman giving him the willies the way they sometimes did, taking his mind right off of what he should be keeping his mind to.

And Pretty Water was just that sort of woman. The kind that would steer a man's mind off of near everything but coupling with her.

He felt his flesh stir here in the darkness at this remembrance of her. Of lying with her beneath blankets or robes as he healed from his wounds that terrible autumn. Her gentle touch mending all those places where his flesh was slowly knitting. And by the time she had come to ask him why he did not want her for his wife, he knew a smattering of Shoshone—just enough to really botch his trying to explain to her why he could not marry her.

How those big cow eyes of hers had pooled and spilled before she'd bit her trembling lower lip, turned, and dived out the lodge door.

For days Pretty Water did not return, her place taken by others who politely pretended not to hear when he asked of her. At last one of the old women told him he was healed. Time for him to rejoin the white men who had returned that very day to follow the Shoshone village through winter while Bass grew stronger. Time, the old woman told him, to forget about Pretty Water. She would never be his.

But how he longed for her again this night.

Wasn't a man really a fool for allowing a woman to entangle herself around him so tightly? Damn—but why had God made them the sort of creatures what smelled so good, their fragrant flesh like downy velvet, all the soft and rounded curves of them rising and falling through hills and valleys?

He craved a woman, but of a time he convinced himself he didn't want one. Oh, how maddening God had made this clumsy dance between the sexes! And in the end, how truly weak a man proved to be in the face of all the tricks and ploys a woman could pull on him.

Those last weeks among the Shoshone had been particularly hard without her. As the days passed, he had grown more and more restive, eager to take to the trail, to be gone from her, anywhere. Keeping to himself by and large so he would not have to chance upon her, until at last that morning arrived when Hatcher had moved out with his small brigade.

Someone stirred there in the black of night. Bass opened his eyes. Hatcher stood, blotting out part of the starshine above them. Nearby Fish and Wood slowly peeled themselves off their beds of cedar boughs and sagebrush. Sleeping right against the cold ground itself could stove up a man, stiffening his joints, paining his bones. Better for him to put some cushion between himself and the cold, bare ground.

What a fool he had been, Titus brooded as he sat up and volved his shoulders slowly. Remembering how ashamed he was when Goat Horn had brought his Shoshone warriors to pull the trappers' fat out of the fire, pitching into the Blackfoot raiders who had the white men surrounded. Ashamed that he had been so demented to actually wonder if Pretty Water might have come along with the Shoshone war party. How reasonable it had seemed—since the village knew the warriors were coming to rescue Hatcher's men, she might well choose to ride along to see for herself that Bass was still alive . . . for a few moments at least he could hope.

But within heartbeats all hopes were dashed. No woman had accompanied the war party. And not one of the Shoshone came up to explain to him that Pretty Water had reconsidered her actions, that she was worried about his safety. That she cared enough—

"Let's get those cinches tightened," Hatcher whispered, puffs of vapor streaming from his lips as he straightened and worked the kink out of a bony knee.

Without a word the others came up from the dark, cold ground, stepped over to their horses, where they threw up the stirrup straps so they could retighten the cinches. Bass shifted the Indian style chicken-snare saddle the others had given him last fall, snugging its high pommel up against the withers before he tugged up on the buffalo-hair cinch and locked it down.

"How you figger this, Jack?" Wood asked.

"We'll ride on down to the stream they camped by," Hatcher began as if he had given it all the thought in the world. "Feel how the wind moves, then see if we can find where them red-bellies put their horses out to graze."

Fish asked, "Come onto 'em from downwind?"

"Only way," Jack replied. "Afore that, best we give some thought to taking care of ary a horse guard they throwed out."

"How many you wager they might have out?" Bass inquired.

"Two, maybe. You?"

"That sounds about right," Scratch answered. "I want one of 'em for my own self afore we put them ponies on the run."

"Awright," Jack said, his eyes glinting with starlight as he stared coldly at Bass. "You and me, Scratch. We'll take care of the horse guard afore the rest of the boys here move in on them others." He stuffed a foot into a stirrup and flung himself into the saddle. "I'll lead out. Single file. Keep quiet as the dead."

He reined away toward the far timber.

Bass rose to the saddle with the others, brought his horse around, and watched Hatcher's back disappear into the dark. "Damn, if it ain't quiet as the dead," he repeated in a whisper.

None of the rest saw how he shuddered in the dark as a lone drop of cold sweat spilled down his backbone.

By the time they had dropped off the ridge and worked their way down to the creek, Scratch could tell how old the night had become, those early hours of morning when the temperature was at its coldest. When both man and animal normally slept their soundest.

Not this night.

The six moved slowly, cautiously, feeling their way upstream through the tall, horseman-high willow and buckbrush so they wouldn't rustle or snap branches, alerting the enemy to their approach. Time and again they stopped, signaling back down their file with an arm thrown up, every man jack of them listening and smelling. More than half a dozen times already they had halted like that, when Hatcher finally cocked his head and sniffed at the cold wind more than usual, then swung his horse around sharply.

When he dropped to the ground, it was clear they had come as far as they were going to in the saddle until the moment arrived to escape with the horses. Jack stepped up to Caleb Wood, handing him the reins to his mount.

"Ye'll see to my horse. Solomon, take the reins to Scratch's pony. Things go the way I plan—the two of us rub out the herd guard—we'll circle back here to join up with the rest afore we all ride in to whoop up a scare in them horses together."

"You smell 'em, Jack?" Gray asked.

"I make the horses off yonder," he answered, pointing north, away from the stream. "But I ain't smelled no Blackfoot yet."

"Mayhaps they're camped on the far side of the herd," Wood replied.

"Things'll sit pretty if they are," Hatcher stated. Then he fixed Bass with his eyes for a moment before he went on. "The rest of ye know what to do . . . if'n one or the both of us don't come back in a bit."

"We get the hell out of here," Rowland declared. "There's more Black-foot camped in spitting distance than I ary wanna see—"

"No!" Hatcher snapped as he took a step closer to Rowland. "Don't none of ye dare run off if things go mad. Ye finish just what we set out to do miles and miles ago."

"We come for the horses," Gray explained.

"Damn right we did," Hatcher agreed. "Something happen to me—ye don't leave 'thout them horses."

Rowland wagged his head, saying, "But if they kill't the two of you—"

"Then that just means they got their hands full for the time being," Bass interrupted. "If them brownskins are busy taking what's left of my scalp, boys—you damned well better see to riding off with their horses."

Hatcher looked a moment into each face. "Ye all understand what Bass is saying? Hell breaks loose, me and Scratch here are on our own. Ye boys just get, and get fast. Ye drive off the ponies, why—Bug's Boys in there won't have 'em nothing to ride and no way to keep up with ye."

"Can we count on you meeting us back to camp?" Wood asked hope-fully.

Hatcher shook his head. "Something goes wrong—don't count on see-ing my mud-ugly mug again, Caleb. Just have ye a drink for me come ron-nyvoo this summer."

Caleb stepped forward, held out his hand to Hatcher in that sudden, shy sort of way. "Don't do nothing stupid, Jack."

"Like jumping more'n thirty Blackfoots by ourselves?" Hatcher snorted with a grin that always made the man's mouth a wide and friendly bow. "Ain't nothing stupid 'bout that, is there, boys?"

The four shook hands with the pair, who silently turned and disap-peared into the willow on foot. Bass followed Jack, a slow step at a time, careful of their footing, toes feeling their way along in the dark, working this maze through the brush a yard at a time until Hatcher stopped and turned.

"This gonna be close-up work."

"I know," Titus whispered. He pulled the old knife from its rawhide sheath.

"Ye done this afore?"

Bass shook his head. "No. Not really."

"Just like sneaking up ahin't someone," Jack explained. "Nothing much to it."

"I figger there's allays a first time," Scratch said.

Hatcher smiled. "Just make sure ye're around for a second time, friend. I come to like ye, Titus Bass."

He laid his hand on the tall, thin man's shoulder. "I come to like you some myself, Mad Jack."

Hatcher held out his hand, and they shook swiftly, suddenly conscious once more of what lay before them. "I'm gonna work on past the herd to yonder where I figger they got 'em a second guard."

"Where's the first gonna be?"

Pointing, Jack said, "Not far, over by that ledge, I'd wager."

"You want me to wait for you to get to the far side?"

"No. Ye kill that son of a bitch, and kill him quick. Sooner he's dead, sooner we're sure that one won't make a sound to rouse the others."

"Meet you back with the rest?"

"Less'n something goes wrong, Scratch," he answered. "Then ye get the hell out of there the best way ye can."

"Same goes for you, Jack. Something haps to me—see yourself that the boys split up what little I got to my name."

He smiled quickly. "I awready got call on yer rifle, Scratch."

"And my mule too?" Titus asked with a grin.

"Hell no, ye lop-eared dunderhead. Who the hell'd want that cantankerous bitch?"

An uneasy moment of quiet fell between them; then Titus said, "Watch your back, now, you hear?"

"Ye watch yer'n."

Bass stared at the black hole among the tall willow where Hatcher had disappeared for what seemed like a long time. The breeze rustled the leafy branches around him as he endlessly tried to sort out sounds, like picking mule hair off a saddle pad, staring now and again at the dim form of the rocky ledge not all that distant. Then back again at the hole in the night Hatcher had punched through to disappear.

Scratch wondered, if it was so cold, then why in hell was he sweating the way he was?

TWO

Scratch thought he heard the horse guard well before he ever saw him.

He stopped, listening intently to the dark. Listening not only with his ears, but with every inch of exposed flesh, his skin alive and prickling at the nearness of danger. He tried to remember to breathe, and when he did, Bass found the air shockingly cold. Sniffing deeply of the gloom, he thought he could smell the dried sweat, the days-old grease that told him the warrior was near. Or was it only his imagination, galloping wildly now that he was inching ever closer to this moment of reckoning?

Not that he hadn't killed before. But this was something entirely different.

When violence confronted a man, it usually did so suddenly, without warning and forethought. One moment a man stood square with the world around him. And with his next breath, things went awry, everything off-kilter and askew in that instant. A man found himself swept up in the immediacy of the moment and responded to protect either himself or those dear to him. Just as he had done when the Chickasaw had slipped on board Ebenezer Zane's Kentucky flatboat.

One moment he's fighting off sleep with heavy eyes and the

gentle bobbing of that flat-bottomed broadhorn laden with marketable goods bound for the port at New Orleans . . . and the next moment he's shooting and stabbing, clubbing and slashing at the heathens who have stolen out of the night.

So this was the first time in his life that Bass ever had time to plan, to think, and to fret on it. Killing had always been what he had done when presented with no other choice. Now it became something altogether different, when he was no longer the one confronted by the violence created for him—now that he was the one slipping out of the dark. Not that these Blackfoot didn't deserve to die, he reminded himself as he took another two steps forward . . . and suddenly saw the shape of the man.

Stopping almost in midstep, Bass held his breath a long moment. Waiting, he watched the warrior, studying to be sure there was no chance he might have been heard. Waiting to be certain the breeze was still in his face. He took another step, paused, then moved to within two short yards of the raider. The horses were just beyond him.

He leaned the rifle against a tree, wondering where Hatcher was. Wondering how long he should wait there before . . . how much time he would have before the warrior moved farther away, or the animals scented him, or all hell broke loose because one of the others were discovered.

Swallowing down the sharp-edged ball of thorny fear lodged in his throat, Bass brought both arms up, his left ready to snare the Blackfoot, the right hand filled with his old knife.

The horses brought their heads up suddenly as Titus was starting the knife back in its arc. An instant later a cry shattered the night. The Blackfoot in front of him visibly jerked, then started to wheel to his right, about to sprint off for camp. He spotted Bass at the same moment Scratch was lunging forward, his arm already swinging down in a frenzy, snatching hold of the Blackfoot's war shirt, yanking the Indian close as the knife became a blur.

In that moment of the white man's hesitation, the enemy managed to bring his forearm up. Bass's wrist collided with it as the tip of the knife grazed the side of the warrior's neck. But the Blackfoot's right arm was free, grabbing for his own scabbard as they danced in a tight circle. The moment the man's knife came up in that free hand, Titus shoved his enemy backward, slamming his knee into the warrior's groin.

Stumbling a step, the warrior sought to protect himself as Scratch pursued him back, back—still holding on to the war shirt—yanking the warrior to the side as he raked his knife across the Blackfoot's gut. He felt the sudden warm splash across his own cold hand.

Until now the enemy hadn't made a sound; but this was something that reminded him of a grunt from the old plow mule, a little of the squeal. Sinking to his knees, the Blackfoot stared down at his hands, found them filling with the first purplish-white ribbons of gut spilling from the deep, savage wound.

Dull-eyed, he looked up at the white man just as Bass heard the rumble burst free of his own throat: stepping forward to savagely slash the old knife from left to right across the enemy's throat.

Deep enough that the man's head snapped back, eyes wide, lips moving bereft of sound this time.

There was enough other noise now.

Scratch could hear the shouts of the trappers somewhere behind him. And off toward the creek came the shrill cries of the rest of the Blackfoot.

Their fat was in the fire now.

Damn if they hadn't managed to stir up the hornets' nest without getting off with the horses.

Of a sudden it sounded as if he were surrounded by the rain-patter of running steps. Out of the gray gloom emerged huge black shadows. Snorting, wide-eyed, with frosty vapor jetting from their mouths, more than two dozen ponies shot past as Scratch dodged this way, then that, to keep from getting trampled. He thought he recognized some of the voices cracking the darkness, yelling to one another as they raced to get ahead of the stampeding herd.

All bets were off now.

He damn well knew he couldn't count on his own horse being back there where he had left it with the others.

As the last of the ponies blew past him in the dark, thundering through the tall willows, Bass knew he was alone, and on foot.

Realizing what that meant for no more than a heartbeat before he heard the Blackfoot cries coming closer and closer. Footsteps, the rustle of underbrush, the strident call of anguish, rage, blood lust.

He looked down at the dead warrior, hoping to find some sort of firearm. Nothing more than that knife and a quiver strapped over his shoulder, filled with arrows and a short bow.

Jerking around at the nearing clamor, Scratch decided the time would never be better to make a run for it—just as more than a half-dozen warriors burst from the far brush on foot.

"Bass!"

The voice yanked him around as he was turning to plunge into the willow thicket for his rifle.

Trying to get any sound free past the clog in his throat was an impossible feat as he stammered Hatcher's name.

Jack burst out of the brush on horseback between Titus and the onrushing warriors. "Up, coon! Heave up now!"

"My gun!"

"Get it, sumbitch!"

By the time he whirled back with it, Jack held out a hand from the back of the Blackfoot pony he controlled with no more than the single buffalo-hair rein. In a frightened circle it pranced around Bass one time, then a second, as Jack struggled for control and Scratch stuffed the knife into its sheath. The two men locked one another's forearms while Titus hopped round and round at the center of the circle.

The cries grew louder, renewed now that the prey was in sight.

"Dammit—get up here or we're both wolf bait!"

"G'won . . . I can't—"

With a mighty grunt Hatcher reared back, dragging Bass off the ground enough that he was able to swing one leg over the hind flanks of the pony, his free hand reaching out to seize Jack's buckskin shirt. Both of them jabbing heels into the horse's ribs, they lunged into the willow thicket.

Arrows smacked the branches around them. Gunfire boomed behind them, the air on either side of their heads alive with the tormented whine of lead balls.

"Far as hitting anything with a gun, never met me a Injun wuth a red piss!" Hatcher roared as the willow whipped their arms and legs and cheeks unmercifully.

Bass's left side burned in the cold—like a sudden, raw opening of tender flesh. Gazing down at the wound while he laid his hand over it, Bass waited a moment, then brought the hand away, feeling the pain already, even before he saw the dark stain on his palm.

"Should've left me behind," he grumbled as he secured a better hold on Hatcher just as they broke free of the willow onto the sagebrush plain.

"Hell with you, nigger!" Hatcher grumbled. "I ain't never left no man ahin't . . . and I ain't about to start now. Mangy as yer carcass is—wuthless, no-good—"

"There they are!" Scratch exclaimed through gritted teeth, fighting the pain in his side where the bullet's path made him want to cry.

"Damn if it ain't!"

Far ahead of them galloped more than forty horses, their hooves hammering the flaky hardpan ground as they were driven by the whooping cries of the other four trappers struggling to keep the Blackfoot ponies from scattering this way or that at either side of their path.

For a moment Bass turned slightly to peer over his shoulder behind them. He was beginning to feel faint, wanting nothing better than to have Hatcher stop so he could climb off, lie down, and sleep. Instead Titus bit down hard on his lower lip—startling himself with the pain that for a moment made him forget the terrible fire in his side.

"W-we gonna make it, Jack?"

Hatcher turned his head quickly to look behind them. "I do believe, Titus Bass!"

"You mean we pulled that off?"

"Less'n them sumbitches got more ponies—and I do believe we got 'em all—they ain't coming after us but on foot!"

Suddenly Titus was growing light-headed and the ground was starting to spin beneath the pony's hooves as it struggled beneath the weight of two men. "I ain't . . . ain't . . ."

"Hang on!"

"Can't hang much more—"

"Ye hit?"

" 'Fraid so, Jack."

"Eegod, Scratch!" he screeched, yanking back on the single buffalo-hair rein.

His eyelids grown so heavy. "K-keep goin'!"

"I wanna see how bad ye're—"

"We're gonna have company soon if'n you pull up."

Hatcher jerked his head around, gazing down their backtrail, spotting the distant figures Bass had sighted only moments before. Horsemen. There weren't many—but enough to make for trouble.

Jack sighed, "Ye gonna hold on?"

"Like a goddamned tick."

"Hep-ha!" Hatcher cried, jabbing his moccasins into the horse's belly, jolting a sudden burst of speed from it.

Burying his face in Hatcher's bony back, Titus drank in deep drafts of air, realizing that it was no longer night. Sometime in the last few minutes, the sky had begun to brighten in prelude to sunrise. Now they'd be all the easier to track for that handful of riders. Ponies the trappers hadn't driven off. And where there was a handful, a man could always figure there might likely be more.

He wondered how Kinkead was doing, remembering the sight of that arrow shaft quivering every time Matthew drew in a ragged breath, shuddering every time he exhaled. How they had struggled to hold the big man down to pull it out. All the blood as Hatcher dug the stone head out of the thick muscle. Arrow or bullet—who was to say what was better . . . what a man could survive . . .

"Help me get him down!"

Some of the black curtain was pulled back, and Bass came awake as the hands grabbed him, feeling himself pulled, allowing himself to fall against them clumsily. The others laid him out as Hatcher slid from the heaving pony's bare back. It was plain the creature didn't take to being so close to these strange-smelling white men. It nearly pulled Jack off the ground with its first lunge, snorting and rearing back.

Hatcher balled up his hard-boned fist and smacked the animal with a powerful haymaker of a blow, landing it right behind the nostrils.

Staggering to the side, the pony righted itself, more wary now of the man who still gripped its buffalo-hair rein.

"Take this, Caleb." Jack handed that rein to Wood. "Solomon, turn Scratch on his side." He knelt beside Bass. "Lemme have a look-see while the rest of ye get ready to welcome Bug's Boys to our li'l hidee-hole."

"That makes only three guns, Jack," Rowland complained.

"Four," Hatcher corrected. "Caleb, tie that jughead off and get yerself a spot to watch the backtrail."

Somewhere beyond them back down the trail, the sun was breaking over the edge of the earth. But here past the mouth of this narrow canyon, it was still shadow. Breath vapor steamed in frosty halos surrounding every head. Bass grunted as he was turned, his eyes struggling to focus as he looked up, around at the faces dancing in a watery haze over him.

"It come clean through, boys," Jack declared, finding the exit wound on Bass's belly.

"Damn lucky, ain't he?" Solomon Fish exclaimed, supporting the wounded man's shoulders.

"Titus Bass lucky?" Hatcher snorted as he leaned close to examine the entrance wound, pushing this way and that with his fingertips. "Any other man I'd call lucky if'n he was hit by a Blackfoot ball that went right on through his side the way this'un did. But from what we know about this son of a bitch, the way he lived to tell of a 'Rapaho scalpin', hung like a tick on the back of that damned bitch of a mule long enough to be in the right place and the right time when the Snakes shot that white medicine calf . . . and then got his fat pulled from the fire with the rest of us last spring when that white medicine calf's hide told them grateful Snakes when we was all about to go under . . . hell, Solomon! I never knowed any man more lucky than Titus Bass!"

Elbridge Gray turned to say, "Born under a good star, that child was."

"Damn if he wasn't," Jack sighed, leaning back. " 'Pears to me that ball went right on through 'thout striking anything but skin and muscle."

Caleb whistled low in amazement. "Almost makes a man wanna keep him around for our own good luck."

Hatcher nodded, pushing some of Bass's long, stringy hair out of his eyes as Titus struggled to focus on the brigade leader. "Damn right, boys—this here's a good man to have along."

"J-jack—"

Hatcher leaned close. "I got bad news for ye, Scratch."

"Bad?"

"Ye're gonna live, ye mangy, flea-bit no-count."

"Gonna make it, am I? By damn that's good news—"

"That is less'n the Blackfoots catch up to us and pin us down till they can finish ye off."

Bass squinted his eyes against the rise of pain. "We ain't gonna let 'em, are we?"

Jack grinned, his overly large teeth the color of pin acorns. "Not by a long chalk, we ain't." He turned. "Caleb—crawl on up there and see what them riders are up to at the mouth of the canyon."

Scratch heard Caleb Wood move off. "I got my pistol, rifle too, if'n any of you can use 'em."

"Hell, Bass," Gray spouted. "You ain't hurt so bad you can't hold on to 'em your own self."

Fish added, "Might be you'll get a chance to use 'em yet."

A few long minutes later Titus fluttered open his eyes slightly, fighting to focus on Hatcher's face hovering over his. "You get your horse guard?"

"Didn't get the chance," Jack replied. "I spooked a horse, so that red son of a bitch jumped out into the meadow on me. Right about the time a second one showed up."

"Second one?" Rowland asked.

"I figger it was another guard coming out to take him his turn at watch," Jack explained. "Boys, there ain't two ways about it: plain as paint I'm 'bout as *un*lucky as Titus Bass born under a good star!"

"Let's hope his star gonna shine down on all of us," Caleb huffed as he crabbed back into that ring the trappers formed around Bass.

Solomon asked, "More coming?"

Wood nodded, licking his dry lips. "See'd 'em. Coming a ways off."

"How many?" Rowland demanded in a rising voice.

"It don't matter how many," Hatcher declared as he rose from his knees. "We can't none of us stay here to let 'em finish us off."

"What about Bass?" Fish asked.

Jack looked down at Titus. "What about it, Scratch?"

He struggled to rise on an elbow and tried out a weak grin on all of them. "Boys, if Mad Jack here says we best be making tracks—then we best be on our way."

"Get the horses!" Elbridge hollered as he wheeled about, sweeping up a rein.

"Put them Blackfoot ponies out in front of us and keep 'em going," Jack ordered. "No matter what, keep them ponies going."

Hatcher was the next up after throwing his saddle onto a fresh mount. He had Fish and Wood heft Bass up behind him.

"Now, get me one of them picket ropes," Jack said. "Wrap it round us both so ye can tie him to me."

"D-do me up tight, fellas," Bass demanded of them, knowing the chances were good that he would grow too weak to hold on to Hatcher by himself. "I don't wanna fall off so them Blackfoot niggers get me."

They made a half-dozen loops around the two men, then knotted the ends in front of Hatcher so he could free himself or Bass if the need arose.

"Get a leg up, boys!" Jack cried. "Move them ponies out!"

Wide-eyed, Solomon said, "Only one way out of this here canyon, Jack."

"We'll run right into them niggers waiting for the rest to come up!" Caleb shrieked.

"That's just what I figger Jack wants to do," Solomon shouted.

Hatcher nudged his heels into the horse. "Right, the first whack! Do our best to run right on over 'em on our way out! Hep! Hep-ha!"

As the horse's powerful flanks surged beneath him, Bass locked his fingers around the loops of rope imprisoning Hatcher's chest. Ahead of them the others were yelling and screaming, driving the horses before them, sure to scare the billy-be-hell out of the half-dozen or so Blackfoot waiting at the mouth of the canyon.

"You really gonna ride right into 'em?" Scratch asked against the back of Hatcher's neck.

"Damn right we are!" he said, turning his head slightly. "A goddamned sit-up, straight-on ride-through!"

Cautiously, Bass loosened the hold he had with his right hand and slid it between himself and Hatcher until he filled his hand with the butt of the flintlock pistol.

"Hold tight, son!" Jack warned. "We're about to do-si-do!"

What few war cries the Blackfoot raised were swiftly drowned out by the hammer of hooves on the flaky hardpan of the earth's crust as the horses and trappers galloped into the open, heading right for their enemy who waited among the sage and buckbrush in the day's new light. Hatcher's men shouted back with their own bravado, hurtling through the few who had dared to follow them.

A lone gunshot. Bass figured it had to be one of the boys. The Blackfoot simply didn't have that many weapons, and chances were good they wouldn't dare try to shoot their weapons from horseback anyway. What Jack had said was true: Indians simply weren't much in the way of marksmanship.

"Take a lookee there, Scratch!" Hatcher called.

He turned his head, immediately catching sight of the warrior racing toward them at an angle—putting himself on a collision course not that far ahead. In one hand the Blackfoot held the elk-antler quirt he used to whip the pony's rear flank. And in the hand that clutched the pony's rein, the warrior also held a long wooden club from the end of which protruded a long, wide knife blade. Two feathers streamed back from his long, unfettered hair while the pony raced around and over the stunted sagebrush.

"Maybe I should ride right into him?" Jack mused.

"You do, you'll knock me off," Scratch replied.

"I'll wager that's what he's fixin' to do."

All the jarring, jolting, side-to-side hammering inflicted on his wound was about to overwhelm Bass. For a moment he bit down on his lower lip again, then said, "You pull up—I'll shoot the son of a bitch."

"I ain't stoppin' for nothing! Not when I got a head of steam behind me!"

It was like a nausea that threatened to surge up his gullet, a blackness doing its best to put an end to the torment in his side. And out of the shrill ringing in his ears, Bass heard the other pony. Opening his eyes, he struggled to focus: discovering the warrior racing just behind them, just over his right shoulder.

"Hatcher!"

"I know, goddammit!"

Bass watched the Blackfoot switch the reins into his free hand, beginning to swing his left arm back. "Can you shoot him, Jack!"

"It's all I can do to keep us on top of this damned horse!"

With a sudden swerving lurch, the warrior brought his pony sharply to the left as he swung the long club forward. Both Hatcher and Bass ducked out of the way as the knife blade hissed past their heads—that sudden shift of weight causing the horse below them to stumble and sidestep at full stride. Both trappers barely held on as the animal dodged through the sagebrush: Hatcher locked on to the saddle, Titus locked on to him.

Bass cried, "Son of a bitch's coming back for another go!"

"He'll keep it up till he gets one of us," Hatcher growled, "or he drops us both!"

"Can you ram your horse into him?"

"S'pose I can," Jack admitted grittily. "But it might spill us!"

"He comes close enough—just give 'im the idea you're gonna."

For the next few moments Bass was able to watch the look of grim determination on the warrior's face as the Blackfoot inched his animal closer and closer to the white man's horse. He saw how the man's hair was cut with long bangs that tossed in the wind, the hair on the top of his head tied up with a few feathers, like a bold challenge to try taking that topknot. And he saw how those black-cherry eyes glittered with hate.

Titus wondered how anyone could ever possess such hate like that for someone he didn't know. Besides the horses—why would these warriors carry such rage for the white men? After all this time, were they still licking their wounds after being driven off by the Shoshone last spring? To Scratch's way of thinking, even that could not account for the unadulterated hatred and contempt he read in the Blackfoot's eyes as the warrior drew closer and closer.

"Now!" Bass screamed.

Hatcher was right on the money, yanking hard on the rein. Their horse twisted suddenly, just as Jack yanked back to the left to correct it. That sudden lunge did the trick: enough to make the warrior pull off.

And when the Indian realized what the white men had done, even more rage clouded his face.

"I gotta get rid of the son of a bitch," Jack grumbled.

"This horse ain't gonna last long under us both," Bass said into the back of Hatcher's neck, feeling himself breaking into a fevered sweat. "Maybe we get a chance, you get us stopped, tie me on another horse. This'un can't carry us much—"

"Shuddup! I ain't about to trust ye to make it on yer own."

Off to the right, the warrior was coming at them again as they reached more open ground, the land falling away gently toward the distant river valley, that beckoning vale rushing at them with its wide border of green disclosing its meandering course to these battle-weary travelers.

"Then gimme a chance to shoot him," Bass demanded.

"How in the devil's eggs are ye gonna shoot 'im?" Hatcher snorted, getting a new grip on the horse's rein. "Ye can barely hang on to me as it is, child!"

"J-just . . . g-get him on the other side of us."

"Don't let go of me, Bass!"

"I ain't, Jack," he vowed weakly. "Just get him on our left. Cross over, hard and sharp."

"An' put him on our left," Jack repeated. "If what ye got in mind don't work—that nigger likely to take off the top of yer head with that club on his next go-by."

"You just keep us both on this here horse—I'll do the rest, Hatcher."

Whooping and wagging his head in astonishment, Jack kept looking over his right shoulder as the Blackfoot urged his pony closer and closer to their horse, and when he figured the warrior was close enough, Hatcher yanked hard to the right.

But the Blackfoot figured this was another feint and didn't go for the bait. Instead, he spurred forward, the nose of his animal nearly crashing into the rear flank of the trappers' horse as it shifted sides. As the startled enemy straightened himself on his war pony, Bass found that Hatcher had done it. The warrior was now inching up on them from their left.

Closer.

He struggled to bring the pistol out of his sash in a sweating palm.

Closer still.

They were lashed so tightly together that he grew scared the weapon might go off wedged there between them. Kill one of them, if not the horse under them both.

Close enough now that he could see the ribbons of sweat coursing down the enemy's face.

Freed at last—he felt the muzzle move between them, tight against his belly as he pushed his hand forward.

Swinging the club back, the Indian grinned, his teeth glittering as he closed on what had to be a sure kill. Two white men at once. What a prize—

Shoved across his body, the pistol suddenly popped out between the two men as Titus raked back the hammer with a thumb.

The club had already begun its arc downward as the Blackfoot's eyes suddenly locked on the pistol just then popping into view between his enemies.

In his sweat-slickened hand the pistol nearly bucked itself loose as Bass pulled the trigger. The ball slammed into its target midchest, right under the warrior's arm that held the war club aloft. As if disbelieving, the Blackfoot kept the arm and club frozen there, reluctantly tearing his eyes off the white men as he looked down at his side . . . weaved—then pitched off the back of his straining pony.

"Sumbitch!" Hatcher cried exuberantly.

Drops of salty sweat stung Bass's eyes as he blinked, trying hard to clear them, straining to see if there were any other pursuers who might pose a threat now that he had emptied his only weapon of the only bullet it had held. Behind them two other warriors slowed and brought their ponies to a halt in the sagebrush, circling back for the body of their fallen comrade.

"Maybeso the niggers are giving up," Titus said, more hopeful than certain.

"Not Blackfoot," Hatcher snorted. "Bug's Boys don't give up."

"How long they gonna keep after us?"

It was a moment before Hatcher answered. "Till they take all the horses they can from us, and they got our scalps hanging from their belts, Scratch."

"Ain't healthy for a man up here—this hard by Blackfoot country— is it?"

"No, I don't reckon it is."

Weakness was like a thick cloud overtaking him now that the hot adrenaline was no longer surging through his veins. "Tell me, Jack: is the beaver so good up here that you're willing to put your hide on the line ever' day you got left in your number?"

"What say when we get back to Isaac and Rufus—we all talk about working our way south to more friendly country?"

"South . . . south is good."

"Rest of them niggers been after our hair won't be follering all that quick—seeing how we put 'em afoot the way we done," Hatcher said. "So we can see to Kinkead and you proper and get this outfit ready to tramp south back to the Windy Mountains after we g'won to ronnyvoo at Sweet Lake. How's ronnyvoo sound to Titus Bass?"

Jack waited a minute for an answer from Bass, and when he didn't get one, he turned slightly to peer at the man roped behind him. "Scratch? Hyar ye—Scratch?"

Up ahead of them the others were driving the horses across the wide creek, threading the animals through the young cottonwood saplings and between stands of willow. How beautiful were the drops of water spraying up from each hoof, countless glittering gems iridescent in the bright spring sun as the four other horsemen shouted and urged the horses across.

"Ronnyvoo . . . just the sound of it shines," Bass finally said as he closed his eyes again, so heavy had they become that he could no longer keep them open.

"There'll be whiskey, Scratch!" Hatcher cheered as he slowed the horse in nearing the ford. "And womens!"

His side burned with a terrible, prickling pain. And for a moment Titus wondered on just how much blood he had lost. Would he make it to rendezvous? Or would he be one of those who went under? Then Scratch couldn't fight it any longer.

"Just lem' . . . lemme sleep now, Jack."

Not all that far overhead the calliope hummingbird's wings blurred in frenetic flight—hovering, darting, then hovering once more as it sought out its nectar.

Bass froze, motionless there in the icy water, the five-pound steel trap and float-stick in hand. Enthralled with the bird's dance on the gentle spring breeze, he watched the hummingbird bob and bounce from flower to flower until it was long gone down the streambank. He sighed in contentment. And arched his back, feeling the tug of tight new flesh slowly knitting along the bullet's path through his left side. Especially taut across those two small puckers of wrinkled skin. It was good to be back working the banks of these streams. Good for a man to know where he belonged.

For days following that scrap with the Blackfoot horse thieves, the others had joshed about keeping him around for no other reason than that Titus Bass was a good omen, perhaps even the old Shoshone soothsayer's most powerful charm.

"I had me a uncle once said to me that a few folks is like cats," Solomon Fish had said beside a campfire one twilight as Hatcher's brigade made their way south toward the Owl Mountains, working to put more and more country between them and the Blackfeet who seemed determined in their chase.

"Merciful heavens," Caleb Wood grumbled as he swayed up with another armload of wood. "How people like cats?"

"Never had me a cat was wuth a red piss," John Rowland observed. "Only good for mousin'."

"Go ahead on with yer story, Solomon," Jack prodded.

With an indifferent shrug Fish nudged some of his blond ringlets out of his eyes and said, "Ain't much of a story, really. Just my uncle said some folks got 'em nine lives, just like cats s'pose to have."

Hatcher turned to Kinkead. "What ye think of that, Matthew?"

"Sounds like Solomon's uncle kept hisself filled with bilgewater to me."

"Maybe not a fella like you," Fish snorted testily. "But just think about Titus Bass here."

Hatcher grinned across the fire, asking, "Say, Scratch—figger ye used up any of yer nine lives?"

"Damn right I have," he answered, feeling the certainty of it down to his marrow. "Figger I had a few whittled off me back in St. Louie, back to the time when I was doing my best to spit in death's eye."

"How 'bout with them Arapaho down near the Little Bear?" Elbridge Gray asked.

"Them," Scratch replied, painfully shifting his position, "and a few times since."

Jack turned back to Kinkead, asking, "So don't it sound like Bass got him a cat's nine lives?"

"Solemn," Matthew used his favorite expression, then spit a brown stream of tobacco into the fire, where it hissed. "But if Scratch truly be a man with nine lives, I reckon he's just 'bout used 'em all up, Jack."

"Long as he don't use that last one afore ronnyvoo at Sweet Lake!" Hatcher roared.

Time was drawing nigh when the company brigades and bands of free trappers would begin to gather, marching farther to the west every few days, stopping now and again when the sign along the streams convinced Hatcher's men the trapping might be worth their efforts. Wandering slowly as the days lengthened and warmed, they neared the southern end of the Wind River Mountains—where a man jumped west by southwest over that easy, sloping divide to find himself in a country where all the waters now flowed toward the Big Salt far, far beyond the horizon.

When the hummingbird finally flickered out of sight, Titus waded another half-dozen steps and stopped there at the base of the long strip of creekside grass growing along the bank, reaching for the knife at his back. With it he plunged his arm under the water, clear up to the elbow, and began hacking away at the side of the bank until he had carved away a shelf big enough on which to set his trap. From beneath his arm he grabbed the bait stick: a section of peeled willow, one end sharpened for driving into the bank just above the surface of the stream where he had hidden his trap at the end of the beaver slide.

Here the animals repeatedly entered the water, usually dragging their limbs and saplings they were using to slowly construct a rugged dam across the stream, or swim underwater with their provender, taking it to their beaver lodge to feed mate and kits. The slides were a good place to count on beaver coming close enough to that stick where the rodents would catch a whiff of the bait Scratch smeared on that portion of the limb suspended over the readied trap.

After driving the stick into the bank at the proper angle with the small head of the belt ax he carried, Scratch pulled the stopper from the wooden vial suspended from his belt. The sudden strong, pungent odor of the casto-reum rose to his nostrils, making his eyes water as he smeared a little of the thick, creamy liquid on the exposed end of the bait stick, stuffed the vial away, then washed his fingertips there at the foot of the slide.

Two more traps still to set before sundown.

Looking over his shoulder at the falling sun, Bass reckoned it would be twilight before he made it back to camp, unsaddled, and picketed the horse on some good grass until it was time to curl up in the blankets for the night.

Despite the hightailing they had done to stay as far ahead of the Black-feet as they could, they had nonetheless made a good spring of it for them-selves—both before that first attack when they were burying Joseph Little, and after as Hatcher led them farther and farther north toward the southern reaches of that country the Blackfoot jealously guarded and protected as their own hallowed ground.

"Man's a fool what'll go where he's bound to lose his hair over a little beaver fur," Caleb Wood had grumbled the farther north they had gone.

"Man's a fool if he don't go to see for his own self if the plew is as prime as some say it is," Jack retorted. "But don't ye worry none. We'll turn around and hightail it out if'n them pelts ain't as big as blankets . . . or if Bug's Boys turn out to be thicker'n summer wasps."

Soon enough they found Hatcher right on both counts. No wonder the Blackfoot got so fractious with white American trappers slipping around the fringes of their country—the beaver up there grew bigger, their pelts more sleek, than anywhere else a man trapped in these mountains.

Moving on upstream, Titus kept his eyes moving, searching for another slide, perhaps the stumps of some young saplings the beaver had felled, any sign that an area was frequented by the big, flat-tailed rodents hunted by the Rocky Mountain fur trapper.

Decades before, the big companies had first enlisted men to come far up the Missouri River for the purpose of trading with the tribes to obtain their fine and coarse furs: not only the seal-sleek beaver and river otter, but mink and lynx, some buffalo and wolf at times too. The British pushed down from the north, and the Americans prodded farther west each year until men like Ashley and Henry decided they would do better hiring a hundred enterprising young men to catch the pelts themselves. The American fur trade was never the same after the Ashley men began to spread out across the far west—from the Milk and the Marias, the Judith and the Mussellshell on the north, to the Gila, the Rio Grande, and the Cimarron down south in Mexican Territory.

But beaver had already been feeding the economy of the New World for more than two hundred years by the time the Rocky Mountain fur trapper appeared on the scene. And beaver continued to turn the wheels of commerce as the big companies and the small bands of free trappers moved farther and farther into the wilderness, searching deeper and deeper for virgin country yet untrapped.

Scratch stopped there in the cold stream fed by last winter's snows, far, far overhead among the high peaks, surveying the banks on both sides while he pushed some of the long brown curls out of his eyes. As a trapper grew in experience, he came to recognize just what the possibilities of finding beaver would be from the type and amount of vegetation sprouting along a certain stretch of a creek or river. Down at lower elevations some of the animals would feed on young cottonwood and alder, while up here above the foothills beaver worked on aspen, willow, and birch.

Crossing the stream to the far bank, Scratch bent and scooped up a handful of the wood shavings thickly scattered at the base of a stump within reach from the water. Rolling the chips in his fingertips to check for moistness, then bringing them to his nose to smell—the more fragrant, the fresher they were—Bass calculated it was a recent cutting. No man had ever taught him this: not Bud, nor Billy, nor even the savvy Silas Cooper—none of the three who had gathered him under their wings and taught him not only what it would take to make a living as a trapper, but how to keep hold of his hair in Indian country.

No, seasons ago Scratch had learned this trick on his own hook. The fresher the shavings, the more recent the activity in that section of a stream, and consequently the greater the possibility of a concentration of flat-tails consumed with building dams, flooding meadows, and constructing lodges for their families.

A trapper counted on the probability that any beaver curious enough to be lured to the bait stick would put a foot in the steel trap waiting for it at the bottom of a slide or near the entrance to its domed lodge. Unable to free itself from the weight of the trap, the beaver would drown quickly, leaving its pelt unmarred, ready for a careful skinning.

After being stretched, fleshed, and dried on round hoops of willow, the hides were bundled in packs for eventual transport to the summer rendezvous. This annual gathering, another invention of General William H. Ashley, was conceived as a means of resupplying his brigades who spread out through the mountains from late summer until the following spring when they would begin their trek down from the high country to a prearranged valley, there to meet with the caravan come all the way out from St. Louis laden with powder and lead, sugar and coffee, beads and trinkets, calico and wool stroud—everything a man would need to live for another year in the mountains, even what that man might employ to entice an Indian squaw back among the brush for an all-too-brief and heated coupling.

No money ever changed hands between trader and trapper, white man or Indian. None was needed. Beaver was the only currency in the mountains. With it a man would eventually buy himself a head-splitting drunk, a raucous series of couplings with a string of agreeable Indian maidens, and he might possibly have enough left over to outfit himself for another year in the high lonesome without going into debt to the company.

No matter that most men had little to show for their years and their miles and their wrinkles. To search out the wily Rocky Mountain beaver, a man might willingly risk his hair, his hide, and perhaps his very soul.

After braving months upon months of bone-numbing streams both fall and spring, after enduring a long, spirit-sapping winter in some isolated, snowbound camp, the trapper would eagerly look forward to summer when he could trade off his packs of beaver for another year's gamble in the wilderness. When the last man had turned in the last of his beaver, when the whiskey kegs had run dry, the traders threw their bundles onto the backs of the very same mules that had hauled the trade goods out from St. Louis, that caravan now to spend the next ten weeks making its return trip to the Missouri settlements. There, or farther east in Philadelphia or even New York, the pelts would be sorted further. While those of average grade would eventually be used for the tall-crowned gentleman's hats so fashionable not only back east but especially in Europe, the finest furs would be sold to brokers who exported them to frigid countries the likes of Imperial Russia and feudal China.

A single pelt of Rocky Mountain beaver might weigh between a pound and a half to two pounds when dried and fleshed of excess fat. The skin of a kit might weigh only half that. Over that brief, meteoric period of the American fur trade, the going rate for plew went anywhere from three to six dollars a pound back in the St. Louis market. So what eventually made Ashley his fortune was not his initially organizing fur brigades to operate in the mountains, but his newest venture: supplying those fur trappers with goods brought out to rendezvous planned for a prearranged site. There the reveling, raucous trappers overly eager to celebrate would be content to receive half the value of their beaver in St. Louis prices, while they wouldn't mind paying many times the "settlement" price of those staples and supplies transported from Missouri.

After holding his first rendezvous three years earlier in 1825, General Ashley continued to refine his rendezvous system until the price of beaver would eventually become standardized at somewhere around three dollars a pound—a figure that earned a trapper some five to six dollars a plew. It was hard, cold, lonely, and ultimately dangerous work for the few hundred men who chose to make their livelihood here in the wilderness, and perhaps on the edge of eternity.

From the northern rivers bordering the Canadian provinces all the way south into territory claimed by Mexico, at any one time less than four hundred Americans scattered their moccasin prints across a trackless wilderness, migrating seasonally across a mapless terrain, confronting a bewildering array of climatic conditions, geography, and native inhabitants. Here in these early years of the nineteenth century, in these opening days of the far west, for a special class of man there simply was no other life imaginable.

To take your life into your own hands, not beholden to any other man, to test your own resolve and mettle against all the elements God or the devil himself could hurl at a puny, insignificantly few bold men . . . ah, but that was the heady stuff of living!

True freedom: to live or die by one's own savvy and pluck.

Such was the nectar that lured these bees to the hive. Freedom was the sirens' song that enticed this reckless breed of men to hurl their fates against the high and terrible places.

Despite the cold and the Blackfoot—despite the odds of sudden death.

After constructing two travois for Kinkead and Bass, the other seven trappers had reloaded their pack animals and pointed their noses south for the Owl Creek Mountains, driving the extra Blackfoot ponies along behind them. Scratch was the first to knit up after their ordeal.

Twice a day one of Hatcher's men would make a poultice of beaver castoreum mixed with the pulverized roots or pulp of one plant or another, smearing the smelly concoction into the wounds troubling both men. It wasn't long before Bass could move about camp without tiring out too quickly. But for the better part of two weeks he contented himself by remaining in camp with Kinkead when the others went out to trap—staying busy by fleshing the beaver hides, then stretching them on willow hoops, or untying the packs to dust the plews and check for infestation before rebundling them in their rawhide cords. Eventually the raw, red flesh around his wounds became new, pink skin that he could gently stretch more each day. Inside, however, he was knitting together much slower.

Nowhere near as slow as Kinkead.

For the longest time Matthew continued to cough up bright-red blood, later on bringing up dark, half-congealed phlegm. With as little as the man ate, over the following weeks the others began to notice the gradual change in their friend as his huge face thinned, accentuating the dark, liver-colored bags beneath his eyes.

"I wanna see Rosa," Kinkead declared quietly one night as the rest joked and laughed around their nighttime fire, that simple plea coming right out of the blue.

The others fell silent immediately, some choosing to stare at their feet or the ground or the fire. Only Hatcher and Bass could look at the man still imprisoned on his travois.

"Natural for a man to wanna see his wife," Jack consoled as he knelt beside Kinkead.

"W-wife?" Titus asked, surprised. "You married?"

Hatcher explained, "She's a good woman."

"She back east?"

Kinkead shook his head. "Taos. She's a Mexican gal."

"I'll be go to hell," Bass exclaimed. "What the devil you doing trapping beaver up here in the mountains when you got a wife waiting for you down in the Mexico settlements?"

"Don't make sense no more, does it?" Matthew declared. "One time it did. Now—it don't make sense to me no more. God, I ache in my bones I wanna see Rosa so bad."

Scratch did not know what to say—struck dumb just watching the way Kinkead's eyes filled with tears. "Man has him someone who loves him, someone he loves . . . I'd sure as hell feel same as you, Matthew—wanting my woman with me if I was healing up."

Dragging a hand under his nose, Matthew's voice cracked as he said, "I decided today . . ."

Hatcher asked, "Decided what?"

Kinkead couldn't look at any of them. "Figger to quit the mountains."

"Qu-quit the mountains?" bawled John Rowland.

Hatcher asked, "What ye gonna do if ye plan on staying back in Taos?"

"Rosa and me, we'll be fine," Kinkead protested. "I figger I'll find something."

"Where you gonna live?" Solomon inquired. "Where the two of you set up home?"

With a shrug Kinkead responded, "I stay with her at her papa's house when I'm back in Taos. S'pose that's what we'll do till we find us some li'l place of our own."

"Damn," Caleb Wood sighed. "If that don't take the circle! I can't believe you're quitting the mountains."

"I'd do it this minute if I could get back down there," Kinkead complained.

Hatcher explained, "We ain't tramping that far south till fall hunt's over."

"All the way to Taos?" Bass inquired.

Suddenly Matthew's tired face grew more animated as he turned toward Titus. "That's prime doings! You're gonna see Taos shines, Scratch! Purely shines!"

"We got us some more trapping to do afore spring is done," Jack confided. "And then we'll be making for ronnyvoo over at Sweet Lake. After that we was planning on moseying down to the Bayou Salade for the fall hunt afore climbing on over to Taos."

"Where's this Bayou Sa . . . Sa—"

"Salade," Elbridge Gray recited. "Way south of here, Scratch. Not far from the Mexican country itself. Up on the headwaters of the Arkansas it be. Pretty place—and full of beaver too."

Now Bass turned to Kinkead. "So, nigger . . . you're married to this Mexican gal named Rosa."

He watched how it made Matthew smile.

"Yep, a purty lady she is too."

"But near as I can callate, you ain't been back there in more'n a year already."

Just that saying of it appeared to take some more starch out of Kinkead. He stared down at himself, lying helpless in that travois. "Makes me hurt more, Scratch—thinking just how long it'll be till I see her again. That'll make it near two years by the time I hold her. We left Taos end of winter a year ago."

"But you knowed we wasn't going back till this winter," Caleb said.

"I knowed . . ." And Matthew's voice trailed off.

"It don't matter if he knowed it was gonna be a long time when he left Taos," Bass said firmly. "Things is different now. The man come close to going under to Blackfoots. Ain't onreasonable to me for Matthew to be getting so homesick."

Caleb turned back to the fire, grumbling, "Homesick ain't no sick for a free man to have."

"Can I get you anything, Matthew?" Bass asked. "You had enough to eat?"

"Ain't got me much of a appetite no more," he replied. "You're coming with us to ronnyvoo, ain'cha, Scratch?"

"Planned on it."

Hatcher turned around at the fire to ask, "Ye got plans for the fall hunt, Scratch?"

"Like to see me this Bayou Salade you boys talk of. Yeah, I figger I'd throw in with your bunch."

"How 'bout Taos?" Kinkead asked, almost breathless with excitement. "You coming there with us when I get back home? Get to meet my Rosa!"

Bass dug his fingernails at his beard. "Taos for the winter, is it?"

Rufus hurrawed, "A man can't do him no better for winter!"

"Senoreetas and lightnin'," Hatcher chimed in. "A man can keep hisself real warm down in Taos come winter!"

Titus asked, "Lightnin'?"

"Mexican drink they make down there to the Taos valley," Caleb Wood explained. "Take the top of your head off like a tomahawk."

"That ain't no bald-face lie neither," Hatcher declared. "So, ye figger to stay on with our bunch till next spring?"

"Winter in Taos?" Bass repeated. "From the sounds of it—a man'd be plumb filled with stupids if'n he passed up the chance to ride into Mexico with this outfit!"

THREE

"They ain't gone and pulled out on us awready—are they, Jack?" whined John Rowland.

"I dunno, boys." Hatcher shook his head in consternation. "That down there's s'posed to be the place—right where we come together last year."

"Where the blazes is our ronnyvoo?" Isaac Simms growled as he shaded his eyes and squinted into the distance.

Digging frantically in the possibles pouch hanging at his hip, Caleb Wood roared in alarm, "Cain't see a goddamned camp down there!"

"You reckon we're late?" Elbridge Gray groaned, his big bulb of a nose looking all the bigger for the morose look on his face.

Scratch peered up at the sky, reckoning from the track of the sun just what part of summer it was right then. "I don't callate as we're late, Jack."

"There!" Caleb Wood suddenly cried, the short brass-cased looking glass stretched out from his right eye. "I see some horses, way off yonder!"

Squinting in the high sunlight, the rest shielded eyes to peer into the distance, eager for that reassurance.

"A herd?" Hatcher asked skeptically.

Wood shook his head. "Not no big cavvyyard, but there be a bunch."

"Hope to shout they're white men," Solomon Fish prayed, sweeping a hand under that long beard of blond ringlets.

Wood went on to explain, "And I see some white spots back in the brush and trees, Jack."

"Take 'em to be tents?"

"Reckon they are," Caleb replied, his eye locked against that brass telescope.

"Bring up them packhorses," Hatcher ordered as he gave heels to his own animal. "Move 'em on down torst the bottom, where we'll get us a better look at things there along the shore of the lake."

"I was here my own self," Bass commented as they descended off the low hills at the southeast shore of that inviting body of blue water reflecting a patchless summer sky. "Back to twenty-six."

"The Willow Valley," Rufus Graham replied. He was missing his four front teeth, two top and two bottom, which gave him an appealing lisp. "Leastwise, that's what the fur outfits call it."

At that moment several figures emerged from the tall willow and cotton-wood far ahead of them at the bottom of the gentle slope.

Hatcher groaned with disappointment. "Figgered there'd be more coons come in by now."

Titus assured, " 'Pears we're just a mite early, is all."

"Longer we wait," Hatcher snorted, that wild smile there of a sudden, "the thirstier Mad Jack gets!"

"Been two year for me," and Bass wiped the back of his hand across his lips. "You ain't the only child half-froze for whiskey!"

"Whiskey, or rum—don't make me no never-mind," declared Graham. "Long as it's got the kick of a mule when it hits the bottom!"

Isaac said, "Trader ain't in yet, so it looks to be we got us a leetle more wait afore you get your eggs kicked, Rufus!"

On down into the lush meadows of that fertile bottomland at the south end of Sweet Lake, Hatcher's brigade whooped, called, and whistled, wrangling their cavvyyard of pack animals and Blackfoot ponies. The closer they drew toward the narrow creek that fed itself into the lake, the more figures stepped from the shade and shadows, all carrying rifles. Suddenly one of those men raised a shout, lifting his long weapon into the air. Bass saw the puff of muzzle smoke appear an instant before the low boom reached their ears.

In concert more of those distant figures raised their rifles and fired them, then went to waving hats and bandannas at the ends of their outflung arms.

Off to Bass's right, Elbridge Gray was the first to fire his rifle in reply. In the space of three heartbeats the shooting became general as Hatcher's brigade was welcomed by some thirty men streaming into the open. Screeching wildly with the whole lot of them, yahooing and whooping, keerawing like Missouri mules, or hoo-hooing with a hand clapping over their mouths in the manner of attacking Indians, Scratch lifted his fullstock Derringer flintlock and yanked back first on the rear set trigger, then barely touched the front trigger. The rifle went off—a universal sign of peace for those who traveled the early far west. To empty one's gun upon approaching a camp was the surest way to show one's peaceful intentions.

"Boys, let's keep these here horses of our'n from mixing in with theirs," Hatcher hollered to his men as they approached the figures that had emerged from the groves of shady trees. Just beyond that camp dotted with canvas pyramid tents and blanket arbors grazed a herd of horses and mules.

"What say we cross the crik and raise our own camp yonder?" Titus asked, pointing off to the west.

For a moment Hatcher stood in the stirrups, gazing this way, then that. When he plopped back down in the saddle, he agreed, "Follow Scratch, boys! Yonder—cross the crik!"

In a matter of seconds the others were bellowing and screaming, slapping coils of buffalo-hair ropes to turn their herd of horses, whistling and calling to the animals, shouting at one another, congratulating their companions on surviving another year, every last man among them busting his buttons to have made it through to another rendezvous with his hair.

On came those who rushed afoot to welcome the new arrivals, some loping through the tall grass, others strolling more casually, most every one of them stripped to the waist in the midsummer heat, their flesh about as white as white men could be—save for the oak-browned tan of their hands from the wrists down, the same leathery look from the base of the neck up. Their leather flap-front trousers and pantaloons were blackened with seasons of grease and blood, smoked by countless fires. At the end of their arms they waved their low-crowned, big-brimmed wool hats, many of which were nearly shapeless after countless soakings by rain and snow. A few had red-and-blue bandannas tied about their heads, while some had tied the popular black silk handkerchiefs to keep their long hair from spilling into their eyes. Even a handful had their tresses braided or wrapped with strips of fur in the fashion of Indian warriors.

"Where from you bound?" cried one of the closest ones who plunged right into the creek, approaching Bass as Hatcher's men urged their animals off the east bank, crossing to the far side.

Hatcher shouted back, "Up to Blackfoot country for the spring hunt!"

"That bunch of motherless sons chased us right on out!" Bass added.

The squat, powerful stranger cried, "Har—with your tails atween your legs I'll wager!"

Rising immediately in his stirrups, Scratch looked behind him in mock surprise as he patted his own rump with a hand. "I'll be damned, Jack! Them Blackfoot bastards done bit my tail off!"

They all roared with lusty laughter as the greeters loping up on foot splashed out of the creek right alongside those on horseback, their leather and nankeen britches soaked above their knees.

The short trapper trotted up to Bass's side, holding up his hand, grinning like a house cat caught with feathers still tangled in its whiskers.

"Name's Porter," he announced. "Nathan Porter."

"Who you with?" Caleb Wood called out.

"Smith, Jackson, and Sublette," the man answered, holding a hand at his brow to shade his eyes in looking up at the arriving horsemen.

Wood asked, "You was one of Ashley's men, eh?"

"Till two year ago."

"Trader ain't in yet?" Jack inquired.

"Hell—Ashley sent his supply train out early," Porter explained as Hatcher's horsemen came to a halt and some began to drop to the ground. "Why, Billy Sublette and Davy Jackson brung us out our necessaries last winter, fellers."

"L-last *winter!*" squeaked Elbridge Gray.

Graham lunged in closer. "Summer's nigh the time for ronnyvoo!"

Porter drew back a step as the others closed in menacingly. "You fellers ain't with the company?"

"Hell, no," Hatcher spat.

"You ain't American Fur neither?"

Jack roared with laughter, dropping his head back and letting go at the sky. "Wouldn't take orders from Pilcher if'n he was the last outfit in the mountains!"

"We're free men," Solomon explained, slapping John Rowland on the back. "And we don't owe no man our allegiance."

"November, it were, when they come early with supplies," Porter started, apology in his voice and eyes. "Damn, I reckon I know just how you boys feel—no way to hear word they brung out our necessaries early. We wasn't in winter camp yet ourselves."

Two summers, come and gone, and still no rendezvous for him. Bass heaved a mighty sigh of disappointment, " 'Thout no trader, not gonna be no ronnyvoo now."

"Just what you boys come here to do if not for ronnyvoo?" Kinkead demanded.

"Not all the brigades got 'em provisions back to winter," Porter stated. Then he threw a thumb back in the direction of their camp. "Our bunch didn't get us a chance to take on supplies with the rest in the spring."

Now Hatcher's face was growing crimson. Gritting his teeth, he growled, "Winter and spring . . . and now it's the goddamned summer! So ye're telling us there ain't gonna be no trade goods come to ronnyvoo?"

"Ashley ain't figgering to be out his own self," Porter explained as more of his bunch came up to stand nearby in the bright midsummer sun among Hatcher's men.

"Each one of the big brigades we still 'spect to come in all got 'em supplies they can trade off to you fellers for your skins, I s'pose," a new and taller man declared, coming to a halt at Porter's shoulder. "What outfit you men with?"

"Like we just told him—we ain't with no outfit," Scratch declared, surprised to discover just how proud that made him to state it so unequivocally. "We are an outfit."

"This bunch is on its own hook," Caleb Wood emphasized.

"Thort you might be some of American Fur coming in," the second man said. "They been dogging near every one of our brigades since last summer."

"This here's Mad Jack Hatcher," Scratch exclaimed proudly, sweeping an extended arm toward their leader. "He's the one what heads this outfit of free mountaineers."

"Hatcher, is it?" Nathan Porter asked, extending his hand to Jack. "From the sounds of it, you got a passel of furs to trade."

"We got plenty of plew," Hatcher agreed as they shook. "But where's my men to find something to trade them furs for?"

The taller of the company men said, "Just as soon's the rest of the brigades ride in, we'll start the trading."

"At mountain prices, I'll lay!" Scratch snarled.

Porter nodded. "After all, this here's the mountains—"

"Wagh!" Hatcher snorted with the guttural roar of the grizzly boar. "Mountain prices, he said, boys!"

"Get ready to get yourselves honey-fuggled by them company booshways!" Caleb Wood cried as he pounded a hand on Porter's back, both of them laughing easily.

But the second man was clearly uncomfortable as Hatcher's men guffawed along with many of the company men. "Mountain prices is what we all take in exchange. Ain't no man better'n any other."

"No, I savvy you're right there," Scratch said as he stepped up before the tall trapper. "But just as long as we get what's fair for our plew here in the mountains, a man don't mind paying mountain prices for his necessaries."

"Hold on!" Rowland jumped forward, his face drawn and gray with concern. "Y-you mean . . . if'n there ain't gonna be no trader come out— there ain't gonna be no whiskey?"

"No whiskey!" shrieked Rufus Graham.

Now it was Porter's turn to roar with laughter. "Ain't got enough to float a bullboat back to St. Louie, boys . . . but we have us enough to wash the dust out'n your gullet!"

"Whooo-haw!" Bass shouted with glee, sidling up to fling an arm over Porter's shoulder. "How smooth it be? Like a Natchez whore's baby-haired bum?"

Nathan Porter turned and looked at Bass in alarm. "Smooth? Hell, it ain't smooth!"

A new trapper stepped forward. "Ain't no such a thing as smooth likker in these here mountains, friend. Ever' drink'll cut'cha going down and land like a bar of Galena lead when it hits bottom."

"I wanna know if it can take the shine off my traps," Hatcher said.

"An' can it peel the varnish off my saddle tree?" Bass inquired.

"Hell if it can't!" the man replied with a near toothless grin.

Bass looked over at Hatcher, and they both smiled so broadly, it nearly cracked their faces in half.

Scratch screamed, "Then bring on that there likker, fellers—'cause I got me a two-year thirst to rid myself of!"

Although there was indeed a small supply of crude grain alcohol at the south shore of Sweet Lake, that summer of 1828 there would be no great and boisterous revelry because Sublette and Jackson had already reached the mountains with some twenty thousand dollars in supplies the winter before. Despite the shortage of trade goods and liquor, the air of excitement, camaraderie, and fellowship swelled as the sun began to drop and twilight approached each evening.

Rendezvous was rendezvous. Make no mistake of that. A man worked a whole year to journey off to some prearranged valley for this reunion with faces and friends he had not seen in all those months of grueling labor in freezing streams, fighting off the numbing cold of the past winter, defending himself against horse-raiders and scalping parties. This July a double handful of the new company's men would be missing.

Survivors of one more year in the wilderness, Hatcher's men joined other free trappers and brigade men at their fires for swapping stories, generously lathered with exaggeration bordering on lies, catching up on any fragment of the stale news brought out from the settlements by the traders last winter—news seemingly as fresh as these men in the wilderness wished to make every report and flat-out rumor.

As night eased down, black-necked stilts called out softly from the rushes in the nearby marsh bordering the lake.

"Listen to that, won't you?" a stranger said to Bass at that cluster of fires in the brigade camp where all of them had gathered.

"A purty sound," Titus replied, hearing the birds' calls fade across the water.

"If'n you think that's purty," Rowland said to the stranger as he strode up, "then you ain't never heard Jack play his fiddle."

The man whirled on Rowland. "One of your men has him a fiddle?"

"We do," Bass declared proudly.

A new stranger with a big red nose leaped up from the ground where he had been lying. "He can play it?"

"Damn if he can't," Rowland declared.

Bass nodded. "Plays so damned bad, it hurts more'n your ears when you're nursing a hangover!"

"Hey, Squeeg!" the man with the big red nose roared across the fire. "One of these here free men plays the fiddle!"

"Who's the one with the fiddle?" demanded a tall, barrel-chested man.

"I am," Hatcher volunteered, standing from his stump. "Jack Hatcher's the name."

"Mine's Brody."

Then Jack warned, "But I don't play for free."

"That's right," Solomon Fish agreed. "None of us play for free."

Brody wheeled around on Fish. "What's it you play?"

"Gimme a kettle an' a stick," Solomon said with a straight face.

"The hell with you," and Brody turned back to Hatcher. "You play for a drink, won'cha?"

"The devil hisself got a tail, don't he?"

The tall man took a wide, playful swing at Hatcher. "Go get your fiddle, coon! This bunch is half-froze for sweet music!"

That twilight as the sky grew dark and meat broiled on the end of sharpened sticks, spitted and sizzling over the leaping flames, Jack Hatcher returned with the scuffed and scratched, journey-weary oak-brown violin case.

"I'll be dogged!" some man quietly exclaimed. "He do have him a fiddle!"

Another voice asked across the fire, "Can he really play it?"

"Your toes'll be tapping in less time'n takes to lift a Blackfoot's hair!" Caleb Wood explained.

"By doggy! Lookee thar'!" one of them marveled as they all bent over Jack when he knelt beside one of the numerous fires. One at a time he took the narrow straps from their buckles until he slowly folded back the top to expose the violin.

Gently taking hold of it by the slim neck, Jack retrieved the instrument from the case and with his right hand took out the bow. Several wild strands of worn catgut sprayed in all directions as he stood. Scratch smiled at the sight of Hatcher turning slowly toward the others, his face beaming with crazed anticipation of this moment: rendezvous, his music, and that wild revelry he brought other men at these all-too-short summer gatherings.

With his bow hand he shoved an unruly shock of black hair from his eyes, then swept the bow around in a wide arc, describing the greater part of a circle.

"Stand back, boys!" he warned ominously. All of them obeyed, eagerly retreating to give him wide berth. "I gets to playing—Jack Hatcher needs him plenty of room!"

"Back, you dogs!" Caleb repeated, nudging a couple of men back a bit further.

How handsome Hatcher looked at that moment, Scratch thought. He was proud to be here, proud it was this very time in the seasons of man. These borning days in the mountains. Most proud to stand among these iron-mounted men, proud not only of this breed—but most proud to be one of those whom Jack called friend.

As Hatcher dragged that ragged bow across the strings slowly, tightening a peg here, another there, dragging the bow slowly again and again until he had each string to his liking—then suddenly kicked off with the wild, appealing strains of a high-pitched Kentucky reel . . . Bass felt a lump grow in his throat. Never could he remember Hatcher looking so happy, so content, so—complete. Not even when the man was well into his cups.

Scratch had only to gaze around the fire at the others, the greater of them strangers, to see just how true was the expression that music calmed the savage breast. Here were the roughest cut of mankind, every last one of them sitting in rapt attention, struck silent in unabashed awe, their eyes every bit as big as the smiles that creased their hairy faces. Slowly, step by measured step, Hatcher moved through them, in and out of the crowd as he swayed side to side with the tempo of his reel, circumscribing a sunwise circle around this largest of the fires. More figures appeared out of the deepening darkness to stand or kneel at the edge of the light thrown off by the leaping flames.

How it seemed Jack thrived on this hypnotic sway he could command over groups large and small when he began to caress the crying strings of his fiddle. Then that first song was done before any of them realized, and the summer night fell quiet for a matter of heartbeats before any of them stirred, or spoke, leaving it up to Caleb Wood and Titus Bass to slap their hands together.

In an instant the others were hooting as well, whistling and roaring their approval. They finally fell quiet when Jack jabbed the violin beneath his chin once more.

"There's one I'd like to play: a song that makes this child remember where we all come from, where it is we're all bound," Jack explained when all had grown completely still.

"Is it loud?" a man demanded.

"No," Solomon Fish roared angrily.

A new voice declared, "We want something loud we can stomp to!"

"You want the man to play for you or not?" Wood asked the assembly as Jack lowered the violin from beneath his chin.

"Play, goddammit!"

Another bellowed, "Just let 'im play anythin' he wants!"

They were shoving and shouldering one another now that he had them expectant. Hatcher knelt, starting to lay his violin back in its case.

"Hatcher!" cried Brody as he tore away from a knot of others. "I've got me likker for your gullet, but only if'n you play that fiddle o' your'n."

"Likker?" Jack asked, holding the violin suspended in midair over the battered case.

Isaac Simms lunged up a huge step into the merry dance of light. "Real lik . . . likker?"

"Traders' likker?" John Rowland wanted to know.

"Right here," Brody said. "Right now. So you gonna play?"

Standing once more with the violin and bow clutched in one hand, Jack drew a forearm across his mouth. "Fiddle playin's hard work, coon. Dry work too. What say ye: pour me a tin of that traders' likker, and I'll see what I can do to play a while for ye niggers."

While the others set to hollering in merriment, Brody turned to wave two men out of the dark at the edge of the grove where they had been waiting offstage with their prize: a small five-gallon keg constructed of pale oak staves clamped together with three dark iron bands. The pair hobbled forward with it slung between them until they reached an open spot near the biggest fire and eased the keg to the grass. Then, as Hatcher stuffed the fiddle beneath his chin, one of the pair stuck his hand into his shooting pouch and pulled out a wooden spout.

"Punch 'er!" Brody ordered.

And with that the trapper ripped the camp ax from his belt, using it to drive the spout into the bunghole. The keg was tapped.

As the notes from Hatcher's fiddle climbed higher still, and the fires spat sparks into the coal-cotton night, the men clamored to fill their cups with the clear grain alcohol David Jackson and Bill Sublette had freighted west from St. Louis after sealing up a small plug of tobacco and a handful of red peppers inside each diluted keg. While the plug had dissolved to give the potent brew the pale, imitation color of sour-mash whiskey, the peppers lent this Rocky Mountain libation its peculiar bite. Not that the pure grain liquor wouldn't already have the kick of an unrepentant Missouri mule.

Squeeg Brody was the first to shove his cup beneath the spout and the first to take a sip of the night's squeezin's. Smacking his lips with approval, he turned and parted the rest as he stepped back to the fire, cup held out, and stopped before Hatcher. Jack stopped playing immediately, looped the bow at the end of a finger on his left hand, and accepted the offered cup.

"Thankee, most kindly!" and he bowed graciously.

When Hatcher brought the cup to his lips, the rest of his outfit came to stand around him, all of them staring at that magical vessel, some unconsciously licking their lips, most of them gone wild-eyed with whiskey-thirst. Jack sipped in a manner most genteel, then brought the tin from his mouth and savored the taste of it a moment, eyes closed.

At last he declared, "That's some!" And with that, Jack threw back his head and went to guzzling the cup dry without drawing a breath.

Fish, Wood, Simms, and the others joined Bass in screeching like scalded alley cats as they leaped away from Hatcher, lunging for the keg themselves. Among the company men there were suddenly tussles, shoving, and some playful wrestling as they all jockeyed to be the next in line to have their cup filled.

"Keep on playing, Jack!" Titus hollered as he knelt with his tin beneath the spout that the keg keepers never had to turn off.

"Get me some more, then, dammit!" Jack flung his empty cup at Scratch, then resumed sawing the bow back and forth across the strings as he dipped and swayed, wriggling his hips, prancing about on his skinny legs, cavorting this way and that like the madman he was.

As the men had their cups filled and rose to return to fireside, each of them swayed or tapped a foot, some stomping harder than the others as they sipped or guzzled at their pint tin cups of grain. Among them a man plopped to the ground with a beaver skin still stretched tightly inside a willow hoop, crossing his legs before him. Snapping off a short piece of kindling a little bigger than two of his stubby fingers, he set about slapping the stiffened, dried flesh of the beaver hide with his make-do drumstick right in cadence with Hatcher's merry tune.

As soon as he heard the loud thumping, Jack himself turned and jigged over, giggling like a child on a lark as his head wobbled from side to side, humming and grunting with the music he was urging from the singing strings. At the drummer's side Hatcher began stomping one foot dramatically, lifting his leg into the air as high as he could before driving it down into the grass and the dust, over and over and over again.

Of a sudden a realization came over Titus as he stood with Hatcher's cup refilled. He knew that song. Hurrying over to Jack, he held the cup in front of the fiddle player's face. "Where you want me to set it down?"

"Don't set the son of a bitch down!" Hatcher snapped as he went right on playing and bobbing without missing a note.

"I ain't gonna hold on to it all night—"

"No ye ain't, Scratch. Here, pour it in my mouth."

"P-pour . . ."

"Right here in my mouth, dammit!"

The tall, skinny Hatcher bent a little at the waist, squatting slightly and contorting himself as he continued to play, lolling out his tongue as Scratch brought the big cup to his lips and slowly began to pour. He was amazed at just how little spilled out, what few drops dribbled down Jack's chin, off his whiskers, and onto the fiddle.

When Hatcher began to sputter, Bass pulled the cup back.

"Now ye set it down on the rocks," Jack instructed.

When he had that done, Bass straightened and yelled into Hatcher's ear over the loud screech of the fiddle, the laughter and hooting of the men, "I know me that song."

"Ye know this?" Jack shouted in reply. "Sing it with me."

"Cain't sing—"

"Sing it!"

"Told you—I ain't no good—"

"Sing, goddammit, Scratch. Ain't no one listening but me!"

Titus cleared his throat self-consciously, his eyes darting left, then right, nervous as a bride on her wedding night.

Hatcher prodded him, "Sing the song with my fiddle notes."

Reluctantly, Scratch began.

Down in the canebrake, close by the mill,
There lived a yellow girl, her name was Nancy Till.
She knew that I loved her, she knew it long.
I'm going to serenade her and I'll sing this song.

Titus never had thought he had a bad voice. Rather, he was merely shy of using it in the hearing of others. He couldn't remember the last time he had sung when folks were around. That is, except when his mam took him and his brothers and sister to Sunday meeting and they all were raised singing those songs settlers on the frontier memorized in early childhood. But this tune was something he had heard others sing around campfires those long-ago summer evenings at the Boone County Longhunter Fair, heard again while rocking on Amy Whistler's porch of an early autumn evening, heard even at his family's hearth before a merry fire as the long winter night deepened in the Kentucky forest around their farm.

This was a song not about church and ancient biblical characters in a time distant and dim, not a song about things religious and mysterious . . . no, at this moment he was singing a song about a subject most boys came to understand as they grew to manhood. A song about women—a matter even more mysterious than religion.

Come, love, come—the boat lies low.
She lies high and dry on the Ohio.
Come, love, come—won't you come along with me?
I'll take you on down to Tennessee.

"Damn, if ye don't have ye a fine voice after all, Titus Bass!" Hatcher roared over the cry of his fiddle.

Now he blushed, made all the more self-conscious as Hatcher kept right on scratching out the melody to the song. He took a drink to hide the flush of embarrassment.

"Gimme drink," Jack ordered.

When Bass took the cup from Hatcher's lips as the song sailed on, Jack asked, "What else ye know?"

"Songs?"

"Any other'ns?"

"A few I might recall, if'n I heard the tune."

"How 'bout this'un?"

And with that Hatcher immediately slipped into a new melody without lagging a note. After a few moments Bass realized he knew this one too. As he began to sing, Simms and Rowland came over with their cups; then others began to walk up, stopping to listen to Bass's singing.

I'm lonesome since I cross'd the hill,
And o'er the moor and valley;
Such heavy thoughts my heart do fill,
Since parting with my Sally.

How he had come to love this song in that first youthful blush of manhood—if not for the lament expressed by those melancholy words he had come to know by heart so many years ago, then he loved the song because of the delicate way the notes slid up and down the scale, all of them blended this night by the bow Jack Hatcher dragged across those taut gut strings.

I seek no more the fine and gay,
For each does but remind me
How swift the hours did pass away,
With the girl I've left behind me.

More company men came up now, falling quiet as they came to a stop in a loose ring around Hatcher and Bass, listening intently. From the looks on their hairy, tanned faces, the glistening in their eyes as the firelight danced across them all, it was plain to read that every last one of these men had someone special left far, far behind. Many miles, and perhaps many years, behind.

Oh, ne'er shall I forget the night,
The stars were bright above me,
And gently lent their sil'vry light,
When first she vow'd she loved me.

Hardened men, all—softened for only a moment as the wistful notes of the fiddle blended with the plaintive words of one who has left behind a loved one oft remembered in quiet moments around a crackling fire here deep in the heart of the mountains, where only a bold breed dared live.

But now I'm bound to Brighton camp,
Kind Heav'n, may favor find me,
And send me safely back again
To the girl I've left behind me.

For long moments the last note hung in the still, cool air of that summer eve at the south shore of Sweet Lake, men struck dumb by the sweetness of the song, by its mournful sentiment. Some of the trappers chose to put their cups to their lips, there behind the tins to blink their moist eyes clear; others chose to snort and hack, clearing throats clogged thick with sentiment.

Nathan Porter pierced the ring formed by others to shove a cup at Hatcher. "Drink, friend!" When Jack took the tin, Porter turned to Bass. "That was fine, the way you singed."

Embarrassed, Titus sipped at his liquor.

Porter asked Hatcher, "You only play the fiddle?"

"I been knowed to strum my hands across nigh anything with strings." He handed the empty cup back to Porter. "Why, ye got a song ye want me to play?"

"No, not no song," Porter replied. "But we got us this squeezebox belong't to one of the boys—"

"Squeezebox?" Hatcher interrupted.

"That's right," Porter stated, biting a lip before he went on. "Fella name of Ryman, went under this past spring to some of Bug's Boys."

Jack's eyes lit with a merry fever. "He had him a squeezebox?"

Nathan grinned hugely. "He did."

"Elbridge!" Jack bellowed over the heads of the others with a childish glee.

In a moment Gray emerged through the cordon of trappers knotted around Hatcher. "What you hail me for?"

"Porter here says he's got him a squeezebox."

"That true?" Gray demanded, wheeling on Nathan.

"Never thort to try it out," Porter explained. "Cain't none of us play it anyway."

Gray snagged one hand on Nathan's collar, fairly screaming in glee, "Get it for me!"

"Grimes! Get that squeezebox you been packing along!" Then Porter turned back to Gray and Hatcher. "You ain't bald-facing me, now, are you?"

"This nigger can play," Jack testified.

Porter seemed dubious. "So where's your own squeezebox if'n it's the true you can play?"

"Lost it," Gray began, his face gone morose. "More'n a year ago now. Damn, but it broke my heart."

"Just up and lost it, did you?"

Hatcher explained, "Didn't rightly lose it. Elbridge got it crushed a'neath a packhorse when the critter slipped off the trail and took it a slide down the mountainside."

"Had to shoot my packhorse," Gray added morosely. "And then I found that squeezebox smashed like fire kindling when I untied my packs to carry 'em back up the slope."

Hatcher leaned forward and whispered, still loud enough that most men could hear. "The man sat right down, then and there, with what was left of his squeezebox broke all apart in his two hands . . . and took to bawling like he was a babe."

"I loved that thing," Gray defended himself in a squeaky voice, hands fluttering helplessly before him.

"Here!" Grimes shouted as he burst back onto the scene.

"Gimme that!" Gray screeched as he lunged to his feet, reaching for the concertina, ripping it from the other man's hands. "Oh, J-jack—ain't she 'bout the purtiest sight you've ever see'd?" he gushed, running his fingers over the oiled wood of both octagonal end pieces and the wrinkled leather bellows.

Hatcher turned and winked at Bass. "Damn sight purtier'n that'un ye got smashed under a dead horse what took a tumble long ago."

"It is purtier, ain't it? It is for the truth of God!" Gray shouted in glee as he hitched up his leather britches before stuffing both hands inside the wide leather straps tacked to the wooden ends of the concertina.

Scratch whispered into Hatcher's ear, "He really can play?"

"This boy can play like the devil his own self," Jack replied. "Eegod! He's better'n me!"

Nodding in amazement, Bass turned to watch Elbridge Gray's merry face as the trapper slid up and down some scales, listening intently to the instrument's tuning. For the moment Scratch was amazed to find himself in the fastness of these mountains—where he had been put afoot, where he had lost three friends to the savages somewhere downriver, where he had been scalped and left for dead, then resurrected by Jack Hatcher and his buffalo-worshiping Shoshone—out here in the great beyond to find not only did Hatcher have along a fiddle he could play tolerable well . . . but now he discovered that Elbridge Gray could make all sorts of sweet sounds emerge from that hand-me-down concertina.

Here in this intractable wilderness, he had found music. Real music. Not just the dimming memories of tunes he carried inside his head, off-key and little used, whistled or hummed in tattered fragments as he went about his icy labors . . . but real, heart-stirring music.

" 'Hunters of Kentucky'!" Gray cried above the whooping and clapping of those crowding close.

"Get back, there—give us some room, dammit!" Hatcher demanded from the gathering as he dragged the bow long across the strings in prelude. Turning to Gray with as big a grin as Jack ever had on his face, he roared, "Do it, 'Bridge!"

Elbridge yanked the two ends of the concertina apart and began to stomp about in a tight circle, thumping the grassy ground with his floppy moccasins, his eyes squinted shut, fingers flying in a blur as he wheezed life into that instrument, squeezing sweet music from it, pumping the magic of song into the lonely lives of lonely men in a lonely wilderness.

With the second playing of the chorus, Caleb Wood started to sing at the exact moment Jack Hatcher raised his own croaking voice.

> We are a hardy, free-born race,
> Each man to fear a stranger;
> Whate'er the game we join in chase,
> Despoiling time and danger,
> And if a daring foe annoys,
> Whate'er his strength and forces,
> We'll show him that Kentucky boys
> Are alligator horses!
> Oh, Kentucky—the hunters of Kentucky!
> Oh, Kentucky—the hunters of Kentucky!

By then two of the company trappers had joined in to sing along with Wood and Hatcher. A few of the words Titus could remember, having learned it during his years in St. Louis following the War of 1812—each time recalling that autumn journey down the Ohio and Mississippi with Ebenezer Zane's riverboatmen. A stirring frontier ditty that recalled the courageous backwoodsmen who had stood with Andrew Jackson against the British at the mouth of the Mississippi.

I s'pose you've read it in the prints,
How Packenham attempted
To make old Hickory Jackson wince,
But soon his scheme repented;
For we, with rifles ready cock'd,
Thought such occasion lucky,
And soon around the gen'ral flock'd
The hunters of Kentucky!

Eventually a few more joined in, accompanied by the trapper beating his taut, willow-strung beaver hide.

You've heard, I s'pose, how New Orleans
Is fam'd for wealth and beauty,
There's girls of ev'ry hue it seems,
From snowy white to sooty.
So Packenham he made his brags,
If he in fight was lucky,
He'd have their girls and cotton bags,
In spite of old Kentucky!

Then Hatcher began to prance and bob right around Gray in a quick, whirling jig of a dance, both of them kicking up dust and bits of flying grass as their feet flew.

But Jackson he was wide-awake,
And was not scar'd at trifles,
For well he knew what aim we take
With our Kentucky rifles.
So he led us down to Cypress swamp,
The ground was low and mucky,
There stood John Bull in martial pomp
And here was old Kentucky!

Back to back the two weaved and swayed, then began to do-si-do around and around one another.

They found, at last, 'twas vain to fight,
Where lead was all the booty,
And so they wisely took to flight,
And left us all our beauty.
And now, if danger e'er annoys,
Remember what our trade is,

Just send for us Kentucky boys,
And we'll protect ye, ladies!

After two more songs one of the company men hollered, "Meat's cut. Time for the fire!"

Night had deepened while a handful of trappers had butchered loose, bloody slabs of venison and elk. The trappers surged forward now that the supper call was raised, knives in hand, waiting for their portion. Jabbed on the end of long, sharpened sticks, the rich red meat sizzled over the flames, juices dripping into the crackling fire. Men grunted and groaned with immense, feral satisfaction until their bellies could hold no more; then once again their thoughts turned to liquor. With pepper-laced alcohol warming their gullets, many of the men brought out pipes of clay or cob or briar burl, filling them with fragrant Kentucky burley, lighting them with twigs at the fireside before settling back against saddles and packs and bedrolls.

"I ain't heard a squeezebox played that good since I floated the Mississap," Scratch declared with pure appreciation as he eased down beside Elbridge Gray, his tin cup in one hand, a second helping of thick tenderloin impaled on the knife he clutched in the other.

Around a big bite of rare meat, Gray replied, "I'm rusty."

"If'n that's rusty," Nathan Porter snorted, "I'd sure as hang wanna hear you when you're oiled!"

Without benefit of fork, Bass held the slab of meat up, snatched hold of a bite-sized chunk between his teeth, then, holding the meat out from his lips, cut off that bite with the knife. Hardly the best of proper table manners, it was nonetheless an efficient way for a man to wolf down his fill of lean, juicy meat in less time than it would take most men to fill a pipe bowl and light it. While some ate more, and a few ate less, the standard fare in the mountains was two pounds of meat at a sitting.

Eventually Titus grew stuffed and well satisfied, ready at last for the coffee some of the company trappers had set to boil at the edge of the fires. As he wiped his knife off across the thigh of his buckskin legging, Bass turned to Elbridge. "You'll play some more for us tonight?"

Gray asked, "You're up to it, Jack?"

Hatcher replied, "Dog, if I ain't. When ye're done coffeeing yerself, Elbridge."

Minutes later the two were at it again, the potent liquor continuing to flow, both company trappers and the free men frolicking with total abandon: dancing, singing, beating on the bottoms of kettles or banging two sticks together in time to the music. They whirled in pairs or stomped about in a wild jig, knees pumping so high, they near grazed a man's own chin.

The night had ripened and the moon had risen before Jack shushed them all.

"Gonna play ye one last song," he told them as he stood wavering back and forth, clearly feeling his cups.

"It be a foot stomper?"

"No," Hatcher growled with a snap.

Someone else yelled, "I wanna foot stomper!"

"Shuddup," Caleb Wood grumped at the complainer.

"I allays play it," Hatcher explained as the group fell quiet. "Allays . . ."

Solomon quickly explained to the others, "It's his song, boys."

Quietly, Gray asked, "You want me play with you?"

Jack nodded. "Sure do. Sounds purtier with ye siding for me, Elbridge."

Hatcher led into the tune with a long, melancholy introduction. After a few bars Elbridge joined in, quietly, echoing Jack's plaintive notes like the answer a man would hear to a jay's call, the faint reply returning from the distance in those eastern woodlands where they had all been raised.

Closing his eyes as he dragged bow across strings, the tall, homely trapper began to sing to that hushed, respectful, firelit crowd.

> I'm just a poor, wayfaring stranger,
> Traveling through this world of woe.
> Yet there's no sickness, no toil, no danger
> In that bright land to which I go.
> I'm going there to see my father,
> Who's gone before me, no more to roam.
> I'm just going over Jordan.
> I'm only going over home.

For a moment Titus tore his eyes from Hatcher's expressive, lean, and melancholy face, glancing quickly about at the others, every last one of them spellbound by the sad, mournful strains of the two instruments, by the plaintive, feral call of Hatcher's voice as he climbed atop each new note.

> I know dark clouds will gather round me,
> I know my way is rough and steep.
> Yet beautiful fields lie just before me,
> Where God's redeemed their vigils keep.
> I'm going there to see my mother,
> She said she'd meet me when I come.
> I'm just going over Jordan.
> I'm only going over home.

One by one the ghostly wisps of people from his past slipped through his mind as Jack and Elbridge weaved their magic spell in that firelit darkness. A father and mother left behind in Kentucky what seemed a lifetime ago. Good men like Ebenezer Zane and Isaac Washburn, dead well before their time. Billy and Silas, and even Bud Tuttle too—those three who had come into Bass's life, then gone to their downriver deaths.

Death so sudden in this wilderness. A man's end come so in the blink of an eye on this unspeakable frontier. Every day was to be savored and cherished and fiercely embraced for all it was worth—a fact that every last one of these few gathered at the fire understood, knowing theirs would not be a Christian burial. No, none of these was the sort of man forever to lie at rest beneath some carved stone marker where family and friends could come to visit. Instead, theirs would be anonymous graves, an unheralded passing . . . their only memorial the glory of their having lived out their roster of days in the utter ecstasy of freedom.

> *I'll soon be free of every trial,*
> *My body will sleep in the churchyard.*
> *I'll drop the cross of self-denial,*
> *And enter on my great reward.*
> *I'm going there to see my brothers,*
> *Who've gone before me one by one.*
> *I'm just going over Jordan.*
> *I'm only going over home.*

To die where the winter snows would lie deep in seasons still in the womb of time, their bones gnawed by predators, scattered to bleach below endless suns . . . to sleep out eternity where only the wind would come to sing in whisper over this place of final rest.

FOUR

By the time Jack Hatcher's bunch began to straggle back to their bowers and bedrolls across the creek from the grove where the company men had raised their camp, a strip of sky along the eastern horizon had begun to relinquish its lampblack, noticeably graying. Dawn was not far behind.

As he stumbled along, Scratch's head throbbed, tender as a red welt. Barely able to prop his eyes open any more than snaky slits, his toes groped their way through the grass and brush. Scattered among the outfit's packs and belongings, he finally located his blankets and lone buffalo robe. Sinking to the ground, Bass rolled onto his side and dragged the old Shoshone rawhide-bound saddle toward him to prop beneath his head. As he lay back upon it, the saddle's wooden frame momentarily creaked beneath the weight of his shoulders, then suddenly split apart and collapsed— smacking his head against the hard ground and the saddle's sideboards.

"What in hell are you about over there?" John Rowland demanded as he sat up, a disheveled sight to behold. He had come back to his blankets some time before the others.

Groaning as he gently rubbed the side of his skull with two fingertips, Bass slowly sat up. Struggling to catch his breath against the hammer pounding inside his brain, he carefully adjusted the greasy, sweat-salted blue bandanna he tied over the top of his head not only to keep his long hair out of his eyes but to protect that bare patch of exposed cranium where he had lost his hair to an Arapaho horse thief.

"Shit," Caleb Wood grumbled as he stretched himself out once more, "Scratch cain't even lay down quietlike."

Bass held up the chewed wooden frame pieces. "My goddamned saddle come apart on me!"

"Come apart?" Hatcher repeated in disbelief as he rolled onto his knees and crabbed over to Bass's blanket.

"Look at it!" Titus shrieked in horror as he ran fingers over the ruin of his old saddle.

"I'll be go to hell, boys!" Jack cried. "Come see for yer own selves!"

"See what?" Kinkead asked as he loomed over them.

"Right there," Hatcher instructed. "See where the damned critters been eatin' at it."

"C-critters?" Titus squawled. "What critters?"

Hatcher's eyes narrowed, looking over their encampment. "Go see to yer outfits, boys. Likely Scratch ain't the only one chewed up."

"Critters?" Bass repeated.

Hatcher watched the others scurry off to their own belongings before he turned back to Titus. "Wolves, more'n likely."

"Wolves done this?" he asked, letting the ruined saddle spill from his hands.

"That ain't the least of it, I'd wager," Jack replied, nodding at the rest of Bass's gear.

"Damn," Scratch groaned as he turned to follow Hatcher's eyes, discovering the mauled tatters of his buffalo-rawhide lariat, the scattered remnants of bridle, hackamore, and cinch, and even the remains of a leather-bound gourd canteen, all of it chewed into hardly recognizable shreds.

"More'n one of 'em done this, Jack!" Isaac Simms called out.

"Likely so," Hatcher echoed. "They come in here in a pack."

Titus shook his head as he stared at the firelit debris. "Wolves dare come this close to a man?"

"Hell," Caleb growled, "likely was a pack don't know enough to fear a two-legged man yet, Scratch."

"Cale's right," Simms added. "Most wolf packs ain't had enough run-ins with men to be scar't off from us."

"Chances be this pack hasn't run across any big guns neither," Hatcher explained.

"So them damned dogs just come waltzin' in here?" Bass whined. "While'st we was off for supper?"

Rowland roared with laughter, slapping a knee. "And the critters had 'em their supper on your outfit!"

"Lookit all they chewed, Jack," Simms clucked, wagging his head sympathetically.

"Bass ain't got him near nothing left what don't need some fixin'," Rufus Graham declared.

"In a bad way too," Titus grumped as he sat there in the midst of what debris remained of his leather tack and gear.

Hatcher knelt beside him. "Where's yer pouch?"

"Jehoshaphat!" Bass swore as he whirled in a crouch, lunging for the tight roll of his extra blanket where he had secured his rifle and shooting bag before they had strolled over to the supper fires—for no other reason than to guard them from a quick-moving thunderstorm while they were gone from their camp. Yanking at the edges of the blanket, he rolled the weapon free, quickly inspecting the strap and bag, the narrow thongs securing the two powder horns to the strap, finding no damage.

"Ye're a lucky man," Hatcher intoned.

"Ain't that the solemn truth," Kinkead whimpered. "Look how they got to mine." He held up what little remained of his bag, spare balls and a ball screw, his bullet mold spilling from the huge, ragged hole gaping in what Matthew had left of his chewed pouch.

"My only pair of spare mocs are gone," Simms groaned as he picked through his few belongings.

Graham held up his old smoothbore, showing the others those vivid teeth marks deeply scored up and down the shrunken, translucent rawhide wrap where in a time past he had repaired the cracked, weakened wood along the wrist of the stock. "They even tried eatin' on this here. Just 'cause it's leather."

"Shit," Bass said as he gazed round at the wolf pack's destruction the others held up for view. "Maybeso this means we ought'n have a man stay in camp all the time, Jack."

"Hell," the outfit's leader snorted, "come ronnyvoo, I don't know a single man jack of these here yahoos be willing to stay ahin't while the rest of us go traipsin' off to have us whiskey, women, and song!"

"Not me!" Wood bellowed. "You ain't leavin' me behin't!"

"Not me neither!" Rowland said. "You each watch over your own outfits!"

Hatcher turned back to Bass. "See. Any other time of the year, a man be willing to stay back to camp for the rest. Be it trapping time, fall or spring—a man don't mind taking his turn hanging back at a trappin' camp."

"Maybeso we ought'n go cross the creek there," Titus said, pointing. "Go yonder there with them company boys and put our camp with them. That way we ain't gotta worry 'bout—"

"We don't have to move camp," Hatcher interrupted.

Bass couldn't believe what he had heard. Did these lean and experienced trappers mean to tell him they were willing to take the chances of wild creatures slipping into their abandoned camp, to chew on anything and everything made of leather again in the future?

"S-so you're telling me we sit and wait for these here wolves to come back and ruin some more?"

As straight-faced as he could say it, Jack stepped up to Scratch and declared, "No . . . we pee."

Titus wasn't sure he'd heard Hatcher clearly. "Did you say . . . p-pee?"

"Pee. Piss. Spray. Same thing, Scratch."

"P-pee?" Bass noticed most of the others smiling, some with hands over their mouths, trying to suppress their guffaws.

"Eegod!" Jack roared. "So I gotta show ye how to pee now?"

Hatcher whirled on his heel and stepped away, raising the tail of his long cotton shirt and tugging aside the blanket breechclout as he went purposefully to the bushes at the north end of their camp. Titus stood rooted to the spot, unsure just what he was to do.

"G'won," Caleb instructed, flinging a hand in Jack's direction. "Rest of us be right behin't you."

Suspicious that he was having his leg pulled but good, Scratch reluctantly followed in Hatcher's steps, stopping nearby as the outfit's leader pulled out his penis and began to spray the base of the thick brush with urine as he sidestepped to his left, still spraying a thin stream in the cool dawn air.

"What the hell you peein' for?"

Hatcher inched away from Bass, doing his best to control the amount of urine he sprayed on the brush, slowly sidling in a wide arc at the far edge of their encampment. "Keeps the wolves away."

Bass laughed with how ridiculous that sounded. But the moment he began, he noticed that no one else was laughing with him. "How a li'l bit of your piss gonna keep wolves away?"

"Wolf and other dog critters piss here and there to lay out their own ground," Jack explained as he moved off a bit farther. "They tell others of their own kind what belongs to them, and what don't."

"That means when we spray round our camp," Simms declared, "chances are the wolves won't come in to bother our gear and truck."

Wagging his head, Bass said, "But Hatcher ain't got him enough pee to wet clear round this here camp."

Jack stood shaking his penis, empty. "Maybe not—but, Caleb, come on up aside me and mark our camp from here."

Wood stepped up, pulling at the antler buttons on the front of his leather britches to begin peeing right where Hatcher had left off. As Titus watched in amazement, the others began roaring with laughter, hopping drunkenly toward the bushes, where they each took their turn at this duty, circumscribing their camp with the smell of urine, marking off their territory, staking it out as if to declare to the wolves that this was a boundary not to be crossed.

"Ain't no little bit of your piss gonna make no never mind to no wolf pack," Scratch snorted cynically as he watched the other eight having themselves far too much fun for him to take this seriously.

"Ye can go piss yer likker away anywhere ye want, Scratch," Hatcher stated. "Or ye can piss where it just might do all of us some good."

"Awright—you had your fun with me," Bass replied lamely. "I'm certain you boys just laughing inside on my count."

"I'm dead to rights serious," Jack argued.

"This is one critter to another," Caleb declared.

"Wolf'll stay away," Solomon agreed. "I seen it my own self."

Kinkead held up the ragged remains of his shooting pouch. "Wish't we'd done it afore we went off to supper. Where 'm I gonna get me 'nother bag now?"

"If'n there ain't one to trade off these company fellers," Rowland said, "we make you a new one, Matthew."

Hatcher turned to Bass as the edge of the sun broke over the nearby hills, spreading day's light into the valley. "Ye gonna pee . . . or ye gonna stand there gawkin' at me like a idjit?"

With a gust of easy laughter, Scratch stepped away toward the far bushes, pulling aside his breechclout as he said, "I'll take my turn at it, Jack Hatcher. Then I'm sleeping out the day."

A damned good idea that had been: to sleep out the day there in the shade of their grove after last night's drinking and raucous carousing at the brigade fire.

But near midday another of the company's brigades hoved into sight along the eastern hills, the noise and excitement electrifying the valley. Among them rode the merry Daniel Potts.

"It's been two year since last I saw you," Bass cried with joy as Potts unhorsed himself among the early arrivals.

"That really you, Titus Bass?"

"Damn if it ain't, Daniel."

"Thort you might'n gone under, friend."

"Came close," Scratch replied, tapping a finger against the taut blue cloth tied over his head. " 'Rapahos raised some hair an' left me for dead."

"But you're standing here flapping your ugly mug just to show me you pulled through!"

"Damn right I pulled through, Daniel!" Scratch bellowed. "I been working on me a thirst for two year now . . . but we come riding in here to hear the traders's already been out here and gone!"

"We'uns got our supplies back to early spring our own selves," Potts explained, his merry eyes twinkling. " 'Stead of you doing without come time for the fall hunt, I'll see what I can spare you."

"No, I don't want you to go short of nothing—"

Daniel interrupted, "I won't, Scratch. But likewise I won't see no friend of mine go short neither. Not when I can help it."

Craning his neck here and there, Bass glanced over the rest of the new arrivals. "Where's that dandy goes by the name of Jim Beckwith was with you two year ago?"

"He ain't with us—"

"Beckwith go under?" Titus asked gravely.

"Nawww," Potts replied. "He's riding with 'nother brigade this spring. Are you here with them three what looked down their noses at Negra Jim?"

Wagging his head, Bass explained, "Them three . . . they went under."

"How?"

"Rubbed out somewhere's on the Yallerstone."

Potts's face went sad as he said dolefully, "Likely Siouxs they were, Scratch. Maybeso Ree got 'em."

"Let's pull your truck off your horse and get it over to the shade, Daniel Potts!" Titus suggested, wanting nothing more than to shake off the gray cloud brought him by that remembrance of those three. "You're the child what's got two year of stories to catch me up on!"

Late that afternoon the growing encampment of white trappers witnessed the arrival of a large band of Flathead who announced that a sizable party of Americans would likely be reaching them sometime the following morning, as they were traveling not all that far behind the migrating village. By sunset the southwestern sky was dippled with the concentric swirls of rope-bound lodgepoles over which the women had stretched their smoked buffalo hides. Bright fires glowed at twilight outside each lodge as supper was prepared, a time when the young men were the first to venture into the trapper camp.

"They're a pretty people, don'cha think?" Potts asked as he settled in beside Bass at a large fire.

"Handsome warriors they make, that they do."

Invited to sit around the fires, the Flathead men joined the Americans for supper, then for many cups of hot coffee and much smoking of the pipes that made the circles time and again. And finally the old men showed up out of the darkness, two of them dragging a large drum between them. Setting it down within the firelight's glow, the two squatted, quickly joined by others who likewise sat cross-legged and removed sturdy drumsticks from their belts.

One coarsely wrinkled man began to sing at the first thump of the huge drum, the others joining in as the songs and the celebration and the night went on.

It was near dawn that second morning when Bass and some of the others dragged back to their camp across the creek. He stumbled forward to his knees on the bedding, more weary than he could remember being in a long, long time. Then he collapsed onto the blankets and let out a long sigh.

"Wolves come back an' chew up anything else of yer'n, Titus Bass?" Hatcher called out as his head sank back against his saddle.

"Not that I see, Jack."

Hatcher chuckled. "Damn right they didn't."

Then Caleb said, "And they won't neither—not with us peein' a line round our camp the way we done."

"That what kept the wolves away from our plunder, eh?" Scratch asked.

"One of these days, maybeso ye'll believe," Jack advised as he rolled onto a shoulder and let out a contented sigh.

"Right now all I wanna believe in is sleep," Bass replied. "I got cut out of my sleep yesterday and again last night—so I'm aiming to sleep right on through to sundown today."

From across their small camp Kinkead asked, "What 'bout the wolves slipping in to chew on your possibles while you're napping, Scratch?"

"To hell with wolves. Long as the sonsabitches don't gnaw on me, I'm sleeping right on through ever'thing."

But undisturbed they were not to remain.

"Blackfoot to the north!"

It was near midmorning on that third day when the distant voice bellowing the terrible news split into Bass's hazy dreaming there in a patch of shade where the breeze rustled the brush overhead.

"Blackfoot got some of our boys pinned down!"

His mind still numbed with half-baked, interrupted sleep, Bass rolled off his hip and onto his knees, blinking against the glare of bright summer light, trying to focus on the middistance where two horsemen were approaching out of the north, their lathered animals racing along the eastern side of the lake as they bellowed their warning.

Reluctantly, he joined the rest as they quickly splashed across the stream to stand with the company men as the two riders reined up in a shower of dust and grass clods. Both of them had stripped to the waist in the heat, tying black silk bandannas around their heads.

Some man on foot called out, "Damn if we didn't take you for Injuns at first!"

One of the riders gulped, saying, "We throwed off our clothes to look the Injun when we rode through the Blackfoots what got us surrounded."

"Who you fellers with?" Porter demanded as he lunged up to seize hold on one of the reins.

Brody answered for the dry-mouthed riders, "He's with Campbell!"

Someone hollered, "Bob Campbell's bunch?"

Brody explained to the anxious group, "Campbell's brigade was up to Flathead country last winter." Then he squinted into the bright light, staring right up at the breathless rider. "You boys taken any dead or wounded?"

Wagging his head, the second rider answered, "Don't rightly know. There was some thirty of us to start with, I s'pose. Campbell sent us riding soon as we was jumped."

"You sartin they're really Blackfoot?" a man cried out.

"Nary a man in this company don't know him Blackfoot from Digger!" someone shouted angrily. "Bob Campbell says they're Blackfoot, then they're Blackfoot, by God!"

"Where?"

The first rider pointed north. "Fifteen mile, maybe."

"That's a long ride," Porter replied. "A hard one at full-out too."

Brody nodded. "Best we get started, boys! Let's leave back a dozen or so to stay with camp and the extra animals."

"Bring in them horses and mules what we ain't riding!" Porter ordered.

Brody turned, his eyes scanning the crowd until he found Mad Jack. "Hatcher! Your bunch planning on throwing in for this fight?"

"Don't see why not," Jack responded. "We ain't the kind to let Blackfoot have their way with no American. To hell with Bug's Boys!"

An instant and spontaneous roar erupted from the seventy-some trappers knotted around those two weary riders and played-out horses.

Bass pushed through the throng to reach the knee of one of the horsemen, saying, "Get yourself down and watered. We'll bring you up a fresh horse afore we're ready to ride out."

"You comin' with us, Titus Bass?"

Turning, Scratch found Daniel Potts headed his way, followed by a handful of familiar faces. "You boys riding out to the fight?"

"No booshway gonna order me to stay back to camp and nursemaid no cavvyyard when there's Blackfeets to fight! Damn right I'm going!"

Bass cheered, "I'll ride with you."

"Be quick about it," Daniel ordered. "I don't want the others to have the jump on us!"

Splashing his way across the creek and sprinting into the meadow, Bass hurriedly freed the long halter rope from the iron picket pin he had driven into the ground near their camp, leaped atop the pony's bare back, and loped it back to his blanket shelter at an urgent trot. After dropping his shooting pouch and horns over his right shoulder, then gathering up his pistol and the fullstock Derringer rifle, Scratch vaulted onto the warm, bare backbone of his saddle horse. This time he would ride far and hard without that secondhand

Shoshone snare saddle. Without stirrups, he kicked his heels into the pony's ribs.

"Hep! Hep-hawww!"

By the time the first of the trappers were streaming north along the eastern shore of Sweet Lake, Flathead warriors were mounting up at the edge of their village. Women and children darted here and there, bringing their men shields and bows and quivers filled with war arrows. Everywhere dogs were underfoot, barking and howling, somehow aware of the importance of this moment as the Flathead men quickly completed their personal medicine, got themselves painted and dressed for battle, then sprinted off to fight their ancient enemies.

What a sight that determined cavalcade made that summer morning! Beneath a brilliant sun the colors seemed all the brighter in the flash of wind-borne feathers and scalp locks and earth paint, the showy glint of old smooth-bore muskets and shiny brass tomahawks and fur-wrapped stone war clubs waved high beside those long coup-sticks held aloft in the mad gallop just as any army would carry its hard-won banners before them as it rode against its foe.

Mile after mile Scratch raced at the head of a growing vee of horsemen as more trappers burst out of camp, mingling with the mounted Flathead warriors, the widening parade streaming behind Bass and Potts leading the rest at the arrow's tip. Here and there the land rose gently, then fell again until they reached the bottom of a draw, where they had to leap their horses over each narrow creek feeding the long, narrow lake from the hills beyond. After urging all they could out of their horses for more than the hour it took them to cover the fifteen miles, those at the head of the cavalcade heard the first of the gunshots in the distance.

And moments later the rescuers galloping in heard the first war cries of the Blackfoot raiders.

As they reached the top of a gentle rise, the low plain spread out before them: less than a mile away the scene was easy to read. The Blackfoot already had possession of most of the trappers' horses and mules, having driven them to the northwest, off toward the shore of the lake where the herd was pro-tected by a handful of their warriors. On their broad backs were still lashed the fat packs of beaver—the fruits of two long, lonely seasons of backbreaking labor by Robert Campbell's brigade.

The rest of the attackers clearly had the white men surrounded in a small cluster of rocks. It was hard for Bass to tell just how many men were hunkered down within that tightening ring he could see was drawing closer and closer.

Suddenly a lone warrior stood up in the grass, waving his arms wildly, pointing at the middistance. He had spotted the first few rescuers: more white men joined by Flathead horsemen.

One by one more than a hundred warriors quickly bristled from the brush and grass, beginning to sprint in an effort to meet boldly the new assault showing itself on that hilltop Bass had just abandoned as he and the first riders raced down the slope toward the raiders, toward that small ring of boulders and stunted brush where Bob Campbell's men fought for their hides.

"Ride right through 'em?" Potts hollered at Titus.

With tears streaming from his eyes as the dry wind whipped them both in the face, Scratch glanced behind him at the dozen or so others, then nodded. "Don't you dare pull back on that rein as we shoot through, Daniel!"

"Whooeee!"

"Heya!" Bass hollered himself at the sudden new surge of adrenaline warming his veins, kicking the tired horse in the ribs, leaning forward as they bounded over the tall grass, heading straight for the enemy, who began to clot together to form a phalanx on foot that was inching its way toward these new targets.

Scratch felt his empty stomach knot as more and more of the warriors joined the numbers already headed their way. His head pounded with more than the lack of sleep, more than a hangover from the potent grain alcohol, more than the hammering of the last hour's race to lift this siege.

As he neared that wall of Blackfoot, Bass spotted the dark carcasses beyond the warriors in the tall grass—the bodies of dead horses lying here and there around those rocks where the trappers had just spotted the approach of their rescuers. Closer and closer he and Potts sprinted for the Blackfoot line . . . close enough now to hear their shrill war cries, close enough to hear the whooping of the trappers whose mouths O'ed in celebration as the first of them stood within their rocks, waving rifles and broad-brimmed hats.

Less than eighty yards remained between Bass and the Blackfoot.

A ball whined past, splitting the air between him and Potts. Then a flying covey of arrows arched out of the grass, bursting from half a hundred bows, speeding across the stainless blue of the summer sky, quickly reaching their zenith before they began to fall.

Fifty yards from the enemy.

The bowmen were many, but the horsemen were quicker. They were already ahead of those first arrows, which hissed into the grass at their heels.

No more than twenty yards remained as Bass leaned forward, pressing himself against the pony's withers, laying his sunburned cheek along the damp, lathered neck, his toes digging into the animal's ribs.

Ten yards . . . a matter of two swift strides.

And Bass was there before them—close enough to see paint and color and dark eyes beneath the greased hair tied up in a provocative challenge to raise a scalp lock.

Swinging clubs and bows and an old fusee, more than eight surged toward him as he burst into their midst. The frightened pony sidestepped, then lunged forward again as the warriors swung and leaped and cried out to frighten the animal, to scare their enemy. First one bow, then a stone club, smacked his legs, raked along the horse's ribs, grazed along its bobbing neck as he shot past.

Suddenly Scratch became aware that he had plunged into the most dangerous moments of their dash through the enemy's lines.

He twisted to look over his shoulder, beyond the pony's flying tail. More than half of the Blackfoot had turned, stringing arrows to shoot at him and Potts and those first few Flathead warriors, to shoot them in the back at the moment they streamed through the enemy phalanx.

"Watch your backside!" Bass screamed, the words ripped from his mouth as the riders closed on the rocky fortress.

"Damned buggers!" Potts growled. "Gonna shoot us in the ass!"

Behind them streamed more than sixty mounted trappers, both free and company men. At least that many Flathead horsemen were mixed in among them as they galloped toward the Blackfoot, who were quickly realizing that the odds were beginning to tip from their favor. In the rocks ahead, black forms became men, and faces took shape beneath the shadow of hats. Sounds became words: cries of joy and shouts of challenge flung back now at the enemy.

As a handful of arrows clattered around them, Bass and Potts crossed the last few yards as three of the besieged trappers emerged from the rocks, hollering, reaching for the horses, eager to drag the horsemen to the ground and back to the safety of their tiny fortress.

"Potts!" a tall, full-faced man bellowed as he dashed up. His left cheek was bleeding, having been grazed by the stone tip of a war arrow. "Is that really you, Potts?"

"Campbell?"

"Aye—it's me, lad!" the brigade leader shouted, jumping forward to seize Potts in both arms and pound him soundly about the shoulders.

"Good to see you standing, Booshway!"

"They'd had us all eventually," Campbell said gravely as he stepped back toward the rocks. "Had all of you not shown up."

Bass agreed as he stepped up. "If ronnyvoo wasn't close—you'd all gone under."

Then Scratch knelt suddenly, peering about him at that scene within the crude oval of rocks. More than a handful of half-breed children, at least that many Indian women, all huddled next to some of the white trappers as they helped their men reload weapons, these stoic mothers preparing to sell their lives dearly come a final assault on that narrow compound. Bass's eyes stopped here and there, looking over the bodies sprawled on the ground within the fortress. Three of the dead had a blanket, a hat, or their own leather shirt pulled over their faces. At least three more were having their wounds attended to by comrades who washed off blood with water dipped from the trickle of a spring that issued within the rocks. A few others firmly held bloody compresses against their bright, bleeding injuries.

"W-would I know . . ." Then Daniel took a deep breath before gesturing at the dead and continued quietly, "Do I know any of these?"

With a doleful cloud passing over his face, Campbell replied, "You know every one of them, Potts."

Immediately sinking to his knees, Daniel dragged back the edge of a greasy blanket, stared a moment at the familiar face, then gently replaced the blanket. His shoulders quaking in grief and rage, he suddenly tore at the bloody grass with both hands as a guttural cry burst from his throat.

"Damn these thievin' bastards!" he roared.

Bass stepped up to stand beside the man, placing a hand on his trembling shoulder.

"Fools they were!" Daniel's voice cracked. "Just like me, Scratch! Fools just like me for coming out here where there ain't no God to watch over a man!"

"Damn right, Potts," one of the wounded said in a small voice grown weak from loss of blood. He had a bandage wrapped around his head, the bloody cloth covering one eye and all but concealing half his face.

"That . . . that you, Scott?"

Hiram Scott nodded. "God don't dare come out this side of the Missouri, Potts."

Daniel looked up, eyes imploring as his clenched fists slowly opened, allowing the broken blades of bloody grass to spill from them. "I ain't staying here no more, Cap'n Campbell."

The brigade leader protested, "We get these Blackfoot run off, we're moving on to rendezvous—"

"I don't mean staying to ronnyvoo, dammit!" Potts spat to interrupt. "I ain't staying out here in this country!"

Campbell started, "It's natural for a man to be bitter—"

"God don't look down from heaven on this country!" Potts shrieked. "Not for no white man, He don't!"

On the ground the wounded Scott agreed, "Not a man gonna convince me God's looking down on this land . . . this place fit only for the devil's kind!"

Raising his face toward the sky, Potts roared in grief, "Man crosses the Missouri an' leaves the settlements behind—there ain't no angels watching his back then, and there ain't no God to drive off Satan's whelps clear away out here!"

"Look here around you, boys—there, there . . . and there. Look and you'll see the proof of it." Scott winced in pain as he straightened, then continued, "No God in this sky out here! No God a'tall!"

Bass watched the tears stream down the wounded trapper's bloody face as he went to sobbing, quietly.

Why some were spared, and others heard their number called—Bass figured he would never know. Likely this was something only someone like his mother could answer, if not one of those circuit-riding preachers. No reason and no rhyme could he put to it . . . yet one thing was for certain: out here he had discovered that the choices were simpler and more sharply drawn than at any time in his life. And out here in this unforgiving wilderness, the consequences became all the more sudden and stark for those who chose to chance fate beneath this seamless dome of endless sky.

"Lookit 'em!" a man shouted nearby. "Bug's Boys turning tail!"

In the middistance gunfire rattled as the onrushing horsemen fired their rifles at the retreating Blackfoot raiders, white man and Flathead alike, all whooping the moment they shot past the rocky fortress to the cheers of Campbell's survivors.

"I see you brought us reinforcements, Titus Bass!"

Bass turned at the distantly familiar drawl to the voice, finding the tall, handsome mulatto stepping up through the tall grass, gunpowder smudged across his mud-colored face, that black shoulder-length hair tightly braided and wrapped in trade ribbon.

Titus asked, "Beckwith?"

"None other!" and he held out his hand. "Thought you was dead when we didn't see you last summer."

"Some tried!" Bass roared as he pumped the arm of that Virginia-born son of a white planter and a Negress that planter eventually married before moving his family to frontier Missouri. "Where you been in this fight, Jim? Laying low?"

"Right out there in the grass," Beckwith explained, and pointed. "Didn't like the feel of these here rocks. Never felt easy about being closed up in a fight. Always figure to have me a way out."

"Look at 'em!" Campbell declared loudly as he waved both arms at the passing horsemen. "Look at all those lovely white faces."

Scratch reminded, "Flathead too!"

"See how them devil's sons scamper!" cried another man, pointing at the retreating warriors.

At that moment the enemy had begun their wholesale retreat from the fight, able to see they were soon to be on the losing side. Easy to realize that now was the time to get away with their stolen plunder and captured horses while they could.

"Sonsabitches got their hands on more than five thousand dollars in beaver!" Campbell fumed as he angrily dragged some fingers across the ooz-ing cheek wound.

A clerk stepped up and added, "And two mules with some of our trade goods too, Cap'n!"

Robert Campbell whirled on him, glowering. "How many horses they get?"

"They're running off with more'n forty head."

"Damn their black hearts!" Campbell cursed.

Then, as if to rally his own flagging spirits, the brigade leader quickly tore the shapeless hat from his head and waved it aloft at the last of the rescuers racing their way, those horsemen shooting past the little fortress like a spring torrent. Campbell joined the rest in clambering atop the low rocks to wave and whoop and whistle as the last of the Blackfoot hurriedly mounted and started to tear away with their booty, driving the brigade's horses and mules before them.

"When'd they hit you?" asked one of the horsemen who had circled back, bringing his horse to a halt just outside the rocks.

"Not long after we put to the trail this morning," Campbell explained. "All told, must've been more than two hundred of 'em dogging our backtrail for the last day or so."

"Likely picked up your scent day before yestiddy."

Nearby, Hiram Scott added, "We made a run for it to get this far."

"Lucky these rocks were here when we needed 'em," Campbell added. "I spotted these willows and made for 'em. Then we found the spring. At least we'd have water. So I prepared the men for a long siege of it."

The rider glanced over the dead and wounded. "You kill any of 'em your own selves?"

"Maybe a half dozen," Campbell declared. "Knocked a bunch out of the saddle, but the others come in and rode off with every bastard we knocked off a pony."

Titus turned back to say, "Wouldn't have mattered to have you water in here, Booshway. Looks to be they was whittling your side down a mite fast."

After a long sigh Campbell blinked his eyes as if they smarted and said, "When I sent the riders out, we were running low on powder and ball. Truth be, we were all preparing for the worst. If these Blackfoot had jumped us any farther from your camp—we'd been finished but good."

"Not a chance you'd hung on again' that many," the rider said as he wheeled his horse about, giving it the heels to speed away after the rest of those chasing the retreating raiders.

Beckwith stepped up to Campbell. "There's another one of our dead out in the grass. I made sure none of them Blackfeet got close enough to scalp him."

"I know," the brigade leader replied. "It's Boldeau—a damned good cook he was too." He nodded toward one of the women. "His Flathead wife made it in on the run, but Louis was just too old, just too slow. I watched him drop—praying he was playing rabbit."

"His woman's gotta grieve proper, in the way of her own people," Bass said, turning to Beckwith. "Why'n't you take her to the man's body, Jim."

With a nod the mulatto stepped over to the Flathead woman and made sign for her to follow him. Bass watched them scramble over the rocks and hurry out through the tall grass.

"Let's get what horses we have left and see how best to get our wounded and dead into camp," Campbell ordered, directing some of the men to bring up the few horses they still possessed. He turned to Bass. "How far to camp?"

At the moment Titus opened his mouth to speak, the Flathead woman raised a mournful wail from the prairie. With the hair prickling on the back of his neck, Scratch turned to see her crumple down to her knees, bending over the body of Louis Boldeau. There she rocked back and forth as Beckwith stood nearby, his hat held in both hands. For the life of him, Bass didn't know what was a more pitiful sight: Potts mourning over the body of an old friend, or the squaw keening over the body of her man.

"Not far, Booshway," Bass finally answered, tearing his eyes from the woman yanking her knife from its scabbard, dragging it across the first clump of hair she held out in the other hand as she hacked it from her head. This she held up toward the sky, slowly opening her left hand to let that hair spill into the wind. "You ain't far from camp now."

Then, as the other survivors began to pick their way out of the rocks, Scratch turned his face to gaze at the sky so immense overhead, wondering— wondering just how far a man was from God out here now.

"Mind my word, boys: I ain't gonna pay these scalpin' prices to no man, no booshway, no goddamned company!"

Scratch stepped up to the outer fringe of that gathering of free trappers who were loosely circled around a bareheaded older man intently haranguing the swelling crowd beneath a hot summer sun that late morning four days after their scrap with the Blackfeet.

"Damn the mountain prices!" someone called from the crowd.

"But that's just what they are!" Jack Hatcher bellowed as Bass stopped at his elbow. "These here are mountain prices, Glass—and a free man pays or a free man don't dance!"

"You . . . you say his name is Glass?" Scratch asked in a whisper.

From the side of his mouth, Hatcher said with an admiring grin, "Yep. Glass be that ol' wolf-bait's name."

Turning and taking a step closer to Mad Jack, Glass grumbled, "I'll wager you're the kind what figgers it's fair for the traders to charge us twice or three times what things is wuth just for 'em bringing the goods all the way out here to us, eh?"

"Every man's entitled to have hisself paid for his labor," Jack argued. "Even a damned double-backed, gobble-necked trader!"

Glass wagged his head, sputtering, "B-but, you're a free man!"

Bass whispered, pursuing his question, "That really Hugh Glass?"

"And I'll die a free man! A free man what don't pay no tariff to no company, and no tariff to you neither!" he hollered back at Glass. Then Hatcher quickly turned his head to look Titus square in the face. "Ye heard tell of that ol' coon?"

"I do," Scratch replied in a hush. "First heard of him clear back to St. Louie. Friend of mine told me 'bout that ol' feller dragging hisself back to the Missouri after a sow grizzly chewed him up an' he was left for dead by the bunch he was traveling with."

Hatcher grinned. "That's the man awright. One and the same. Have him show ye his scars after he steps down from preachin' hellfire to this short pew of sinners."

"What's the rub he's greasin'?" Scratch asked.

"Like Glass is saying: all these here men ought'n take a stand against being dangled at the mercy of the traders. Him and a few others trailed in here with him yesterday and called all the free men together out of the camps to grouse about the tall prices we're faced with payin' to Smith, Jackson, and Sublette."

"For the life of me, sounded there like you was coming down on the other side of this fight," Scratch replied.

"Nawww," Jack explained with a widening grin. "Hell, Glass does have him a good point. An' he's right on most every count. I'm just the nigger what likes to argufy with that ol' buzzard ever' now and then 'cause it gets him so riled—'bout as steamed as a unwatched tea kettle over the fire."

"So what's Glass figger we can do about what toll the traders charge us for their goods?"

"And for what they give us for our plews," Hatcher added. "Don't forget they got us two ways of Sunday!"

"Like I told you—them three friends of mine got rubbed out with my furs last summer, they figgered to float downriver to the first post they come onto and trade there, 'stead of packing our plew into ronnyvoo, where a trader can skelp us both top and bottom."

As the heated discussion continued among the gathering, Jack wagged his head. "Ye saying we should pack our furs all the way to a fort, Scratch? Ye know how far the closest post is nowdays?"

"Why—we ride in all the way to ronnyvoo," Bass explained. "Ain't nothing more to ride our plew all the way to a fort."

"Damn—closest fort's clear over to the Missouri—taking a man right through Sioux and Ree country, Scratch!"

Glass shushed the crowd and stepped toward Titus and Jack. "Did I just hear you fellers talkin' 'bout taking your furs to a fort clear over on the Missouri?"

"As crazy a notion as I've ever heard!" Hatcher snorted with a wry grin.

"Then again, maybe not," Glass declared, turning his eyes to gaze at Scratch. "Way you're talking, friend—must be you heard of the new post they're building at the mouth of the Yallerstone."

With a shake of his head Titus answered, "No—I ain't heard no such a thing."

"That's old news, Glass!" cried someone in the crowd.

Another man called out, "No man's had the balls to open Henry's old post in many a year!"

Whirling on the naysayers, Glass roared, "You dumb, Digger-brained idjits! I ain't talkin' 'bout Henry's old post!"

"What fort at the mouth of the Yallerstone ye speakin' of?" Jack demanded, glaring at the old trapper.

"Mackenzie's post."

Amid the sudden noisy murmurs in the crowd, Hatcher asked, "The same Mackenzie been on the upper river for some time?"

"That's the nigger," Glass declared. "The one what runs the Upper Missouri Outfit for American Fur now."

His head bobbing, Caleb Wood shouted, "That's a man knows what he's doing!"

Titus asked, "Where you hear all this news, Glass?"

Glass turned back to Scratch. "From Mackenzie's own tongue hisself."

The mumblings and murmurings grew louder among the free trappers until Glass waved his arms and got the crowd shushed.

"This last spring I run across a bunch of pork eaters raising their stock-ade walls up there on some high ground just above the mouth of the Yaller-stone," Glass explained after he had those curious men completely quiet. "Mackenzie his own self was there—seeing the place was built proper. Said he was naming it Fort Floyd."

"That's still a hell of a trip up to that country," Solomon Fish complained, scratching contemplatively at his beard of blond ringlets.

"Then come to ronnyvoo year after year," Glass replied with a shrug, "and pay mountain prices."

Hatcher demanded, "Mackenzie's prices gonna be better?"

"Yeah!" Scratch protested. "And is he gonna give us a better dollar on our plew?"

Stepping back toward Titus, Glass explained, "Mackenzie didn't say much more'n asking me to come down here to ronnyvoo and tell you he was open for business, even while they're building the post."

Some of the men looked at one another, almost as if calculating the journey they would have to make then and there that very summer if they chose to pack their beaver all the way north to where the Missouri River issued out of the badlands.

Matthew Kinkead stepped up to ask, "If'n you come as a courier for this Mackenzie and the American Fur Company—what you get out of it, Glass?"

"I got me a new rifle, and a hundred pounds of bar lead, boys," Glass admitted, then began to tap his chest with a gnarled finger. "But more'n that—I come away from this here meeting knowing I done right by all the free men in these mountains."

Isaac Simms asked, "So what's a man left to do who don't see going all the way to the mouth of the Yallerstone to trade with American Fur?"

"Way I figger it," Glass replied, "least a man oughtta have him a choice."

"If'n Mackenzie didn't tell ye to guarantee he'd beat mountain prices," Hatcher began, "what's to come of us when we get all the way there and this here Mackenzie turns out to be just as much a thief as Ashley, Sublette, or any of 'em?"

Bass held up his arms for quiet, and before Glass could reply, he said, "Maybe you ought'n go back to Mackenzie and tell him we're interested, but . . . but he should bring his trade goods to ronnyvoo, where we'll have us two traders to sell to on the same spot."

"Two traders!"

"That'd keep prices down!"

Then another voice bellowed, "And plew prices up!"

The roar was unanimous. Excitement energized the congregation as they babbled about the possibility of actually having competition among traders: competition in the dollar given for beaver, in those prices charged for a man's necessaries once a year. No longer would they be at the mercy of one trader who kept the price of beaver low, and the cost of goods sky-high.

"Is that the word what you fellers want me to carry back to Mackenzie at Fort Floyd?" Glass inquired after the crowd fell quiet once more.

The first man yelled, "Tell the Upper Missouri Outfit to come to ron-nyvoo!"

"Tell Mackenzie the free men in the mountains will make it worth the trip!"

And a third cheered, "Tell him men like us ain't at the mercy of traders no more!"

•   •   •

That summer of 1828 none of those double-riveted, iron-mounted free trappers had any idea that the invitation they were extending to Alexander Mackenzie of the American Fur Company's Upper Missouri Outfit would prove to be akin to the sort of dinner invitation the inhabitants of a henhouse would extend to a hungry fox in a well-known children's fable.

For now, the only men truly standing between the free trappers and their being at the mercy of American Fur's total monopoly in the mountains were St. Louis traders William Ashley and Billy Sublette. In less than a decade, however, John Jacob Astor's company would be trading without competition in the far west, able to dictate what it would pay for fur, to demand what it would for supplies. In less than a decade American Fur would be king of the mountains.

But for now . . . for the next few glorious seasons of an all-too-brief era in the early west, the free men would rule the Rockies.

As it was, things did not look all that bright for the American Fur Company that hot July. The previous fall Joshua Pilcher and his partner, William Bent, led a party of forty-five men west from Council Bluffs, their supplies and trade goods provided on contract by Astor's company. Then somewhere on the upper North Platte, the Crow struck and drove off most of their horses. Pilcher was forced to cache most of his trade goods before proceeding over South Pass and on to the Green River, where he planned to winter his brigade.

Having traded for horses from the Shoshone with the arrival of spring, Pilcher sent some of his hands back to raise their cache—only to find most everything destroyed by water seepage. With what little he could salvage, the booshway didn't have much to offer those coming to rendezvous at Sweet Lake. Showing up late, and hampered by his pitifully small supply of goods, Joshua Pilcher succeeded in trading the free trappers for a paltry seventeen packs of beaver before the fur hunters began drifting off in all directions. As the grasses browned and the land baked late that summer, Pilcher and Bent dissolved their partnership.

While Bent started back to St. Louis with their miserable take for the year, Pilcher and nine of his trappers left rendezvous following David Jackson and Thomas Fitzpatrick on their way north to the land of the Flathead, that brigade bolstered by a good share of the trappers who had deserted Pilcher at Sweet Lake. That next morning the brigade led by Robert Campbell and Jim Bridger departed for Powder River country and the home of the Crow.

Company partner Jedediah Strong Smith hadn't shown up at Sweet Lake that summer. The carousing men drank toasts to him and his California brigade, hoping that Jed's boys had not bumped up against disaster. Maybe next year they would all be together once more.

"It's been a good season!" cheered William Sublette as he started his caravan on its return trip to St. Louis. "We're out of debt, and in control of the mountain trade."

"Let Astor have the rivers," Davy Jackson had proposed.

"Damn right," Sublette agreed. "The mountain trade is ours."

"See you on the Popo Agie next summer, Bill!"

"See you on the Popo Agie!"

This business was growing, slow and sure. And rendezvous had proved to be the way to supply the company men, the way the partners could secure the biggest return from the trappers' dangerous labor in the mountains. That first day of August, Sublette turned east with more than seventy-seven hundred pounds of beaver that they had purchased for three dollars a pound, fur that would bring them over five dollars per in St. Louis. In addition Sublette had forty-nine otter skins, seventy-three muskrat skins, and twenty-seven pounds of castoreum aboard his pack mules.

After paying off General Ashley the twenty thousand dollars they owed him for the year's supplies, the three partners were left with a profit of more than sixteen thousand dollars.

It had indeed been a good year in the mountains.

FIVE

"Say, Mad Jack!" the fiery-headed trapper cried as he tottered up atop one good leg, the other a wooden peg, his face rouged with the blush of strong liquor.

"Tom! Ye ol' she-painter!" Hatcher shouted back as he took the fiddle from beneath his chin. "Thought ye'd took off with Jackson or Bridger awready."

"Nawww," the peg-legged trapper said as he came to a weaving halt, his bloodshot eyes glassy. "Me and some boys are moving southwest in a few days. See for our own selves what lays atween here and California."

"Yer favorite tune still be 'Barbara Allen'?"

"Damn right," Tom Smith replied. "That squeezebox feller know it good as you?"

Jack laughed. "Elbridge knows it better'n me!"

"Sing it for me, boys," Smith said as he collapsed onto the grass, stretching out that battered wooden peg clearly the worse for frontier wear. "Sing it soft and purty."

> *In Scarlet town where I was born,*
> *There was a fair maid dwellin',*

Made ev'ry youth cry, "Well a day,"
Her name was Barb'ra Allen.

'Twas in the merry month of May,
When green buds they were swellin',
Sweet William on his deathbed lay,
For the love of Barb'ra Allen.

"I ain't never see'd a man stand so good having him only one good leg," Titus whispered to Matthew Kinkead.

"Peg-Leg Tom?"

Scratch nodded. "How he come by it?"

Isaac Simms answered, "Cut it off hisself, Scratch."

"The hell you say!" Scratch replied in amazement, staring at the crude whittled peg.

He sent his servant to the town,
The place where she was dwellin',
Cried, "Master bids you come to him,
If your name be Barb'ra Allen."

Well, slowly, slowly got she up,
And slowly went she nigh him;
But all she said as she passed his bed,
"Young man, I think you're dying."

"Isaac speaks the bald-face truth," Caleb Wood stated with one bob of his jutting chin.

"Injun's rifle ball broke both bones in the leg, right here," Kinkead declared as he bent over and tapped his own leg just below the knee.

Simms snorted, "Figger on how much that'd pain a man!"

She walked out in the green, green fields,
She heard his death bells knellin',
And every stroke they seemed to say,
"Hard-hearted Barb'ra Allen."

"Oh, father, father, dig my grave,
Go dig it deep and narrow.
Sweet William died for me today;
I'll die for him tomorrow."

"Lookit the man just sitting there easylike, tapping the end of that ol' peg on the ground like it was his foot," Solomon said.

Scratch prodded, "So tell me who really cut it off him."

"Isaac tol'cha: Smith done it his own self!" Kinkead declared. "Well, most of it anyways. First off he got good and drunk afore starting down through the meat with his own scalping knife."

"Shit," Bass whispered with a shudder.

"Passed out by the time it was to cut on bone," Simms took up the story. "Two other'ns had to finish the job for him. They burned the end of that stump with a red-hot fire iron to stop the bleeding, then went off and buried the leg far 'nough away that Smith could never go lookin' for it."

"Go looking for it?" Scratch repeated.

"Damn, if that ain't what I seen happen with ever' man lost a arm or leg," Solomon Fish stated. "Like something pulling, an' yanking 'em to find that missing part of themselves."

> *They buried her in the old churchyard,*
> *Sweet William's grave was nigh her,*
> *And from his heart grew a red, red rose,*
> *And from her heart a briar.*

> *They grew and grew up the old church wall,*
> *'Til they could grow no higher,*
> *Until they tied a true lover's knot,*
> *The red rose and the briar.*

"Most ever' man I know of in the mountains calls Tom by the name Peg-Leg Smith now," Caleb said.

"Never have I seen a man get around so good on a peg," Bass observed with fascination.

As Hatcher and Gray finished the song, Smith clapped and hooted, then asked, "How 'bout something a man can get up an' stomp to, Jack!"

Hatcher thought a moment, then suggested, "Say, Tom—how 'bout a tune writ special for all of us bachelors?"

Smith asked, "Bachelors? What the hell's that?"

"What *we* are, ye stupid nigger!" Hatcher roared. "Any man ain't married, he's a bachelor!"

"Then sing it, by God!" Smith cried merrily as he struggled to rise, clambering clumsily onto his leg and peg, clapping and hobbling about in exuberance. "Sing it for all us happy bachelors!"

> *Come all you sporting bachelors,*
> *Who wish to get good wives,*

And never be deceived as I am,
For I married me a wife makes me weary of my life,
Let me strive and do all that I can, can, can;
Let me strive and do all that I can.

She dresses me in rags,
In the very worst of rags,
While she dresses like a queen so fine;
She goes to the town by day and by night,
Where gentlemen do drink wine, wine, wine;
Where the gentlemen do drink wine.

When I come home,
I am just like one alone;
My poor jaw is trembling with fear.
She'll pout and she'll lower, she'll frown and look sour,
Till I dare not stir for my life, life, life;
Till I dare not stir for my life.

When supper is done,
She just tosses me a bone,
And swears I'm obliged to maintain her;
Oh, sad the day I married; Oh, that I longer tarried,
Till I to the altar was led, led, led;
Till I to the altar was led.

"Hooraw, niggers!" Tom cried as he spun round and round a few times, pivoting on the peg as his axis. "Let's hear you beller for bachelors!"

Hatcher guffawed, "Ain'cha a marryin' man, Peg-Leg?"

"You're full of vinegar and prickly juice, Mad Jack—if'n you think any mountain man is the marryin' kind!"

Caleb Wood spun up, grabbing hold of Smith's left arm to do-si-do two spins round with him, shouting in glee, "Not too many Injun womens got 'em a hankering to bed theyselves down with that peg leg of your'n, eh?"

Balancing on the peg for a moment, Smith gave his wooden leg a sound kick with his moccasin, declaring, "This here peg ain't the only thing on Thomas L. Smith them Injun womens know will stay stiff and hard as a tree trunk all night long!"

"Listen to this here ol' firecracker head!" Matthew Kinkead crowed. "Spouting like he was the answer to every woman's prayers!"

Puffing out his chest like a prairie cock on the strut, Smith snorted, "The hell if I ain't!"

"I damn well know ye'd have women prayin', all right!" Hatcher said.

"Prayin' for mercy!" Smith shouted. "I'm a hard-user on the womens, I am!"

"No, Thomas!" Jack replied. "They're prayin' ye'll just stay away from 'em with that li'l willer switch of yer'n when a real man like me carries round a oak stump in his britches!"

"I swear, Mad Jack Hatcher—you go spreadin' talk like that, why—I'll sit down right here, unbuckle my wood leg, and take after you with it! Whup you like a poor man's field hand—whup you about the head and shoulders!"

"Ye take yer peg off, Smith—ye'll never stand no chance of catchin' a sprightly fella like me!"

"I can move when I wanna," Peg-Leg argued, then smiled hugely in that flushed face. "In the robes an' out!"

Fish roared, "Ain't no way you're ever gonna catch a squaw, Tom—less'n she wants to be catched."

" 'Nough of 'em still want me to catch 'em!" Smith gasped, his face red with easy laughter. He held out the peg and bent his good leg, collapsing again to the grass, where he rolled onto his back to thrash around, screaming as if in a fit, "Oh, me—I'm dyin' o' thirst, boys! Hoo-yoo! I'm dyin' o' thirst! Rum me quick! Rum me!"

Hatcher scissored his legs so he stood directly over the man, his fiddle and bow tucked beneath his left arm, peering down as somber as a settlement undertaker. "Maybeso ye ought'n dig poor Tom his grave, fellers. He's sure to die of thirst, don'cha see?"

With a small whimper Smith asked, "W-why, Jack?"

"We ain't got us nary a drop of likker left in our camp!"

Smith bolted upright like he'd been gut-shot, his eyes gone wide. "You ain't g-got no more l-likker in camp?"

"Mad Jack said it true!" Caleb declared.

His eyes glaring in anger mixed with disappointment, Smith sputtered, "T-then what the hell are you f-fellers so gay about?"

Solomon Fish waved an arm toward the mountains, explaining, "Tomorrow we're off for the high country and our autumn hunt!"

"That's all?"

Hatcher nodded. "That's all I need to make me happy."

"Where you going this year, Jack?" Smith prodded, and he relaxed back on an elbow.

Jack chuckled. "We ain't none of us tellin'."

"Awww, c'mon now," Peg-Leg pleaded. "Don't reckon to foller you anyways—"

"I can't be sartin of that," Hatcher grumped.

"You know I'm headed to Californy, Jack."

Isaac Simms inquired, "What's way yonder in Californy, Peg-Leg?"

"Dark-skinned womens."

"Hell, child," Elbridge argued, "they got dark-skinned women where we're headed to winter up in Taos."

Gazing at the sky, Smith got a wistful look in his eyes as he said, "Not like the dark-skinned womens I heard tell of live out to Californy."

"Ain't they Mexicans just like the folks down to Taos and Santy Fee?" asked John Rowland.

Wagging his head, Smith said, "No, sir. Them down that way just be poor Injun and greaser half-breeds."

"So tells us what sort of dark-skinned women they got in California," Hatcher demanded.

"Womens there got royal Span-yard blood in 'em."

Rufus said, "That so?"

Peg-Leg nodded. "The truth of it. And I hear them gals is looking to show a good time to any American rides their way."

Jack roared, "Hell, the womenfolk down to Taos show an American a mighty fine time, Tom!"

"You boys go and winter up to Taos now," Smith advised. "As for me and my band—we're headed for Californy to see just how hot them high-toned Span-yard gals can get when a outfit of real men come riding into their country!"

"Hell, the real men will be riding into Taos come this winter!" Hatcher roared as he propped the fiddle under his chin.

"Real men?" Smith asked, cocking his head to the side and grinning as he looked around him at each of Jack's trappers. "Real men would've saved a last drink for their old friend, Peg-Leg Smith! Afore we all hit the trail!"

"Har!" Jack snorted. "Any man claims he has a real wood peg for a cock wouldn't come beggin' in my camp for no last drink!"

His face turning sad and downcast, Smith puffed out his lower lip and moped, "Looks like you found me out, boys! I ain't got no hardwood cock that will pleasure a gal all night long." Then immediately he grinned as he began to boast, "But this here's one child what can still outride, outshoot, outbeller, and outthump the lot of you weak sisters! Mark my words, fellers—there's comin' a time when all the fun will be gone in these here mountains. And on the day you sorry niggers come dragging your sorry asses into Californy—don't 'spect Thomas L. Smith, the king of Californy, to be waiting there with open arms for any of you!"

"You gonna own all of Californy?" John Rowland asked.

He turned on Rowland, one finger jabbing at the sky. "I damn well will own it, child! When the Mexicans have everything south of the Arkansas, when Sublette's company rules the Rockies and American Fur owns the Missouri, 'cause Hudson's Bay lays its claim to everything else west of here . . . then all that's left for likely fellers like me to do is plant my stake out to Californy, where the pickin's is good."

"But the price of beaver ain't fallin', Tom," Hatcher argued.

"I see more niggers coming out here every year," Smith replied in a quiet, grave tone. "Every summer they bring more trappers into these here mountains. One day they'll bring a train of wagons. Then they'll bring out white womens! And you boys know what comes next, don'cha?"

Isaac asked, "What, Tom? What comes next?"

"Everywhere white womens go, they build churches an' towns, stores and schools! They bring in the constables an' the lawyers—all of 'em telling men like us, 'You cain't do this! You cain't do that!' "

"Too damn much room out here for to worry 'bout any of that," Titus finally spoke his piece.

Smith turned to regard the stranger he did not know. "Maybeso, mister. Maybeso. But I do know there's a passel of folks back east—likely enough to fill up all of this out here if'n the first ones come out and spread the word."

"I figger a man can just keep moving ahead of 'em," Scratch observed.

He hobbled toward Bass unsteadily, his eyes squinting in the bright summer light. "S-stay ahead of 'em, you said?"

Bass nodded. "Yep. Stay out front of all them what come west to raise their houses and towns."

With a wag of his head Smith said, "What kind of life is that gonna be for niggers like us, boys? What good is life for a man just to be pushed on ahead of the crowds . . . knowing them settlement folks is ruining everything we left behind when we moved on?"

"Maybeso a man don't have to turn around and see what they're doing to what he's left behind," Bass protested.

"No," Smith said quietly. "No, he don't. Just like he don't have to cry when he loses a good friend neither. A man just don't have to give a damn when them farmers and white womens and towns come out here and ruin all this for the likes of us."

"So that's the reason ye're haulin' yer plunder to California, is it?" Hatcher asked.

"For the life of me, I don't think I can bear to watch this country get ruin't, Jack. I'll go on to Californy, where there ain't too many greasers, where I can steal some horses and trap me some beaver too."

"Can't make me believe it," Titus said solemnly. "Look around you. There's too damn much room out here for all this ever to get ruin't on us."

Smith wagged his head, a great sadness come into his eyes. "The folks are comin', boys. They always have . . . an' I guess they damn well always will."

How long did they have? Scratch wondered.

He raised his eyes to gaze at the late summer blue and wondered, How long would it be before numberless columns of smoke would smudge the skyline the way it had in St. Louis? How long before the dust of wagon wheels and plowshares and thousands of feet and hooves would clog up a man's nose and make it hard for him to breathe normal?

How long before what he had found out here was no more, and he had to climb higher and higher, up from these rolling prairies and plains, to escape those who always came in the wake of the first to open a land. Smith was right about that. They always came.

They always would.

The longhunters had pushed over the Cumberland, down into the cane-brakes when the stalks stood twice as tall as a man, when the game was plentiful and the buffalo still haunted the eastern timber. But in the wake of those lonely individuals came men with their families following the same narrow footpaths and game trails into the virgin forests until they came to a meadow, a grove of trees by a stream—a place where those men and their women decided to set down their roots then and there. They built cabins and turned the soil, planted their seeds and fought off the Indians there beyond the edge of the frontier.

And eventually they watched others come, leapfrogging over them to inch back the dangerous edge of that frontier a few miles, a few more days farther to the west. Season by season, year by year, farm by farm. They had always come.

And there was no reason for Titus to believe that they wouldn't always continue to come.

On his way west Scratch had seen them with their toes dug in, clinging fast to the country along the Missouri River. Settlers and widows, families and farms. Merchants and towns. How far would they push before they ran up against the buffalo country? And what then?

That land wasn't fit for farming, he convinced himself, hopeful. That soil wasn't rich and black like the ground he had turned over with a plow back in Kentucky. The domain of the buffalo was nothing more than poor grassland, not at all fit for raising corn or tobacco, hemp or squash or potatoes. The settlers who came to raise crops would eventually discover that they couldn't grow anything in that ground and would therein refuse to venture farther.

So men like Tom Smith were wrong, Bass told himself.

Farmers would not dare probe very far beyond the hardwood forests. Surely the buffalo ground would serve as a buffer, as a no-man's-land where the great plains blanketed by those shaggy beasts would forever protect these high prairies and tall mountains from the masses of humanity he had seen streaming across the Mississippi on their ferries, rumbling right on through the byways of St. Louis, hurrying their wagons west.

It just wouldn't happen here.

This simply wasn't a quiet, closed-in country like that back east of the river. This land was too damned wild, too open and unruly ever to be tamed the way that country had been. Like a horse broke to saddle or a mule to plow, like a man broke to marriage . . . that was the kind of country folks could tame.

Not this. Not here and surely not now.

This was a land no man could tame, and these were men every bit as tough to break to harness.

"We got visitors," Fish announced just loud enough that the others could hear.

He didn't point, but the others just naturally looked left to Solomon's side of their march. Up the far side of a gentle slope Bass caught sight of them. He had been so wrapped up in lazily musing in the hot afternoon sun that he might well have been asleep on horseback.

"How many ye make it?" Hatcher asked.

"Maybe a dozen," Fish replied. "But you can bet there's more we don't see."

"That's for sartin," Caleb warned.

"Maybeso they're just watching," Kinkead said, faint hope in his voice.

"For now anyway," Jack stated. "They'll keep their eye on us and figger a place to make their play. If not today, then tomorrow."

"What are they?" Titus asked.

For a moment they all looked at the horsemen sitting passively at the skyline atop their ponies, just far enough away that a rifle shot would not reach them, close enough to see the long, unbound hair lifting in the hot wind, some feathers and scalp locks fluttering beneath the chins of the horses.

"Bannawks," Jack declared.

"Likely so," Elbridge Gray agreed.

"This here's Bannawk country," Rufus Graham put in his vote.

"They good to Americans, like the Flathead?" Scratch asked. "Or they devilsome, like Blackfoot?"

"Man can't allays callate that," Hatcher explained. "But more times'n not, Bannawks don't mind running off yer horses, taking yer plunder, and raising yer hair if ye give 'em a chance."

Wood said, "You ask me, they ain't to be trusted."

"Bannawks ain't as brave as Blackfoot," Hatcher explained, "and they ain't as sneaky as Crow. But this bunch is likely to make a run at us sooner'n later."

"Two of 'em just turned off back of the hill," Graham declared.

The rest of the horsemen continued to watch as the party of white trappers and their remuda of pack animals pushed on by, plodding slowly up and down the low swales in the rumpled bedsheet of this land baking under a late-summer sun. It raised the tiny hairs on the back of Scratch's neck just to look up at those motionless statues . . . until as one the warriors reined their ponies to the right and disappeared from the skyline.

Dusk would arrive all too soon.

"We better be looking for a place to make camp and fort up," Kinkead declared.

"We'll find something ahead," Hatcher said. "Keep yer eyes peeled for water."

That was most important in something like this. No one had to explain that fact of life and death to these men. In seeking out a place to camp most nights on their journey south from Sweet Lake, they looked for a spot that promised wood and water and some open ground all round, not only for grazing their animals until dark when they would be brought in close, but open ground any enemy would be forced to cross in pressing their attack, making themselves good targets in the bargain.

A couple hours later as the sun was sinking toward the low range of western hills, they discovered a narrow stream issuing from a ravine where a small spring bubbled up from a green and grassy haven of thick brush and saplings.

"Likely this is the best we're gonna find," Hatcher stated after he had halted them and dismounted alone to explore the ground nearby. "Let the animals drink, then graze 'em close in. Hobble every one, and tie 'em up two by two."

"You 'spectin' trouble tonight?" Rowland asked.

"I figger they'll make a run at our horses, first whack," Hatcher replied. "With Injuns, the horses always come first. Whether they try for us and our plunder tonight, or wait till tomorrow morning, I'll wager they try to run off the animals right after dark."

Without a word the other eight swung down off their ponies and went about their business. Some stepped off a ways to relieve themselves, others squatted up and down on sore, trail-worn knees, loosening up kinks and cramps. No man had to ask what needed doing. Each of them had been through this sort of preparation before. And they all knew their mutual safety depended upon the weakest link in their chain being ready to protect the rest of the group with his life.

As it had turned out, Hatcher's band was the last to abandon the Sweet Lake rendezvous site. They watched one company brigade head north, the other turn east, while small outfits of free trappers drifted off to the four winds. Every group had its own particular medicine to try for the fall hunt. A few of the bands had even paid for a private session with a Flathead shaman camped near rendezvous, in hopes of ascertaining a likely spot to find a rich lode of the flat-tailed rodents that were the currency of these mountains.

While the white men waited patiently, the dark-skinned diviner burned his smudge of sweetgrass, smoked his pipe, consulted his special buffalo bones tossed onto a piece of rawhide, or even peered into the gutted carcass of a badger or porcupine or rock gopher the trappers had brought in for just that purpose. There in the blood pooled at the bottom of the creature's cavity the old man could fathom the best course for the white men to take, just as folks back east might pay to have their futures foretold by an all-wise sooth-sayer reading the pattern of damp tea leaves whorled at the bottom of a china cup.

So off the many groups had journeyed in just as many directions, by and large keeping their destinations to themselves, disclosing no more in their leave-taking than that fearless call, "Meet you on the Popo Agie!"

A fall, a winter, and then a spring but to come before then.

Another year of travel, trapping, and hanging on to one's scalp before another rendezvous would bring them all together.

Hatcher's outfit had tramped almost due south for several days before they struck the Bear River and from there headed east on a climb around the southern end of a range of low mountains, finally dropping over the hogback into an arid bottomland where they began to angle to the southeast. Striking the Green, and crossing to its east bank, they plodded south along the river's path, stopping only to rest through the short summer nights, again to eat and graze the animals briefly at midday.

With the high green country beckoning to them, pulling them onward, Hatcher's men kept their noses pointed toward the west slope of the Central Rockies. South of the Uinta Mountains they finally left the Green behind, and upon striking the ancient Strawberry-Duchesne Indian trail, the trappers turned directly east as the ground began to rise below them.

In that great basin lying at the western foot of the White River Plateau, the Bannock had found them.

Scratch sat in the tall grass, some drying clumps of brush right against his back—all but hidden from any intruders until that enemy would be on top of him. He had volunteered to wait here, some distance out from their camp as the sun disappeared and the light began to fade. When the raiders came for the horses, they would have to pass right by him. Then he would be at the enemy's back—alone when the shooting started.

The worst that could happen, Titus figured, was that he would have to grab up a horse and race back to camp if things got tight.

As the air began to cool, the deerflies began to rise, buzzing and droning through the tall grass—seeking some fleshy creature to bite and bleed. As much of the springwater as he had swallowed upon reaching the spring, he found himself thirsty now, still parched from their long, dusty day. From his pouch he pulled a twist of dark tobacco leaf, cutting from it a small knot about the size of the end of his thumb. Just enough to stimulate his salivation. Stuffing it inside his mouth, Titus returned the twist to the pouch, then suddenly slapped his right cheek.

The sting, the burn, the heat of the deerfly's bite spreading through that tiny knot of flesh—Scratch seized the painful site between a finger and thumb, pinching as hard as he could. It was about all a man could do when the devil creatures bit: squeeze for all he was worth to flush the poison back out. If he didn't, the bite would go on stinging for days. Pinching the skin until it grew numb, Bass finally swiped a finger over the site, smearing what blood he had oozed out of the tiny wound into his brown beard.

He licked the blood from his fingers. And as he did, Bass remembered he hadn't eaten since early that morning, just before light when they had prepared for another long day on the trail. Back among the two skimpy packs he had pulled off Hannah was his share of some meat they had dried yesterday after dropping two antelope. He chided himself for not bringing some along to chew on, if only to remind his stomach that he wasn't forgetting to feed it.

There hadn't been all that much in the way of supplies the company brigade leaders or Pilcher could lay out on blankets before those free trappers assembled there at the southern end of Sweet Lake. Only natural that they would hold back the lion's share of most everything for their own. So he and Hatcher and the rest had looked over what was offered: the powder and bar lead, spare flints and hickory ramrods, some flour and a little coffee. No Indian trade goods here. Everything Sublette and Jackson brought out early last winter they intended their trappers to use firsthand.

As it turned out, Hatcher's bunch ended up bartering with men who knew directly the value of a trapper's labor. Jack and the rest traded for a little more of everything, enough perhaps to hold them over for several more months until they put the fall hunt behind them and reached the Mexican settlements far to the south beyond the Arkansas River.

"We still got furs we ain't traded, Jack," Rowland had complained.

"So we'll keep 'em," Hatcher declared. "These company men don't have anything more what we can use to trade us, so it looks like we've got us a start on next fall's hunt awready."

Back at their camp that last evening before they would head out, the nine of them took serious stock of what would have to last them on this long trek to the Bayou Salade, and into a longer autumn trapping season.

"I can't tell a man not to smoke or chew," Hatcher began as he stood from looking over the packs with the rest of his men, "but as for me, I'm saving my 'baccy for fall. Most of my coffee too. Saving 'em both for a time when the air turns cool and I hear the first whistle of them elk in the high country."

It was a damn good idea, Bass remembered thinking. A man didn't really need tobacco and coffee until then. What a treat they both would be when the quakies began to turn gold on the hillsides of those high places, when a man finally saw his breath halo before his face, when the water began to ice up along the banks of the streams where they were laying their traps—

A bird called. With a sound that just didn't belong.

Then he saw the first half dozen or so of them reach the brow of the hill just beyond him. They had no idea he was there, watching them as the warriors stealthily poked their heads above the gently waving crowns of grass so they could watch the rest of Hatcher's men down in their camp far behind Scratch.

Bass felt just as he had back in Kentucky a time or two when he and friends were about to pull a prank on others. He grinned. This surprise would be good.

As the handful of Bannock turned and stealthily retreated back into the tall grass, Titus turned his face back to camp, cupped his hands around his lips, and whistled like a red-winged blackbird. In a heartbeat the gentle reply of a dark-eyed junco floated back to him from below on the long, gently falling slope. Although the others went about giving the appearance of being totally unaware of danger, that birdcall confirmed that the other eight were ready.

Scratch jerked around at the sudden hammer of the many hooves on the ground. As his eyes met the grassy skyline, some two dozen or more horsemen bristled against the blue dome like a mirage for no more than the instant it took for them to break over the hill, spread out in a widening formation. Not a sound had burst from their mouths as they poured off the high ground, racing toward him—strung out to his right. Only after they shot past him at the gallop did they start to holler and yelp, waving pieces of leather and rawhide and blanket, all those fluttering shapes raised to dance on the wind at the ends of their arms in the rose-lit air of dusk.

In another heartbeat they had torn past him.

He saw Hatcher come out from behind a tree, raising that big smoothbore to his shoulder. Kinkead was off to the left, already sighting down the long, heavy barrel of his rifle.

Bass shot to his feet, feeling his heart surge into his throat. As much as he had tried to calm himself while waiting in the grass, he knew it had done no good. Fighting was fighting. And killing was killing. Any man who approached such life-and-death struggles as these with anything less than fear was a man Titus Bass failed to understand.

Caleb Wood was the first to yell as he burst out of the grass halfway down the slope between Scratch and the camp. The first horseman reined aside as he bore down on the lone trapper, but Caleb blew him off the back of his pony.

Titus held on the narrow, copper-skinned back, squeezed on the set trigger, then eased his finger down on the front trigger. Through the pan and muzzle smoke he watched the warrior pitch forward, spinning slightly to the side as his legs came loose of his pony to go tumbling into the tall grass.

Immediately reversing his rifle, Scratch blew hard down the muzzle to clear the breech of any remaining powder embers—a thin, faint stream of smoke jetting from the touchhole. Yanking the plug from his powder horn with his teeth, he quickly poured enough of the coarse black grains up to the right crease in his left palm, then dumped them hurriedly down the muzzle. Bringing the muzzle back to his lips, he spat one of the four balls squirreled in his cheek down the barrel, at the same time dragging the long wiping stick from the iron thimbles at the bottom of the full stock, which he used to ram the unpatched ball home against the powder charge.

Grabbing up the small horn that hung from the strap to his shooting pouch, Bass quickly sprinkled some of the fine grains into the cupped recess of the pan and snapped the frizzen back over it.

The hair bristled on the back of his neck as he heard the yelps and cries behind him. There weren't supposed to be any behind him.

But suddenly the skyline sprouted four, five . . . then six more—their arms raised, bows and clubs and axes in their hands as they pounded heels into their ponies' ribs and rushed toward the fight in a second wave of terror.

Here he stood out in the open now, a good half of him poking above the tall grass, with nowhere to run for cover. The way they swerved as they burst over the top of the rise, Scratch was sure they saw him, sure they must have realized he had been part of a trap laid for them all.

Down below along the gentle slope three more rifles cracked, friends hollered, and those men hit with ball or pierced by arrow grunted and cried out.

Flicking a look at his belt, he saw the big horse pistol stuffed in the side of his wide belt, reassured. That would make two dead niggers, he figured as he slapped the gracefully curved rifle butt into the hollow at his shoulder. He had a tomahawk at the back of his belt, there beside the knife scabbard. That might account for two more when it came to the close and dirty of it.

But that meant there were two more who might swallow him up, fill his lights with arrows, hack off the top of his skull, or pound him beneath their ponies' hooves as they rode right over him while he was busy fighting off the rest.

As a big-chested warrior leaned off the side of his pony a ways, raising the arm clutching a long shaft, over the top flat of his rifle barrel Scratch spotted the two knife blades planted in the end of that swinging weapon. Plunging downhill at him . . . he raised the front blade a little higher, there at the notch where the Bannock's neck met his chest.

And pulled the trigger.

The Indian's cry was shrill as he was shoved off the back of his pony. Scratch took the rifle into his left hand, letting it fall at his feet as his right yanked the big-bore pistol from his belt, dragging back the hammer to full-cock as it came up. The next one bearing down on him already had his bow strung, the arrow drawn back as he leaned off the side of his animal racing on a collision course for the white man standing alone in the grass, its onrushing eyes and nostrils wide.

Using both hands to steady the pistol, Titus held high on the chest, then pulled the trigger. The weapon bucked back and upward at the end of his arms. Again his left hand dropped the weapon as his right reached round for the small-bladed tomahawk he pulled from his belt.

Three of them were turning his way.

Where was the fourth?

His left hand emptied of the pistol, Bass filled it with the handle of the old skinning knife and dragged the weapon from its rawhide scabbard just at the moment his left leg burned. He looked down, feeling the gorge rise in his throat, knowing he was going to be sick from the pain of it—seeing the arrow stuck clear through the meat of his thigh. At the back of his leg the stone tip glistened in the falling light, bright with his blood. Against the front of his legging the shaft's three rows of fletching quivered as his muscles tensed and shuddered in pain.

He wasn't sure how long he could continue standing before his stomach revolted and he threw up. But swallow it down he did as a warrior bore down on him. Twenty feet . . .

Then, as the Bannock swung back a stone club, he was knocked side-ways, the roar of a rifle surprising Scratch.

Jerking to his right, putting most of his weight on the one strong leg, Bass spotted Solomon Fish hurrying through the grass as he blew down his muzzle, reloading on the move. Behind them, on down the slope, those raid-ers not knocked off their ponies were ascending the far side of the shallow bowl, scattered and demoralized that their surprise had not succeeded.

"Bass! Behind you!"

Scratch whirled at the thunder of hooves.

A pure wonder, Bass thought. The son of a bitch boldly sat straight up atop his pony—drawing back the bow's rawhide string with one hand, a clus-ter of arrows in the other that gripped the center of the horn bow.

All he could do now was wait—wait and anticipate when the bastard would release that arrow. When he saw the string snap, Bass lunged to the right, landing in the grass, tumbling over onto the wounded leg—crying out as the shaft broke at the back of the thigh and splintered at the front in his clumsy roll. It hurt so damn bad, he wanted nothing more than to get up and yank the rest of the shaft from his flesh.

Struggling to his knees, then raising himself on that good leg, Scratch heard one of them yell again. And the hoofbeats—

He only had time to get his arms up to catch the warrior flinging himself off his pony as the animal raced on by the trapper. Together Bass and the bowman pitched into the grass, tumbling over one another, grunting and groaning as the warrior struggled to dig fingers into his windpipe and gouge his eyes while Titus flailed away with his weapons.

The thick-chested warrior stuffed a thumb into the side of Scratch's mouth and started to rip downward against the cheek and jaw. To his tongue that thumb tasted like smoke and dirt as Titus bit down hard, grinding the back of his teeth against the sharp pain as the enemy worked at ripping his jaw off.

Striking out with his clenched fist, the Bannock knocked the tomahawk out of Bass's hand, then seized the white man's upper arm in his grip.

Unable for the moment to make use of his knife, Scratch flung both arms around the powerful chest, locking his free hand around the other wrist, starting to squeeze as he bit down all the harder on the thumb.

With a shrill wail of agony the Bannock popped his head forward savagely, smacking his broad forehead against Titus's brow. Bits of shattered glass and fractured, mirrored light spun outward from his eyes as he jabbed a knee into his enemy, again, and then a third time—hearing the man grunt with each blow, feeling each strike shudder through that bare, sweaty chest he gripped within his arms.

As the Bannock cocked his head back, Titus released his grip, the fingers on his free hand shooting past the Bannock's hair, immediately snatching hold in time to yank back as the warrior tried again to smack his forehead.

At the same instant he felt the Indian's fingers close around his ear. Digging, tearing with almost as much pain as there was in that quivering thigh of his as Scratch lumbered onto his knees, sweeping the knife in a huge arc toward his enemy's back. He sensed the blade drag along a rib for a moment before it plunged on through the taut muscle there in the lower back.

Scratch yanked it free, then drove the knife downward again, this time fighting to drag it to the side as the warrior stiffened, his whole body gone rigid while Titus struggled to turn the weapon this way, then that, twisting the blade through the soft tissue below that hard-strap muscle.

The enemy pitched to the side suddenly, stared up at the white man with glazed eyes as he took three quick gasps of air, then breathed no more.

It was quiet for a heartbeat; then Bass became aware of the fading hoofbeats, the raucous shouts of the others as they trudged his way up the slope. Off to his right he watched Isaac Simms rise out of the tall grass, lift an arm with a tomahawk in his hand, then swing it down savagely.

"Ain't none of these alive now, Jack," Simms called when he finally stood fully.

Fish and Wood were the first to reach Scratch.

"Who . . . who else hurt?" he asked.

Solomon dragged up one of Bass's arms, and together with Caleb, they lifted Titus out of the grass. "No one. You're the only nigger got enough stupids to wait out here for 'em to 'sprise you the way they done."

"Everyone awright?"

Wood replied this time, "Maybe a scratch or two."

"The horses?" Titus asked. "An' my mule?"

"They didn't get a damn thing for their trouble," Fish growled.

Bass tried to turn partway around in their arms. "Get my guns—"

"We'll get yer guns," Hatcher snapped as he came up out of the deepening gloom. "Get him down to the fire, boys."

"Damn, if I ain't the ailin' one again, Jack."

"That's right," Hatcher said quietly. "But this time we ain't got time to sit around waiting for ye to heal up."

Solomon asked, "What you aimin' to do, Jack?"

"We'll build us a big fire and cut that arrow out'n his leg—so we can be long gone afore morning light."

SIX

Two of them brought all their stock right into camp and began to load the pack animals in the bright glare of that roaring fire Bass was certain would mean the death of them all, backlighting the white men as some went about preparing for the trail, others busy with heating a little water in a kettle to use in Jack's surgery.

"Hold 'im down, boys," Hatcher ordered when he finally dragged his thin-bladed skinner from the edge of the coals.

Bass struggled for a moment as five of them seized him, shoved him back onto the grass there beside the fire pit. He knew what was coming.

"Sorry we gotta do it this way, friend," Hatcher explained, his merry green eyes gone dark with concern. "We ain't got time to soften yer brain on whiskey."

"Hell, you ain't got no whiskey left anyway," Scratch said between gritted teeth, struggling slightly against the others as his eyes narrowed on the blade headed for his leg. Then he quickly glanced at the other faces hovering near his—knowing there wasn't a lick of sense in fighting them all.

Hell, he realized he'd do the same for any of them—whatever it took to save a friend's life.

"Get that legging off'n his belt," Hatcher commanded, his lean face gone taut and gray in the firelight, eyes narrowing on the job at hand.

It all went so slowly after that. Brutally, brutally slow. With the legging straps unknotted and the tube of deerskin tugged down around his knee, it was clear to see the ends of the splintered arrow poking from the two blackened, bloody holes.

Hatcher dragged the back of his hand across his dry lips and murmured, "Gimme yer ramrod puller, Caleb."

In a moment Wood returned with the small pair of anvil-forged pliers a trapper used to give himself leverage on his hickory ramrod in pulling a ball back out of the long-barreled flintlocks that were the constant companions to these men far beyond the frontier.

With the fingers of his left hand, Jack pressed down on the bloodied skin around the hole on the front of the thigh, spreading the edges of the wound a little, and began digging into the torn flesh with the narrow, open jaws of the puller. Each time he squeezed down on the handles, thinking he had a bite on the shaft, all he dragged out was reddened splinters.

"Dammit," he grumbled quietly. "Roll 'im over for me."

Bass gritted his teeth as they twisted him onto his belly and sat back down on his shoulders and legs.

Jack tapped Rowland on the arm. "Get outta my light, Johnny."

Rowland shifted his weight on the wounded leg.

"That's better," Hatcher said. "Ye're a lucky nigger, Titus Bass."

"T-this don't feel like lucky." Then he twitched with the sudden flare of pain.

"Didn't hit that big bone," Hatcher explained as he leaned over the wound, pressed down on the flesh around the hole with his weight, and dug in with the puller.

Scratch ground his teeth together as the pain continued to swell, rising to a feverish red heat, glowing in overlapping waves that rose right up through his buttock and into the pit of him, spreading deep through his belly. Again and again Hatcher dug—yanking and swearing with each attempt, only to dig again. Each time coming up empty-handed.

"Sumbitch!" Jack grumbled, the bags under his eyes going liver-colored with frustration. "Caleb Wood! Get me my pouch yonder."

When the shooting bag was laid on the ground next to Scratch, Hatcher began digging through it all the way to the bottom as Bass raggedly caught his breath while the sharp pain slowly subsided. He watched Hatcher drag a short ball starter out of the pouch.

"Roll him on his right side, fellas," Hatcher said, of a sudden his voice much calmer than it had been since this operation had begun.

While they gently rolled him onto his right hip, Titus stared at that ball starter: a short six-inch length of hickory ramrod embedded in a small hardwood ball that fit comfortably in a man's palm.

"Wha—what you gonna do now with that?"

"I can't pull that arrow outta ye," Jack explained, holding the starter in the light, "so I figger to hammer it out."

"H-h-hammer?" Titus squeaked.

"Hold him down," Hatcher said, refusing to answer the question. "This is gonna hurt him, bad."

As much as he tried to keep his muscles relaxed, Scratch felt them tense as Hatcher set the brass-tipped end of that short ramrod into the hole on the front of his leg. He didn't like the idea of what he knew was about to happen, watching Hatcher take his knife from its sheath, grip the blade, and prepare to swing the weapon's handle at the round ball. He figured Hatcher was right about this, if nothing else: it was gonna hurt.

The last thing Bass remembered was hearing the antler knife handle whack hollow against the hickory ball . . . then sensed his stomach rise, twisting itself into a fiery knot that hurled against his tonsils before he lost all sensation, the searing red flames of pain mercifully dissipating in a cool blue rush of blessed unconsciousness.

Slipping down, down—scolding himself for ever having thought the pain was going to be unbearable, that it was going to be so bad he'd wet himself there in front of his friends . . . because right where he was at that moment, Scratch didn't feel a goddamned thing.

It wasn't until the following morning that he learned how the others had hoisted him up on the back of a horse behind the muscular Matthew Kinkead, then tied the two of them together before setting off in the dark, riding south and east at a good clip toward the foothills lying tangled at the base of the western slope of the Rockies.

The sun had felt good that morning, despite the fever he was running. Its touch was warm and reassuring there on the back of his neck as he awoke slowly, bouncing gently against Kinkead's broad shoulders, gradually sensing the rub of the thick hemp rope wound across his ribs and back, slowly realizing what they had done because he didn't have the strength to cling to the back of a horse by himself, much less hang on to consciousness during their perilous starlit ride.

"Seen any sign of 'em?" he whispered in a hoarse croak that sunup, his words mumbled against Matthew's back.

"Nothin'," Kinkead replied wearily.

That one word was spoken loud enough to alert the others that Bass had come to.

Hatcher eased his horse up on the off-hand side, the direction Bass faced with his cheek rubbing Matthew's shoulder blade. "Mornin' to ye, ol' coon!"

"Wh-where we . . ." Then realized his mouth was terribly dry.

"Where we headed?" Jack finished. "To Bayou Salade, Scratch. Right where we been heading since we pulled away from Sweet Lake ronnyvoo."

"Mornin', glory!" Caleb came up on Jack's off side, smiling hugely as he leaned forward so Bass could see him. "How's he doin', Jack?"

"Don't look to be bleedin' no more," Hatcher said. " 'Bout all I know is the nigger's awake and thirsty as the burning pits of hell itself. Let's see if'n we can find us a cool drink for him up ahead at that line of green, yonder."

"Likely a crik there," Wood said, urging his horse into a lope so he could take the lead.

"This time of year," Kinkead declared, "I hope it ain't a crik what's dried up already."

"Nawww," Jack said, his eyes smiling at Bass's pasty face, "there's bound to be water for this here arrow catcher. Even if we have to scratch for it."

What there was had been a trickle. Still, enough for the men to water the animals downstream after they untied Bass and eased him down into a patch of shade among the trees where the buzz and drone of summer's insects accompanied the rustle of the leaves brushed by an intermittent breeze. They brought him the cool water a cup at a time. No matter that it was a little gritty, what with flowing so close over the sandy bottom of the creekbed—it tasted better than he could remember water tasting on his tongue in a long time. They bathed his face and neck, washed off some of the dried blood around the crusty strip of cloth binding up his wounds, and some of the men dozed as the sun rose.

After a couple hours of fitful sleep, Scratch awoke to hear Hatcher rustling the men into motion. They had been off the trail long enough, he told them. They'd get a chance to sleep more that night if they put a few more miles, a few more hours, behind them.

Back onto the horse went Kinkead. Up they hoisted Scratch again, two of them, a third cradling the leg as gently as he could, raising him to his rocking chair behind the saddle, where they retied him to Matthew; then all went to their horses and drove the pack animals away from that narrow little stream.

Not until sundown did Hatcher select a secure place for a cold camp. No fire that night—but not one of them grumbled. They were either too tired to complain, or they damn well understood the stupidity of lighting a beacon that might well call down a reinforced Bannock raiding party on them again. That night Bass grew cold not long after moonrise.

"We're climbing a bit," Solomon Fish explained as he knelt and laid another blanket over Titus. "Natural for you to get yourself a chill."

They kept on climbing the next morning, and for every day across the next two weeks as they tramped through the long hours of sunlight, winding into the high country. From time to time one of the group would point out a recognized landmark to the others. By the fourth day after the scrap with the Bannock, Scratch was staying awake longer as he rocked against Kinkead's back. And by the end of that first week, he was finally able to move about on the leg, finding he could stuff his left foot into a stirrup and hoist himself onto the back of his horse without the muscles in that leg crumpling, collapsing, spilling him onto the ground.

This matter of getting himself forked astride a horse was something a mountain trapper quickly learned was an affair of life or death. To ride was not a luxury, not some mere convenience. Having an animal and the ability to ride meant survival. To be without a horse, or to find that one could not stay in the saddle, might well be a death sentence.

So again, from somewhere deep inside this determined man, came the strength and dogged resolve to mend himself. Mule-headed stubbornness even more than pride drove Titus to test the leg, to swallow down the pain and push beyond what he had known before as his limits of endurance. At each night's camp Bass found himself almost too weary to eat as the fire was kindled and meat set to broil at the end of long green sticks driven into the earth around the fire. The ride, that work it took pushing up into the high country, picking a trail along the mountainsides, up and down, then up and down again—it all took its toll day after day. At night he slept so soundly, he rarely rolled over, slept until someone nudged him with a toe, announcing it was time to water the stock, pack, and move out again.

"How far now to this Salade of your'n?" he asked Hatcher of a morning when they were both throwing bundles onto the sawbucks strapped onto the backs of their pack animals.

"Ain't far now."

"Take a guess for me."

"Don't know for sure," Jack replied, his eyes back to being merry sparkles of green light. "Can't say. Soon, though."

By that time they had climbed east into the heart of the southern Rockies, following the tortuous path of a winding river ever higher as the late summer days continued to shorten by a matter of heartbeats every evening, the air cooling more quickly at twilight, the streams and freshets colder than they had been since spring, fed by those snowfields suspended just overhead above timberline where the marmots squeaked and the golden eagles drifted upon the warm updrafts, searching for another meal.

Up, up as the hooves of their animals crushed the dried, golden grasses having cured beneath the late-summer sun, on across the slopes as they picked their way through stands of rustling aspen, past the wide, bristling boughs of blue spruce, mile after shadow-striped mile of lodgepole forests. Finally near timberline, they turned almost due south, climbing from the headwaters of that westbound river, crossing over to the slopes where a new river system was given birth.

"This here where the Arkansas has its start," Jack explained late of an afternoon as they topped out on the brow beneath a jagged series of hoary granite peaks scratching at the clouds on both left and right.

Here they let the horses have a blow.

"The Arkansas what flows into the Mississap way down south?"

"The same, friend."

Bass wagged his head, unable to comprehend it. "Why—I'll be go to hell and et for the devil's own tater, Jack."

"Ye been on the Arkansas, I take it?"

"Never. Just by it, once," Bass explained. "Never did I figger that water come all the way from these here mountains."

"Snow from the *Shining* Mountains, Scratch—'cause they allays got snow on 'em. Every li'l flake, every damned drop of rain, falls up here makes its own long, long trip till it reaches the sea."

"We must be getting close to that valley now, ain't we?"

Pointing east with his left arm, Hatcher replied, "Right over them high peaks."

"You figger we'll climb over them?"

"Nawww," Caleb finally spoke. "Too much work on the animals."

Hatcher pointed south, down the long, narrow valley crimped between the two ranges. "We follow the Arkansas down till we reach the foot of the hills on our left. Ride right around 'em and we're in the south end of the Bayou Salade."

"Some of the best trapping a man can do him," Isaac Simms said as he patted the neck of his horse.

"Best trapping anywhere in all the Rockies," Rufus Graham added.

Scratch asked, "Even good as the Three Forks country?"

Nodding, Hatcher said, "I'll put this country up agin' that'un any day, Titus Bass. Ye ain't been where we're going—so I'll 'llow ye're just plain ignernt about the Bayou. But the beaver ye'll pull out of the streams yonder, right over them peaks . . . those beaver some of the best a man can trap hisself anywhere south of English country, or north of Mexico."

"They shine, that's the bald-faced truth," gushed Elbridge Gray.

"Worth the trip, are they?"

"The trip?" Hatcher echoed Bass. "This bunch gonna winter down to Rancho Taos—so South Park is right on our way."

Caleb declared, "And South Park gonna be right on our way north come spring green-up."

"When the flat-tails be some, so seal fat and sleek!" John Rowland crowed.

Hatcher said, "Come spring, them big water rats gonna have 'em a winter plew knock yer eyes out, Titus Bass!"

"Swear on my own heart! Way you niggers are talking," Scratch observed, "makes a fella want to lift his tail up and get high behind to ride on over there right now!"

"Titus is right, boys," Hatcher said. "Let's cover ground while we still got light."

Perhaps it was only the air's tingle hinting at the arrival of autumn, but his skin goose-bumped as they all whooped, hollered, and cheered, urging the animals south downslope along those headwaters of the Arkansas, no more than a matter of days now from their goal. Up here so close to the sun, Bass found himself in awe once more how warm were the rays caressing his bare skin, how cool was every breeze that whispered out of the thick timber.

His anticipation grew over the next week, what with the way the others talked every night of the Park, glorying on the promise of its beaver, on the herds of buffalo, elk, and deer said to blanket the valley floor. Just to sense the rising excitement within the other men as they crossed to the east bank of the Arkansas, each day hoping to reach the end of the mountain range where they could finally sweep around the foot of the hills and drop into the Bayou Salade.

Of one golden afternoon, with the high sunlight gently kissing each early-autumn breeze, Bass slipped away into that place a man goes with his thoughts when he really isn't thinking of a thing. They had been pushing hard since the first gray light of predawn, squeezing every mile they could out of the day. While all of them had been quiet for the most part, each man off in his own thoughts that afternoon like so many gone before, Scratch suddenly became aware of a change coming over the others. Gradually the men appeared to grow restless, shifting in the saddle, unsettled and anxious. Eventually some of them began to murmur to one another, tugging at their sweaty clothing, resetting their shapeless old hats atop their heads. It reminded him of a bunch of Kentucky schoolboys in those last few moments before the schoolmaster called for midday recess, or in those last breathless heartbeats every afternoon before the entire schoolhouse was freed at the end of the day—

"Lookee yonder, Scratch. This be the end of the hills!" Hatcher exclaimed, pointing as they eased up the side of the slope toward a low saddle fringed with dark emerald timber. "Other side lays the Bayou Salade."

Feathers suddenly took swirling flight within his belly, like the flapping beat of huge wings. Sudden whoops startled him as John Rowland and Matthew Kinkead burst past him, hooves hammering by on either side as they drove their horses the last few yards to the top of the saddle there between stands of blue spruce, shot over the rise, then were gone from sight. Only their exultant voices reverberated off the hills.

Then Isaac Simms shot by. And Rufus Graham careened past Hatcher and Bass, until Jack had time only to remind Solomon and Gray that some of them needed to stay back momentarily and see to the cavvyyard of horses and mules. At that reminder Scratch tightened his grip on Hannah's lead rope, pulling the mare closer to his saddle mount. They were about to enter a special place by all accounts. Such magic was to be shared with all of a man's friends.

"That it?" he asked Hatcher almost breathlessly as they crowned the saddle, pulling Hannah's rope so the mule came up right alongside him.

Below the crest, down the smooth, treeless hillside, he watched the others race, zigging and zagging, waving hats and standing tall in the stirrups, passing one another in curving swoops, signaling back at those yet to come down the slope. Beyond them on the valley floor lay the slowly undulating clots of buffalo milling, grazing, lowing among the belly-high, mineral-rich grasses.

"This is it," Jack said quietly, his eyes twinkling with a peaceful contentment.

"The Bayou Salade." Spoken almost like a prayer of thanksgiving.

Hatcher reached over and touched Scratch's arm. "Way ye said it, I can tell ye feel the place awready."

Tugging at the back of the blue silk bandanna he had knotted over his skull, Titus replied, "I can't remember seeing a valley near so purty, Jack. Not in all my days out here. Strange as it may sound to folks what ain't never come to this here place, looking up to see such sculpturin's as these all around 'em—I doubt their kind would ever understand if I tried to explain just how I feel right here an' now."

"How's that, Scratch?" Hatcher asked with a smile as wide as South Park itself.

"You told me yourself the other night, Jack."

"Told ye what?"

He rubbed the back of the bandanna over his missing scalp and hair, saying with a quiet, but keen, anticipation, "You told me I'd feel like this here's one of them few places where a man can know just why it was he ever come out here to the Rocky Mountains."

It was the marrow of the world.

Scratch realized at last that this was the bone and sinew to which everything else in his known universe had always been attached.

From these tall peaks where the snow never fully melted flowed the lifeblood of a whole continent. This truly was a place where a man found confirmation in the reason he ever dared to venture on past those folks back east not willing to risk all they ever had, continuing on by those not willing to dare enough in placing their very lives on the line . . . here suddenly to sense the close kinship a man could feel with a patch of ground, with a stretch of open country, with an entire virgin land that had embraced him.

Welcoming him home.

Into a small protected bowl the rest had taken their pack animals, stopping only when they had reached a secluded meadow ringed by thick timber and outcroppings of granite dotting the hillsides. A place big enough to afford enough pasturage for their remuda over the next two months or more, yet a place small enough to afford them ample security from chance discovery of their fires and shelters by roaming bands of raiders. More than enough wood—a litter of deadfall back in the thick groves . . . and water too: a narrow stream gurgling along its mossy bed right through the middle of the bowl. The stock would want for nothing as the last days of summer waned and the seasons turned.

Here they would be sheltered by the timber on the surrounding hills and the rock outcroppings. The stone faces of the granite would reflect the heat of their small fires on the nippy mornings to come, again each cold evening that autumn was bound to bring anyone venturing this high. As well, these rocky faces would serve to better hide the entrance to their small bowl from any who might pass through the valley itself.

"We used this here same place a couple seasons back," Isaac Simms explained. "Oughtta be real safe here."

"Off the beaten road," Hatcher added. "Not on any trails the tribes use when they crisscross the Park, coming and going as they please."

"Fella should keep his eye peeled for brownskins?" Scratch inquired.

"Just look down there," Jack advised. "See all the buffler. Then ye tell me if ye figger this be a place where the Injuns'll come to hunt."

Titus nodded.

And with every day that followed it made him marvel all the more just how alive was this valley. The variety of wildlife were drawn here for the natural salt licks. They came for the abundance of grass, itself rich with natural minerals. And, too, the creatures came for the cold, crystalline waters tumbling down from the high, treeless places like streamers of sunlit glitter itself.

From time immemorial man had followed the four-legged creatures into this valley. Where the game went, so followed the hunters after meat and hides, after tongues and survival. From one end of the valley floor to the other ran the boggy salt marsh that had led the French trappers and voyageurs to first give their name to this place, a sparkling series of ponds where beaver had dammed the creeks and streams into a necklace of quiet water. With the arrival of autumn an untold variety of ducks appeared overhead every day, sweeping in from the north across the autumnal blue skies to join the great long-necked geese in a brief migrational layover in this magical place.

Their first morning in South Park, they had moved away from their breakfast fire into the stands of lodgepole to select and fell a number of long, thin trees they dragged back to camp, where they trimmed off branch and stub, then cut each pole to length. One by one the shelters took shape, most no more than lean-tos made from bowers laid across their lodgepole frames, finally covered with pack canvas and old blankets. More than a dozen were there: some men pairing up, a few of them preferring to sleep on their own, along with four large shelters built to protect the outfit's supplies.

That night, well after dark when they completed their camp-making chores, Hatcher joined the weary men at the fire to run over the well-worn sequence of trapping in hostile country.

"Caleb, I want you and Rufus to hang back the first day." Jack waited until the pair nodded. "Next day gonna be Scratch and Matthew."

He went on and on, pairing the men, then waiting while each pair nodded to one another in recognition.

"That just leaves you again," Elbridge stated.

"Ain't no different'n it was after Little went under to the ticks last spring," Jack explained. "With him gone after that bad scrape with the Blackfoot, we had us one odd man out."

"I remember that," Fish replied.

"So, boys—I'll be the one what will hang back on my lonesome when it's my day to stay in camp."

It was not the practice of all Mad Jack Hatcher's brigade to depart every morning to set traps along the streams and slides, down at the valley ponds.

With the exception of their solitary leader, in rotation two men took their turns lying back to camp for one day out of every five: using their time to repair tack and saddles, doctor the sores and saddle ulcers on riding and pack animals, trim hooves and mend bite wounds that a man had to expect among half-wild horses. From hides traded off the Flathead back at Sweet Lake, some spent their camp day, even nights, around the fire, cutting and sewing additional pairs of moccasins. On occasion a man would tinker with a trap he found not working properly, or he might fashion himself a rawhide sheath for a knife, perhaps add some brass tacks to a belt or the stock of his rifle.

Never was there any end to the lot of a camp keeper. When more interesting work was finished, there was always more than enough to do tending the plews: fleshing the freshest beaver hides scratched with each man's distinctive mark . . . cutting, trimming, and tying willow limbs into a wide hoop . . . finally lashing the day's pelts onto the willow hoops—stretching, tightening, then stretching some more. With each new day these huge, round red dollars of Rocky Mountain currency dotted the campsite, stacked against every tree trunk, sapling, and clump of brush. More were brought in every afternoon by the seven who took their turn at the streams and slides and pools.

As the weeks passed, even Scratch grew astounded by their take. Rich as some previous seasons had been for him, he had never seen anything quite as bountiful as this. Large beaver, thick fur, not one empty trap any day. And nary a sign of brownskins about.

Most mornings he had thrown the much-worn, oft-repaired Shoshone saddle onto Hannah's back, tied his two greasy trap sacks on either side of the horn, where they would hang at his knees, and move out with the other six who would be trapping that day with him. On those mornings when it was Bass's turn to hang back to tend to camp duties, the mule had proved just as restless and out of sorts as he was when not allowed to venture into the pristine beauty of the valley.

If she wasn't picketed on those days, Hannah came right into camp even before the rest pulled out—seeming to know that the other animals were being saddled and prepared for departure while she was not. Until he eventually trained her better, having to swat at the mule with a switch and scold her, driving her out of camp, Hannah would turn over kettles and coffeepots with her nose, braying loudly to show her deep displeasure.

Many were the times on those chilly mornings when he'd grab the mule by her ears, yanking her head down so he could glare into one of her defiant eyes and growl an endless rash of words strung together to convince her just how angry he was with her impish antics. Later that day she'd slip up behind Titus as he was concentrating on one chore or another, suddenly shoving her muzzle right against his shoulder blades to knock him off balance, sprawling on the ground.

"You're a she-devil all right," he growled. "Times are I've thought to strangle you. But I can't bring myself to it—not when I recall how you saved my life . . . twice already."

Seemed as if she somehow knew what he was saying at those times, for Hannah would eventually come up to stand over him, lowering her nose right against him softly, her big eyes half-closed, twitching those peaked ears of hers as if in apology for her childish stunts. Lord, if she didn't know just how to get herself back on his good side again.

As if he could ever be angry enough with Hannah to kill her. Maybe a man like Silas Cooper could have shot her easy as spitting . . . but not Titus Bass.

The days continued their march into autumn, each one imperceptibly shorter than the one before it. The mornings grew colder, a film of ice forming in the kettles and at the edges of the creeks until enough of the high, glorious light warmed them each day. Even a blind man would know that summer was over, that the seasons had turned, that they were beginning their headlong tumble toward winter.

A man with a good nose would surely know. Autumn mornings had their own unmistakable fragrance—that sharp, crisp tang to the air. The smell of this high country dying, or its life already dead for another cycle of the year. Grasses and brush had grown dry and brittle beneath the increasing bite to every breeze that knifed its way down from the high and hoary places. It smelled of winter on its way.

Autumn advanced with an amazing swiftness above their camp on every mountain slope. Each morning he found the descending line of gold-smitten aspens had inched a little farther down the hillsides toward the valley floor . . . as if autumn were creeping down upon them from above, a few yards more every night.

No more were there any of the hardy wildflowers tucked back in the protected meadows—swept away by the falling temperatures and the harshness of the winds, joining the summer-browned grasses in parched oblivion. Each day brought the deer and elk farther down the forested slopes toward the safety of their winter pasture in the valley. And these days of waning light brought the constant accompaniment of whistling elk calling other bulls to combat, or the slapping crack of bucks' antlers locking, twisting, slashing in an ages-old combat. Males battling for the right to the harem, that struggle played out on the nearby slopes of dark pine-green and sun-splotched gold quakie.

Farther below in the valley itself, the cottonwood and willow would be the last to give way before the mysterious forces of nature and time and season. But ultimately their leaves began to shrivel with age, dried with the passage of time and the invisible hands of nature's clock. Trees stood bare, stark, and skeletal against the golden, browning backdrop of the hills. Autumn's breath was seizing hold of this land.

And so much of the rhythm of life appeared to grind slowly to a halt like a miller's wheel brought rumbling to a stop by an unseen hand.

Yet as suddenly as life seemed to breathe its last, the Bayou Salade burst into frenetic activity across a week or more. Swarms of migratory birds blackened the skies now. Over the lower peaks and passes, formation after formation of the spear-headed migrations paraded across the crystal-clear autumnal blue. Each formation transformed itself from black specks spotted far off in the sky to become a low-swooping V of geese and ducks, angling in to settle across the ponds and still water of the valley with a thunderous concert of honking and splashes. First the longnecks circled, their heads craning, searching for a landing spot before making their long, graceful figure-eight loop across an open spot of marsh water. Then the huge geese slanted down in formation, banking sharply before they hit the skylit water, kicking up rooster tails of spray, squawking to one another, to the ones they were joining, or to those still descending from the sky above.

On those mornings that Bass found himself out in the autumn chill to set his traps, he would stand and stare for long periods of time at the pageant of sky and water and wing—there were so many of the ducks and geese that there could not possibly be room for any more out on the huge marshes and icy bogs. Yet still they came as if spewed out of the sky.

From this direction and that, the smoothbores echoed from the far hills, his fellow trappers out hunting, their guns loaded with shot instead of a huge round ball. And every night the men roasted the rich, fat meat over their fires, this a welcome change from a diet of elk and venison and buffalo.

Other, smaller songbirds feasted before the coming onslaught of winter on those insects, locusts, and beetles clinging cooled and torpid on those grasses dried by the slash of autumn winds. Time hung in the balance here, and fall was clearly a time when it was decided just what creatures survived, what creatures would not. Each species was making ready for the coming change in its own ages-old dance of the seasons, each life-form readying itself for the time of cold and death that was winter in this high country.

True, the coming winter would decide just what would live, and what would not. This intricate rhythm that hummed around him each new and glorious day was a rhythm begun so long ago that aeons had still rested in the womb of time.

The first storm came and went, not yet cold enough for the snow to stay longer than a couple of days. Then the second and third storms rolled through the valley, each snowfall lasting a little longer before it finally melted, soaking into the soggy ground, dripping off the thick spruce boughs, feeding every creek, stream, and freshet a sudden, final burst of life before winter would squeeze down hard.

"When you figger for us to pull out?" Elbridge Gray asked one evening around their fire as the wind came up, beginning to blow off the high slopes with a wolfish howl.

Standing to stretch, Hatcher said, "Trapping's been so damned good— I'd like to stay right to the last day afore the passes close up."

Caleb Wood declared, "Trouble is, a man can't never tell when he's gonna stay a day too long . . . till he tries and finds the passes are all snowed in."

"Ye saying it's time to go south?" Jack asked.

With a shrug Caleb replied, "I dunno. Last week or so I been thinking real hard on Taos—"

"Ain't a one of us ain't been thinking real hard on Taos," Matthew Kinkead interrupted.

Hatcher stepped over and laid a hand on Kinkead's shoulder. "Ye'll be there afore the hard cold sets in."

Matthew's eyes softened, and with a hound-dog expression crossing his jowly face, he sobbed, "Wanna see my Rosa."

John Rowland looked up and asked, "You ever get the feeling she might one day figger you for dead, Matthew? That you been gone so long from her . . . she goes out and gets herself 'nother husband?"

Slowly wagging his big shaggy-bear head, Kinkead gave that considerable thought, then answered, "I don't figger her the kind to do anything of the sort . . . not till one of you boys rode into Taos and tol't her your own self I gone under."

"And even then Rosa's the sort of woman what just might expect one of us to bring her something special of yer'n, Matthew," Hatcher explained as he knelt by the coffeepot. "Something what would show her ye was really gone."

Isaac Simms asked, "What would that be, Kinkead?"

"Yeah," echoed Solomon Fish, "what would be the one thing we'd have to show your Rosa to prove to her you been rubbed out?"

He scratched his big onion bulb of a nose with a dirty, charcoal-crusted finger, deep in thought. Then he said, "I s'pose it'd be this here kerchief I wear round my neck." Using a couple of fingers, Kinkead lifted the soiled black cloth, emblazoned with a multitude of painted red roses in full bloom.

"Rosa give you that, didn't she?" Titus asked.

He nodded, looking down at it a moment. "Winter afore last, when this bunch was all in Taos—afore we come north last two year. She and me, we bought this here kerchief down to a poor woman's blanket she had spread out in a warm spot there in the sun, over to the Taos square."

"I remember that ol' brown Injun gal!" Rowland crowed with excitement. "I see'd that same kerchief my own self that morning and was coming back to buy it."

Kinkead nodded, grinning. "Yep: that were the first time I met this here skinny son of a bitch." And he pointed at the rail-thin Rowland.

"We got to talking," John began.

Then Kinkead continued, "And you said you was done with that bunch you'd been trapping with for more'n a year."

"Some folks just ain't meant to run together," Rowland agreed.

Matthew said, "You told me your outfit was breaking up that winter, picking sides then and there in Taos."

"Yep, some fellers following Ewing Young, and some others saying they was gonna tag along behind Antoine Robidoux. Only me and McAfferty didn't take no side when the outfit tore apart."

"McAfferty?" Hatcher inquired. "That when you two come and hooked up with us?"

With a nod Rowland looked up at their brigade leader and answered, "Damn—but that nigger never was the same since't he killed that Ree medicine man. He started to get . . . strange after that. Strange and . . . downright spooky."

"Damn if he didn't after he killed that medicine man," Fish replied.

"Just the fall afore we run all the way south to Taos—two year ago now."

"All the way from Ree country. That was a far piece to travel just to winter up," Graham observed.

"McAfferty, he was a nigger what wasn't gonna stay in that country where he'd just killed the ol' rattle shaker," Rowland recalled. "Hell, he told us it wasn't healthy for a man's hide to be caught in country anywhere close to where the Ree stomped around."

Scratch found that long trek hard to believe. "Just for him killing a Ree medicine man you tramped all the way down to Taos?"

"Don't you see?" Rowland tried to explain in a quiet voice that hushed the others. "This here McAfferty had him dark hair—shiny like a new-oiled trap and near black as the gut of hell itself—afore the night he had to kill that Ree medicine man."

Bass asked, "What you mean, *had* to kill the Ree?"

For a moment Rowland pursed his lips as if he were trying to pull out the particulars of that memory. "Something to do with what feller had the strongest medicine . . . to do with that medicine man fixing to steal McAfferty's Bible."

"He carry a Bible hisself?" Scratch inquired.

"Yup," John answered. "The man left us with hair black as charred hickory. An' he come back with it turned."

"No shit?" Titus asked. "So that's when his hair become white?"

Turning to Bass, Rowland explained, "McAfferty's hair is as white as new snow."

"What turned his hair?" Titus inquired.

John stared into the fire for long moments before answering. "Maybeso the hoo-doos."

"Hoo-doos!" shrieked Rufus Graham with a gust of sudden laughter.

"That's right," John said, nonplussed. "Like I said, McAfferty left our bunch with black hair . . . and come back with it and his beard turned white."

Rufus declared, "Like the man see'd a ghost!"

With a shrug Rowland continued, "The man never told any of the rest of us what scared him so. Said he wouldn't talk about it—claimed that he'd always counted on God to watch his backside agin' the devil."

"Not a word of what hoo-doo spooked him, eh?" Caleb asked.

"Nary a peep did we pull outta him," John explained dolefully. "All the way down to Taos that fall, I don't recall the nigger sleeping much at all."

"How's a man get by 'thout any sleep?" Scratch asked with a yawn.

"All I can tell you is on our trip south that white-headed nigger was awake when I closed my eyes ever' night, and he was awake when I opened my eyes again come morning."

Skeptically, Scratch asked, "Awake, doing what?"

"Just looking up at the sky near all the time, moving his lips like he was talking to somebody, keepin' a tight hold on his Bible."

"That's spooky right there," Hatcher declared.

"He packed that ol' Bible along in his possibles ever since I knowed him. Never saw him pull it out much," Rowland explained. "But after that night when he come back with his head turned white, McAfferty was one to keep that saddle-worn Bible right in his hand or laying by his side . . . ever since."

"McAfferty sounds to me like a man what got hisself spooked but good!" Bass observed.

Hatcher agreed, "Right from the very first time I laid eyes on him down to Taos, I knowed in my bones there was something a mite odd about that child."

"Yep," echoed Solomon. "Young as he was—to have his hair turn like it did."

"Don't matter how young a feller is when hoo-doos reach out an' grab hold," Rowland protested, stretching out his arm, making a claw of his fingers. "Hoo-doos gonna leave their mark on you."

Bass snorted. "Sounds to me like you believe in ghosts your own self, Johnny."

"How 'bout it, boys? Any of ye see'd any of McAfferty's hoo-doos yer own selves when ye was with him?" Hatcher added.

Shaking his head, Wood said, "I ain't never seen none for myself . . . but I rode many a mile, and many a moon, with Asa McAfferty. I saw what become of a man who did see a hoo-doo. A man what see'd a Ree Injun rattle shaker's hoo-doo!"

"Damn! If that don't give me goose bumps the way Johnny's talking!" exclaimed Isaac Simms, rubbing both of his forearms as if he had just suffered a sudden chill.

"Shit!" roared Elbridge Gray. "Johnny's got you jumping at shadows now too!"

Hatcher turned to Rowland, asking, "Whatever come of McAfferty that winter we rode back to Taos, John?"

At that moment in the timber above their protected valley, a wolf raised its voice to the clear, starlit autumn sky.

All nine of them turned and listened as the morose howl drifted away slowly, the sound swallowed by the utter, black immensity of that night.

After a bit of reflection Rowland answered, "Like I said, he didn't figger to join up with Young or with Robidoux's outfit. Hell, truth was both of 'em made it real plain that they didn't want him along come spring."

"So he go north with another outfit?" Scratch inquired.

"No," Rowland answered. "Near as I know, he never looked for a bunch to trap with after that. Like he knowed others down that way was talking about his hoo-doos that winter, like he knowed there wouldn't be a man wanted to trap with him."

Rufus asked, "What happened to him?"

"Dunno," John stated. "I heard tell he up and pulled out of Taos late two winters ago. There in Mexico one day. Gone the next."

Wood asked, "By hisself?"

"Yup. I heard he was all on his lonesome."

"Damn," Hatcher grumbled. "Here I was first thinking he become a strange goat . . . an' now I'm feeling a mite sorry for this McAfferty. Feel sorry for a man what no one wants around."

"How 'bout you, Johnny?" Elbridge asked. "Would you want to trap with McAfferty now?"

Shaking his head emphatically, Rowland answered, "Not a whore's chance in Sunday meeting I'd ever travel the same trail with that one. Something 'bout him killing that rattle shaker, something 'bout that ol' rattle shaker's hoo-doo medicine made McAfferty go . . . go real soft in the head." Then with a sudden, uncontrollable shudder of his body, John added, "This coon'll stay as far away from that crazy bastard as I can."

"He's trouble," Rufus added.

"Nawww, not like he's a bad sort," Rowland explained. "Just that . . . well, let's say trouble follers on his backtrail ever since the rattle shaker's hoo-doos come after him. Way I see it: McAfferty's gonna have trouble dogging him the rest of his days, for here on out."

"Man's got enough to worry about in Injun country," Solomon declared. "He don't have to take on a partner what's been turned soft in the head."

"So how 'bout you, Hatcher?" Bass inquired with a grin. "You ain't gonna get soft in the head an' keep us here till all the passes outta this valley are closed in, are you?"

"Nawww," Jack replied. "I figger we each have us one more turn at camp keeper—five days more—and we'll get on outta here."

"To Taos!" Kinkead roared with renewed enthusiasm.

"Damn right," Hatcher answered. "We push on over the high side and make for the mud-house Mexican settlements."

"Ah! Women got skin the color of smoked leather," Isaac Simms growled, a hunger glistening in his eyes.

Rufus Graham agreed, "And Workman's likker, clear as a summer sky and as strong as the kick of a mule."

"I'm half-froze for corn an' beans," Caleb Wood said wistfully, then licked his lips. "Don't make me no never-mind that their bread is flat as it can be—it's still bread to this here starvin' nigger!"

"I ain't had me no greaser bread since we put Taos at our rumps!" Rowland grumbled.

"This here nigger can't wait to get me some of that greaser tobaccy," explained Elbridge Gray. "How 'bout you, Jack? What you wanna get when we shine in Taos?"

"Music . . . music I don't have to make for everyone else," Hatcher explained, looking up at the cold sky dreamily. "I wanna listen and dance to such music them greasers play . . . while'st holding my arm round the waist of a thin gal or a plump one—hell, it don't make no matter to me! My, my, my: how I look forward just to spin a woman to some music and look down at her purty face, seein' right there and then in those eyes that she wants this here child to plant his wiping stick atween her legs."

"Stand back, you damned greasers!" Rowland shouted to the heavens. "Bow your brown heads to American free men come riding in from the mountains! Get back you damned *pelados* an' make way for free mountaineers come to shine in Taos!"

SEVEN

With each shrinking day Hatcher's brigade pushed man and beast alike from the first gray stain of predawn until past the coming of slap-dark, putting behind them every mile they could—every man jack anxious for Taos.

Halting at midday only to water the animals, the trappers doggedly pressed on as the winds grew stronger and the snows fell deeper, like mules with the scent of a home stall strong in their nostrils. Grown restless around their night fires, where they began to talk more and more of the Taos valley, more and more of the spicy food and heady liquor and that strong native tobacco. And as the men pulled their blankets and robes about them with the dropping temperatures, they spoke each night of the dusky women and that particular fragrance of Mexican skin.

"Not like no Injun woman I ever knowed," Caleb Wood advised Titus Bass.

Hatcher snorted. "An' sure as hell like no white farmer's gal back to the settlements."

Wasn't Amy Whistler a white farmer's wife by now? Likely she had her a brood of her own, tugging at her skirt, the newest tucked in her arm, suckling at its mama's breast. He remembered those breasts at times, how they broke the surface of that swimming hole back to Boone County, Kentucky. Firm and high, slicked with summer cool water, just begging him to fondle, to excite, to kiss each one.

How about Marissa Guthrie? Had she given Able Guthrie a grandchild yet? Why, the way that girl threw herself into the coupling, Titus was dead certain she was the sort could end up with a man of her own not long after he had pulled himself free and run off for St. Louis that autumn of 1815. Slipping away by the skin of his teeth—for he had fallen in love for the first time in his life . . . and if he hadn't escaped, he'd be there still. Working the land, planting seed, tilling the ground, and raising walls around them . . . just like Able Guthrie, like his own pap, Thaddeus.

How much better could those greaser gals be than was Fawn, the Ute widow he bedded that first winter in the Rockies? His first Indian, so warm and fragrant with the smells of grease and smoke, bear oil and old soot, had she been. Very much like Pretty Water, the Shoshone woman who had cared for his wounds and sated his hungers that third winter before it came time to leave as the high country began its spring thaw.

In their own way, each one of them hard to leave behind.

"Just be keerful you don't end up like Rowland or Kinkead," Elbridge Gray warned.

Scratch would grin every time one of the others chivvied him about the Mex gals. "Don't you worry none about me, fellas. I ain't the marrying kind."

"I wasn't neither," Matthew protested.

Hatcher would always roar, "Kinkead wasn't till he met up with Rosa!"

At which Kinkead would nod in affirmation and agree, "That's the solemn truth."

Moving south over the low ridge of the Bayou Salade, the outfit dropped west to strike the Arkansas once more, following it downstream for two days until they left the river behind to climb south slowly toward the lowest pass compressed among those mountains surrounding the narrow northern reaches of a valley that eventually widened its funnel into a fertile, verdant floor carpeted with autumn-crisp grass crunching beneath the icy remnants of winter's recent snow.

"You're in Mexico now," Rufus Graham explained as he brought his horse alongside Bass's saddle mount.

"Don't look no different to me."

Solomon Fish explained, "Been in Mexico since we come 'cross the Arkansas."

"How far north the greasers ever come?" Scratch asked.

With a spill of raw laughter Hatcher declared, "Never would they come this far north, Titus Bass. This still be the land of the mountaineer and the Injun. Ain't many a greaser gonna venture far outta their villages."

Down, down through the heart of that high valley they hurried against the lowering storms that gray-shouldered the peaks on their left and right. Finally they struck the river flowing into the valley in a tangle of streams given birth in that high ground to the west.

"A blind man could foller this all the way from here clear down to Taos," Caleb instructed Bass that afternoon as they began winding their way along a dim trail some distance back from the brushy banks.

Hatcher said, "The wust of the ride's over now, Scratch." Then he sniffed the cold air deep into his lungs. "Eegod, boys! Why, I swear I can smell tortillas and beans awready!"

Two days later Bass spotted his first herd of wild horses racing along the bench a short distance above them. None of the creatures appeared to be the least bit concerned about men capturing them—often loping along the outfit's line of march for hours at a time. On those occasions the trappers had to be very wary that none of their pack animals broke loose to follow the wild herd. The farther south they pushed, the more of those mustangs they encountered crossing their trail day after day. This had to be a horse thief's paradise, Scratch thought.

"Injuns in these parts?" he asked of the others one night at their fire as the men unfurled their robes and blankets, settling in for a few hours of sleep.

"Not many what a man might worry about," Jack replied.

Then Elbridge added, "Less'n the Comanche ride down on the town."

Hatcher nodded. "The Comanche been known to cause considerable trouble for the Mexicans."

Throwing his arm in a wide arc, Bass inquired, "This here Comanche country?"

"Not rightly," Jack declared. "They just come here to raid the poor *pelados*, to carry away everything they can. Horses, cows, mules, anything they take a shine to."

"That means they'll carry off Mex young'uns too," Solomon stated.

"What the hell they want with the young'uns?" Scratch asked.

"Turn 'em into good Comanche," Caleb said. "The boys they make into warriors, and the girls—well, down the line the girls gonna start having Comanche babies."

Rufus wagged his head sadly. "The greasers ain't all that good at putting up a good fight of it."

"Ain't they got any soldiers?"

"They got soldiers, Scratch," Isaac said. "But they ain't allays the sort to be any help."

"What these soldiers good for?"

"Sometimes they dare ride out on the Santy Fee trail what takes a man back to Missouri," Hatcher said. "But there's Comanche out there in that water-scrape hell. So most times them yellow-backed polecats are hanging round where they can be safe when they stare real hard at traders come in from the States. Making sure they're always somewhere they don't have to worry 'bout no Comanche."

"Mostly, them *soldados* gonna be where they find lots of women and pass brandy and some fandango to take in," Caleb said.

"Fandango?" Scratch asked.

"Mexican for dance," Rufus said with a generous grin. "A real hurraw an' stomp—with plenty likker and womens!"

Turning back to Hatcher, Titus asked, "So how bad these Comanche be?"

Jack's merry eyes darkened. "The Blackfoot be the devil's sumbitches up north. And down here the wust a man run up against be the Comanch'. Ain't no red nigger any finer on the back of a horse."

That night it snowed, right on into the pale, murky dawn as the sky continued to lower off those craggy mountain slopes rising on either side of them as they flung the fat, icy flakes off their robes and blankets, quickly rolling up the bedding and lashing it atop the packs they hung across the backs of their animals. The wind stirred just before sunrise, hurling itself at their backs all that day, whining and whimpering around them on into that night when they made camp just as the sky muddied and the snow finally let up.

"How far now, Jack?"

Hatcher ruminated on that a moment, then said to Scratch, "Less'n a week, give or take."

"Five days, I'll wager," Solomon declared.

"Ye're up to making a bet?" Jack asked.

"Five days," Fish repeated. "An' I said I'd wager."

"A week," Hatcher stated. "No less."

"Anyone else?" Solomon asked, gazing around at the others huddled shoulder to shoulder at the edge of the flames as he shook Hatcher's lean hand.

"Can't be soon enough for me," Kinkead groaned. "No matter how many days."

It began to snow again the following morning as the nine of them rolled out and stomped around to stir up some warmth in their limbs. Bass, Kinkead, and Fish went out to take the horses down to water, finding the narrow creek beginning to ice up along the banks. Using a dead limb he found beneath an old cottonwood, Scratch hammered away at a thin crust, breaking a large hole where the animals could drink before taking to the trail.

As he stood there shivering slightly, huddled within his soot-smudged, grease-stained red blanket, Bass watched the frosty halo over the herd slowly change from a misty gray to a delicate rose as the sun climbed briefly until swallowed by a thickening boil of snow clouds. As he watched, that tint of crimson gradually faded to pewter as the sun continued to rise, hidden once more behind the lowering of the heavens.

"C'mon, Scratch!" Caleb hollered as he and the others drove the horses back toward their camp. "We only got us five days till we reach Taos."

"Seven days!" Hatcher bellowed like a calf hamstrung by a pack of prairie wolves as he struggled past, huffing as he hefted a pack onto the back of a horse.

Wood waited a moment, then leaned toward Bass. "Five days," he whispered, and held up all the fingers on one bare hand. "Five."

It didn't matter to Titus. This close, those two days they argued over truly didn't matter. They were drawing nigh, near enough that Scratch could sense the keen edge to the anticipation building in the others, an anticipation that ignited an excitement of his own.

As long as he had been out here already, in the last few days Bass was coming to realize that everything would be brand-new in this country south of the Arkansas. Not just the peoples—both Mexican and Indian—but their food and drink as well, along with another new and foreign language bound to fall about his ears. As much as he had been swallowed up in the varied cultures and races at the international port of New Orleans back in his youth, or lived at the St. Louis crossroads of a nation busy with its westward expansion, Bass was surprised to find himself growing as anxious to reach this Mexican village as he had been to enter his first Indian village back in twenty-five.

But more than anything else, he was finding the country itself different from what lay to the north.

This mountain southwest was truly a land of extreme contrasts. While spring would give birth to richly flowered valleys, so too did high, snowcapped peaks rise well above the desert floor. Green, rolling meadows carpeted the slopes of hills all the way down to sun-hardened desert wastes speckled with ocatillo and barrel cactus, mesquite trees and frequent reminders of an even more ancient time in the sharp-edged, black lava fields that occasionally cluttered the landscape.

Always the land of the lizard, horned toad, prairie dog, and rattlesnake, this was also a country where he found cottonwood and willow bordering the infrequent gypsum-tainted streams where that "gyp" water might well cause most unaccustomed travelers to grow sick, stricken with a paralyzing bowel distress.

These vast, yawning valley plains stretched upward toward the purple bulk of hills, from there up to brick-red mountainsides timbered with the ever-emerald-green of pinion pine and second-growth cedar. At sunrise a man would find the treeless ridges staring back at him like some swollen, puffy, fight-ravaged eye. But by the time the sun rose high, that same vista would be painted a hazy blue, eventually turning to a deep purple as the sun finally sank to its rest. In such a land there was sure to come the summer heat of hell, the bitter cold of an unexpected and uncompromising blizzard in winter.

For much of the last few weeks, the nine and their animals had threaded their way through this high land of brilliant color and startling contrast by following the Rio Grande River itself as it flowed due south. Eventually, of an early afternoon, they stopped to water the animals for midday at the mouth of a narrow river that flowed out of the hills to the east to mingle its snow-melt with the Rio Grande.

"That there be the Little Fernandez," Caleb Wood instructed as he pointed toward the Sangre de Cristo Mountains.

Come evening, with the sun setting across the valley, those hills themselves would take on a crimson hue so realistic that it had reminded the early Spanish explorers of the blood Christ Himself had shed on the cross.

Isaac stepped up as their horses drank at the icy stream. "There be a pass up there a feller comes over. Just follow the crik down into this here valley, turn south yonder there . . . and you'll run onto the village called Taos."

Overhead the last of a winter storm was spending itself among the high places, while on the valley floor where they put their animals back on the trail, the snow fell gently. Here a man might find refuge from winter's harsh fury that battered the northern plains and Rockies. From spring until well into the fall here, green pastures welcomed the heat-jaded prairie traveler who stumbled in from the dry and dusty Santa Fe Trail. Here the shadows of the Sangre de Cristos offered a man respite from the harshest weather meted out by both summer and winter.

The valley had long been a refuge to weary sojourners.

As early as the 1300s the Indians had begun building the massive multistoried Pueblo de Taos, raising the thick mud walls near Taos Mountain at the northernmost end of the valley. Successive pueblos had been added over the centuries. Finally, after the threat of frequent and deadly attacks by roving bands of Comanche raiders had diminished, a new Spanish settlement was given birth. Named after a seventeenth-century Spanish pioneer who settled in the valley and made it his home, the tiny village came to be known as Don Fernando de Taos.

Up ahead in the lengthening shadows of late afternoon raced Kinkead and Rowland, kicking their horses into a gallop to shoot past Rufus and Isaac. At the top of the bluish, twilit rise covered with snow, the two yanked back on their reins, settled their horses, and pounded one another on the back. As Hatcher led the others up this last gentle slope, Bass heard the excitement in how Johnny and Matthew yelled back and forth with childlike eagerness, pointing this way and that, pulling their caps from their heads to signal the others to hurry, their long hair tormented with each gust of wind.

Bass stopped at last, gazing south, staring down into the valley for the first time. What with all the snow and those whitewashed adobe walls, it was hard for him at first to make out the village. Soon enough his eyes spotted the faint glow of candles and lamps brightening more and more windows as afternoon light oozed from the early winter sky.

"That there's Taos, Scratch," Hatcher said quietly.

"Welcome," Kinkead added, his eyes beaming. "My Rosa's yonder!"

Jack turned and asked, "Ye'll keep your head down tonight, Matthew? You too, Johnny?"

They glanced quickly at one another and nodded.

Kinkead declared, "We're going our own ways, Jack. This first night I'm laying low with Rosa's folks."

"How 'bout you, Rowland?"

"Me too, Jack," he answered, his happy face gone serious. "Don't wanna dance with no trouble—not after two years."

Hatcher nodded. "That's the chalk of it, boys. Slip into town quietlike, and don't let many folks see ye. We'll catch up to ye down to the square in a day or two."

"You'll see to our animals and plunder, won't you, boys?" Matthew asked the group.

"G'won now," Jack coaxed the two. "Ye got wives waiting for ye down the hill in Taos. Get yer gullet shined with lightning and yer stinger dipped in sweet, warm honey tonight!"

Rowland turned to gaze at Kinkead. "Jack don't have to ask me twice!"

They started to whoop like wild men as they kicked their horses into motion, but Hatcher hollered at them to be quiet. Instead, the two men raced down the snowy slope toward the distant village without another sound out of them but the hammer of the hooves, and the pounding of their excited hearts.

"Look at them two, won't you?" Caleb asked as the others sat in silence. "Like a pair o' bulls in the spring—"

"You'd be bellering like a scalded alley cat if'n you had you a woman tucked away down there!" Rufus scolded Wood.

Caleb wheeled on him. "Who says I don't have me a woman tucked away down there?"

"They really got wives down in that town?" Titus asked. "Mexican wives?"

"Yup," Jack replied, then winked wickedly.

"So what we gonna do when we get down there tonight? Find us some women and whiskey?" Bass inquired, the tip of his tongue licking his cracked lower lip.

"We ain't going to Taos tonight," Jack explained as he raised his face to the sky, peering this way and that at the onrushing darkness.

Down in the valley the distant peal of a solitary bell drifted up the slope.

After two rings a second bell took up the faint chorus. Back and forth the two rang for the space of a half-dozen heartbeats, then faded off into the cold as silence replaced their joyous song.

"What was that?" Scratch asked.

"Church down there," Isaac said. "Got two towers. A bell in each tower. They ring 'em at break o' day, then at noon. And again at eventide."

"Bells," Bass repeated. "I'll be go to—"

Caleb said, "Looks like we got here about the right time of the day."

"Right time of the day for what?" Scratch proclaimed.

"To get ourselves round to the far side of town 'thout the Mexicans seeing us come in," Hatcher declared, raising his right arm and pointing with his rifle to the hills west of the village.

"Them greasers cause us trouble?"

"Not the plain folks," Isaac said. "Just the greasers what run everything. The soldiers and the tax fellers what don't want Americans to trap no Mexican waters."

"How the hell they gonna know if we pulled our beaver outta Mexican streams?"

"They don't," Jack said with a shrug. "So they tax all the beaver we got—no matter where it come from."

This was startling news. Titus continued, "How's a man s'posed to pay a tax when he ain't got no money to begin with?"

"Them tax collectors and the soldiers what ride around with 'em take the government's cut from yer beaver."

"My beaver!" Bass shrieked. "They ain't gonna take any of my beaver— not after I lost those last packs when Bud, Silas, and Billy went under!"

"That's just what we're trying to explain to ye, Scratch," Hatcher said. "Them greasers working for the governor ain't gonna have a chance to take none of our beaver."

"Not a plew," Caleb echoed.

"H-how we keep 'em from it?"

"By taking our asses on over yonder there to the west now that it's dark," Jack explained.

"What's over there?"

"Workman's caves," Caleb answered. "That child makes good corn whiskey."

"W-whiskey?" Bass stammered.

"Taos lightning," Hatcher said. "Take the top of yer head off cleaner'n a Blackfoot tomahawk!"

"Lemme at it!" Bass croaked, his dry throat constricting in excitement.

"Ooo-hoo! Looks like Titus here got him a thirst, fellas!" Elbridge barked.

"Time we got down off this hill anyway," Jack advised. "A cold night like this, best thing a man can do is to find him a warm place where the wind won't blow—"

"Like Workman's caves!" Caleb interrupted.

"Damn right," Hatcher continued. "A warm place where he and his companyeros can pour some whiskey down their gullets!"

"Cómo la va?"

The loud voice came booming out of the night, echoing and reechoing off the narrow canyon walls. It was enough to cause Scratch's skin to prickle with cold despite his layers of clothing.

"Workman?" Hatcher called out after he had thrown his hand up and stopped them all as they were slowly picking their way along the dry creekbed in the inky darkness. "That you, Workman?"

"Who the hell's asking?"

"Jack Hatcher."

They heard sounds from the night—above and to their left: stones clunking together, pebbles ground underfoot.

"Mad Jack Hatcher, is it?"

Suddenly a figure emerged out of the gloom here at the bottom of the deep, dry creekbed.

Jack sang, "So there ye are, Willy!"

"You don't smell like no ghosts," the stranger said as he stepped to within a rifle's length of the muzzles of their horses. "And for sartin you don't look to be Mexican soldiers neither."

With a shrug Hatcher explained, "Just a bunch of fellers need a place to spread out our robes and hide away our packs for the season, Willy."

"Done for the winter, are you, Jack?" the man asked. "If'n that be so, kick off there and give me a proper greetin'."

Quickly dismounting, Hatcher stomped up and the two of them embraced, pounding shoulders and backs as Bass strained to get himself a better look at this William Workman. With nothing better than dim starshine it was hard to tell more than the fact that the man kept his face shaved and his hair cropped short, looking no different from a settlement storekeeper back in the States. Across his arm lay a rifle; in the wide belt that encircled his blanket coat were stuffed a pair of pistols. He wore no hat despite the cold, his pale face smiling as he turned from Hatcher to look up at the others.

"Who all's with you, Jack?"

"Ye know 'em, Willy," Hatcher explained. "All here with me 'cept Kinkead and Rowland."

Workman moved up another two steps, peering over the group. "Where's Joe?"

"Little's gone," Caleb replied.

"That you, Wood?" Workman asked. "You still throwin' in with this bastard Hatcher?" He turned to Jack. "How'd Little go under? You run onto some Blackfoot way up there where you was going?"

"He went sick, Willy. Got him the ticks last spring."

Then Isaac added, "Just afore the Blackfoot jumped us."

With a raw snort of humorless laughter, Workman said, "I warned you sonsabitches not to go up there to Blackfoot country when you lit out of here more'n a year ago. But would Mad Jack Hatcher listen to any sane man?"

"Hell, no!" Hatcher answered, slapping Workman on the shoulders. "What good would it do me ever to listen to a sane man?"

Workman brought up the muzzle of his rifle, pointing it in Bass's direction. "So who's the new man?"

"C'mon down here, Scratch."

"Scratch, is it?" Workman echoed as Bass kicked out of the saddle. "This new hand got him a real name?"

"Titus Bass," Scratch said, pulling off a mitten to hold out his hand.

"Good to make your 'quaintance, Titus. Whoa—your grip feels cold. Mayhaps we ought'n get you boys on inside to warm up."

"Ye got lightning? That'll warm me quick!" Hatcher declared as he and Workman turned and started off into the dark.

"You'll dang well play that fiddle o' your'n for every drop, Jack," the whiskey maker warned. "There ain't no free drink at Workman's still."

"Ye gone and wounded me, Willy! No man can't never say Jack Hatcher don't pay his own way."

"What's to eat, Willy?" Elbridge asked, trotting up right behind the two.

"Got me most of a small cinnamon I shot up in the foothills two day back," Workman answered. "That sow was young enough to still be tender."

Isaac asked, "Bet you've got some corn too."

"We can rustle you up some corn cakes to go 'long with that bear meat." Workman stopped and turned as the others came to a halt in a broad semicircle around him. "You boys go on with Jack here and get your packs off them horses afore we draw too much attention standing round here in the dark o' night. You know where you can corral your animals after you've got your beaver underground in the cave. Then you come on over to the mill house where I got the fire going, and we'll catch up on what all you fellers see'd since last you was in Taos."

That bear meat was superb, kept cool hanging back in the cavern across the dry creekbed from the hut and mill house William Workman had built himself out of all the loose stone found underfoot in this broken countryside west of Taos. Some two years previous he and John Rowland had discovered the narrow entrance to the cave just big enough for a dismounted rider to bring his horse through if the need arose. Once through the portal, however, the cavern opened up. Several smaller rooms jutted off that large main room.

After dropping their packs and possibles just outside the cave entrance, Scratch helped Isaac and Elbridge wrangle the horses and mules up the creekbottom another sixty yards to a bend in the canyon where Workman had constructed a post corral big enough to contain the animals a large trapping party would bring in. Against one side of the fence they found a pair of hayricks filled with cut grass, which the three trappers pitched into the corral for their trail-weary stock after removing all the bits and rope halters, draping them over the top fence rail.

By the time they stepped through the rough-hewn door into the low-roofed mill house, the fragrance of boiling corn and frying hoecakes instantly set Bass's mouth to watering.

"I ain't had no corn since . . . since I put the Missouri River at my back in twenty-five," he stated as Caleb Wood handed him a flat tinned plate. Titus brought the johnnycakes right under his nose and drank in their heavenly fragrance, conjuring up memories of a warm hearth, memories of a long-ago home slowly bubbling to the surface within him like a hearty rabbit stew.

"You ain't been out here long," Workman commented.

"Wondered if I'd ever get away from there," Titus replied as he propped his rifle against a stone wall, pulled the strap from his shoulder so his shooting pouch draped from the long weapon's muzzle.

"Settlers moving out toward the Santee Fee Trail at Franklin," the man said. "But I don't think they'll ever put down roots on the prairies. Not anywhere near that god-forsook country a man goes through 'tween here and there. Ain't worth the trouble to plow that ground."

"Too damn hot, that country," Elbridge garbled around a hunk of bear, corn soppings dripping into his chin whiskers. "What fool'd dare try to grow something in that desert, I'll never know."

As he speared a slab of the dark, lean bear loin onto Bass's tin, Workman continued. "I ain't been here much longer'n you, truth be. Got here first of July that year. Me and Matthew," he said, pointing his butcher knife off in the general direction of town, "the two of us and a third one named Chambers was gonna start us our own still."

"Ye see just how far Matt got being a whiskey maker," Hatcher said.

"Door's still open for him," Workman said. "You tell 'im I can always use a partner around here again."

"Ye tell 'im yourself, Willy," Jack declared. "I figger he'll be looking for something to do now that he's give up on the mountain trade for a while."

"He don't figger to trap anymore?"

Hatcher replied, "What he's been saying since spring."

Turning back to the fire to stab another slice of bear from the huge iron skillet suspended on a trivet over the glowing coals, Workman said, "I'll lay that he's off seeing his Rosa."

"Missed her something fierce," Solomon said.

"Don't doubt it," Workman agreed. "My eye's landed on a purty Mex gal my own self."

"Marrying kind?"

"Enough of the marrying kind that I went out and got myself baptized in the Mexican church last June," their host explained.

"B-baptized?" Hatcher stammered, spewing a mouthful of his meat onto the pounded clay floor.

"By Padre Antonio Jose Martinez," he said, laying a slice of bear on Caleb's plate. "In town the folks all call me Julian."

"Hoo—"

"Julian," Workman repeated the name for them. "S'pose that's William in their tongue, eh?"

"My, my," Hatcher exclaimed, then whistled low and long. "To think of another American getting hisself baptized just so he can get hitched up to a Mex gal."

"I don't figger you can ever understand that, Jack . . . because none of you are the kind ever to settle down in one spot long enough to have a wife, raise some kids, maybeso even have a job that means you don't have to look back over your shoulder for Injuns."

"I like my life just the way it is, Willy," Hatcher said, then corrected himself. "I mean, Julian."

"Man oughtta be happy with the way he's living his life," Workman declared as he scooted back from the fry skillet and got to his feet. "If he ain't happy, then he ought'n change something so's he can be happy. Like this new fella here—'pears he left ever'thing behind and come west to the mountains to find what wasn't back there."

"Happy? I'll tell ye what makes that nigger happy!" Jack snorted, pointing his knife at Scratch. "Bass is the sort what ain't happy less'n he's making life hard on me!"

Titus chuckled, saying, "It's for sartin no woman ever want you around long enough to get yourself baptized so you could marry up to her, Hatcher."

"See what I mean, Willy? This nigger's nothing more'n a pain in the ass to me."

Rufus Graham dragged the back of his hand across his lips, belched, then stood to stretch. "When you gonna bring us some lightning?"

"Thirsty?"

"Save for ronnyvoo last two year," Graham explained, "I been thirsty near all the time, Willy."

"I'll fetch us up some," their host stated, dusting his hands together eagerly.

By the time Workman was back with a clay jug in each hand, the rest had finished the last of their supper and had sopped up all the corn juice and bear grease. Some of the men even tipped up their tinware and licked their plates clean, eyes half-closed, savoring the last of the corn.

"Ain't gonna be the last meal you have, fellers," Workman said as he came back into the fire's light.

"Never know when you're riding with Jack Hatcher," Caleb grumbled. "Every meal might be a man's last—'cause you sure as hell don't always know when you're gonna get the next one."

They laughed together as the jugs clunked to the surface of a thick plank table before their host pulled small, crudely formed clay cups from the two big patch pockets on his short blanket coat.

Bass watched as the man began to pour a clear liquid into each cup, filling them about halfway to the top. When they all had a cup in hand, Workman passed the last to Titus and raised his own.

"A toast—to the new mountaineer," Workman said. "And his first trip to Taos."

"Hurraw for Scratch!" Hatcher bawled, slapping Bass on the back of his shoulders.

For a moment he watched the others stuff their clay cups to their hairy mouths, tossing back the cups and their heads at the same time. Then he brought his cup to his lips and tasted. Damn, if it didn't have the sting of distilled corn itself!

"What you think?" Workman asked.

"G'won, drink up and tell the man what ye think of his lightning," Hatcher demanded.

Scratch brought the cup from his lips, licking them a moment. "Tastes like John Barleycorn to me."

"Drink it down and tell me if'n you like it," Workman suggested, crossing his arms.

He had to admit that he did. Having found that first sip quite to his liking, Bass threw back the cup, letting the rest of the clear, potent liquid tumble back over his tongue, right on down his gullet, where it scorched a wide, fiery path all the way to his belly.

Impatient, Hatcher brought his face close, asking, "Well?"

"M-more," Bass stuttered, his voice as raspy as a coarse file dragged over crude cast iron. A bare whispery ghost of its former strength.

"I think he likes it!" Caleb declared.

"Lookit his eyes!" Isaac said as he leaned in an inch from Bass's nose. "This man's gonna be drunk on his ass afore he knows it—ain't he, Jack?"

"If that hoss don't take the circle, Willy!" Hatcher bellowed. "Looks like ye found 'nother nigger what took to yer likker right off!"

"M-more, I said," Scratch repeated, his voice a little less raspy this time. Already he was sensing the heat rise in his throat, his face and forehead feeling flushed and feverish.

Workman complied, pouring a full cup this time. Then the others held out their cups as their host made the rounds of that tight circle, dispensing more of the heady grain spirits he had distilled from wheat and corn grown nearby in the Taos valley.

"Now, s'pose you boys tell me all 'bout them scalps I see you have hanging from your belts and pouches," Workman declared. "And don't forget to tell me how you come to ride back into Taos with this here whiskey-lovin' Titus Bass!"

He didn't remember much about that night, just crumbs of recollection scattered across the empty plate of his consciousness, no more than scraps slowly tumbling round in his aching head as he forced himself out of the blankets before he peed all over himself right then and there.

Someone had put him to bed and covered him up. As he stood unsteadily, Scratch watched the slow spinning of a half-dozen points of light: the flames of low candles reflected against the walls, their pale light flutting against the dark void surrounding the cave entrance, where an ashy grayness told him dawn was coming soon.

How his head swam as he struggled to stay upright, wobbled, then almost went down, catching himself with a hand against the cold cavern wall. The others lay here and there, all six of them dead for all he could tell. But they weren't—because somehow they had gotten him back to the cavern from the mill house and stretched him out beneath his blankets.

This lathering his tonsils with whiskey wasn't as much fun as it used to be.

For an anxious moment he worried that he might have puked on himself while he'd lain there passed out. Sickened with the throbbing of a dull drum in his head, he stopped, braced himself against the wall just beneath one of the low, sputtering candles, and inspected the front of his shirt. Wiping a dirty hand down his chest, across his belly, and then lifting his breechclout to give it a quick inspection, Bass was satisfied he hadn't made a mess of himself.

The air grew chillier the closer he inched to the mouth of the cavern. A stiff breeze drifted down the riverbed the moment he stepped out into the morning air, nudging his wild, tangled hair. As he stood watering the ground, Bass realized the hangovers were beginning to hurt more than they ever had before. Maybeso the older he got, the more his body rebelled at the way he abused it.

Tucking the breechclout back over himself, Scratch fought the dizzying headache doing its best to blind him, then swallowed down a little of the bile revolting from his stomach. How his head pounded, reverberating with the dull echo of distant gunshots.

Then his stomach had finally had enough of his standing upright. What he had left from last night's bear and corn mush flung itself against the back of his tongue violently. Folding at the waist, Titus spilled it onto the ground until he gagged nothing but a burning bile. Slowly he straightened, distressed that his head still echoed with the hammering of those distant gunshots—

"Get them others rousted, goddammit!"

Turning, Bass strained valiantly to focus his bloodshot eyes on where the voice had come from—finding Workman coming out of the gloom of that cold, gray dawn. The man took shape out of the dizzying rocks, that rifle across his arm.

"Get Hatcher!" the whiskey maker shouted, his voice shrill, ringing off the narrow canyon walls. "Roll 'em out!"

Behind him Scratch could hear others stirring, muttering inside the cave. Groggy, he grumbled, "What?"

Workman came to a stop before him there at the entrance to the cavern. "There's trouble in the village an' we gotta go."

"Trouble?" Elbridge Gray asked as he emerged from the dark, swiping a big hand over his face several times.

"Gunfire," Workman said, starting to push past Gray. "Where's Jack?"

"I'm coming," Hatcher's voice was heard. Then he stood in the cold with the rest of them shoving up behind him.

"Hush! Listen," Rufus demanded.

They did, for the space of a few heartbeats until Workman spoke.

"Grab your guns, boys—and foller me."

"We gonna saddle up, Willy?" Caleb Wood asked.

"Ain't got the time!" he ordered. "We gotta go *now!*"

They had led their horses out of the pole corral and were on the cold, bare backs, crossing that dark bottom ground between the cavern entrance and the stone mill house, urging their mounts up the trail cut along the gentle side of the canyon onto the high ground, where Workman led them out at a stiff lope. The wind at their back, the eight rode toward the graying horizon, toward the gunshots, toward the rising screams of the women.

This was something totally new to Bass, this mix of rifle fire and those cries—the shrieks, the fear and horror of women. Never before had there been any womenfolk mixed in with the times he had been forced to spill blood.

But of a sudden he remembered Annie Christmas's gunboat on the Mississippi River. Moored up to the pier both bow and stern, what was once a Kentucky flatboat had been converted by its madame into a floating saloon and brothel. Just the sort of place where a man who drank too much might well never wake up. He recalled how Hames Kingsbury ended up having to gut the whore who came for him with blood in her eye. On Annie's boat the whores were every bit as treacherous as were the river pirates themselves. Leaving dead men and women behind, they had fled Natchez by the skin of their teeth, praising the fates for sparing their lives.

One of those big iron bells began to ring in the chill gray air—not two, as there had been at dusk last night. Just one bell, its tolling both a shrill warning, and a plaintive call for aid and succor. When the hair prickled on the back of his neck, Scratch tugged the coyote-fur cap down a little farther on his wild, unruly hair, hoping to make it more secure over the blue bandanna as they raced toward the outer buildings that gradually took form out of the gloom.

Someone was blowing a horn now—its clear, brassy notes shrill on the air between each resounding peal from the cathedral bell. But by now the gunfire was fading quickly, falling off to a few scattered shots, then a final volley by the time the horsemen tore into the western outskirts of the village. Down a narrow street they clattered across the icy, rutted ground pressed between two rows of low-roofed dirt buildings, the dawn-gray walls like skulls pocked with black-doored nose rectangles and empty eye sockets of lightless windows. Dodging a dog here and there, reining aside for a crude, wood-wheeled *carreta* shoved up against its owner's house, the eight kept on, stringing themselves out into a long file as Workman led them toward the center of town—

Where the screaming grew louder, wails and shrieks of horror and distress swelling like a massive wave rumbling toward them, about to engulf the horsemen, when Bass saw the crowd take shape out of the dark.

"Pray it ain't one of our boys," Isaac Simms growled beside him.

"One of our—"

Simms interrupted, "Gone under, Scratch. Gone under."

As the crowd congealed, become an organic, growing wild thing filling the street's entrance to the town square, that cathedral bell continued clanging its call of danger, the brass horn kept raising its stuttering, clarion call from somewhere else in the village. Perhaps a rooftop, its braying alarm coming from on high, Scratch figured.

They brought their guns up about the time Workman and Hatcher each threw up an arm to signal a halt. For another breathless heartbeat it appeared the crowd was turning to rush them, whirling away from the village square with murderous intent.

"It's the wimmens!" Jack bellowed as he yanked back on the reins, sawing them savagely to the left to spin his horse aside as the women surged toward the horsemen, screaming in utter chaos.

In a swirl of shawl and dress, they poured around the riders, every arm held up to the horsemen, every hand imploring the Americans, eyes wide and fear filled, tears streaming down their faces, mouths chattering a wild, confusing, ear-taunting cacophony of a foreign tongue.

"What're they saying?" Jack shouted at Workman as their horses wheeled about, jostling, bumping into one another as the rest of the riders came to an abrupt halt, trapped in the narrow confines of the icy, rutted street. "Ye make it out?"

"Comanche!" Workman barked the single word the rest of the horsemen could understand.

"Hatcher!"

Out of the milling mass of frightened women emerged the huge figure holding a rifle overhead at the end of his arm.

"Kinkead!" Jack bellowed.

It took several moments for the big man to force his way through the stream of women who flooded round him, and that tiny woman who dared not leave the safety of that shelter right beneath his left arm. They pulled at Matthew's clothing, touched his face with their fingers, stumbled backward in front of him as they screamed and cried out their warnings, their pleas, their prayers.

"Yer Rosa all right?" Hatcher asked as Kinkead and the woman reached the side of his horse.

He pulled her closer beneath his bulk. "Rosa ain't hurt. She came along—helped reload my guns."

Hatcher managed to get his horse close. "Willy says it was Comanche!"

With a nod Kinkead replied, "They hit us in the dark, Jack. Come in on the south side of the village."

Rufus asked, "Where's Rowland?"

"I ain't see'd him," Matthew declared. "But I heard him hollering for me during the fight."

"Heard him?" Jack inquired.

"His gun, heard it," Kinkead explained. "And I thought I heard him yelling for me too."

"Maybeso the Comanch' got him?"

With a shrug Kinkead said, "Could have, Jack. I know he was staying the night on the far side of the village, near where the Comanch' rode out when they was finished with us."

"What'd they get?" Workman demanded, trying to settle his nervous horse as the women shoved against the riders, filling every space between the Americans like water seeping between the boulders on a summer-dry creek-bed.

Looking down at Rosa, Kinkead had to shout to be heard. She appeared to listen a minute, then asked first one of the shrieking women, then another, before she stood on her toes and spoke into his ear.

Matthew gazed up at Workman and Hatcher as they jostled before him in the frightened crowd, his face gray with concern. "They got some women, Jack. And a few of the *niños* . . . chirrun too."

"Women? Some growed women?"

Kinkead nodded, swallowing. "Sounds like they got Rowland's woman . . . his wife."

Hatcher's eyes narrowed. "It don't look good for Johnny, does it?"

Staring at the ground a moment, Kinkead said, "Rowland ain't the sort to let the Comanch' take his wife if he were still alive."

"Let's go find Johnny afore we go after the red-bellies!" Workman hollered.

Hatcher whirled on him. "Ye fixing to go running after them Comanch'?"

"Damn right! We can't let 'em get too far ahead!"

Jack turned to the others in a blur, asking his men above the dying tumult of screams that had become more a sobbing, wailing, whimpering mob of mourners, "We going after them Injuns?"

"If Rowland's wife is took by 'em," Elbridge answered for the rest, "we're going after every last one of the bastards!"

Jack's eyes bounced off the hairy faces, each pair of bloodshot eyes like sunset-streaked portals into their tortured, hungover souls. He asked, "Elbridge speak for the rest of ye?"

Feeling the fear of it rise in a knot from the gut of him, Bass watched them all nod, some of the men growling their agreement like the distant coming of black-bellied thunder.

Hatcher turned toward him. "How 'bout you, Scratch?"

He felt the eyes on him, not just of the men who had saved his hash after he'd been left for dead, but of these half a hundred or more women who looked up at him with their pooling eyes. His belly was empty of everything but the fear, now that he had puked back at the cave. A cold, gut-wrenching fear . . . and the hot, rising flush of adrenaline giving fire to his veins.

"Ain't nothing could keep me from going."

EIGHT

"Ain't a man worth his salt gonna stand for Injuns stealing women and young'uns," Bass told them as they nudged their horses into motion, slowly parting the crowd of wailing women. "I 'member my grandpap telling me about the Shawnee and others what come down on the canebrake settlers way back, not just to kill and burn them folks out, but to steal the womenfolk and the young'uns too."

"This is different," Hatcher groaned as he studied the scene, side to side. "There'd be too damned many of them Comanch' for us to take on from the looks of things here."

Solomon hollered, "But them red-bellies gotta pay!"

"Too damned many of 'em!" Jack repeated, working to convince them. "There's just a handful of us."

"We ain't gonna give it a try?" Bass shouted.

"And get ourselves kill't in the bargain?" Caleb protested.

Titus sighed, his eyes imploring Hatcher. "Awright, Jack. We find John Rowland first—then go out there on their trail and see if we figger out how many we're up against by the looks of the tracks."

For a long moment their leader considered that. "So be it. I don't cotton to no Injun carrying off no woman or child neither, boys. We'll go find Johnny . . . then we'll see what the trail's got to tell us about what we'd be up against."

There erupted a spontaneous, raw cheer among these men yanked from their blankets, heads throbbing with a long-overdue hangover, men grouchy, out of sorts, and damned well ready to do battle.

"Get you yer horse, Matthew!" Hatcher shouted, turning to fling his words behind him as the Americans moved their animals slowly into the noisy crowd filling the village square. "We gotta find Johnny!"

"I'll catch up to you!" Kinkead said, clutching his Rosa tight. "G'won past Rowland's hut, off yonder—I figger we'll cut the trail out by his place."

On all sides of them the devastation increased as they pushed for a narrow street on the far side of the village square. There at the corner squat-ted an old woman, a filthy shawl hanging half on her head, each of her hands resting on the body of a dead man crumpled at her knees. Beneath her fingers lay a bloodied face dotted with a gray stubble, the old man's skull cracked open. At her feet sprawled the body of a younger man, perhaps a son. At least four arrows were stuck deep in his bare brown back. A dog slinked close, cautiously, its feral nose twitching at the smell of blood and gore seeping from the bodies.

Bass gave heels to his horse, reining straight for the cur. The dog's neck ruff bristled as Scratch leaned over, swinging his rifle butt for the canine, smacking it in the ribs. Rolling over and over with a pitiful yelp, the dog picked itself up from the icy ruts and scurried away down the street, tail tucked between its legs.

Here and there in the village around them some of the squat adobe houses smoldered, wisps of ghostly smoke seeping from the rawhide-covered windows, curling up in twisted columns from the portals where the doors hung akimbo on broken hinges. Overturned *carretas*. A dead goat or dog, a pig or some chickens—the refuse of animal carcasses strewn about to mark the Comanches' path through town.

Villagers suddenly converged on the path the Americans were taking, appearing from behind them in the narrow street, flowing in from both left and right to form a noisy mob. Weepy-eyed women and angry men shuffled into that open ground where a handful of squat sapling-and-mud wattle huts stood leaning against the cold dawn sky. There on the snowy, trampled ground three women were hunched over their prey, pummeling the enemy again and again with short pieces of firewood, one wailing hag swinging a long wrought-iron fireplace poker. More of the mob surged forward, eager to join in—shrieking, swinging, and kicking.

"Get back!" Hatcher bellowed above them as he steered his horse into their midst. "Goddamn ye—get back!"

The crowd may not have understood his words, but there was no mistaking the gringo's meaning. Slowly the villagers stepped back, and back some more, until the trappers recognized the bloodied, battered body of an Indian.

He didn't look to be too tall a man, dressed only in a shirt and breech-clout above his moccasins. A blanket had been torn from his waist. Bare-legged, his hair disheveled, the Indian had a face almost unrecognizable as such.

Someone had even begun to decapitate the body. A woman nearby shook with rage, a huge knife trembling in her bloody hand.

"He dead?" Solomon asked as he halted his horse with the others.

"Damn well better be," Caleb growled. "Let 'em work the son of a bitch over, Jack. That dead Comanch' is the only thing they can take it out on now."

"First whack, it's my turn," Hatcher said as he kicked his right leg up and to the left, sliding off the bare back of his horse.

The crowd inched back even farther, muttering in unrequited fury as he strode up without hesitation, yanking his skinning knife from the sheath hung at his hip. Without a word he knelt, whizzed the sharp blade around the head, then wiped the knife off on the Indian's shirt before he stuffed it away. Placing a foot on the warrior's face, Hatcher leaned back against the Coman-che's thick hair until the scalp peeled away, complete with the tops of the ears.

This moist, limp trophy he held up for all to see at the end of his outstretched arm. Slowly he turned, the blood dripping in the dirty snow. Suddenly Hatcher opened his mouth and let out a long primal scream. Noth-ing close to being a word, only a frightening sound—some guttural, wild, and feral noise the people in that crowd understood.

"Wagh!"

With that ear-shattering cry of the grizzly boar preparing for battle against one of its own, Jack pushed on through the crowd, walking up to a wooden door, where he looped the long black hair over the top hinge, took a quick step back, then spit on the scalp.

As others, mostly old men and young boys at first, shoved out of the throng to imitate the trapper by spitting on the scalp themselves, Hatcher turned and pushed his way back through the crowd. At that moment some of the infuriated Mexican women threw themselves back onto the body, resum-ing their brutal, passionate dismembering of the dead enemy.

Jack grabbed a handful of his horse's mane and flung himself onto its back. Taking up the reins, he brought the animal around and began to part the growing crowd that clamored for vengeance upon the raiders. One by one the Americans slipped their horses through that narrow gap in the mob. Alarmed by sudden and wild shrieks from the Taosenos, Bass turned to look over his shoulder—seeing the Indian's head appear above the throng. In the next moment it was hoisted far above the Mexicans at the end of a long, sturdy pike, the people swirling about on their heels like a throbbing mass below this gory, eyeless trophy they began to carry back toward the square.

As the mob washed away, a group of young boys led by a pair of old women stayed behind to tie lariats to the wrists and ankles of the headless body. As the last rope was knotted, the youngsters took off on foot, wildly screaming together as the beaten, bloodied, pummeled body bounced, tumbled, and flopped crazily behind the racing boys. Hobbling along behind the torso came the teetering old women, both of them striking what was left of the enemy again and again with firewood switches.

While the clamor of the mob faded toward the square, from a side street came the sudden clatter of boot heels echoing off the cold whitewashed walls of the village. Suddenly more than fifty Mexican soldiers burst around a corner. The trappers brought up their long weapons. For a terrifying instant, both groups stared at one another provocatively—ready for the other side to open fire. Every bit as disheveled as the Americans, the soldiers looked as if they too had just been pulled from their beds. Very few of them wore a complete uniform—and those who had managed to pull on their coats hadn't taken the time to button them in the morning's cold. Red-eyed, pasty-faced: these were men rousted from their barracks with the toe of a boot or the point of a bayonet.

"Señores!" the thin-faced officer at the head of the formation finally yelled as he took two steps toward the trappers, slapping a sword against his tall boot. *"Americanos!"*

With his eyes locked on the officer, Hatcher quietly spoke from the side of his mouth, "Willy—ye know their talk better'n I do. Tell 'em to get out of our way so we can find our friend."

After a quick dialogue, Workman said, "This one—he's the ensign."

"What's that?" Hatcher demanded.

"The big soldier chief here 'bouts," the whiskey maker replied. "Name's Don Francisco Guerrero. These here are his soldiers 'cause he's Senior Justice and War Captain of San Geronimo de los Taos."

A smirk crossed Jack's bony face. "This bastard's got too damned many names for me, boys! Willy, tell him to get his ass out of our way."

Wagging his head emphatically, Workman protested, "But they ain't fixing to stop us—"

"Damn right these greasers won't stop us!" Isaac bellowed as he came up to stand shoulder to shoulder with Hatcher.

Workman continued, "But this here Guerrero says they found the Injuns' trail."

"Where?"

"Heading north out of town," Workman said to Hatcher, pointing.

"With them red niggers gone, we go find Johnny—"

"They want us to help 'em go after the Comanche."

Hatcher turned to look at Workman now. "Why they want our help trailing after a bunch of Injuns?"

"Guerrero here, he says the Comanche took some women and children with 'em."

"We know that!" Jack snapped.

"One of them women is the wife of the gov'nor," Workman explained quietly. "And . . . they run off with his li'l girl too."

"Why us?" Hatcher demanded, eyeing the soldiers suspiciously.

Licking his lips, Workman sighed, "They figure the only chance they got of trailing the Comanche is using us gringos as trackers."

"Why use us gringos?"

Workman grinned. "These Mex think we're damned close to being 'bout as bad as Injuns anyway, Jack."

"So we work for the Mexican army as trackers?" Jack squeaked in protest. " 'Cause we're the only ones can foller Injuns?"

"To hell with 'em!" Caleb snarled. "They can track the Comanche on their own!"

"There's J-johnny!"

At Isaac's wild cry, Scratch jerked around.

His forehead smeared with blood, Rowland suddenly emerged from a thick veil of smoke that clung close to the snowy ground like the bushy tail of a black cat switching back and forth as it waited patiently for a mouse to come within pouncing distance. Soot smeared his face in broad, grotesque patches.

"T-they got m-my . . . Maria," John sobbed, his eyes pooling, tears spilling down his cheeks, tracking the black soot as he stood before the smoking ruin of the hovel that was his Taos home.

Hatcher held down his hand, grasping Rowland's in sympathy. "We been told they got away with some women, and young'uns too."

John nodded, choking on his sobs. "When I come out of the house, I see'd they had the gov'nor's wife and his little g-girl with 'em," Rowland explained. He turned away suddenly, looking to the north, swiping a hand first beneath his nose, then dragging it beneath both eyes, smearing soot. "The red-bellies knocked me in the head and left me for dead, I s'pose. Afore they took 'em all that means—"

"We're going after your Maria now, Johnny," Rufus said as Rowland looked away, a man clearly uncomfortable with his grief.

"We'll bring her back to ye."

Rowland whirled back around on them, his wild eyes darting between his friends and the soldiers, his lips moving wordlessly for a moment before his voice crackled in its growing rage the moment he lunged forward and seized hold of Hatcher's reins. "I'm going after her with you!"

"Ye're . . . hurt right now," Jack explained, rubbing his fingers across his own forehead there below the front of his badger-fur cap. "Better ye stay behind."

As if he had been unaware of the wound, John touched his bloody brow where the gaping skin had been split with a club of some sort. Rowland said, "Ain't nothing can keep me from killing my share of those red sonsabitches."

"It's gonna be a long ride—"

"You ain't leaving me!" he shrieked, balling up a fist and daring to shake it right under Hatcher's chin. "I can find my own way just as good as I can ride with the rest of you."

Hatcher dropped his reins and with that empty hand gripped Rowland's defiant fist. "Ye ain't goin' on yer own, Johnny. Ye're gonna ride with yer friends. We aim to all go after yer Maria with ye—together."

Bass watched those simple words shake that wounded, grieving man right down to the soles of his moccasins. He stood there trembling, tears gushing from his eyes as he tried to control the sobbing, tried his best not to show his grief in front of these hardened, bloodied veterans of mountain winters and Indian warfare.

"It's awright, Johnny," Solomon reminded him quietly as the wild shrieks of the mob faded behind them. "A man what lost his wife got him a right to get broke up just like you."

Jack reminded, "Ain't a one of us wouldn't cry too."

"Been you got rubbed out, Johnny," Isaac admitted, "I'd be broke up like that my own self."

Rowland suddenly dragged in a deep breath, slowly pulling his fist from Hatcher's grip as he gathered himself together with a trembling shudder of emotion. Biting his lower lip a moment, the trapper blinked his eyes clear, swallowed hard, and said, "Lemme find a horse—just gimme chance to find me a horse . . . they got mine . . . run off with mine—"

"Get you a horse," Jack agreed. "We'll fetch us up some saddles and food out'n the houses here first whack—something for the trail. We'll set off after ye've got a horse."

"How 'bout the soldiers here?" Workman asked. "What we tell them?"

"Tell 'em . . . tell 'em go get their horses pronto, Willy. Tell Guerrero we're gonna lead 'em to them Comanche."

"Sun's coming up," Graham pointed out as Workman turned aside to speak to the Mexican officer.

The trappers turned to gaze east just as that loud cathedral bell pealed its last and the brassy horn's final note drifted into the cold dawn. The top edge of the bright orb was just emerging over the Sangre de Cristos, every bit as red as blood. The blood of Christ, Scratch was reminded as some of them gasped at this vivid portent written there between the mountaintops and the early-winter skies—the underbellies of the cold, bluish clouds suddenly aflame with savage streaks of crimson.

"That's a sign, by God," Isaac whispered while the soldiers turned on their heels and double-timed it back down the rutted street toward their stables.

"Damn right," Elbridge grumbled in agreement. "Gonna be a bloody day for them Comanche."

Bass figured it would be a long and bloody day for them all.

That first night the Comanche didn't stop.

Neither did the Americans and the Mexican soldiers strung out behind them on the backtrail.

Scratch thought Hatcher's bunch was about as prepared for this endurance ride as they could have been even if they had been given an hour to make ready. The only thing that might have been better was to have themselves some more guns. The villagers dug up enough blankets and saddles for the Americans, a few gourd canteens, and some poor cloth bags filled with meager offerings of food. It touched Bass's heart to see how these simple people, who had so little, expressed their gratitude for what risk the trappers were about to take.

As it was, the Americans made good time that day, stopping for a few minutes every couple of hours as the afternoon aged and the winter light waned and night was sucked down out of the eternal sky all around them.

Then they were alone with the land, and the black gut of night, alone with one another once more. Somewhere behind them in the dark the Mexican officer and his men were struggling to force their tired horses into the cold night. They were making a lot of noise, every clatter and voice sounding all the louder here in the dark. At first their clumsy bumbling had angered Titus, but over the long, cold hours in the saddle, he gradually figured that they just might have a chance to turn that bumbling into an advantage, one that might somehow pay off in a big way.

If the Comanche believed they were being followed by soldiers who had no real chance to catch up to them, and even if the Mexicans did catch up, there would be no way in hell Guerrero's men could beat the warriors. . . . Then the trappers might just have a shot at rigging a surprise for the raiders.

There wasn't a whole hell of a lot said among Hatcher's men as they loped their horses north toward the foot of the hills that winter dawn, then found the wide trail of Indian ponies driving along stolen horses, cattle, and a noisy, bleating herd of sheep sweeping around to the south against the upland. The Comanche were doubling back toward the high country, turning east into the difficult terrain of the Sangre de Cristos, striking the narrow valley of Fernandez Creek itself.

Near midmorning Hatcher had called a short halt, turned around, and faced the rest of them, discovering Kinkead catching up to them on their backtrail, the Mexicans strung out down the slope behind him.

"Yonder comes Matthew," Jack quietly told the rest as they came out of their saddles. "We'll let the ponies blow till he gets up—then we'll go on."

Scratch asked, "You figger them greasers gonna stay up with us, we keep humping like this, Jack?"

"They'll stay up."

Then Workman added, "Any soldiers what bring in the governor's wife and daughter—they'll be heroes, don't you know. That Guerrero's gonna damn well make sure his men stay up the best they can, even if he's gotta stick 'em with that fancy sword of his."

For a moment they all fell quiet as the horses snorted and blew, some tearing noisily at the dry grass. A few of the men watched Kinkead approaching, others stared higher into the foothills rumpled against the high mountains.

"Those red sonsabitches going up there, ain't they, Jack?" Caleb said it more than he asked it, for it was as plain as pewter where the Comanche were heading.

"It's for damned sure they ain't tried one lick to blind their trail," Bass declared.

Elbridge agreed, "Not with all them cows and sheep they been driving with 'em."

"Red bastards," Hatcher growled almost under his breath. "They don't figger no one to try following 'em."

"Leastways no white man," Rowland said as he eyed the ragtag formation of more than fifty soldiers struggling up the slope behind them.

Hatcher nodded in agreement as Kinkead came up, hauling back on his reins and letting out a long sigh himself. His eyes landed on Rowland, and he urged his horse over, holding out his hand.

"Johnny."

"Matthew."

Kinkead dragged a hand under his nose. "Damn, but it's good to see your face."

"The others," Rowland started, his voice already cracking with emotion once more, "they tol't me you figgered me for d-dead."

Kinkead touched his own brow below the blanket cap he had pulled down over his bushy hair. "Half-dead anyway, from the looks of you. We ought'n sew that up—"

"M-maybe later," Rowland argued. "After . . . after . . ."

Kinkead's eyes moistened. "I'm glad . . . glad you're with us to go get your Maria."

Hatcher watched Rowland turn away, blinking his eyes. Clearing his throat, Jack used his rifle to point up the creek into the timber and rugged slopes that stood over them. "Looks like they're run off for the highlands, Matthew."

Kinkead squinted, peering into the hazy distance that softened the clarity of those high peaks. "A good escape."

"Them dram-med Injuns knowed just how to make a good getaway, wasn't they?" Isaac said.

"Damn right," Caleb agreed, glancing back at the distant soldiers. "They knew no greaser was gonna foller 'em up there."

"Not when most of them greasers sore afraid of a ambush," Solomon declared.

"But we ain't greasers," Bass argued.

"And we ain't afraid of them Comanche neither," Caleb stated.

Jack nodded. "Them sumbitches ain't counting on no one coming after 'em once they make it into the tough going, do they, boys?"

They all grumbled in solidarity.

Hatcher continued. "Way I see it, only men who can stand any chance at all going after 'em is a bunch of plew niggers like us what can ride the ass end out of Comanche pony in mountain country any day of the week. Any season of the year."

The way he said it made Bass shudder. They hadn't brought along bedrolls, only what poor blankets the villagers had pulled from their mud hovels, donating what little they possessed to the gringos. . . . Then he consoled himself: wasn't a one of Hatcher's men didn't really figure on this chase lasting all that long to begin with. And right then he had the feeling they really wouldn't be sleeping much at all until it was over, one way or the other.

For a fleeting moment Scratch felt the whimper well up inside him, feeling sorry for himself over the sleep he had lost last night by staying up to drink so damned much of Workman's brew—that and the sleep he was bound to lose until this chase was settled, one way or the other.

But, then, a man could always catch up on his sleep, he figured, still as young as he was, what with closing in on his thirty-fifth winter. Besides, if he was given a choice, going without any shut-eye for a few days was far preferable to sleeping out eternity like the dead. Like the men he himself had rubbed out were sleeping right then. Men who did their best to put him under.

These ten were alone with their thoughts while that day grew old and the light began to muddy, then to fade beneath the bony fingers of lengthening shadows. The Mexicans were struggling along behind them, still out of sight behind the last ridge or back beyond that last bend in the canyon. And the Comanche were still somewhere ahead of them, above—where they could likely look down and see the Americans dogging their backtrail. Titus figured the chances were better than good they were watched from time to time throughout that cold day as the clouds hovered among the peaks overhead. Black-cherry eyes peering back now and again to survey the distant, snaking movement of ten horsemen leading those half a hundred soldiers.

No telling what might happen to those white women and children once the Comanche believed their pursuers had halted for the night, no longer pushing the chase . . . when those raiders were free to halt, light their fires, and take a good, close look at the women they'd thrown up on horses and whipped out of the village. Women like Rowland's wife.

It made Scratch shudder.

"We ain't stopping here for long, ye understand," Hatcher declared brusquely at twilight when the sun had receded from the flat land far below them, gone beyond the western hills on the far side of the Taos valley.

"Ain't we gonna rest none?" Graham asked wearily, his face liver-colored with fatigue like the rest of them. Then Rufus noticed at the way the sudden pinch of pain crossed Rowland's face and said, "Hell, forget it, Jack. . . . I s'pose we ought'n keep on long as we can see far 'nough in front of us for the horses."

"Just what I was figuring myself, Rufus," Jack replied. "It's for damn sure them Injuns gonna be stopping somewhere up ahead once it gets dark enough—but they'll keep on climbing long as they can."

"I'll wager them bastards get a mite spooked in these here mountains at night," Caleb observed.

Isaac said, "For sartin the Comanch' ain't used to no mountains, that's for sure."

"They're flatlanders, by whip," Solomon agreed.

"Maybeso we can turn that back on 'em," Bass declared.

"What ye mean?" Jack asked, his eyes narrowing in interest.

"Like you boys said: they ain't on their own ground," Scratch explained. "Even if they ain't spooked by the mountains or the night, leastwise we know they ain't on their home ground where they're used to fighting."

"Bass is right," Workman said enthusiastically. "This is home ground for you fellers. That's gotta count for something."

Hatcher nodded, thoughts clearly spinning round in his head, and he growled, "We'll make it count for something, boys. Willy, turn back down-trail and go talk to that Guerrero soldier. Get him to hurry up his men now that it's getting dark."

"I'll bet they're the sort to stop for the night," Simms grumbled.

"They cain't this night," Hatcher argued. "Tell 'em in Mexican that we gotta use these hours of darkness to close the gap on the Comanche the most we can."

"Right." And Workman began to turn his horse around.

Jack continued, "Ye stay with 'em, Willy—till I send one of the boys back for you."

The whiskey maker sawed back on his reins. "Stay with them soldiers?"

"Yep," Jack advised. "Till tomorrow sometime."

Concern knitted Workman's brow. "Why tomorrow I gotta wait to join back up with you?"

"We eat up enough of the ground atween us and the Comanch' tonight," Hatcher explained, "we'll have us a chance to lay a trap for them sumbitches afore tomorrow night."

The whiskey maker nodded. "You want me to tell Guerrero you're gonna lay a trap for the Comanche?"

"Ye tell 'em we got a chance at getting the women back, only if them soldiers ain't afraid to keep on comin'."

"All right, Jack. I'll wait back with 'em. Wait till you send one of the boys to come fetch me up."

"When I do," Hatcher said quietly, "it'll be time to bring them soldiers up on the run. Time for us to open up the dance on them Comanche."

Workman didn't utter another word, only nodding at two of the men as he reined his horse about and set it off down their backtrail into the mountain twilight. In moments he was gone from view, engulfed by the growing gloom, along with the fading muffle of his horse's hooves, that last vestige of him swallowed by the trees and the boulders, become a part of the night coming down around them.

"Caleb, I want you and Bass to hang back ahind the rest of us." Hatcher waited till the two of them nodded. "Keep yer eyes on the downslope so them red sumbitches don't double back and pull a grizz on us. Let's move out."

They followed him into the dark, across the open ground and past the stands of tall evergreen and spruce, where the shadows seemed to loom all the larger for the coming of night as the stars winked into view overhead. Right then it didn't feel all that much colder than it had been during the day, Bass thought. Odds were good it would be before morning, before sunrise, before the earth ever started to warm once more.

Jack stopped them not long after moonrise some four hours later. He slid from his Spanish saddle, only motioning with an arm that he wanted the other eight to do the same. Gripping their reins, the bone-weary men stepped in close.

"Solomon, you and Isaac good at a sneak," he began in a low voice. "What with the moon coming up and it being dark for some time now, I figger them Comanch' gonna be ready to hold up for what's left of the night so they can get 'em some sleep. You two keep going 'head of us—find out where and when they stop for camp and some sleep."

Bass looked over at Rowland. He knew that the man damned well knew better. If the raiders stopped for the rest of the night, sleep might not be all they stopped for. That brand of cruel worry had already been at work at the man all day—carving deep lines in Rowland's grayish face.

If the warriors had no more than three or four hours head start on them at the most, then what hours remained between now and daybreak could hold the key to freeing the women. Staying on the trail of those ponies and cattle and sheep here in the cold and the dark might well be their only chance of catching up to the raiders before they got over the mountains and down onto the plains. Down onto the flat where they would again be on their home ground, where they and their ponies would again have the advantage of numbers and knowing the terrain.

But up here, across the next few hours, the Americans would have the advantage to use, or lose. Either they would succeed because of how they used the time and the terrain, or they would lose because they had recklessly squandered both.

"Johnny," Hatcher said as Solomon Fish and Isaac Simms disappeared on up the hoof-chewed trail left by the raiders. "Want ye stay near me."

"Sure, Jack."

"See to yer cinches, boys," the leader reminded the rest. "We'll give them two fellers a li'l bit more rope till we foller along."

In something less than an hour, with the moon climbing above the plains to the east, Hatcher suddenly threw up his hand and whispered harshly for a halt. Out of the dark limned two horsemen riding low along the withers until they made out their companions.

Solomon Fish straightened. "Figgered it had to be you."

"Ye run onto 'em?"

Simms nodded as the rest of the bunch came to a halt on Hatcher's tail root. "Looks to be 'bout half of 'em sleeping. Other half up watching."

"They got a fire?"

Shaking his head, Fish said, "No. Not a damned one. They ain't taking no chances, Jack."

"Damn," Hatcher grumbled, scratching at his chin in reflection. "I don't think we're gonna jump 'em this way, fellas."

Between that gap of the missing four front teeth, Rufus asked, "If'n it ain't in the dark—how the hell you 'spect us to su'sprise them red niggers?"

"Lookit the moon," Jack ordered them.

Caleb asked, "What you saying?"

"This is a cagey bunch of niggers, they are," Hatcher told them. "Don't ye figger they're the sort to be up and on down the trail soon as it gets light enough to see?"

"Damn right," Rowland protested, spewing his words. "That's why we ought'n go on in there now!"

Hatcher put his hand out dramatically, grabbing the front of Rowland's blanket coat. "We do that, Johnny—not knowing where them women are, where yer Maria is in that bunch, they'll kill all them prisoners in the dark afore we can get in there to know who to shoot, who to save."

"She's . . . Maria . . . damn—"

"I know," Hatcher said, turning to look at the others again. "So how much time ye boys figger we got till it gets light enough for them Comanch' to go riding off?"

"Not much," Rufus said.

"Tell me how long."

Bass had been studying at the position of the moon hung there a little south of west in the sky, slowly laying one hand lengthwise right above the horizon, then laying the other horizontally atop it, then the other hand on top of that one until he had a count of distance from the horizon.

In that heavy silence Titus said, "We got less'n four hours left."

"Then we gotta get our trap set in three hours," Hatcher said. "I don't wanna take the chance we'll get caught moving, so we'll figger they'll be up and on the trail afore first light."

"Three hours," Rowland repeated. "Then what?"

"Then we'll kill the sumbitches."

"How we gonna do that?" Solomon asked.

"Let's get moving," Jack suggested. "We'll sort the rest out once I find us a good place to spring the trap."

Bass didn't know what Hatcher had in mind; then, again, he figured he did know. Simple enough what they had to do: they were going to be waiting somewhere ahead for the Comanche.

"But before we set off again," Jack said, "Scratch—I want ye to ride back to tell Workman what we're planning."

"Us to get ahead of 'em?"

"Have Willy tell the soldiers to keep on coming, no stops now. That goddamned noisy bunch gotta be coming close enough for to scare the Comanch' into moving outta their camp."

"And us," Scratch replied, "we'll be waiting on down the trail for them Injuns to come running right smack into us—right?"

"Right on one count: we want them soldiers to flush them Injuns into us."

But Bass was confused. "What d'ya say I'm wrong on?"

"You and Workman can't come catching up to us."

"Why not?"

"Someone's gotta keep them soldiers up and humping, high behind . . . or this plan ain't gonna work," Hatcher advised.

"So you want me to stay behind with Workman and the soldiers?"

"You two just make sure them greasers are close enough ahind the Comanch' that ye can jump on in the fight when me and the rest of the boys here start up the band."

"When's that gonna be?" Rowland asked impatiently.

Hatcher turned to him. "I hope we can wait till sometime after we got enough light to see Injun from greaser . . . from American."

"God pray that we have enough light," Kinkead mumbled.

"That's the plan?" Bass asked, not sure if he had it all square in his mind.

"Ye just have them soldiers ready to run up on the back-ass of them Injuns soon as ye hear us lay down the first shots into their faces," Hatcher explained.

"Merciful heavens! We'll have 'em in cross fire," Caleb declared.

"That's a touchy place to put us," Rufus argued. "Out front like that."

Jack fumed a moment, then growled, "Any of ye got a better idea what to do here and now?"

As he glared at them one by one, most of the rest turned their faces away.

Finally Hatcher said, "Awright. Since't none of ye got a idea what's better'n mine, we'll go with my plan. Scratch, ye take off now."

Holding out his hand, he shook with Jack, Kinkead, and three more before he said, "See you boys afore sunrise. Keep your goddamned eyes peeled and don't shoot anything that looks like me, you hear?"

Some of them grinned nervously as Scratch mounted up and reined the horse around, adjusting his position in the Spanish saddle. Its seat was a bit too small, even for his bony butt, but with its stirrups the saddle was better for making a long ride than having nothing at all.

"See you, boys," he said once more.

"We'll find us a hollow piece of ground," Hatcher explained as Bass was bringing his horse around. "Where we can hold out if we have to hunker down and make a stand."

"A hollow?" Bass asked, reining up a moment.

"Low place, not no high ground. We'll wait up the hill from that hollow and open fire when the Comanch' are under our guns."

Scratch grinned. "You boys just remember my purty face and don't shoot at it when the time comes."

He pulled hard on the reins, tapped heels into the horse's ribs, and quickly pulled away from them, engulfed by the brooding dark of the night forest.

"This ain't nothing new," William Workman quietly explained in something just above a whisper as they rode along ahead of the Mexican officer and his mounted soldiers.

Scratch asked, "The Comanche been raiding the greasers for a few years now, eh?"

"Not no few years. They been raiding that poor town even before there was a town."

The whiskey maker went on to explain how the Comanche, even the Navajo far to the west, both had raided the ancient pueblos for food, plunder, and prisoners far back into the telling of any of the ancient stories.

"It's something that's always been. Always will be, I s'pose," Workman declared. "The Injuns come in and steal and kill. So the Mexicans work up enough nerve to go find a camp of Injuns and kill them. So the Injuns come in and steal again. Which means the Mexicans gonna work up a bunch to go kill Injuns again."

"So it never stops?"

"Ain't never stopped," Workman replied dolefully. "And right now—it don't appear it's gonna stop anytime soon."

"Leastways not near soon enough to leave off this here fight," Bass grumbled.

"Like Jack wanted, we'll just have these damned soldiers ready when the rest of Hatcher's boys open up on them Comanche."

The two of them talked quietly from time to time as they rode along, able to hear the murmur of the soldiers whispering behind them each time the cold wind died in the trees. Bass began to grow edgy when he found the moon near to setting at their backs.

Minutes later he thought he smelled something different in the air as the chill breeze drifted toward them. Then he was sure as they came into a small clearing.

"Hold 'em up here, Willy," he commanded as he kicked down from the saddle.

Holding on to the reins, Bass led his horse toward the far line of trees. He let his nose lead him until he was sure, bending down finally when he could smell that unmistakable spoor—horse dung. Using one bare finger, he probed its surface. Just starting to dry, and cold as could be. With the way the temperature had dropped through the night, it wouldn't take long at all for a steaming pile of dung to cool off completely.

Then his nose caught wind of something else. A little different sort of smell. He followed his nose here, then there, the way old Tink would have stayed locked on the scent of a coon back in Boone County. Going to his hands and knees to get closer to the ground as he inched his way back among the trees, Scratch found it. Another pile of dung. But this was left by a human.

Damn, he thought. Now I'm sniffing the snow for Comanche shit.

But just as he turned away, his nose caught the scent of something new, yet something recognizable. He had smelled this before. And instantly he knew. Nothing else quite like that sweetish tang on the air, an odor going old and rancid.

Crouching low once more, Bass moved another two steps, sniffed, then a second two steps. Again he sniffed, moved to his right, and the smell hit him all the stronger. In five steps he was standing over it in the dark.

Whatever it was had attracted him, he was no longer so sure he was right as he knelt over the clump now, the odor growing stronger than ever. Giving it a good sniff, Bass assured himself he was right about the smell, but remained uncertain what the clump was. He poked a finger at it, then a second time to confirm it.

Cloth—a pile of some greasy cloth. Soaked in blood. It was plain from the looks of the area right around the clump of bloody rags that someone had lain here. With the flat of his bare palm he found the snowy ground as cold as the air.

He heard the saddle horse snort quietly behind him, a sound that yanked him back to the urgency of the moment.

Rising, Scratch hurried back to Workman and the soldiers.

"What'd you find?"

"They been here," Bass disclosed. "I s'pect this is where they waited out the night. Moved on not too long ago."

Both of them glanced at the eastern horizon far away, far out on the eastern plains beyond the top of the ridge they were nearing.

Workman said, "We ain't got long. If them Comanche pulled out, they'll be bumping into Hatcher and the boys real soon."

"Get them soldiers moving with us," Scratch suggested as he rose to the saddle.

Once the rest were moving up in tight order behind the two Americans, Bass leaned close and whispered, "I found where one of 'em was bleeding real bad."

"They leave a body behind?"

Shaking his head, he spoke low. "No. Just some bloody rags."

"You look close at them rags?"

"No. Why?" For a minute Workman didn't answer. "I was just wondering if they . . . they was someone's . . . clothes, is all. Some woman's dress . . . maybeso a child's, a li'l—"

"I don't even wanna think about it," Scratch snapped, cutting him off.

They rode on in silence.

Intently listening, they were both anxious to give that long-delayed signal to the soldiers, the strings inside each man strung so tight, they were stretched to the point of popping. Both of them listened to the darkness ahead as it slowly converted itself into that inky gray of dawn-coming.

As the light grew, so did the muttering of the nervous soldiers riding on their tails. Bass realized their fear must be mounting with each passing moment as they pressed on toward the break of that day—these Mexicans who had grown up learning to fear a raid by the Comanche as early in life as they had learned their own language. Hadn't it been that way for his Grandpap? Titus pondered.

For those innocent folks settling at the ragged edge of a dangerous frontier, whether in the valley of the Ohio River or in that Taos valley he and the others had left down below, a person simply came to accept the raw odds of life versus death. Some men just naturally figured they would be brave enough to stare their enemy in the eye if that time ever arose . . . while others prayed they would never have to find out.

He couldn't blame these soldiers for doubting what they had gotten themselves into; the more ground they put between them and their homes, the farther they climbed into the mountains, the colder and darker became the smother of night. Just as he couldn't really blame folks back in America for figuring they could push against the frontier without having to pay the price in blood and lives. It had always been that way, Bass figured. Back to the time of his grandpap. Down through the days of his own father.

Here in his thirty-fifth winter, Titus realized he could no longer blame his father for trying to give his son what he figured his son would want from life. Even though it turned out that Thaddeus's life of peace and quiet and security was about as far away as anything could be from what Titus wanted for himself.

If that man hadn't been the sort to go forth, to push against the starry veil of the frontier, to dare dance on the winds of fate . . . then at least Thaddeus must be the sort of man who could summon up the courage to defend his family, those dear to him. To defend his own kind against those who came to steal from him. Like these Comanche.

He hoped these soldiers would be brave enough for what stared them in the eye this cold morning.

With that first distant shot echoing through the timber ahead, down in his marrow Bass wondered if any of them—American or Mexican—had any idea what they had bitten off.

NINE

"Andele! Andele!"

Workman was shouting, waving for all he was worth, already a horse length behind Bass, doing his best to goad the Mexicans into hurrying their stubborn horses into motion.

It was like dragging a reluctant, harness-sore mule out of its stall to plow a field.

In a matter of moments the air on the other side of a low rise dotted with pine and spruce was cluttered with more gunshots, the yelps of warriors, and shrieks of women and children.

One of the women kept screaming so long and so loud Bass wondered if she would ever take another breath. But as long as she was hollering, he figured she was still alive.

At the top of the knoll he burst out of the timber, the clatter of the Mexican brigade coming up behind him, the noise of the fight rising from below him.

But for their straight black hair and the feathers tied in it, the warriors didn't look any different from the trappers—except that the white men stood back at the edge of the trees and rocks, jamming more powder and ball down the long barrels of their rifles—the Comanche threw tomahawks and knives, fighting to control their frightened ponies so they could rush their enemy as they wildly swung long-handled clubs or dashed toward a target with one of their buffalo lances. Others fought dismounted in the swirl of horses and bodies, seeking a target for their small, strong bows of Osage orangewood, firing their rosewood arrows.

"Save the women! Watch for you don't shoot the women!"

On that far side of the meadow he heard his friends yelling to one another, each of the eight fighting his own battle against more than four or five bandy-legged raiders against every white man. Already the ground was littered with more than a dozen Comanche bodies.

With a mournful anguish Rowland darted from the trees, shouting, "Maria? Maria?"

Where were the women and children?

Then Scratch saw them as the horses jostled and sidestepped. There . . . in the middle of some ten or so Indians the women struggled against the enemy, who clamped on to wrists, yanking them off their horses, dragging them brutally away from the fight. Children clawed and kicked at the warriors, crying out for their mothers.

He shot one last glance over his shoulder as he jabbed heels into the horse's ribs, seeing the whiskey maker working everything he could out of his animal, the Mexican officer and about ten of them right behind him.

Down the gentle slope Bass raced, beginning to yell. All the fear, all the goddamned, paralyzing fear . . . just yelling always got rid of most of it as he reined right for those horsemen in the middle of the pack who had charge of the prisoners.

Somewhere among them would be Rowland's Maria.

The hillside behind him suddenly filled with the garbled commands in a foreign tongue, the depression in front of him a torrent of war cries, gunshots, and the screams of utter terror.

"Bass!"

He was too late in turning: finding the Comanche already driving the sharp blade of a short cutlass down into the top of a woman's skull, part of her head peeling away from the blow like a thick layer of onion. Too late to save her, he brought the rifle up anyway as the warrior whirled about in sheer ecstasy, bellowing full-mouthed, shaking that bloody blade at the end of his arm.

The ball caught him high in the chest, knocking him back the distance of two full steps, his legs churning, before his feet touched the ground again and he collapsed beneath one of the milling, stamping ponies.

Rowland was struggling to fight his way into the open, grassy depression, screaming her name as if it were a battle cry.

"Maria!"

There were at least four rushing John in that next moment, closing in on him as he fired his pistol, then jammed it into his belt to begin reloading the rifle.

Scratch knew the man wouldn't have a chance.

Looking up the slope to where the Mexicans had fanned out behind their leader to charge into the fray, Bass sawed the reins to the right before he stuffed them into his mouth so he could pull the big pistol from the wide belt around his blanket coat. Dragging the hammer back, Scratch chose the one who would reach Rowland first.

The warrior heard him coming at the last moment, whirling suddenly, his face pinched with surprise as Scratch brought the pistol across his body, held it steady on his target that lone moment as he raced past—pulling the trigger to watch the oak-brown face explode into a bright crimson crescent in that cold mountain sunrise.

As his horse carried him on by, Titus watched Rowland turn in his direction, the trapper now seeing the twisted body of the Comanche only steps from his back. For a heartbeat John gazed up at the horseman, attempting to mouth something, only his eyes able to convey the gratitude.

With shouts and screams of their own, the Mexicans flooded into the clearing with a noisy crash of arms. Their crude smoothbores barked, great mushrooms of gray smoke coughing from the muzzles as their horses balked, many spinning to attempt fleeing the melee. For a narrow sliver of time the Indians burst in all directions at once, like a covey of quail exploding from their hiding place among the tall grass. But in the next heartbeat the Comanche must have realized they still had the advantage of numbers and whipped back to hurl themselves onto the soldiers.

Those tortured moments allowed the trappers to emerge from the trees and rocks where they had awaited the Comanche, where the Americans had slapped shut their trap, where they had fired the first shots of this battle— likely spilling as many riders as there were American guns trained on the raiders.

As he clumsily poured a palmful of powder down the muzzle of his rifle, Bass turned to watch the warriors who mingled with the women and children. The Comanche were forcing their captives slowly back toward the center of the clearing, the first of the children being wrenched from the arms of their mothers and thrown onto the back of a pony. Another warrior savagely kicked a woman, at the same time pulling from her arms a small child he handed up to another warrior already on the back of a horse.

"Maria!" Rowland screeched.

There came no answer that Bass could hear above the roar of guns, the slap of lead among the trees and rocks, the neighing of the horses and the shrieking of the prisoners.

Another woman went down, her skull crushed with a stone club as a

Comanche stood over her, swinging the club's handle back in a graceful, deadly arc, preparing to make another blow. Her brown, naked body twitched in the grass convulsively from that first wound.

"Maria!"

Out of the corner of his eye Bass saw Rowland inching toward the captives, swinging his rifle this way, then that—his eyes just as wide with fear as were every woman's.

Spilling a few grains of priming powder into the pan, Bass dragged the frizzen down and brought the rifle up to his hip, yanking back on the trigger without consciously aiming just as the warrior began the deadly downward arc of that club.

The ball caught the Comanche in the lower belly, doubling him over in half as he was knocked off his feet, spinning to the side, tumbling over the naked captive. Rowland collapsed at the woman's side, turned her crushed, bloody skull so he could stare into her face, then stood suddenly, his face one of horror as he peered into the blurry torrent of bodies.

"Maria!"

Bass knew the body wasn't hers. But where was she?

His eyes raced over the naked prisoners herded within a shrinking compound of horses and warriors. Very few left: women struggling to pull their children out of the arms of a few horsemen attempting to escape, women seeking to shelter their little ones with nothing more than their bare brown bodies.

"Juan!"

As Scratch held the muzzle to his lips and blew down the barrel to clear it of embers, he heard the woman's shrill voice above the rest of the screeching and war cries and rifle fire.

She was so close. Closer to Bass than she was to Rowland as she fell to her hands and knees, then rolled under the dancing legs of a pony to scramble back to her feet. Scratch could see she was already bloodied, could see her wrists still bound by loops of crude hemp, two sections of rope still wrapped around her ankles to show how her legs had been tied beneath the belly of a pony that carried her out of the Taos valley, her mouth and chin smeared with blood where they had struck her in anger—perhaps to silence her screams, to quiet her sobbing.

Jamming the plug between his teeth, Bass pulled it from the end of the powder horn, spilling the coarse black grains straight down the muzzle. Racing to reload.

She was struggling back into motion, stumbling toward Rowland, raising in the air those hands still tied together. Begging . . .

"Maria!" John bellowed, focusing his overwhelming relief on the woman.

Titus dropped the powder horn so that it hung suspended there above his shooting pouch as he tongued another ball from the inside of his cheek, pushing it forward with the tip of his tongue.

From his left Bass saw the movement of one of the horsemen as the warrior whipped his pony around, the fourteen-foot-long buffalo lance coming up halfway between earth and sky like a crude splinter against the winter blue. His black hate-filled eyes followed the escape of the woman, spotting the white man rushing toward her.

Spitting the wet lead ball from his lips with a noisy *puert,* Scratch yanked the ramrod free of its thimbles under the big octagonal barrel, ramming the ball home against the powder and the breech.

How Bass wished he would have enough time to finish reloading . . .

Then knew he wouldn't—

Just as Rowland was reaching out for her, the warrior cocked the huge lance beneath his arm, his horse leaping into motion as the arm snapped back, then slingshotted forward.

Both Bass and Rowland watched it hit the naked woman stumbling toward her husband. Piercing her body more than six feet of its length, suddenly erupting from her chest, red and glistening as she stumbled two more steps, staring down at the lance that impaled her, imprisoned her there, on the point of death.

She seized hold of the lance with her two grimy hands becoming slicked with her own blood. Fluid gushed from her mouth, spilling off her chin and onto her small brown breasts as she collapsed forward.

"Juan!"

It was more of a gurgle than a scream of pain or anguish.

With a terrifying scream the Comanche flung the long lance forward, releasing it.

Rowland was a few feet shy of catching Maria as she collapsed onto the long point of the lance, teetering there a moment as if in the hovering flight of a nectar-robbing hummingbird, then keeled off the six feet of lance to fall to the side with more than eight feet of the shaft slapping the icy snow behind her as she thrashed on the ground, gurgling.

Lustily screaming in victory, the horseman was pulling an ax from the back of his belt as Rowland spun to his knees over his wife, shrieking in horror.

Kicking his pony and yanking savagely on the horsehair rein—struggling to get his animal slowed and turned around—the Comanche came about and started to dash toward the grieving white man at the instant Scratch jammed the rifle into his shoulder. At the very moment he realized he'd forgotten to remove the ramrod from the barrel, Bass raked back on the trigger.

Both ball and hickory wiping stick exploded from the rifle as the muzzle spat a bright torch of yellow flame. While the lead sphere smashed through the warrior's breastbone, the long ramrod embedded itself deeply at the base of his throat. There it quivered for a moment before the warrior released his big-headed ax, seizing the wiping stick with both hands as his legs lost their grip on the pony. He slid over onto the snow.

Rowland hunched over the naked, bloody body—sobbing—as Scratch skidded to a stop beside him.

"Gimme your pistol!"

Rowland looked up dumbly, his eyes at once filled with rage, wild and feral, at the very moment they pooled with tears of unfathomable grief.

"M-maria—"

"Gimme your pistol!" Bass shouted again, then crouched and grabbed for the weapon stuffed in Rowland's belt like a goat's hoof.

Dropping his rifle at his feet as he started to rise, Scratch dragged back the huge hammer on the pistol and whirled at the shrill war cry ringing in his ears. Nearly upon them was a warrior whose skin was more mahogany than oak brown, racing toward the trappers on foot.

His finger twitched on the trigger . . . but he held—spotting a second warrior sprinting right on the heels of the first headed their way.

Scratch waited, waited—his whole body tensing as he struggled against the instinct to shoot . . . then fired the big horse pistol—its huge ball cutting a swath through the first Indian and smacking into the second, dropping them both within spitting distance of Rowland.

As the two Comanche tumbled out of the way onto the icy snow, behind them a mounted warrior charged up to skewer a Mexican horseman with his buffalo lance. With so much power behind the impact, the warrior was able to pick the Mexican out of his saddle, dangling the helpless soldier aloft momentarily on the end of that terrible spear, then fling the dead man off into an icy patch of pine needles before the trembling carcass could break the lance.

Realizing that now he was without a loaded firearm, Scratch dropped the pistol beside Rowland at the same time he snagged hold of John's collar and pulled his head back so he could stare into the trapper's eyes.

"Get your goddamned pistol loaded—or you're gonna end up like her!"

Wagging his head slightly, Rowland let the tears pour out.

It was plain to see the man didn't care if he ended up like his Maria then and there. Bass let go of John's shirt, leaving the man to collapse over the bare, bloody body, his own chest racked with silent sobs.

From the back of Rowland's belt he pulled free the throwing tomahawk and leaped to his feet, exploding into a sprint. The Comanche lancer who had speared the soldier was turning his horse, bringing that huge blood-slickened weapon around to find another target. The closest was another of the naked women stumbling away, tripping and pitching into the snow to crawl on her

knees and hands across the frozen ground. Her feet must be as leaden as
adobe bricks, Bass thought as he lowered his head, his eyes locked on the
horseman, flying across the crusty snow.

At the instant the Comanche loped past, Scratch flung himself onto the
pony's rear flanks, his left arm locking around the warrior's chest as he swung
out sideways with the tomahawk—hurling it back in savagely as the warrior
twisted and jerked, trying to free himself from the white man he suddenly
found clinging to him like a buffalo tick.

The tomahawk sank into soft tissue.

Only his gut!

Bass swung out again, this time bringing it against some bone.

Ribs!

Again, and again—hacking the blade higher and higher as the man
coughed and gurgled and thrashed . . . until the Comanche went completely
limp. Scratch yanked the warrior and his lance off the horse. He hopped
forward just as the pony leaped aside, snatching hold of the reins in his left
hand, spinning the animal around in a tight circle.

Some of the Comanche were already spurring their horses into the trees
out of the depression where Hatcher's men had sprung their attack. Nearly
half of the horsemen bolted right past the trappers. Those warriors who were
left to fight were either the very brave, or the very dead.

In his own most private duel Ensign Guerrero slashed and jabbed and
parried with his sword against two Comanche who swung at him with their
clubs and tomahawks, all three of them still on horseback, spinning about and
bumping, throwing the weight of their animal against the others, kicking out
with their legs at the enemy.

Suddenly the officer froze, his face gone pasty as day-old bread dough
the instant a third Indian behind the Mexican pierced him with a long lance.
The Mexican gazed down at the bloody lance protruding from his chest, vainly
pulling at the slick wood with his empty left hand as he began to slip to the
side from the saddle, spilling to the ground. Sprawling there, kicking his legs
futilely, Don Francisco Guerrero finally dropped his engraved sword so he
could clutch the thick, bloody wood with both hands as his eyes glazed over,
staring sightless at the lowering sky.

Bass drew back the tomahawk and hurled it at the closest of the three
horsemen, watching it crack into the warrior's back. The other two wheeled
around immediately as Bass pulled his own tomahawk from his belt, ready for
the charge they were sure to make.

One of them yelled at the other; then both put heels to their horses and
raced toward the white man. He set himself, ready to spring to either side,
ready even to pitch onto the ground when they reached him. But to his
surprise neither one leaned off to swing at him with their club or tomahawk.
Rather, they burst on past, kicking their ponies furiously.

Right on the heels of the rest of those already fleeing the battle with wild shouts.

"Hatcher!"

It was Kinkead's voice he heard as he turned.

Matthew was pointing back into the timber where the Comanche had disappeared. They could still hear the hoofbeats. But instead of that hammering growing fainter, it was becoming louder.

"They're coming back!" Hatcher exploded out of the dawn shadows, hollering and waving.

All the rest were looking back over their shoulders as the war cries and captives' shrieks grew louder.

"Get the women!"

Bass spun to glance back toward the middle of the meadow, where he found three of the captives miraculously still on their feet—naked and shivering, trembling from fear and the cold, huddling and clutching one another.

"Where's the children?" Bass screamed at Solomon Fish as the trapper sprinted up beside him.

The stocky man's face went blank as he swallowed hard and replied, "Ain't none of the li'l ones left."

In disbelief Titus groaned, "They kill 'em all?"

Lumbering up, Graham shouted, "What ones they didn't awready get off with!"

"Watch out!" Hatcher warned.

The three of them whirled around with Jack as a dozen horsemen exploded from the shadows at tree line, horses snorting frosty jets of steam from their nostrils, bearing their riders toward the men on foot, who set themselves for that charge. Behind the trappers arose the shrieks of the three naked captives as they saw the Comanche returning.

Behind the women the soldiers themselves screamed in terror of being overrun and immediately turned on their heels, abandoning the women just behind that last stand being formed by those nine Americans.

Scratch quickly searched for Rowland on either side of him as the horsemen urged more speed from their ponies, coming all the faster across that trampled ground. There, off to the side, he finally saw him—where Johnny was as good as dead, collapsed over the body of his dead wife.

"Stand steady and look 'em in the eye!" Hatcher bellowed.

"Take one of 'em with you when you go down, boys!" Isaac Simms shouted, that tobacco-stained, whitish beard of his quivering with rage.

Bass barely had time to take another breath before the horsemen crashed into them with a deafening tangle of shouts and cries, screams and groans. In that clamor the trappers ducked and dived out of the way, some spinning about to reach up, immediately yanking horsemen down from their ponies as the warriors twisted to this side, then that, on the backs of their horses, attempting to slash at the whites with tomahawks, jabbing with knives of Mexican steel, and swinging stone-crowned clubs or stout bows at their enemies.

Only five of the twelve made it past the desperate trappers; no more than a handful reached that undefended patch of snowy ground where the three terrified women suddenly whirled and sprinted off, with the horsemen right on their heels, scampering like rabbits surprised far from their burrow. Hatcher pulled out his huge knife and in one motion brought it back, then flung it forward with such force that its impact knocked a warrior off his pony.

As if a keg of powder exploded beneath them, the nine Americans sprinted after the Comanche, screeching like demons with the coming of that crimson dawning of the day.

A black-haired horseman reined up beside one of the fleeing women, slamming his horse into her, knocking the shrieking woman off balance. As she staggered to her feet, he leaned from his horse, reached over, and looped a dark arm around her naked body, wrenching the woman against the side of the pony.

She kicked and thrashed her bare brown feet as they left the ground, struggling with what strength she had left in her, pummeling the man with her fists as he yanked the horse around, intending to escape with his prize still dangling off the side of his pony.

As the other trappers swarmed toward the rest of the enemy, Bass shot away at an angle. Dropping his rifle behind him in that headlong dash, he pulled out his knife a breath before he leaped against the warrior, wrapping an arm around the Comanche's dark neck.

With the woman struggling on one side, and the trapper yanking him down on the other, the horseman freed his prisoner and smashed his open right hand into the white man's face—his fingers clawing and tearing, searching for the eye sockets. The Comanche swiftly found Scratch's left eye with a thumb he jabbed savagely into the soft tissue.

At the same moment one of the grimy, char-smudged fingers found the corner of Bass's mouth, where it began ripping at softer flesh.

Jerking his head to the side, Scratch almost pulled that finger free. Grunting in exertion, the warrior clawed his enemy's face with renewed strength as Bass filled his hands with coarse black hair. Bass knotted the hair around his fingers, pulling that face closer, closer to his while he worked to free his right hand and the knife it held.

With a roar the Comanche smashed his head against the white man's temple, stunning Titus. He began to blink his eyes clear as the warrior snapped his head forward again. But this time Bass was ready. Opening wide, he clenched his teeth around the bony, grease-painted nose like the jaws of a trap.

Screaming in pain, the Comanche rammed his thumb all the farther into the white man's eye.

Now the agony in that one eye became so great, Scratch could no longer keep the other open. He squeezed them shut.

With his teeth locked around that big nose, Bass flung his weight this way and that, blindly yanking and tugging, trying to unhorse his enemy. Grinding his teeth ever tighter as he twisted about, he felt the grimy, war-painted skin tear loose across hard cartilage, tasted the sticky blood as it oozed from the torn flesh, warm and thick on his tongue as the hard tissue continued to crackle beneath Bass's powerful jaws.

Twisting, jerking, yanking backward, Titus finally felt his top teeth grind down onto his bottom teeth—and snapped backward from the enemy's face. With the warrior's shrill scream, the smelly claw flew back from Scratch's face: no more did those fingers spear his eye, no more did they rip at the side of his mouth.

With blood gushing from the middle of his face, the Comanche screamed in even greater pain.

With the severed nose still in his mouth, Scratch gave one final heave, leaping again as he yanked savagely on the warrior's hair. Dragging the man's head to the side with an audible snap, Bass felt the warrior's muscles relax, freeing the woman and the pony at the same time.

Spilling backward, Bass fell to the ground, his fingers still tangled in the warrior's long hair as the Comanche lumbered to his knees, grunting and huffing from that sudden hole in his face where blood streamed and air bubbled. With one hand he touched the terrible wound, looked at his fingers, then reached for his own knife.

Lunging out, Scratch slashed his blade across the warrior's blood-splattered buckskin shirt, bright crimson spurting from the wound opened beneath the garment. He raked the knife back again, higher still across the chest, as the warrior clumsily brought his knife out.

Then a third time, now across the side of the Comanche's neck, severing the thick vein and artery in a brilliant spray of blood. The warrior gasped as he fell forward in the throes of a last convulsion, the knife still clutched in that hand held out before him.

As the Comanche plunged toward him, attempting to kill his killer, Scratch twisted aside. The warrior's knife pierced the flap of Bass's blanket coat before it plunged on into the icy ground, buried up to the guard. His eyes already dead, the Indian brushed past Titus, collapsing upon the handle of his own knife, those last terrible spurts of blood splattering across the long tail of Scratch's coat as the body collapsed against his legs.

Shocked to find himself slammed into the snow, Bass tried to roll away, discovering that his legs and one arm were pinned beneath the dead man. He twisted and yanked desperately, trying to free himself . . . when a shadow flitted over him.

From the corner of his eye Bass watched arms drag the body back so he could roll away. He rose onto his hip and elbow, turning back, prepared to thank one of his friends—but his mouth froze open in surprise. Scratch found his rescuer a woman in her midforties, naked and blue-lipped, her arms, back, and face bloodied and tracked with swollen welts.

Embarrassed for her, Scratch was on his feet and yanking at the buckle to his belt before he was conscious of dropping the wide leather belt and its knife scabbard on the ground. Quickly he tugged the blanket coat from his shoulders and swept it behind the naked woman. After stuffing her arms down the sleeves, she wrapped it securely around her and looked up at him, muttering something in Spanish as her red, puffy eyes began to seep again.

It took only a moment before her voice faded to a shrill, tiny squeak of unutterable pain and the woman collapsed to her knees, pitching slowly forward until her brow pressed against the ground as she wailed inconsolably.

Not until that moment when the woman began to wail did he become conscious of the sudden quiet in the narrow depression where Hatcher's men had sprung their trap. Nothing more on the cold wind but the soft noise of horses snuffling, the whimpers of the wounded, the soft crunch of footsteps across the icy ground.

And with the next gust of breeze, the quiet was gone. More of the Mexicans were strutting down the slope toward the battleground now, yelling and screaming of a sudden. A few of them loped through the pack on horseback, carrying their own spears. These riders roamed the ground like a pack of dogs, searching out any of the enemy still alive. Once found, a wounded Comanche was pierced with two, three, or four of the Mexicans' spears while those on foot rejoiced and shouted, rushing in to hack at the body until it was dismembered, even before the enemy's heart had beaten its last.

Going to his knees, Scratch scooted close to the woman, then laid an arm across her shoulders. She raised her head, looked into his face, then nestled her cheek against the hollow of his neck and began to quake. Some forty yards away Isaac Simms had wrapped a large horse blanket around a small woman, and Kinkead was talking with the third captive in her native tongue as he clutched a large Mexican blanket around her trembling shoulders.

Suddenly the small woman with Simms turned, crying out in anguished Spanish, causing the woman Bass was comforting to lift her face, holding out her arms and screeching for the small woman who was rushing her way.

Bass helped her stand, then steadied the woman as she hobbled forward on bare, frozen feet. Closer and closer sprinted the small woman, closer still until Scratch could plainly see she was not a woman at all, but a young girl barely on the threshold of her teen years.

Kinkead and some of the others stepped over dead bodies of Indians and a soldier, following the girl and the other woman toward the oldest of the three, who continued to clutch Bass.

"Mi Jacova!" she shouted at the girl.

"Mama! Mama! Mama!"

How they embraced, forgetting their wounds. They kissed and kissed again, hugging and squeezing their arms around one another as the trappers came up.

"That's the gov'nor's wife," Kinkead said. "Her name's Manuela."

"And that's her girl?"

"Yes, Scratch," Matthew replied. "Her name's Jacova. For all her papa's treasures, she's his prize. He'll be some punkins to see they both come back alive."

At that moment Bass felt a tug to turn, finding Hatcher at his elbow. He pointed.

Rowland lay across the body of his dead wife, wailing.

"Get me a blanket," Jack told Isaac.

Simms understood and nodded, turning away toward the battlefield, where he knelt beside a dead Comanche wearing a bloodstained blanket tied around his waist. With it Isaac met Bass at Rowland's side.

Hatcher helped Bass lift the grieving husband off the woman so Simms could spread the blanket over the naked body. Then Scratch slowly turned the woman over, dragging the blanket up to cover her face.

"Isaac, get her ready to travel," Hatcher requested in a whisper. "Pull some rope off one of them dead horses."

As Rowland sat sobbing between Bass and Hatcher, Simms prepared the body for their journey back to Taos. Lashing the rope around and around the blanket-wrapped shroud, Isaac tied his last knot just as one of the soldiers strode up to Kinkead. The Mexican spoke in the clipped tones of a man who clearly thought he was talking to someone occupying a lower station in life.

Caleb hobbled up, a leg bleeding, to ask, "Who the shit is this nigger?"

"Sergeant of this here outfit," Kinkead grumbled. "Name of Ramirez. Sergeant Jorge Ramirez."

"What's he saying to you, Matthew?"

"Says it's time for him to take the women and the girl back to the gov'nor in Taos."

"Take 'em back?" Elbridge Gray echoed. "Why, them damned *soldados* didn't do nothing to save 'em!"

Hatcher nodded, giving his order: "Tell him that, Matthew."

Behind the sergeant, what others weren't tending to their own wounded or their dead continued to mutilate and dismember the enemy dead. Matthew brought himself up to his full height, casting a shadow over Ramirez as he repeated the declaration.

Then Kinkead told the other Americans, "Says he demands the women—'specially the woman and her daughter—so he can turn 'em over to the gov'nor when they get back to Taos."

Hatcher stood. "Didn't ye tell him we figger these soldiers didn't save the womenfolk, so we don't figger they got any right takin' the womenfolk back?"

"Just what I told him."

"Tell the sumbitch again," Jack growled. "Then tell him we're taking the women back on our own. They can come along, or they can stay here and tear these here bodies apart like they was the ones what won the fight."

When Matthew's words struck the Mexican's ears, more of the soldiers stopped their butchery and moved over to join the sergeant arguing with Kinkead.

"He says they have more guns than we do."

"This bastard brung it right down to the nut-cutting, didn't he, boys?" Jack snorted. "Awright, Matthew, tell him he sure 'nough does have him more guns right now . . . but we got more balls, and these yellow-backed greasers ain't going to back down no American!"

With that answer to his bold demands, the sergeant's eyes darkened in fury. Suddenly he shouted at the other Mexicans—silencing their angry murmurs. In the uneasy quiet Ramirez glared at Kinkead as he spoke.

"This one says he's asking us one last time to turn over the women afore he orders the men to kill . . . kill us all."

At that challenge several of the Americans pulled back the hammers on their firearms as they stepped backward around Rowland and his wife, slowly ringing the three freed captives. Those who did not have loaded weapons pulled knives or reached down and scooped a tomahawk or club from the ground. In a moment all eight had their backs together, the women and Rowland at the center of that tiny circle.

Close to shaking with rage, Hatcher growled, "Matthew, ye tell this sick-dog, sad-assed, whimpering greaser that I wanna know what right they got to take the women back for themselves . . . when these here yellow-livered cowards wasn't even brave enough to jump footfirst into the fight to save these here women!"

As Kinkead translated, the eyes of nearly all the Mexicans glowed with even more hatred—but not a one of them dared initiate an assault on the trappers. Their spokesman trembled with rage as he spat out his words.

Matthew said, "He says they're not cowards—"

"Like hell they ain't!" Bass interrupted with a snort of derision.

Sputtering in anger one moment, Ramirez fell to wheedling the next, attempting to explain the lack of action and courage of his men during the fight.

Kinkead translated, "Says he wasn't able to get the rest to keep fighting after Guerrero was killed. The rest were . . . were—but I don't think he can find a nice word for them being scared."

Hatcher shook his head in disgust. "Then tell that sumbitch to have his men either start this fight right now—or get back outta our way, and make it quick!"

With that said to the Mexican, he waved his men back a few yards, then turned once more to growl at Kinkead.

"Just who the hell is this greaser to take on these high airs?" Bass inquired.

Matthew explained, "Now that Guerrero's dead—this one takes over, I s'pose."

Watching the soldiers inch back a short distance, Hatcher repeated, "That give this Ramirez nigger the due to rub up against us the way he is?"

As the soldiers closed in around their leader once more, Matthew said, "They don't figger these here women any safer with us than they was with the Comanche."

Most of the Americans laughed at that declaration, a few even jabbing one another with elbows, some wagging their heads in amused disbelief.

But while the others guffawed, Caleb Wood stepped up to demand, "Merciful heavens! Why the hell aren't these here women safe with the men who saved 'em?"

"Because he don't figger us for Christians," Kinkead said. "Leastwise, none of the rest of you."

"How you so special?" Simms grumbled, pulling at a blond ringlet in his beard with a grubby finger.

"Remember how I got myself baptized in the Mexican church some time back," Kinkead explained.

"Don't mean to stomp on yer Rosa's church, Matthew," Hatcher began, "but the way we see it, ye tell this son of a lily-livered bitch that I don't give a damn if he's Christian or not. . . . Tell him his bunch wasn't in this fight enough for me to call 'em brave men."

When Kinkead turned back to Hatcher after delivering those inflammatory words, he said, "Seems you're dishonoring not just him but the other soldiers who died here this morning if you don't let 'em take the prisoners back to their families in Taos."

"Eegod! Honor? That what this is all about?" Hatcher spat. "How the hell can this here greaser talk to me about honor when he and his men didn't have the honor to fight like men? To fight like their dead leader fought? Maybeso to die like a man, instead of standing right here in front of real men and whining like alley cats about their goddamned honor!"

It was plain to see how those words slapped the sergeant across the face like a sudden, unexpected challenge. His eyes glared like black coals; his lips curled, stretching taut over his front teeth as he struggled for words.

"When we get back to Taos, he says he'll let you tell the gov'nor what all we done to help his men in this fight."

Jack whirled on Kinkead in utter disbelief. "That what he said, Matthew? That we . . . only *helped* in this fight?"

"Yep—says we just helped his men."

Flecks of spittle crusted the corners of Hatcher's lips as he sputtered, "Tell that sumbitch Ramirez to step out of my way or I'm going to cut him up into pieces small enough that the jays can eat what's left of 'im!"

"Jack," Kinkead said with a soothing tone, his words almost whispered. "Maybe you ought'n figger us a way to do this 'thout anyone else getting killed. They got us near surrounded now."

"I'll gut my share of 'em afore—"

"Lookee there, Jack," Caleb interrupted Hatcher as his eyes flicked about of a sudden. "The greasers sure as Katie do got us circled."

"Goddamned Mex," Isaac growled. "Only time they figger to fight is when they got the enemy outnumbered."

Scratch added, "And when they got the drop on us!"

"Listen up," Jack told them. "What say we leave it up to the women here?"

"You mean let the women decide who they ride back to Taos with?" Elbridge asked.

"That's right," Jack replied. "Matthew, tell this greaser we're going to let the women decide."

After a minute of coaxing from Kinkead, the sergeant nodded in agreement, a smug look of victory already apparent on his face.

"He says he'll let the women decide."

"I'll wager he thinks the womens will pick him," Jack declared.

"He's probably right," Kinkead replied. "After all, the womens are Mexican like these here soldiers."

"So ask 'em, Matthew," Hatcher ordered. "Ask 'em who they're riding back home with."

Scratch watched Kinkead pose that question. Instead of answering immediately, the daughter clutched her mother, burying her face against Bass's coat. And the younger woman looked at the governor's wife a moment, then stared at the ground before she muttered something. Finally the older woman held her chin high and in a soft voice gave her answer. Her words visibly caused a dark cloud to cross the soldier's face.

"What'd she say?" Hatcher demanded in a harsh whisper.

Kinkead cleared his throat and said, "Says she's been listening in on ever'thing we been saying, Jack."

"So what's her answer?"

"She's telling Ramirez that they all three agreed the same together,"

Matthew began. "Says they are going to ride back to their homes with the men who had risked their lives to save 'em—the Americans."

"I'll be go to hell," Rufus whispered in shock.

"Then maybe we better get the bodies of these here other women wrapped up and ready to ride back," Jack said as he turned away from the sergeant.

Ramirez held out his beefy hands, saying something quietly to the women, his tone imploring, but instantly the oldest woman snapped at him angrily, one of her brown arms poking from the capote sleeve, pointing at the bodies of the other captives lying across the battlefield—both women and children. Hostages and prisoners dragged from their homes only to be brutally murdered in this attempt to save them all.

"She just told him that she had her no doubt he and his soldiers wouldn't never come along on this ride if it wasn't for the Americans leading the bunch," Matthew translated as the soldiers turned away, shamed by the woman's strong words. "Said she's sure there wasn't no chance for any of them to come out alive if only the soldiers come along . . . because the coward soldiers likely wouldn't come to rescue them at all."

As he and the others watched the haughty Mexicans shambling away, grumbling among themselves as they caught up their horses and shouted orders among their numbers to mount their wounded and load up their dead, Scratch asked, "That what finally made them soldiers back off from us?"

"No," Matthew answered quietly. "It's what she told 'em there at the last."

"What was that?" Hatcher asked.

Kinkead said, "The woman told 'em she figgered it would be far better for any woman to live the rest of her life being a slave to the Comanche . . . better that than to live as the wife to a coward dog what wasn't ready to fight and die to save his woman."

It took the rest of that day and on through the long, cold night, when they camped on their way back over the mountains and down to the Taos valley, for Bass to begin to forget that pitiful, solitary wail that escaped from John Rowland at the moment Kinkead translated the Mexican woman's declaration: how a courageous man would fight and die to rescue his wife.

Better to live as a slave to the savage, heathen Comanche than to live ashamed and married to a coward who wasn't prepared to give his life to save his own woman.

That afternoon as they recrossed the divide and began their descent toward the valley, storm clouds clotted along the western horizon. Thick as a blood soup, they made for an early sunset as the procession continued east, clouds drawing closer with every hour, dragging down the temperature, giving the wind a cruel bite. Both Rufus Graham and Solomon Fish each managed to kill an elk close to twilight. Food for them all, and in as good a place as any to hunker down for the rest of that night they would have to endure.

As darkness sank around them, Hatcher had Kinkead instruct the sergeant that his men must put out a night guard not only around their camp but around the horse herd too. While the Comanche might be too wary to attack the trappers and Mexicans in the dark, they wouldn't be at all skittish about rushing in and riding off with some or all of the enemy's horses. There were four fires that night, three of them placed close together where the Mexican soldiers gathered to fight off the cold and gloom. And the fourth fire where the nine Americans huddled with the three Taos captives. Clear enough was it that the line had been drawn. Just as clear enough that were it not for the wife and daughter of the governor, Ramirez's soldiers might well have tried to wipe out the upstart trappers.

For the longest time that night as the cold deepened, young Jacova Mirabal kept her eyes fixed on the American who had rescued her mother, watching Bass move from place to place as he brought in wood, or stirred up the fire, or cut and cooked slices of the meat for the women, or even helped them with the cold, damp horse blankets—all that the Americans had to offer as protection from the terrible temperatures as dawn approached.

That storm rushing out of the west was at hand. Winter's clouds hovered just overhead as the sky paled enough to travel.

"Matthew," Hatcher called across the fire to the big man with his back propped against a tree, dozing fitfully. "Get them greasers up and moving. We're lighting out soon."

A little rest and the chance to sit around a warming fire wasn't near enough to improve the disposition of the soldiers. Sullen and bleary-eyed as they slowly dragged themselves out of their blankets on the snowy ground, the Mexicans glared at the trappers with even more hate than they had the day before. A very sinister loathing was reserved for Scratch when young Jacova chose to ride alongside him again that cold dawn as they continued their descent down the western slope of the Sangre de Cristos, smoke from the distant villages already visible on the far horizon below the approaching storm clouds.

As the sun rose against the peaks at their backs, it spread a soft light into the Taos valley below, brushing its rosy tint across the gray smudge of morning cookfires that would be warming every home, hut, and hovel. But all too soon that cheery glow was gone as the sun continued to rise behind the thickening clouds, swallowed by the oncoming storm as the riders made their way toward the valley floor.

By the time the party reached the first of the northernmost ranchos, word began to spread of the rescuers' return. Riding at the head of the cavalcade were Ramirez's soldiers, each of them triumphantly waving their weapons—lances or swords or muskets—as they drove ahead of them what cattle and sheep they had managed to recapture after the ambush. Some distance behind the Mexicans trailed the Americans, the ten of them led by the trio of captives who, by choosing to ride with the trappers, made it apparent to the growing throngs who gathered to watch their procession that they would rather ride among the gringos than with their own countrymen.

Field-workers and wranglers from those first ranchos streamed onto the road, joining the procession on its way toward Taos itself, more and more people joining in to scurry along both sides of the march—shouting and cheering, waving hats and shawls and scarves over their heads, singing praises for the deliverance of the three still alive. Others wailed and sobbed, crying piteously for the captives brutally butchered by the Comanche—an eerie, discordant cacophony that loudly battered Scratch's ears, one that suddenly swelled in volume and intensity when they drew within sight of the walls of the village itself.

Suddenly the cathedral bells began to toll wildly. On rooftops stood young boys holding aloft thick streamers of colorful cloth billowing on the cold wind. Girls of all ages pushed forward on either side of the procession to hold up offerings of bread, fruit, and even a live chicken to the victors. The soldiers eagerly snatched up all that was given: life in the army was not far from abject poverty. Bass himself took a loaf of warm bread, then passed it back to Jacova, who thanked him with that sad smile on her lovely brown face smudged with soot and grime and blood. Some of the villagers rushed up to Jacova and her mother, bowing their heads respectfully while lifting a corner of the blanket each held around them, these impoverished people kissing the dirty wool with such reverence, such gratitude that both mother and daughter had been spared.

No more than fifty yards ahead lay the town square. And at its center waited Padre Jose Martinez; beside him stood the governor, Don Frederico de Jesus Mirabal. How stoic the man is, Titus thought as he watched this official calmly gaze at his loved ones returning. Were these his own wife and daughter, Bass was certain he would be shoving his way through the gauntlet himself, unable to wait patiently on the cathedral's low steps as the bells continued their joyous peal.

Here and there among the crowd were those already dressed in black—a rebozo that fully covered a woman's head and shoulders for some, was no more than a poor shawl for others. These were the mourners crying and wailing as they searched among the survivors and did not find a loved one—abruptly realizing that one of the blanket shrouds covered a family member or friend. The shrill keening grew all the louder as the procession drew closer and closer still to the church, then stopped . . . when all fell quiet but for the muffled sobs of so many mourners, the uneasy snuffles of the weary, hungry horses.

In a loud voice that rocked from the sides of the tiny square, Governor Mirabal spoke.

"Welcome back, my family!" Kinkead translated as the governor moved off the steps and hurried to his wife's side.

Holding up his arms, Mirabal pulled his wife down from the horse, kissing both her cheeks, her forehead, enthusiastically before he embraced her savagely and wheeled about to do the same in helping his daughter from her mount.

With his wife, Manuela, beneath one arm, Jacova under the other, the governor climbed back to stand atop the steps of the small cathedral, where he spoke to the murmuring crowd.

In a whisper Matthew repeated, "He says he wants everyone to be quiet while the padre gives a prayer."

For long minutes the brown-robed priest droned on, his eyes closed and his face turned heavenward as he gestured first with one arm, then the other, and eventually made the sign of the cross, bowed his head, and kissed the crucifix around his neck—at which point all the crowd raised their heads.

Again the governor spoke in his loud, stentorian voice.

"He says he wants to do something important to show his gratitude to the soldiers who returned his family to him—"

But Kinkead interrupted his translation as Bass and the others watched Manuela turn to her husband, raise her face to his ear, and whisper to him as he bent toward her.

The moment she began speaking to him, the governor's gaze shifted to stare at the party of gloating soldiers; then he straightened, and his eyes darted farther back in the square to find the small party of Americans. Mirabal bent slightly and spoke in hushed tones to his wife. Both she and Jacova whispered something to him before he pulled them against him all the more fiercely and began to speak to the throng.

Matthew said, "Now he says he wants to do something very, very special for the men who his wife and daughter say put up their lives to save his family. He wants to . . . to . . . ."

"To what, Kinkead?" Hatcher demanded as Matthew fell silent.

With his chin quivering, his eyes moistening, and a big smile splitting his bearlike beard, Matthew answered, "The governor wants to give the Americanos a very special *baile*!"

Solomon Fish asked, "A *baile*?"

"A dance!" Kinkead roared, then went to laughing lustily, sweeping up his Rosa and swinging her around and around while she giggled like a young girl.

"A dance?" Rufus asked.

Matthew joyously cried, "The governor his own self is gonna thank us niggers for saving his family! By holding a dance in our honor!"

TEN

Jehoshaphat, if that liquor didn't taste good!

Despite the remembrance of how this evil brew had lopped off the top of his head the last time he had settled down to put on nothing more than a nice, rosy glow. It had been that first night at Workman's, when he'd ended up waking the next morning feeling as if his head were clamped in the jaws of a huge trap, his mouth tasting as if Ramirez's *soldados* had marched across his tongue in muddy boots.

"Best you go at it slow this time, Scratch," Kinkead warned. He stood before Titus like a jolly monolith, his arm wrapped securely around Rosa's shoulder.

"This here stuff is pure-dee magic, Matthew!" Bass replied, licking his lips as he refilled his clay cup with the ladle. "I'll be go to hell if it don't beat that Monangahela rum I was broke in on back to the Ohio country."

"Bet this here wheat brew of Workman's does pack a bigger wallop too!" Hatcher declared as he stepped up to get himself a refill at the table placed a'straddle the corner of the long *sala,* the parlor where valley folks had begun to arrive and all was gaiety beneath the huge fluttering candles and smaller mirrored lanterns.

Besides that fermented grain beverage manufactured by William Work-man at his new distillery west of the village, Governor Mirabal and his wife, Manuela, were serving what was variously known among the American trap-pers as "Pass brandy" or "Pass wine"—given that name from the fact that this grape product was routinely brought up from Chihuahua through the "pass" in the mountains, those fine spirits transported as far north as Santa Fe and Taos in oaken kegs and earthen jars.

"Scratch—just you be careful that Taos lightning don't whack you in the back of the head when you ain't looking!" Caleb cried as he held out his cup for another ladle of the heady concoction.

"*Aguardiente* I hear it's called," Bass declared with an expert roll of his *r*.

"Ah-wharr-dee-en-tee! Listen to this here nigger spit that out so smooth!" Hatcher snorted. "Picking up on the Mex talk, he is."

"Only a little," Scratch admitted.

"Maybeso just enough to get yourself hunkered atween the legs of some purty senorita," said Solomon Fish as his eyes studied those comely maids moving about the room.

Quickly gazing over the small knots of dark-eyed, rosy-cheeked young women, Scratch wagged his head and replied, "Maybeso this child's gonna learn enough of their Mex talk to dig hisself down into one helluva lot of trouble!"

Slipping his knife from its scabbard hung at the back of his belt, Titus plunged the narrow tip of it into the open clay crock sitting on the table among stacks of clay cups, huge basket-wrapped jugs, and crystal bowls. Spearing some clumps of coarse brown sugar on the flat of his blade, Scratch dumped the grains into his cup, stirring a bit before he licked both sides of the knife and returned it to the scabbard—then took himself a long drink he let lay on his tongue, savoring the hearty burn.

Jumpin' Jehoshaphat! If that Mex way to drink this here liquor didn't make his sweet tooth shine!

Back at Workman's place that first night in the valley more than two weeks before, Rufus Graham had introduced him to the way many Taosenos sweetened and softened the locals' favorite potion. As strong black Missis-sippi River coffee became a dessert with heapings of cane sugar, this Mexican *aguardiente* went down all the smoother after a man sweetened it with a coarse brown sugar transported all the way north from Mexico's southern-most provinces.

As new as these villages in northern Mexico might be to gringo traders from the States, the Taos valley had been settled well before the arrival of the first English to the eastern shores of North America. From the time the Spanish first ventured north to the Rio Grande country, the simple people of this valley had celebrated the annual tradition of the Taos Fair in late July or early August. Drawn by the prospect of riches, traders of many colors flocked to this high land locked beneath the dark snowcapped peaks of the Sangre de Cristos.

To Taos came merchants from the Spanish provinces far to the south, their poor *carretas* piled high with the treasures of Chihuahua and beyond. Other traders laid out wares brought on tall-masted schooners to the coastal cities of Mexico all the way from Spain: cutlery of the finest Toledo steel, butter-soft leather goods, perhaps bright tin objects to dazzle the eye, or those large silver coins so valued as ornaments by visiting Indians who bejeweled themselves in grand fashion. From all those remote provinces of New Spain came hundreds of traders who sought the riches to be bartered at these fairs. While some might bring Spanish barb horses to trade, others brought the handiwork of faraway native craftsmen—everything from earthenware and furniture to saddles, harness, and tack. Upon their trade blankets many displayed the shiniest of finger rings, bracelets, and objects to enhance the slender throat of any woman.

And when those traders came to this land of the Pueblo dweller every summer, so came the more nomadic tribes from the surrounding region: Arapaho, Kiowa, and Navajo, Pawnee and Ute, even the more warlike Apache and Comanche bands. Perhaps it was the presence of the other tribes, perhaps even the desire not to be counted out in this annual fair, that kept a secure lid on the powder keg—suspicion and hostilities suspended for a few days of merriment and bartering. Instead of raising scalps and seizing captives, the warriors had to content themselves with growling and trading, blustering and bartering. By a long-standing tradition, each of them held to a temporary truce despite the bloodiest of intertribal wars, despite their uninterrupted depredations on these same Mexican villages.

But for that brief time at the height of summer, the tribes brought their hides: huge, glossy buffalo robes; the silklike chamois of antelope and mountain goat; the luxurious pelts of wolf, badger, and fox. And they brought slaves. Human misery, so it seemed, had become a staple of this annual trade with the Indian bands at the Taos Fair. With their prisoners stolen in raids made on rival tribes, the visitors traded their captives for trinkets, blankets, kettles, beads, and weapons . . . and always the Indians traded for their share of the Mexican's alcohol.

For more than two hundred years they had come here like bees to the hive—both the suspicious Mexican from Chihuahua and the wary warrior from the Llano Estacado—forging an uneasy truce while they took what they needed most from the other.

Everyone knew the warrior bands would return to the killing soon enough. Would return to Taos for the sheep and horses, for the women and children soon enough.

Although Don *Fernando* de Taos was the village's proper name, some of the Mexicans themselves had come to call this sprinkling of whitewashed adobe huts and walled compounds by the name Don *Fernandez* de Taos. Still others corrupted it further to *San* Fernandez or San Fernando de Taos. No matter what expensive two-dollar name the Mexicans chose to hang on it . . . to the mountain trappers who learned of its existence—the breed who flocked here come the brutal winters raging farther north in the Rocky Mountains— this place was known simply as *Touse.*

Here the residents were far more willing to trade with the Norte Americanos who brought their wares from back east in Missouri all the way down the Santa Fe Trail than they were to trade with the trappers for their pelts. After all, the trade goods came from elsewhere—items that could not be had anywhere in Mexico. But those beaver hides . . . now, those might well have been pulled right out of Mexican waters! So though most Taosenos enthusiastically tolerated the American traders who came with their wares, traded them off for specie and mules, then turned around for the States without lingering, these trappers were something quite different altogether. They arrived late in the autumn and stayed on until winter itself was retreating from the high country.

Which meant that most of this reckless breed of unwashed, crude characters were underfoot and causing trouble for the natives of this sleepy village until the prospect of trapping prime beaver plews eventually lured the foreign interlopers from the valley once more.

It was a clash of two distinct cultures—in so many ways no different a story from when the trapper confronted the Indian's way of life. Yet here in northern Mexico there was one essential ingredient added to the volatile mix that wasn't thrown in when the beaver men met Stone Age Indian in those early days of the mountain west: liquor. To the Americans their beloved Taos lightning greased the wheels of international commerce, while the Mexicans found any trapper in his cups more likely than not a quarrelsome and overbearing creature all too often quick to pick a fight. In short, it didn't take too much of the potent *aguardiente* stirred in with all those months of pent-up deprivation before many minor conflicts were aggravated into potentially deadly clashes.

In the two weeks following their rescue of the captives, Hatcher's Americans made Workman's caverns their base camp. From time to time they would mosey into town with a handful of the pesos they had bartered off the whiskey maker for a few of their plews. With that hard money warming their pouches, the trappers looked over the rich variety of goods offered by the cart vendors and blanket traders who cluttered the open-air verandas surrounding the village square every day from dawn until just after dusk. More than any American-made goods, the gringos coveted such items as thick Navajo blankets almost impervious to water to fine hand-painted scarves; from sturdy saddles and tack to crops harvested just that very autumn; from select cuts of beef, pork, and lamb to the slimy organ meats hung from open-air racks; from coarse Mexican tobacco to the natives' fine linen shirts, pantaloons, and stockings.

Why, Titus hadn't been around such a place with so many pungent odors and curious sights since he'd floated to New Orleans eighteen long years gone now.

The narrow, sometimes off-kilter and mazelike, streets laid out in their tiny grid were more often than not teeming with roaming dogs, burros shuffling past beneath their loads of firewood, bleating sheep and goats being driven to a new patch of grass, and the ever-present gaggles of chickens and roosters wandering aimlessly about, feeding where they could on that refuse pitched from every door into the rutted, stinking byways. Occasionally a yoke of oxen or a brace of Missouri mules were herded past by American traders, more often by some young boys or very old men, all of the *pelados* dressed alike in their loose peasant clothing, a blanket serape for their only warmth.

While most of the squat adobe buildings strung out from the town square would never impress a traveler from the old French dominion of St. Louis, the municipal building and the towering cathedral nonetheless stood as two of the most recognized landmarks in the tiny town. Hand in hand, these institutions of church and state alone ruled the daily lives of this valley's simple people as each was born, baptized, raised, married, sired their young, then died and were laid to mortal rest within the church cemetery. More and more it struck Bass that these were a people accustomed to accepting, a people who had learned not to ask for much from each day. To lead their simple lives, that might well be enough to ask of the divine.

Behind each low-roofed hut sat the domed beehive of a baking oven, where each day the peasant women made their loaves of bread, where on cold winter nights the family dogs slept among the warm embers. While the poorer mud-and-wattle homes were no more than a single small room with blankets hung to section off a tiny sleeping area, most of the adobe dwellings in this village were a bit more spacious, some even built large enough to encompass a small central patio where narrow plank doors led the inhabitants to each of the few rooms. In a corner of every room sat a squat mud fireplace filling the house with the pungent fragrance of burning cedar or piñon.

From the poorest *pelado* to the richest landowner, no Taoseno laid down plank flooring in his home. Instead, hard-packed earth sufficed, over which the woman of the house would throw a series of coarse, woven mats, since the thick Navajo wool rugs served only as blankets at night, rolled up each morning and used in the place of chairs during the day.

In these mud houses each small window was paned with a sheet of translucent mica and frequently barred with wrought-iron or carved wooden bars. On the sills of many windows this winter sat empty flower boxes that come spring would display a bevy of colorful red geraniums—clearly the favorite flower of the Taosenos.

Kinkead had explained that the villages in this valley were not always painted in such drab, dreary colors of winter. With the arrival of spring the tiny towns would burst with vibrant colors just about the time the trappers were seeing to their final preparations in departing for the mountains. Looking about now, Titus found that hard to believe, what with the pale and pasty colors this season brought to Taos: the grayish white of dirty snow smearing sun-washed adobe, the monotonous pastels of ocher and sienna earth, along with the ever-present black buckskin pantaloons and jackets favored by the *caballeros* in from the ranchos for a spree, or those black rebozo shawls most women pulled over their heads for warmth whenever they ventured from their homes.

Isaac walked up to the table, pouring himself some more *aguardiente*. He asked, "Scratch, you wanna come see the cock fight Mirabal's getting started back out to the stables?"

"I've see'd cock fights afore," Bass replied, sipping his drink as he continued to peer around the room over the rim of his cup.

"Ain't you a gambling man?" Simms inquired.

"Scratch got better things to take a look-see at than no stupid cock fight!" Hatcher advised, wagging his eyebrows knowingly at Simms, nodding his head toward a small group of comely young women who were coyly studying the Americans from behind their lace fans.

"Hell," Isaac admitted as soon as he sorted out his priorities, "I s'pose a man can allays find hisself a cock fight in Touse . . . but there ain't allays senoritas to gander at!"

"Scratch, don't want you to feel bad now if most of these here gals don't give you the time of day," Kinkead declared. "Their papas and mamas don't want their daughters having nothing to do with no gringos."

"I knowed their kind back in St. Lou," Titus replied. "Snooty stuff-shirts—look down their noses on the rest of us."

"Here it's the ones with all the money, mostly, what look down on us," Matthew replied. "My Rosa's folks—now they're better off than most, but they're the sort who understood she fell in love with me, so it weren't gonna make no never-mind to Rosa that I was a gringo."

"Bet it helped a hull bunch you getting yourself baptized in their church," Bass commented.

Kinkead nodded that massive head of his, smiling. "You wanna marry a Mexican gal, you wanna live your life down here in Mexico—why, a man best figger on doing things the Taos way."

"You're happy, ain'cha, Matthew?" Titus asked.

"Damn right I am," he answered, then went solemn as he whispered, "I thank God in heaven Rosa wasn't took by them Comanche like Rowland's woman."

At that very moment Scratch was reminded that John Rowland had elected not to join them for the evening's fandango.

Caleb Wood finally cleared his throat and turned to Matthew, asking, "How's he doing these days?"

"Has him better times, and he has him some low times . . . when he's down in his mind over losing her," Kinkead replied. "Ever since we got back, Rosa and me had him stay over to our li'l house so he won't have to lay up in no place gonna remind him of his Maria."

"Damn fine of you, Matthew," Scratch said. "Keep a friend under your wing till his heart heals up."

Kinkead responded, "No more'n what ary man does for them he cares for."

"When you figger a man gets over grievin' for a woman?" Rufus asked quietly after a few moments of quiet and contemplation.

It was a question that struck the others dumb, many of them staring at the floor, or into their cups, reluctant to let their eyes meet another's.

Finally Hatcher whispered, his voice clogged with sentiment, "I figger the only way a man gets better is with time. After all what his friends can do . . . and a lot of time."

Bass had come to this celebration bent on having himself a good time: to drink until he was numb and to pound his moccasins on the floor until he could no longer stand. To hop and whirl and bounce wildly to the music the others explained was a major part of these gatherings.

But now the Comanche raid and the kidnapping and that final, bloody, all-too-quick fight of it came flooding back over him. Maybe it was Rowland's own damned fault, he brooded as he turned from the others and moseyed toward the other side of the room, where a knot of young doe-eyed women had been watching him over their lace fans. No two ways of Sunday about that: it was a man's own damned fault when he let a woman get down under his skin and something terrible . . .

Long as he didn't let that happen to him, Scratch figured he'd never have to go through all what he knew John Rowland was suffering.

From time to time he stole a glance at one or the other of those five women who whispered to one another behind their fans, nodding their heads slightly as they spoke, the mantillas on top of their heads swaying gently, the long lace scarves brushing bare brown shoulders. He finally had to admit he wasn't all that good at sneaking a look without being caught.

Reluctantly, Titus moved away a few feet, sipping from his cup and trying desperately not to turn around and gaze at the senoritas again. Better to study what was hung on every wall completely encircling the long *sala:* joining the many portraits of the governor's family ancestors were those customary portraits of famous religious figures and dramatic biblical scenes.

From a large central chandelier and just overhead on all the walls blazed a dizzying assortment of colorful candles, their light fluttering gently as the guests moved about the room, stirring currents of air that caused the soft light to dance.

Titus turned back, recrossing the room to his friends, doing his best to keep his eyes from climbing to the wall right over the table bearing the liquid refreshments. It was enough to give serious pause to any drinking man bent on having himself a real spree—for right there above the clay jugs and crystal bowls hung the biggest wooden crucifix Scratch had ever seen outside of a church. On it hung the naked Christ, His side and forehead vivid with the red paint of His final tortures, His head hung in the final release of death.

Indeed, the sacred holiday celebrating the birth of the baby Jesus was fast approaching, little more than a week away now. Festive decorations were already hung at the front of most shops and carts in the village square where traders sold their wares and vendors offered a warm tortilla made from blue Indian corn filled with a ladle of frijoles spiced with green chiles. More than anything else here in Mexico, it had been the food that Bass took an instant liking to—far different from anything he had ever known back east, even since reaching the Rocky Mountain west. Never was it dull to the palate. Scratch had yet to find anything handed him on a plate that he didn't care for, all of it either spicy or sweet. Truth be, as the minutes rolled past and the room grew all the more crowded, Titus wondered if he might be wearing down a groove in the earthen floor between the table bearing the Taos lightning and another table weighed down with trays of sugar-coated treats.

"Here comes the music, boys!" Caleb suddenly yelled.

Hatcher slapped Scratch on the back of the shoulders as Bass whirled in surprise. Jack hollered, "Time coming to let the wolf howl!"

"You dance, Titus?" Elbridge Gray spoke up for the first time since they had arrived.

Jack snorted, wagging his head. "Hell, don't ye remember this here nigger didn't wanna dance with us for his last birthday?"

"Ain't never felt like dancing when I got me a hangover," Bass grumbled. "And you boys just wouldn't leave a man alone to sleep off his case of the shakes."

"You fixing to tie on a case of the shakes this night?" Solomon asked.

"I'm due, don't you think?" Scratch replied. "Hell, I ain't had me a good drunk since . . . since—"

"Since a few nights back when we first rode in to Workman's place!" Caleb roared.

Jack turned to him and said, "There be yer dancing music, Scratch!"

Down at the center of the huge *sala* six musicians were taking their places on a low wooden bandstand the servants had set in place on the earthen floor just for the *baile*. Right in the center at the back of the plank platform the first player seated himself, cradling a huge Indian drum called a *tombe* between his legs. On either side of him sat a pair of chairs where two others settled in with their oversize guitars known as *heacas*. Beside each one of them sat a man who played a violin, while in the middle stood a musician holding a mandolin across his left arm as he wiped his entire face with a bright white kerchief he stuffed back into the left wrist of his jacket.

"Maybeso there'll be trouble tonight, boys," Hatcher warned a few moments later as the musicians were tuning their instruments.

"I see 'em," Solomon grumbled. "Damned *pelados!*"

All eight of them and Rosa turned to look across the long room at the doorway where at least a dozen men had come in, stopping to stand at the elbow of Sergeant Jorge Ramirez. Seven of them wore uniforms freshly brushed for this evening. As many as a half dozen were clearly civilians. Young men all, talking among themselves as they first spied the Americans at the end of the *sala*. Dark eyes glowered below dark brows as tension instantly charged the room. Between the buckskinned gringos and the Mexican dandies stood the prize: those handsome young women who first looked in one direction, then in the other, their seductive glances bestowed upon all rivals.

"Don't they look to be fancy niggers tonight!" Bass declared. "That head soldier got him a new uniform too."

"That's right," Kinkead agreed. "He ain't a sergeant no more. I heard Mirabal made him a lieutenant. Ramirez is gonna be head dog here till they send up a new ensign from Santa Fe to take over for Guerrero."

Scratch watched how Ramirez and the men with him began to strut, puffing out their chests like prairie cocks. In a whisper he asked, "They gonna cause trouble, Matthew?"

Kinkead shook his head. "Nawww. But those greasers gonna be right there when *we* start the trouble."

"We?"

Matthew smiled. "Hatcher and the rest ain't about to let them *pelados* buffalo 'em and keep them senoritas all to themselves."

"Trouble comes, we'll be ready," Jack declared confidently. "Because we'll be the ones get in the first licks."

"Don't go get yourself too drunk, Bass," Graham warned. "Need to have you ready to kick and gouge, soon enough."

"Damn," Scratch muttered. "Here I come to this here *baile* to have myself a hoot and a headache come morning. Then you niggers tell me you're gonna get me in a fight and all my fun's over!"

"Plenty of time for fun afore the fighting starts," Caleb explained.

Bass inquired, "Why there gotta be any fighting anyways?"

"That soldier bunch been wanting to trim our feathers ever since we caught up to them Comanch'," Hatcher declared. "Ain't no stopping what's been coming ever since that morning up in the mountains."

" 'Sides, Scratch," Elbridge said, "it ain't a real fandango less'n there's some head-banging on them greasers."

"Man can't come and have himself a drink and a dance?"

Caleb shook his head, grinning. "Not when there's more fellers here than there is wimmens!"

"Ye figger on dancing with their women," Hatcher explained, "ye best be ready to put yer fists to work."

"They don't like me dancing with their gals, eh?"

"You'll get a whirl or two in," Kinkead stated. "But they don't put up with us dancing with their women for long at all."

"I was looking forward to some likker and a dance with a soft-feeling gal or two," Bass grumped. "Might as well be spending this night in some Injun camp since't I can't enjoy my likker and my dancin' neither . . . 'thout some Mex soldiers wanting to put their thumbs in my eyes, or stomp on my shins!"

"Matthew, go take ye a look around the room," Jack instructed as he put a fraternal hand on Bass's shoulder. "See if'n ye can spot a likely gal for Titus to dance with afore the fighting starts."

"And once the fighting starts," Scratch kept on muttering with deep disappointment, "then all the rest of my fun's run dry too."

"I'll be back straight-'way," Kinkead declared as he steered Rosa away into the bustling room.

As he sipped on his clay cup of liquor, Bass looked over the growing crowd, beginning to notice how the men and women openly flirted with one another. While the more demure and younger women stayed behind their wide fans kept fluttering before their eyes, most of the older females boldly began conversations with the men passing by them. Much the same with the rougher sex, anxious and unsure young men scrunched up against a wall, perhaps talking only with male friends as they furtively eyed the young women, mortally afraid to chance striking up a chat with one of the black-eyed beauties.

As his eyes bounced over this group and that, Scratch groaned, "What you go and do that for, Jack?"

Hatcher asked, "Do what?"

"Send Kinkead off to go find me a gal—"

"Ain't you gonna dance tonight?"

He finally turned to look at Hatcher. "I am."

"Eegod! Won't it feel good to have your arms round one of 'em for that dancing?" Jack inquired.

"Damn fine," Bass replied.

"Then it's settled: we'll find you a likely gal for dancing," Jack explained. "And maybeso . . . a li'l courting too when the night grows old."

"Courting? I ain't in no mood for courting one of these here women!" Scratch bellowed a little too loudly. Then, realizing his transgression, more quietly he said to the others, "I ain't like Matthew there. I don't aim to get married off to no gal—Injun or Mex."

"Dancing . . . even courting don't mean you're getting yourself married, Scratch!" Caleb guffawed.

And Isaac declared, "But some sweet courting talk just might get you bedded down with some soft-skinned gal!"

"Just like you got yourself a warm one to sleep with while you was healing up with the Snakes," Solomon declared.

"Hush!" Jack declared, waving his arms suddenly.

At the center of the long room Governor Mirabal stepped atop the low platform in front of the musicians, bowed gracefully in his velvet uniform trimmed with silver braid, the crowded room applauding politely, then began to speak. As Kinkead hurried back to the group, Hatcher asked him to translate.

"He's saying he's proud to have everyone as a guest in his home," Matthew explained as the governor turned, holding out his arm. "Says that this is a special night for celebration . . . his wife and oldest daughter are back under their roof . . . not again to have to worry about Comanches."

"T-that's them?" Rufus Graham asked as the woman and her daughter glided up to the low platform in their wide-hooped dresses, both of vivid color, the long lace of their mantillas spilling from the tall bone combs fastened at their crowns, hair ironed into tight ringlets around both faces.

"Damn if them women don't shine!" Hatcher exclaimed.

Caleb declared, "I can't believe it's the same two we brung back from the mountains!"

"Can't be," Scratch agreed. "They don't look a thing like the two what Matthew here said was relations of that governor."

"It's them," Kinkead testified. "You niggers don't recollect them two been yanked out'n their homes afore sunup by the Comanche . . . and now you see 'em in all their finest glory."

"Damn if them women don't shine!" Hatcher marveled again.

"You said that awready once't!" Wood cried. Then, as he peered over at Hatcher, he added, "Lookee there, boys! Mad Jack's got him pup-dog eyes for them gals."

"Shut that bunghole of your'n!" Hatcher snapped, then turned to Kinkead. "What else is he saying now, Matthew?"

Just then the governor motioned off to the far side of the room, waving up the sergeant of that detail of soldiers who had followed the trappers along the Comanche trail.

"Telling everyone how much a hero they were to ride after the Injuns what took the cattle and sheep, what took the women and children of our valley," Kinkead translated.

The new lieutenant stood on the floor just in front of the governor as the official continued speaking.

"He wants the rest of the soldiers to come up so everyone can know who were heroes after their captain was killed in the fight with the Injuns."

The seven uniformed soldiers came out of the crowd, joined by at least a dozen more men dressed in their finest civilian clothing, resplendent in braid, silver conchos, and ornamental buttons from ankle clear up to collarbone.

"That ain't all of 'em is it?" Isaac asked in a whisper.

"I figger some of 'em still covering guard watch, maybe," Jack replied. "They ain't all here."

"Hol't on!" Kinkead blurted, waving both his arms in a downward motion to quiet the others.

Hatcher asked, "What's he saying?"

"I'd tell you if I could hear!" Then Matthew moved forward a step, cocking his ear as the governor's eyes scanned the crowd. "Jack—he's saying he wants you and me to come up there with them soldiers."

"Me?"

Kinkead nodded, starting off with Rosa beneath one arm, his huge hand snatching hold of Hatcher's sleeve and tugging him along. "Governor wants all of us."

"Why, goddammit?"

Matthew grinned. "He says we're the heroes what brung his family back to him. We're the heroes he says kept the soldiers from getting all killed by the Injuns."

"C'mon!" Hatcher growled with a sharp gesture of his head. "If'n I'm going up there, rest of you are too!"

"Likely he's got that right," Solomon said.

"Got what right?" Bass asked.

Fish replied, "When he says them soldiers get killed if'n we hadn't come along."

The group shyly followed Matthew and Rosa to the front of the low platform, where Rosa slipped out from beneath her husband's arm and joined the front row of spectators who were applauding with their approval. Most everyone in the room smiled enthusiastically as the eight Americans strung themselves out at one side of the platform . . . everyone but the soldiers and those in attendance who hated every gringo, no matter what they had done to rescue the governor's family.

As Bass shoved in between the shoulders of Isaac Simms and Rufus Graham, his palms began to sweat something fierce, especially when he looked up from the toes of his muddy moccasins to find the soldiers glowering at him and the others beneath their dark eyebrows. Quickly he turned away, glancing over the rest of the room, finding hate flickering in the eyes of so many males, adoration glittering in the eyes of so many of the females. Old and young. Especially the young who held hands and fans at their breasts, that rounded, dusky flesh half-exposed in their bloodred, black, sunset-blue or buttermilk-yellow gowns that barely clung to their bodies.

At that moment he couldn't remember ever seeing a woman out in public in so provocative a manner, her clothing exposing so much of her neck, her shoulders and arms, even unto the top half of her breasts. Swallowing hard, Titus wondered how the dresses stayed up. But then he figured those firm, soft-skinned mounds were what held everything in place. So much of those breasts exposed that it wouldn't take much at all for a man to just reach his hand right in there and—

"Titus Bass! Step up there, nigger!"

"Uhh?"

"Matthew just called your name," Rufus said in a harsh whisper. "He's calling out our names for this here party to clap for us."

Glancing quickly to his left, he found Isaac Simms and the others beyond him grinning sheepishly, motioning him up with them. He immediately took a step to join the others as he heard Matthew call out Graham's name. Rufus was there at his right shoulder a heartbeat later, so that all eight of the Americans stood before the group as the governor, his wife, and daughter stepped off the platform and right up to Rufus Graham. There the governor held out his hand, shaking it before he moved on to Bass.

As Titus released Mirabal's grip, he had but a moment before the governor's wife stepped up to him, her hand suspended between them.

"What'm I to do?" he whispered to Isaac, frantic.

"Bow your damned head, nigger!" Simms said in a husky whisper.

Nervously shoving his hairy chin against his chest, Scratch watched Manuela Mirabal give a short curtsy before releasing his hand and stepping on to do the same with Isaac. But the moment the woman moved on and relief began to wash over him, he discovered the pretty, cherry-eyed daughter stopping right in front of him, toe to toe, staring up at him as soft-eyed and wet-lipped as a young fawn.

"Bow again, goddammit!" Rufus reminded him with a growl.

As Manuela Mirabal moved by Isaac, he nudged Bass with an elbow. "This'un's sweet on you, Titus, ol' boy! Better give her hand a kiss too."

On the other side Graham chuckled softly. "Just like them proper Frenchmen do in St. Louie!"

"Kiss her h-hand?"

"Do it!" Isaac ordered.

As instructed, Titus bowed his head and brought the small, smooth hand to his lips obediently, brushing it with his parched lips, embarrassed that his entire mouth and throat had just gone dry. Raising his head, he found Jacova's eyes brazenly locked on his. Instead of immediately removing her hand from his once he had completed his bow, the girl held on to his hand as he straightened. Her mother reached out and gently nudged her young daughter, as if to remind Jacova she was to continue down the receiving line. Just as she was about to step aside, the young woman squeezed Bass's hand, lingering for a heartbeat longer.

While she turned to present her hand to Isaac, Bass felt both ears growing hot beneath his long curls.

Barely able to breathe, Scratch found he couldn't take his eyes off her—helpless as he studied the way Jacova held out her delicate fingers to Simms, how she curtsied politely, the way she spoke to Isaac as she furtively glanced at Titus. He suddenly realized just how quickly she pushed her limp hand into Isaac's, allowed Simms to bow, then immediately yanked her hand away while she had let it linger in Bass's grip.

Was he crazy? Or had she really sought to hang on to Bass until the very last moment they might have to share, the last moment they would have to touch, to gaze into one another's eyes?

As he watched Jacova float back across the front of the room to rejoin her parents, Titus suddenly became aware of the hateful glare in the eyes of all those young soldiers arrayed just behind the governor, his wife, and daughter as the Mirabals stopped before Matthew. Mirabal motioned for Rosa to join her husband. While she shyly stepped to Kinkead's side at the center of the *sala*, Bass noticed the governor's daughter looking at him from beneath her long eyelashes.

"Maybeso that young'un's got the idee to make herself your wife," Rufus whispered, leaning into Bass's shoulder.

With a reflex jerk Titus jabbed back with his elbow, planting it deep into Graham's belly. Giving a noisy *ooomph,* Rufus stumbled back a step, snorting with laughter.

"What's he saying now, Matthew?" Gray asked.

Kinkead translated in a whisper, "Says they're gonna bring in the lamb and the calf now. I don't figger there's gonna be a empty belly in the whole house!"

At the far end of the room the crowd parted as four men stepped through the cordon, on their shoulders a large pewter platter atop which lay the roasted carcass of an entire lamb. Right behind them came four others, these carrying a roasted calf. Whistles of approval and cheers arose as the fragrance of the steaming meats washed over the room.

With his mouth already watering, Scratch had his knife halfway out of its scabbard before Kinkead locked his hand around Bass's wrist.

"You'll get your turn, pilgrim," Matthew warned. "Let the women get their meat first."

Suddenly shamed and remembering the long-ago social manners his mother had worked so hard to teach him, Bass dropped the knife back into its sheath. "I'm sorry, Matthew."

With a wink the big man replied, "Don't you need feel sorry, Titus. Folks like us, we ain't got much call to show our proper manners what with the life we have in the mountains."

When, if ever, had he gone and bowed to a gal . . . much less kissed a woman's hand? But in the last few minutes, here in a foreign land, he had just done both! Right in front of a whole room filled with gawking folks watching him as his face grew hot and his eyes smarted with embarrassment.

This was all something so different, so completely new to him. Oh, to be sure, many of the women he'd known could be brazen in their own way, usually when he found himself alone with them. Amy Whistler, even Abigail, the Ohio River whore. And Marissa wasn't shy at all about letting him know exactly what she had on her mind when she came sneaking out to where he had his blankets laid in her father's barn.

Now, those Injun gals, Fawn and Pretty Water, they had never appeared to worry about the niceties of preliminaries nor concerned themselves with social appearances. Behind the dropped door of their lodges, neither had a problem showing Titus just what they wanted from him of a sexual nature. There was no clutter of polite manners to get in the way of man and woman taking what they needed most from one another.

So it struck him as all the more flattering that this young woman had made her thoughts abundantly clear through nothing more than that steamy look in her eyes and the way she gripped his hand until her mother demanded she move on down the line.

Through the early part of the evening Bass had danced one lively *jota* after another with a succession of young women brought up and introduced to him by Matthew and Rosa. There had been a Carmelita, a Maria, and a Linda, those three somehow rememberable among all the faceless others who came to sway at the end of his arms in that Mexican dance so reminding him of a country reel, each of those perfumed females smiling politely through their song, then turning away before he could escort them back to their side of the room.

"Don't you know Jacova's mama is gonna keep a close eye on that girl now, Scratch," Kinkead warned hours later after the lamb and calf were no more than greasy platters heaped with bones, long after the musicians were beginning to tire and the room had grown unbearably warm from all the heated bodies pulsing to those most ancient rhythms of the courtship ritual.

Bass turned to Matthew. "Whose mama?"

"Jacova's mama," Kinkead chided. "The governor's wife. It's his daughter you gone and got all moon-eyed over."

"I ain't moon-eyed," he snapped.

"Well, she sure as hell is," Matthew snorted with a wink. "Best you just forget that girl afore she spells trouble for you."

"I ain't about to do a thing to make for trouble—"

"G'won and set your eye on one of them others," Kinkead suggested. "Like Hatcher there."

"Jack ain't about to sit out a dance!" Caleb gushed as he came up, a clay cup in one hand, a rib he was tearing meat from in the other.

"See how I got him a good woman to take a whirl with and he's a happy man, Titus," Matthew boasted. "Now, whyn't you do the same and forget that Jacova Mirabal."

"I ain't thinking 'bout Jacova!"

Kinkead jabbed an elbow in Caleb's side. "Looks to me you gone all soft-brained over her."

"Then bring me 'nother girl to dance with or leave me be!" Bass grumbled, his forehead hot as all-night coals—already sensing the long evening's potent liquor. "To hell with what's right and what's wrong with these here Mex folks. Can't think of nothing better to do than drink till my own feet don't hold me up no more."

"You're damned near that now!" Rufus said as he came back to the group at the end of a song.

"That Hatcher," Bass said, watching Jack standing near the center of the floor, holding both hands with a comely maid until the next song started. Just beyond them stood at least a dozen young Mexican men glaring at the lone American.

"Tell me, Matthew—she a gal gonna get Jack in trouble?"

"Nawww, she's the sort gonna get us *all* in trouble," Kinkead replied. "That's Consuela Guerrero."

Bass licked his lips, thinking how lucky Hatcher was to be getting all that attention from such an alluring woman arrayed in black lace stretched tight against her dark-brown skin. "She's a purty one."

Matthew clucked, "Her husband was the officer what got hisself killed by the Comanche when we brung back the women."

"That's her?"

Kinkead nodded. "The widow Guerrero her own self."

"What's she doing here after her husband got hisself kill't?" Caleb asked.

"Why, lookit there—the widder is wearin' black!" Elbridge said, patting the beginnings of a potbelly slipping over his belt.

"Wonder if she's gonna be wearing black all night?" Bass snorted with a grin. "Or if she's gonna shuck herself outta them widder's weeds for Mad Jack Hatcher!"

In a flurry the following moment, Kinkead pushed away from the rest of them, leaving his Rosa behind as he warned, "Jack ain't never gonna know now!"

Their eyes followed Matthew into the crowd, finding the dancers at the center of the floor suddenly shoving backward, getting themselves as far as possible from the spot where Hatcher stood imprisoned by two large Mexican soldiers as Lieutenant Jorge Ramirez yanked the widow away from the American, whirling her back by her arm. She screamed, swinging out with her flat hand. But the lieutenant caught it, held it prisoner while he shouted at her and the room grew hushed, the music ending in discordant notes.

"What's he saying to her, Kinkead!" Hatcher bellowed, twisting this way and that, trying to free himself from the two men who had him stymied.

"Telling her she ain't got no business dancing with you—not when her husband is in his grave because of us gringos."

Every set of American eyes snapped to Ramirez as the trappers came to a stop arrayed on either side of Matthew Kinkead.

His eyes narrowing into a feral wildness, Jack echoed, "He said her husband's dead 'cause . . . 'cause of us?"

"Shit!" Caleb growled. "The rest of them li'l wooden soldiers be nothing more'n buzzard bait right now if'n it weren't for the likes of us!"

Jack tried again to twist away from his handlers. "Tell these sumbitches let me go!"

Matthew spat some of the foreign tongue at the soldiers being joined by young men in civilian clothing. In their sashes were jammed pistols, and from their wide belts hung stiletto knives and short swords.

The lieutenant howled with a derisive laugh, then snarled something in reply.

"Caleb—get these greasers off'n me!"

Speaking low, Caleb said, "Elbridge, you and Scratch come with me to get Hatcher free."

"That'll start the dance!" Gray said.

"Fight now, or fight later," Caleb snapped. "We damn well ain't gonna show the white feather to these here greasers tonight!"

With those words still in the air, the trio descended upon the two soldiers so suddenly, the Mexicans let go of their prisoner on reflex to reach for their weapons. Hatcher whirled on one of them like a wild blur, his bony fist cracking into the soldier's jaw like a twenty-pound sledge colliding with solid hickory. Bass was right behind Hatcher as Elbridge and Caleb leaped into the second soldier.

In the next heartbeat Matthew and the others surged past Titus in a blur, lunging toward bystanders on all sides the moment the Mexican males jumped out of the crowd to resist the gringo attack. Women screeched. Furniture was overturned and crumbled. Clay and glass shattered against walls and the hard earth floor. Men grunted as bodies slammed together.

Isaac was suddenly there beside Bass, grabbing Scratch's hand—shoving into it a thick piece of a broken chair that felt as big as a horse's leg. An instant later the stocky Simms turned aside, slapping another chair leg into Rufus's hand. That done, Isaac began swinging two chair legs over his own head as he hurtled toward the worst of the fighting.

First one, and a second, then more heads cracked loudly in that noisy room as the three of them cleared a swath right into the soldiers and their civilian friends. Joining Hatcher and the rest, they kept swinging their crude weapons as they retreated to the center of the room, eyes quickly darting this way and that. The trappers crowded back together, each of them facing out like herd bulls protectively surrounding the cows and calves against a pack of wolves snarling, yapping, dodging in to slash at a hamstring.

"No guns!" the governor bellowed in English from the platform.

His futile warning was hardly heard above the frightening clamor as the soldiers warily inched toward the ring of eight Americans, their pistols and knives, swords and shards of broken glass, held before them as they closed the noose.

"No guns, señores!" Mirabal warned again, louder still, as the Mexicans came within striking distance.

"Get ready for the nut-cutting, boys!" Hatcher bawled, his arm slowly waving his own knife back and forth as he went into a crouch, preparing for the coming clash. He took a quick feint toward the closest adversary—getting the soldier to leap back—then Jack rocked onto the balls of his feet, body swaying side to side as he laughed.

Bass knew Hatcher was laughing at death.

Hell, he could smell that stinking odor of death all around them in this room.

Suddenly certain he was about to die.

Instead of making a life for himself within the bosom of the high and lonely places, he was going to shed his life's blood here on this clay floor in a foreign land, cut to ribbons by greasers, perhaps with a Mexican bullet in his heart.

Where was his mother's god now?

Why would any god leave him to die after he'd somehow survived those long years rotting in St. Louis, lasted long enough to make it to the Rocky Mountains on his own hook? Why would a god that ruled from the heavens above abandon him now after the Arapaho had tried twice to kill him? Blackfeet done their best too. . . .

So he was to die among these Christian people whose eyes were filled with such hate.

ELEVEN

As Mirabal's daughter rushed onto the platform, lunging across the last two steps to clutch her father's arm, screaming at him, the governor shoved Jacova behind him and continued yelling into the pandemonium.

Suddenly Mirabal drew his own pistol from the wide red sash there beneath the short-waisted *chaqueta*.

At that instant the screaming women were falling back toward the walls, leaving the two rings of antagonists alone in the middle of the long *sala:* that small knot of outnumbered Americans at the center, a thick ring of Mexican rivals surrounding them.

Firing his weapon into one of the thick wooden beams above their heads, Mirabal instantly silenced the entire room. The soldiers spun with a jerk. And the trappers looked up in alarm.

Bass wondered, Was this the signal for the killing to begin?

When he had their attention, the governor began to speak again in his loud, certain voice.

"He just ordered them *soldados* to put their pistols away," Kinkead translated breathlessly.

For a moment no one moved; then the first of the soldiers

began to comply . . . as if they had weighed the odds of disobeying not only their governor but their gracious host. The haughty Mexicans stuffed their pistols back into the colorful sashes tied around their waists, still brandishing their knives and short swords with unmasked glee.

"If one of us falls," Hatcher growled, "the rest get round him—don't let them greasers drag him off."

"How many you figger we can take on?" Caleb asked.

Elbridge was the first to answer. "Many as they wanna throw agin' us!"

Just as the soldiers took another cautious step toward their rivals, Mirabal hollered again.

Jack demanded, "What's he saying?"

"Something about the knives," Kinkead declared. "He don't want no killing here."

The governor hollered to some older men at the foot of the platform. Reluctantly two of them handed up their pistols to Mirabal. He immediately held them right over the heads of those standing below him on the clay floor, pointing the weapons directly at Ramirez.

Matthew swallowed hard, saying, "Mirabal just told 'im he'd be the first to die. If there's gonna be blood, then Ramirez's blood's gonna be the first on this floor."

"He—he's really pulling them soldiers back?" Fish asked in that hushed room.

Kinkead nodded. "Says he won't let the lieutenant and his men dishonor him twice."

It was plain as sun how the governor's words slapped the officer and his men every bit as hard as if he would strike them across the cheek.

"Says them soldiers dishonored him when they didn't fight hard enough to save all the prisoners," Matthew explained to his stunned companions.

"Weren't their fault the bastards was yeller polecats," Isaac grumbled.

Continuing, Kinkead declared, "He won't stand for the soldiers dishonoring him again by killing in his . . . in his house . . ."

Bass listened to the way Kinkead's voice dropped off. "What . . . what is it, Matthew?"

"He said there won't be no killing in his house, 'specially no killing the men what brung his wife and daughter back to him safe."

The lieutenant whirled on the governor, red-faced as he spat out his words, gripping the huge butt of that pistol stuffed into his sash. The officer's whole body trembled with rage.

"He says that's twice Mirabal's shamed him and his men," Matthew warned gravely. "Says they're due the right to wipe off that shame, or there is no honor in this house."

Slowly the governor lowered one of the pistols, pointing the other directly at the lieutenant's head.

"If there's gonna be killing, that Ramirez gonna be the first to die here. Mirabal ain't gonna let them soldiers disobey him."

Even though the room was as quiet as a convent at dusk, the governor bellowed like a bull, flushed with anger from the neck up.

"Told 'em to put away ever'thing," Kinkead translated. "Knives too."

"Why?" Hatcher asked.

Pausing before he answered, Matthew eventually explained, "Told Ramirez if they wanted to show they was honorable men, then they could fight like real men—'thout no guns or no knives."

"No knives?" Simms repeated.

For a long time no one moved.

Then suddenly the lieutenant turned away from his men and stepped right to the foot of the platform, where he passed both his pistol and his long stiletto to Jacova. The governor's daughter took the weapons as the rest of the Mexican males reluctantly handed over their weapons to women lining the adobe walls where candles flickered in the still air.

Mirabal hurled his voice over the heads of the others, speaking to the trappers.

Matthew translated, "Says it's our turn to put our guns away—"

"Cache our guns?" Hatcher replied in disbelief. "Ain't no way in hell I'm letting go of this pistol of mine—not when these sumbitches got us outnumbered the way they do."

Silence fell heavy about them once more. And finally Mirabal spoke, filled with apparent regret.

"Governor says we ain't the honorable men he thought we was when we brung his family back . . . not if we don't put our guns and knives away like his soldiers done."

"If we do," Wood demanded, "then what?"

Matthew drew himself up hugely, "Then we'll have us our fight."

"Us agin' alla them?" Isaac inquired.

"Just our fists, boys!" Kinkead cheered as he turned and passed his weapons to Rosa.

"Who's gonna hold the rest what we got?" Hatcher demanded.

Graham said, "Yeah—I ain't trusting no one with my gun and my knife!"

"Lay 'em on that table by you," a voice cried out in plain English from somewhere beyond the thick ring of Mexicans. "They be safe right there."

"Damn," Bass muttered as the slight figure poked his way through the last layer of soldiers and stepped into the open between the two groups of rivals.

"Johnny!" Hatcher bellowed with glee. "Come to fandango with yer friends?"

Rowland's eyes bounced over the crowd a moment before he answered. "I s'pose you might say I come to fandango, Jack."

"We was 'bout to have us a do-si-do with these here greasers," Caleb explained.

"That's what I was tol't," John replied. "My Maria's mama—she come to get me over to Matthew's place."

"She come for ye?"

With a nod Rowland answered bravely, "Tol't me there was trouble aplenty 'tween the soldiers and my companyeros. Said I should come help my friends—since they was such good boys to go help me get my Maria back from the Comanch'. M-my Maria."

At Rowland's pained words a flame burned gently in Scratch's chest, a sharp warmth lodged just behind his breastbone. He felt the salty sting at his eyes.

"You gonna fight with us?" Elbridge asked, tugging manfully at his leather britches.

"I didn't come to dance with the likes of you, you ugly nigger!"

Then Rowland moved past the trappers, laying his two pistols on the long table. He didn't turn until he had taken his knife from its scabbard and propped it between the two pistols shoved in among the clay jugs of lightning and crystal bowls of sweet brandy.

Johnny turned back to the Americans, his eyes damp. "Yeah, boys—I come to fight 'longside my friends."

Hatcher suddenly raised his chin and let loose a shrill wolf howl. The rest instantly followed suit, clearly unnerving the soldiers as John Rowland stepped up and squeezed in between Hatcher and Kinkead, both men making room for him in their tight circle.

Matthew ordered, "Rest of you—put your guns and knives away, fellers . . . just like Johnny done. Because—by God—we're gonna give these here greasers the thrubbin' they been needing ever since't we come back from fighting the Comanche for 'em!"

One by one, wary and watchful, the trappers stepped over to the table, laid their weapons down, then quickly resumed their place in the tiny ring. Now there were nine of them. Nine against many times their number. But as the last of the Americans, Jack Hatcher himself, stepped back to that circle of defenders, the lieutenant growled a command of his own and the soldiers started forward.

But this time there were only the seven in uniform, and no more than nine in civilian clothing. Realizing he no longer had the great numbers behind him, the lieutenant halted right in his tracks, whirling around on his heel to glare back at those who no longer joined him.

Hatcher turned to Kinkead as Ramirez began shouting.

Matthew said, "The rest of 'em he's calling cowards."

"I figger 'em for smart fellers," Bass declared.

"How you figger on that?" Solomon asked beneath that sharp hatchet of a nose dotted with huge pores forever darkened with fire soot and ground-in dirt.

Titus explained, "They're smart enough to know that they ain't got near as good a chance taking us on when they don't have all them guns and knives."

"Give 'em the thrubbing they deserve!" Caleb bellowed as the lieutenant turned around to face Hatcher.

With a sudden screech of rage Ramirez lunged forward, his arms raised, both hands stiffened like claws over his head. Jack was the first to swing his chair leg as the others rushed in behind the lieutenant.

Scratch didn't see when his friends got into the melee—he was already swinging the thick chair leg he clutched in his sweaty hands at the first of two soldiers rushing him. That burly Mexican reached up, seizing the chair leg in midarc as he leaped up toe to toe. Bass brought up his knee in that instant the soldier was setting himself to strike, savagely driving it into the Mexican's groin. But he had little time to enjoy watching the man crumple before him, clutching his genitals, his dark face gone pasty in pain.

For the second soldier had grabbed the end of the chair leg and rocked back with a jerk, then made a second attempt to loosen it from Bass's grip. Instead, Scratch drove his heel down onto the Mexican's shin, stabbing the man's instep with all his weight. As the soldier lunged back, releasing the chair leg, Bass was already swinging it behind his shoulder—

—just when he felt a huge fist slam into his lower back.

The pain was so immediate, so severe, that he sensed the breath rush out of his lungs, sensed his knees turning to water.

Then came a second blow to his back, harder than the first. His legs went out right under him as if they weren't there.

As Scratch went down, he heard the women's screams for the first time. They almost drowned out the grunts of men colliding, bone and muscle and sinew crashing together, might against might. So loud was the screaming and that thunder of bone striking bone that he almost didn't hear the sharp gust of wind rush from his lips as he struck the hard clay of the earthen floor.

Gasping for breath, he twisted about to look up—finding that shadow looming over him become the first soldier he had kneed as the Mexicans rushed them. While Scratch drew himself into a ball, the soldier drove his cowhide boot into Bass's ribs again and again. With each blow great bubbles of air exploded from Titus's lungs, replaced by searing pain. Moccasins and boots scuffed around his head as he fought to curl himself tighter . . . struggling not only against the Mexican's boot, but fighting down the frightening remembrance of that brutal beating at the hands of Silas Cooper.

Suddenly the Mexican's foul breath was in his face as the soldier grabbed a handful of Bass's shirt, raising the American slightly, then driving his fist into Titus's face. A second time the man pulled Bass halfway up off the floor, only to slam his jaw back down with another blow.

He was going to kill him, just as Cooper tried!

But this time Scratch vowed he would not lie there and take a beating like a whipped dog.

From somewhere at the marrow of him Titus found the strength to seize the Mexican's left wrist in both of his hands. He jerked it up at the same moment he opened his mouth, instantly clamping down with his teeth on that soft web of skin between the thumb and forefinger. Grinding, sawing, chewing on the hard thumb bone and musky tissue that tasted of days'-old dirt and spilled *aguardiente*.

The Mexican smashed his other fist into the side of his head again as the man cried out in pain.

Bass bit down harder.

Again the soldier hammered a fist into Scratch's cheek. But not near as hard as before.

Through every blow Titus locked down harder on the skin, feeling that single bone grind beneath his teeth, feeling the flesh tearing away and the gushes of warm blood oozing over his tongue—thick and salty.

Of a sudden the fist opened and clawed at Scratch's neck, a thumb pressed against his larynx so hard, Bass wasn't sure he would breathe again. Freeing his right hand from the Mexican's wrist, Bass lashed out clumsily, finding his enemy's face. Seizing the fleshy jowl, his fingers crawled up the whiskered cheek until he found the eye socket. Remembering his struggle with the Comanche, Titus plunged his thumb past the edge of bone, stabbing into the soft, pliant tissue.

Above him the man flinched, yanking his head to the side—unable to free himself of Bass's terrible thumb. Instead, all the Mexican could do was tighten on the gringo's neck.

As Scratch watched the first sharp pricks of light shoot from the center of his head with that convulsive pain crushing his throat, he flexed his thumb spastically, digging deeper and deeper into the eye socket. Each time he did, he sensed the Mexican relax that iron vise on his throat just a little, before the man clamped down once more.

His decision was made—knowing he would either die without drawing another breath . . . or he would have to disable the Mexican and possibly kill the soldier outright.

With another sharp jab of his thumb, Scratch felt the bony rim of the socket, realizing he had reached the corner of the man's eye. As he struggled to draw a breath into his tortured, quaking lungs, Bass scooped his thumb to the side with what little resolve he had left.

Beneath his thumb soft membranes tore away from the socket. A sud-

den gush of warmth spilled over his thumb and hand. The Mexican's unearthly cry stung his ears as the soldier jerked backward, releasing that mortal
grip on the American's throat.

Scratch was unable to focus at first; all the movement around him was a
watery blur, like that deafening cacophony of noise—unable to pick out any
one sound, any single voice. He struggled to breathe: for him every gasp was
filled with such exquisite pain. Air! How it hurt to suck it in . . . but it was
air!

Then his vision cleared enough that he saw the Mexican stumbling
backward against other soldiers, both hands held at his face, his mouth open,
screaming in agony. That black hole within a black mustache and beard—with
a sound so shrill, it reminded Bass of a wild animal.

Blood slicked down the Mexican's cheek as two soldiers rushed to
him—

Then someone grabbed Scratch, snatching hold of the back of his collar,
dragging him backward.

On instinct Scratch whirled clumsily, still fighting for breath, locking his
hands around the arm that yanked him across the trampled floor.

"Easy, goddammit!" Elbridge bellowed.

It was Gray's face. And his arm pulling Titus back toward the others,
who were again drawing into a tight circle. Their faces and heads and knuckles bloodied. Two of them still holding their heavy chair legs.

"Bass put his goddamned eye out!" Kinkead yelled with glee.

Jerking back around the moment Elbridge got him to the others, Titus
looked for the soldier—found him. Someone had a white handkerchief out
and was pressing it against the man's cheek, where a wide ribbon of crimson
shimmered in the candlelight. Above that bloody handkerchief the eyelid
fluttered loosely over the socket. Empty was it, like a grave yet unfilled, black
as night.

Several women burst out of the crowd to join the two soldiers helping
their own stumble away toward the door. The sound the blinded man made
was one of excruciating agony, a shrieking warble slowly dying in that suddenly hushed room. Mingled with the muted murmurs of the crowd were the
gasps for air and grunts of newfound pain from nearly all the fighters taking
stock of their own injuries.

Suddenly the ring of Mexicans around the gringos appeared to shrink.

"Ye done good, Scratch!" Hatcher cheered, slapping him on the shoulders.

"I—I really put his eye out?"

"Ain't nothin' but a hole there now," Caleb answered. "I see'd that a
few times afore. Leastways, he's lucky you didn't kill—"

Kinkead shushed them as the governor began speaking again. "He's
asking them soldiers if they had 'em enough."

Their only answer was a sudden shriek from the lieutenant and those left standing with him as they rushed the Americans again. Both forces met with a mighty noise, the wooden sound of hard bone meeting hard bone. Men grunting and cursing in both languages. Bodies slammed to the floor.

Scratch saw the lights again, felt himself sinking to his knees, watched figures swimming before him in an inky pool. Like the summer night he first laid between Amy's soft thighs beside that old swimming hole. This was just as black, just as liquid as that.

He caught himself with one arm, starting to blink as he looked up, turning to gaze back over his shoulder—finding the Mexican lunging over him with most of what had been a huge chair still in both his hands.

Bass tasted blood, wondering if it was the eyeless soldier's blood . . . or if it was his own. It was dripping down his neck, along his jaw and cheek, through his beard and onto his lips. Must have opened up the back of my head, he thought in a blur as he blinked again, trying to focus on the Mexican bringing down the chair against his head and shoulders a second time.

That blow sounded exactly like one of his mother's heavy churns dropped onto their puncheon floor, back in Kentucky. Hollow, ringing, and with the same dull echo as he felt the cool, earthen floor smack against his cheek.

He shivered so hard, he thought his teeth were going to rattle out of his mouth. Clacking so loud, they sounded almost like those bone dice in that ivory cup of Ebenezer Zane's—the way the old riverboatman shook them whenever he gambled with his flatboat crew on its float down to New Orleans that autumn of 1810.

Bass was certain his cheek still lay against the clay floor in Mirabal's *sala,* so cold it felt. And he wondered how long he had been out as he attempted to open his puffy eyes.

"Lookee there!" Jack's voice sang beyond the foggy, black curtain. "The nigger's coming to, boys!"

Then he felt a cool, damp rag brush his forehead, down his cheeks, as he struggled to pry open his eyes again. They remained so heavy.

"Maybe not, Jack. His eyes jumpin'—that's all."

That sounded like Elbridge.

"Likely had all the mortal sense knocked out of him clear back to the Wind River, I'd wager."

Caleb.

"What with that wallop he took, I don't reckon the child's gonna wake up for a week."

Bass tried to say the name, "R-rufus?"

"Eegod—ye hear that, fellers?" Hatcher said. "He called for Rufus."

The damp cloth brushed his face again as he forced his eyes open into slits. There were people before him—at least he took the milky forms to be people. It hurt to move his eyes. Not that there was any real pain right in his eyes—just the dull throb everywhere in his head. Moving his eyes hurt about as bad as anything.

Then he suddenly smelled something strange. Different. Sweet and alluring. It damn sure wasn't the odors of those men he had ridden miles and months with.

This was the smell of a woman!

Slowly prying open an eye a bit farther, Bass rolled it so he could peer first in one direction, then in the other. His eyes fluttered open as soon as he saw her.

Recognizing that small, smooth face with its high cheekbones. The large, dark eyes. The lips she had rouged with crimson *alegría* juice. The lips moved—she was talking to him, speaking with that gentle voice of hers so like a soft breeze.

Trying to speak himself, all Bass could do was get his dry lips open and a few strange sounds past them. Nothing that made any sense.

"Matthew, tell the man what she's saying to him."

"Scratch—the governor's daughter here come to see how you was after the fight last night."

Sure felt like he'd been down in the black a lot longer than that.

"M-morn . . . ing?" he croaked.

"It's near evening now," Hatcher replied, coming up beside Kinkead to peer directly down into Bass's face.

"The girl come out here special with her servant and her driver too," Kinkead explained. "She was afraid you was dead, what with the way we dragged you out of there last night."

Elbridge Gray was chuckling, then said, "The way we tied you over the backbone of your horse like you was gone under for sure."

"Wa . . . ter?"

Someone gave the young woman a half gourd of water, into which she dipped her fingers, then laid them against Bass's parched lips. Time and again his tongue licked the droplets off as she continued to brush water there until his throat no longer felt so dry. Filled with a sickening pain, Scratch knew his throat was bruised severely. Yet he was relieved to find he nonetheless could speak with a raspy harshness.

"My h-head . . ."

"Likely gonna hurt for some time to come too," Hatcher warned. "Solomon here sewed ye up."

"My head—sewed?"

Fish answered, "Yep. Ain't never sewed so many stitches afore neither, Scratch. You was a awful mess."

Then Hatcher and the rest began to laugh.

Jack declared, "Nigger, was ye ever a tolerable mess! Just laying there on that floor—out colder'n a preacher's wife on her wedding night. But soon as I had Solomon here get down to take a look at ye, he pulled that blue bandanny off'n yer noodle, and that's when the hull room got scared!"

"S-scared?"

"Hell, yes!" Kinkead replied as he came up to stand beside Jacova. "All them soldiers and guests thought somehow you'd had your hair knocked right off with that chair the nigger hit you with."

"My hair?" he asked, none of it making sense right then.

"Ye stupid idjit!" Hatcher roared. "Solomon scalped ye again—right where you was scalped by them Arapaho!"

Unable to contain his amusement, Caleb gushed, "Them Mexicans was all worried you'd been hit hard 'nough to knock off a big knot of your hair!"

"So we brung you on out here," Kinkead continued. "You been sleep till now."

Scratch inquired, "What come of the greaser's eye?"

"I s'pose one of their own got the feller fixed up best they could," Kinkead answered. "But he was bound to lose the eye for good—no two ways of it."

Rufus clucked, "Made all of 'em mad as a spit-on hen."

"I s'pose that's why that soldier hit you so damned hard with the chair," Elbridge explained.

He swallowed a gob of saliva, finding it hurt terribly. When he opened his eyes again after that wave of pain had passed, Titus found Jacova hovering over his face.

"How long she been here?"

Matthew said, "Soon as she could get dressed at sunup, she come on out to see 'bout you."

"Told ye," Hatcher said, "this'un's sweet on ye."

"Too damn sweet on you for my notion," Kinkead replied sternly in that solemn way of his.

With a squeak Scratch protested, "I ain't done nothing to make her sweet on me, Matthew."

"Hell, I know that, Titus," he responded. "S'pose she just don't know no better'n to fall for a wuthless gringo."

"Rosa got herself a good gringo," Bass replied.

Kinkead was visibly touched, his lower lip quivering slightly. "And you been a good friend to Rosa's gringo."

"Maybeso tell the girl go on back home now," Scratch said, his eyelids falling. "Tell her I'm gonna be fine now but I wanna get me some more sleep."

Eyes closed, he listened as Kinkead spoke low to the young woman. Then, without a single word from her, Bass felt soft fingers lightly touch his swollen cheek before they briefly squeezed his hand. And she was gone. It grew quiet as he heard the voices of the others move off. Bass shivered once in the growing cold, then quickly slipped off to sleep.

When next he awoke, Scratch found himself ravenous. Opening his eyes, he found the cavern still lit with a number of thick candles, the gray of dawn at the entrance to the cave no more than a thin sliver from where he lay. But he also discovered that the back of his head still throbbed mercilessly—worse even than when he had been scalped. Just beyond the room where they had placed him, he heard low voices.

It hurt too much to try raising his head, what with the way his neck and shoulder muscles protested, that wide band of painful stricture wrapping itself around his head like the jaws of a huge iron trap. Bass closed his eyes and welcomed the sleep that allowed him to leave the pain behind.

Sometime later the voices grew louder.

He awoke with a start, irritated at first that they weren't letting him sleep any longer. Then he concentrated: slowly discerning the different voices, able to tell that they were angry.

"Hatcher!"

Oh, how it hurt to call out!

Those angry voices fell quiet as he shut his eyes, trying to squeeze off the throb in his head. Feet shuffled into the cavern.

"Scratch? Ye call me, Scratch?"

Looking up, Bass saw most of the faces around his bed. "Why you so all fired mad?"

At first no one answered.

Then Hatcher glanced at the others and eventually looked at Bass. "Goddamn Mexicans wanna come throw us out of the country."

"But they ain't," Workman asserted.

"Willy here just come from town with Matthew," Hatcher continued. "He heard from Padre Martinez that the soldiers and most of the folks in town was talking about coming out here to try flushing us out."

"Flush us out?" Bass echoed. "They figger to kill us?"

"Sounds like it," Matthew said. "But Mirabal and the padre wasn't about to let 'em. Fire's out for now."

"Then . . . everything's fine."

"No," Workman answered sadly. "None of you fellers can trade off your plews in town. Fact be, the governor wanted the padre to tell us that he could do all in his power to make sure no mob come out to kill us . . . but he couldn't have us coming in to Taos no more this winter."

"Means we gotta stay out here," Caleb grumbled.

"That ain't so bad, I s'pose," Bass figured, relieved.

Solomon snorted, "What the hell use of a man coming to Taos if'n he can't drink till he's shit-faced drunk!"

"Or dance with the gals!" Graham shouted.

Elbridge roared, "And get his pecker soaked with poontang!"

Slamming a fist into an open palm, Hatcher growled, "Maybeso we just should'a kill't our share of them greasers when we had us a chance and been done with it!"

Workman wagged his head. "From the sounds of things—you'd never got out of Mirabal's house, you gone and done that."

"What's so bad 'bout them not letting us go into Taos no more this winter?" Scratch asked.

Caleb said, "We don't go in—we can't get all our plew traded off for supplies."

It was quiet a moment before Workman replied, "Maybe you don't need to trade all them plews."

Hatcher guffawed. "With what we gonna get our truck and plunder for spring?"

"What you need?" the whiskey maker asked.

"Powder and lead!" Caleb answered. "I know we need that."

"All right—see just how much you need," Workman declared, something clearly going on between his ears. "I'll see what I got here. See what I can get my hands on too."

"We better have us some of that Mex coffee afore we head out," Hatcher demanded, skepticism still on his face.

"What else?" Workman asked with growing intensity. And when the others began to suggest flints and wiping sticks, blankets and awls, the whiskey maker suddenly shushed them all and said, "I'll tell you what, Jack. You boys figger all what you're needing to get you through the spring hunt till ronnyvoo up north—maybe we can see you're outfitted when you take off come the break of winter."

Solomon knelt close to Bass and said, "They keep us outta town—looks like you ain't gonna see that li'l senorita what's sweet on you."

Kinkead looked down at them. "I figger Scratch here's part of our trouble too."

"Bass?"

He started to raise his head to protest, but it hurt too damned much. From his pillow he demanded, "How I'm to blame for all this?"

"That were a fair fight, Matthew!" Hatcher suddenly leaped into the argument.

"That's right, Matthew," Elbridge said. "I see'd lots of men lose a eye—"

"Had to be *that* man's eye," Kinkead explained. "Hell he was a Montoya. One of the richest families down the valley."

"So tell me what a man s'pose to do when a nigger's trying to kill him?" Scratch asked.

"Bass here ain't to blame for our troubles," Caleb protested.

"Course he ain't," Kinkead agreed, laying his big paw of a hand on Scratch's shoulder. "But it's for certain Mirabal hisself knows his daughter's sweet on an American gringo—and that makes for a bad case of things, no matter what."

Rufus asked, "Thort the governor liked us after we got his wife and daughter back from those Comanche?"

"He likes gringos when they help him out all right," Kinkead declared. Then he slowly moved his eyes down to look at Bass. "But he don't want no gringo in his family."

Suddenly Hatcher burst out in laughter and finally bowed elegantly. "Here he is—his own self, boys!" he roared, then straightened and saluted. "This here's Governor Mirabal's new son-in-law!"

"I ain't no such a thing!"

Elbridge got into the ribbing. "You're sure 'nough caused us a heap a trouble: going off to court that man's li'l girl!"

"Ain't been courtin' nobody!"

"Maybe you just better leave the womens alone," Graham joked.

"I told you stupid niggers—"

"Speaking of women," Hatcher said suddenly, quieting the rest. He turned quickly to Workman. "What the hell we gonna do for the rest of the winter here 'thout women?"

"Glory thunder!" Caleb roared as it struck him like a load of adobe bricks. "No women to dip my stinger in?"

Isaac grumbled, "See, Scratch? All your damned fault!"

"Hold it," Workman hushed them, waving his arms. "Maybe I can get Louisa to bring some of her girls out here ever' now and then."

"Sure," Caleb cheered. "We got the likker here!"

Then Solomon joined in, "And Willy'll bring the womens!"

"Workman says he's gonna round us up some plunder for the spring hunt too!" Hatcher added.

"Maybeso we'll make a winter of it after all!" Elbridge agreed.

"But ain't none of this my fault," Bass protested. "Ain't done nothing to make that Mex gal go sweet on me!"

"Hell, Titus Bass," Hatcher said, laying a hand on Scratch's shoulder, "I might be mad as a swarm of wasps at ye for making eyes at that woman—"

"I didn't make no eyes at her!"

With a loud laugh Hatcher nodded. "Simmer down, Scratch. I know ye ain't done a damned thing to put us in this fix. Truth is, ye're too damned mud-homely for any but a blind woman to fall in love with!"

Just like Caleb Wood and his saddlebag filled with notched sticks, William Workman kept track of such things. Keeping count, knowing what year it was, even what month it was. Hell, the whiskey maker was as hard about such things as was the padre and his church. Ciphering such things as if they really mattered—marking off days on some calendar.

When all a man had to do was watch the sky, feel the change in the air. Maybe even see how the sun was pushing a little more toward the north in its track now that it didn't snow near as hard or as often as it used to. One might even believe the days were getting longer too—if a man believed in such superstition.

But the whiskey maker told them it was drawing close to the end of February, in the year of eighteen and twenty-nine. With the coming of that spring, Bass realized he had been gone from St. Louis four years.

In those quiet moments of remembrance and reflection, Scratch looked around the cavern at what any of them had to show for their seasons in the high country. Especially him. Nearly wiped out more'n twice. But at least he still had the rifle he'd come west with . . . and he had Hannah too. She'd grown seal fat and sleek over a winter of leisure. Their saddle horses and pack animals all healed up too—those niggling sores and bites and skin ulcers gone the way of the Mexicans' holiday celebration in Taos. Gone the way of the new year too. Another raucous, liquor-soaked, wenching new year of it they had with Mama Louisa's whores and William Workman's finest squeezings to welcome in eighteen and twenty-nine.

Which meant he was thirty-five now. Nowhere near as young as most of those he had watched head upriver from St. Louis. Not near as young as he hoped he could have always stayed. But, he figured, if a man had him only a certain number of winters—if the years were indeed allotted out to each man—then a man must surely choose on his own hook just how to spend what was given him. Indeed, over time Scratch had made peace with that. A man who asked too much out of life was clearly an unhappy sort.

But a man who discovered the richness in every new day he was granted . . . the sort of man who gave thanks at every sunset—now, to Scratch's way of thinking that was a man who was doubly blessed.

They weren't in all that bad a shape when they got down to going through all their plunder right after the turn of the year. Not that they couldn't use a little more of this and some of that. But with what Workman already had—and what he could buy either in Taos or on down the road to Santa Fe, where most of the merchants didn't know word one of the trouble-some Americans up at Taos—Hatcher's bunch laid in all of what they figured they would need to get them through to rendezvous slated to gather that year on the Popo Agie.

Lead and powder, a lot of coffee and a little of that Mexican sugar, sixty-weight sacks of salt from the Chihuahua mines, flints and wiping sticks and assortments of screws for their guns, along with some repairs Bass made to all the aging and broken traps the outfit packed along from season to season. Sure did keep himself warm sweating over Workman's forge through winter's coldest days while the others repaired packsaddles and tack, sending the whiskey maker out to buy what he could of Spanish horse gear for the coming trip.

Returning from the nearby Pueblo, Workman brought back his mule loaded high with the colorful wool blankets traded from the Navajo who lived far to the west—woven so thick they were all but impervious to water. And with some two dozen woolly skins the whiskey maker bartered off sheep ranchers, hides that the trappers could stretch and tan to a supple softness, Hatcher's men now had ideal pads to place beneath their packsaddles.

Over the long winter Kinkead hadn't changed his mind about staying, no matter what any of them said, no matter the growing excitement as the time to depart drew nigh. Matthew was staying behind this trip out. Perhaps for good. His narrow brush with the Blackfeet had only made him pine for his Rosa all the more. Kinkead was determined to stay behind and do what he could to support his wife right there in Taos.

Workman explained that it was likely time to be breaking for the north—it being the second week of March—when Hatcher rushed into the cavern one fine afternoon and demanded they all come outside and take themselves a whiff of the air.

"If it don't smell like spring's coming!" Hatcher gushed as they all hurried out into the sun, a chill breeze wending its way down the creekbottom. "If it ain't time to light out—then . . . I'll eat Caleb Wood's longhandles!"

"That sure as hell is a safe bet," Elbridge assured. "Can't doubt it's spring!"

Rufus agreed, "And a man sure don't wanna take a chance on losing that bet—having to eat that man's longhandles!"

"Really time to go, Jack?" Bass inquired.

"Damn right it is."

Solomon asked, "When you figger?"

Hatcher turned and looked them over. "How long it take ye boys to be ready?"

Caleb asked the others, "Day after tomorry?"

They all nodded.

"Then it's settled—day after tomorrow," Hatcher affirmed. Then he looked at Workman. "Anything ye need us to do here for ye . . . afore we pull out?"

"Can't think of anything needs doing, nothing needs fixing neither. 'Bout time you niggers got out from being under my feet!" the whiskey maker said with a hint of sadness.

"Gonna miss ye, Willy," Hatcher said, slapping Workman on the shoulder.

"Been good having you boys here too," Workman admitted quietly.

Solomon asked, "Even what with all the trouble we caused you?"

"What trouble?" he repeated. "What trouble was that?"

"The trouble Titus Bass brewed up for us at the governor's!" Elbridge roared.

"Wasn't no trouble," Workman replied, turning to look at Scratch. "The girl stayed away just like her father warned her to, and likely things be all settled down come next winter when you boys come back."

"Likely won't be back till winter after next," Hatcher explained, seeing the disappointment it brought Workman. "We'll stay north, trap long as we can, Willy."

The whiskey maker nodded a little sadly. "All right then. You all got work to do, I'm sure of that. And I have me some kegs to fill for you."

"Some l-likker for us?" Rufus asked.

"Ain't gonna let you boys go 'thout nothing for your trip!"

Early the next morning they began work on their saddles and tack, assuring themselves that all their equipment was trail-ready. That done, they all gathered in a circle with their firearms—each man to show the others that his weapons were cleaned, locks tight, and everything in top order. This was no drill without life-and-death necessity: the entire outfit might well depend upon the weapon of a single man.

From there they broke out the powder and lead, coffee, salt, and sugar, along with what other heavy items they would be carrying—placing it all into small packs that could be divided among the animals following them north.

That finished just past sunset, Workman called them in for supper and some lightning, along with some sugar- and cinnamon-coated treats he had purchased in town.

As Hatcher's men settled on the floor with their cups of *aguardiente* and their mugs of steaming coffee, Workman went to the corner and returned with eight bags, each the size of a man's thigh.

The first was accepted by Jack. "What's this, Willy?"

"Look inside your own self, nigger," Workman replied, handing out the lightweight burlap bags.

"Tobaccy!" Hatcher roared with loud approval. He pulled out a dark, fragrant twist of rolled and dried tobacco leaf, sniffing it hungrily.

"How much all this cost you?" Caleb asked as he accepted his sack.

"Not that much down in Santy Fee."

"This much Mexican tobaccy had to cost you some," Solomon declared.

"I already got my due out from your plews," Workman explained.

Jack asked, "Ye saying we're even?"

The whiskey maker looked at Hatcher. "We're even, boys. I got more'n enough plews from you to cover everything else and this tobaccy."

"You done a lot for us this winter, Willy," Scratch said.

"Whiskey and women and now some smoke," Caleb cheered.

"It ain't only the things ye traded for us," Hatcher explained. "You and Matthew saw to it them greaser soldiers didn't come try rubbing us out."

"Where is Matthew anyways?" Rufus asked.

"Here it is our going-off hoot and Matthew ain't here," Isaac said.

Workman replied, "Kinkead said to tell you he'd be here afore first light. Said he knows how Jack hates to burn daylight—so he'll be here afore you pull out."

Matthew Kinkead was good at his word. Always had been. And that cold mid-March morning was another painful tearing away for Titus Bass. They had fought Blackfeet together, covered more miles than any man back east might imagine, slept and ate and talked around countless fires in what had been more than a year of scuttling across trackless wastes and climbing over never-ending mountain ranges. But now Matthew was staying behind with his Rosa.

Titus knew he would miss the big bear of a man as much as he had ever missed anyone in his life of wandering.

"You listen up to what Mad Jack Hatcher tells you," Kinkead instructed as he released Bass from a terrible squeeze.

"That's right, ye best listen to me," Hatcher echoed as he took up the reins to his saddle horse.

But Matthew continued as if he hadn't heard Jack say a thing. "You listen to Hatcher . . . and then you damn well go do just the opposite!"

They all laughed together, but this time it wasn't the easy laughter that comes from camaraderie on the trail. This was the strained laughter of men parting from good companions, longtime friends, compatriots in battle, men who had survived long, harsh winters together. Slowly Matthew made the rounds of those riders gathered in what was a long oval of horses and pack animals. Then he finally stepped back to join the whiskey maker at the stone threshold to Workman's hut.

"We got miles to go, pilgrims!" Hatcher cried as he turned back to his horse, his voice cracking with sentiment. "And you sumbitches are burning my daylight!"

"Let's ride!" another cried.

A voice called, "Hep-hepa, you trail niggers!"

"To the Shining Mountains!" Matthew Kinkead cried, dragging a hand beneath his big bulb of a nose and raising his arm overhead as the others filed out of the creekbottom, up the wide trail to the prairieland above.

"To the . . . the Shining Mountains!" Bass roared, his throat clogging as he leaned far out of his saddle to quickly shake Kinkead's and Workman's hands while he moved past.

"There's beaver waiting!" Hatcher sang out from the head of their column.

Caleb hollered, "Here's to likker-lovin' coons like us!"

"Billy Sublette better hide his whiskey!" Isaac bellowed.

"Injun bucks better hide their daughters!" Rufus cheered.

As they went on and on like that, their loud voices careening off the stone walls of the creekside, Bass turned in his new Spanish saddle with a groan of stiff leather . . . gazing back at Workman and Kinkead. He pulled off his blanket mitten and raised a bare hand in the shocking cold of that dawn. Saw them both wave to him one last time as the trail took him around a bend and they fell out of sight.

Farewells never got any easier. No matter how old he got, farewells damn well never got any easier.

TWELVE

"H'ar ye now!"

Bass and Elbridge Gray turned at the sudden call of that strange voice, their hands gone to their pistols.

Out of the quakies emerged a horseman in gaily ornamented buckskins pulling behind him two more ponies, their packs gently swaying from side to side as they were brought to a halt near the two trappers on the grassy creekbank. Mexican conchos dotted the outer seam of his leggings dyed with red earth paint, the same color as the sleeves on his war shirt. Over the fringed shirt he wore a faded, soot-stained waistcoat complete with pewter buttons.

With the way this stranger had his stirrups buckled real short and high along the ribs of his horse, he appeared to be perched atop a saddle far too small for his long, bony legs. From both ears dangled large sky-blue rocks of turquoise suspended on narrow wires that bobbed and jiggled as the man turned this way and that, looking first at Gray, then at Bass.

"H'ar yourself," Scratch replied as he relaxed the grip on his pistol. "You ain't no Injun now, are you?"

"Ye took me for Injun, did ye?"

Elbridge pointed to his cheek with a finger, saying, "Why's a white nigger wear Injun war paint?"

The stranger's narrow, slitted eyes suddenly came to life, twinkling within a tanned face of well-soaped saddle leather as he studied the pair for what seemed like the longest time. Then he spoke.

"Been living with Injuns for lotta moons."

"You paint up like 'em?" Gray asked.

"I paint up like 'em, yeah," the stranger replied matter-of-factly as he pulled his massive wolf-skin cap off and pointed to the bright purple of the vermilion pigment he had rubbed along the part in his hair.

"You're sure a purty Injun, for a white man," Scratch declared.

He turned to Bass. "I h'aint see'd a real honest-to-God white man in just shy of a year, boys. Where ye hail from?"

"The Illinois," Gray answered, taking a step closer to the horseman. "By way of Taos this past winter."

He nodded, his eyes quickly coming back to rest on Bass while he spit a thin stream of brown into the grass beside his saddle horse. "An' you?"

"Kentucky, by way of St. Louie . . . and a winter in Taos."

"Taos a good place for winter doin's," the stranger agreed. "Wha'chore names?"

"Titus Bass," Scratch answered as he stepped up beside the horse and held a hand up to the rider. "And this here is Elbridge Gray."

"Ye on yer own hook, ye two?" asked the stranger.

"No," Bass replied, sensing his guard hairs bristle as he glanced past the horseman to the timbered hillside, wary. "S'pose you tell us your name."

"Williams. William Shirley Williams," he answered, innocently smiling.

"Sweet Marie!" Elbridge exclaimed. "That there's a hull passel of Williams in that goddamned name!"

The smile faded as the horseman turned his straight-faced, expressionless stare back to Gray. Then, with a droll purse to his lips, he replied, "That be my name. But my friends call me Bill. I figger any white man up here got a good chance to be my friend—so whyn't you two call me Bill?"

"Be pleased to call you Bill," Bass replied, already liking the cut of the tall, skinny trapper. "My friends hale me as Scratch."

Craning his neck to look up the aspen-choked hillside, Gray asked, "More niggers with you?"

"Nope. I ride alone now'days."

"Leg on down here," Bass proposed, stepping back. "We're bound to finish setting our last two traps straight-away, then you can ride on up to camp with us. Make a night of it."

Elbridge declared, "One of the t'others dropped a elk cow this morning. Some mighty fine eating—"

They both watched Williams visibly shudder, his whole body trembling, his face pinched.

With a wag of his head the rider said, "Good it weren't no bull elk."

"Bull ain't near as good eating," Bass stated.

"Don't ye fellers never go kill a bull with one antler broke off and a'hanging like so," he said, a sudden sharp and warning edge come to his voice as he balanced his long fullstock rifle across the tops of his bony thighs and raised both his arms to their full length on either side of his head, spreading his fingers as if they were antler points. Then he crooked the left arm at the elbow, swaying it crazily.

"Why?" Elbridge asked, cocking his head slightly. "He a bull in these parts what you got your own sights on?"

"No," Williams said evenly, his eyebrows lowered meaningfully. "One of these days I'll go under my own self, boys. And spirits awreddy showed me how I'm coming back."

In utter disbelief Gray squeaked, "C-coming back?"

"My medeecin showed me in a vision I had this past winter," Williams declared. "Coming back as a bull elk."

Gray glanced over at Bass with a wink and a wry twist to his smile. "A bull elk, you say?"

"With his left antler growed crooked, jest like I showed ye," Williams explained. "What's wrong with ye two? Don't tell me ye don't believe in Injun medeecin?"

"Damn well don't," Bass declared. "But that don't mean you can't, William Shirley Williams."

For a moment the older man regarded Titus before a smile eventually came to that well-tanned, leathery face. "So, tell me, Scratch. How long ye been out here to these mountains?"

"Since summer of twenty-five."

"I come out west the y'ar afore that and laid in my first winter up near Salish House in Hudson Bay country," Williams explained as he rocked out of the saddle and landed on the ground. "Ye both been out in these hills for any time at all, boys—a shame ye h'ain't learned much from the Injuns here 'bouts."

Gray demanded, "What you mean—we ain't learned from the Injuns?"

" 'Bout life . . . and dyin' . . . and all the magic what lives all round us," Williams said, his voice quieting, gesturing his right arm in a full half circle. Then he went to rubbing a sore knee as he continued. "There's more for a man to learn hisself and unnerstand than most folks can ever start to know. But it takes a smart man to own up to not knowing about all the magic what lives around him."

Titus scratched at his beard a moment. "Don't reckon I savvy what sort of magic you're talking 'bout."

"He's telling us about the sort what makes a coin disappear from a man's hand," Elbridge explained. "Magic what pulls that coin from ahind a man's ear."

Stroking his horse's muzzle, then bending to pick up a front hoof to inspect it, Williams replied, "Ain't that kind of magic at all, boys. Magic . . . like the spirits all round us. The ghosts of them what gone afore. Powerful beings—warriors and such. Hoo-doos what we can't see 'cause we ain't got our own magic strong enough yet."

"And when we get our own magic strong enough," Bass inquired skeptically, "you're saying we can see them hoo-doos? See them spirits you talk about?"

With a wide smile Williams set the second forehoof on the ground and straightened, stretching his back. "Man makes his own magic strong, Scratch—then that man don't just hear them spirits talking to him, he can *see* 'em too."

"Shit!" Elbridge groused in total disbelief. "You been sipping at the cider jug far too long, Williams!"

The old horseman calmly turned from Elbridge without showing the slightest contempt for the man's disbelief. "The spirits are around us alla time, Scratch. They show theyselves to me. They palaver at me. And I listen. I h'aint ashamed to tell ye listening to 'em has saved this nigger's hash a time or two."

Elbridge snorted, "How them hoo-doos save your hash?"

Without acknowledging Gray in the slightest, Williams continued. "Like it's no more'n a curtain, Scratch—there's nothing more'n a breath of air atween us and the world of them hoo-doos."

"So you hear them spirits all the time, do you?" Titus asked, amazed that he sensed something more than sheer lunacy in the older man.

"No, don't hear 'em not alla time," he answered, gazing up at the clear blue of springtime's fading light. "It's . . . it's like there's that spirit world, and there's our world right here. They're two differ'nt places. But there h'aint nothing more'n a curtain up atween us and the other world. Atween us and all what we don't unnerstand."

Wagging his head, Titus asked, "So how's a man ever hear or see these hoo-doos?"

"Only when there's a rip in that curtain atween our world and the rest of what is."

"Only then?"

"When there's a tear in that curtain I tol't you about. Maybeso think of it like . . . like a crack," he declared, waving that arm of his at the horizon, describing a jagged line rising from the earth and ascending toward the darkening dome overhead. "A crack that goes all the way from here, where folks like us walk . . . clear to heaven."

"A c-crack in the sky?" Elbridge chortled.

Now at last Williams turned to Gray and nodded emphatically. "That's right, nigger. A man what opens hisself up to hearing the real world all round him—then that's the man what can see right on into the world of spirits and hoo-doos by looking through that ol' ragged crack in the sky."

For the moment Bass wasn't sure just how he felt about this ghosty horseman as he and Elbridge went about setting the last two of their traps here along a stretch of a new stream they hadn't visited during last autumn's stay in the Bayou Salade. But one thing was for sure—Williams had given him something to think about, something with some real heft to it. Titus figured the talk around the campfire that night wasn't destined to be the usual fare of senoritas and Taos lightning and how big a carouse they would have come rendezvous on the Popo Agie. If no one else got this William Shirley Williams to talking about his magic and his hoo-doos and that crack in the sky, then Scratch vowed *he* sure as hell would.

More than three weeks of hard riding out of Taos had brought them into the southern end of the Bayou once more. How different the high, narrow mountain valley appeared this time. Last year they had reached South Park from the north near the tail end of summer, when the grasses were burned and curing beneath a relentless and high summer sun, just before the turning of the leaves.

Here in early spring the snows were only beginning to retreat up the mountainsides. The trees only starting to bud, the willow and alder giving no more than a hint of what would soon be their green glory. The streams were just opening up after a long winter's rest beneath thick blankets of ice, every tiny freshet beginning to throb with snow-melt as the days lengthened, their narrow threads meandering through every meadow, adding their strength to the creeks that spilled from the snowfields overhead, continuing through the darkened stands of spruce and fir and lodgepole as they descended toward the great, long valley where the beasts gathered and took their nourishment.

Come this the season of prime plew. Early spring when the beaver possessed its finest coat. When the flat-tails were their busiest: warily emerging from the security of their winter lodges to labor through the short daylight hours constructing new slides and dams in every meadow. After three spring seasons stalking this high country, Bass knew down at the very marrow of him just how important was the spring hunt to a trapper.

When beaver were easiest to spook and hardest to bring to bait—spring was the time a man discovered if he had what it took to be a master trapper.

During the fall was another matter entirely: the animals had been out of their lodges and active since the melting of the high snowpacks. They were less guarded and careful in the autumn, when their activities were nudged into an even higher intensity than they had been during the summer. With the cooling of the days and the chilling of the nights, the beaver became more animated, roaming farther, extending their territory with the arrival of fall.

But for now—this season of rebirth—the bucktoothed rodents were extremely wary, watchful, and suspicious of the castor set out to lure them to their deaths.

"I come outta Boone County, on the Ohio River, northern Kentucky," Bass answered the newcomer's question. "Where you from back east?"

Brushing the hair back from his shoulder, so long it oft tangled in the beard that fell halfway down his chest, Williams said, "Borned in a cabin on Horse Crik, tucked up under Skyuka Mountain."

Hatcher asked, "Where's that, Bill?"

"Rutherford County, in Northern Carolina."

"How long ago was that?" Isaac inquired.

"I'm forty-two this last Janeeary."

Scratch commented eagerly, "I'm born in January. When's your day?"

"The third."

Bass nodded. "Mine's the first."

"New Year's, eh? Two of us start the year off right, don't we?" He held out his cup as Caleb Wood started around the fire with a blackened coffee kettle.

"Scratch says ye travel alone," Hatcher declared.

"Last time I rode with others, I come north out of Taos with Pratte and Savary." He sipped at the steaming coffee a moment, then continued. "Pratte died that trip out and Savary took over. We went on trapping and wintered up in Park Kyack afore we come back to Taos the spring of twenty-eight. After that I swored I'd never ride with a outfit again."

"Ain't so bad," Scratch explained. "When you ride with the right outfit."

"Said you come west in twenty-four?" Gray repeated.

"Up to Blackfoot country, where the Englishers play," Williams snorted.

"God-blamed Blackfoot!" grumbled Rufus Graham. "Too many good men gone under at their hands!"

"I quit that country come spring—damn them Blackfoot," Williams growled. "Got my carcass back to live with the Osages, where I run onto the surveyors gonna mark the road from the Missouri clear down to Santy Fee. They needed 'em a feller what knew how to talk sign—so I was took along."

"When you get back to trapping?" Solomon asked.

"That fall—pulled out'n Taos and headed down the Rio del Norte, then moseyed on over to the Heely. Plew down in that country weren't near prime as they was up where them Blackfoot roam."

"Plew is prime in Blackfoot country," Caleb agreed.

"I fi't me more'n my share of Blackfoot," Williams said with clear disgust. "They deviled me for a time the next year—when I set off on my lonesome. Niggered me clear down to the Wind River Mountains. Didn't did get shet of Bug's Boys till I made it far up the Bighorn."

Hatcher asked, "So ye stay in these parts now?"

With a wag of his head Williams replied, "H'ain't been healthy for this coon up north there in Blackfoot country. And the 'Paches caught me flat-footed of a time down on the Heely."

"Apache?" asked Rowland.

"That's right. When I tried the Heely a second go-round. Bastards stripped me, stole my guns, my horse and mule, ever'thing. Then they pointed me out to the desert and laughed as I took off barefoot."

"How'd you pull yourself out of that fix?" Bass inquired.

"Pointed my nose torst the Spanish country. Only place I could reckon on. Way I lays the set—it were just shy of two hunnert miles afore I run onto some Zunis. They took me in like I was some special kin. I spent some time with them folks, healing up. Then went on over an' stayed with some Navajos."

Elbridge said, "Eventual' you come back Santy Fee?"

"Taos—that's when I hooked up with Pratte and Savary," Williams said dolefully. "This nigger's had him good fortune to pull out'n the thick of it a time or two. So I figger my luck runs high 'nough I don't dare travel with no brigade no more."

"You fixin' on trapping the Bayou now?" Scratch asked.

He stared at the fire a moment, then answered, "Nawww, I'll mosey on. You fellers busy here this side of the Park. If'n I take a shine to it, I'll lay some traps on the far side. It don't pay to crowd 'nother man."

"Enough beaver in the mountains for us all!" Isaac cheered.

"Damn right there is," Williams said. "If'n we don't trap 'em out, the Englishers do."

"Trap 'em out?" Bass echoed. "How we ever trap out all the beaver?"

Of a sudden Williams grew animated, his eyes alive with the loathing and hatred he felt for the huge Hudson's Bay Company. "Them Frenchie brigades the Englishers put out up north go right on into a stretch of country and trap ever' living flat-tail there is. Strip that country clean: ever' stream, ever' beaver too—not matter that they catch some kits while they're at it."

"Sons of bitches," Rowland grumbled.

"They h'ain't got no business in our country," Williams declared. "I plan to stay north of the greasers and south of the Englishers and all their Frenchie parley-voos. 'Sides, I've come to be partial to the Utes. But watch yer ha'r when there's 'Rapahoes about."

"The hell you say?" Bass growled. "Last time I run onto Arapaho my own self, I damn near went under."

Williams grinned in the fire's light. "Ye're a lucky man. Them 'Rapahoes can be bad as Bug's Boys when it comes to a white man. They'll kill ye flat out and run off with all ye had. They leave ye 'thout an outfit?"

"They took that—'cept for the rifle they didn't find, run off with all my animals but for my dear mule," Scratch explained.

"Leastways ye come out of it with yer ha'r," Williams observed, his leathery brow wrinkling in remembrance. "Live to fight 'nother day. Jest like I done a time or two—did ye lay up in some rocks a'hiding till the red niggers quit the country?"

"Weren't so lucky as you, Bill," Scratch replied, reaching for the knot at the back of the bandanna he tied over the top of his head. "One of the black-hearts took part of me with him."

Slowly nudging the large knot upward, Bass removed the bandanna and a circular scrap of beaver fur in one smooth motion, turning his head. As he did so, Williams could see the results of the scalping that had removed a crude circle some six inches in diameter from the crown of his head late in the summer of twenty-seven.

Setting his coffee tin down and wiping a forearm across his lips, Williams scrambled to his feet and stepped right up to loom over Bass. He took Scratch's head in both hands and turned it gently toward the firelight, peering at the skull plate from all angles, then inspected the wound so closely, he was almost rubbing the end of his nose against the yellowed bone.

"It pain ye any?"

"Not after I learn't to keep it covered."

"With that patch o' beaver plew?"

"Found this here fur is the trick," Bass replied. "Sun does a powerful evil to my skull if I don't keep it covered."

" 'Magine it would, Scratch." He continued to study the bone closely. "Back east where I was raised up from a kit, I heard me a time or two of fellers getting scalped and living to tell the tale of it."

"They done their best to kill this nigger off," Hatcher said. "But I figger Scratch here just born under a good star."

Williams gently patted the bare bone, then shambled back to his place at the fire and settled down with his cup. "Way I figger it, Bass—ye been told plain as sun that there be a heap more living in store for any man what lost his ha'r but wasn't put under by the niggers what took that skelp from him."

"Maybeso," Gray replied with a cynical wag of his head as he quickly tallied the befuddled reactions of the others around the fire and began to grin widely. "But only if you're a coon what believes there's hoo-doos hiding behin't every tree!"

"Hoo-doos, is it?" Hatcher asked with a snort, animated once again.

Elbridge gushed, "Don't that beat all, Jack? Williams here says after he's dead, he's coming back as a bull elk what got it one bad antler." And he showed them, mimicking what the old trapper had told the two of them near sundown. "If that ain't the kicker—he says the Injuns are the ones show us how to talk to ghosts."

But instead of laughing right off, Jack appeared to study Williams, then finally brought his gaze back to Gray and said, "Sounds to me like Bill Williams here savvies things same way as Asa McAfferty."

"O-o-o-o! That name just give me the trembling willies!" Isaac shrieked.

"Me too," Rufus agreed with a shudder. "That crazy coon gone and rubbed out a 'Rikara medicine man—"

"Damn!" Williams exclaimed, leaping to his feet so suddenly, he startled all of them into stunned silence. "Ye really know a nigger what kill't a medeecin man?"

In amazement they all watched the skinny man shuffle-footing it there by the fire, restless as a bull in spring, very much like a man walking over a bed of coals, trembling uncontrollably every few moments as if he had come down with the ague.

"Like Jack said," Caleb was the first to dare speak, "feller's name is Asa McAfferty."

"He really kill a medeecin man?"

Hatcher nodded. "His hair turned white after rubbing out that Ree."

Another convulsion shot through Williams's body as he attempted to hold his arms and hands still over the fire like a man in dire need of its warmth. "Ye sure it weren't just a Ree warrior?"

"Medicine man," Hatcher agreed.

And Solomon added, "A real rattle shaker."

Rubbing his hands together over the flames, Williams asked, "An' his ha'r turn't white?"

"McAfferty's did."

Williams looked straight at Bass. "Just as I tol't ye, Scratch. Mark these words. I'll lay that McAfferty these boys talking about is the sort what don't just hear the hoo-doos through that crack in the sky yonder. He's gone an' see'd them spirits too!"

Graham asked, "Say, Bill—you figger that's what turned McAfferty's hair white?"

Slowly Williams turned so his rump faced the flames. As he rubbed the breechclout covering his bony posterior, Williams said, "Only thing I ever heerd of turning a soul's ha'r white is coming eye to eye with a hoo-doo."

Caleb whispered solemnly, "Don't say?"

Williams pursed his lips in reflection for a moment, then said, "That McAfferty must be a nigger with some strong magic."

Leaning toward Hatcher's ear, Gray whispered, "Here he goes with his magic talk now!"

"If'n the rest of you don't wanna hear what Bill's got to say," Titus snapped at Elbridge, "s'pose you g'won and have your own talk on your side of the fire."

Elbridge started to rise suddenly. "You ain't gonna tell me where I ought'n go—"

Hatcher suddenly put his hand out and grabbed hold of Gray's arm. "Maybe ye ought'n go fetch yer squeezebox. And bring me my fiddle too."

"You figger on some music tonight?" Rufus asked as Gray reluctantly nodded and moved off, glaring back at Williams.

"Music's better'n my men squabbling over hoo-doos like some puffed-up prairie cocks."

"Didn't mean to cause no trouble here," Williams said.

Still edgy, Bass watched Elbridge as he grumbled, "Ain't your doing, Bill."

With a wag of his head Bill declared, "This here's why I travel alone now, boys. Can't allays count on folks caring to listen to what 'nother man's gotta say—even after they gone and asked me to tell 'em what I think."

"Elbridge just be the sort don't want ye to know he's unnatural scairt of ghosts and such—even the talk of it," Hatcher whispered, glancing over his shoulder to be sure he wasn't heard. "Scratch—I want ye to know he didn't mean nothing by what he said."

"No harm done," Williams volunteered.

"Yeah," Bass agreed, nodding. "No harm done. Didn't know he was scared of such."

"Elbridge allays makes fun of ever'thing he's afraid of," Hatcher explained.

"Ye're friend's awright being 'fraid," Williams declared. "Something wrong with a man what ain't afraid of nothing."

Jack nodded, staring at the flames for a moment more before he admitted, "Truth be, I ain't so sure I wanna have any more talk of ghosts around me too."

Williams said, "Ain't nothing ye be scared of with a little talk, Hatcher."

"That's right, Jack," Bass replied confidently as he laid the beaver fur back over his skull and tugged on the blue bandanna. "Only things a man should be scared of are them what a man can see. Like Injuns. Or grizz. Even a whiteout blizzard."

"To hell with fearing what I can see," Hatcher declared sourly, staring into the fire. "Only things this child's ever been afraid of are what I *can't* see."

Spring was all but done warming the earth in advance of summer, carpeting the hillsides with a new color every day as wildflowers of bewildering hues raised their heads to sway in the breezes drifting along the slopes where snow-melt raced toward the valley floor. More than a moon had passed since Bill Williams had departed as he said he would—leaving at sunup the next morning, the old man had crossed to the far side of the Bayou where he disappeared into the shadowy timber. And was gone.

Better than a month of hard work trapping first one creek, then another, trying every stream that showed some promise by its beaver dams, slides, and lodges. As diligently as the beaver labored to fell the young saplings that forested their watery meadows, the trappers worked all the harder still. Time enough for a man to fit in a little sleep here and there after setting the traps at sundown, rising early to check the line at sunrise the next day. After dragging the pelts and traps back to camp, scraping and fleshing and lashing them onto willow hoops, a man might catch a little shut-eye before the sun began to fall and it was time to haul the traps back out as twilight brought a delicate rose-colored alpenglow to this high valley.

"Billy Sublette damned well better get his ass to the Popo Agie this summer," Rufus Graham often grumbled, reminding them how the trader had distributed supplies to company men well before last July's rendezvous.

Hatcher agreed, "All this prime beaver gonna stake us to one big hur-raw!"

"If Sublette brings out the likker," Isaac argued in that overly solemn way of his, scratching aimlessly at his whitish beard stained with dark, yellow-ish-brown streaks that characterized the man's careless tobacco chewing.

Was that all a man worked for? Bass wondered. Did a man force himself through endless hours standing up to his crotch in the icy streams only to earn himself some two weeks of revelry with whiskey and women and wildness? Was there nothing more to what days were granted a man?

Such brooding thoughts troubled his head as Titus chopped down aspen saplings for float-sticks, peeling each before sharpening one end, then lashing them together in a bundle for the next day's sets. These were matters rarely considered by most men adrift here early in the far west. By and large they were of a breed who existed in the here and now, and that was all that concerned any of their kind. That day, perhaps the next, maybe even those thoughts of how fast the summer rendezvous was approaching . . . those were the only concerns of most trappers: survival, and that which lay on the immediate horizon for a man—what to eat the next time their bellies rum-bled, where to lay their blankets and robes the next time they grew weary, where to find water and grazing for their stock . . .

But never, never, never did any of the rest want to talk again about what Bill Williams had stirred up within Titus Bass. And as the days rolled past in slow, easy succession, Scratch was beginning to believe the others refused to talk about those uncertain, frightening matters because such talk stirred up feelings better left untouched within each of Hatcher's men. Simple men. Iron-hard, hand-forged men. The sort not easily given to ruminations on life and death and what might exist beyond one's grasp.

A man lived. Then a man died. So be it.

Yet as many times as Bass tried to convince himself he should put such notions out of his mind, those notions grew more troublesome. After all, he spent so damned much time alone every day. Hours alone with only his thoughts, with matters that deeply pricked a man who had begun to fear he hadn't spent near enough time listening to the stories his mother read her children from her Bible.

Did a man's life tally up for no more than dumb luck? How else could he account for one man going under to nothing more than ticks . . . when he himself had been shot, scalped, and left for dead? Was it a roll of the dice or a lay of the cards that determined who lived and who died? Or . . . was it something more?

Was it as Williams explained it: that Titus Bass had been told plain as sun that there was a heap more living in store for the sort of man who survived a scalping by those intent on killing him?

For some reason unfathomable to a simple man, had Titus Bass been chosen not to die? Had he been somehow plucked from the grasping claws of death itself? Why had he been spared a fate that befell other men? Who were these capricious and fickle spirits deciding such things?

Who had yanked him from the gaping maw of death?

Were they at his shoulder then and there? And if he listened hard enough, would he hear them?

Climbing down off the bank, he waded upstream with the trap, float, and bait sticks.

So many questions.

Quickly scraping out a shelf for the trap a few inches below the surface of the stream, Scratch positioned the trap and strung out the chain, driving the long, pointed sapling into the graveled creekbottom. Returning the small ax to the back of his belt beside the knife scabbard, he moved downstream toward his rifle and pouch.

At the sharp-sided bank he hoisted himself onto the grass and sat there dripping, finally settling back against the tree trunk where his rifle leaned.

Too many questions.

He would try listening. Williams had claimed a man might just hear the other side if he listened hard enough. The breeze stirred the leaves around him a moment; then the quakies settled. In that momentary silence he strained to listen. Then felt the air move around him unexpectedly. Almost as if it were something of substance . . . some*one* touching his shoulder.

Scratch turned, expecting to find . . . but there was nothing.

He sighed and went back to listening. The breeze came up again, rustling through the aspen leaves overhead. Stirring all the trees around him as he gazed out upon the floor of the valley. When his eyes began to droop, the wind chuttered among the leaves—murmuring, almost whispering.

"Bass."

Alert anew, eyes open, Scratch turned this way, then that. Listening. The breeze stirred again.

"Bass."

Slowly he raised his face to peer overhead into the branches cluttered with tiny, trembling green leaves.

"Bass."

Only the breeze nudging the leaves just gently enough that he had imagined they were murmuring his name.

When he brought his gaze back down, Scratch spotted them.

Two riders across the valley floor. Not where he would expect to see any of the rest of Hatcher's outfit. And the two were close enough . . . for him to see their long, loose hair and the feathers tossing on the breeze that had whispered his name through the branches overhead.

"Bass."

The hair bristled at the back of his neck with that next chutter of the leaves.

For a moment he studied the sky above the two horsemen, on either side of them, the very air between them. Hopeful he would actually be able to see the ragged tear rent in that filmy curtain between the other world and his. Wondering if he would indeed be able to see for himself that crack in the sky through which these riders had suddenly appeared.

As the riders slowly approached the far bank of the stream, Titus leaned to the side and brought the rifle into his lap—snapping the frizzen forward to assure himself that the pan was loaded. Next he saw to the charge in his pistol, then stuffed its barrel back in his belt. The pair of horsemen stopped when he rose from the ground holding the fullstock rifle at his right hip, his finger gently nudging back the rear set trigger until he felt the sear engage.

Titus stared at them for what seemed like a long time, waiting for the two warriors to declare themselves as friend or foe, ready for when they would plunge off the far bank into the stream and rush him. Then as one of the horses began to paw and bob its head impatiently, a rider spoke, gesturing with his bow.

Bass let him finish what he had to say, then tried to explain, "I don't know your tongue."

Scratch put the fingers of his left hand to his lips, moving them directly out toward the warriors as he shook his head vigorously.

Passing the bow over his head, the horseman stuffed it within a quiver half-filled by arrows. With his hands freed, the Indian began to sign.

But those gestures weren't making any sense, their being this far apart. Bass shook his head.

Apparently frustrated, the sign talker said something to the other, and they both nudged their ponies into motion.

Bass took a step forward, planting his feet as they entered the stream. He brought the rifle up, the cheekpiece braced between his bottom ribs and arm.

"Stop right there!"

Yanking back on their reins, both horsemen halted their ponies near the middle of the stream. Down the creek Titus heard the warning slap of a single beaver near that dam the creatures had been building over the last few days. More tails slapped the surface of the water; then it gradually grew quiet again.

So quiet, he heard the air nuzzle the quaky leaves above him.

"Bass."

Again the sign talker tried. But now that he was closer, Scratch could see just what the warrior had to say in sign: with only the first two fingers of his right hand extended, the others closed in the palm, the Indian held the hand momentarily in front of his chin, the extended fingers pointing at the sky. Then he slowly moved the hand up until it was about level with the top of his head, slowly bringing them down to point at the white man. Several times he repeated the same gesture while Titus stared quizzically at the two.

"Oh, damn!" he gushed, suddenly remembering. "*Friend*. Why—you're saying friend."

Bracing the rifle against his hip, Scratch mimicked the sign with his left hand. Then he tapped the rifle with his hand, pointing to himself and making the sign for friend again.

Finally the warrior nodded.

"That's right, fellers," Bass murmured to himself. "This here gun's my friend."

Scratch formed a fist with his left hand, extending only the index finger, and held it out in front of his body, finger pointing upward. *People*.

"What people are you?" he asked aloud.

The two looked at one another and shook their heads. They weren't understanding. Perhaps he had it wrong.

Then he thought of asking it another way. Again the hand with only the index finger went up, pointing at the sky, but now he brought it downward in a graceful arc, in the path taken by an arrow shot straight into the sky.

"What band are you?"

Through it all he studied the way the riders wore their hair, the feathers, their clothing and horse trappings—anything that might give him a clue. Here in South Park, he realized this pair could be anything from wandering Comanche or Kiowa or Southern Cheyenne come a distance to hunt. But then he realized if they had come from so far away, chances were good more warriors were somewhere close at hand. They didn't look all that much like Ute, he decided, regarding their hair and the elaborate face painting.

Painted. Maybeso they were from a warrior band foreign to this part of the mountains, come here with a large raiding party, painted for battle. Not some local fellas, out hunting for their families, to take meat and hides back for their village.

Painted.

Locking his eyes on them, Scratch intently studied their faces for any betrayal as to their intentions.

Again he signed slowly, saying aloud the words: "What band are you?"

One of them wagged his head, and the second horseman repeated the sign for "friend." Again they talked low to one another, both of them gazing this way and that, upstream and down. It began to make him more than a mite nervous, what with the way they peered all around more than look at him . . . as if they were assuring themselves he truly was alone.

Tapping their heels against the ribs of their ponies, both warriors eased toward the bank, where Bass stood some twenty feet back from the water's edge.

He licked his lips, feeling his right palm begin to sweat, anxious to put his trigger finger inside the guard. But with the trigger now set to go off at a touch—he knew he must hold the finger there against the trigger guard.

The animals lunged onto the bank, and their riders brought the dripping ponies to a halt less than fifteen feet from the white man.

One made the sign for "friend" again, then both peered upstream and down, their eyes quickly darting into the trees behind the trapper, able to see his saddle horse and the pack mule.

Again he signed "friend" too, his gaze darting back and forth between the two copper-skinned horsemen . . . making mental pictures of their loose hair, the handful of feathers tied at the crowns of their head. One had his coup feathers arrayed in a cock's spray at the back of his head; the other tied his so they descended down the side of his hair as it spilled over his shoulder. Metal conchos were riveted on the belt of one; a stone war club hung from the front of a snare saddle, a big metal ax swung by a rawhide thong from the other saddle.

One of the horsemen signed something new and baffling. He made a fist of his right hand, only the index finger extended upward, held along the right side of his nose. In this position the warrior moved the hand up and down slightly there next to the nose.*

Bewildered, Bass shook his head, gesturing helplessly with his left hand briefly before he returned it to grip the forestock of his rifle.

Once again the warriors glanced about them. One grinned wickedly and nodded to the other. Their eyes flicked past the trapper to those two animals grazing in the trees, then returned to the white man. Now one of them made another new sign.

This time he formed a claw out of his right hand, fingers and thumb held apart, bent and cupped, which he brought a few inches away from his heart at

---

Sign for Southern Arapaho.

the left side of his chest—where he repeatedly tapped the clawlike fingertips against his breast.*

Bass had never seen that sign ever before. Once more he shook his head and wagged his left hand in that gesture of nonunderstanding.

The warrior who had done the lion's share of the signing nudged his pony closer, his lips pursed in frustration, giving a minute gesture of his own for the other warrior to advance beside him.

"Hold it, fellers."

He immediately took a step back so that he would still be able to make a wide arc with the rifle if they suddenly rushed him. For the first time he realized his heart was hammering beneath his breastbone, his mouth gone dry and pasty. He watched the ponies come to a halt, dripping—wishing he had a drink from that stream right then.

The warrior repeated his sign of that right hand cupped and tapping the left side of his breast, but he did so as he urged his pony to the right a little, separating himself from the other rider. At the same time, the second horseman inched to his left a little and they both came to a halt. Now they waited some ten feet apart—the sort of gesture that did nothing to inspire his confidence in their good intentions.

His hand grew sweaty there on the wrist and forearm of the rifle, his heart thundering in his ears as the warrior on his left finished tapping his breast.

Bass shook his head and, from the right corner of his eye, saw the other warrior inching his pony more to the left. The niggers get far enough apart, they can rush me from two sides—put me under.

No more than twenty feet now . . .

Taking another step backward, Bass wheeled the rifle to his right, aiming it at the second Indian. Then his eyes suddenly narrowed as they locked on that wide strip of porcupine quillwork sewn along the man's legging. His gaze slowly climbed up the legging, then dropped back down to that moccasin.

Rocking onto the balls of his feet, Scratch felt everything inside him go cold. Glaring up at the face, quickly looking over the war paint, the way the man tied the feathers in his long, free hair. Then Bass's darkened eyes ran back down the wide strip of porcupine quillwork sewn along the outside seam of the legging . . . once more to that moccasin stitched with the same central rosette, sewn with quills of the same colors.

And he was sure.

After the better part of two long years . . . he was sure.

The burning gall rose like a flood, flinging itself through that cold core of him in a rage.

---

* Sign for Northern Arapaho, symbolizing the pockmarks scarring the chest of long-ago chief who had survived a bout of smallpox.

"You red son of a bitch!" he roared as his left hand flung up the barrel of that fullstock rifle, finger stabbing inside the trigger guard, jerking back in a burst of blinding fury.

Even as the huge .54-caliber ball smashed the warrior in his face, spraying a corona of blood that haloed his head, Bass was already bellowing.

"Raised this child's hair, you brown bastard!"

Through the gauzy veil of powder smoke Titus watched the warrior spill backward onto the rear flank of his pony, pitching off as the animal bolted, sidestepping and spinning away on its rear legs.

With his next heartbeat Titus heard the loud, shrill screech of the second horseman as the Indian savagely kicked his pony into action. Pounding his heels into the animal's ribs, the warrior charged the lone trapper, swinging up the long-handled ax from where it hung just in front of his right leg.

Bass dropped his rifle at his feet, rocking forward to brace himself, bending at the waist the instant he yanked that huge pistol from his wide leather belt, his left palm dragging back the big hammer. Without consciously aiming he brought the muzzle up just as the warrior crossed those few yards, firing at the black blur leaning off the side of the pony, at that shadow swinging his ax in a great, hissing arc.

When the bullet struck the horseman in the upper arm, the ax spun loose from his grip. Already on its way, the heavy, bladed weapon began to tumble, careening crazily toward the trapper. Too close and no time to duck now.

The handle slapped him on the front of his right shoulder as he started to twist aside, knocking Bass off balance, spinning him violently, pitching him on around to the side like one of his sister's stocking dolls no more than a breath before the warrior leaned completely off the side of the horse, arms outstretched, his legs releasing their grip on the pony as he collided into the white man.

With his weight the Indian speared Bass into the ground, driving the air from Scratch's chest in a great explosion. The man immediately jerked back, sweeping a leg over him to straddle the trapper as Titus fought for breath, blinking to clear the star shower from his eyes . . . realizing the warrior had a knife in his hand and was starting his lunge forward with a cry of blood lust.

Seizing that thick brown forearm slashing the huge knife downward, Titus braced himself, trying to squirm free beneath the warrior's weight and those muscular legs pinning him to the slick grass. As he twisted this way and that, Bass suddenly felt the fingers seize his throat like a claw closing down his air supply.

Remembering how death had loomed at the hands of the Mexican soldier.

A hot pain spread down across his chest where the Indian squeezed with his knees, where Scratch realized he wasn't able to draw in another breath—

no chance of air getting past the searing agony of that claw shutting down his throat.

Drops of the Arapaho's sweat mixed with greasy earth paint plopped onto Scratch's face as he flung his head back and forth, trying desperately to free himself from the warrior's grip on his neck right below the jaw. As he arched his back violently, one leg suddenly broke free and he flung himself up against the warrior. Scratch drove the knee into his enemy, then a second, and a third time, feeling the warrior's grip on his throat weaken with each blow.

At the same moment he drove his knee up, Bass relaxed his own grip on that brown wrist . . . fooling the warrior.

Reacting immediately, the Indian yanked back the arm clutching the knife. Already Scratch was driving the arm back with his own weight and with the might in his two arms, hurling the top of the handle right into the Arapaho's temple with a resounding thunk. The large round base of the elk antler used for the handle split the flesh, instantly spraying blood over the trapper. When the warrior jerked in surprise and pain, Titus yanked the brown arm forward, then hurtled it backward again, this time into the corner of the eye socket.

At that moment the strong legs began to loosen from their spider-lock around his middle. He savagely drove the knife handle into the bloody face a third time—smashing the forehead just above the eye. The skin opened up, oozing at first; then blood gushed from the ragged wound.

Weaving a moment, the Indian gurgled something as his head bobbed back loosely as if it hung by disconnected wires. Scratch twisted to the side, tearing himself free of the claw at his throat, spinning himself loose, releasing the knife arm before he rolled away across the grass.

Tumbling onto his knees, he vaulted forward, leaping onto the warrior's back just as the bloody face spun around. Bass seized the wrist of that hand holding the knife, squeezing, struggling from behind the Indian to jab the weapon back into the enemy's belly, to rake it across his chest, spear it deep between the ribs. With every attempt the Indian fought to control the blade, yanking it upward. His own undoing.

With a sharp blow the knife handle smashed against the warrior's jaw, and all fight went out of him. Like a wet sack of oats he spilled to the side, his eyes rolling back—out cold.

Rocking to his knees, Bass grabbed a handful of the black hair, jerked the face toward him, and drove his fist into the sharp nose. Again. Then a final blow of fury as he tasted the sting of bile that had been at the back of his throat all along.

Standing at last over his enemy, the trapper kicked the warrior in the ribs, then the gut, and finally drove his moccasin into the man's jaw. The Indian gurgled on his blood, his jaw moving slightly as if trying to speak.

The breeze murmured through the leaves.

Alarmed, Scratch immediately knelt, prying the knife from the warrior's hand and whirled in a fighting crouch, expecting the approach of another.

But he found himself alone on the creekbank. Save for the two fallen warriors, Bass was alone. The only sounds around him were the chuffing of the animals, the hammer of his heart against his ribs . . . and that breeze slipping through the aspen overhead, calling out his name.

Whispering it in celebration.

Carrying his name forth in victory.

THIRTEEN

Ol' Make-'Em-Come had done its work slick as scum on blood soup.

That much was plain to see when Bass hurried over to the warrior he had blown off the back of the pony.

Not all that much left of the man's face, what with the way the soft lead ball had flattened as it smashed right on through the bottom of the jaw. Nearly all of the lower half of the Arapaho's face was gone in a shredded, bloody pulp. Only a small part of the jawbone and some slivers of flesh still hung from the front of the skull below the hole where most of his nose had been.

Little wonder, Scratch thought. The bastard was sitting no more than five times the length of his fullstock from him when he pulled the trigger.

The wonder of it was slowly beginning to soak in.

His eyes crawled on down the muscular frame of the younger man. Perhaps somewhere in his midtwenties, no older than thirty, for certain. Bits of dried grass and dust furred his dark and sweaty body, fuzzing what bloody smears were left of his war paint. A strong man.

Suddenly Titus thought how outsized he would have been if he had been conscious enough to make a fight of it that day after being wounded and knocked from his horse. Instead, the warrior had figured him for dead, taken the prized topknot, and left the white man where he lay beside the river.

Funny how things worked out . . .

Cautiously, Titus looked around him, turning this way . . . then that, his eyes roaming, carefully scanning the horizon for any movement, any life . . . any crack in the veil between this world and that.

Maybeso there was some spirit, some power, some being watching over and protecting him back then. Watching over him even now.

He tore his eyes away from the tree line behind him, listening to the hush of the wind creeping through the quakies. And stared back at the Arapaho he had killed. The man who had left him as good as dead.

Something decorated with fringe and beads lay partially hidden by the warrior's body. Bass planted the toe of his moccasin under a hip and gave a shove. There at the waist hung a long bag looped through the side of the man's belt—something on the order of eight or so inches wide, it lay there twisted in the fall of the body. Bass knelt, turning it over, feeling the large brass beads and the strands of thick hair as he pulled it free.

Brown hair. Loose, wavy curls. A white man's. There was no mistaking that.

With the bag draped over one hand, he brought his fingers up and touched the curls hanging at the side of his head. Then rubbed the scalp and his own hair at the same time.

This was his hair.

Those brown, wavy locks more than a foot long clinging to that shriveled circle of a topknot were crudely stitched to the front of that belt bag. Like some of the fringe, many strands of the hair had been gathered and decorated with tarnished brass beads.

He shoved aside two strands of animal sinew loosely stitching the scalp to the bag and slipped a single finger beneath the dried flesh. It was hardened to a rawhide stiffness with age. Nothing much left of his topknot now but this coup of a dead warrior.

He gently caressed those long waves of brown hair lying across his palm. This scalp had nearly cost him his life. And it might well have saved his life too.

So Bass stared at the dead man for a long time before he flipped the body over with his foot. With the warrior resting on his stomach, Scratch carefully laid the long fringed bag across the dusty small of the bare back. He squatted beside the Indian's shoulder, picking up that big knife he had wrestled off the second warrior. Looping his fingers through the long black hair, Scratch tugged back on the head, laying the big blade against the bare flesh of the forehead an inch below the hairline.

There his hand froze a matter of heartbeats, his breath coming quicker.

Suddenly he decided to lay the Indian's knife aside, placing it atop the buckskin bag. Instead, Titus pulled the head back again and slipped his old skinning knife from its scabbard at the back of his belt.

Only fitting, he figured.

What he clutched in his hand was the only knife left him, back when this warrior took nearly everything from him. Its curved skinning blade had been sharpened so much by ol' Gut Washburn that the metal had gradually been worn down over years of use until it was no more than an inch in width.

Laying his right index finger along the top flat of the blade, Bass again pressed the sharpened edge on the warrior's brow. Slicing through that thin layer of flesh, he quickly dragged the old skinning knife back toward the temple, right on through the middle of the right ear, and after tugging aside the warrior's long hair, Bass finished that first cut just below the hairline at the nape of the neck. Yanking the long hair aside, he pulled the head over so it rested on the right cheek. Again he dragged the knife from the brow, down across the middle of the left ear, and on back to the incision he had left at the base of the skull.

This would be a full scalp, complete with the tops of his dead enemy's ears. No mere topknot as this warrior had taken from him. This day was clearly the doing of strong medicine.

Bracing his knee at the back of the Arapaho's neck, Bass gathered the hair in both hands and started pulling from the brow back. Slowly, the scalp began to give way, peeling from the skull with a crickling sound as it tore loose, tops of the ears and all, until there wasn't much flesh left on the bloody cranium—nothing much left on the dead man's head at all.

Standing again, Scratch stared down at the scalp hanging limp from his hand, then gazed at his own scalp sewn to that belt bag while the warrior's dripped the last of its blood and sticky gore across the toes of his moccasins. With the flush of a sudden impulse he began to whirl the fresh scalp vigorously round and round at the end of his arm, slinging off the last of the thick fluid and blood from the drying flesh.

Remembering how he had awakened in that thick, hot fog. How he had watched the Indian scraping his scalp with the edge of his knife through the blood oozing into his eyes.

There and then Bass knelt beside the Arapaho's body, just as the warrior had knelt beside him on that riverbank so long ago. Laying the whole scalp, flesh side up, atop one of his thighs, Titus began to carefully drag the side of the skinning knife's sharp blade back and forth across the flesh, scraping it clean the way he fleshed an animal's hide.

Twilight continued to deepen as he worked at his task, the air cooling until he finally stood again, turned, and looked in the direction where he had left the second Arapaho.

Unable to see the warrior, Bass narrowed his eyes, fingers tightening on the scalp. And he listened.

The son of a bitch was trying to crawl away through the grass, slipping into the buckbrush bordering the creek. Quiet as the Injun was, Bass still heard him. Swapping the scalp to his left hand, taking the knife into his right, Titus moved along the creekbank, finding the warrior's horse grazing on the far side of some bramble. Then he saw him.

"You fixing to make it to your pony?"

In the middle of pushing himself across the grass, the warrior jerked his head around, discovering the trapper coming up behind him. His eyes instantly filled with a dangerous mix of fear and hatred, the Arapaho tried to lunge forward in escape, grunting in pain as he dragged his broken ribs across the ground.

"Come back here, nigger," Bass growled, slamming his moccasin down on the warrior's ankle.

Clearly in agony, the Arapaho attempted to twist back far enough to grab hold of the trapper's foot, to swat it off his leg. Amused at that effort, Titus cocked his foot back and slammed it under the Indian's jaw. The warrior crumpled back on the grass, groaning low as blood oozed from his lips.

"Easy, now—I ain't gonna kill you," Titus said quietly as he knelt, realizing how much it hurt where the ax had smacked his shoulder minutes ago. "That'd be too damned easy, don't you see?"

He leaned down and rolled the warrior onto his back. The eyes fluttered a little, as if the man was struggling to stay conscious.

"I wan'cha alive, you red bastard. Just enough alive so you can earn your miserable life back."

With that he raised his right foot into the air, momentarily suspending it directly over the warrior's lower leg, then slammed the foot down with savage force halfway between knee and ankle, shattering both bones.

The sudden, excruciating pain wrenched the warrior off the ground in an arch of agony—screeching. Half-coagulated blood spewed from his mouth as he sputtered some garbled oaths, whimpering in pain and spitting out pieces of his teeth and blood to clear his mouth.

"Good," Scratch muttered as he knelt beside the warrior's head. "I want you wide-awake for what comes next."

As the Arapaho writhed, Bass held the scalp inches above his face and shoved the bloody skinning knife right under the man's nose—pressing up, up, up as crimson drops beaded along the blade. The warrior quickly stopped writhing.

"That's better," he said as he got to his feet. "Now you're coming with me."

Laying the skinning knife in his left hand with the scalp, Bass filled his right with the warrior's hair, dragging up the man's head and slowly bringing the body around in a wide circle to begin slowly, foot by foot, tugging the Arapaho's deadweight through the grass. Towing him back toward the dead scalper.

Each time he tugged the warrior forward with a lunge, the Indian grunted low in his throat, a guttural sound of deep pain that always ended with a quiet, shrill whimper. Then Bass would drag him another three or four feet through the tangle of grass, the man's head suspended by his long hair, and he would groan in pain again. On and on, until they crossed better than sixty feet of creekbank to stop at the outflung arm of the dead warrior.

"This here's the son of a bitch what scalped me," Scratch told him, releasing the man's hair.

Then he knelt where the wounded warrior could watch his pantomime of removing the Indian's scalp. That done, Bass reached up and took the blue bandanna from his head, turning slightly to point to his own bare skull—tapping the bare bone to be certain the wounded man understood. Next he pointed his gnarled finger to that brown hair stitched to the dead warrior's belt bag. Back to his skull his finger went a second time, then once more to the bag. Over and over that blood-crusted finger moved slowly as he continued to gaze straight into the Arapaho's hate-filled eyes.

At last he saw something register there, some understanding, perhaps a recognition that only increased the pain and fury in the eyes.

After tugging on his bandanna, Bass held up two fingers. Then he positioned both hands in front of him at waist level, palms and fingers pointed up, fingers waving gently as he raised them slowly.

Again he signaled two.

And once more he made the grass sign for "summer."

The Indian's eyes came away from Scratch's hands to meet the trapper's eyes. Sure enough sign the warrior understood.

"That's right. Two summers ago."

Then he tapped the end of his finger on the dead Indian's chest. And when the wounded man's eyes came back to his, Bass said, "This nigger. That's right. Two summers ago, this here red nigger."

As before, he used both hands to sign. Extending only the forefinger on the right hand, Titus held out his left arm, the first two fingers on that hand pointing down, symbolizing the legs of a man. Now he struck that man repeatedly with the right forefinger.

Coup.

"Good. This friend of your'n counted coup on me two summers ago. You savvy that, you bastard?"

He signed all of it over again.

Two.

Summers.

Counted coup.

Then he ripped off the bandanna a second time, pointing to the bare skull bone. And finally to that patch of long, wavy brown hair loosely sewn to the buckskin bag.

When those black, luminous eyes locked back on his, Bass resumed signing. He tapped his own breast with his right hand, then placed the back of that hand against his forehead, the first two fingers extended and held apart, slightly curved. He raised the hand slowly, moving it round and round in a simulated rise of smoke from a fire.

"My *medicine,*" he spoke softly as the breeze nuzzled the leaves overhead.

Making a fist of that right hand, Titus slapped it against his chest, right over his heart, then brought the fist down to almost waist level with a bold, confident gesture.

"It is strong. My medicine's strong."

Now Scratch opened his hand and placed it near the right side of his forehead, fingers open, separated, and slightly curved into a cup as he twirled the hand back and forth, back and forth in a tight spin to resemble mental instability.

"That's right: I'm *crazy,*" he explained, the volume of his voice rising. "A damn fool, crazy. You go tell your people they best not mess with me. I'm a crazy nigger!"

The eyes glared back at him, unflinching.

"Now I'm gonna prove to you just how crazy I am, you son of a bitch," Titus growled. "When you get back to your people—you be sure to tell 'em all what you see'd here today."

Leaning to the side, Bass quickly laid the belt bag and the dead man's knife where they would be safe, more than an arm's length away, then took out his own skinning knife. It made a faint crackling noise as he drove the narrow blade deep into the base of the dead man's throat, blood seeping out as he dragged the blade along the flesh and muscle stretched over the breastbone. At the bottom of the sternum he plunged the knife into the abdomen, all the way to the handle. Sawing through the thick rawhide belt that held up the leggings, Titus flung aside the front of the leather breechclout and continued down, down in a ragged line, drawing the full length of the blade through the gush of blood and spill of purple intestines until the knife struck hard bone just above the warrior's penis.

After wiping the blood from the blade on the dead Indian's legging, Scratch drove the weapon into the ground beside the body. He rocked forward, rising onto his knees over the warrior. Giving the wounded Arapaho one last, long look of devilish insanity—the trapper stuffed both hands into that wide, grisly incision.

Again and again he ripped apart the gaping slash, pulling out long lengths of that purplish-white intestinal coil, heaving it to the far side of the body until no more remained. Then he retrieved the knife from the ground and went to work on the rest. Bladder and both kidneys he hacked loose, flinging them onto the growing gut-pile. The stomach, and liver, then the gallbladder—chopping it all free with savage slashes of the knife, splattering himself with the Indian's blood, painting himself in crimson, reveling in the warmth of his victim's body like some wild, feral beast gorging itself up to the snout in its prey.

He growled, grunted, whooped, and shrieked in shrill exultation every time he pulled some new organ free and hurled it onto the expanding gut-pile there in the grass near the body. Chopping and jabbing, hacking and sawing with the knife, Scratch repeatedly stuffed his arms past the elbows into the chest cavity, tearing free the lobes of lung from the connective tissue on the interior of the chest wall, ripping them from their last grip on the windpipe's branching forks.

With all those warm, quivering organs lying beside the sundered carcass, empty from downstream anus to upstream voice box, there remained but one last organ for him to cut free from that bloody hollow.

Seizing the soft, sticky, warm globe in his left hand, Scratch slipped his knife under the rib cage and hacked it free. Bringing it out from beneath those last, lower ribs, he gazed at the heart, turned it over and over, thick blood continuing to ooze from those butchered vessels. So small and weak and defenseless, he thought as he studied it.

Then for the first time during his mad, crazed orgy over the body, Bass turned to look at the wounded man. And when he saw how transfixed the warrior's eyes had been on him throughout it all, Bass knew what he must now do.

Cradling the quivering heart in his left hand, he scrambled over to where he could squat right beside the wounded Arapaho. Rolling the organ over in his hands, Bass suddenly shoved it forward, until he held it suspended no more than two inches from the warrior's face, blood still dripping onto the brown skin stretched taut across the Indian's frozen, grim countenance.

"You tell your people what you see'd here today," Bass grunted, realizing his anger fired his every vein with hot surges of adrenaline, his voice little more than the sound an animal would make after making its kill.

His eyes never leaving the wounded man's, Scratch slowly turned the heart over and over in his hands, slowly bringing the slimy organ closer and closer to his opening mouth. Then he shoved the heart between his teeth, clamped down, and savagely tore off a symbolic hunk of his enemy's power.

How warm the soft, elastic tissue felt between his teeth, against his tongue—yet no different from the elk liver or buffalo heart he had been eating for years. So strong was the muscle, he knew as soon as he began to grind it between his back teeth that he wasn't about to chew it up fine enough. Instead, he swallowed hard, gagging at first, then tried again—this time sensing the hunk of raw flesh glide past the back of his tongue. He swallowed once more to make sure it would stay down.

And stood, grinning madly, staring wild-eyed at the wounded man—then suddenly cocked back his arm and flung the heart across the creek. It landed with a bounce on the open and grassy bank the horsemen had come down to make their crossing.

Quickly pointing at the dead Indian, Bass made the sign for "medicine" in front of his forehead: bloody, slimy fingers rising slowly in that symbolic spiral of smoke. He concluded by slapping his own chest with that crimson hand—painting himself with that red handprint.

"His medicine," he uttered the words now as he repeated the signs. "It's now *my* medicine!"

Swiping the back of his red hand over his mouth, Bass made the signs onc last time, not taking his eyes off the enemy who lay there in pain, breathing in short gusts, watching the crazed trapper.

"You're gonna live to tell 'em," Titus growled as he turned back toward the mutilated carcass.

Dropping to one knee near the dead man's hip, Bass swiftly made two slashing arcs with the skinning blade, freeing both penis and scrotum together in one ragged trophy.

"Here's all this bastard's got left for power now," he said, shaking the warrior's manhood.

Then he violently stuffed it into what was left of the dead man's face. He adjusted it there, ceremonially, not having the lower jaw to clamp it in place. Bass stood to admire his handiwork: how he had carefully laid his enemy's manhood across what was left of the bloody face, how he had gutted the warrior. All of it would speak a powerful message to any man who happened across this scene . . . that is, before the predators came and finished what he had begun.

After wiping off the knife and stuffing it back into its sheath, Scratch retrieved the buckskin bag from the ground and stuffed it under his own belt. Then he stopped and studied the dead warrior one more time. Those leggings weren't all that bloodied. And the moccasins might be serviceable.

He knelt and dragged the cut ends of the rawhide belt thong from the knotted loops at the top of the leggings, then scooted himself down to the dead man's feet, where he grabbed the heel of the moccasins and yanked them off the dirty brown feet. One at a time he urged the soft buckskin sheaths down the legs until they were both free and slung over his shoulder. He got back to his feet, stuffing the decorated moccasins inside his shirt.

"Go. Go on back to your people now."

Holding his arm out toward the distance, pointing across the creek in the direction the riders had come, Bass sensed the hot fire in his veins beginning to subside. Moving over to stand above the wounded man, he watched those black eyes a moment longer, then looked down at the blood smearing the warrior's legging where he had crushed the lower leg.

"Gonna have to drag yourself from here on out," he said quietly, a strange calm come over him now. "G'back and tell your people what happened here. Show 'em that busted leg of your'n. Tell 'em I got the bastard what took my hair. You tell 'em his medicine's mine now."

"Damn—but would you look at Scratch!" Elbridge Gray said as he slowly rose from their circle of downed timber where they had spread their sleeping robes.

Titus slowly came into the fire's light and reined his saddle horse to a halt.

Hatcher scrambled to his feet too, his eyes narrowing in concern. "Ye awright, nigger?"

"He looks hurt, Jack," Caleb declared, stepping closer. "Lookit the blood all over 'im."

"Ain't mine," Scratch explained. "Ain't none of it mine."

Isaac craned his neck to look back at the pack mule. "Hannah ain't carrying no game. How you come to have so much blood on you?"

"I had me a scrap," Bass answered as he leaned back and peeled the moist scalp off the saddle horn where he had placed it for his ride back to their camp. Placing his fist inside it, he raised the long, glossy hair into the firelight.

"What the hell is that?" Solomon asked, the farthest away at the other side of the fire.

"*Whose* the hell is it?" Hatcher corrected.

Kicking his left leg to the right to clear the saddle horn, Bass dropped to the ground. "The bastard what scalped me."

He watched the sets of eyes flick to the blue bandanna, then come back to rest on his face.

"Ye made some mess of yerself," Jack advised as he stepped closer, reaching out to brush the hair with his fingers.

Wood was next, moving up just before the rest crowded in. "How you so dad-blamed sure this was the one what got your scalp?"

"Yeah?" Rufus agreed. "That's coming on two year ago."

"I know," Titus reassured them as he pushed through the group and settled onto a downed log at the fire's edge. "A man just knows."

"I be damned: Scratch got him back the warrior what got him," Caleb declared as he came up to sit beside Bass.

"I knowed one day I'd kill the bastard what took my hair."

"Awright, Scratch," Hatcher said sympathetically. "We're yer friends: we'll believe you when ye say you know it was the one—"

"It *was* the one," he snapped. Yanking the leggings from his shoulder, Bass flung them to the ground at his feet. "There, see for your own damn selves."

Graham asked, "You . . . you took the red nigger's leggings?"

"There," and Titus pointed at the quillwork illuminated by the flickering firelight as the last of twilight seeped to black of night. "That's just the way I been remembering them colors every night since the son of a bitch cut my hair off my head. Every last blessed night I see that strip of quills in my sleep. See them colors sewed up just like that."

"Warrior wears his colors," Hatcher agreed thoughtfully, nodding. "Every red nigger has his own design too."

Solomon looked askance at the legging. "That really come off the one what took your topknot?"

"Many a time I told you boys since you found me in that buffler valley— I was knocked out to the world, but I come to while the son of a bitch was scraping off my scalp. I saw with my own damned eyes the colors on them leggings. He was hunkered right by my head." Titus reached inside his shirt, tore out the moccasins, and hurled them onto the leggings by his feet. "I saw the nigger's mockersons too!"

"I 'member ye telling us," Hatcher assented.

"Every damn night since . . . I seen that nigger's leggings, seen his mockersons in my head, and nary of it would go away and leave me be."

"Now we know why," Fish replied. "You was bound to get your chance at the nigger."

"Solomon is right," Jack agreed. "Ever' man should have him his chance at those that done him wrong. Just one chance to even the score."

Caleb snorted, "Looks to me like Titus done better'n just even up the score! I'd say Titus gone and got the better of it all!"

"Where'd you leave 'im?" Rufus asked.

"Right where he and 'nother jumped me."

" 'Nother'n?" Hatcher asked. "How many red niggers did ye lay into?"

And as Elbridge brought him a scalding cup of coffee, Bass told them of the horsemen's approach, how they attempted to outflank him and run him down about the time he noticed the warrior's leggings and moccasins. He told it all—everything from breaking the second man's leg, to gutting and butchering the scalp taker.

"Then ye just up and left that other'n to crawl off?"

Bass nodded. "He ain't going anywhere very fast. I don't figger that brownskin's gonna drag hisself outta the Bayou afore we set off ourselves for the Popo Agie."

"Rendezvous ain't long now!" Rufus cried.

"Wha'cha gonna do with that scalp?" Caleb asked. "Make you some hangy-downs, some scalp locks to sew to your shirt, maybe 'long your shoulder and down the arms?"

"Dunno," he said. "Ain't thought that far."

Hatcher handed the scalp back to Bass as Scratch tugged nervously at the blue bandanna. Wagging his head, Titus said, "Lost my patch o' beaver fur, boys. Can't for the life of me . . . I took off the bandanny to show the one nigger where his companyero skelped me. Must've lost it then."

"You want me to see to cutting you 'nother from a poor plew, Scratch?" asked Solomon.

"No," Hatcher responded instead as the others turned to regard him with curiosity. "Bass won't be needing no more beaver fur to wear over that little skull spot on his noodle no more."

He studied Jack cautiously. "I won't?"

"That's right," Jack replied, kneeling at Bass's knee, using one finger to describe a circle around the Arapaho's scalp. "Ye won't need that plew no more because ye got 'sactly what ye need to make a new skelp lock for yerself."

Scratch gazed down at the glossy hair and the drying flesh he held in his lap. "For myself?"

Hatcher reached out and seized the trophy. "Take off that goddamned bandanny for me."

"Why you want me to—"

"Take it off so I can have me a good look at that head bone of yer'n. G'won, do it."

Quickly glancing at a few of the others, Bass's eyes eventually landed on John Rowland, who sat alone at the side of the fire, staring morosely into the flames—totally without interest in what the others were doing. John looked up at Scratch for a long moment, then went back to gazing at the fire.

"Awright," Titus agreed quietly, standing as he started to drag off the dirty bandanna.

"Sit back down right where ye are," Hatcher commanded, stepping right to Bass's side, where he could peer down at the bare bone. With one hand he gently turned the back of Scratch's head toward the fire's light.

Bass started to look up a moment. But Jack locked Scratch's head in his hands and turned it back to the side so he could examine the patch of bone while holding the Arapaho's scalp beside it.

"Eegod! There it is, boys," Hatcher declared eventually. "Bass can wear this nigger's hair for his own!"

"How he gonna do that when we know the bastard's skelp gonna dry up?" Rufus asked.

"This here scalp ain't gonna dry up," Hatcher said. "Not if Bass takes care of it."

"Just how'm I gonna take care of it?" Bass inquired.

"First whack, ye're gonna salt it," Jack explained.

Titus wagged his head. "Awright, then what?"

"Ye're gonna tan it just like the squaws do all their hides."

Scratch had to grin, what with the way the others were beginning to smile as if Jack had lost a few of his pebbles. "I . . . I'm gonna tan this nigger's scalp."

"Injuns do it alla time," Hatcher declared. "Take ye some brains and water . . . get that worked down into the skelp. In no time at all it's gonna be ever' bit as soft as them skins a squaw used for yer leggings last winter."

He stared at his leggings for a long moment, rubbing the brain-tanned, fire-smoked hide between a thumb and forefinger. "You really s'pose it'd work?"

"Mad Jack Hatcher says it'll work?" Caleb Wood cheered, "It's gonna work!"

Jack himself boasted, "Less'n a week from now, ye'll be wearing this nigger's hair for yer'n."

"The hull thing?" Solomon asked.

"Hell, no," Hatcher growled. "We gonna cut that skelp down so after it's cured, it'll be just a li'l bigger'n that bone on the back of Bass's head."

"Fit right over it?" Scratch inquired.

"Like it was made to be there," Jack said enthusiastically.

"Jumpin' Jehoshaphat!" Bass roared, slapping his knee as he stood. "I'll wear the nigger's hair what got mine, boys!"

"Gonna look a li'l strange to me," Isaac said.

Bass whirled on him. "What the hell's gonna look so strange 'bout it?"

"Ain't same color as your'n."

He peered down at the scalp, a disappointment sucking the wind right out of him. "Damn, if you ain't right. It don't look like—"

"It don't have to," Jack interrupted, shouldering Simms aside. "The nigger's hair is yer'n, no matter that it don't look like yers. It's the medicine what counts!"

With Hatcher's contagious enthusiasm, he felt cheered anew. "Damn right, Jack! It's the medicine what counts."

"But Scratch's hair is brown," Solomon grumped, "and that there's black as night."

"Scratch's ain't gonna be brown much longer anyways," Caleb declared.

Bass cocked his head, asking, "What you mean by that?"

"You ever look at your hair since we moseyed down to Taos last winter?" Wood tried to explain. "Ever give that beard of your'n a good look too?"

"This child sure is getting gray awready, ain't he?" Rufus said.

Grabbing a hank of hair at the side of his head, Titus held it out before his eyes in the firelight. "This here ain't gray!"

"That ain't where ye're going gray right now, Scratch!" Hatcher bellowed. "Up there on top of yer head. Down there on yer beard. Here," and he grabbed some of the silver-flecked hair hanging right there at the temple. "Lookee there."

Sure enough, if those strands didn't radiate some gray in the firelight.

"Get me a mirror, you sonsabitches," he grumbled at them. "I wanna see this for my own self."

Hatcher turned to the rest. "Get the man a mirror, boys. He deserves to see just how he's getting on in years."

"But I ain't a ol' man," Bass whimpered as he sank down upon the log with the scalp in hand.

Hatcher took the scalp from him and handed it back to Caleb. "Here, get that salted down real good for me. Roll it up like ye'd do a skin, and tie a whang around it till we can start on it in a couple of days."

Caleb turned away as Isaac returned with a small mirror the size of a large man's palms put side by side. Bass shifted on the log so he could look into the mirror with enough light to inspect his graying hair. Still, his eyes always came back to his mustache and beard. In a stripe of gray that ran down the middle of the brown mustache, on below his lower lip and down the extent of his brown beard, the hair stood out like that white band running down a skunk's back.

"Damn, if I didn't notice," he confessed as he studied the gray hairs spreading back from his temples, the graying of that hair hanging from his brow.

"Ain't getting old," Hatcher declared. "Just getting gray earlier'n most, Titus."

"Sometimes . . . it feels like old," Bass explained as he peered at himself in the mirror, examining his first wrinkles, the spread of those deeply furrowed crow's-feet.

"Chirk up, friend!" Jack cheered. "Why, ye got plenty to bark about this night!"

Isaac leaped in front of Bass, there between Scratch and Hatcher, grinning wildly. "Don't you figger it's 'bout time to punch some holes in Titus's ears?"

"A damned fine idee!" Hatcher roared.

"P-punch some holes in my ears?"

"Hang some purties from 'em," Rufus said, leaning in to tap his earrings with a fingertip.

"Y-you said . . . a hole?"

"Get me my awl!" Hatcher bellowed, ignoring Titus completely.

Scratch nearly came off the log as Rufus whirled away. "Your awl?"

"I could do it with a needle, Scratch," Hatcher said, stepping right up beside Bass to grab hold of Bass's earlobes, tugging on them to turn Titus toward the light. "But a needle makes it a round hole, ye see?"

"Which means it takes longer to heal," Caleb explained.

Hatcher nodded. "We'll get some glover's needles from the trader this summer: they got three sides filed on 'em like a awl."

"Awright," Titus replied with no small measure of relief. "L-let's just wait till we got the proper needle—"

"But don'cha wanna have it done on the night ye killed that red nigger what took yer hair two years back?" Jack asked.

Everyone came to an immediate stop around him, turning to look his way, expectantly awaiting his answer.

Clearing his throat nervously, Scratch explained, "It's a mighty fine thing you wanting to celebrate with me—"

Solomon hollered, "Birthdays too!"

"But I ain't so sure 'bout putting holes in my ears—"

"Nothing to it," Jack assured. "Why, ye had bigger holes shot in you with G'lena lead, bigger holes poked in yer hide by Injuns. Hell—don'cha 'member?"

"By jam," Isaac said. "We can hang some wires in 'em!"

"Maybeso Scratch don't wanna," Caleb came up to say, patting a hand on Bass's shoulder protectively. "S'awright—we can just wait till ronnyvoo an' do it."

"No," Titus answered of a sudden. "By Jehoshaphat's drawers: let's punch them two holes!"

As if a horn of powder had gone off, there was a flurry of frantic motion as Rufus returned with the awl held aloft triumphantly. Hatcher began giving instructions while he stuffed the awl's point down in the hot coals for a few minutes. Elbridge brought over a scrap of oiling rag to lay over the shoulder while they punched through Bass's flesh. And Solomon went off to fetch a small coil of brass wire out of his plunder.

"Cut me two pieces," Jack explained to Solomon as he returned. "Not too long neither."

In minutes the others were ready, all of them crowding in on either side of Hatcher to get themselves a firsthand look at the operation on one of the ears.

"Turn this way," Hatcher instructed, tugging on the right ear to turn Bass's head.

Elbridge draped that old piece of oiling cloth over the right shoulder beneath the ear where Hatcher was pinching the lobe tightly between thumb and forefinger.

"Damn—how much you gonna hurt me like that?" Scratch growled, rolling his eyes back to try peering at Jack's hand.

"I don't pinch it like this," Hatcher explained, "it's gonna hurt worse when I punch the hole." He looked up at Isaac. "Got that chunk of pine from the woodpile for me?"

Simms handed him a small sliver of kindling wood about six inches long and some two inches wide.

Jack held it near the tip of Bass's nose momentarily. "This here pine's good and soft, Scratch."

His brow knitted suspiciously. "What you use it for?"

"Gonna put it ahind yer ear like this," he answered, slipping the flat piece of kindling behind the lobe. "I do this so yer hide don't tear on the backside. Keeps that skin flat when I'm punching through."

"Y-you ain't gonna tear my skin, are you?"

"Eegod! I done this more times'n I can 'member." Hatcher turned to Simms. "Time to make some blood, boys. Gimme the awl, Isaac."

Simms bent and retrieved the awl from the glowing coals. He swiped it free of ash across his longhandle sleeve, then blew on it for good measure.

"Them ashes don't hurt nothing," Caleb declared. "They're cleaner'n most anything."

Hatcher took the awl from Isaac. "Gonna punch the hole now, Scratch."

"Awright. Go right on ahead."

Looking at Fish to see that he held the two short sections of wire, Jack delicately placed the awl's sharp point at the center of Bass's earlobe. Only then did he move the fingers he had been using to pinch the lobe and numb all feeling from the tissue.

Although he did feel the awl's point penetrate the lobe, Scratch heard the sound of the piercing more than he felt it.

"You hit it center, Jack," Caleb said with approval.

"Damn if I don't always hit center," Hatcher replied. "Here. Gimme a wire."

Jack passed the awl off to Isaac and took from Solomon a short length of thick brass wire the trappers employed for making a variety of repairs around camp: all the way from wrapping about cracked wrists and forestocks on their rifles to making strong, long-lasting repairs to saddles and other tack where sinew would likely break down and unravel.

"Isaac, set that awl back to the coals for me," Hatcher instructed as he seized the short piece of wire near its end.

After wiping off a little blood that oozed from the new hole, Hatcher carefully poked the wire through to the back side. Quickly he bent the wire into a crude hoop without tugging on the lobe too much, then looped and twisted the ends back on themselves so that the hoop wouldn't be falling out by any accidental rubbing.

"How's that feel?" Jack asked as he began to pinch the left ear, nudging Bass's head in the opposite direction toward the firelight.

"Don't feel much of a thing," Bass confessed, surprised.

"Awl," Hatcher said as Elbridge dragged the cloth off the right shoulder and draped it over the left.

"He's sure gonna be one pretty nigger!" Gray declared.

Hatcher placed the awl tip against the earlobe right where he wanted to make the hole. "Shit! Ain't no pair of goddamned brass ear wires gonna make this mud-ugly son of a bitch into a pretty nigger!"

He rolled his eyes up at Jack. "Who you calling mud-ugly?"

Hatcher punched the awl through the lobe into the soft pinewood stop, yanked the awl out, and when he had handed it off, took the second piece of wire and slipped it through to loop it off. Then he stepped back, cocking his head from this side to that, back and forth, first inspecting one ear, then the other.

"A right fine job, even if I do say so my own self. Get Scratch that mirror again."

He gently touched the brass wires that dangled from both ears while Rufus brought up the mirror. Turning it toward the light while he twisted about the log, Bass gazed at one ear in astonishment, then turned aside to inspect the other ear, his grin beginning to grow within that gray-striped beard.

"Well, Mad Jack Hatcher," he declared, showing nearly all his teeth in glee, "you said you couldn't—but you sure did make this mud-ugly nigger one purty feller."

Through the heads and shoulders of the other trappers Bass again spotted Rowland squatting at the far side of the fire, scuffing up small clouds of dirt with a peeled stick he used to dig at the ground near his feet.

"Say, Johnny," Scratch said, "don't you think I look real purty now?"

"I s'pose," Rowland mumbled so quietly, his words almost went unheard against the sough of the wind in the trees and the crackle of their fire.

The others moved aside as Titus clambered to his feet and stepped through them. He stopped at Rowland's elbow. "Something eating a hole in your belly, ain't it, John?"

Without looking up, the man answered, "Nothing wrong."

"He's been like this last few days," Caleb explained, coming up at Scratch's shoulder.

"Man can act any way he wants to," Rowland snapped.

"We been friends long enough for me to know that something's kicking around inside you and it won't give ye no rest," Hatcher said when he came to a stop on the other side of Titus.

Suddenly Rowland looked at the three of them. Then he blurted out his confession: "I wanna go back to Taos."

"Go back?" Rufus repeated as he knelt nearby.

"I done decided it," John declared. "Don't wanna be up here right now."

Jack inquired, "What's pulling ye to give up on these here mountains?"

"You got me wrong," Rowland protested. "I ain't saying I've give up on the mountains from here on out, Jack."

Jack settled on a log next to Rowland. "You and me, we fought more'n our share of red-bellies, Johnny. I figger ye can tell me what's on yer mind."

"I-I really dunno what this is all about," Rowland admitted. "I ain't never . . . never had me a feeling like this, Jack."

"You had a hole cut outta your heart," Bass explained quietly, sympathy flooding up inside him. "When you lost your Maria—it cut out a big hole from your heart."

When Titus said it, Rowland looked up. Wagging his head, he said, "Ain't none of this the same no more, Scratch. Not like it was before: when I didn't have me no woman. Not like it was when I had Maria waiting for me back in Taos."

"You turn back for the south, what you aim to do?" Solomon asked.

With a shrug Rowland admitted, "Don't rightly know for now. Something'll come by that I can do."

"Sure of that," Hatcher agreed. "A likely man such as you can do most anything he puts his mind to."

"Maybe I can watch some sheep, do some hunting for other folks too," John replied. "Pay for my keep till I get all this sorted through."

"Maybe you figger you ain't done with the mountains?" Bass inquired.

"No," and John shook his head. "I don't figger I'll stay outta the mountains for the rest of my days. Just that . . . for now—I ain't a damn bit of good to none of you."

Hatcher clamped a hand on Rowland's knee. "Johnny, ye damn well know we'll ride with ye come what may. Not a man here gonna say ye gotta go out and trap when ye're nursing that hole in yer heart. Don't make me no never-mind if ye stay back to camp and watch over our plunder and the stock while the rest of us go set traps. You just do what ye can till things get better, and we'll stay together till they—"

"I don't know when things'll get better, Jack," he interrupted. "Don't know . . . *if* they'll ever get better."

Hatcher glanced up at the others when Rowland went back to staring at the fire. "Awright, Johnny. All I'm gonna ask of ye is ye leave us yer license."

"Sure," Rowland said. "I'm the only one of us with a license to trap in these parts since Matthew ain't along this time out. Might be you could use it when you bring some fur back to Taos."

"Won't be till winter after next, I 'spect," Jack declared.

"One of you gonna have to be me," Rowland explained, rubbing his palms down the tops of his thighs in that manner of a man who has come to a difficult decision. "Now that I be a Mexican citizen, they call me Juan Roles. Who's gonna be me?"

"I will," Rufus volunteered as he squatted near Rowland.

"You'll do," John replied, trying out a weak smile, then gazed at the flames.

After a long, uneasy silence Hatcher asked, "Tomorrow, Johnny?"

"Don't see me no reason to hang on when I've made up my mind to go."

Caleb said, "Want some whiskey, for saying our fare-thee-wells tonight?"

"You fellers go right on," Rowland answered. "I don't much feel like drinking. I found out whiskey just don't kill this hurt no more."

"Come a time," Bass said, "you'll be back in these hills with us. Back to skinning beaver and fighting Injuns. Come a time when you're ready to get on with the living."

"Right now it don't feel like I'll ever wanna do much of anything ever again," Rowland declared. "Thing of it is: a man what don't care much if he goes on living . . . that man sure as hell gonna end up dead lot sooner'n he should."

FOURTEEN

The sun was content to hide its rise the following morning as the seven of them bid their melancholy farewell to John Rowland. Clouds had gathered through the night, blotting out the last shimmer of starshine as they stirred in the cold gloom, kicked life back into the fire, and went about seeing off one of their own.

No longer were there ten.

Joseph Little lay in a shallow grave scraped from the forest floor high in the Wind River Mountains.

Matthew Kinkead had stayed behind, vowing he'd had him enough of the wandering and the womanlessness, choosing instead a life among his Rosa's people in Taos.

And now Rowland—turning back himself, unable to salve his grief among these good friends in these mountains. His final hope might be to find a healing to those deep wounds of his heart among Maria's people.

That was just what Bass wished for him when it was Scratch's turn to step up and fling his arms around another old friend in farewell. Quickly he whispered, "Johnny, I pray your feet'll take you back where you can be happy once more."

Rowland inched back in their embrace and looked into

Bass's eyes. "I find me what makes me happy again—I'll be back to these here mountains. Lay your set on that."

"Just make sure our trails cross afore too long," Titus replied, slapping John on the shoulder and stepping back.

"Count on it, Scratch."

By the fire's light in the last hour before dawn that murky, gray morning, they had seen to it that Rowland was outfitted with what he would need to see him through the passes and down the high side all the way back to the valley lying at the foot of the Sangre de Cristos.

"I ain't gonna listen to none of yer back talk, John Rowland: ye'll take yer rightful share," Jack Hatcher had declared when he had the rest begin to divide out Rowland's portion.

"Ain't right that I take more than I need to make it back," John protested, laying a hand on Hatcher's arm before his eyes touched those of the others. "I'll be fine once I get there."

For a long moment Jack did not move, nor did he speak. Then, with a voice clogged with regret, he said, "Yes, Johnny Rowland. I figger you will be fine once ye get back to Taos."

So they had split off only what Rowland himself said he would take, everything else spread among those friends he was leaving behind, split among those men who one day soon would push on north themselves for rendezvous on the Popo Agie. And then Rowland had climbed into the saddle, waved as he turned his mount and packhorse, then never looked back as he reined out of the trees.

As the seven stood watching the man and animals grow smaller and smaller against the immensity of the Bayou Salade, the sky slowly began to seep . . . a gentle, cold spring rain. And with the way the weeping clouds continued to lower down the mountainsides around them, Bass sensed they were in for a long day of it.

As empty as his belly was that morning, Scratch hadn't been hungry enough to eat like the others as they huddled over their tins of coffee at their smoky fire. Coffee was all he wanted to warm his gut that morning until he figured he could put it off no longer. Taking Hannah's lead rope, Bass mounted up and rode off across the valley toward his half-dozen sets placed along a stretch of narrow stream that spilled into a wider creek tumbling toward the valley floor.

He tugged the soggy wide-brimmed hat down more firmly on his head, sensing the way the greasy blue bandanna rubbed that patch of bare skull. As soon as he returned to camp that morning, Bass vowed he would start work on the scalp he was to wear in place of his own. Cutting it down to a workable size, curing and tanning it over the next few days—then making the final trim so that it would lay over that lopsided circle of bone.

Then he decided. Instead of retracing his way back through yesterday's sets, he turned downstream toward those last traps he had baited. Curious now to find out what had become of the two.

Something had been at the butchered Arapaho's body. Some of the gut-pile was gone; some creature had attempted to drag off the corpse.

His eyes quickly scanning the scene, Bass slipped to the trampled grass, knelt by what remained of the man who had taken his scalp, and inspected the soppy ground. A free meal had drawn two of the lanky-legged beasts here. Sign of their pads tramping around the body, yonder around what they hadn't finished of the gut-pile. It was enough to show him the wild dogs hadn't been here too long ago.

Looking up, Bass figured they were somewhere close enough to be watching him. He had scared them off, but not far enough away that they wouldn't be ready to return when he was gone. Standing, he gazed around at the wall of forest there beside the creek. It was fitting, he decided. Fitting that the wild predators of this high land would come to reclaim the warrior's remains. Just as Bird in Ground had begun to teach him winters before—that great circle of life and death, then life again.

Of a sudden he remembered the second Indian, looking over to the grass and brush where he had left the wounded Indian. Hurrying back into the saddle, Titus brought the horse and Hannah around, moving them slowly across the soggy streambank as he leaned off the side, watching the ground and buckbrush for sign. In a matter of yards it became plain that the warrior had begun to crawl north, something pulling him on, something driving him out of the valley.

Maybe he spent the whole night crawling. Then again, maybe no farther than he could force himself to go with that broken leg while it grew slap-dark and the night sky began to clot with rain clouds. The farther Bass went, following the trampled grassy path, the more he marveled at the warrior's stamina.

Scratch saw him ahead at the same moment the Arapaho heard the horses or felt their hooves on the ground—turning his head suddenly and peering behind him at the approaching white man. For but a moment the eyes showed fear . . . then slowly they narrowed into slits through which nothing but hate could show.

Reining up, Bass sat in the saddle for several minutes, looking this way and that from time to time, his eyes always returning to the wounded man, who had refused to budge any farther. Scratch wasn't sure, but he thought he could hear the warrior's raspy breathing in the midst of that rain battering his hat, splatting on the nearby willow leaves.

Finally he dropped to the ground, slowly moving back toward Hannah, always keeping his eyes on the Arapaho now. Reaching the mule's side, Scratch quickly laid the rifle within the cradle of her packsaddle and made sure the oiled leather sock was secured over the lock's hammer, frizzen, and pan. Patting the animal on her rump, he circled her flank and stepped toward the Indian.

By the time Scratch reached the other side of the mule, the Arapaho was flopping back onto his belly, attempting to crawl away, clawing futilely at the wet grass, his fingers digging desperately into the muddy soil. But when the trapper drew close, the Indian gave up and slowly rolled onto his back. Pain fleetingly crossed his eyes again as he prepared to meet his attacker. Then the look of unmitigated hate returned as Bass set a moccasin on one of the warrior's brown arms.

Kneeling, Titus took hold of the man's other arm and flung it out to the side of his body—then pressed his other moccasin on it. As he slowly settled onto his haunches, he firmly had the warrior pinned to the soggy ground. But even as Scratch dragged the skinning knife from the back of his belt, the Arapaho did not resist, did not struggle, did not move in the least. Instead he only stared, transfixed on the white man's hand as it shifted the knife into position.

Planting the tip of the blade high upon the man's right breast, Bass slowly dragged it down in a straight line until he reached the last rib, just above muscles banding the taut solar plexus. Again he pierced the skin up high on the chest, right next to that first bloody laceration, and crudely dragged the knife downward again, widening the superficial wound. As he began to carve a third stripe of crimson, Scratch watched the warrior's eyes, watched how the lids fluttered as the man fought to ignore the pain, doing his level best to show the white man how he refused to exhibit any weakness.

With five long vertical cuts that together formed a bloody wound more than an inch wide, now Titus punctured the brown skin out near the hollow of the man's right shoulder. Here for the first time he noticed how the brown flesh was goose-bumped with the soggy chill. After suffering through a night without the blanket that had been tied behind his simple snare saddle, after enduring this cold soaking—Bass felt a begrudging admiration for this Arapaho he pinned to the wet earth, a man who did not struggle as the white trapper began to drag the skinning knife vertically across his right breast . . . putting a top on the huge letter *T*. Four more times he scraped that blade across the brown flesh, opening the skin, moving glistening metal through oozing blood until he was satisfied with his work.

Then he began to mark this enemy with his second letter. Down the left breast he dragged the blade in a wide gash, making it as long as he had the *T*, this new incision opened right beside the breastbone. After it too had been widened four more times, Scratch added two crude semicircles to that vertical line, forming a huge *B*.

He finished by picking up a handful of the warrior's hair in his left palm, splaying it out between his fingers a moment as he watched the Indian's eyes move toward that hand.

"No," Scratch said, not much above a whisper. "I ain't gonna scalp you, nigger. Save that for someone else to do. For 'nother time."

Instead, Bass slowly dragged one side of the bloody knife blade across that clump of hair, then flipped the knife over to wipe off the other side on the hair. He placed the weapon back in its sheath.

"Figger I marked you 'nough awready," he said to the Indian. "Them's my letters."

Taking his right index finger, Titus scraped his fingernail down the bloody cuts to retrace both letters, watching the warrior grimace as Bass opened up the wide lacerations and got them to oozing all the more.

"Want you to remember me, nigger. Want you to remember what you saw me do to your friend yesterday. I ain't gonna make sign for you like I done yesterday when I told you that nigger scalped me. Want you go back to your people and tell 'em what happened here. Go back and show 'em my letters I put on you."

He wiped off the bloody fingertip in the warrior's hair and stood, finding his knees had stiffened in the time he had been squatting over his enemy. Bass stepped off the warrior's arms.

"That's gotta be some big medicine to your kind. You come crawling back to your people . . . telling 'em the story how I killed and cut up the man what took my hair. He your brother? Your friend?"

After Titus waited a moment, staring down at the Indian's face, studying it for some betrayal, he sighed.

"It's good you hate me now. Hate me for what I done to your friend. Hate's good and clean . . . much better feeling than someone what just don't give a shit. I understand hate lot better'n I can understand a man what ain't got a heart big enough to feel big feelings. I figger a man what don't hate big ain't the sort what feels anything in a big way."

Slowly dropping to one knee beside the warrior's shoulder, Bass pushed an unruly sprig of his own hair out of his eyes.

"I had folks what took from me. It hurt so bad I wanted to hate some-one, just one someone for it. But . . . I didn't know who to hate, so it ate at me inside. Maybeso it still does."

Holding his fingertip just above the wounds, he quickly traced the letters again.

"So you know that's me."

Then he tapped the index finger against his own chest. And quickly retraced the letters again before tapping the finger against his own blanket capote once more to emphasize.

"That's my letters. That's *me*. Want you tell 'em *I* killed the nigger took my hair. And I marked his friend with my letters. I could kill you, kill you for trying to kill me. But . . . I figger this gotta be bigger medicine."

He stood again.

"G'won now, nigger. And remember what happened here. Remember who marked his letters on you . . . 'cause I want you to hate me. Want you to hate me bad as I been hating that nigger what stole my hair."

Bass turned and started away, then stopped and looked back at the man sprawled on the ground, unmoving.

"Can you hate me bad as I been hating your friend? Maybeso that's worse'n me killing you right off. Letting the hate eat you up the way it's been eating at me."

Then he smiled crookedly at the warrior. "I'm gonna wear that nigger's hair for my own now. And I carved my hate into you. So I don't figger I got no more hate to eat me up now. Leastways, any hate for the one what stole my hair. That hate's all gone now."

Scratch turned away and dragged the rifle off Hannah's packsaddle, then stuffed a wet moccasin into a stirrup and rose to the wet saddle. Bringing the horse around, he led the mule down to the creek and crossed the water, its surface dippled with huge drops the size of tobacco wads.

The hate was finally gone.

Dragging the chill air deep into his lungs, Bass suddenly sensed how light he felt.

So light he just might float right up through that jagged fracture forming in the clouds way out yonder in the sky. Right up through that crack in the heavens where the sun's first rays were streaming through.

Summer had a way of suddenly appearing there at your shoulder one day.

The long spring had actually started with the last heavy snows of winter as the land renewed itself, then drifted past the soaking rains come to bless this high, parched land, and finally gave way to the here-and-gone-again thunderstorms that formed along the western horizon nearly every afternoon.

Only a matter of weeks after Scratch put the Arapaho warriors behind him, summer reached the high country, and with its arrival came the time to begin their march southeast from the Bayou Salade. Following what Hatcher explained was the southern fork of the great Platte River, they turned north-east at the far end of the Puma Mountains, staying with the river canyon as it tumbled toward the far western edge of the great plains.

There were days when they stuffed their bellies with elk, mule deer, and antelope. At other times they feasted on migrating duck and geese, or scared up an occasional fantailed, redwattled turkey roosting in the low branches of the leafy trees blooming along the Platte's meandering course.

At the emerald foot of the front range they left the gurgling river behind as it meandered onto the plains while they hugged the base of the mountains in a course that led them due north. After more than two hundred miles, some eight long summer days of march, Hatcher's band struck the North

Platte, swam the animals over to the north bank, then turned their noses to the northwest.

"I figger we come almost half the way," Jack declared that evening as they went into camp beside the North Platte. "Maybeso 'nother ten days is what it'll take us to get where they told us Sublette's gonna hold ronnyvoo."

They crossed better than 230 more miles, another eleven hot days of travel across the broken wastes—trudging up the North Platte to reach the mouth of the Sweetwater, climbing that river north by east toward the base of the Wind River Mountains, passing timeless monuments formed aeons before in a glacial age: the incredible hump-backed shape of Turtle Rock, then on to Split Rock as the high ground, buttes, ridges, and low mountain ranges continued to rise on either side of them. Where the Sweetwater angled off toward the southwest to begin its gradual climb toward the Southern Pass, the seven sunbaked, hardpan wayfarers crossed to the north bank of the stream and pressed on into the verdant foothills of the Wind River range. One after another of the tiny freshets rushed together out of the grassy meadows in sparkling braids to form narrow creeks that tumbled east toward the widening streams until they reached that low divide above the Popo Agie, or Prairie Chicken, of the Crow.

In the broad valley below him, Bass spotted the narrow wisps of smoke rising from the leafy cottonwood canopies, eventually smeared and smudged by the cool breezes drifting down from those high places above them where thick mantles of snow still remained despite the advance of the seasons.

He had figured there would be more camps.

"Ain't many of 'em here 'bouts," Titus grumped.

"Not yet, there ain't," Caleb Wood replied.

"Don't look to be no trader's tents," Hatcher complained. "We beat Sublette in to ronnyvoo."

Solomon declared, "Damn sight better'n getting here after all the whiskey's been traded off!"

Beyond the creek, on the far side of the tall green mushroom of trees, stood some two dozen browned hide lodges, their blackened smoke flaps pointed toward the east.

"Sho'nies?" Rufus asked.

"This here be their country," Hatcher said. "Though I figgered there'd be more of 'em."

Bass said, "Maybeso it's early for them too."

"Let's camp!" Isaac Simms roared.

Now, after all those weeks—the hot, dusty leagues—that curling blue ribbon of the Popo Agie beckoned them across those last two miles, down into the grassy bottom where the stalks rubbed a horse's belly, brushed a man's stirrups as the trappers fanned out in a wide front to make their presence known as white men upon nearing the camp. Again at last to see faces old and new, trapper and trader alike after so many months with only the earthy hues of Spanish skin or the coppery sheen of Indian flesh, both friend and foe alike . . . not to mention how they had tired of the sameness to one another's drab, familiar faces.

"Ho, the camp!" Jack was the first to bellow as they drew close, attracting the attention of those relaxing back in the shade of the towering cottonwoods.

From up and down a short stretch of the river, more than twenty-five men appeared from the tall willows and brush, stepping into the brilliant sunshine of that midafternoon, the land grown so hot that shimmering fingers of heat wavered above the valley's wide meadows. They shaded their eyes with flat hands or squinted up beneath the brims of their weathered hats to watch the strangers approach.

"Where from, fellers?" a large man prodded the riders.

Caleb Wood dragged his big hat from his head and smacked it across his dusty thigh, stirring an eruption that drifted off on the warm breeze. "Wintered down to the greaser country in Taos. Come up by way of Bayou Salade for spring trapping."

"Mexico, you say?"

And a second man in the crowd asked, "Did I hear 'em say they rode up from Mexico?"

Inquired another of those moving up on foot, "Are the plew prime down there?"

" 'Bout as sleek as I ever see'd 'em," Jack replied as his group came to a halt near the trees and the others crowded close to the horsemen.

A man came up to stand below Hatcher. "First thort you mought'n be some of Davy Jackson's outfit."

"He ain't working to the south last season, is he?" Jack replied.

"No," the man declared, "but some us figgered he was sending fellers over from the Pilot Knobs with his catch, like him and Sublette planned he would."

Isaac asked, "What's the price o' beaver this summer?"

"Sublette ain't come in yet," the first man answered. " 'Spect him any day now."

"Who you boys?" Solomon inquired.

A tall, ruggedly handsome figure of a man Bass recognized had worked his way through the gaggle of greeters, scratching at a bearded cheek. He held up his hand to Hatcher, and with a distinct Scottish burr he announced, "I'm booshway of this brigade. Name's Robert Campbell. We're down from Crow country up on the Powder."

"Crow country, eh?"

"But the Blackfeet were devils this year," Campbell explained. "Lost four of my men to the bastards at the Bad Pass in the Bighorns." They finished shaking and he dropped his hand. "Did I hear right that you're not from Davy Jackson's bunch?"

"On our own hook," Jack stated. "Hatcher's my name."

Another man declared, "Heard of you afore. Welcome. Drop your leg and let's camp!"

"What's your name, mister?" Caleb asked as he leaped to the ground and presented the stranger his hand.

"Jacob Slaughter."

Campbell stepped over, waving his arm toward the trees. "C'mon, then—any man's always welcome in Robert Campbell's camp!"

"Yonder looks good for us," Jack explained, pointing upstream. "We'll picket the horses, then mosey down for supper."

That evening the company trappers hosted Hatcher's outfit. Over the flames broiled juicy quarters of elk and antelope, as well as two bighorn sheep that hunters had brought down to camp earlier in the day.

"Ain't never had me no sheep afore," Scratch told the man who served up a slab of the red meat thicker than two of his fingers. He stuffed the end of the sliver in his mouth and sliced off a healthy bite, finding the texture and sweet taste of the meat entirely pleasant.

The company man settled on his haunches right at Bass's knee. "And I ain't never knowed no one gone to Mexico afore. Heard tell the food's every bit as hot as the sun can boil a man's brains there. Any of that true?"

"A feller can get hisself a pepper belly, that's for sartin," Isaac piped up on the far side of Titus.

"Forget the goddamned food!" A second of Campbell's men squatted near them. "The women—tell me 'bout them."

"Nawww," Scratch said, shaking his head. "You don't want us to go and tell you 'bout them Mexican women."

"Hell if I don't!" he roared in mock wounding.

"We been dry since we come in to ronnyvoo," explained that first of the company trappers who pointed across the stream. "Them Snakes over there ain't bringing out their wimmens for none of us."

"Course they ain't," grumbled the second man. "Leastways not till Sublette gets here with shinies and foofaraw what can make any Injun woman plop on her back and open her legs for an American!"

"So go right ahead and tell us 'bout them greaser gals!" a third man exclaimed as he strode up, grease dripping from his lower lip into his chin whiskers.

"Why, now . . . they ain't like no white gals I ever poked," Bass said, trying his best to emulate that knowledgeable tone of the backwoods school-teachers he had suffered under for so many years. "Not like no Injun women neither. My, my—"

"That's a crock of shit!" Wood blurted out. "And this nigger's full of it up to the bung!"

Bass whirled on him, growling around a chunk of bighorn sheep, "Careful who you say is full of shit, Caleb!"

"This here pilgrim ain't never bedded down no Mex gals but one," Wood continued. "Nary but that one."

"It ain't cause I didn't wanna—"

"Must'a took a shine to her since you humped just her all winter long!" Caleb interrupted.

Scratch shrugged, explaining, "She was a good whore. Good 'nough to last me the winter."

"You had a Mex whore?" asked one of the company men.

"Mama Louisa's fine Taos whores," Caleb declared. "I been through 'em all—forwards and backwards, boys. I can tell you anything you wanna know 'bout them greaser womens."

Another company man lunged in anxiously. "They any good?"

"Good? You ask me if them bang-tails is good?" Wood replied. "Just how good a willing woman gotta be when a man's been 'thout for nigh onto half a year?"

They were attracting more of Campbell's trappers as Caleb warmed to his task before this attentive audience.

"They really good, eh?"

"Good ain't the word for it," Caleb declared matter-of-factly. "Better'n any red gal, twice't as good as any white whore I poked."

One man licked his lips unconsciously; another dragged the back of his forearm across his mouth, eyes wide, glistening in primal stimulation.

"G'won, Caleb," Hatcher said as he walked up, a curved and meaty rib in hand. "Tell 'em how good them greaser women are for American men."

Wood nodded, leaned forward, and said in a low, dramatic voice, "You boys know them Mex folks cook most of their food with hot peppers in it?"

He waited until most of his audience bobbed their heads in eager agreement.

"Well, now—I s'pose it's them peppers."

"What 'bout them peppers?" demanded a Campbell man.

Caleb looked at him straight-faced. "I figger the peppers they eat just makes them Mex gals naturally eager to jump on a likely American. Makes 'em just 'bout as hot to jump on your wiping stick as them peppers they eat in their food!"

Some of the men whooped in glee; others stomped a moccasin on the ground or slapped a thigh, while a few whistled with lurid approval. This was just what they wanted to hear. More fantasy to feed their womanless dreams as brigades of men roamed this far and lonely mountain west. Fanciful dreams to warm a man on cold winter nights, trapped in the fastness of the wilderness, far from Indian camp or white settlement or Mexican village. Sometimes dreams might just be enough for a man to make it through to spring, on till rendezvous.

If he made it, then a man had cause to celebrate—what with waiting and yearning all year long to find himself a gal who would fulfill even the slightest of his inflated fantasies . . . for after a long autumn, a terrible winter, and an endless spring of fevered, womanless dreaming, it damn well didn't take much at all for most any woman to fill those wildest of cravings.

As Bass leaned back against a pack of company beaver, Campbell's men leaned in attentively, totally captivated by Caleb Wood's exploits with one Mexican maiden after another: tales of bared shoulders, filmy camisoles allowed to hang so loose, they barely covered the rounded tops of a woman's breasts, how those Taos females shamelessly flaunted their ankles and calves beneath a swirl of short skirts, their cheeks reddened with a bright-red berry juice, clenching corn-husk cigarillos between their full and provocative lips.

How brazen were those brown women, he explained, women who called out to the Americans whenever they passed through the town's narrow byways. Women actually beckoned a man to join them for a drink, a meal, and often more . . . for some modest payment. Women eager, perhaps, to find and catch themselves a likely American husband rather than some poor, earth-grubbing *pelado*.

"Ain't none of 'em got any money?" asked one of the company men.

"Most don't have much at all," Hatcher explained as he came up and sat. "Only a few got anything to call their own. Their kind looks down their noses at the rest of their people, not just Americans."

A Campbell man turned to Caleb. "You ever poke one of them rich gals?"

"Nary a one what was real rich," Wood admitted with a wag of his head. "They wear too damn many clothes—just like our own gals back in the States. Almost like they don't wanna show no skin on their bodies. So them poor gals is the only ones ever showed me a good time . . . they're the kind of woman what gonna show you ever'thing on their bodies!"

As Bass dragged out his tiny pipe, then retrieved a small chunk of tobacco carrot from his belt pouch, he listened to Caleb and Jack go on to tell the company men about the wonders of Mexican women. Between a finger and thumb he crumpled a bit of the dried leaf over the bowl, tamped it in with a fingertip, then crumpled in some more until he had the pipe filled. After retrieving a twig from the fire, he lit the tobacco, inhaled, then sighed, ruminating again on Kinkead and Rowland.

John must surely have made it back to Taos by now, he decided. Likely Rowland went straight for Matthew's place—stay there for a time till he sorted out what he figured to do. Till he figured out how he could get himself over the miseries for his Maria.

As much as he had made peace with himself for leaving those two women in the past, Scratch wondered how a man ever came to feel so much for a woman that he found himself grieving and lost without her. Then he remembered sensing more than a twinge of that sort of strong, undeniable feeling for Marissa Guthrie. Admitting that it was possible to feel that way about a woman . . . because it was just that sort of feeling that compelled him to leave Marissa before that feeling grew into an unmovable thing, before his need for her outweighed his hunger to see what lay beyond the next valley.

More than likely it was possible for a man to care about a woman and stay to one place with her as much as a man could be lured to see what lay over the next hill, what beckoned from the far valley, what adventure awaited him far away from the bothersome nattering of a woman who rarely gave her man room to breathe, room to be.

Poor Rowland, having give up so much for that woman . . . only to have what little he had left of a sudden took from him by the Comanche in those mountains above Taos.

How sad it made Titus to remember the melancholy of that dreary, rainy morning when John parted company from old friends.

Rowland had taken the small folder of waxed paper from the crude pocket sewn inside his blanket capote, thinking on it a moment before handing the folder to Rufus Graham.

"You keep this now," he told Graham. "You boys get stopped here or there by some Mex *soldados,* just show 'em your paper here, Juan."

"Juan?" Rufus echoed.

"That's the name on that paper what says you can trap in Mex waters," Rowland instructed. "I don't need it . . . leastwise not for some time to come."

"So that's your license?" Elbridge asked, tapping a finger against the corner of the waxed envelope Rufus held.

"To the greasers my name is Juan Roles." He repeated what they all knew. "Now you carry the license for the rest of these here men, Rufus."

"I'll hang on to it till you need it again," Graham replied. "You just ask for it back."

With a shrug John continued, "They give it to me 'cause I got married to Maria. Padre Martinez baptized me in their church and married me the same day to her. That's why they give me a license last winter after we come back . . . come back from fighting them Comanche and why they ain't gonna ever give the rest of you a license."

"No, Johnny," Hatcher said, stepping up to tap his finger against the envelope, the huge dollop of an emblazoned wax seal growing brittle and cracking. "They give ye that license 'cause you was a brave man."

Rowland shook his head. "I become a Mexican citizen, so they give it to me—"

"They didn't give it to ye when you was baptized, did they?" Jack demanded.

"N-no."

"And they didn't give it to ye when you got married neither, did they?"

"No," Rowland admitted.

"You was a brave man, going with the rest of us to get them women and children back from the Comanch'," Hatcher explained. "They give ye that license for being a brave man with the rest of us."

"You think they knowed the rest of us was going to use Johnny's license?" Elbridge Gray had asked.

"Damn right they did," Jack said. "And I don't figger it made 'em no never-mind. It was the governor's way of saying to us—saying to Johnny—he was grateful for what we done to bring his family back to him."

Throughout the winter there had been other expressions of gratitude for the men who had risked their own lives to rescue those who meant nothing to them, to rescue women and children who weren't even American. The tax assessor had turned his head and looked the other way, or had conveniently been busy or out of Taos when William Workman rode into town to trade. For gringo trappers who expected to trade off their furs in barter for supplies from Mexican merchants, the local officials normally levied a tax of 60 percent on every beaver plew brought into Mexican territory. After all, to the government's way of thinking, there was simply no way an American could prove that his packs of fur weren't Mexican beaver.

But throughout that long winter in Taos, they hadn't suffered any hefty governmental tax. And by disposing of the beaver a few pelts at a time, Workman was able to see that Hatcher's men were resupplied by the time they prepared to set off north for another trapping season. In fact, the $3.50-per-pound price the whiskey maker was able to wrangle in pesos for their plews in Taos actually turned out to be a half dollar higher in American money than they figured they would have made packing those furs to rendezvous where they would trade them off to Billy Sublette. That meant Hatcher's men earned at least five dollars per hide in Taos.

Perhaps for no better reason than because John Rowland's Mexican wife had been slaughtered with a Comanche lance.

Scratch stared off through the trees, gazing across the stream at that cluster of buffalo-hide lodges, watching the fires kindled out in front of each one, studying the shadowy figures passing this way and that in the Shoshone village.

As Campbell's men carried on with Hatcher and Wood, Titus suddenly interrupted them to ask, "Any you fellas know what band that be over yonder?"

Some of the company men turned to look at him in surprise, wagging their heads.

Jack glanced across the creek, then turned back to ask, "Ye don't figger it might be Goat Horn's bunch, do ye?"

"Nawww. That camp ain't near big enough," Bass replied. "But maybeso that bunch knows where Goat Horn's people are . . . knows if they're coming in for ronnyvoo too."

Hatcher asked, "Ye fixing to see about it?"

"Morning be soon enough, I s'pose."

This here was Snake country, no doubt of that.

But that wasn't Goat Horn's band.

Two of the headmen in the village across the creek did know of the chief and his oldest son, Slays in the Night. But in sign and little of their spoken tongue, the two explained they did not know where Goat Horn's band was that spring, nor if he would bring his people to join in the white man's rendezvous.

Last night had been a restless one for Scratch. First he had grown too warm, kicking off his blanket and robe. Later he became chilled. Then warm again as he tossed and fought through dreams and remembrances of Pretty Water.

A great, gray disappointment settled upon him when he discovered there would be no familiar faces, no joyful reunion with Slays in the Night, nor with the old, blind shaman, Porcupine Brush, nor a chance to gaze upon, perhaps to embrace, that woman who had cared for him as his shoulder had knitted, as he had nursed his rage in losing his topknot to the Arapaho. Not a young woman, but he had found Pretty Water all the more desirable because of her experience in the robes. She knew what it took to satisfy herself, and more so, she practiced what it took to satisfy a man.

He had crossed the Popo Agie on foot that summer morning as soon as it was light enough for a few of the Shoshone women to emerge from their lodges and go about kindling fires, preparing breakfasts, seeing to infants bundled tightly in their cradleboards.

Only two of Campbell's men stirred when a dejected Bass recrossed the stream and slogged onto the east bank. Their coffee was just beginning to boil as Scratch walked up.

One of the men pulled the kettle to the edge of the flames to slow its roiling. "Coffee?"

"Never passed up a cup," he admitted with a sigh, settling to the ground by the fire. "Either of you fellers know a man named Potts?"

"Daniel?" replied the first.

"That's him."

Asked the second, "How you know Potts?"

"Come to meet him my first ronnyvoo out here, back to twenty-six."

The coffee maker tossed Bass a tin cup. "Potts give up on pulling the tiger's tail. He's gone back east."

"East." Bass said it as if that land were a far and foreign place now after these few short years.

"Daniel figgered he ought'n made his fortune out here already," the second man explained. Then he peered into the smoky fire. "Ain't none of us gonna make ourselves rich men."

The coffee maker wagged his head. " 'Cept maybe the booshways like Smith or Jackson—like Sublette his own self."

"Diah Smith's gone under," the second man claimed. "Ain't no man see'd him since he took his men to Californy two y'ar ago now."

"Davy Jackson ain't the kind what'll make hisself a rich man neither," the first man declared. "He'll allays be a working man like the rest of us."

"But that Sublette—now, he's gonna make hisself a tidy nest egg afore long," the second trapper said as he began to carve thick slices of red meat from the rear haunch of an elk.

"Plain to see that some men come out here to this high land for the money," Scratch commented as he brought his coffee tin to his lips. "Dame Fate does end up smiling on some of them what come for the money."

"Like Billy Sublette," the coffee maker replied.

But the meat carver commented, "Then there's most what your Dame Fate might as well spit on—like poor Daniel Potts."

"I met a couple other fellas that same ronnyvoo," Bass explained, suddenly remembering faces. "I ain't seen either of 'em here. One was named Bridger."

"Jim Bridger?" the first trapper asked. "Bridger did go back east with Sublette last year—see his ol' home and family some . . . but he ain't give up on the mountains."

"He's got him some family he wanted to see back to Missoura," the other man explained.

And the coffee maker said, "Likely Jim'll be back out with Sublette's pack train when it shows up in the next few days."

For a while Titus watched the flames in the fire pit as more men began to stir in their blankets, some rising to move out to the bushes, where they relieved themselves. A few came over to join the three at the fire, while most simply returned to their bedrolls and drifted back to sleep as the chilly air brightened with the sun's first appearance in the east.

"Knowed me 'nother fella—his mama was a slave and his daddy was a Virginia tobacco grower," Bass began to explain. "They come out to Missouri when he was a tad. That feller had him his mama's dark skin and curly hair—"

"And he wore it long and fancy," interrupted one of the new arrivals to the fire as he came to a halt. "Fact be, all his clothes was damned fancy, wasn't they?"

He turned to the stranger. "You know him?"

"Sure sounds like Beckwith. He was half-Negra, if'n that's what you're trying to get at with the talk of his mama being a slave."

"Jim Beckwith, that's him," Titus replied, remembering all the more now. "So what become of him? He off north with Davy Jackson's outfit?"

The meat carver shrugged. "No. Beckwith signed off the books with Campbell middle of the winter last. Decided to go out on his own and live with the Crow."

Scratch asked, "Why'd a man like him wanna go off and live with them Crow 'stead of staying with his own kind?"

The new arrival looked at Bass. "Beckwith said he figgered them Crow was closer to his own kind than we white folk was."

"Seems that last fall some of us boys played a joke on him, figgering to have us a hoot making them Crow think Beckwith was one of their own what was stole from 'em when he was just a child," said the coffee maker.

The meat carver chimed up, "Don't you know Beckwith even had him a mole on his eyelid, just like a li'l child what was stole from them Crow years back! So when we told them Crow that Beckwith was their own kin, why—one of them ol' squaws spotted that mole!"

"And she was dead sartin Beckwith was her long, lost boy come back home to roost once more!" roared the coffee maker, slapping his knee.

"Beckwith figgers to be something big on a stick with them Crow now," explained the new arrival at the fire.

The round-faced meat carver said, "Could be you 'member some others, eh?"

Staring into the smoky fire, Titus wagged his head and grumbled, " 'Cept for them friends of mine what ride with Jack Hatcher, ain't a man around I know anymore."

FIFTEEN

Near everyone he knew was gone. Hatcher had said that's what become of most of them what ventured out to the far mountains.

Some time ago Jack declared theirs was the sort of man who discovered they wasn't cut out for what it took to make a life for themselves out here . . . so they skeedaddled back east. If they were lucky enough to keep their hair until they fled, like Daniel Potts. Bass figured there was a lot of men who had no business being out here, men who hadn't been fortunate enough to get back east before their luck ran out.

Even Jim Beckwith—giving up on the mountain trade and throwing in with them Crow. Much as he liked Bird in Ground's people, Titus couldn't imagine himself staying on as a full-time member of the tribe. It was getting to be all he could do to stay on as a member of Jack Hatcher's little brigade of free trappers.

Maybeso he just wasn't the joiner sort. Perhaps by the time winter arrived, he might decide to go his own way, see how his stick would float all on his lonesome. Maybe he'd be able to rendezvous with Mad Jack's men every summer. Leastwise, it sure didn't seem none of them were the kind to give up and skedaddle back east like Potts, not the sort to turn over and go to the blanket like Beckwith done. Hatcher's bunch was cast-iron, double-riveted beaver trapper, all the way to the muzzle, by damned.

But he suddenly remembered Kinkead and Rowland. Both of them Hatcher's men, both of them the hardy, hang-on sort who wouldn't turn around for the backtrail. Yet they had given up the mountains in exchange for a life among the inhabitants of a foreign people in a faraway Mexican village.

For every man who ventured west beyond the Missouri, perhaps there did indeed come a time when that man had filled his life with all the mountain peaks and ribbons of valleys, with all the sparkling beaver streams and snowy, untrammeled meadows that his soul could contain. Perhaps he realized his kind needed something more that only the settlements could offer: something that only women and crowds, buildings, clutter, and closed-in skies could give him.

But damn the settlements while there was still beaver in the mountains!

Damn them white women and their whiny ways, getting a man all bumfoozled the way they could so a man didn't know fat cow from poor bull and damn well didn't even care a cuss!

And damn them all them tight places where folks back east chose to live, crawling all over themselves with a racket of wagons and carriages and surreys too, shoving down narrow streets, squeezed in by buildings so tall a man was hard-pressed to see all the sky a man was made to see.

Not to mention the smell of such places where folks lingered far too long!

Not that he wasn't glad most folks were content to live that way, satisfied to stay back east in their settlements and towns and big, sprawling cities. Better for them that they kept themselves back there beyond the rolling prairies where the buffalo ruled. And damn well better for men like Titus Bass that the crowds were so content to huddle together back east rather than come swarming out here.

Bringing along their white women with those harsh stares they shot a man just about every time he got set to have himself some fun. On their coattails came the constables and preachers with their Bibles too. Raising jails and schools and churches right alongside one another . . . till the crush of them drove near all the joy right on out of life.

Always seemed that in the wake of wagons came white women. Where a wheel could roll, some high-necked, glary-eyed white gal was bound to show up before a man really had himself a chance to snort and prance. Wagons and white women—why, they'd be the ruin of the West!

This wasn't no land fit for the likes of them, he thought. This was a man's country, a man's country fit only for a certain type of man, at that. Now that land back east, all closed in with little bumps of hills and all the crush of trees . . . now, that was a woman's country if ever there was one.

But out here where the hills had grown on up into huge, hoary chains of impenetrable granite and ice and mazelike passes . . . this was a man's country, by the everlasting! Back there the country was all closed in, and a person damn well couldn't see very far: just the way things ought to be in a land where little minds reigned.

Not here! Where only a man with a heart big enough, with a soul mighty enough, could expect to take it all in. From horizon, to horizon, to horizon and back again under an endless blue dome.

He could only hope that Bridger would be back. Likely Jim was the sort to stay on out here, no matter what. Maybe a man like him had to return east just once in his life after he had eventually discovered where his heart was truly at peace. To return east so he could put things to rest with his family, to settle with all that was so he could get on with living all that was to be. Perhaps Bridger had him just that sort of healing and burying the past to accomplish . . . and then he'd be back.

Titus hoped, figuring that the young fella was the sort who could no longer live back in the States. After all, it seemed Bridger was the sort to take life on its own terms, the sort to take each day by the horns, the kind who could build himself a bullboat, wave fare-thee-wells to his friends, and take off floating downstream into an adventure and a salty lake of such great proportions that few believed him when he finally returned with his tall tales of a land never before touched by the eyes of a white man.

Bridger would be back, he told himself. While others ran from the danger and the risk and the challenge, men like Jim Bridger and Titus Bass would run to embrace the danger and the risk and the challenge each new day brought them with the rising of the sun.

Of a sudden in his reverie there intruded a clamor of activity as company men burst into the groves where they had tied up their blanket and willow-branch bowers, scooping up their saddles and bridles with an excited chatter.

"What's going on?" Titus asked as he got to his feet at the shady base of the cottonwood where he had been watching the lazy passing of the Popo Agie.

All around him more and more of the company men were hurrying to saddle up their mounts, the first beginning to sweep up their loaded rifles and pistols.

Should he seize his weapons?

Someone had to answer him—"Injuns?"

But before it appeared any of them had heard him, Campbell's men were whooping at the top of their lungs, gushing in unbounded joy.

Finally one of the brigade stopped long enough to blurt out to the free trapper, "God-bless-it—the trader's come in!"

"Trader?"

Trembling with excitement, the skinny whiffet of a man whirled and shot out his arm toward the red-rimmed southeastern hills that framed this verdant, emerald valley. "Sublette's train comin' in!"

Squinting into the resplendent midsummer's light, Bass stepped to the edge of the shade and stared expectantly at the upvault of those crimson bluffs where a long file of horsemen and burdened mules were fanning out across the skyline, backlit by the late-morning sun. More than fifty riders were up there now, all gawking down at the valley below them. And there had to be at least three times that many pack animals, every last one of them reluctant to hurry before their eager masters. Despite the distance, Scratch could almost hear the newcomers barking and bawling at their contrary charges.

A gray mushroom puffed from the end of a distant rifle, a tiny blot against the summer's blue—a heart's throb later came the low boom of that rifle held aloft by the pack train's leader.

Good thing, too, that was. Out here in this country a man never rode up silently on a camp. Prudence dictated that you always announce your arrival, and even discharge your weapon to show peaceful intentions. That gunshot only confirmed Bass's fervent hope.

"Trader!" he screeched wildly as his feet lurched into motion beneath him, almost as if they were in that much more of a hurry to be off announcing the news to Hatcher's outfit.

But Jack and the rest were already caught up in a flurry of saddling and mounting by the time he reached them.

"Comin' to find you!" Elbridge Gray shouted as Bass sprinted up through the trees. Red-faced, the big-nosed trapper tugged on the reins to his own horse with one hand, which also held his rifle, while in the other he gripped the reins to Scratch's saddle mount.

"Thankee, Elbridge!"

Gray turned and vaulted into the saddle, kicked his toes into the huge cottonwood stirrups. "Get high behind, Scratch! That's Billy Sublette and he's bringing likker to ronnyvoo!"

"Likker, Titus Bass!" echoed Hatcher himself as he goaded his horse past them at a trot, then kicked it in the ribs the instant he reached the edge of the meadow. The pony was off like a shot.

By the time Bass swept the rifle from his blanket and stuffed a foot into a stirrup, swinging his horse around, the rest were already on their way across the grassy flat, a wide fan of company trappers and free men gradually streaming together toward that grassy point where the first of those arriving riders were making their way down a gentle slope slanting off those far red hills.

Those dark horses and indistinguishable riders were no more than five hundred yards away now as the last of the pack animals lumbered off the top of the ridge, spilling toward the valley.

"Likker!" Scratch cried as he kicked the horse into a gallop.

"Likker!" he bellowed when he caught up with the rest of Hatcher's bunch.

"Likker!" was the cry echoed by another two dozen free trappers and nearly the whole of the Campbell brigade.

At four hundred yards Titus could recognize how the nervous green-horns were bringing up their weapons, waving rifles in the air, shouting at one another.

"Goddamn pilgrims!" Bass growled as he kicked the horse in the flanks again, urging even more speed from it so he wouldn't be among the last to greet the supply train.

Past three hundred yards the dry-throated riders raced at a full gallop, that wide fan narrowing as the frantic horsemen galloped full tilt, their wide hat brims whipped back by the run, some hats whipped right off their heads, careening back into the belly-high grass.

At Bass's left a trapper was shouting, "Get ready to give 'em a salute!"

Most already had their rifles in the air by the time those in the lead sprinted past 250 yards.

"Give them pork eaters a mountain how-do!" a voice called out some-where in that cluster where Bass found himself as the trappers funneled closer and closer together with every yard.

Horses' nostrils flared as big as their frightened eyes, straining at the bits and hackamores, lunging forward across the uneven ground at a maddening gallop.

At two hundred yards the rider at Bass's elbow shouted, "Whiskey for my whistle!"

That journey to the last hundred yards took no more than a matter of heartbeats. . . . Then he could see their faces.

The pilgrims' eyes and mouths grew as wide and gaping as were the eyes and nostrils of the trappers' horses. And those leaders of that pack train were already standing in the stirrups, shouting something to the first horsemen racing their way. They raised their long rifles into the air and fired: mushroom puffs of smoke immediately followed by the dull echo of a half-dozen scat-tered booms carried off on the summer breeze.

Immediately echoed by a gunfire greeting from a handful of the charg-ing riders . . . then another ten . . . and now two dozen more. Gray smoke hung in tattered shreds just above Scratch's head as he raced on.

The headman coming down off the slope toward them was warwhoop-ing and waving his rifle like a fiend. Suddenly he reined up in a flurry of dust and leaped to the ground, his horse wheeling away in the excitement. Snatch-ing the broad-brimmed felt hat from his head, he started sprinting on foot toward the oncoming riders.

One of those horsemen just ahead of Bass yanked back on his reins, his horse's head twisted to the side as it stiff-legged to a halt and the rider lunged to the ground, nearly spilled, then was up and finding his gait, running those last few steps until he and the leader of the pack train met one another with a violent collision, banging into one another, then dancing round and round as they pounded on each other. As Scratch shot on by, beginning to rein back his own horse, he recognized Robert Campbell as one of the two. Then, as the pair continued their spin, he recognized Bill Sublette—the trapper chief called Cut Face by Washakie's Shoshone, whom Sublette had helped fight against the Blackfoot back to the summer of 1826.

All around him now the free trappers were popping their hands against their open mouths, *whoo-whoo*ing and *hoo-hoo*ing like attacking savages, not slowing in the slightest as they exploded through the ranks of the pack train— bawling mules, rearing horses, and frightened men fresh from the settlements, all of them gone white-faced and gulping at the long-haired, buckskinned, half-naked mountain men wheeling round and round the long train as if they were attacking their quarry.

On all sides more guns went off. Puffs of gray clouds hovered in the hot air, barely dissipating on the gentle breeze as old hands shrieked their war cries and Sublette's greenhorns grumbled and cursed, fighting their frightened, balky mules. More and more of the company men breathlessly slowed their attack, reining up and leaning off their horses to shake hands, calling out their greetings, some even managing to hug a newcomer here or there in the ragged procession.

As he reined about, Bass saw that Campbell and the pack-train leader were remounted and loping on toward the brigade encampment, where a few well-browned lodges bordered a small glade.

By then more than three dozen Indians had splashed across the Popo Agie—warriors, women, and naked brown children, along with half a hundred barking, baying half-wild dogs who weaved between the legs of man and horse alike, adding their voices to the excitement as Campbell and Sublette slid to the ground, the reins to their horses taken by one of the company men who led the animals away.

"By damn, it's Billy Sublette his own self!" Hatcher roared as he reined his horse from a gallop to a walk beside Titus.

"Any man know if he brung likker this year?"

Jack's head bobbed like a young child's on Christmas morning. "Some of them greenhorns say Sublette brung him some likker all the way from the States!"

"Damn if I could ever feel this dry again!" Scratch bellowed.

Hatcher himself dragged a forearm across his lower face. "Let's get these here horses tied off, then get back afore that trader opens up his packs!"

But tapping those whiskey kegs wasn't the first item of business.

As Hatcher's men sprinted back through the trees toward Campbell's lodge and that scattering of bowers tied here and there among the saplings, those shelters made from oiled Russian sheeting or thick Indian trade blankets, the last of the pack train reached the company camp. As the newcomers dismounted, Sublette ordered them off in one direction or another. Back in the trees the unloading of the first mules began, while at three other points to the north, east, and south more divisions were made, particular bundles dropped at each location according to the trader's instructions.

Only then did William Sublette have one of his clerks unlash the two leather trunks from the packsaddle atop a weathered old mule the booshway kept close at hand. With both of those three-strap trunks resting at his feet, the trader knelt to unbuckle the straps across the first chest.

Quickly flinging back the top and reaching inside, Sublette said, "Bob—get that other'n open and we'll give out the mail."

The moment Campbell crouched over the second trunk, the anxious crowd of boisterous men began to shove close.

"Get back! Get back, there!" Sublette growled at his eager employees. "You'll all get mail if'n you got mail comin'!"

"You heard the man!" hollered a young, clean-shaven trapper as he shouldered his way toward the center of the mass. "You damn well waited more'n a year for mail—you niggers can wait a li'l more!"

Damn, if that wasn't Bridger himself!

"Jim!" Bass hollered, lunging toward the younger man known among his brigades as the "little booshway."

He hadn't given up on the mountains!

Bridger turned, his eyes squinting in the bright light, giving measure to the onrushing trapper.

"Titus Bass!" hollered Scratch as he held out his hand and came to a stop. "You 'member me from twenty-six?"

Bridger held out his hand, saying, "Titus Bass. I do recollect meeting you. Twenty-six—was it that long ago?"

"You tol't me all 'bout your float down to the big salt, Jim!"

"Damn, if that wasn't a time to make my bung pucker!" Bridger roared. "Good to see ol' faces here, Titus Bass! Three y'ar now, and you still got your ha'r too!"

"Not all of it," Bass replied, patting the back of his head, sweeping off the blue bandanna and the tanned Arapaho scalp lock without ceremonial preliminaries.

A sudden hush fell over those men in that immediate area, followed quickly by an excited murmur as even more pushed in to have themselves a look at Bass.

For his part, Bridger stood on his toes as Titus bowed and turned his head so his friend could inspect the bare skull. "Man's gotta keep that bone covered, don't he?"

"I do for certain, Jim!"

Sublette began calling out names, his left arm cradling a mass of folded, sealed, and posted letters as well as small wrapped packages, while Campbell unbuckled the last strap securing the top of the second trunk. He threw back the lid and stuffed both hands down into the masses of old newspapers and correspondence from loved ones and family far, far away.

Bridger's fingers brushed the long scalp Bass held. "Injun hair?"

"Arapaho," Scratch answered. "Last spring it happed I run onto the same nigger scalped me two year ago."

Bridger rocked back on his heels, grinning widely. "Damn, but that's got the makin's of a windy tale!"

"Ain't no bald-face to it!" Jack Hatcher cheered as he came up to slap his arm around Bass's shoulder. "Ever' word's the truth!"

"The hell you say," Jim declared. He pointed at Bass's head. "Get that topknot of your'n covered, or you're like to burn your brains."

Holding the scalp on with one hand, Scratch slid the bandanna onto his head, smoothing it back from the forehead. "Out here a man's gotta pertect what little he's got left for brains."

"I better see camp's set up for the train like Billy asked me to do," Bridger said as he began to turn away. "I figger you'll be round for a few days afore pulling out?"

"There's whiskey to guzzle down my gullet, Jim," Bass exclaimed. "I ain't pulling out till Sublette's kegs is empty or I'm gone bust and don't have no more beaver to trade!"

Jim asked, "Where you camped?"

"Yonder," he answered, pointing upstream. "You'll find us there a ways—two, maybe three rifle shots."

"Camped just close enough to get in trouble with Billy Sublette's whiskey!" Hatcher bellowed. "Far 'nough away for us to sleep it off when we do!"

Although Sublette announced he would not be hammering in the bungs to those whiskey kegs until the following morning, there was no dearth of gaiety that evening as twilight broke across the valley of the Popo Agie. Whiskey would be pouring soon enough, they knew, but for now the booshways stored the potent grain alcohol in Campbell's lodge, where a rotation of trusted guards would be stationed throughout the night.

Meanwhile more of the newcomers were assigned the task of picketing the pack animals, some to erect the five large awnings under which Sublette would conduct his business from the shade. A pair of greenhorns assembled a large balance scale beneath the oiled sheeting that was to be Sublette's headquarters, while a few trusted clerks began to unpack the trade goods, checking off every item as it emerged from those canvas and paper and blanket bundles wrapped up back in early spring, back in St. Louis, back in the far, far States of America.

Fires roared and meat roasted, coffee boiled and men laughed, pulling uproarious pranks or puffing unbelievable windies for the newcomers fresh off the prairie who suddenly found themselves here now among these half-wild veterans of the wilderness, those hivernants who had wintered in the fastness of these terrible mountains inhabited by never-before-seen savages and unimaginable beasts. This first night always served as an initiation of sorts—a tradition none too kind but always applied in good humor to those greenhorns struck dumb to suddenly discover themselves in the company of these hard cases who had survived Blackfeet and blizzards, scorching deserts and dry scrapes, men who had outlasted loneliness and deprivation . . . yet were willing still to risk it all again for another roll with Lady Fate's dice.

Here and there in the bright, flickering flames, the few among them who could read each sat with a cluster of those who could not, reciting those undecipherable words written by mothers and fathers, sisters or brothers, or even more moving—soul-wrenching prose and promises written by sweethearts left behind when men abandoned hearth and homes, daring to challenge these mountains. Letters of yearning and words of caring scribbled on small sheets of foolscap, stories from home counties read from yellowed newsprint. Lockets of hair sent west many, many months before, sent beyond the wide Missouri with faith and a prayer that it would reach a beloved son, would make it to a beloved brother, by the hope of some aching heart that it might just find its way to a beau known to be somewhere out west beneath a wide and faraway sky.

Stories and news of the east were dragged from the newcomers, tales of places and rivers and towns left far behind, a long time ago. Some men laughed at themselves and traded jokes on others, while more sat on downed logs and listened with red-rimmed eyes to what was read them of home another world away. Men who sat in abject silence, listening, men who sat remembering those dim-lit faces once more, remembering the black-earthed closeness of those gently rounded hills and hardwood forests, men who thought back to how long it had been, how far they had come since choosing to leave all that had been, since choosing to cast their lot with the few, with these bravest of the brave.

Like men become so crazed, they dared not consider the odds against them. Men torn by not knowing if they ever would return to what was left behind . . . men not able to understand why they didn't really care if they ever did go back.

Night came down on that far valley, the sun hiding its face beyond the Wind River Mountains. Although he had no letters, although he had no loved ones who knew where to write him—Scratch felt that here he was among his chosen brotherhood. Families were no more than a matter of chance. Here he felt himself embraced in the bosom of those who were his family of choice.

Men who expected no more from him than they were willing themselves to give in return.

Songs of old leaped from those strings that Jack Hatcher pressed beneath his dancing fingers, tunes came wheezing and wailing from that squeezebox of a concertina that a weaving and bobbing Elbridge Gray clutched at the end of his outstretched arms.

Into that wide circle of fires' light, pairs of hardened men came. Turning to bow to one another, they readily clasped hands and danced with festive abandon: whirling recklessly—ofttimes spinning one another so robustly they landed in a heap at the very edge of the merry flames, where they guffawed at one another until bounding to their feet, stomping and shimmying some more. While some preferred to imitate the fancy steps learned long ago in polite white company back east, others stomped toe and heel round and round, swooping low and howling in their own earsplitting rendition of the scalp or buffalo or war dance.

And at the border of that open-air dance floor stood those copper-skinned spectators who looked on in unabashed amazement at this unfettered celebration by men who had survived another year in the mountain trade, witnessing this raucous revelry of those who had journeyed west to join that small fraternity of white men come to challenge an unforgiving land. Shoshone males brought their women and children across the creek, here to watch impassively this annual gathering of the white man's own noisy, strutting warrior bands.

A few like Bass turned their gaze upon this young woman or that, wondering just what it would take in the way of foofaraw to talk one of those dark-skinned beauties into the willows, to convince her to join him back into the shadows where a few minutes of fevered coupling might ease this aching woman-hunger he suffered, might quench his parched thirst for a moistened coupling with a woman soft, a woman smooth, a woman as eager as he.

Which of them might he convince that she simply could not live without a clutter of shiny beads in his palm, without a strand of red ribbon, without a tin cup filled with trader's sugar?

Which one of those cherry-eyed squaws would eagerly hike up her short leather dress and let him spend himself inside her before he grew one day older?

The next morning Campbell's trappers had first crack at the treasures excavated from Sublette's packs.

Company men were first when it came to trade goods brought west by the firm of Smith, Jackson, & Sublette.

"The rest of you gonna have to wait till tomorrow," Sublette warned the small knots of free men who had gathered by the trader's awnings. "Might so have to wait long as the day after till we get our company business taken care of."

There weren't all that many free trappers in yet, nowhere near as many men as the combined brigades—considering the number Campbell brought down from the Powder River country when coupled with the fifty-four hands Sublette brought out from St. Louis. Close to a hundred men already.

And no more than two dozen free trappers on the Popo Agie.

So all Bass could do was grumble. Sit in the shade and watch the company men come and go about their company business, come and go with their company kettles filled with Sublette's whiskey.

It was enough to make a saint cuss a blue streak, had there been a saint in that valley of the Popo Agie.

"By damned, they better leave enough wet for our whistles and a good drunk or two outta this ronnyvoo!" Hatcher snarled.

Caleb added, "That trader better leave us enough plunder to see this outfit through 'nother winter."

"Likker!" Jack snapped at Wood. "The rest'll take care of itself. Long as we get some likker."

Most of the other free trappers hung close by the trader's awnings too—watching as Sublette's greenhorn clerks sorted through each company man's hides, graded them into three stacks, then lashed each stack into a bundle they hung from that huge wooden balance arm where another clerk carefully added weights until both sides swung evenly. That tally was entered in a tall leather-bound ledger—then Sublette informed that mountain employee what he had earned for the year. After the trapper had paid off what he owed from the last rendezvous, after he had settled up for any broken traps, lost tack, or busted saddles, after he had paid for a horse run off by the Crow . . . he would find out just how much, or how little, celebration he had in store for himself.

Lowest of the three stations of company men were the camp keepers.

"Mangeurs de lard," Hatcher instructed Bass in the mountain man's hierarchy.

"Parley-voos?"

"Damn right," Jack growled with disdain. "Frenchy pork eaters. Most of 'em, leastwise."

Hatcher went on to explain that this bottom rung had received its name because those camp keepers who had accompanied the earliest expeditions forging up the Missouri River had been French laborers who ate salted sow-belly while the Americans dined on the lean red meat of game hunted on either shore. No better than slavery, Bass figured—forced to perform every dirty, menial task the booshway ordered.

"Company trappers are up from there a big notch," Jack continued. "It's where a man with any pluck at all got him a chance to show he's up to

Green River," referring to that company's name engraved right at the guard of their knife blades, clearly meaning a trapper who made the supreme effort to plunge into any effort clear up to the hilt. "That man's got him a chance to prove he's got the makings of a mountain man."

While company trappers still had to do whatever task the booshway assigned, their reward nonetheless remained the coming season to show their brigade leaders that they could make a profit for the company as well as hanging on to their hair.

And if a man survived, then someone like Campbell or Sublette or Jackson could promote that man to the top rung of "skin trapper." Such a man signed on with the company but with no guarantee of wages. When he moved up from company to skin trapper, a man indebted himself for company equipment at the same time he swore to sell his furs only to the company at what price the company quoted. And if there was anything left over when his accounts were settled, then the skin trapper could more than satisfy his thirst for whiskey, or have enough in trade to buy himself a squaw for a night or two, perhaps enough to purchase himself a wife, who would accompany the brigade wherever it wandered in the coming seasons.

But above all three ranks of company men stood the most coveted class of all: the free trappers.

While they might be forced to wait until the trader dispensed with his hirelings, those free men had what Sublette desired most: the finest of plews brought to rendezvous by the "master trappers," men who traversed the high country on their own hook, beholden to no booshway, in debt to no company.

While the Smith, Jackson, & Sublette men still wore a frontiersman's wool or leather breeches and some sort of linen or calico shirt, most free trappers gaily sported Indian leggings and war shirt, the twisted fringes of which were caparisoned with tiny brass hawk's bells, steel sewing thimbles, or strewn with Indian scalplocks, leather garments decorated with wide bands of brightly colored porcupine quillwork. Beneath that outer layer of warrior's clothing they wore a greasy, soiled, and sooted cloth shirt and woolen longhandles when the seasons turned cold.

Many plaited their hair in two long braids, tied up in bright ribbons of red trade wool or wrapped with otter skin. They daubed purple vermilion down the center part in their hair, often smeared earth paint on their severely tanned faces, and trailed long fringes or small animal skins from the heels of their moccasins. Some ambled about camp wearing a colorfully striped blanket belted around their waist in the fashion of a tribal chief, while others brandished a wide wool sash finger-woven back in eastern woodlands, where they stuffed a brace of pistols, a tomahawk, and perhaps the long stem to their personal smoking pipe.

How plain it was that this breed prided themselves on just how much like an Indian they appeared—but for the long, shaggy, ofttimes braided beards. Oh, how they seized this chance to swagger and strut before Sublette's gaping greenhorns and mule-eyed pilgrims come fresh-as-dew to the far west.

It was just as clear that such men would never again feel comfortable setting their feet down among civilized company. Doubtful was it that any of their breed would ever return east. Little, if anything, remained for them back there in what had been.

As the long morning dragged on, Titus returned to wait out the hours in camp with Rufus, Elbridge, and the others. To kill some of the time, he brought both Hannah and his saddle horse into camp, securing them to a tree branch while he went to work fancying them up in the fashion of an Indian warrior. First he tied up their tails just as a man would do when about to ride off on the warpath. Then he braided their forelocks with narrow strips of varicolored Mexican ribbon he swapped from Caleb Wood for a single plew of beaver. Next Scratch braided the manes of both with more of that ribbon and looped in a half-dozen feathers from a golden eagle that Bird in Ground had killed during his first winter with the Crow. And finally he made a thick paste from the white clay he discovered in an alkali bed along the creek, using it to paint crude lightning bolts and hailstones, even pressing his own handprints along the neck and flank of both horse and Hannah.

That task complete, Bass collapsed against a huge cottonwood, where he dozed as the air warmed and the flies droned.

Later that afternoon he meticulously honed his knife and camp ax on a stone and steel, then cleaned his weapons before he finally decided to run some balls for both pistol and rifle: melting bars of soft Galena lead in a small pot from which he dipped tiny ladles of the molten silver and poured the liquid into the round cavity of his bullet molds. Hot work this was at the edge of a fire in this midsummer heat, but that sweaty job was one task more that helped him pass the hours while the free trappers waited for their crack at Sublette's treasures.

After supper of elk tenderloin, buffalo tongue, and prairie oysters, he joined Hatcher, Fish, and Wood as they moseyed off for the company camp at twilight.

"I would've figgered a bunch the size of Campbell's outfit would've had 'em more beaver took in," Jack appraised as they came to a halt near Sublette's awnings, where a handful of men still clustered around the stacks of blankets and crates of goods, arguing this point or that with the trader's clerks.

"Maybeso that Powder ain't so prime a country as it be back toward the mountains," Bass observed.

"Not for beaver, it ain't," Solomon added.

"If'n a man wants to hunt him prime plew," Caleb declared, "that nigger's gotta stick his neck out some."

"I ain't never been afraid to stick my neck out some," Jack said. "Way I see it—to get us the best fur, we gotta trap the edge of Blackfoot country . . . but I don't aim to lay a trap where I'll get my hull damned head cut off!"

Bass spread his fingers and ran them through the skins at the very top of three tall stacks of pelts under the wary eye of a Sublette clerk. "Our fur looks a damned sight better'n this here, fellas."

"It ought'n be better," Solomon grumbled. "We damned near lost our hair to Bug's Boys trapping that beaver!"

"Bug's Boys?" the greenhorn behind the beaver pelts repeated.

Hatcher gazed at the man fresh out of the settlements. "Ye ever hear tell of Blackfoot, mister?"

"Blackfoot? I heard tell of 'em, yeah. Sublette says the Englishers set them Blackfoot out to kill off Americans like his men."

"Damn them black-hearted bastards," Solomon growled. "Too many good men gone under at their hands."

"Sublette says the Blackfoot is why Davy Jackson ain't come in to Popo Agie yet."

Titus asked, "Trader figgers Jackson's gone under?"

The man's head bobbed, his fleshy jowls quivering like the wattle at the neck of a tom turkey. "Maybe his whole outfit too. Just like Jed Smith—the other'n who's a company partner. Word is he's dead somewhere far west of here with all his men. Been two years now, and Smith ain't showed up at rendezvous."

"So Sublette figgers Jackson's been rubbed out too?" Solomon repeated.

Leaning an elbow on a stack of pelts, the clerk said, "Jackson was up in Flathead country. And Sublette says that's right near Blackfoot country. I suppose it ain't hard to figure Jackson's run into trouble and got himself killed too."

Caleb clucked, "Damn well might be a real stroke of luck, for that leaves Sublette the whole company, don't it?"

"Maybe, but Mr. Sublette figures to wait on here for a week or little more, then if Mr. Jackson doesn't show, Mr. Sublette said he's going to head on west to the Snake River with what he's got in supplies to search for some sign of Jackson's brigade before he turns back for the fall hunt."

"That Smith feller's gone," Hatcher observed flatly. "This long and ain't none of his bunch showed . . . why, it's for sartin he's been rubbed out. But Jackson, now, that's a savvy booshway. I reckon he could pull his fat out of just about any fire."

Caleb asked, "Sublette say if he figgered this was a good year for beaver?"

"I saw him just twice today, when he come around my tent with Campbell." The clerk wagged his head and rolled his eyes heavenward. "Mr. Sublette just shook his head each time he looked through them furs his men brought in over the last season."

"Don't sound like he's a happy man to me," Bass observed.

"Not when he don't have near all the beaver he was counting on taking in," the clerk stated.

"And now he figgers he lost him his two partners," Solomon added.

"So tell me if Sublette's gonna trade for our furs come tomorrow?" Titus asked.

"He ain't said nothing 'bout it, neither way," the clerk admitted. "But from what I see, he'll likely open up trade with all you fellers come morning. There ain't any more company fur to take in. Leastways, not till he finds Jackson's brigade."

"If he finds 'em at all," Hatcher declared.

"What's your tobaccy?" Scratch inquired of the hawk-nosed clerk who stood impassively writing down the value of the pelts another of Sublette's employees was reciting from his weighing of Titus Bass's plews.

"You buy your supplies down there." The man jabbed a finger at another awning. "I just record your take."

Bass felt as if Sublette and the company had everything arranged just so they could skin a cat every which way of Sunday. No matter if a man worked hard trapping, skinning, fleshing, and packing them beaver plews all the way through from last autumn, the St. Louis trader always held the high cards. But for those suspicious Mexicans down in Taos, there wasn't another trader for better than eighteen hundred miles of the Popo Agie.

"This all you're trading in?"

Bass looked up at the second of the clerks, a moon-faced man without distinguishable characteristics: he looked like every other settlement sort, town hanger, and citified nabob.

"That's all I'm trading with you."

The man went back to peering down at his ledger, dipped his quill, and went back to writing. "Not a good year for you, was it?"

"That ain't all the fur I got."

The clerk stopped his hand and glared at Scratch with the crimson creeping up from his neck. "I just asked you . . . if this was all you was trading."

"It is," Scratch repeated, flashing the man his teeth. "But it ain't all I caught. Only what I trapped this last spring."

Now the clerk was clearly angry at the confusion caused him. He sputtered for a moment, his face growing as red as the Indian paintbrush that dotted this high valley in early summer. "Do you want to do business with us or—"

"I ain't got no more furs to trade to *you*," Titus explained, eager to settle the dust. "The rest I sold in Taos last winter."

With a great rush of air the clerk sighed as if he had been asked to coax milk from a stone. "Very well."

Back to his ledger he went, wagging his head slightly as he added and carried numbers from column to column. While the clerk finished his computations, Bass gazed over at the rest who had finished this grueling part of the process. Hatcher and the others already stood among the stacks and kegs, crates and boxes of trade goods—fingering this and that, chattering excitedly about most everything they picked up and held to the light. There remained no more than a handful of other free men waiting patiently behind Scratch for their turn at the trader's scales.

The clerk carefully tore a strip from the bottom of his ledger page and handed it to another man, who stuffed the strip of paper beneath the rope holding together Bass's beaver skins. Then the hawk-nosed man wrote a little more and tore another strip of paper from the bottom of the page.

He held it out to Bass.

"Here's your credit."

"My credit—for over at the store?"

The clerk looked past Scratch at the trapper pushing up behind him. "Next! You're next, now—come along lively!"

Pressed from behind, Bass stepped aside, trying to hold the rustling strip of paper still enough to read it in the breeze. It was hard for him to make out that writing scratched on the white foolscap beneath the glare from the summer sun. Stepping into the shade beneath the edge of an awning, Titus studied the marks again. Several words were scrawled there, that much he was sure of. And beneath each of them a number. In addition, at the far end of the strip was a fourth number, written bigger than the rest, and circled as well.

"Scratch—how much you got to spend?"

He looked up, finding Rufus Graham before him. "You read this?"

Rufus shook his head. "Can't read a't'all."

"Near as I make it, I got me a few hundred dollars for supplies."

"How much hundreds?"

"That looks like a nine," he answered, squinting his eyes as his dirty fingernail pointed out a number. "Damn, but I never was a good one at ciphering numbers. Could do it once, but it's been too long since I done any of that."

"None of the others can help you neither," Graham admitted. "None of us read."

"S'all right," he sighed, looking up. "Only place I can spend it is here anyways."

" 'Cept you go back to Taos."

"Ain't a chance of that," Titus said, starting toward the rest, who were dickering with a pair of clerks beneath a far awning.

"This here tobaccy ain't half-bad!" Caleb declared as he turned toward Bass when the two walked up to the others.

"Better'n Mexican," Hatcher agreed.

Scratch asked, "How much?"

The clerk perched behind the wooden crates holding several hundred-weight of twisted brown carrots of tobacco declared, "Two dollar the pound."

"Same as it's been for the last two year," Isaac stated.

"Damn good thing too," Bass grumbled. "Missed out on American tobaccy last year."

Asked the clerk, "You're ready to buy?"

"I damn well waited the better part of a day and a goddamned half to buy," Titus snapped. "If'n that don't take the circle! You better believe I'm ready—"

"Where's your paper?" the clerk interrupted.

Handing the man his slip, Bass watched the clerk glance quickly at the numbers, then look over at the first of Sublette's men. "This here right?"

"What's right?" the other civilian asked.

"This says five hundred fifty-nine?"

The man glanced at Bass a moment before he remembered. "Five hundred fifty-nine is the right amount."

As the first clerk went back to grading and weighing pelts, the store clerk said, "Take your pick," and began to write in his own ledger. "You got enough to near buy what all you want."

"Damn," Titus said as it began to hit him. "I ain't really had no chance to buy nothing but what it took to live on for so long now—I . . . I don't know how to act, boys."

"What you need?" Solomon said as he came up and laid a hand on Bass's shoulder.

Hatcher chuckled, bursting out with, "The nigger needs just 'bout ever'thing!"

"I got me a gun," Bass said.

"You need a pistol?" asked the clerk.

"I got the one Hatcher loaned me," he replied. "How much are those you're selling?"

"They're smoothbore, sixty caliber—sell for fifty dollars."

"Ooooo!" exclaimed Caleb. "That hurts."

Hatcher came up to stand beside Titus, saying, "You go ahead on and keep that'n I loaned ye long as ye want."

"If I can buy me my own, I'll do that. Much 'bliged, Jack," he said, then turned back to the clerk. "Gimme one of them pistols to look at."

After he started inspecting the weapon, slowly dragging back the big hammer to check the crispness of the lock, holding it against his ear to listen to the action, Bass had the clerk hold up this or that, quoting one price after another.

Closing his eyes in sensual pleasure, Scratch sniffed at the bag of green coffee beans below his nose.

"Two dollar a pound."

"Better weigh out twenty-five pounds. How's your powder?"

"Best grade is two-fifty the pound."

Titus turned to Hatcher and Gray. "You figger it's better'n that Mex powder we got along?"

"Gotta be," Jack replied.

"It's American," the clerk asserted. "Du Pont."

"All right," and Scratch nodded. "I'll take fifty pounds. What's Galena?"

"Lead's only a dollar and a half."

"We got us some of that Taos lead from down in the Mexican mines," Rufus said.

Bass cogitated a few moments, staring up at the underside of the awning over his head as the sun baked down on them. "I'll take me a guess and go with seventy-five pounds. And I need me some good awls."

The clerk spun around and swept up a sample from the boxes behind him. "These are three for fifty cents."

They appeared sturdy with their fire-hardened steel points and hardwood handle. "Gimme six."

Solomon asked, "You want 'nother blanket?"

So Bass looked at the clerk, "How much?"

"White blankets for twenty dollars."

"That's a lot just to keep a man warm," Bass grumbled.

The easterner said, "You want it sewed into a capote, them are only twenty-five each."

"How much your striped blankets?"

"They ain't near as much," Hatcher explained. "He's charging just fifteen dollar for striped ones."

"Because they ain't as big as the white ones," the clerk declared.

"Better gimme a white blanket."

As the clerk returned with the neatly folded blanket, he asked, "Need any pepper or salt?"

Scratch shook his head. "Got plenty of that down to Taos last winter."

"Beads or ribbon?"

"What do them hanks of beads cost a man?"

Shoving forward that heavy tray containing thick hanks of the big colored variety commonly called pony beads, the clerk answered, "Five dollars a pound."

"Show me how much a pound is," Bass requested.

In a moment the man had weighed out several hanks of the various colors. "That's five pounds. So it'll be twenty-five dollars."

"All right," Titus said with a smile. "I'll take them five pounds, but put back them white and black'uns—gimme only them real purty colors: like that green and blue, the yellow and that blood color too. See that brown, gimme that too."

"You need nails?" the clerk asked after he had laid out the long hanks of beads atop the white blanket.

"Lemme see what you have."

After inspecting the various sizes of short brass nails a man used for both repair and decoration, he asked, "How much?"

"Fifty cents a dozen."

"Let's see—five dozen of 'em oughtta do."

"You want any ribbons?"

"Show me what you got to trade."

The clerk brought out a box containing a rainbow of cotton ribbon. "It's six bits the yard."

"Better let me have my pick of ten yards."

"I figure you'll want some bolt cloth too, won't you, mister?" and he patted a stack of different patterns and colors.

"Tell me how much that'll cost me."

As he started down the stack of bolts, the clerk called out the prices. "This here scarlet is the best grade. Mr. Sublette likes it best too. It's a wool. Goes for ten dollars."

"Ten dollars a yard?"

"A yard. The coarse blue is eight dollars. But the calico here is only two-fifty."

"What's that on the bottom?" he asked, pointing.

"Striped cotton. It's a soft material like the calico."

"Sounds like I can get me a lot more of that 'stead of the coarse cloth," Bass declared. "Let's say . . . ten yards of each of them two. Show me how much cloth that'll be."

After Scratch had seen just how much twenty yards of material would be, he felt himself growing more excited about the possibilities—staring again at the various colors of the beads, figuring gifts like these would be able to communicate where his rudimentary talents with the Shoshone tongue left off.

"You got some vermilion, don't you?"

"Chinee, I do," the clerk replied. Returning to the rough-hewn plank, he held up a wooden tray that contained a profusion of small waxed packets the size of a man's fist, one of which he opened to show the deep-purple pigment. "It ain't cheap."

"How much?" Hatcher asked.

"Six dollars a pound."

Bass scratched the end of his nose, sensing the eyes of the others riveted on him. "Better make it five pounds."

"All that red paint for you, Scratch?" Rufus asked.

"Shit!" Caleb snorted. "It ain't all for him, you idjit! Scratch's gonna get his stinger wet with that Chinee vermilion!"

Graham wagged his head in doleful confusion. "How's Scratch gonna get his stinger wet with . . . " Then it struck him like a bolt of summer thunder. "Say! You're gonna get yourself one of them Sho'nie gals, ain'cha?"

Bass winked and turned back to the clerk. "Show me what you got in wiping sticks and flints."

"Good hickory, these be," the clerk replied, turning back to his crates. "And for flints: we got English and French."

"Get them French ambers," Hatcher suggested. "Likely we'll pay more for 'em, but they'll last longer'n the English."

By the time he had picked out a bundle of two dozen straight-grained hickory wiping sticks, as well as three pounds of the pale amber flints imported from France, along with several handfuls of assorted screws and worms for gun repair and cleaning, he finally asked the clerk to total it all up. He looked again over at his stack of pelts beneath that first awning, remembering just how many plews he had sent downriver with Silas Cooper. Then he suddenly squeezed his eyes closed in that way he hoped would shut off the terrible memory.

Letting out a long sigh, the trader's employee came back to the free men and announced, "That all comes to four hundred seventy-three."

Several of the others whistled low, but Bass remained undismayed. "What's that leave me?"

"Eighty-six."

Scratch licked his lips and asked, "So how much is your whiskey?"

"He don't just wanna get his stinger wet!" Caleb hooted behind him. "Bass wants to get his gullet scrubbed too!"

"Damn right I do!"

The clerk cleared his throat. "Whiskey sells two dollar the pint."

He squinted again, trying to imagine how much a pint was. "How much is that a gallon?"

"Eight dollars."

For a moment more Scratch looked around at the other six trappers. "I got enough for three gallons start off with?"

"That's twenty-four dollars. And you'll have a little money left over for some more."

"That's the way I want it," Bass said with satisfaction. "Go get a kettle, one of you."

"I ain't gotta go anywhere to get a goddanged kettle," Caleb yelled with glee, leaning over to retrieve the kettle he had purchased from the ground. "Here, mister—put a gallon of that likker right in here."

The clerk looked at Bass.

At which Scratch roared, "You heard the man. This here's a free man, master trapper in the Rocky—by God—Mountains. So you better pour us some whiskey in that kettle and give me my trade goods . . . then step back outta our way, 'cause these here cocks o' the walk are struttin' bold and brassy tonight!"

SIXTEEN

He had forgotten just how good an Injun gal could smell, all earthy and fragrant with her own body heat, skin smeared with some bear oil, maybe some crushed sage or flower petals rubbed in her hair.

Quite different from them Mexican gals, who stank of cheap *aguardiente* and corn-husk cigarillos just like their menfolk. But the Taos whores sure did know how to raise hell and put a chunk under it to entertain a mountain man wintering down their way!

Still, he was glad to be back in the mountains, back to Injun gals what didn't chatter that much at all like them Mexican whores while they serviced their customers. These Injun women knew what they were about when it came to earning that handful of beads, that cup of Mexican sugar, or that yard of calico he held out to finally entice one of them to follow him back toward a spot he had prepared in the middle of a patch of willow.

She grasped his rigid flesh in the moonlight as he centered himself over her and began to lunge forward hungrily as she half closed her eyes.

Starved as he was, Scratch did his best to go at it slow. Knowing that after having gone so long without, this was bound to be over with all too soon anyway. Best savor it while he could.

Squirming, the woman adjusted herself on the buffalo robe he had spread beneath the wide strip of oiled sheeting Titus had tied up in the event the sky decided to cloud up and rain on them that night. Right at dusk a few clouds had begun to clot at the western rim of the valley, there against the mountains, ominously backlit by the falling sun.

Titus thought he could smell her excitement. Its strong pungency rose to his nostrils on the warm night air. And that stirred him to jab himself into her with all the more urgency.

How long had it been . . . too damned long to calculate, to wonder about, now. The drought was over. He had bought himself a woman for the night. At least he hoped it was for the night, praying suddenly that she would not get up and leave once he was done in her. Because he realized he would be done all too soon.

It was always that way when he went so long without—

Then he was exploding inside her in great rushing waves of relief, flinging himself against her, almost whimpering that it hadn't lasted longer.

Slowly, slowly he sank atop her, filled both with regret and immense satisfaction, savoring these few minutes while his breathing slowed and his heart quieted itself, listening to her breathing and the night sounds so close around their crude shelter. When he grew soft, the woman slid out from under him, then scooted back against his body, nestling her head on his shoulder as she reached out for her dress and that blanket she had wrapped around her shoulders when she'd followed him there.

He unfurled her blanket over them both and closed his eyes.

How warm was the night air, despite that hint of a chilling cloudburst carried in from the horizon on an occasional breeze.

After completing his purchases and carrying his supplies back to camp, Scratch and the others had carved up the remains of an elk cow shot two days before and put the steaks over the fire. As the meat sizzled at the end of sharpened *appolaz,* they eagerly dipped their tin cups into the three kettles, sipping at the amber-colored grain alcohol that burned a man's goozle raw.

Scratch near choked with that first great gulp.

Sputtering, he found the others guffawed and knee-slapped at his fit of coughing.

"Ain't smooth as lightning, is it?" Hatcher asked, grinning so widely one could see all of that rotted tooth.

No, it sure wasn't smooth. Nor had Bass chosen to sweeten the liquor's raw bite with Mexican brown sugar as he had learned to do with the Taos *aguardiente*. But soon enough his tongue and gullet grew accustomed to this particular recipe. So with supper out of the way and his head feeling light and easy, Bass cut free enough beads to fill a pint tin cup half the way to the top, sliced himself off an arm's length of striped cotton cloth with his belt knife, then bid the others farewell for what he hoped would be the rest of the evening.

"Ye be back afore morning?" Hatcher cried.

But before Bass himself could answer, Elbridge yelled, "Shit, Jack! His blankets and robes is gone!"

"Eegod! Ye got yerself a little hidey place picked out, don't ye?" Jack asked before Scratch could utter a word.

He was really beginning to feel the numbing tingle radiating across his forehead now that he was standing, doing all he could to remain standing. "My night to let the wolf loose, boys!"

"See you tomorry," Caleb replied with a slur and a wave.

He weaved past their merry fire as some of the rest grabbed their crotches and hooted profanely. An exuberant Hatcher blew him a kiss before Bass turned toward the banks of the Popo Agie.

That's when he heard the loud voices of men mixing with the lighter giggles from women. Instead of wading on into the creek, Scratch decided to stay with the east bank. After crossing less than fifty yards he came upon an open piece of ground within the willow and cottonwood, where more than two dozen people milled about in the light of the rising half-moon. Trappers sauntered among the warriors and squaws who had come across the Popo Agie with one thought in mind: no two ways about it, there were treasures to be bartered from those white men hungry to lay with their dark-skinned women. Cloth and coffee, beads and bells, knives and awls, vermilion and ribbons.

And all these beaver men wanted was a few minutes' time to rut with a woman!

Were there no females back in the land of these white men?

For a few minutes Scratch stood shuffle-footed on the fringe of that merry gathering, watching the company men and a handful of free trappers mosey in and out through the group. They circled, appraising, then circled again, stopping now and then to have themselves a close inspection of this or that woman beneath the moonlight. He ought to have himself a look, Titus decided, just so the others wouldn't pick over all the best there was before he got around to choosing.

The warrior warily watched the white man approach, saying something quietly to his woman from the corner of his mouth. She nodded as she looked Bass up and down. Then smiled faintly. He set down the cup of brown Mexican sugar at his feet and asked How much? in sign, ending with that simple gesture of male readiness: a stiffened index finger on one hand sliding back and forth between the wide-spread Y of the first two fingers on the other hand.

"A knife and some powder too?" he asked when the warrior gave his answer.

He showed the man the calico, but it was the woman who fingered it with approval.

"Listen—you go and offer 'em too much," one of the company men growled as he lunged up to Bass's elbow, "gonna make it miserable on the rest of us here on out!"

"This free man giving these red whores too much?" grumbled another who lumbered up to stand at the other elbow.

In the meantime the squaw knelt and retrieved the cup from the ground. Sniffing it first, she plunged a finger into the sugar.

"Lookee thar'. He offers her a bunch of that smooth cloth, and see? She's took her a shine to that cup of his," the first man snorted. "What's in that damn cup?"

"Sugar."

"Shit—you're giving 'em sugar!" the second trapper shrieked, and turned away, throwing his hands up in disgust. "Better get your whore quick now, boys. That free man's riding up the price of a man's poke but good!"

The first warrior had snatched the cup from his wife and stiffly handed it back to Bass, wagging his head and pulling the woman away toward the other side of the clearing. Pursing his lips in frustration, Scratch began to circle again, feeling the glares of the company men hot between his shoulder blades. A second time around the glen he stopped before another warrior who had a woman stationed at either arm.

"You have two wives?" he asked as he watched the plain-faced woman bend to retrieve the cup.

But the warrior signed that he had one wife. The other—and he gestured to the woman who licked the brown sugar from the finger she had plunged into the tin cup—was the sister of his wife.

"How much you want for her?" Scratch asked aloud as he signed, then indicated the warrior's wife. She was clearly the better-looking of the two.

The Shoshone put his arm on his wife's shoulder and shook his head. Next he laid his arm on his sister-in-law's shoulder and pointed to the cloth on Bass's shoulder. And the tin cup. And then he used a finger to tap against the butt of the new pistol Titus had stuffed in his sash.

"No," Scratch said emphatically.

The warrior glowered, turning both the women away so quickly, Titus had to lunge to snatch his tin cup back. But he promptly stepped in front of the warrior and stood his ground, forcing the trio to stop.

"Here."

He handed the cup to the sister-in-law and freed the antelope-skin bag stuffed beneath his belt. From it he pulled a handful of the big pony beads. First he pointed to the beads, then to the cup the squaw held, and finally to the calico.

"That's too goddamned much to pay for a quick hump in the brush!" a voice snarled somewhere close behind him.

Ignoring the grumblings of those around him, Bass inched his hand closer to the wife, holding the beads right under her chin, then slowly moved the hand so he could hold them right under the nose of her sister.

"It ain't too much for a goddamned woman," Titus said, flinging his words over his shoulder at those behind him, the men he knew were watching his negotiations.

The Indian shook his head again, tightening his arms around the shoulders of the two women and saying something to his wife's sister. She handed the cup of sugar back to Titus.

"You ain't getting my pistol," Bass snapped at the warrior. "Now, here's a fair trade."

But the Indian pulled the women away again. This time he let them go, standing right there watching their backs, his hands filled with beads and sugar, his heart despairing.

"Serves you right, nigger!"

He turned on a group of them sniggering at him.

"That's right," another bawled. "Serves you right for stacking up the price of a hump that'a way."

From the corner of his eye Bass saw them moving his way: an older warrior, leading four women. Halting in front of the white trapper, the wrinkled Shoshone with an expressive face stepped aside and gestured in turn to each of the four. Scratch quickly appraised them in the silver light.

"No men," the man signed.

Maybeso he means they ain't got no husbands.

Setting down the cup and dumping the colorful beads back into the small skin pouch, he asked, "No men?"

"Killed," the warrior replied with his hands. "Rubbed out by Blackfeet."

"Your daughters?"

He nodded, then spoke in Shoshone. "Show me your beads."

Handing the old man the pouch, Bass watched the Shoshone pour out some of the beads and inspect them in his palm. Then he held them out so his four daughters could appraise them.

His deep, dark eyes gazed into the white man's. "The cup?"

Bass picked up the tin and waited while the man licked the tip of his finger, dipped it in the Mexican sugar, then licked the fingertip once more.

"I got the cloth too," Scratch said in English, taking the strip of calico from his shoulder as the grumbling from the white men around him grew louder.

One of the women stepped forward, and immediately a second, both of them fingering the cloth. But the old man motioned them back suddenly, then nodded. Moving aside, he gestured again to his four daughters in turn, moving his arm from the trapper to each woman as if asking that a decision be made before a price was negotiated.

The oldest looked a lot like Fawn, and the youngest, a mere slip of a girl, looked very similar to Slays in the Night's daughter. That one couldn't be any older than fourteen, maybe fifteen, summers. But the warrior had said they all had been married. An immediate tug at his heart made him feel sorry for the girl, for the old man too. He hoped she would not be chosen this night . . . but realized that was muddle-headed thinking. She'd likely be the first to go to one of the others, a man who might not treat her near as kindly as he would.

Then he wondered if he was feeling sorry for her, or if he was trying to talk himself into picking her instead of the others.

"How many summers?" he asked.

"Seventeen."

Titus peered closer at the girl. She had to be younger than that. Why, Amy Whistler was that same age when she and he . . .

So Bass repeated the number. "Seventeen."

With a nod the old man reached over and inched the young woman forward as if about to consummate the deal.

Jehoshaphat! That's half my age!

Still clutching the skin pouch, the old man upended the bag and poured out all the beads into the hands of another woman standing behind the youngest, who kept her eyes fixed on the ground. Then the warrior gave the pouch back to the trapper at the same time he took the tin cup from Bass's hand. His final gesture was to take the folded strip of cloth from where it hung over the white man's arm—leaving Scratch with nothing more to hold.

In a whisper the young woman turned slightly and said something to the man. Instead, it was the oldest of her sisters who answered curtly. Chastised, the young woman turned back, glanced up at Bass for a brief moment, nodding her head at him before her eyes returned to the ground at her feet.

Shooing the trapper away, the old warrior turned on his heel, pulling a soft pouch from his belt. Spreading its top and holding it out as he shuffled away, he had the oldest of the sisters pour the beads into it while the other two women took turns licking sugar from the fingers they repeatedly plunged into the cup. With his bag poked back under his belt, the old Shoshone unfurled the long strip of cloth and draped it around his own shoulders, swirling this way, then that, admiring it on himself in the moonlight.

"Gonna make himself a shirt, I'd reckon," Scratch said to no one at all.

"Damn you, free trapper!"

Turning slightly, he found that group of company men glaring at him anew.

"That's right—we oughtta cut your goddamned oysters off right here and now!" a second one bellowed menacingly. "Then you'd never go daubing no Injun gals again!"

For a moment he measured them in the moonlight limned through puffy clouds embroidered with silvery borders. If they meant him real harm, they wouldn't be blustering—he figured as his heart began to beat faster with this challenge, uncertain if it did so out of anticipation for the woman, or from the danger the four company men presented with their swagger.

That's likely what it was, he decided. Nothing more than strut and swagger. Nonetheless, he laid his left hand on the handle of his knife for a moment while he wrapped his right hand around the curved butt of the new pistol. Squaring his shoulders as the four continued their hooting and catcalls, Bass turned and grabbed the woman by an elbow. She let him guide her through the rest of the Indians and trappers crowding the glen.

And she did not protest as he led her back along that east bank of the Popo Agie until they reached the bower he had constructed over his sleeping robes. He prayed she understood what was expected of her when he came to a halt and let go of her arm. For a moment she watched him as he freed the knot in the wide, colorful sash, then laid the pistol on it near his blankets, just within reach.

The minute he sank to the ground and began to untie his moccasins, she flung her own blanket aside, then seized hold of the fringed bottom of her hide dress with both hands—pulling it up over her thighs, her bare hips, the flat of her belly as he stared transfixed at that dark wedge of hair there at the crown of her legs . . . on up she dragged the dress, pulling it inside out over her shoulders as her small breasts bounced free and he swallowed hard, suddenly so dry-mouthed he could barely swallow—watching every shimmy of her flesh as the woman slipped the dress down one arm, then another, and finally tugged it off over her head.

Sweeping both hands down the length of her long, loose black hair before she tossed it over her shoulder, the woman knelt onto the rumple of blankets he had prepared, folding her own neatly at the side of the bed, then laid her skin dress upon it. At last she sank onto her back, and gazed over at the white man staring mule-eyed and slack-jawed at her provocative, bare-skinned beauty.

Scratch sensed the urgency suddenly seize hold of him, realizing any self-control was no longer possible. More quickly than she had, he wrenched up the bottom of his leather shirt and ripped it from his arms, yanking it over his head, flinging it into the brush. Where the shirt landed, it mattered not.

Reaching beneath the front flap of his breechclout, Titus's fingers flew at the knot tied in the wide rawhide whang that secured the wide strip of wool around his waist. That whang came whipping off in one hand at the same time the other hand ripped the breechclout from between his legs. He heaved both of them into the surrounding brush.

Still wearing his leggings, Scratch knelt at her knees. She spread her legs and held her arms up to him, grasping one of his wrists and pulling him toward her gently as she reached out with a hand, fingers searching for his manhood.

He nearly choked on readiness when she wrapped her hand around him, guiding him down, down, then forward, ever so gently as the woman sought to place him against her just so.

Lying here now with the woman as his heart continued to slow, Titus remembered how she had half closed her eyes while he had driven himself into her. Not sure if that had been pleasure for her, or merely pain with his fury to plant himself fully, completely within her moist warmth.

Barely opening his eyes from time to time as they lay together, Scratch became aware that time was passing only because of the journey taken by that half-moon limned behind the silver-framed cotton puffs in its climb from there to there across the cloudy sky. He wasn't really aware he had been sleeping until he felt her rustle beside him, bringing him fully awake.

For a moment she peered over a shoulder at him, her narrow, naked back only inches from his face; then she reached out to drag her dress into her lap. As she began to pull the hide garment right side out, Bass propped himself up on an elbow and studied what he could see of her, finding himself stirred once more. Just as the woman was about to stab her arms into the sleeves of the dress, he seized her, twisting her down onto the blankets.

In her first words to him, these spoken in a low, husky voice, she began to give him hell, shaking her head emphatically as he flung the blanket off himself and rolled over to position himself between her legs. With one arm shoving upward against his chest, the woman clamped her other hand over herself so he could not enter.

"Now what you doing that for?" he groaned, rocking back on his knees in distress, his hardened flesh wagging forlornly.

Pushing herself backward, the woman slid far enough away from him that she could sit up and reach for the blanket, which she yanked into her lap.

"You was all for me crawling on you afore," he groaned, dejection thick in his voice. "Why not now when I can make it last a little longer for us both?"

After a pause she shook her head, then motioned that she intended to head over to her village across the creek.

He tried to inch forward, eager to grab one or the other of those small breasts. "Lemme crawl on you one more time . . . then you get on back to your camp."

Curling her legs up defensively, she put out an arm to hold him at bay. Then she made the sign for no trade.

"No . . . no trade?"

For a moment he was confused; then it struck him. "What I give your father was for just the first time, that it?"

She continued to stare at him. At least she wasn't moving to get away.

Good enough for the first time—all right, he thought. If he was going to convince her to spread her legs for him a second time, Bass figured he was going to have to come up with something to give her that she would not have to share with her older sisters. Something for her and her alone.

Turning to stare at the free trappers' camp some sixty yards away in an attempt to divine what he could offer her, Bass heard her moving of a sudden. When he whirled back, he found her dragging her dress over her head and arms.

"No, stay," he begged in desperation, his hardened flesh still insistent, his heart in despair of finding something to offer her.

But then he lunged to the side, flinging back the flap on his shooting pouch to dig around inside until his fingers found one of the awls he had traded for that afternoon. Scratch scooted back on his knees to present it to her in his flat palm.

After a moment of consideration she took it from his hand, tapped a finger pad against its sharp tip, and considered his offer a moment longer . . . before she laid it back in his hand and went back to pulling the dress down over her breasts.

Jehoshaphat! What did he have that would make her eyes shine enough to lay back down for him!

Glory!

He dived back at his shooting pouch, stuffed a hand into the pocket at the back, and swept out a long length of the wool ribbon generally used to bind an edge on blankets. This he held out in his hand for her to inspect.

By that time she wasn't watching him—rising to her knees so she could tug the dress down over her hips when she suddenly spotted the selvage ribbon and froze. Despairing that it was not enough, he moved that open hand closer to her, bringing it up beneath her chin so she could see just what it was that he offered her. The woman lifted the narrow strip of wool from his palm, inspecting it in the moonlight. Then shook her head and dropped it back across his hand.

"Please, don't . . . don't go," he implored with that urgency of the flesh.

Then, with her two hands, she pantomimed poking the index finger of one hand into an invisible something she held in the other. For a moment he imagined she was making the sign for copulation. . . . Then he understood.

"The awl!" he whispered. "You want the awl too!"

He retrieved it from his pouch and laid it in one hand, grabbing the ribbon in the other, and presented them both to her.

For a painful moment the woman stared down at the awl and ribbon. Just stared.

And finally she removed the two objects from his palms, placing them to the side atop her blanket, then rose on her knees to grasp the bottom of her dress once more, shimmying out beneath it as he suddenly went desert-tongued at the sight of her quivering breasts freed again for his touch . . . sensing his own renewed hardness, his own feral heat about to overwhelm him.

As savage as he attacked her that first time, now he discovered he was able to savor this delicious anticipation of delay rather than feeling himself hopelessly swept up and helplessly hurtled forth by a mysterious force he could in no way control.

Again she reached out to wrap her fingers around his swollen readiness, easing him forward to rub against that moistening cleft in her flesh for a time while she gently gyrated her hips, gradually driving him mad with desire. With one volcanic lunge he was finally inside her, feeling his groin locked against hers as the woman clamped both of her hands on his buttocks, arching her back as she began to gyrate more violently beneath him. He was certain he would explode if she continued flinging herself up at him—

Instead, Bass locked his hands on her hips and rocked back, lifting her completely off the blanket as he sank backward until the woman straddled him. For a sudden, frightening moment she did not move, gazing down at him in shock. But when he ground his hips up against her, raising her off the blankets, he got the notion across to her. The Shoshone woman apparently liked the sensation of their position so much that she herself began to buck and dance there atop his upright flesh, clamped tightly about him as she moved forward and back, side to side, and even tried slowly to grind herself round and round in small, and very insistent, circles.

Of a sudden she was recklessly bouncing on top of his hardness, rocking up so far on her knees that she stroked the entire length of him, so far, in fact, that he feared she would pull him out . . . yet each time she slammed herself back down onto his hips. Up and down she pumped him, her eyes compressing into half slits, her breathing become ragged as he felt himself rising toward a furied crescendo.

Then she was whimpering, and for a moment he became afraid he had hurt the young woman with the vigor of their coupling. He stopped and seized hold of her shoulders, worried—when she opened her eyes and stared down at him. Shaking her head, she smiled as she hadn't ever smiled at him before . . . and immediately went right back to bouncing atop his rigid manhood.

This time they rose together, climbing toward a fiery release. The initial whimper that had begun low in her throat was now a keening, breathless, raspy cry. And that grunt of his beast on the verge of achieving its primal satisfaction became like shrill hammer strikes on an anvil.

Slamming herself down onto his penis, the woman instantly began to shudder and quake, little high-pitched wails squeaking past her lips. . . . Then he was thrusting himself against her every bit as forcefully, clawing at her breasts, seizing her upper arms and pulling her close as he roared into her like a ferocious torrent dammed for far too long.

She collapsed against him, sinking weak and drained, at just the instant he felt that last explosion rocking him to his core.

Bass cradled the woman atop him until their flesh cooled and the air chilled with the coming of morning there beside the Popo Agie. He pulled her blanket over them both and let her sleep atop him. Surrendering to complete and utter exhaustion, Scratch sighed and closed his eyes, feeling the weariness washing over him, sensing sleep flooding every part of his body.

A woman like this was clearly a poison for a man: exactly the sort of creature who confounded, confused, and ailed a simple man with simple needs, just those very needs that made him crave a woman like her in the worst way . . . yet at the very same time, she was just the sort of cure for that very poison she inflicted—a soothing balm for all that ailed him. A poultice drawing out all the months of pent-up hunger and despair with such satisfaction that Scratch knew he would never again find such complete and utter relief.

Bass went to sleep as the sky far to the east began to gray, realizing that if he ever again found a woman who could bring him the sort of satisfaction he had just experienced, he wouldn't hesitate a moment to trade his pistol for her.

Almost two weeks later, William Sublette and Robert Campbell parted company on the Popo Agie. The Irishman was intent on returning to his native soil—much disturbed at a number of letters that had reached him in the mail his good friend had packed overland to rendezvous. Instead of accompanying the mule train bound for the States himself that July, Sublette installed Campbell as booshway over those he assigned to see those forty-five paltry packs of beaver all the way to St. Louis.

By any measure, a miserable take for a whole year in the mountains.

Of the three company owners, it appeared only Sublette had secured any profit for their joint efforts—and all of that through the dogged efforts of Campbell's Powder River brigade. It was hoped that David Jackson was still somewhere north in that Flathead country where the Blackfeet were wont to go, but after two years no one expected ever again to lay eyes on Jedediah Smith and his outfit . . . not this side of the great by-and-by.

At the same time Campbell was to backtrack east toward the Sweetwater and the Platte, Sublette dispatched his younger brother, Milton, along with German-born Henry Fraeb and Frenchman Jean Baptiste Gervais, north—leading a forty-man brigade to hunt the Bighorn basin in three smaller outfits that fall. Now William could himself lead the rest of his hardened veterans and a crew of green recruits to search for some sign of what had become of his long-overdue partner—reported to be somewhere in the country of the upper Snake River.

The Blackfeet hadn't rubbed out the industrious Jackson!

After more than a week of revelry beside the Popo Agie, word had come that the ever-enterprising brigade leader would be waiting on the Snake instead of coming to the prearranged valley of the Prairie Chicken—news of that change in plans arriving with Tom Fitzpatrick, who weeks before, as Jackson's brigade had begun to work its way south from Flathead country, was dispatched as a lone express rider sent to reach Sublette east of the Wind River Mountains.

"Tell Billy I'll meet him on the Snake below the Pilot Knobs."

With that electrifying report Sublette had promptly hurried to wrap up the last of his trading with what free men wandered in to rendezvous so he could turn west himself. This was great news! Not only was Davy Jackson still alive and kicking—but their company would now have more to show for their efforts than those puny forty-five packs of beaver.

Why—with what furs Jackson was likely to have with him, the two partners might even have enough left over after paying off General William H. Ashley that they could show a profit for the year! Things were looking up.

Jack Hatcher and his outfit of a half-dozen free trappers had decided they would mosey along behind the booshway's brigade, with the idea in mind that they could divide off from the company men after reaching the Snake, laying plans to trap into the autumn season there on the eastern fringe of Hudson's Bay territory.

"That Snake sure is purty country," Mad Jack had boasted the morning Sublette and more than fifty company men were to start into the high country for the headwaters of the Wind River. "Eegod—them three bee-you-tee-full breasties just pointing up there agin' the sky like tits on a squaw ye're thumping! My, but that's country the likes I ain't seen none of anywhere else!"

As the twenty-eight-year-old Milton struck out down the Popo Agie, which would take his outfit north for the Bighorn and Yellowstone country, Campbell whipped the balky mules south by east for the States* that same morning.

An hour later Bill Sublette himself turned his nose north by west, ascending the Wind River with some free trappers in tow until he crossed over the mountains and dropped down the Buffalo Fork to strike the Snake River in the northern part of what was already widely known as Davy Jackson's Hole. On the shores of Jackson's Lake, the booshway allowed his outfit to

---

*In St. Louis those furs he had traded $9,500.00 in supplies for would garner the company a return of $22,476.00. Campbell would not return to America and his beloved mountain west until the famous Rendezvous of 1832 in Pierre's Hole.

recruit and recuperate for a few days before he would set off again in his search.

Where was Davy? He sent word that he would meet Sublette on the Snake below the Pilot Knobs!

Trouble was, by the time he reached Jackson's Hole, the booshway realized there were *two* sides to that narrow mountain range. And to top off the dilemma—the Snake River tumbled through a valley on *both* sides of the Tetons.

So when William Sublette struck that river and failed to find any sign of Jackson as he doggedly continued on down the Snake, the booshway came to the conclusion that his only hope lay in crossing the mountains to continue his search on the western slope.

There in what the mountain trappers were just beginning to call Pierre's Hole . . . the dead were about to be resurrected.

"Who is that up yonder?"

Those company men at the head of the caravan with Sublette ignited a buzz that shot back the length of their pack train eventually to reach the half-dozen free trappers led by Jack Hatcher.

Bass squinted into the morning light, anxious with alarm—suddenly spying the distant horsemen. "Didn't bump into a Injun war party, did we?"

A half a mile ahead along the foot of those peaks still snowcapped here late in summer, a force of more than half a hundred was spotted riding their way out of the north, several leaders immediately spurring away from the rest as they put their horses into an easy lope. At two hundred yards Sublette's men could see that the oncoming riders had hairy faces.

At a hundred yards out, those buckskinned strangers raised their rifles and fired a joyous salute into the air.

Now the company men were roaring in delight up and down the caravan—recognizing old friends of the trail.

"Tom Fitzpatrick says it looks to be Davy Jackson hisself!" came word from one of the excited brigade men as the caravan was whipped into a lope.

Immediately a curious Hatcher and the rest gave heels to their mounts, spurring toward the action.

Caleb Wood roared, "Fitz oughtta know if it's them—he wintered with Jackson's men!"

"Davy Jackson's brigade, by God!" Elbridge cheered as they hammered toward the reunion.

Then, just about the time Sublette, Bridger, and Fitzpatrick all fired their rifles and reined to a halt to greet the overdue Jackson . . . they had themselves another shock that rattled each man jack of them all right down to the soles of his moccasins.

There beside Davy rode none other than Jedediah Strong Smith his own self! Come back from the land of the dead!

Why, there was more back pounding and hooting, hurrahing, and bear hugging that late morning in the shadow of the Tetons to last any man a lifetime!

Then and there the three reunited partners decided they'd camp and hold themselves a *second* rendezvous. Even if Billy Sublette didn't have but a third of his supplies left, there would never be a better reason to hold a celebration in the mountains than when one of your own was come back from the dead!

"Hatcher? Is that you, Jack Hatcher?"

Bass got to his feet as the impressive stranger came to a halt on his horse some five yards away from where the seven were occupied unlashing packs and preparing to make camp themselves.

Hatcher stood, shading his eyes to stare up at the man who had the high sun at his back, his snowy mane radiant in the summer light as it spilled from beneath the wide, rolled-up brim of a crumpled felt hat.

Caleb Wood was the first to utter a sound as he came up on the far side of the stranger. "McAfferty?"

Then Hatcher bellowed, "Th-that really you, Asa?"

As the stranger slid from his saddle, Elbridge turned quickly to Titus and declared, "That's the preacher fella we tol't you of—one what kill't that Ree medicine man."

Scratch watched alone while the others knotted around McAfferty like acorns around an oak, shaking hands and pounding one another on the shoulder, all laughing and talking and jabbing at the same time in their joyful surprise.

"Didn't ever figger to see you again!" Rufus confessed.

McAfferty asked, "What? Me rubbed out, Mr. Graham?"

"Nawww!" Jack roared. "I figgered ye give up on the mountains and run back east with yer tail tucked up atween yer legs!"

"Oooch! Mr. Hatcher, you sting me to the quick!" McAfferty shrieked, then started to laugh with an easy, contagious mirth that got the rest of them laughing with him.

Scratch had to admit that this McAfferty did have him an elegant, booming voice the likes of which would have enthralled and captivated far-flung frontier congregations and revival-camp meetings, without a doubt.

"Where in these hills ye been hiding yerself lately?" Jack inquired.

"Been up to Flathead country. Where I run onto Jackson's men when they was riding south to find Sublette."

Solomon slapped McAfferty on the back. "From the looks of it you still got all your purty white hair, Asa! And here I thort Flathead land was up there where them Blackfeets get a chance to lift that hair from you!"

Asa nodded, his dark eyes merry in that face starkly tanned against the radiant white beard. Then those eyes landed momentarily on the stranger who stood back from the others, observing the reunion of old friends.

"Up there near troubled land was I, that be God's truth! *'And I will give peace in the land, and ye shall lie down, and none shall make you afraid.'*" McAfferty said, quoting Biblical scripture. Then he looked at Hatcher, saying, "Who this be, Jack?"

They all turned and found Bass standing back, waiting alone.

Hatcher vigorously wagged his arm. "C'mon over here, Scratch. Want ye meet this nigger what use to ride with this bunch."

"Scratch, he called you?" McAfferty asked as he held out his strong hand.

"Titus Bass," he explained. "Scratch just the name what got hung on me not long after I come to the mountains."

Asa winked at Caleb. "I'll bet there's a story there to tell, eh, Mr. Bass?"

Titus grinned. "Nothing more'n a bad case of the graybacks I had to get rid of."

"Wait—" McAfferty said suddenly, his eyes flicking this way and that, the merry smile disappearing. "Where's . . . ah, hell—they ain't gone under, have they? Not Matthew and Johnny Rowland?"

Isaac spoke up, "Them two still kicking!"

Asa cranked his head around the others. "Where have they gone? Off on some errand?"

"Ain't with us no more," Hatcher explained.

McAfferty's eyes narrowed. "Not rubbed out?"

"No," Caleb remarked. "Both of 'em stayed down to Taos."

McAfferty asked, "Women?"

"Yeah, women," Rufus answered with that knowing nod to his head.

His own eyes half-closed, McAfferty pronounced, "This gentler sex: what a curse they be to a man . . . and what a balm those sweet creatures are to all that ails us! *'For the lips of a strange woman drop as an honeycomb, and her mouth is smoother than oil.'*"

"Asa—we had us some Snake women!" Rufus began. "Back at ron-nyvoo in Snake country."

"There'll be more fornication here next day or so," McAfferty declared.

Hatcher grinned. "Injuns coming?"

Asa nodded. "Flatheads was follering Jackson south. Likely make it a day or so behind us."

"How many's the lodge?" Solomon inquired.

"Enough to keep this bunch of hydrophobic wolves busy for some time!" McAfferty roared. "Least sixty . . . seventy lodges."

"Whoooeee! Flathead girls!" Isaac sang.

McAfferty continued, "Jackson got word there was a big village of Snakes coming here to the valley too."

"Gonna be some shinin' times now!" Caleb cried.

" *'Do not prostitute thy daughter, to cause her to be a whore; lest the land fall to whoredom, and the land become full of wickedness,'* " McAfferty snarled.

"Weren't but a few gals on the Popo Agie," Hatcher explained.

"That where Sublette opened up his likker kegs?" Asa inquired.

"Ain't all that good on your tongue," Rufus said. "But it can sure 'nough kick you in the head!"

"Sublette have any likker left him?"

"Near as I know," Hatcher said, "he's got him least half of what he brung out from St. Louie."

McAfferty wiped some fingers across his lips. "I got me a hankering to end this longtime dry, boys. Sublette's up to trading, is he?"

"Damn right he is," Caleb said. "You got plews?"

"I got plenty of plews, Mr. Wood. *'The Lord maketh poor, and maketh rich: He bringest low, and lifteth up.'* "

Hatcher turned to Bass and gestured a thumb at McAfferty. " 'Sides allays spouting his Bible talk, Asa here allays was one of the best for bringing flat-tails to bait. Why, hell—I'll bet he's almost good as you, Scratch!"

Asa asked, "This here new man that good, is he?"

"Notch or two better'n you ever was, Asa," Caleb bragged.

"That so?"

"McAfferty allays was the best at finding prime beaver country too," Jack continued. "Shame when ye up and decided ye was leaving us to ride out on yer own hook, Asa."

Slowly tearing his measuring eyes from Bass, McAfferty stated, "Man goes where a man is called to go. And if the Lord calls him to come alone . . . a man must listen to the commandment of the Lord his God."

"Damn—but you still preachify as purty as you ever did!" Elbridge cried in glee.

Hatcher laid an arm over Bass's shoulder and asked him, "Don't that oily tongue of his'n just make ye wanna ask Preacher McAfferty to bring hisself on out to yer place for dinner on church meeting day?"

"Dear Lord, *'Preserve me from those who would trouble me!'* " Asa roared.

"So you camping with Jackson's bunch?" Caleb asked.

"I go only where the breath of God leads," McAfferty answered. "Usual', that keeps me off on my lonesome."

"Throw in with us for a few days," Isaac suggested.

For a moment Asa looked them over; then his eyes landed on Bass. "Mr. Hatcher—you say this nigger's better trapper than me?"

"That's gospel in my book, McAfferty."

The others muttered their agreement, and Caleb echoed, "The only man I ever knowed better'n you, white hair."

"Awright then," McAfferty confirmed. "I'll camp with you boys for a few days . . . and see just what I can learn that makes this here Titus Bass the finest trapper any of you devil's whelps ever see'd."

In two more days it came to pass that the Flathead camp and a large village of Shoshone reached the pastoral valley where some 175 company men and free trappers had thrown up tents, lean-tos, and blanket shelters at the western foot of the Tetons. The Indians arrived right about the time that the renewed celebration was working itself into a genuine lather.

For better than a day now Sublette had had his kegs opened for trade beneath his canopies. Jackson's Flathead brigade were as eager as any men could be to have themselves a real blow, and the company owners themselves rejoiced in this unexpected reunion.

Like so many others, both skin and free trappers, Titus Bass joined those who gathered in the shady grove where Jedediah Smith captivated his audience with tales of crossing the Mojave desert, the terrible blow of losing ten men to the treachery of those Mojave Indians, and dealing with the capricious Spanish who ruled that land from their Californio settlements and ranchos. Hour after hour he described his confrontations with the haughty and suspicious Monterey officials who kept his men under custody until ultimately releasing them upon Smith's promise never to return to California. From there he described how they had hurried north, selling some of his furs to an American captain who anchored his ship in the Bay of San Francisco before Smith's brigade continued its search for the mythical but famed Buenaventura River that was rumored to carry a man from the west slope of the mountains all the way to the great Pacific Ocean.

But along the southern coast of Oregon country,* Jedediah's company clerk and men let down their guard and allowed a band of seemingly peaceful and childishly curious Kelawatset Indians into their camp one morning—only to be savagely set upon and brutally butchered as the warriors pulled knives, axes, and clubs from beneath their blankets. A lone man, Arthur Black, managed to escape into the forest with his wounds. In addition, due to the fact that they had been out of camp on some duty or another at the time, Smith and two others survived the attack. At first Black believed himself to be the only one alive as he stumbled north to Fort Vancouver. Smith as well believed his little party to be the sole survivors, pushing north themselves with only what they had on their backs, knowing too John McLaughlin's Hudson's Bay post lay on the Columbia River.

---

*At their camp on the Umpqua River in the present-day Oregon, near the site of old Fort McKay—July 14, 1828.

Horses, mules, weapons, traps, blankets, buffalo robes—everything was gone in that senseless massacre.

By early August the four reunited within the bosom of McLaughlin's generous bounty. Through the autumn and into the winter, Smith explained to his awestruck listeners now, the gracious post factor sheltered the Americans, treated them with every courtesy, and even dispatched a sizable brigade to punish the Kelawatsets. What his employees were not able to recover from the severely chastised tribe, McLaughlin promised to do everything he could to repay.

After one of the survivors elected to stay on at Vancouver, and another journeyed east with an English brigade, Smith and Black finally set off for the Rocky Mountains once more in early March, beginning their epic and solitary journey of more than a thousand miles that took them across the entire extent of the great northwest. Passing Fort Colville at Kettle Falls and on past Flathead Post on the Clark's Fork, the pair finally stumbled onto their old friends in the Kootenai country. Familiar faces! At last—back in the arms of their own countrymen!

So here in Pierre's Hole, Smith stood before that gaggle of Americans and reached inside his well-soiled, smoke-smudged shirt to pull forth a leather envelope, from which he took a folded parchment. As one of the few in that assembly who could read, Jedediah clipped off the words scrawled by the hand of no less than Chief Factor John McLaughlin—a draft on the great and powerful Hudson's Bay Company itself!

"I didn't have an idea one you had such a paper on you!" Davy Jackson exclaimed as he and Sublette pounded Smith on the back. He turned to Sublette and explained, "When 'Diah come upon me, we was camped by the shore of the Flatheads' lake, all he and Black was carrying on their skinny, crow-bait horses was a few otter skins they brung all the way from the western ocean! Them, and the hide from a moose he shot last winter up near the Englishers' fort. Now, don't you know 'Diah here looked like one poor digger Injun, that's for sure!"

Because of McLaughlin's kindnesses and his evenhandedness in making those reparations to the destitute Americans, Smith now told the hushed gathering that, although the Snake River country was by treaty jointly held by the U.S. and Britain, he had taken it upon himself to promise on behalf of his company that no American trapping brigade would trouble any waters on the west side of the Rockies.

"But—damn! This here's prime beaver country!" Jackson shrieked in protest.

"Trap over on the other side," Smith suggested in that polite, preacher's-son tone of his. "In *Jackson's* hole!"

Round and round that afternoon the partners argued the question, but in the end the resurrected Smith's Christian charities prevailed upon the other two.

"Maybeso it's a hard country, after all," Sublette relented. "We're liable to lose good men, horses, and traps up there to the goddamned Blackfeet anyway."

"There isn't anything to be gained south and west of the Great Salt Lake either," Smith informed the crowd. "No beaver of any worth down there."

So Sublette prodded, "What you say of California, Jed?"

"Nary any sign there, and the Spanish soldiers are near as bad as Blackfeet."

And in the last few seasons the valleys of the southern Rockies were being trapped by various brigades based out of Taos and Santa Fe: the Uinta and Wasatch front were trapped out by the likes of Etienne Provost and Ewing Young.

Compelled to decide just where they should concentrate their efforts now, the partners determined they would claim that country east of the mountains, on the southern fringe of Blackfoot country, in the land of the Madison and Gallatin, even crossing over to the Yellowstone to trap the rivers west of where Milt Sublette's brigade was at work.

Jedediah Smith's crossings to the Pacific coast had cost the company thousands of dollars in animals and equipment. Accounting for both desertions and massacre, only two of the original expedition who had bid farewell to friends as they departed Sweet Lake back in 1826 were returned to this land of the shining mountains.

While some might eventually say that these expeditions were nothing less than catastrophes, at that moment in the late summer of 1829, there beneath the shadow of the Tetons in Pierre's Hole—let no Englishman doubt that the Americans had come, once again stretching their arms from sea to shining sea.

Call it "manifest destiny," call it what you will—the Americans had come to tramp and map, lay their traps and eventually conquer all of what lay between the Atlantic and the far Pacific.

By that summer of 1829 it was plain the Americans had come to stay.

SEVENTEEN

Pushed up against the late-summer sky stood over a hundred hide lodges, brown as a Snake woman's breast. While both the Shoshone and the Flathead bands chose to spread the horns of their camp circles across the valley floor itself, the white trappers had spread their blankets and raised their canvas shelters back against the trees that bordered this stream flowing right out of the snowfields still mantling the Tetons like a creamy shawl.

Here tarried the morning shadows, and cool mists clung to the surface of every narrow thread of water draining both the Teton and Big Hole ranges that defined this long, narrow valley. There was wood and water and graze enough for those hundreds of Indians and something on the order of 175 white men. With those who had followed Milt Sublette into the Bighorn country, all told, Bass reckoned that there was no more than 220 Americans working the mountains of the far west. A damned rare breed what wandered about in all that lonesome country.

The face of a white man wasn't so common a sight—not yet, he figured that August morning. And he thought back to all those days and weeks and more he had spent on his own—alone by choice, or made lonely by chance. How many times in the past two years had he just wished he could go without hearing another human voice? If only for a whole day. If only to go for enough days with nothing but the soothing quiet of the wilderness itself until that quiet became so overpowering that he could then seek out his own kind.

As long as he had yearned for that rendezvous on the Popo Agie, as much as he had reveled in this even bigger, bawdier Pierre's Hole rendezvous, Bass awoke before sunup this morning, unable to go back to sleep. Restless, unsettled, not knowing what it was plaguing him with a nagging itch he'd have to find some way to scratch.

On the Popo Agie and again here, there had been enough copper flesh pressed against his to sate the woman-hunger until another winter had arrived. Enough too of the numbing alcohol to remind Titus of just how much a fool it could make him and the others as they rolled and wrestled and romped like the young pups none of them were any longer.

Two years now, he thought again—awakened and restless in that predawn darkness. And peered at the six long mounds that were Hatcher and his men cocooned in their blankets. Good men. Men who had saved his life, taken him in, made Bass one of their own. Men who had shown him the very best of the beaver ground in the Bayou Salade, then introduced him proper to Mexican territory, Taos lightning, and those gringo-loving senoritas.

Two years now . . .

Was there such a thing as too much companionship?

He grappled with that dilemma as he stared into the dark and impatiently waited for morning to come. Was this an itch to strike out on his own, or only that annual itch to be done with this summer fair and on to the autumn hunt, planning his winter ground, cogitating on where spring would find him breaking ice to set his traps?

So Scratch watched the light come creeping across the horizon, nothing more than a graying of the sky behind the jagged spires of those Pilot Knobs that rose so stately there could be no denying that a man must surely feel himself anointed to be here in this high kingdom, must surely consider himself one of the chosen to step foot in this virgin land . . . in some way embraced as one of the few who would ever get a glimpse of what lay beyond this world and into the next. So high, so high did they travel that such men as he should surely see right on through the sky.

For too long he had lived in one place. Was it only that his moccasins grew itchy, and he grew anxious to be on the tramp again? Trapped back east among so many people for most of his life, to discover so late what a balm the aloneness could be for his soul. To discover just what the silence in all that was outside of him could do to create serenity for all that rested inside at the marrow of him.

Gone to the banks of the stream as the sun brushed the sky to blue and the Indian camps came alive, Bass splashed cold water on his face, then pushed himself out over the water on locked elbows, dipping his chin right into the bracing liquid so shocking it made him gasp. On the far side sat some women bathing their tiny naked ones in the grass, the children stoic and mute as the sparkling droplets tumbled from their shivering bodies onto the lush green blanket of trampled grass. As he stood, and finally turned to move away, the giggle of children drew him past some tall, concealing willow to find a trio of girls busily chasing a huge bullsnake with their sticks through the grass and brush.

They reminded him of little ones in those camps of the Ute, Crow, and Shoshone where he had passed winters at peace. During those long cold moons the warrior bands were content not to move until the village decided to pick up and find another valley when the wood ran low, or the game disappeared, or the ponies required more of the autumn-cured grass.

Perhaps the warrior had it right, after all, Scratch brooded as he headed downstream toward the Flathead camp.

Indian males celebrated their togetherness in many ways: in the buffalo hunt, at pipe ceremonies, making war, and with those informal talks on all manner of things as they sat in the warm sun while their women went about the camp chores. But, too, many were the warriors he had known who would set off on their own for the hunt, or eager to earn themselves a battle honor, perhaps to steal horses, or only to find an answer to their seeking somewhere on high.

Suddenly stopping dead in his tracks, Scratch nodded emphatically. Although he was alone, he spoke out loud.

"Yes."

Having decided answers came only to those who took their own path.

All a man found among others was the noisy answers that fit only those other men: a garbled babble of talk that was hard to divine.

To find his way back to that serenity he had first discovered in this huge land, Bass realized he had to make his way back toward solitude.

Barefoot and dressed in nothing more than tiny strips of cloth that served as breechclouts held around their waists by narrow rawhide strings, a half-dozen little boys came chasing after another handful as he neared the outer lodges of the village. Yelling taunts and shouting encouragement to one another, flinging their sapling lances or shooting their boyhood bows, they played at these deadly lessons of warfare, this study of dying and death learned so young.

At the edge of a morning fire sat a young woman who glanced up at the white man walking past. In her lap she cradled the head of her free-trapper husband, his eyes closed in exquisite relaxation. Carefully the Flathead squaw parted her husband's coal-black hair, inspecting the scalp painstakingly—until she found another louse, which she seized and cracked between her teeth before tossing it into the fire, then continued her search for the next.

Men and women came and went on foot, or on horseback. Warriors rode past bareback, the expressive eyes in their impassive faces locked on some nether point and never touching his. Girls of marrying age watched him pass as they whispered to one another, their sparkling eyes gleeful above the hands they held over their mouths as they shared secrets about him, giggling coyly, playful at the arts of catching themselves a mate.

"Mr. Bass!"

He stopped, turning toward the sound of the voice, searching for the caller. Ahead in the shadows stood a small group of Flathead warriors, busy with some concern near a lodge door. One of the men waved, called out.

"Ho, Mr. Bass!"

Only then did he see how that warrior differed from the others. While the rest wore their hair plaited, braided, adorned, and unmistakably black, the one who called wore white.

"McAfferty? That you?"

Asa stepped away from the Flathead men. "You was up early—gone afore I rolled out this morning."

"Didn't sleep in."

"I see'd such is the way about you," McAfferty said as he came to a halt before Bass. "That what makes you so damned good a trapper?"

He grinned. "Maybeso, Asa. Get them flat-tails afore the day gets old." Then, with a gesture, he asked, "What brings you to the Flatheads so early of the day?"

Shrugging, McAfferty replied, "I happed to spend me some of last winter with this very bunch. Stayed on in their country for spring trapping."

"Spring gotta come late that far north."

Shuddering slightly, Asa declared, "No truer words was ever spoke. I was hunting on my own hook and about to mosey south for ronnyvoo when I run onto some of Davy Jackson's boys. Said they was soon to start back to join up with their booshway so to make their way to ronnyvoo their own selves. Sounded like a fine notion to me."

Bass felt the sensation grow strong deep within him: something snagging his curiosity, pulling at it like the hooked claw of a golden eagle tearing at the body of its prey, peeling it back and making him suddenly aware of what lay beneath.

"You said you was . . . was on your own hook?"

McAfferty looked at him strangely a moment before answering, "Didn't none of Jack's boys tell you how I come to part company with 'em?"

"S'pose they did, yes."

Asa stared off toward that far border of trees where the white men had their camp. "I ain't one to stay with a gaggle of fellers, not for long I ain't."

"They said you up and had to take your own way."

"Now, don't go getting me wrong, Mr. Bass. Ain't but a few men near as good as Jack Hatcher to lead a bunch of niggers what want to go their own road and do things their own way. And the rest . . . why, I likes some better'n others, but that's a bunch what'll be there when it comes time for the nut-cuttin'."

Scratch nodded. "They've been at my back ever' time I've needed some backing up. Never let me down, not once."

"And they won't. That just ain't their way," Asa argued. Then he seemed to regard the man before him carefully until he said, "You ain't really the sort what cottons to a lot of folks around either, are you, Mr. Bass?"

"S'pose I'm not," he admitted.

"How long you say you been with Jack's outfit?"

"Almost two years now since I got my hair stole and Jack's bunch run onto me up by the Wind River hills."

With a cluck McAfferty replied, "That's a long time for a man such as yourself to stay hooked up with others."

"Maybeso. Then again, maybe not."

"For some men, like the rest of them what been together for years and years now, it ain't nothing to run in a pack with others winter after winter."

Scratch looked deep into McAfferty's icy blue eyes. "But for you?"

"For me?" he asked, then sighed. "I ain't like most. Had my fill of faithless folks long time back. East it was. For winters now I ain't been the sort to stay on with this bunch or that very long at all. Sets better by me to have my friends, spend time, trap, and winter up with 'em . . . then move on afore we find we ain't friends no more. Maybeso that makes me a hard one to live with, eh, Mr. Bass?"

"None of 'em claimed you was a hard keeper, McAfferty."

"I 'spect they wouldn't—that's why I moved on after a couple seasons with them boys. Took off afore we wasn't friends no more. Do you figger it's wrong to ride off before being round others starts to stick in my craw? Is it wrong that I pack up plunder and plews and get high behind down my own trail?"

"Don't sound onreasonable to me, if'n a man's made of such," Bass declared.

"You the sort what likes to mosey on his own, Mr. Bass?"

"I . . . " And Scratch paused a moment, reflecting, "I s'pose I am. Truly."

"Never was much a joiner, was you?"

"Can't say I was."

Then McAfferty's eyes narrowed as he gazed at Titus. "The trapping's better when there ain't so many to split the take."

With a shrug Bass said, "We allays worked our own places on the stream. Never was a problem for me."

"Just give yourself a shake or two and think on it. How good you'd do 'thout all them others working that same stream."

"It ain't all about the beaver—"

But McAfferty grabbed hold of Bass's elbow and turned him so they directly faced the west slope of the Tetons. With an arm, he waved slowly across their granite ruggedness, saying, "Now, look up there and tell me how good you'd do in beaver country, if you was the only one working a stream. Maybeso it's only you and 'nother trapper."

He turned to appraise Asa. "I had me a good spring what got me a fine hurraw on the Popo Agie. Had me 'nough plews last fall to get me a fine winter down to Taos too."

"Fine place, ain't that Taos?" McAfferty said in a low voice, letting go of Bass's elbow and licking his lips almost as if remembering the taste of *aguardiente* and Mexican tobacco.

"Catched all the beaver I needed to outfit for me 'nother year, 'long with a little likker—"

"But think of what you'd have if all them beaver been your own."

Wagging his head, Scratch said, "A man don't need all the beaver to hisself."

McAfferty stepped right around in front of Titus again, toe to toe. "But there's some men what need one hell of a lot of country for their own. Now, you just try to tell me I got you wrong, Mr. Bass. You tell me you ain't one to wanna drink up all that big space out there for your own self."

"I . . . I ain't never thought about—"

"You tell me you ain't the sort what wouldn't jump at the chance to see new country, country where *you* chose to go—not where you foller along behind the rest."

He shook his head, as if it didn't make sense. "Much as I fought me Blackfoot, I ain't so damned certain a man on his lonesome ain't a crazy nigger just waiting to die."

Asa rocked back on his heels a moment. "So you're the sort figgers you wanna die in a tick bed back east somewheres, white folk' sheets pulled up around as you go off to sleep, eh?"

"Damn well don't."

McAfferty's booming voice beginning to rise dramatically, Asa stated, "Then set off on your own hook—and say to hell with Blackfoot country when there's more land to see than you and I both'll ever lay eyes on in our natural lives."

If it wasn't downright contagious, just the way this ex-circuit-riding preacher man stirred up the juices within him.

"You understand that, don't you, Mr. Bass?" McAfferty said. "You don't have to trap Blackfoot country, less'n you cotton to the idee of losing more of your scalp."

"Lost all I wanna lose—"

"There's country far south of here what ain't had a trap set in it. Ever."

"There's country like that down to Taos?"

McAfferty wagged his white mane vigorously. "I ain't talking about Taos, or that Santa Fe country. I've heard tell of other rivers what take a man off torst the Californios."

"There's beaver there?"

"There's beaver on the Heely!"

Scratch swallowed hard, considering, weighing, hefting it the way he would hoist his trap sack first thing of an evening as he went out to make his sets.

Eventually Titus asked, "Ain't a white man been there afore?"

"Not one I hear tell of ever set a mokerson down out in that country."

Bass finally tore his eyes from McAfferty's convincing gaze to stare again at the deep-purple-hued peaks. "Sounds to me like you're talking about a couple fellers throwing in together, Asa. Them two fellers what Jack and the rest of his bunch says're the best trappers in these here mountains."

Asa stepped up so close that Scratch could feel the warmth in the man's breath as he spoke, their noses all but touching as they locked eyes. "I'm saying you throw in with me, Mr. Bass—and you ain't ever gonna wish you hadn't. There's streams out there so thick with beaver, a man don't have to . . . but you said it ain't the beaver you're here for, is it, Mr. Bass?"

"The plews keep me in coffee and powder," Titus declared. "The fur buys the geegaws for a squaw or two—"

"But the beaver ain't what brought you," McAfferty interrupted, a single finger tapping against Bass's breastbone. "And that beaver ain't what keeps you here either."

Right there, staring into the depths of that man's blue eyes, he was certain McAfferty was peering right on down into his very soul. Finding the truth there that he himself had rarely considered, if ever admitted to. Perhaps this was the same powerful pull that he had seen drag grown-up folks out of those crowds gathered on the banks of rivers back east in Kentucky where he had grown up, the lure that pulled men and women right out of the crowd to join a preacher man standing waist-deep down in the stream, the same seductive call that caused those people to turn themselves over to that preacher and have themselves laid back in the water within the cradle of his arms. . . .

"I ain't so sure—"

"You're certain enough that you don't belong in no outfit no more, Mr. Bass," Asa interrupted, his voice softer now.

"Don't mean I can just ride off from Jack and the others—"

"And I ain't expecting you to," McAfferty whispered. "You wanna hook up with me?"

"Hadn't thought 'bout it afore."

"But you're thinking 'bout it now."

He finally nodded.

"Telling 'em's a simple thing," Asa explained. "Jack Hatcher's the sort what understands. Time came for me to go, I set it by him and he didn't stand in my way."

Bass nodded again, then said, "So did Matthew Kinkead, and Johnny Rowland too."

"Them too, yes," McAfferty echoed. "Comes a time when a man must make his own way and don't follow the shadow of others."

"I'm a better trapper'n any of 'em," Scratch declared, surprising himself.

"You ought'n be showed for just how good you are!"

Scratch turned and gazed at the distant trees across the creek, off in the direction where he had pitched camp with Jack Hatcher's bunch. Where Asa McAfferty camped too. Then he peered back at the white-head. At last he spoke.

"Where's that country you said ain't never had a trap laid down in it that you know of?"

"On the Heely."

"I s'pose you're right that if nary a white man ever set a foot down in that country," Titus confirmed, "then it bears out that there ain't never been no traps set along those rivers."

McAfferty's eyes widened, a smile crinkling that stark white beard. "No one there, Mr. Bass. No one . . . but Injuns."

It felt as if the very air around him were sucking him dry.

Not anything like the steamy country back where Bass had grown up along the Ohio and the Mississippi: where a man slowly simmered in his own juices.

Out here far beyond the western slopes of the southern Rockies they had confronted an unimaginable heat, the air around them so hot, Scratch figured it could boil fat off a flea. The sunlight grew so intense that several times a day Scratch swore his skin was shriveling, becoming just as crisp as those cracklins his mam used to fry up for him back in Kentucky . . . so stark and white was the radiance all around him that it felt as if his eyes were melting while he struggled to focus them on the dancing horizon, everything shimmering in the distance through the midst of that incomprehensible heat.

And the farther south they pushed, the hotter it became.

They desperately needed to find water for their animals, for themselves, before there was nothing left of him but a cracklin like those pan-fried pork rinds his grandpap had so loved to eat. Just to find a pool in some stream deep enough for him to sit—even to lie right down in—submerged right up to his chin so every square inch of his body could soak up that blessed moisture.

Titus didn't know what was worse: sizzling beneath his thick buckskin war shirt as they plodded on hour after hour, or how the sun's powerful rays penetrated right on through that old linsey-woolsey shirt he wore under the buckskin, soaking up the sweat. This morning both he and McAfferty had decided to strip to the waist about the same time, lashing their garments behind their saddles as they kept on moving. It didn't take long for Scratch to realize just how big a mistake that was.

By midafternoon, with the sun still hanging high and seemingly reluctant to begin its slide into the west, Bass realized he was growing lightheaded. Strangely . . . dreamlike. Everything he peered at around him had an unreal quality to it, shimmering, all the edges ill defined and watery, every object pale, all but translucent as they were swallowed up in the endless waves of heat rising from sand and rock and brush alike.

Up ahead of him a few yards McAfferty slowly keeled to the side in his saddle, tipping so far this time that he spilled off in a heap, sprawled on the hot-baked hardpan.

Of a sudden it became an insurmountable struggle for Bass to get the reins pulled back and halt his horse. He sat there a moment, huffing with exhaustion, wavering in the saddle himself, staring at McAfferty's body lying just as twisted as one of his sister's sock dolls on the sand-flecked, sunburned grass while he sorted out just what he would do to get himself off his horse.

His head swimming, Scratch leaned until he felt all his weight shifted to his right leg, pain crying out in that foot stuffed in its wide cottonwood stirrup. As he brought his free leg up, he lost control, spinning out of the saddle, losing his balance, careening onto the ground, landing on his back to stare at the pale, fiery sky and that unblinking yellow eye, with that one foot still tangled in its stirrup.

It took only a moment for him to realize that the ground beneath him was on fire, so hot he wasn't sure he might not just burst into flame himself. In a dizzying surge of effort, Bass kicked his foot free, rolling to the side so he could rock back onto his knees. That accomplished, he brought one leg under him, reached up for the stirrup, and pulled himself onto his feet—gasping for air. Lunging forward on legs that weren't quite heeding his commands, Scratch stumbled across the last few yards to McAfferty's side, where he gratefully sank back to the burning ground.

After a painful struggle he managed to get Asa rolled onto his back. Sand and flecks of the gold, withered grass clung to the man's oak-brown cheek and forehead, plastered there above the stark white whiskers. As Bass bent over McAfferty's face, hovering above it to peer closely at his partner, he put Asa in a shadow. Almost immediately the eyes fluttered open into no more than crusted slits, grains of sand embedded in his damp eyelids.

Asa's cracked lips quivered for a moment, his parched, bloated tongue trying to form the words until he spat them out. "C-cut me."

"Cut you?"

"Knife," the bleeding lips instructed. "Cut my wr-wrist."

"Use my knife?"

Slowly McAfferty nodded as if his head weighed more than their trap sacks. "Here." But it was some time before Asa urged some movement out of one of his red, burned arms and pointed at the other wrist. "You cut. I'll suck."

It still didn't make sense. "Cut you so you'll bleed?"

"Suck . . . bl-blood."

"I can't cut you—"

With what had to be the last vestige of the man's strength, McAfferty grabbed a handful of Bass's long brown hair and tugged on it hard enough to pull Titus right down toward his face.

"Only ch-chance," Asa croaked with a voice so dry it sounded like a dry rasp being dragged across coarse cast iron. "Blood . . . save me . . . till we . . . get to the river."

Then with an exhausted gasp Asa released his hair, and Scratch slowly raised his head, squinting below that wide brim of his hat to peer off at first one horizon, then another, and finally in a third, endless direction. Nothing of any promise in sight.

"Yeah, Asa. You just hol' on. The river ain't far now."

But he knew McAfferty wouldn't make it . . . unless he cut the man. With a trembling hand Scratch reached around to the small of his back to drag the skinning knife from its rawhide sheath. His vision was blurring, his eyes stinging more and more from the sweat and the blowing sand: red, raw, bloodshot. Scratch didn't know for sure if it was the salty drops seeping into them, or perhaps that his eyes were simply starting to melt, oozing out of their sockets and right on down his cheeks into the thick beard.

After he had blinked, and blinked some more, to clear them for a moment, Bass peered down to find McAfferty's head slumped to the side, the man's eyes half-closed, only the whites showing in that glare of brutal light.

Painfully, Scratch dragged his knees across the hardpan earth, scooting right up to Asa's shoulder, where he jabbed his left arm under his partner's neck. With his fingers locked under McAfferty's armpit, he heaved against the dead weight. That effort made his stomach threaten to hurl itself against his tonsils. He bent over the body, gasping as he squinted his eyes shut, then groaned, gritting his teeth the moment he heaved against the weight once more.

Succeeding in getting McAfferty's shoulders propped against his thigh, Bass shuddered from that last terrible exertion. With a raspy sigh that felt as if he had swallowed cactus needles, Scratch dragged Asa's far arm across his lap. Clamping the wrist in his left hand to steady it, he laid the sharp edge of the blade against the inside of the wrist . . . then suddenly found himself staring at that line where the dark saddle-leather-brown hide of the hand ended and the sunburned crimson began as it climbed up the man's white skin.

He gritted his teeth, resolute.

Across that tan line he compressed the blade into the reddened flesh, struggling to focus his eyes again, to whip his mind back to the task before him . . . until he suddenly realized he was watching the man's blood oozing from the laceration.

"Asa," he gasped in hope. "Here, Asa."

Letting the knife spill from his right hand, Titus grasped hold of McAfferty's chin at the same time he raised the bleeding wrist toward Asa's mouth.

Rubbing the wound against the cracked lips, Scratch murmured, "Here. Suck, Asa. Suck, dammit!"

But his partner did not move.

In despair Bass rubbed the wrist back and forth over the dry, cracked lips, still without response from McAfferty. Titus dropped the wrist and slapped a flat hand across Asa's cheek.

The eyes fluttered, clenched, then slowly opened as McAfferty's thick, blackened tongue came out to lick at the lips.

"That's your blood, dammit!" Scratch whimpered down at his partner. "Suck . . . suck it now or you're . . . you're done."

It took all he had left in him to grab the wrist again and drag it to Asa's mouth, holding it there against the lips as McAfferty's eyes closed and his lips parted, tongue flicking out to taste the blood. Then Asa finally began to suck on the wound, swallowing slowly.

For the longest time Titus watched McAfferty draw at his own blood before Asa turned his head and attempted to gaze up at Bass, his eyes slowly swimming, rolling.

"G-get us to . . . water. Get water."

With the deadweight of a sack of meal, Asa's head went limp across Bass's arm.

Unable to support it any longer, Scratch pulled his arm free, gasping for air as if his lungs were filled with hot coals. Squatting there by the body of his partner, Titus stared down at his own wrists. Then he peered over at the bloodstained knife lying by his knee.

The antler handle had a strange, foreign feel in his hand as he scooped it from the ground. A sensation not quite real as he laid the knife lengthwise along his own wrist and without hesitation pressed it down until his watery eyes finally noticed the blood seeping up on either side of the narrow blade already crusted with sparkling particles of sand.

Surprised that there was no pain, Scratch continued to ease the blade down into his skin, opening himself up even more. As the dark fluid began to bead and tumble off his forearm, Titus yanked the wrist to his mouth, began sucking noisily. His eyes fluttered half-closed in that feral way of an animal savoring the warm, moist nourishment of its prey.

Blood thick as his mam's Kentucky sugarcane molasses. So warm against his lips, oozing back upon his tongue. He swallowed, sensing himself gag, feeling his stomach lurch in revolt. Desperate, he shoved the bile back down, his throat stinging with the acid's burn, its fiery aftertaste, and kept on sucking.

At the back of his neck he became aware of the fire against his skin. Revived enough now to raise his head, Bass turned and glanced at the path the sun was taking into the west. They might just stand a chance now . . . make it through till nightfall. But they damn well needed shade until the sun had limped from the sky.

"H-hannah," he whispered, able to coax no more out of his throat.

Sucking some more on his wrist, Titus used the tip of his tongue to smear that blood over his lips until they were moistened, then tried to whistle. Nothing more than a faint shrill sound. Beginning to feel hopeful at this small success, Bass watched the half-dead mule roll her big head to the side and peer over at him.

He licked the lips again and whistled. This time she obediently started to turn his way. Then stopped.

"Hannah," he croaked.

She came on around with his coaxing. The mule worked unsteadily at those next few steps, turning slightly, picking up one hoof at a time beneath her burdens, finally drawing close enough that he could reach out with his bloody arm and grab for the lead rope. On the fourth try he captured the braided rawhide and looped it around the hand. Now he was able to nudge her closer, eventually turning her so that she stood nearly on top of them to block the bright light. So hot had the direct rays become that this sudden shadow seemed like the cooling breath carried by a spring breeze.

It surprised him when his saddle mount came over to join the mule. Nor was it long before one of McAfferty's packhorses came over to join the others. He let himself collapse to the side in relief. A good thing it was, he thought as he let his head rest atop his elbow on that hot ground—good that horses were a damned sight more sociable than he was.

There in the collective shade made by those near-dead animals, Scratch closed his eyes and sighed, letting his mind drift now that his tongue wasn't near so swollen with thirst, now that he could feel some saliva beginning to work up at the back of his throat, around that tiny pebble he had stuffed under his tongue back near sunup. In a while he figured he just might have enough strength to get up and cut a horse's ear for McAfferty.

Not . . . right now.

In a while.

On that August morning—what seemed like ages ago now—he and McAfferty had hastened back to Hatcher's camp, eager to announce their plans to set off on their lonesome to the others, who were trudging over groggily to settle by the fire and swill down some steaming coffee.

"Here I thought you was a happy man being part of us!" Caleb Wood sputtered, the first of them to protest.

Elbridge Gray shook his head woefully, pursing his lips until he exploded, "Can't believe you'd up and leave us now, Scratch—after all we been through together for the last two years!"

Isaac agreed. "And after all we done to take you in with us!"

Their reactions making him feel the first pangs of regret, Scratch nodded and said, "I'll always be a grateful man, fellas—for all you done by me. But don't get it wrong just 'cause I aim to make my own tracks now. I'm beholden to you, for always."

With that sentiment encouraging them, Caleb, Isaac, and Elbridge did their best to caution Scratch against pulling up his stakes and setting off alone with Asa McAfferty.

"Goddammit, Bass," Simms growled, smearing drops of coffee collected in the broom bristle of his whitish-blond mustache. "You damn well know how many times we had a scrap with the Blackfoot our own selves in the last two years."

Gray nodded vigorously. "And now you wanna set off with just the two of you niggers!"

"We ain't going nowhere near Blackfeet country!" McAfferty protested after remaining silent for so long.

But Wood ignored the white-head, jabbing a finger at Bass instead, just as that turkey-wattled schoolmaster back to Kentucky had jabbed once too often. "Pick up and move off from us, Scratch? And here I thought you was our friend!" Caleb glared a moment at McAfferty.

"This don't mean I ain't your friend no more—"

Wood fumed, "But I guess you ain't our friend, are you, Scratch! I s'pose now I can see just how your stick floats—"

"A man does what he thinks best," Jack Hatcher interrupted the tongue-lashing, immediately shushing them all. "Bass allays been that sort to take the circle. Even though I don't agree with him one whit . . . I'll trust to what Scratch thinks best for hisself."

"Y-you mean you're gonna let him go off like this, Jack?" Rufus asked, his voice rising an octave in disbelief.

Hatcher didn't answer all that quickly. Instead, his unwavering gaze landed on McAfferty. Then he said, "I'll trust in both of 'em, boys. Ye 'member we rode with both of these men of a time." Then his eyes came over to fix on Titus. "And now it 'pears that the time for us to ride together's come to an end."

"Don't mean we reached the knot at the end of our days together," Bass replied, his throat filled with sentiment, suddenly sensing the ghostly presence of so many of those who lived on now only in his memory.

"Ye leaving us . . . it's been coming for some time," Jack explained. "I seen it plain as prairie sun. Some folks need others around 'em all the time—like the rest of these boys. Then . . . there's folks like you, Titus Bass. The sort of man what does best left on his own."

Those words reverberated someplace within him now, like the waves of heat rising off the cast-iron surface of this land.

Scratch didn't know how long he had been lying there with his eyes closed, his half-cooked mind numb from the dizzying heat, his thoughts running in this direction, then that, just the way Hannah would urinate on this baked and flinty ground, the hot yellow piss streaming off in one little rivulet, then a second, and then another speeding there, finally a fourth narrow dribble fingering across the merciless, endless crust of the flaky sand.

With a cold seizure of his heart, Scratch wondered if he had made a mistake—come so far into this devil's fry pan to die with McAfferty. Maybeso he came only to prove something to himself.

Could he make it on his own hook?

Or was the real problem that he doubted he would ever be able to trust in another man as fully as he had trusted in those three before they disappeared with near everything he had labored for?

And while he was questioning himself and what he had done: should he have followed McAfferty out of rendezvous back in August? Or had he only been blinded by the prospect of virgin beaver streams where no white man had ever laid a moccasin?

In the end, was he cut out for making it on his own hook?

Hearing Asa groan, Bass reluctantly opened his eyes. It was still shady on him. Peering up, he could see that all of their five animals remained around them. What a sight he and Asa must make, and he tried to chuckle in that taut, sunburned face of his. Out here where nothing green grew tall enough to brush a horse's belly, their little tableau would stand right out on the flat, baked desert for many miles around. Those horses and that mule ringing two near-dead, completely stupid niggers . . . a pair of men waiting for the buzzards to come circling above them in the clear, pale, steamy sky. Waiting for those naked brown Apache to pick up their trail again.

"B-bass."

It took some doing, but Titus slid his head off his arm, raised himself on an elbow, and made his face hover somewhere over McAfferty's.

"Night c-coming?" Asa asked as the shadow crossed his eyes.

"Not near soon 'nough."

McAfferty's brow sagged with despair. "God d-deliver us . . ."

Bass waited a while, then admitted how likely it was that McAfferty was sleeping again. As much as he wished he could, something down inside his gut nagged at him the way a tiny cockleburr got itself hitched under a saddle blanket and chafed the animal, irritating the horse's hide until that animal fought to throw off its torment.

Licking his lips, Scratch again tasted the blood. Blinking, he found that this time his eyes did not sting with sweat, nor swim with blurry images. Grunting, Titus straightened, sitting right up beside McAfferty in that shady ring of horseflesh. Alongside his head hung the wide wooden stirrup on Asa's Mexican saddle. It would do about as good as anything.

Seizing it first in one hand, then with the other, Bass took a deep, hot breath and began to pull himself onto his knees. The weakened horse whinnied, protesting at the sudden shift of weight on its saddle as the animal peered back at him.

"There . . . there, there," he tried to coo.

Astonished to discover he was already up on one knee, Titus pulled with his arms, pushed with his legs, lunging up with an arm to snag that wide dish of the saddlehorn. Pulling still more as his knees began to straighten, his head suddenly fuzzy again, light as cottonwood down.

He gasped in surprise, relieved to find that he was standing.

Forced to squint into narrow slits now that he was no longer protected in the horses' shade, Scratch peered across the distance—struggling to focus through the shimmering, dancing heat waves streaming up from the monotonous ground and that ocean of low brush struggling just to survive beneath a fiery sun. Then he turned slightly, clinging desperately to the saddlehorn with that one hand, the other arm draped around the cantle. Slowly he turned a little more, gazing far, far out into the distance. Checking for a smudge of dust, looking for any betrayal of black, beetlelike forms swimming watery along the shimmying horizon. He did not allow himself another deep breath of the superheated air until he had peered in all directions.

Nothing. Almost as if he and Asa and their animals were the only living things for hundreds of miles around. But, then, he knew better. The Apache were somewhere out there. Following on foot through the broken country. Likely the red bastards had already reached this flat, endless stretch of valley at the base of the rocky mountainside and were coming on. Tracking the white men and their half-dead animals.

Should they drop the animals now and fort up, preparing for the inevitable?

There wasn't any question that the Apache would follow them, relentlessly. Both he and Asa knew it. The warriors had been dogging their trail for the better part of five days already. Pursuing the trappers right on through the cleft in the mountains, across the plateau, driving them right on down into this sea bottom of a desert.

There wasn't a reason in all of God's creation why the Apache would give up now. Especially when the trappers' horses were slowing, when the white men hadn't come across water in three days . . . when the sonsabitches could waltz right in on him and Asa come nightfall.

More than ever, Bass realized he had to get them to some shelter. Trees . . . not a prayer of finding that much cover out here. Maybeso some rocks to hunker behind. By a miracle perhaps they would happen upon some animal's den out of the sun and out of sight near a narrow stream. Water and shelter, both.

Which did a man need more right now? he brooded hopelessly, his mind unable to cling to one thing for too long.

Plain enough to see they needed water and shelter, both.

But to get the strength to push on as long as it would take to find that water and shelter, Scratch realized he needed more blood. He needed to open up one of the horse's ears. Maybe even open up a leg back of the pastern.

Daringly, he hobbled away from Asa's saddle, inching his way toward his own horse's neck and up to its head, struggling to focus on the ear. But of a sudden he stopped, stumbled to the side and made for McAfferty's packhorse. Its ears were bigger. He ran his hands over one of them, finding it all the thicker, jug-headed cayuse that it was. Best to cut Asa's animal. Besides, he rationalized, if it meant that he might have to coax some additional bottom from his own horse in the hours to come, then the smart thing for him was to bleed McAfferty's mount.

Wobbly there beside the big head, Scratch pulled out the skinning knife while he positioned the ear in the flat of his hand. As he brought the knife close, one of the big eyes rolled back as if to inspect what the human was about to do.

"Easy, boy," he murmured at the gelding.

It was all he could do to keep his balance on those watery knees, to hold the horse's twitching ear steady as he drew the knife down one of the fat veins.

The blood burst readily from the wound as he yanked the knife away, immediately poking his head beneath the ear, his dry mouth flung open, its blackened, bloated tongue protruding like a huge strip of half-dried buffalo liver, doing his utmost to catch every precious drop of that hot stream of life. Milking the ear from the wide base, he continued to steadily stroke toward the cut he had made, squeezing gently below the wound as the horse began a

slow, circling sidestep. For every one of its moves, Bass moved—always staying right with that drooling wound as he licked and swallowed until the
animal finally relented and stopped so Scratch could pull gently down on the
base of the ear, urging the big head closer to his own face. Now he pressed
his lips right against the open vein, lapping every bit as greedily as any man
would suck at fresh marrow bones pulled warm and toasted from the fire.

The hot, thick liquid dribbled from his lower lip, down his chin into his
gray-brown whiskers.

Suddenly he drew back for a moment, gasping for breath—as his lungs
felt the shock of the heated air. He clenched his eyes shut and sucked some
more of the warm blood.

Finally sensing his stomach lurch in revolt of the warm fluid, Bass
pulled away, gasping again.

It was a few moments before he realized he was standing there on his
own. No longer was he barely holding himself up, braced against the horse.
As he tugged down the floppy brim on his felt hat, Scratch felt his stomach
slowly settle. Perhaps it had made peace with the blood.

To straighten his shoulders now, draw himself up, and flex his arms and
knees—all made him feel one hell of a lot better than he had for days.

He blinked his eyes and stared off into the distance: first here, then
there as he licked his lips, conscious of the blood's sharp metallic tang coating his mouth. They had maybe as much as three hours till dark. Less until
sunset . . . but something more than that until it would be dark enough for
them to venture forth without being spotted by the Apache out there, somewhere in the distance.

No sign of a dust cloud, but then—the Apache wouldn't be the sort to
raise a cloud of dust, would they?

Squatting beside his partner in Hannah's shadow, he slowly raised
McAfferty across his leg again. "We gotta push on, Asa."

"G-go on 'thout m-me." The voice sounded hollow, thick with despair.

"Help me get you up," Scratch demanded.

"Leave m-me. Lo, I travel through the deserts—"

"I ain't leaving you," he argued, shifting himself beside McAfferty.

"Just y-you go on 'thout—"

"Shuddup, you stupid idjit."

Pulling Asa's arm straight out from the shoulder, Scratch ducked his
head under it. Looping his right arm around McAfferty's thigh, he rolled his
partner and struggled to get both his legs under the man's deadweight as he
rocked back—settling as much of the load right over his shoulders, then his
legs, that strongest part of his body.

Weaving, wobbly at first, he quivered as he steadily rose with Asa
slumped across his shoulders. Steadying himself, Bass lurched those few

steps to the side of McAfferty's mount, braced a shoulder against the animal, then heaved with all he had to shove the man's upper body across the saddle.

Asa grunted, half-delirious, as he slid across the hot leather.

"That's right, nigger," Titus grumbled. "Hope it hurt you bad as it hurt me to get your flea-bit, crow-bait carcass throwed up there."

Tossing McAfferty's reins back over the flat, saucer-shaped horn, Scratch turned, exhausted, then caught his breath in the blazing heat of that unforgiving southwestern desert. Weaving forward, he patted the mule's neck, murmuring assurance to her.

"I ain't 'bout to die here. Not now."

Then stumbled on by to take up the reins to his mount.

Stuffing his left foot into the stirrup, he gripped both hands around the horn—about the size and shape of a large Spanish orange—and managed to drag himself into the saddle. After he had shifted his weight back against the cantle, he brought the horse around, then leaned across to catch up the reins to McAfferty's mount.

Urging his horse away, Bass clucked at Hannah to follow, his lips too dry again to whistle anymore.

He raised his eyes to the blazing bone-yellow sky overhead, praying his thanks that the mule and McAfferty's horses chose to follow.

Where they were going, he didn't have a goddamned idea.

But they had less than three hours to find water, or they wouldn't last through the following day.

As much as he tried, Scratch couldn't squeeze away the realization of what that came down to: they had less than three hours to keep their lead on the Apache who were following.

The Apache who wouldn't be stopping for anything as long as they had a white man's trail to follow.

EIGHTEEN

Just what hell would be worse?

Dying of thirst? Or dying at the hands of those Apache?

One was slow . . . painful to the point of sheer, unbearable agony it was so slow. While the other was nothing short of a real gamble. It could be fast: taking a stone arrow in the lights, or through the heart, maybe having his head caved in by a war club or his throat slit with a knife as those pursuing warriors closed in for the dirty eye-to-eye of it.

Then again . . . from what they had decided some days back, the Apache likely could make a white man's dying such a slow and exquisitely unimaginable torture that he might yearn all the more for this slow death from thirst as his tongue bloated until he could no longer swallow, no longer breathe. A savvy man might just have to prefer this agonizing broil right out under the sun itself to having the Apache hang him upside down over a low fire so that his brain slowly cooked and the blood that pooled in his head was eventually brought to a boil, his own juices so hot steam escaped from his ears.

At least that's the way Hatcher's bunch had described some of the most delicious ways the Apache could make a white man linger in his dying.

And all the way south from Pierre's Hole, Asa had told him even more stories he had heard from other trappers who had worked the southwestern streams out of Taos and Santa Fe. Men who rode with the likes of Sylvester Pattie and his son, James Ohio Pattie, other men who trapped with Ewing Young or Etienne Provost. While the southern trapper did not have to concern himself with the horse-thieving Crow and the scalp-hungry Blackfoot, McAfferty made it plain that they would have to cross the land of the troublesome Diggers—so poor they ate insects and dressed in rabbit hides, a people who shot small rock-tipped arrows at the white trappers and their horses, arrows the Diggers used to hunt their small game and birds, rock-chip points nowhere big enough to cause death—just big enough that the Diggers would be a nuisance to their remuda of horses.

Pushing south from there a man entered the land of the Apache.

He realized the horse below him was beginning to move more slowly now, almost rocking from side to side as it plodded ahead. Bass did what he could to keep his head tucked to the side, his eyes closed. As the late sun dipped below the big brim of his hat, it still had enough glare to peel a man's skin back. As he rocked atop his saddle, his thoughts slid back and forth, in and out of dream.

He desperately tried to remember, scolding himself that he must open his eyes every now and then to scan the horizon behind them for sign of the Apache—perhaps no more than a telltale spiral of dust barely discernible as it rose into the buttermilk sky.

Ahead or to the side he was forced to squint to cut out the glare in his search for some dark border that hinted at enough moisture to be a creek-bed, murmuring something on the order of a prayer that he might locate that river bottom. Praying that they would again run onto the meandering course of the Heely they had abandoned days ago when they sprinted away to escape from these warriors who wore long breechclouts and tall leather boot moccasins, wide bandannas of colorful Mexican cloth tied around their heads. And poor skin quivers rattling with arrows.

Scratch hadn't really seen them up close, not yet anyway.

Days back McAfferty had run across the sign late one afternoon—fresh tracks that suggested there were Apache in the area. Moccasin prints only, no pony hooves.

"That much be the Eternal Lord's blessing," Asa had exclaimed. "This ain't a riding bunch. Ain't stole no horses from the greasers east of here. Maybeso we got a chance to outrun 'em."

That's when Scratch had chortled. "Outrun 'em? Jehoshaphat! Have your brains been fried down in this country? Course we can outrun 'em—bunch of poor Injuns ain't even got no horses to ride—"

"You stupid idjit!" McAfferty interrupted with a warning. "On foot them Apache can damn well keep up with a man on horseback."

He had stopped his chuckling when he saw the serious pinch on Asa's face. "You ain't blowing a bald-face windy?"

"This is the Lord's truth," McAfferty swore. "I see'd it once my own self. Heard of it more'n a handful of times from others what saw it with their own eyes. *'Arise, O Lord; save me, O my God: for thou hast smitten all mine enemies upon the cheek bone; thou hast broken the teeth of the ungodly.'*"

So those bastards could near keep up with a white man on horseback. And what little lead a man might gain through a day of riding was most times eaten right up when he stopped for the night, stopped to water and graze his done-in mount, stopped because it got just too damned dark to attempt crossing that unforgiving stretch of near-barren rock.

After crossing the Snake as they headed south from Pierre's Hole, Scratch and Asa struck out for the Soda Springs northwest of the Sweet Lake before pushing on down along the foot of the Wasatch front, which took them through the valley of the Great Salt Lake. Skirting the eastern edge of that first, startlingly flat desert, they trapped the narrow streams draining the Pahvant Range, able to bring nothing more to bait than some miserably small beaver, their poor plews hardly worth skinning out. They plodded on, day by day, remaining hopeful that by working this far south, that autumn would last all the longer, that they could trap the Heely country right on into the middle of winter.

Resolutely they continued past the brilliant colors and haunting, wind-sculpted bridges and monoliths that made Scratch uneasy as he imagined those tall formations to be the ancient haunts of petrified monsters of a bygone era that might just return to life come dark, freed to roam this strange canyon and land of high desert until the next sun would rise.

Every distant sound, every changing shadow cast upon the rocks rising about him—it all pricked his imagination to conjure up fierce hoo-doos and formless wraiths.

Bass didn't sleep near as good as Asa those nights they were forced to wait out the hours of darkness in this frightening journey through such an evil country. Without fail he sat up awake with their fire blazing, weapons in his lap, ears attentive to every groan of the incessant wind as it carved its way through the canyon, listening to every rolling rumble of the distant rocks tumbling off some nearby precipice, listening to the fading echoes of what might be footfalls of nameless beasts, the hair standing at the back of his neck.

As the sun itself arched farther to the south with each day, they tramped on, climbing through a high country before crossing a great river and striking across part of its desert, making for the green, lofty mountains they watched rise in the distance.

Choosing not to tarry at all to set their traps in those hills visited by Taos brigades, they put that high land behind them, pressing on south by west, guided every plodding step of the way by those landmarks Asa McAfferty had set to memory, recited firsthand from the lips of those who claimed to have looked down from those foothills at the basin below, where a man got his first glimpse of the Gila as it spilled southwest across a virgin land.

"No man you know of ever trapped this river?" Scratch had asked that first night they'd camped beside the Gila. This sure didn't appear to be beaver country the likes of which he'd ever seen before.

"No one I heard of ever gone on down toward the Mex desert to see what lies in that country," McAfferty had asserted. "The trapping outfits turned back from here."

There had to be a cause, Bass reasoned. After all these weeks and, lo, the endless miles—surely there was something that had caused those hardy brigades to turn about and search for more hospitable country to the north and east of the Heely. At first he had figured it was only the heat and the yawning maw of the desert the farther south they rode that gave him a sense of unease . . . as they stopped here, then there, whenever they came upon beaver sign.

On their fourth day moving downstream the partners ran onto the beginnings of a lush valley fed by untold creeks spilling into the main river, a long and meandering country verdant enough to support a rich population of industrious flat-tails busily damming up their world into an endless series of ponds as the Gila continued its path between the foothills of two mountain ranges.

For more than a month they worked through the slowly shrinking daylight hours, trapping the unwary beaver never before chivvied in that country. Then McAfferty had spotted the moccasin prints late of an afternoon. After returning to camp, then taking Bass to study them with him, they both decided there was sign of enough warriors to cause them concern—no matter that those warriors were prowling about the country on foot.

"I heard tell from one of Pattie's men that a man can foller the Heely upstream into the mountains," Asa had asserted.

"How far them mountains be?"

"Far enough," and McAfferty had pointed to the east. "A good ride will put ground atween us and them red heathens. *'Pour out thy wrath upon the heathen that have not known thee, and upon the kingdom that have not called upon thy name.'*"

McAfferty had gone on to describe how he was told they could continue up the Gila, following it into the foothills, and eventually the mountains—saying all a man had to do was continue north by east from there in making his crossing of the high country, up and down through a series of broken ridges until he eventually dropped into the valley of the Rio Grande del Norte.

"The river what leads us right on into Taos for to winter up," Asa had declared, gesturing dramatically with an outswung arm as he pointed to the northeast.

"You figger we ought'n load up and set off soon as it's dark?"

But McAfferty had shaken his white head as he considered the plateau above the brushy draw where they had made camp the night before. "Nawww. Each of us take our watch tonight, go out come morning to collect our traps and turn back upriver for the mountains. The Lord my God will watch over and deliver us."

Instead, they had spotted the warriors approaching from the rocks above just before first light. Abandoning what traps remained in the waters of the Gila, the white men fled, doggedly pursued right on into a country that reminded the ex-circuit-riding preacher of that land where Moses had led his Hebrews in their escape from a vengeful Pharaoh.

"Verily—that ol' King of Egypt watched the destruction of his army beneath the hand of the one true God!" McAfferty had declared optimistically. "But God still had to punish His people with years of wandering in the desert because they turned from His voice."

At their backs now, the sun was sinking behind the low, jagged, rocky bluffs that passed for hills in this desert country. Scratch remembered how three days before he had begun to wonder if he and McAfferty hadn't themselves turned away from God's voice—punished by being driven into an unforgiving desert, pursued so relentlessly by the Apache that they had eventually abandoned the Gila in a vain hope of eluding the warriors.

Leaving the river and crossing a low, rocky divide, Bass and McAfferty had fallen headlong into a basin where little but stunted brush and withered cactus struggled above the sun-baked hardpan. A sandy soil dotted with wide patches of golden, heat-seared bunchgrass broke up the monotony of the landscape as they pressed on for that thin, jagged line of purple beckoning from the distance.

In those mountains he knew they would find water, shelter, escape from their pursuers.

But on the morning of their second day without water they had spotted a second band of Apache off to their right in the distance—and were forced to turn sharply away from their goal. Forced to plunge deeper into a desert tracked only by jagged scars of waterless, scorpion-infested arroyos. At the bottom of one after another they had stopped only long enough to scrape down through the powdery sand with no luck, finding not so much as any damp soil before remounting their thirsty horses and urging their pack animals on behind them. Relentlessly keeping an anxious eye on the country at their backs, Bass was sure they had passed through the gates of hell itself.

Too many days. More waterless miles than he could recall. So much of his hope shriveled and drying the way the stunted plants in that land curled up and died. There had been no turning back. In every direction the prospects looked much the same. But only to the east did there appear the promise of cool, beckoning shade beneath that jagged scrap of autumn sky, while over their heads, hour after hour, hung nothing more than the sun, hovering like a sulled mule refusing to budge. It made his mouth water to gaze at that distant line of purple high country where a ragged batch of black-bellied clouds cluttered the eastern horizon.

Autumn rain. Bright green streaks of hot, phosphorescent lightning cracking the distant sky. Offering no more than a remote hope. Perhaps nothing more than despair for the man gradually dying of thirst now forced to watch those faraway thunderclouds, realizing he might never again feel the caress of cool rain upon his cracked, peeling, sunburned face.

Yet enough light flickered from heaven, streaking down through each jagged crack in the sky with every burst of that pale-green heat lightning, enough to give him renewed hope as they struggled on now, struggled on past the falling of the sun at their backs.

Suddenly the horse beneath him jerked its head, tugging the rawhide reins from his loose grip. In that next moment he heard Hannah snort. Instantly afraid the animals had winded Indians, Bass peered quickly to the right and left, painfully twisting his aching, thirst-ravaged body to gaze behind them. Nothing but a spiny dust column here and there as tiny whirlwinds zigzagged their way across the barren wastes. Nothing but those capricious spirals of the same alkali dust coating his nostrils, seeping into every pore, gumming up his swollen, blackened tongue and parched throat, making it hard to swallow around the tiny pebble he held beneath his tongue.

As he watched, the horse bearing McAfferty's body suddenly sidestepped, pulling at the reins Scratch was holding—yanking them right out of his hand. Before he could get his own legs to respond, to kick his mount into motion, Asa's horse was lumbering away, rolling into a clumsy lope with that deadweight of the trapper slung sacklike over its saddle.

Much as he might want to keep making for the distant mountains, Bass let his horse have its head as he followed vainly behind McAfferty's animals. In their midst waltzed his ever-loving Hannah, her loads shimmying from side to side as she struggled to keep her footing on the uneven sands.

Wide-eyed were every one of the creatures, their dust-caked nostrils swelling all the bigger as they loped on yard after yard up a long, low rise toward a band of striated white and ocher bluffs looming in the middistance.

Up ahead of him some fifty yards at the top of that rise, he watched Asa's body slipping to the off side, spilling headfirst onto the hard ground after the horse took another half-dozen steps. His body cartwheeled away from the hooves and came to rest on its back.

Struggling to stop his own resistant mount, yanking back repeatedly on the reins to get it halted, Bass had barely begun to swing his offhand leg over the saddle when the horse suddenly bolted, yanking his hands from the braided loop of rawhide, snatching the big cottonwood stirrup from his left moccasin and spilling him onto his hip.

Dazed, Scratch crawled to his knees and crabbed over to his partner.

"As-Asa," he croaked, his voice disused in those last dry hours of the chase.

Gripping McAfferty's chin in one hand, he pulled off the sweat-soaked hat and shook the white head.

" 'I am forgotten as a dead man out of mind: I am like a broken vessel,' " he gasped as Bass's shadow came over his face. "Figgered to lay here till I was dead, Mr. Bass."

"You ain't dead."

"I can see by the looks of your face you ain't St. Peter waiting for me at the gates of heaven neither."

Bass watched McAfferty's eyes close, then flutter open again in the fading light as day slowly gave way to night. "Sundown, Asa."

"What happened?"

Scratch looked up. "Animals bolted on us."

"Might as well be dead now. No horses. Been this long, and no horses."

"You been out of your mind, Asa," he explained. "We been . . . been covering ground."

"Don't matter, I s'pose. 'Thout them horses," he whispered wearily. " 'For my life is spent with grief, and my year with sighing: my strength faileth because of mine iniquity, and my bones are consumed.' "

How he wished McAfferty wouldn't keep on spouting about their being without horses now. Peering behind them, Bass declared, "I don't see nothing. Maybe they give up."

" 'Pache don't give up," said the cracked, swollen lips.

"We're in a fix anyways you set your sights," Bass admitted as he rocked up onto one knee and started to stand. "Damp powder and no way to dry it, that's our fix here and now."

"Leave me," McAfferty demanded. "Find some water."

"Night's coming on. Ain't gonna leave you—"

"Best leave me when it gets dark."

He brooded on that, again measuring horizon after horizon, then brought his eyes back to that bluff ahead of them where the rise of land lay smeared in contrasting layers. "Maybeso I'll figger to go see where them horses run off to. Foller tracks. Catch one up. Come back for you."

" 'Give us help from trouble: for vain is the help of man,' Mr. Bass."

Scratch started to rise onto the other leg, painfully. "You rest. I'll . . . find us some water."

"Get water or there ain't no sense coming back for me."

Something strange in the voice yanked him back to stare down at McAfferty's face once more. There was a new, distant look in those dust-caked eyes. The haunted look of a man teetering on the precipice of the eternal and staring into the bottomless void at the instant his feet were about to give way.

Titus briefly touched Asa's shoulder, laying his hand there in the hollow, where he swore he could feel the rattle of each of McAfferty's shallow breaths.

"I'll be back," he whispered. "Shortly."

After watching the eyes close within that dark, sunburned face, Bass struggled back onto his wobbly legs, uncertain of each step as he commanded his feet to shuffle forward beneath his weight. Yard by painful yard he slowly ascended what remained of the gentle slope toward that rise from where he figured he might look over enough ground to spot the runaway animals disappearing toward the striated bluff, its hues beginning to darken as the light continued to fade from the desert sky.

A soft breeze met him in the face as he neared the top of the slope. Something more than a choking, sand-dry wind—bearing with it a hint of some new scent on that warm air as he dragged it into his nostrils.

At the top his legs stopped beneath him suddenly of their own accord. It was better than lunging on over, only to have to come back up, he figured. His eyes began to descend to the base of the bluff as he drew in another of those mercifully blessed breaths of that new air. Then spotted the five animals below him.

No more than three hundred yards away at the bottom of the gentle slope, they stood among a scattered profusion of belly-high brush and boulders that had tumbled from the side of the nearby sandstone bluff. At least the animals had found some cover for the two of them to hole up in—someplace where they could make it a little tougher for the Apache to get at them than it would be out on the open flat.

He needed to get one of the saddle mounts and lead it back for Asa. Couldn't leave him out there now that night was coming. No matter that the dark might conceal him from their pursuers. The Apache would likely have no trouble following tracks beneath the stars and that thin rind of a moon until they bumped right into the half-dead white man.

"Then they'd make me listen to your screams all night," Bass brooded to himself as he forced his legs to wobble down the slope toward the animals huddled in the brush. "Damn you anyways, Asa McAfferty—for making me listen to them cut on you slow while them bastards tear you gut from gizzard like one of their goddamned animals they was getting ready to eat. Maybe even hang you over their fire."

One leg at a time, he braced a knee and swung the other leg forward.

"You ain't gonna make me listen to that, you son of a bitch. I'm gonna

get you down here with these damned animals . . . if I have to drag you in
my own—"

He lurched to a halt. Watching the horses and that pretty mule of his,
all with their heads bent low, snuffling, as if they were grazing.

Then, as the warm breeze quieted its evening sigh, he heard their noisy
drinking.

Water! They were drinking *water.*

A whimper broke free of his throat as his feet lumbered forward on
their own, hurrying him on down the slope toward the animals. Now he saw
how they stood up to their knees in the stream. Its semiglossy surface lured
him on, glittering in the dim, silvery shine of those first stars and rind of
moon.

Shoving his way past the huge, dusty rumps and heaving sides of the
burdened animals, Bass waded ankle-deep into the dark liquid ribbon some
fifteen feet across. Not just water—but one helluva lot of it!

Collapsing onto his knees, Scratch flung himself forward, landing face-
first into the cool stream. Wagging his head back and forth deliciously beneath the surface, he drank and drank and drank as he remained submerged.
Then yanked his head out and sputtered, sucking in a long breath, the warm
evening air singing past his tortured membranes as his lungs swelled to
bursting.

Down under he dived again, reveling in the glorious sanctuary this
much water gave him, feeling it finally soak through the thick buckskin of his
war shirt, wetting the linsey-woolsey shirt, making it all clammy against his
sunburned chest and back.

Flipping his head back, he yanked off the soppy hat and hurled it back
toward the bank, suddenly aware of just how much his long, curly hair
weighed as he flung the mass of it back over his shoulders. In the next breath
he rolled over onto the sandy river bottom. Now he leaned back, slowly back,
until he was submerged right up to his chin—just the way he had dreamed he
would when his last vestige of hope seemed about as far away as those distant, jagged lines of lightning that savagely split the sky asunder.

Now they would survive the night. Here they could fort up the next day
until they regained their strength. They could drink their fill until the following night, when they would press on toward range after range of the distant
mountains dark against the twilit sky. Perhaps they stood some small chance
of making it back to Taos. Perhaps they . . .

They.

Bass sat upright in a noisy gush of water, feeling the liquid sluice off
him as he gazed up the long slope toward the high ground. Beyond that rise,
somewhere on down the other side, lay Asa McAfferty.

Feeling renewed, strong enough to clamber out of the water, Scratch seized up the reins to his own animal as he dragged its muzzle out of the water.

"Don't want you getting loggy on me," he scolded it as he yanked on the reins.

For a moment the horse protested, then reluctantly allowed Titus to pull it around and climb into the saddle, water pouring out of his leggings and off the twisted fringes at the bottom of the war shirt, spilling in sheets down over the saddle as he tapped his heels into the ribs before stuffing his moccasins into the stirrups.

"Hep-hep! Let's git!"

The horse was slow getting him back up to the top of the rise, but it was far better than trudging up the slope on his own two legs. At the top his eyes began to search the sandy ground for a dark object large enough to be McAfferty.

Bass spied something to the left, and a few moments later he hauled back on the reins, staring down at the body a heartbeat before he dragged himself from the saddle, wet leggings gluing themselves to wet saddle. His leathers weighed as much as a trap sack.

Going to his knees beside his partner, Scratch bent over Asa's face as he yanked up the long flap of his own breechclout and rubbed the wet wool across McAfferty's hot face.

With a groan Asa stirred fitfully beneath the insistent rubbing.

Clenching a fist around a corner of the trade wool, Bass squeezed some water out of the thin cloth he held right over his partner's swollen, blackened lips. Then he wiped the breechclout against the cracked lips, parting them with his fingertips and squeezed some more. When there was no more water left in the wool, he yanked up the fringed bottom of his war shirt, pulling it aside so he could grab the long tail of the linsey-woolsey shirt. From it he squeezed more water between the slack lips until McAfferty finally sputtered. Then coughed as the tiny stream of water pooled at the back of his throat.

But Asa managed to get it down, swallowing with a harsh, raspy, choking sound while his eyes blinked open. "W-water?"

"I found some."

"Wa-wa-water," and he licked his swollen lower lip with the tip of his blackened tongue. "Praise be."

For some time Titus remained there beside McAfferty, squeezing what was left in the breechclout and shirttail until there was no more. Eventually he raised his partner off the ground, across his shoulders, and stood shakily with the larger man for the second time that day. Stumbling forward, Bass got Asa over to his horse and thrown over the saddle.

"Ain't far, long as you don't go and fall off on me again," he assured as he gently patted McAfferty on the back and took up the reins. "I figger I ain't got no bottom left in me to get you pulled off the ground again."

There was no answer but the whisper of the night breeze as darkness seemed to suddenly grip the desert the moment he turned to nudge the horse into motion, like a huge black wing silently passing over the land. Back up that rise he led the animal, straining to reach the crest, where he finally peered down again at the dark meandering line of that narrow river, on over to begin their descent.

He led the horse into the midst of the others about the time Hannah raised her snout and announced her satisfaction with a watery snort. Up to his knees in the river, Bass stopped the horse, dropped the reins then and there, and turned back to grip a hand under each of Asa's armpits. Leaning back with his own failing strength, Titus tugged far enough to get McAfferty's legs over the wet saddle with a struggle—then the man's deadweight took over, and Asa spilled headfirst into the water.

Sinking to his knees, Bass snagged hold of the back of his partner's long white hair and dragged his head out of the water. Asa sputtered helplessly, so weak he couldn't raise his own head. He stared up at Scratch, eyes blinking, those swollen lips moving wordlessly at first until he finally got the words out.

"P-praise God for our deliverance."

"Better you praise these here goddamned horses for smelling water, Asa McAfferty," Bass grumbled as he turned his partner's head to the side, supporting the man so his tongue could lap right at the river's surface.

McAfferty drank, then drank some more, and finally cocked his head so he could peer up at those animals standing about them in the dark river while he shoved long, dripping tendrils of his wet, white hair out of his eyes.

Finally his gaze came to rest on Scratch, those eyes of his glowing once again like twelve-hour coals. "God made these here dumb brutes under us to be thirsty critters, Titus Bass. Verily I say, that same God led these brutes to find us this water."

Funny thing how a little water could change a man's whole outlook. Enough that he didn't mind being clammy and cold as the wind came up and the temperature dropped as if all that day's heat was nothing more than a long-ago memory.

The desert had a way about it of pointing out to a man just how fickle nature could be. Almost as fickle as damn near every white woman he had ever known. At sunrise the earth began to warm, the cold air slowly dissipating in the mists clinging back in low places. But long before sundown, a man might well vow all he possessed and half his soul in exchange for a patch of shade and a pool of tepid water. And by the next sunrise that man would be shivering, his teeth rattling like bone dominoes in a hardwood box, praying for the sun to rise once more so it could warm the chill from his bones.

For the longest time the two of them had remained in the shallow river, soaking in the cool water as if it were life's elixir. And by the time that Bass suggested they get to the far shore and find a place to fort up beneath the bluff, McAfferty was able to clamber to his feet with a little help. His arm locked over Scratch's shoulder, he hobbled toward the bank.

Titus left him there with his rifle while he went upstream in search of a likely spot among the rocks. And when he got Asa and the animals moved that two hundred yards farther along the north bank, Scratch pulled their buffalo robes from the packs. With them both he wrapped McAfferty against the deepening cold of the desert night, then settled down beside his partner, clutching a pair of blankets around his own shoulders.

He had begun to shiver as the moon rose late, spun toward the west, then fell quickly. Only after it set had he finally warmed within his wet clothing, snug enough that he no longer trembled. Through the long hours his shivering had served to keep him awake, too fitful even to doze. Beside him now in the first graying of the night, McAfferty snored softly, another sound among all the others magnified on the wind that came to him off the desert, moving up the river valley.

He wondered if the Apache had followed close enough to reach them just before dawn. Wondered too if those strong, bandy-legged warriors were the sort to stop now and again in their pursuit just long enough to sleep for an hour or so before they would again take up the chase.

Bass felt his eyes close as the cold breeze sank off the shoulder of the bluff overhead. He hoped he would hear the Apache as they crept up out of the gloom. Maybe even smell them on the dry desert night air.

Fawn's hands were cool on his skin where she had pulled back the buffalo robe to expose him to her eyes, to her touch. She wasn't the sort to tease him, moving her fingers across his belly or down the inside of his thighs. Fawn went straight to his manhood: caressing it without preliminaries, massaging it into readiness, stroking it insistently, often impatiently, until she herself took him and drove his manhood within her. Often would he keep his eyes closed until he felt her moving to straddle him, gazing up to find the Ute woman settling atop him like an ember-lit shadow in the winter darkness of her lodge.

He gazed up now, surprised to find Pretty Water staring down at him. As her moistness clamped around his rigid flesh, he wondered for a moment where Fawn had gone. Wondered where the Ute village had disappeared. Wondered why he had never found them that summer he went looking for them . . . the summer he was scalped.

This woman riding back and forth slowly atop him was Shoshone. He found her so different from Fawn. Pretty Water was the sort to tease him to the point where he wanted to cry out, to growl at her with her playfulness that he flung her back onto the blankets and thrust himself into her out of the fiery hunger she aroused in him as her fingers barely brushed the flesh around his manhood, but never really caressed it. How she grinned as she watched his penis twitch and grow, even though she wasn't touching it directly. How she sighed as she gazed upon the growing excitement she had caused. How she groaned when he shoved her legs apart and madly drove himself within her, so crazy had she made him.

There above him she rocked up and back, up and back, raising her buttocks from his thighs just enough to slowly pull him out, then slowly seating him deep within her again. . . .

He felt himself ready to explode as he gripped her small, soft breasts in his hands, wanting so badly to lick the nipples again just as he erupted—

Hannah's snort brought him awake.

Frantically he dug a knuckle at his eyes, listening.

The mule snorted again, more loudly.

He smelled it too. A change in the air.

What direction was the wind coming from? Bass turned his face into the breeze, drinking deep of all that it could tell him. Upstream. They were upstream . . . and likely on his side of the river already. Perhaps they had crossed upstream after finding the white man's trail descending to the bank.

And now they were closing in. Waiting for dawn.

Tightening his grip on the rifle's wrist, Titus ground his knuckles into his gritty eyes a second time and blinked. Sore and prickly from lack of real sleep, burning from the relentless glare of endless days beneath that wide brim of his felt hat—they felt as if he never would get the grains of sand flushed from them. Red, swollen, so gritty that he wondered if he would ever focus them again.

Upstream. He kept staring upstream through that cleft in the low, waist-high rocks. Watching the light change as he gazed across the gray, shadowy, dreamy texture of boulders and brush and the river's silvery path through it all.

Behind him one of the horses accompanied Hannah with its own plaintive whinny. They likely felt boxed in back against the tall overhang of the bluff—helpless now with that scent of the enemy growing strong in their nostrils.

Different this must be from anything they had smelled on the northern plains. Thankful too that these animals never grew accustomed to the odor of Indians—no matter where, no matter what tribe.

The light began to bubble a little more, defining edges to the gray of low boulders scattered on either side of the river, giving depth to the black splotches that were the low clumps of brush dotting the banks.

From between the brush and boulders emerged the angular shadows stepping into the midst of the silver ribbon. First there were two, then another pair, then six fanning out in an arrow pointed at the white men.

There surely had to be more.

"Asa!" he whispered harshly, shaking McAfferty's shoulder.

As the trapper worked at opening his eyes, Bass grumbled, "We got company!"

Sputtering something with his thick, swollen tongue, McAfferty shoved his rifle toward Bass. "Take it."

Turning quickly to stare at his partner, Scratch asked, "You got you your pistol?"

Painfully, McAfferty worked his fingers around the curved butt and struggled to hold it aloft. "I'll get one of 'em for sure—they get close enough."

"Get that other pistol of your'n too."

"Saving it for me."

"For you?"

McAfferty licked at his cracked, bloodied lips. "Don't let these here 'Pache bastards take you alive, Mr. Bass," he implored. "Better to go under by your own hand—"

"Shoot myself?"

"They'll roast you over a slow fire if they take a notion to—"

"Shuddup!" Bass snapped. That was the last thing he wanted to hear. Suddenly his mouth was again as dry as it had been for the last three days.

Chastised, Asa closed his eyes and began to mutter, " 'Though a host shall encamp against me, my heart shall not fear.' "

The six slowly crept their way. He had to make each of the rifle shots count. His own. McAfferty's rifle. And Asa's big-gauge smoothbore. Along with Bass's own flintlock pistol. And if Asa used his two pistols, they could account for all six of the bastards.

Pebbles and loose sand skittered down the side of the bluff over his left shoulder, jerking him around—

An unearthly cry raised the hair at the back of his neck.

Whirling, Bass watched the black wisp of shadow materialize out of the ashy gray of that line formed by the rocky outcrop thrust up against the dawn sky just above them. As he brought up his rifle and squeezed back on the trigger, he heard the others let out with their catlike calls from the stream behind him. With the weapon's roar the warrior let out a shrill shriek as the Apache plunged on through the air, slamming against the muzzle of the rifle an instant after the soft lead ball plowed through his chest. Dead before he spilled to the ground at Bass's feet.

Knocking Titus backward against a boulder.

McAfferty was kicking against his robes, shrieking, "God's wrath falls on the necks of the Philistines!"

"Shoot the bastards!" Scratch bellowed as he wheeled about, dropping his rifle and sweeping up McAfferty's rifle: dragging the hammer back to full-cock.

Breaking into a run, the six were yelping, slogging as fast as they could through the knee-deep river, making straight for the boulders where the white men waited.

Jamming the rifle against his shoulder, Titus aimed into the dim light at one of the black shapes bobbing atop the silvery surface of the water. Pulling back on the trigger suddenly, he felt the gust of wind at his back as the weapon roared, hearing behind him the grunt from his partner.

Squinting his eyes with that second brilliant glare of muzzle flash, Scratch whipped about on his heels, finding an Apache rising from McAfferty, rocking back on his knees and pistoning back an arm. At its end a huge stone club hung in the air.

Asa sat dazed from the first blow from the Apache, who leaped upon him from the narrow shelf of rocks directly behind them.

Wheeling, Titus lashed out at the warrior with the heavy octagonal barrel, slamming the Apache on the shoulder as he began his swing at McAfferty. But only enough to shove the warrior to the side, rolling him onto a hip to glare back at Scratch.

Springing to his feet like a mountain cat, the Apache cried out hellishly as he dived headlong for Bass, almost as if he sought to spear the trapper in the middle of the chest with his head.

They fell backward together against the boulder, catching Bass at the back of his hips, bending him on across the curve of the rock. Arcing the muzzle around a second time the instant the warrior drew back to make a try for his own belt knife, Scratch caught the Apache along the temple with a crack as loud as a maul colliding with a tight-grained hickory stump. Titus never watched the warrior settling into the sand at his feet.

He was already spinning back to find the rest.

Yanking back on the hammer—then suddenly remembering that he held an empty rifle.

Hurling it aside as McAfferty scrambled to his knees, wagging his head groggily, Bass scooped up the smoothbore. He was snapping back the huge goosenecked hammer as he caught sight of Asa rocking forward on his knees, the pistol coming out at the end of both arms—a jet of bright, incandescent yellow spewing from the big muzzle.

Shadows loomed even larger in the coming light of morning, playing off the gray of sky and dull shimmer of river surface. The first lunged into the air and landed in a crouch atop the low boulders, his wet moccasins clawing the surface, coiling instantly, then springing on toward the white men.

"Other pistol—"

Bass raked back on the smoothbore's trigger as he shouted his command, watching the warrior rock sideways. As the Apache fell between the two trappers, gurgling, clawing at the damp sand, Titus turned aside. Lifting the empty smoothbore into the air by its barrel, he brought it down savagely on the warrior's neck, then smashed the brass-plated butt three more times into the back of the Apache's skull.

McAfferty cried, "My last shot!"

Pulling back from that last, sodden crush of the enemy's head, Scratch turned in a crouch the moment McAfferty fired that second pistol of his. As he dropped the smoothbore into the sand beside Asa, Bass lunged for the handles of two of the tomahawks they had laid out in readiness beside the white-head.

Just as he rose and straightened, one of the last two Apache leaped out of the stream like a panther, howling in a crouch as he landed on the rocks, immediately snapping his bow string forward. On the dry air Scratch heard the *thwung* as Asa gasped, a moment before Scratch swung the tomahawk sideways through the air like a scythe, catching the warrior's belly, slashing through soft flesh, sensing the hot blood gush across his sunburned wrist as the Apache crumpled backward, nearly cut in half.

A searing cry warned of another behind him.

Spinning around, Titus had no more than a heartbeat before the eighth warrior sprang from the narrow shelf, falling spread-eagled out of the dawn sky for the white man. From the corner of his eye, Bass watched Asa's arms jab forward, both hands clutching a skinning knife, blade pointed skyward as the Apache plunged downward.

The knife caught the warrior just below the breastbone, where the Apache's weight and McAfferty's sudden twist to the side drove the weapon deep, opening up the warrior's abdomen as he collapsed against Bass, writhing on his knees.

The Apache's arms flailed helplessly, a knife spilling out of one of the brown hands that clutched his wound. Stumbling backward, Scratch collided with the rocks. For a terrifying moment the warrior's face seemed to hang in front of his, a dark river of black blood oozing from his lips as the eyes locked on Bass's . . . then rolled back to whites as the body continued its slump to the sand.

His heart thumping, hot adrenaline coursing through his veins, Scratch stared down at the warrior crumpled around his knees as if merely resting there, half in a squat. He cocked back with a foot, knocking the Apache free, and leaped aside. Spooked by those eyes that had locked on to his for that moment in time, eyes that were already dead even in that instant.

His right hand wet with drying blood, he shoved the tomahawk into his left, snatching his pistol from his belt. He was dragging the hammer back to full-cock as the last screaming Apache vaulted over the top of the rock downstream suddenly. The warrior lunged forward, knocking Scratch's right hand out of the way the instant the pistol came up, swinging his own brown hand out wide in a savage arc that showed a glint of steel.

Collapsing back suddenly, Bass sensed the burn of the blade as it raked past his belly. Sensed that sudden cold of the dawn air against the wound, that seep of icy warmth as the blood beaded and oozed.

Already the warrior was beginning a second sweep, coming from Bass's right this time.

Yanking the pistol back, Titus suddenly shoved the right hand upward, flinging the Indian's wrist aside as he brought the short barrel's muzzle under the brown chin and pulled the trigger.

With the Apache's knife hand crookedly imprisoned beneath the man's chin, the top of the warrior's head exploded in a glittering spray of crimson as the first orange rays of light seeped over the edge of the gray desert.

Gripping the tomahawk handle all the tighter in his left hand as he spun back toward the river, Titus stared over the low boulders, ready for the rest.

Everything was quiet but for the murmuring river.

And McAfferty's raspy breathing.

Nothing moved. Nothing but the light on the water as the ribbon's surface lost its silvery glitter in those moments . . . became a river once more. Brush and rocks no longer shadows.

And along the banks, there lay those brown bodies half-submerged in the shallow water, one of the warriors bobbing up to the foot of the waist-high boulders, slowly turning in the gentle current until the Apache stared at the dawn sky with glazed eyes, a great dark smear on his chest as he bobbed to the side, wedged in the eddy that lapped against the rock.

So quiet suddenly, so quiet that he thought he could hear the water lapping against the dead man's body.

"That . . . that all of 'em?" Asa croaked.

Bass finally turned and glanced at his partner before his eyes studied the rock ledge behind them. He sighed, "Looks to be. Any more of 'em—they'd be all over us now."

" *'That thy foot may be dipped in the blood of thine enemies, and the tongue of thy dogs in the same.'* "

Scratch knelt, so weary, he wasn't sure he would ever stand again.

McAfferty watched Titus settle. "You're cut."

"Could be worse," he said, peering down at the slash that yelped in pain with every brush of the dawn breeze.

"Best see to it soon as you can."

"Let's just damn well get these guns reloaded," Bass growled, not wanting to look again at that torn flesh.

"You do that, then you take the scalps."

Wagging his head, Titus quietly said, "Leave the goddamned scalps."

"We gonna take the scalps," McAfferty prompted wearily, rising to his knees. "They're ours now."

"I don't give a damn," Scratch replied. "I don't ever figger to be back here—"

"You don't take your scalps," McAfferty blurted out as he snatched hold of the front of Bass's half-damp war shirt, "the ghosts come back for you one day."

"Ghosts?"

His icy blue eyes squinted half-closed as they slowly volved down to stare at the half-naked bodies there among them in the rocks. "You don't take this hair—the ghosts come back for you."

With a snort Bass shook his head. "Of all the soft-headed, school-child—"

McAfferty jerked down on Scratch's shirt, shutting him up. "You listen," he rasped, his dark eyes filled with terror. "Only one scalp I never took, Mr. Bass. Only one. The hair of a Ree medicine man."

"Hatcher told me . . ." and then his voice trailed off as he watched how pale his partner's face became.

Asa's blue eyes had gone to slate as they flicked left and right, as if he were expecting to catch something more hurtling at them out of the gray of dawn's light. "Should'a took the hair of that'un . . . but I didn't. And now the old bastard's ghost is gonna come for me."

Scratch swallowed hard. "You don't believe—"

"One day he'll come for me."

NINETEEN

They had waited out that short autumn day there beside the river, watching for more Apache.

Better to fight them here, Bass thought, than have them catch you out there on the desert. Here—where a man at least had water, and a few rocks around him, along with a little shade slanting down off the rocky bluff once the sun began its dip into the last quarter of the sky.

By the time Bass turned to move back toward the animals so he could retrieve some bear grease to smear on his tender belly wound, he sidestepped through the rocks to watch one of McAfferty's packhorses go down. Its knees buckled as the animal snorted, kneeling into the sand clumsily. Arrows bristled from its neck and front flanks. More shafts quivered from the other animals, their packs, and saddles.

He quickly counted—finding one of them missing.

Dropping to one knee, Scratch peered under Hannah's legs, finding his saddle mount already down, on its side and unmoving—more than a dozen arrows sticking from its bloody ribs and belly, all of them fired from above where the three warriors had crawled along that narrow shelf.

With a groan he let his head sag between his shoulders.

Right then the two of them had tougher problems than Asa's god-damned ghost.

For a while Titus brooded on just what they could do with all the plunder and supplies without adding to the burden the animals were already carrying. To put any more weight on Hannah and the last of McAfferty's horses was unthinkable—not with the heat and the desert and all that distance still to go before they would reach Taos.

Another option would be for him to walk those hundreds of miles, wearing out one pair after another of his moccasins. But even in the cool of that desert morning, Titus doubted he could ever accomplish that journey on foot.

Their only choice lay in separating wheat from chaff: packing only what was absolutely necessary on Hannah's back, caching the rest here beside this river—as if they would one day return to reclaim what they would abandon.

Bass knew he never would.

"I ain't digging no hole for it," he growled at McAfferty. "Let the Apache have it all."

Once the sun rose high enough to warm the air, Scratch settled back against the side of the bluff to wait out the rest of the morning. He simply didn't have enough strength left to work any longer in the immobilizing heat. By midafternoon, when the sun's direct rays slid behind the sandstone butte—bestowing a little shade upon their side of the hill—the dead horses had already begun to bloat. Now and then expanding gases whimpered and hissed from the arrow wounds and anuses.

In the cool of twilight, after an entire day with no further sign of more Apache, Bass felt confident enough to stand and move around in the dimming light. Managing to free his saddle from the carcass of the dead mount, he propped it atop the boulders while he went to work pulling the supply packs from the dead packhorse. After removing the last of the packs from Hannah and McAfferty's second horse, Titus began to tediously go through all that they possessed—setting aside what was essential. That done, he put everything else in two stacks: what they would readily put to use, and what was more luxury than necessity. This last pile they would leave here in the shadows of the bluff, beside the Gila, come nightfall.

Titus stood and looked down at the rest when he was done, wagging his head at how pitifully small was what they could carry away from this place. Without those two extra animals and their four packs—why, what they were taking along now might just outfit a small band of Digger Injuns. No more than that.

But he and Asa had their lives back in their own hands, and that was a damned good feeling for a man who had no hankering to turn over his fate ever again to another, nor to the desert. His life was back in his hands, and his hands alone.

As soon as it was nearing full dark, Bass was already strapping the rebuilt packs back on Hannah and on Asa's packhorse. Kneeling, he nudged McAfferty awake, and together they hauled themselves into the saddle and reined away from the boulders, following the river toward those mountains looming in the distance. Swinging loosely from the ropes lashing both bundles carried by Asa's packhorse were the nine Apache scalps. Every bit of the long black hair, and the tops of the ears too. Titus wasn't about to let any hoo-doo haunt him from here on out.

With the arrival of dawn Bass was half dozing in the saddle. McAfferty lay asleep, slumped forward against the withers of his horse. It wasn't until some time after the sun came up that Scratch found them a place out of the light among some small but shady paloverde trees.

Another day out of the sun, followed by another long autumn night of relentless riding—pointing their noses northeast, keeping the North Star at the corner of his left eye. Pick out some feature of the land in the dark and ride right for it until they got there. Then select another landform in the distance and make for it. Again and again while the stars continued to wheel overhead and the night turned cold enough to turn their lips blue and cause their teeth to chatter.

Night after night of riding. Waiting out each day, keeping a rotation of watch between them, their eyes constantly searching the horizon for pursuit until sundown again marked the hour for them to pack up and remount.

How much longer? he had often wondered. How much farther did they have to go? . . . Until he scolded himself and forced his mind to think on something else. Day and night Bass tried hard to remember the look of Taos from afar, remember the smell of the rutted streets littered with refuse and offal. Were the women really as pretty as he remembered them? Was the village as gay as his memories painted it? Or had he only grown so sick and lonely for the sight of another human face, desperately yearning for some sign of those whitewashed walls, that the Taos he conjured up was far more than it really was?

"How ol't a man you be, Mr. Bass?" Asa asked early of a morning after they had snuffed out the moon and rolled into their robes to sleep out the frosty day.

He thought a moment, tugging at the figures the way a man might tug at the strings on his moccasins to knot them securely. "I'll turn thirty-six this coming birthday."

"When will that be?"

"First day of the year."

"A noble day, that," McAfferty replied. "Meself, I'll be turning thirty-six next year too. Late of the year, howsoever."

Bass turned in the growing light and pulled the edge of his robe from his face to peer over at his partner. "You're younger'n me?"

" 'Pears to be."

"S'pose it's that white hair of your'n," he said finally. "Makes you . . . seems you're older'n me."

"My years out here make me a old man to some," Asa confessed. "But I'm a young'un to others."

"Never asked where you come from."

McAfferty hacked at some phlegm, then answered, "I was bred and borned in North Carolina."

"I ain't never been there. Was down along the Natchez Road, clear to the Muscle Shoals—but never got that far east."

"A purty country, so my pappy said. He come to America back in eighty-nine. He always told folks he got here when this here country got its first president. I be full-blooded Scot, you know. A Scot I am—and most proud of that. Though I was borned this side of the east ocean, I'm a Scotsman like my pappy's people."

"My grandpap was a Scot his own self," Bass announced. "You come west to the mountains from Carolina country?"

"By the heavens no," McAfferty snorted. "I was on the Mississap when it come time to point my nose for these shining hills. Wasn't too old when my family up and moved west from the Carolinas, clear across the Mississap to the Cape, south there from St. Louie."

"I know of the Cape," Scratch replied. "So you was the firstborn to your mam and pap?"

"My folks had three boys awready to bring along with 'em when they come to America. The family come in from the coastal waters, on to the deep forests where my pappy started off trading with the wild Injuns for their skins. He brung to the villages blankets and axes and mirrors and paint, goods like coffee and sugar too. It was a hard life, but a good one for my folks. After them three boys, they had 'em three girls. Then I come along there at the last."

"If you was a young'un when you come to the Cape, it must've been a wild place back then."

"Not many a white man had come across the Mississap to settle. Oh, there was folks up around St. Louie, but only a few French farmers down at the Cape. Good, rich ground that was too."

With no school within hundreds of miles, McAfferty had come to learn his reading and writing as most did on the frontier, if they were fortunate: studying at his mother's knee, copying words every night, following supper, from their old Scottish Bible, by the light of the limestone fireplace.

"By summer of 1810 more and more folks was coming in, so my pappy itched to move us on to a crik near the Little White River—a place more'n a week's ride on west of St. Louie."

"That was the fall I left home," Bass admitted, watching his words drift away in hoarfrost. "Run off and ain't ever been back."

"You was sixteen then—a time when a boy figgers he's just about done with all his growing," Asa confided. "Likely you figgered you was man enough to set your own foot down in the world."

Scratch turned to his partner. "You 'member the day the ground shook so terrible the rivers rolled back on themselves?"

"I do," McAfferty said. "I was turned seventeen that fall. By the prophets, I do remember the day the earth shook under my feet. 'O Lord, be not far from me!' "

"I was working on the Ohio—a place called Owensboro. Where was you?"

"On the Little White," Asa replied. "That first day the shaking started early off to the morning, afore the sun even thought to come up. I woke up, me pappy yelling at me, 'Asa! Asa! Get up, boy! Fetch the dogs! They under the floor after a coon, boy! Fetch them dogs out!' "

Titus inquired, "Them dogs of your'n was chasing a coon under the house that very morning the earth was shaking?"

"No—my pappy thought the rumbling and the roaring under the floor come from the dogs chasing a coon critter under our cabin. We all come right out of our beds—hearing the dogs outside the window, in the yard—all of 'em howling and yowling. Wasn't a one of 'em *under* the floor!"

"You all knowed right then it weren't the dogs?"

"Pappy hit the floor with his knees, and my mama was right beside him—and they both started praying like I ain't ever heard 'em pray afore or since. Their eyes so big—saying they was sure the day of judgment was at hand."

"I was up the Ohio a ways that cold day," Titus explained. "Remember my own self how the ground rolled and shook so hard, the river come back on itself."

"We was all on our knees—praying our hardest together," McAfferty continued his story. "Soon as my mama went to singing 'Shall We Gather at the River,' the might of the Holy Spirit come right over me, commanding my tongue to speak words right from the Bible: *'Thou are my hiding place; thou shalt preserve me from trouble; thou shalt compass me about with songs of deliverance.' "

"You knowed those words by heart back then?"

"I never paid me much attention to the lessons my mama gave me from the Bible," Asa admitted. "But there I was—watching my pappy pray like he never done afore, the trees outside our window swaying this way and that, big limbs snapping off like they was fire kindling, my sisters caterwauling like painter cubs . . . when my mama up and tells us all she see'd it all real plain, see'd it as a sure sign that I was to preach God's word to his wayward flocks."

Scratch nodded, enthralled with the story. "You knowed back then you was made for speaking them Bible words."

McAfferty snorted and rubbed the raw end of his cold nose. "No, Mr. Bass. I was a idjit nigger back in them days. This child just laughed at the notion of me taking up the Lord's work. *'Blessed is the man that walketh not in the counsel of the ungodly, nor standeth in the way of sinners, nor sitteth in the seat of the scornful.'*"

"You didn't turn to preaching then and there with that ground shaking under you?"

With a wag of his head Asa declared, "No, not till later on that year when we had us a great shooting star come burning 'cross the sky. The ground shook under my feet. But that star was something made me look right up at heaven. Something made me behold the power of the Lord. *'The God of glory thundereth.'* Maybeso the ground shook for there is the dominion of the devil hisself . . . but to have me a sign from above, from the realm of God!"

"That's when you knowed you had a calling then and there?"

"That shooting star come back night after night," he explained. "Made it plain I had the Lord's calling."

For the next few years Asa studied the family's Bible, investing nearly every waking hour not spent in the McAfferty fields in reading, prayer, and long walks in the woods as he talked to his Maker.

"Wasn't until eighteen and sixteen when I felt the burning in my heart that set me on the path to tell others of the word of our redeemer."

It wasn't long after that the young circuit rider took a proper wife. For more than a year his heart had been the captive of Rebekka Suell's beauty. Finally, as the eldest in the family of nine children he visited once a month on his lonely circuit, sixteen-year-old Rebekka's pa agreed to Asa's marriage proposal.

McAfferty dolefully wagged his head now as darkness came down on the valley. "I can see how it weren't no life for a woman—that riding the circuit from gathering house to gathering house. What few days a month we was home, she tried her best to keep up a li'l garden, and I done my best to bring game to our pot . . . but we never had much more'n my trail of the Lord's calling and that tiny piece of ground where I scratched us a dugout from the side of a hill."

By 1819 two interlopers came in and filed for ownership on the land where Asa had neglected to make his claim formally. Amid rumors that they accepted "donations" from rich landowners, the slick-haired government folks issued a demand that threw Asa off his place.

" *'Behold, these are the ungodly, who prosper in the world; they increase in riches.'* Losing what little we had took the circle for Rebekka," Asa declared with bitterness. "With her gone, I put what little I had in my saddle pockets and set to drifting."

Asa preached where he could, wheedling a meal here and there, sleeping out in the woods or slipping into some settler's shed when the weather turned wet or cold. Those next two years were a time of sadness, loneliness, despair. Still—he had his Bible, and his faith that the Lord was testing him for something far, far bigger.

In the late spring of twenty-one he found himself among the outflung Missouri settlements, hearing news that two traders by the name of McKnight and James had cast their eye on the villages of northern Mexico.

"Asa McAfferty had no home in the white diggings," he said. "And this was one nigger what had him nothing or no one to leave behind. Even the tiny flocks I was shepherd to didn't heed to my warnings that the world was near its end. *'For God speaketh once, yea twice, yet man perceiveth it not!'* "

"That when you come west? Twenty-one?"

"I was a man broke down, ground under the heel: ready to look west for my salvation, Mr. Bass," and he nodded. "The west—where a man depends only upon the Lord . . . and mayhaps a rare friend, for his daily salvation. *'This poor man cried, and the Lord heard him, and saved him out of all his troubles.'* "

On through the late autumn Bass and McAfferty continued their crossing of the craggy mountains and the desert wastes as the days continued to grow short, as the nights lengthened beneath each starlit ride, pushing hard for the Rio Grande. It was snowing the night they reached its banks—a light, airy dusting, the air around them filled with the sharp tang of a harder snow yet to come.

"Santy Fee ain't far off now," Asa said, nodding to the east.

"We going there?"

"Not 'less'n we want to cut out more trouble for ourselves," McAfferty replied. *" 'They wandered in the wilderness in a solitary way; they found no city to dwell in.'* "

Downstream at a ford they crossed that black, shimmering ribbon in the dark and rode until the sky began to lighten in the east before locating an arroyo where there were enough leafless cottonwood to provide some shelter, branches to disperse the smoke from their tiny campfire, modest protection from any distant, any curious, eyes.

So they skirted Santa Fe and its seat of Mexican territorial power, wary of the frequent army patrols the officials sent out—*soldados* instructed to detain any gringo careless enough to be caught on Mexican soil with beaver but with no Mexican license to trap that fur. Better was it for them to stay with the Rio Grande as they continued north each night rather than make for the well-traveled road that lay between the territorial capital and that string of villages in the Taos valley itself.

By the time they drew close to the Sangre de Cristos, Scratch imagined he could actually smell the burning piñon on the cold winter air in the gray light of a rosy dawn. At the knob of a hill they halted, their noses greeted with more of that smoke carried on a wind working its way out of the north, their eyes falling on the welcome sight of those clusters of mud-and-wattle huts, those neat rows of adobe homes arranged along a maze of narrow streets, all of them nestled across a whitewashed, snowy landscape.

McAfferty took in a deep breath, sighing. " *'Hungry and thirsty, their soul fainted in them. Then they cried unto the Lord in their trouble, and He delivered them out of their distresses. And He led them forth by the right way, that they might go to a city of habitation.'* "

Watching the keen fire in the man's icy-blue eyes, Scratch shuddered with a gust of that cold wind and followed the white-head down the snowy slope.

Los Ranchos de Taos was the first village the trappers reached at the bottom of the broadening valley. Beyond it lay the largest of the local villages—San Fernando de Taos—lightly veiled this sunup by a low cloud of firesmoke. Farther still they could make out the squat buildings of San Geronimo de los Taos.

"I'll lay it's San Fernando where Jack Hatcher and his boys brung you," Asa proclaimed, pointing out the prominent church steeple.

"We didn't come in to town all that much," Bass admitted. "Stayed out to Workman's place, mostly. When we first come in, he said it was a far sight better if we didn't show our faces in town too much. After we went for them women took by the Comanche—things was better for us."

" *'And if a stranger sojourn with thee in your land, ye shall not vex him. But the stranger that dwelleth with you shall be unto you as one born among you, and thou shalt love him as thyself,'* " Asa quoted.

Wagging his head, Titus declared, "Much as they appreciated what we done, them greasers wasn't about to treat us like one of their own. 'Specially after that fight we had with them soldiers."

"We'll go round and lay up at Workman's our own selves," McAfferty instructed. "Be best we don't make too much a show of ourselves. Not just yet. Till that whiskey maker tells us what be the temper of these here greasers."

As they reined away from the road leading into San Fernando, Bass gazed longingly at the buildings still shuttered against the cold of the winter night, at the piñon and pine garlands draping the doorways and windows, at those ghostly wisps of smoke starting to curl from the chimneys of each low-roofed house as its inhabitants began their day.

"They prepare for our Lord's blessed birthday," McAfferty commented as they pitched toward the hills west of town. "Even these Mex celebrate the Lord's sacred birth, Mr. Bass. Might'n be some hope for these people yet."

A land of extreme contrasts this: dotted with flowering valleys in the spring, shadowed by high, snowcapped peaks year-round, with green rolling meadows butting up against the sun-baked hardpan, desert wastes speckled only with cactus, lizard, and scorpion. Along the banks of each of the infrequent streams grew borders of cottonwood sinking their roots deep to soak up the gypsum-tainted water that rumbled through the bowels of many an unaccustomed American come fresh from the States.

Here in dawn's first light the snowy valley lay like a rumpled, cultured-folk bedsheet, rising unevenly toward the purple bulk of the surrounding foothills, farther still to that deep cadmium red of those slopes the sun's first rising would soon ignite, mountainsides timbered with the emerald cloak of piñon, blue spruce, and fragrant cedar. How quickly the light changed as night gave way to day, as deep hues softened and the last of winter's stars flickered out in the brightening sky right overhead.

The bruised-eye black of night faded around them, and Scratch said, "Caleb and them others, they didn't tell me much at all 'bout the time you run with 'em."

"Some men keep their own counsel, Mr. Bass," McAfferty eventually replied.

"Will you tell me?"

Asa turned to look at Bass for several moments, then answered. "Been trapping for two years already by the time I hooked up with Johnny Rowland, Jack Hatcher, and the rest in Taos. That first season we worked our way north across the Arkansas."

"That's a good bunch," Bass said.

"Johnny Rowland," McAfferty said with fond remembrance. "Now, he's a Welshman—almost like me own kin. Yes, I took to Rowland, right off."

Two years of trapping and Indian fighting, wenching and wintering in Taos, found the free trappers up close to Arikara country.

Asa clucked. "Them critters never really took to a white man, Mr. Bass." Then he growled bitterly, " 'Let death seize upon them, and let them go down quick into hell: for wickedness is in their dwellings, and among them.' "

Jack Hatcher's brigade made the mistake of crossing the homebound path of a Ree war party returning from raids in Sioux country to the south. When both sides drew up, keeping their wary distance, the warriors signed that they sought only to trade with the white men. In order to buy themselves some time to slip off after dark, the trappers said they would open their packs—but not till morning.

"Night come on, and us fellers all gathered up round our li'l fire we made inside our packs where we figgered to fort up there at the edge of that

Ree camp, ever'one of us ready for what be coming—knowing Rees're good ones for hair stealing."

Hatcher and McAfferty sent Joseph Little out to determine just how well the Arikara had them surrounded. He returned well after darkness with distressing news that there lay but one path for making good their escape without alerting the enemy. In the dark that would take them along a narrow prairie goat trail that switchbacked up the side of a thousand-foot bluff.

Bass exclaimed, "Sounds to be your powder was damp!"

With his mitten Asa smoothed his long white beard. *"'Though a host shall camp against me, my heart shall not fear. And now shall my head be lifted up above my enemies round about me. Deliver me not over unto the will of my enemies.'"*

But just as the trappers were gathering at their fire to lay plans for their flight, who should show up to speak to McAfferty but the war party's medicine man himself, signing that he wanted to speak with Asa alone. The two stepped away toward the black belly of the timber, stopping just beyond the ring of faint firelight, in that darkened no-man's-land between the two groups.

"When we got stopped in the dark, off from the other coons, that Ree nigger made it plain he wanted me Bible!" McAfferty roared in indignation. *"'Regard not them that have familiar spirits, neither seek after wizards, to be defiled by them; I am the Lord your God!'"*

"What happed?" Scratch asked. "Did that nigger get your Bible?"

"When I told him he wasn't 'bout to get my Bible—the heathen tried to rip the book right outta me pouch—signing that he wanted the power of me own medicine!"

When McAfferty refused a second time, the Indian threatened that he would have the Bible before sunrise anyway . . . along with Asa's scalp, which he said he would hang from his belt pouch.

"'And they shall no more be a prey to the heathen, neither shall the beast of the land devour them; but they shall dwell safely, and none shall make them afraid,'" Asa declared. "I wasn't 'bout to be buffaloed by no red nigger. No matter he was a medicine man or not!"

But the trapper's strong protests caused the Arikara to explode. At that moment the Indian suddenly yanked out his tomahawk, lunging in close . . . but McAfferty was just a little faster with his skinning knife.

"Parted that red nigger's ribs, I did," Asa admitted, patting the handle to his knife. Then he shuddered slightly, although the air had begun to warm with the sun's coming. "Dropped him where we stood. *'And that prophet, or that dreamer of dreams, shall be put to death.'* But . . . I didn't take his scalp, Mr. Bass. I left him be where he fell."

"You raised them Apaches' hair. Why didn't you take *his* hair?" Titus inquired.

"That was afore I knowed better." Then McAfferty turned to gaze at

Bass with a mortified look. "I wasn't 'bout to cut off the hair of no medicine man! There's been many a thing I done in my life I'm sure the Lord don't look kindly upon . . . but I wasn't gonna raise the scalp of a medicine man, Mr. Bass."

"Way it looks, your horn was empty."

"By damned—I was in a proper fix then and there," McAfferty agreed. " 'Yet the Lord will command his lovingkindness in the daytime, and in the night his song shall be with me, and my prayer unto the God of my life.' "

"How'd you come to get your leg outta that trap you fixed to close around it?"

"Shaking just like the trembling earth come Judgment Day, I creeped on back to our camp and told them others real quietlike what just happened with the medicine man. Said I knowed for sure now the Rees was getting blackened up for morning. But Hatcher, Rowland, Kinkead, and the rest acted like they wasn't listening to me—all of 'em just looked at me with the queer on their faces."

Titus nodded. "They told me how you come back with your hair turned white."

Slapping the top of his thigh, Asa said, "Damn if my head weren't as white as the fur on a winter snowshoe hare! And that sure scared all them boys something fierce."

Scratch asked, "Didn't it scare you none?"

McAfferty quietly replied, "I was more scared than all the rest put together. I'd be damned for crucifying through all eternity if I didn't admit it was the truth. The Almighty Hisself had turned my head to white—done it to show me the power of the Holy Ghost! 'For the Lord most high is terrible; He is a great King over all the earth.' It was plain as paint to me, Mr. Bass: Asa McAfferty had set his foot on evil ground! I figgered I'd even had a hand in setting free them Rees, the devil's own hellions, myself."

"Hatcher said you all made tracks that night."

"Somehow we got our horses up the side of that canyon in the dark and slipped off 'thout getting caught by them Rees. But it never were them warriors I was 'fraid of while we was running south."

"What?"

"It were them evil spirits I could feel all round me—clawing at my shoulder, breathing on my neck, hanging just at the corner of me eye every time I turned to look."

"Ghosts?"

"Maybeso," he eventually answered as they reached the foothills. "They was the spirits from the beyond, Mr. Bass. The same spirits that ol' Ree medicine man was carrying with him . . . them devil's whelps what come after me then and wasn't 'bout to let go their hold on me. 'Wilt thou shew wonders to the dead? Shall the dead arise and praise thee?' "

"Sounds like you was more scared of them spirits than you was scared of that Ree war party what was bound to be coming after you."

"Abominations, Mr. Bass!" he began with a voice that shriveled to an ominous quiet. "Asa McAfferty ain't never been 'fraid of anything he can see. What I can't see be the only thing what scares Asa McAfferty!"

As they picked their way across the snowy landscape toward Workman's caverns, he went on to explain to Bass how the trappers had galloped south from Arikara country. Weeks and many miles later, a restless, frightened Asa split off from the rest, and returned to Taos for the winter. The next spring he ventured north on his own.

"For the first time I liked the lonesome. And for the most part I been alone ever since I kill't that medicine man. *'And the soul that turneth after such as have familiar spirits, and after wizards, to go a whoring after them, I will even set my face against that soul, and will cut him off from among his people.'* "

McAfferty was quiet for a long time as they pushed on, expectant of the sun's appearance on the mountain peaks above them. Finally he sighed when they came to a clattering halt on the rim of the prairie looking down at the canyon where Workman had erected his distillery. "Ever since that winter, seems most white fellers I run onto don't take to traveling with a man what speaks the Bible, a nigger like me what begs the Lord for forgiveness ever' day and night. I s'pose such folks just don't care to be with a man who listens real hard to the voices of them spirits what be all round us."

"Your Bible talking ain't bothered me none," Bass admitted. "And I figger a fella gets lonely enough for real company . . . he's bound to start talking to any damn hoo-doo and spirit what'll listen to him."

"Listen to you now, Mr. Bass," Asa snorted, then chuckled as he pressed his heels into the pony's ribs and started down the side of the canyon toward Workman's stone house. " *'The Lord bringeth the counsel of the heathen to nought.'* "

"So you figger me for a heathen, Asa McAfferty?"

"No, I don't," he answered after a pause. "I figger you for the sort of friend what puts up with a very, very troubled man. A tormented man like me. An inflicted man what the Lord has set adrift in a world of woe and despair."

"But you ain't alone, Asa."

Ahead of Titus on the trail descending into that dark canyon where the sun's first rays still refused to shine off the icy granite flecked with snow, a somber McAfferty replied, "That's where you're wrong, Mr. Bass. In the end, no matter what . . . every one of us is alone."

They'd limped into Taos with little more than it would take to outfit a band of Diggers. But they had their hide and hair. And—by damned—it was Nativity time in ol' Taos town!

A holiday when every Mexican male appeared to turn and give the long-haired gringo a second look, when every cherry-cheeked, black-eyed senorita seemed to smile and flutter those long, dark eyelashes at him and him alone.

This second winter among the Mexicans was proving all the more joyous than the first, perhaps because there weren't all that many Americans around. From what Workman reported, most of the gringo trappers had spent only a few days here earlier in the month, then moseyed on down the road to Santa Fe. Those who remained behind were the quiet sort—not at all like Hatcher's bunch, not the sort given to stirring up a ruckus among the Taosenos. A few here and there even remembered Scratch, remembered how he had been one of those daring Americanos who had risked his life to bring back the Comanche captives.

A few of the hard-eyed soldiers glared at him whenever he came to town. Bass figured they were just the sort to remember the faces of those gringos who'd stood their ground at last year's grand *baile*. Scratch didn't figure he could blame them—not since he had himself been the sort to nurse his thirst for revenge for some two years until he ran across the Arapaho buck what took his hair. Just the same, he never put the *soldados* at his back and always made sure there were folks around, along with an escape down a side street, or up a set of outside stairs, or was always near a likely runner of a horse. A man always needed him a way out of a tight spot when he found the odds stacking against him.

One thing for sure, no handful of soldiers was going to jump him anywhere near the Taos square. Not while Ol' Bill Williams was around to help.

That morning of his third day out at Workman's, Titus decided he would give the village a try, figuring he would stroll about the tiny plaza where he could mingle with Mexican folks, maybe buy himself a sugar-sweetened treat or two. After knotting his horse's reins to one of the iron rings sunk deep along the walls of adobe lining the treeless square, Scratch turned at the strong fragrance greeting his nose on the cold, chilling air. There, near the center of the plaza, he spotted several of the vendors gathered around their communal fire, each of them roasting coffee beans and brewing a thick, heady concoction.

His pouch a peso emptier and his fingers wrapped around a clay mug he peered over to take in the holiday scene, Titus sipped at his coffee and began to wander. He hadn't taken but a few steps toward the north side of the square, when he suddenly stopped and turned at the cry of a familiar voice.

Unsure at first, Bass squinted through the fingers of thick smoke curling from every one of the many fires where vendors warmed themselves or prepared kettles of frijoles, baked their crepelike tortillas, or offered customers freshly slaughtered chicken and lamb, each selection hanging from the rafters of their huge-wheeled carts. It was then he heard that voice call out again in greeting to someone across the square, and laugh.

Sure enough. The smoke danced aside, and there stood Bill Williams his own self, slapping a vaquero on the shoulder, sharing a lusty story between them.

How good to see an old face!

Immediately Scratch cried, "Ho! Bill!"

Williams turned, finding Bass headed his way. He quickly said something to the Mexican before beginning his long-legged way across that corner of the square.

"You remember me, Bill?"

"Scratch, ain't it?" he asked as he came to a halt and held out his bony paw. "We run onto one 'nother up to the Bayou, didn't we?"

"Right on both counts," he replied, shaking the offered hand vigorously.

"Down to Taos for the winter, are ye?"

Bass said, "Me and a partner come in three nights back." Then he whispered. "Laying up out at Workman's."

With a nod Williams rocked back and roared, "Sometimes it's best to stay low around these here *pelados*. But as for me—I damn well let 'em all know I'm in town for a spree!"

"You're here for the winter too?"

"Been here for more'n a month now," Williams answered.

Gesturing toward the canvas-draped stall filled with bright, gaudy, eye-catching trade goods, Scratch said, "This here fella appears to have him quite the geegaws and hangy-downs, that's for sure, Bill!"

Williams started them toward his sales stall. "Ye see anything catch yer fancy?"

"You don't need my help trading off your plews now," Scratch snorted as he glanced at the way a couple of Mexican men looked him over, figuring the pair for the shop's keepers. "How's this here feller's prices?"

Williams grinned as if it were going out of style and brushed some of the long fur on his wolf-hide hat back from an eye. "This here nigger's prices is allays low as they can be and him still make a decent living. Lookee here, Scratch." He stuffed his hand into a wooden tray and brought up strings of huge varicolored glass beads, each one bigger than his thumbnail. "Won't those make some senorita's eyes shine just to look at 'em?"

"You got your sights on a likely gal, have you?"

"Hell, no, Scratch! I thort ye might get yer wiping stick polished yer own self, seeing how ye're here to winter up." Then Williams slung an arm over Bass's shoulder. "And we both know winterin' is a time for a man to get hisself a hull passel of polishing!"

Scratch hooted, "Better polish it enough to last him through till next year!"

"Lookee here too. The man's got tin cups and American blankets. Brass wire for them ear hangy-downs of yer'n, child. You could string ye a big bead or two on them wires ye got awready—it'd purty ye up real good."

Scratch's eyes bounced over some of the rest of the trade goods displayed against the stall's three sides as the cold breeze tugged at the canvas walls and roof. "Almost sounds to me like you're wanting me to buy something from this here trader, Bill."

Williams dug at his chin whiskers with a dirty fingernail. "Sure as hell am! How ye 'spect a man to make him an honest living?"

"You know the trader?"

"Know him!" Williams snorted. "The god-blame-med trader's *me!*"

"You?"

"This here's *my* plunder!"

Wagging his head in disbelief, Bass sputtered, "W-why the hell you selling your own plunder?"

"Decided I'd give a offhand shot at turning trader, Scratch. Brought my plews in last month. Traded 'em to a Kentucky feller here what come in with a train from St. Lou. He give me good dollar for my beaver, so I'm pounding my bait-stick in right here in Taos."

"Ain't you gonna trap no more?"

"Not if I can make a living right here, sitting in the sun 'stead of wading in icy streams up to my *huevos* and cock-bag!"

They both chortled; then Williams retrieved his own china cup of coffee from the rocks surrounding a nearby fire where the two of them stood warming themselves as Taosenos crisscrossed the plaza in their daily shopping excursions.

"Bill Williams—trader," Bass announced, testing the feel of it.

"Don't sound too bad, do it?"

"You're happy with staying put to one place, Bill?"

"Wouldn't *you* be happy?" he asked. "Happy not to worry about having yer hair raised, or yer bones gnawed on by some wild critter back up in that high lonesome where no man might never again set down another mokerson?"

Scratch raised his coffee mug in salute. "Then I'm glad for you, Bill Williams. Here's to your success this winter."

"How's trading sound for you?"

"For me?"

"You, become a trader like me," he answered. "Like the rest of these here damned *pelados.*"

"Titus Bass—trader," he rolled the words off his tongue. "Naw. Don't taste right."

"Ye don't mind living yer life on yer fingernails, eh?"

"Don't get me wrong, Bill," Bass explained. "There's been many a piece of ground where I wondered then and there if I was about to leave my bones bleaching in the sun. But I figger a man takes him a little bad with all the good of living free like I do."

"I'm a free man! I can pack up my truck and ride off any time I want," Williams bristled in protest. "I just don't have to worry 'bout no red varmit putting a early end to my days, afore my time."

"Damned Apache almost put me under this fall," Bass admitted.

"West of here? Or was they roaming north?"

"Over on the Heely. Bastards follered me and my partner for days," and Bass went on to relate the tale as Williams poured more coffee for them both.

When Titus finished the story with their arrival at Workman's place a few days back, Williams said, "This McAfferty—he's the one I heerd tell of got his hair turned white."

"One and the same."

"And folks call me a strange one!" Williams chortled. "From what I hear, that McAfferty takes the circle."

"He may talk strange and have him his spells a'times—but he's never let me down."

"That's all a man needs in a partner," Williams agreed. "Find a partner what don't ask for no more than he's ready to give his own self. So"—and he turned, ready to change the subject as he gestured toward his stall—"ye had yer wiping stick polished yet since ye come in to Taos?"

"Naw: this here's my first trip in from Workman's."

Williams draped a long, bony arm over Bass's shoulders and urged him toward the stall as he confided, "Hmmm—let's us see what a man like you could need, what with him figgering to get his wiping stick polished!"

Despite the coffee, Scratch's mouth was going dry. "You hap to know where a feller might go to . . . to find him a likely gal—"

"A bang-tail whore?"

Embarrassed at Williams's loud response, Bass flicked his eyes this way, then that.

"Hell!" Williams roared loudly. "These here greasers don't know much American talk! And they sure as hell don't know sheep shit from bang-tail whores!"

Several of the Mexicans nearby turned at Bill's loud voice, but they as quickly returned to their own affairs.

"See, Titus Bass?" he asked. "Ain't a one of these here *pelados* know any American!"

Speaking in a hush, Scratch asked, "You know where I can find me a gal might be happy to let me crawl her hump?"

"There's two places in the village," Williams explained. "But, for my money, the gals over to the Barcelos house are the finest American money can buy!" And he smacked his lips in delight.

"Barcelos, you say?"

"Senora Gertrudis Barcelos," Williams repeated. "She ain't here herself no more, but she's got her sister running the Taos house since she went down

to Santy Fee. Older gal—'bout as tough talking as a Yankee sailor, she is . . .
but she runs the best knocking shops and saloons here 'bouts in north
Mexico."

Grabbing hold of Bass's shoulder, Williams turned Scratch and pointed
off to the east side of the square. "Off yonder, that way takes ye to a street
where ye'll come to a fork at the corner of a low building—been whitewashed
just this fall. Go on down past it to the left, and ye'll come to a place allays got
horses tied up out front, morning and night. Allays busy with soldiers, them
gals is."

Bass marked it in his memory the way he would a piece of ground he
figured to remember. "Barcelos."

"Barcelos," Williams echoed.

"And it might be worth yer while to ask for Conchita," Williams advised.
"If she ain't busy with no soldier."

"She a looker?"

Williams expressively held his cupped hands out in front of his chest as
his eyes got big as saucers. "A likely gal with lots for a man to enjoy kissing on,
if'n ye catch the way my stick floats. But this here Conchita ain't young as
most of them others at the Barcelos house. Still, she knows her business, and
her business is pleasuring a man like he ain't been pleasured in a long time."

"Good, eh?"

"For my money Conchita is the gal to ride yer wiping stick till ye're
panting like a played-out mule and yer eyes roll back in yer head!"

TWENTY

Conchita was everything Bill Williams said she would be.

Of course, it wouldn't have taken much to satisfy a man with as wild a woman-hunger as he was nursing about the time he and McAfferty banged the huge iron knocker against the cottonwood plank door that very next evening.

Stripping his wide-brimmed hat from his hair he had tied in braids for this special occasion, bowing low in his freshly brushed and dusted buckskins, Bass used a few of the sparse words Williams had taught him to greet the fat, moon-faced woman who answered the door—light and warmth, music and laughter, pouring out around her ample form.

"Buenas tardes, Senora!"

"Sí?"

"Senoritas?" he asked, working hard to get the right roll to it.

Her red, liquor-puffy eyes shifted to McAfferty and took their measure of them both. "Gringos, eh?"

" Sí," Scratch answered, thinking he might get this Mexican talk licked yet. *"Senoritas* for us. Two. *Dos senoritas."*

She poked a grimy finger at the corner of her bloodshot eye and rubbed as she stepped back out of the way, then motioned for them to enter. The sudden warmth of the place surprised him as they stepped into the entry. On two sides of a large parlor flames danced in tall fireplaces. Rugs and blankets lined the walls where a half-dozen men sat, each of them accompanied by a woman. As the Americans followed the large one toward a small bar in the corner, the room fell hushed of a sudden, merry laughter and happy voices disappearing as if swallowed in one great gulp of silence. Only the two guitar players in another corner played on a few more measures before they too looked up in wonder and fell quiet.

The fat woman stopped and snarled something at the musicians, and they began to play again as she pointed the way for the Americans to accompany her to the bar.

Behind the broad cottonwood plank a woman set down two clay cups and poured the gringos a drink from a wicker-wrapped gallon jug. McAfferty pulled a single coin from his belt pouch and slapped it down on the plank. The fat woman held up four fingers to the woman behind the bar, then turned away.

Dragging his cup from his lips, Titus reached out to grab the fleshy arm of the large one who had answered the door that evening as twilight gave its way to night.

She looked at him with disdain and sighed as she pulled her arm free of his hand.

"Barcelos?" he asked.

"*Sí.*"

"I want Conchita."

Her brow furrowed. "Conchita?"

"*Sí,*" he replied, nodding. "Conchita."

For a moment she looked him down and up. "*Bueno,*" and then she turned to the woman at the bar, to speak rapidly in Mexican before turning away once more.

Bass watched as she left, about to speak when the woman at the bar spoke.

"I am Conchita."

Bass whirled, his throat suddenly constricting. "Conchita?"

" *Sí.*"

"Bill Williams . . . he said I should ask for you."

"Conchita . . . me," and she tapped a finger into that cleavage between the full breasts that strained against the low-slung camisole she wore with nothing more beneath it to conceal her fleshy charms.

"He said . . . Bill said I should ask for you."

"Conchita, me," she repeated, a little confusion crossing her face.

"You don't know much American, do you?"

"Gringo . . . Conchita," she explained slowly, as if to make the trapper understand, while pouring McAfferty some more of the pale *aguardiente* from the wicker jug. "Gringo . . . pesos, Conchita go gringo." And she pointed toward a darkened hallway leading from the parlor.

"Mayhaps she don't know much American, Asa," Bass said, "but this is a gal what means business."

"Lo, but a woman's heart is wormwood, Mr. Bass," McAfferty warned as his eyes flicked around the room. "Best you watch your backtrail with this'un."

As the barmaid came around the end of the short plank resting atop four large oak barrels, Bass looked over the room with a growing worry. Wasn't natural the way everything had come to a stop and everyone was studying the two Americans.

"Ain't this Mex gal I'm worried 'bout, Asa. Looks to be these soldiers don't want us here."

"Aye, Mr. Bass," McAfferty replied, and threw back the rest of his liquor. " *'To keep thee from the evil woman, from the flattery of the tongue of a strange woman.'* These here whores don't mind taking American money, but their men don't cotton to having gringo dogs dipping their stingers in Mexican honey pots."

The barmaid slipped her arm in his and Scratch beamed with anticipation. "I s'pose it's time to dip my stinger."

" *'And upon her forehead was a name written,'* " McAfferty called to Scratch's back as Titus left with the woman. " *'MYSTERY, BABYLON THE GREAT, THE MOTHER OF HARLOTS AND ABOMINATIONS OF THE EARTH!'* "

Conchita led him back to the portal of that darkened hallway, stopping for a moment to pull a candle from an iron holder hammered into the whitewashed adobe wall. On down the hallway she stopped and pulled open a sagging door, then held back a thin blanket to let Bass into the tiny crib where she plied her ancient trade.

Setting the candle in another wall-side holder, Conchita turned to the bed, where she flung back the layers of thick Indian blankets, then stepped right up to the American and proceeded to help him off with his pouch, then his coat. Next she yanked up the long tail of his buckskin shirt, tugging it over his head.

Hurling his garments aside piece by piece, without any preliminaries the shorter woman surprised Scratch when she stood on her toes and ran her lips across his chest, the hot tip of her tongue circling his nipples before she dragged it up the side of his neck.

While Titus threw back another long swallow of his fiery Taos lightning, her fingers yanked at his belt buckle, then dragged aside his breechclout as the belt dropped. Suddenly she pushed him toward the thick pad of mattress and blankets tucked in the corner of her tiny cell, so abruptly that he spilled some of the liquor from his clay cup, drops spilling onto the back of her head as she went to her knees in front of him as Bass eased back onto the bed.

As her sure hands flew over the knots lashing his moccasins around his ankles, then tugged at the top of his leggings to pull them off his feet, Scratch found his flesh hardening, stretching, growing just with the sight of her breasts all but spilling out of that loose-topped camisole, growing warm with the sweet anticipation of having himself buried deep within a female once more.

He wasn't sure if it was the heat from the pale, amber liquor, or the closeness of the small room where the single candle flutted against the mud wall. Maybe even the strong odor of lard coming from that poor lamp made of nothing more than a burning wick set within a small cup of pig fat. Perhaps it was the cinnamon oil he could tell she had rubbed in her hair.

But he knew he was ready to explode when she rocked up on her knees above him and thumbed down the top of her camisole, slipping it off her bare shoulders one side at a time, tugging it over each of those breasts the color of smooth milk chocolate stirred into steaming coffee. But when he reached up to grab them, Conchita pushed his hands away and instead rocked forward so that her shoulders were right over his hips. Smiling broadly enough to show her two missing teeth, she gently spread her fleshy breasts apart enough to swallow his hardened penis between them.

Then, with her hands clamping the soft, chocolate flesh around him, the woman began to rock herself up and back, up and back as she rested her chin on his upper belly and gazed up at him devilishly.

Savoring the delicious wickedness of having her watch him as she brought him to climax, Scratch was certain she knew exactly what she was doing. Sure she had done this a hundred times before—even a thousand . . . with a thousand other men. But as he felt the boiling eruption begin all too quickly, those others didn't matter. All that was important right then was the woman-hunger that overwhelmed him every few months . . . thinking back to how it was when he had been a young man and this unimaginable hunger had run hot in his veins more frequently than it did nowadays.

With the sudden explosive release as his hot eruption washed over her breasts, he once again realized that of all the different women in all the Indian camps, and of all the whores in every one of the Taos knocking shops—none of them could come anywhere close to satisfying what he figured he truly wanted. With each passing season, each new moon, with every day's sunrise, he wondered why he was no longer satisfied to have each new woman spread her legs for him and be done with her. In years gone he would have been more than content to take his pleasure and quickly move on.

But of late here he was beginning to get the nagging sense that something was missing from these infrequent grapples with a woman's flesh. Not that this bucking and thrashing of that ol' monster with two backs didn't bring him a moment's peace and contentment . . . but rarely anything lasting.

And even as deliciously wicked as the way Conchita had used her soft breasts on him, the satisfaction of this long-pent release she had just given him began to fade quickly like a cooling breeze come to erase the fever from his skin.

Then, again, perhaps that was the way it was meant to be between men and women—that they somehow coexisted despite never truly giving one another what each really wanted. In the end they were at best able to give one another only what they themselves needed.

With that moist, mindless, momentary compulsion to couple brought to a boiling eruption—men and women retreated from each other, back to truly needing little else the other could give. Although married—as his parents were, as Able Guthrie and his wife were, as were all those who clung to one another in the sight of their God—a husband and wife struggled through their days together as no more than polite strangers come from different sides of the river.

He was certain no woman would ever understand what lay inside him, waiting to be spoken. He was sure no woman ever could. And for him to attempt to fathom the depths of a woman's soul . . . why, he might as well climb to the highest peak in the mountains and with his rawhide lariat try to rope the moon.

Men and women were never meant to live together—that much was plain to him from the painful thrashing life had given him. Hell, there were few men he could live with day after day himself. But he was certain that unanswered, aching loneliness each man and woman must feel a'times compelled them on rare occasions to reach out and somehow touch a private place within one another, no matter how brief and short-lived that intimacy. Still, what troubled him was that as soon as each brief fever had passed, both man and woman went back to walking on alone. Went back to feeling little more than emptiness until they struggled to reach out for one another again.

As he felt his flesh hardening, Bass realized he had been asleep. Conchita was awakening him with her hands. He opened his eyes into slits and watched her in the slowly dancing candlelight as she held him between her two palms, rolling his responsive penis between them like tortilla dough a woman kneaded. Here she massaged his stiffening flesh into readiness.

As Conchita rolled onto one hip and kicked a leg over him, he savored the fleshy sway of those healthy, pendulous breasts as she straddled him, took his manhood in one hand, then settled down upon him with an earthy groan from them both. It fired him anew to find just how moist she was for him, so wet there was hardly any friction as she immediately set about her throbbing dance upon him. With every thrust she took upon him, Conchita became more furied, driving herself more wild, causing her breasts to dance and volve above him until he found himself so maddened, he seized them both—pulling her down savagely so he could suck on one as her hips continued to drive up and back, up and back.

A wild, feral sound was born low in her throat as she pounded herself so fast and hard above him that he knew she was going to flatten out the straw mattress stretched out beneath him on the earthen floor. So savagely did she hurl herself down upon Titus again and again that he knew Conchita was going to hammer him right into the ground itself before she was done with him.

Yet of a sudden he didn't care again. His own rising fever boiled over in those last few moments before the mindless explosion overwhelmed him, causing Bass to lose himself in the soft coffee-brown flesh of her, tugging for all he was worth at her colorful striped skirt she had hiked up over her hips.

Conchita immediately stopped bobbing atop him for those few seconds it took her to reach down, untie the knot in the upper hem, and pull the long skirt away from her hips, flinging it over her head, where it landed against the nearby wall. Now she was completely naked but for her crude moccasins and that silver crucifix around her neck that rhythmically tapped against his cheek as he pulled the other breast to his mouth and began to suck.

"Mr. Bass!"

She tasted so good—piñon woodsmoke and *aguardiente* and cinnamon. Oh, the way she gripped his manhood within that moist, heated crevice of hers—

"Mr. Bass!"

Reluctantly he opened his eyes and gazed into her face, expecting that she would call out his name again in that muffled way he heard her call out before.

But Conchita's head was thrown back and to the side, lost in the delicious passion . . . and she was biting her own lower lip as she continued to hammer herself down upon him so she couldn't have spoken—

"Mr. Bass! Your union with that whore is over!"

Almost there. He felt himself like an overripe fruit about to burst, when more voices suddenly grew loud right at the edge of his consciousness. Exactly the way he might see something flit at the corner of his eye but—when he looked—it would be gone.

Just when he was certain Conchita was moistening even more around him and Bass sensed that first wave of release himself—

—a sudden rush of cold air flooded into the tiny room as the blanket was flung back.

She froze above him as he jerked up on an elbow.

In the darkened open doorway stood a figure wide of shoulder. A man.

"Conchita!"

Although she did not dare dismount from Bass, the woman nonetheless reached over and swept up her skirt, pulling it up to cover her breasts as the man in the doorway lumbered into the room, into the gently flutting candle-light, stirring shadows and hues of saffron as he came in two long steps and stopped, his arms hung at his side, his chest heaving, fists clenched as he snarled low foreign words at the woman.

Bass did not understand anything of what the man barked at her, but his meaning was never more clear. The import of the intruder's words was as shockingly plain as the ominous bark of a strange dog encountered on the backtrails of Boone County, the warning growl of a cornered badger, the hostile grunt of a grizzly boar closing in on him.

The stranger took another step into the room as Titus searched frantically for his coat, his belt that had been wrapped around the coat, the scabbard that had been hanging from that belt—

Then looked up at the intruder.

The lieutenant!

"You son of a bitch!" Bass spat at the soldier who stood above him, bare-chested, wearing only his black pantaloons, held up by wide leather braces.

Conchita suddenly dragged herself off him, both of them still wet from their mutual release. He began to rise to meet the soldier who Scratch knew felt nothing but hatred and rancor for the Americans who had trailed the Comanche into the mountains to save what women and children they could.

In the hallway behind the sergeant shadows darted, voices called out, someone grunted and others screamed as a heavy object struck the wall outside. A man cried out in pain. Then a second, and a third body smacked against the side of the hall. And in those fleeting seconds as he rolled onto his hip, scrambled to his feet, and hurled himself at the soldier, Bass thought he heard the white-head barking in that dark, narrow tunnel of a hallway—grousing with fire and brimstone and a most certain eternity spent in hell's own fire for those he found arrayed against him.

A solid thunk burst through the doorway from that hall, echoing with the sound of a heavy maul striking tight-grained hickory.

The sergeant met him in the middle of the room. Conchita screeched in horror as they grappled, arms and legs a blur. For a fleeting moment Bass was gratified that his opponent had burst into the room without a weapon . . . gratified, that is, until the Mexican cocked back a huge, hard-boned fist and drove it against the American's temple.

With the light of a thousand shooting stars the darkened crib lit up as Scratch rocked back on his bare feet, then shifted his weight back farther still to keep from pitching over, when the sole of one bare foot landed on the wide band of thick leather. He stood there, blinking his eyes to clear them of stars as Conchita burst up from the floor, shrieking, her arms outstretched before her as she lunged for the sergeant's arm curling in the wavering candlelight, in that hand a long double-edged dagger appearing right out of the air.

Ramirez swore at her while she struggled to pull the arm down far enough to seize the knife. Sobbing, she implored him as Bass blinked again, trying vainly to clear the rain-soaked cobwebs from his mind: hearing men banging the wall outside, the grunts and curses in a foreign tongue, McAfferty's cries almost as foreign to his ears.

"'. . . will I lay apart the Philistines like sheaves of wheat!' "

Then, as Scratch sank to his knees, his temple throbbing still but the shooting lights grown dim, he felt the belt beneath one hand. And beneath the other, the rock-hard rawhide sheath.

At the moment Titus seized the scabbard in one hand, gripped the knife's handle in the other—he watched the sergeant clench his beefy left hand into a fist, drag it back as a man would cock the huge goosenecked hammer on a smoothbore, then fling it at the woman's face.

The wide row of hard knuckles struck Conchita squarely across one eye and the bridge of her big nose. Titus watched her head snap back from her shoulders like a withered shaft of the corn he sheared with a huge scythe back on that Kentucky farm so many years ago. As the woman collapsed against the wall, smacking her head into the crude mud bricks, Ramirez slowly quartered around on Bass, grunting from somewhere within his barrel of a chest.

The soldier's long blade shimmered in the candlelight as he held the weapon out in front of him and began to snarl in Mexican.

Just behind the lieutenant's shoulder a knot of shadows congealed against the crude plank door; then a body collided with the door itself, smacking the planks against the mud wall as the man melted to the floor and in stepped a white-headed warrior. His long hair flowing about his shoulders like corn silk in that muted candlelight, McAfferty immediately whirled about, putting his back on the room as he inched inward—a tomahawk in one hand, his long skinning knife clutched in the other. Foot by foot he retreated, holding more Mexicans at bay there in the darkened doorway.

Both Bass and the lieutenant realized McAfferty had his back to them at the same moment.

Like a strip of night torn from a midnight sky itself, Ramirez whirled and brought up his dagger, yanking it into the air as he started to lunge for McAfferty.

And like sunlight glancing off the rushing surface of mountain creek water, Scratch exploded from the floor. Slinging his left arm around the soldier's bull-thick neck, he plunged his skinning knife into the side of the barrel of a chest there below the arm raised to strike McAfferty.

With a piglike whimper of surprise, Ramirez jerked, muscles tensing as Bass felt his thin blade slide along a rib for an instant, then suddenly plunge in clear to the hilt.

He had it buried until it would sink no farther.

The soldier tried jerking away, tried flinging Bass to the side, but the American clung there like a bloated tick to the hump of the herd bull.

Stumbling to the side a step, the Mexican nonetheless swung his knife downward at McAfferty. Missed. Then yanked his huge knife back into the air to try it again.

Bass's arm pistoned only enough to free his knife from the enemy's chest before he jabbed its razor point between another pair of ribs, feeling the warmth ooze over the back of his hand as he twisted the skinning blade this time, working it side to side through the muscle, slashing it on into the man's bellows.

Again from the corner of his eye Scratch watched that huge right arm swing up and down toward McAfferty—realizing too late that the lieutenant's target was not the white-head. The Mexican was arching his knife back at the naked tormentor plastered on his back. Too late—

"Arrrghghgh!"

The pain grew hot as the huge flat blade plunged into the meat of his right thigh, close to the hip.

So much pain that Bass almost went faint, sensing his damp, sweaty grip loosening around the Mexican's neck. Feeling his hand releasing the warm, slick handle of his skinning knife.

"Asa!" Titus cried out desperately as he watched the muscular Mexican yank the knife out of his leg and cock it into the air for a second plunge.

At his call McAfferty whirled in a crouch no more than three feet from the sergeant and immediately raked his left arm to the side before him. The dull oil-blued metal of the tomahawk blade slashed through the Mexican's flesh, which gaped like a bloody mouth opening with bright-red berry juice the way Mexican women stain their own lips with the seductive red of the *alegría*, that honed blade cleaving the entire width of the man's belly in that one smooth motion as the Mexican's arm drove downward, completing his reflex.

Ramirez's knife planted itself into Bass's leg a second time before the big, hard-knuckled right hand tensed into a bird's claw, releasing the weapon's handle. He left it quivering in the meat of the American's thigh.

" *'The bows of the mighty men are broken, and they that stumbled are girded with strength!'* "

Feeling his supper smack itself against his tonsils with the icy pain, Bass slid backward, no longer able to hang on to the lieutenant's neck. Scratch's moist, sticky right hand opened and closed, empty now as he struck the cold earthen floor. His knife still hung in the Mexican's chest as McAfferty whirled away, growling, cursing, spewing biblical invocations at his enemies who crowded against the doorway, working against themselves to get at the white-headed American.

" *'Whoso sheddeth a man's blood, by man shall his blood be shed; for in the image of God made He man!'* "

Asa lunged toward the shadows in the door as Bass sensed Ramirez begin to totter to the side, both his arms clutching his belly, where blood splattered his forearms, the first squirt of purplish-white gut puerting from the wound that had nearly cleaved the huge man in half.

Mumbling moistly around the blood that burbled from his lips, the Mexican lurched to the side, suddenly stiffening as he collapsed to his knees, his eyes opening wide, his chin sagging. Ramirez pitched forward onto his face across Conchita's legs.

She began moaning in that slow, dull-witted, dazed, and wounded way of an animal . . . realizing a dead man pinned her legs to the floor, his warm blood gushing over her bare flesh, pooling on the ground around them, soaking into the pounded clay. But her guttural moans became unearthly shrieks of horror the moment she attempted to free her legs from their prison beneath Ramirez's bloody, eviscerated body.

"Mr. Bass!" McAfferty cried as he backed another step into the room, one moccasin landing in the black puddle as the sergeant's blood pooled near the center of the tiny crib. " 'Lust not after her beauty in thine heart; neither let her take thee with her eyelids!' Cover your nakedness before the eyes of this whore and come help me!"

How it hurt with a cold fire now to slowly drag that hot metal from his flesh, the whole of his leg from toe to hip throbbing with pain . . . just as two Mexicans leaped through the narrow doorway and McAfferty stepped back, a foot slipping in the dark puddle of the dead lieutenant's blood.

In a smooth sweep Bass brought Ramirez's knife up as he rocked onto his one good leg, jabbing forward the moment one of the soldiers cocked his arm over his head, knife in hand. Scratch caught the Mexican squarely in the left side of his chest, low. Dragging the big double-edged stiletto to the side, he felt the blade separate the muscle between two ribs, slash on through the tough muscle of the lung as the soldier recoiled in a jerk, attempting to pull away so violently, he struck the mud wall behind him. Dead, as he struck the floor already littered with another man's blood.

Hearing the crack of metal against bone, Scratch whirled—finding McAfferty yanking the tomahawk out of the side of another soldier's skull, letting the gurgling Mexican sink slowly to his knees before Asa flung the dead man back against the crude table where the pig-lard lamp spilled to the floor, snuffing itself out with a stifling stench of rancid bacon.

In the light of that one small candle, McAfferty spun for the last of the shadows in the door, flinging the knife an instant before pulling his pistol. He fired at the shadows, the sudden light blinding them all in the closeness of that tiny room.

"It's time to find your pistol, Mr. Bass!"

His hands gumming with drying blood, his knees cold on the earthen floor, then suddenly warm as he crabbed through the Mexicans' blood, Scratch searched the darkness for where his pistol had fallen in those frantic, fevered moments as the whore grappled with his belt, coat, and clothing. Beneath the flap to his capote he felt the short, hard barrel. Flinging back the thick blanket wool, Bass seized it with his left hand, dropping the knife from his right to fill it with the pistol butt as he palmed back the hammer with his left hand.

Brought it up just as another shadow burst from the darkness of the hallway. Firing at the black hole the figure made in the dim, flutting candle-light. How his eyes stung with that bright-yellow jet of flame spewing from the muzzle as the shadow hurtled back against the door, its wooden planks slam-ming against the mud wall with a hollow sound.

"Gather your damned clothes!"

Scratch couldn't agree more. He scooped up his leggings and moccasins, stuffing everything inside his war shirt before he jabbed his arms inside his coat sleeves as McAfferty swept out of the darkness and whacked his pistol against the side of a soldier's head the instant the Mexican leaped into the room.

Scratch clambered to his bare feet, trying to balance on that one good leg, flinging the wide black belt around his waist and buckling it as he stabbed the knife into its scabbard, shouting, "Let's get!"

At the doorway a step ahead of Bass, Asa stopped, peered quickly at the three bodies of unconscious men who lay sprawled across the hall, then looked toward the dull, dancing light of the parlor, where women still shrieked and more than four vaqueros stood shoulder to shoulder, squinting into the darkness of the hallway. Their own knives at ready, each one waited half-dressed, their bare-breasted whores clinging frightened to their backs, peering between the shoulders of the men as they clamored and swore and screamed. Behind them flitted a huge, blurry form half-illuminated and back-lit with more than two dozen candles.

As he followed McAfferty from the doorway, Scratch stopped a moment and gazed down that narrow hallway so low a man almost had to duck, peering at those vaqueros, at that gaggle of prostitutes, at that fat and frantic madam who had looked upon them both with such disdain—eager to take their American beaver money, eager perhaps to help the lieutenant and his soldiers take their American lives once she had her fat fingers secured around their beaver pesos.

How he wished he could plunge his knife into her heart.

But Asa grabbed a fistful of Bass's capote and yanked him farther into the darkness, on down the narrow hallway and out a door so low, they both had to duck as they plunged into the shocking cold of that moonless night. Dogs barked nearby on the far side of this mud-walled den of whores. Voices streaked out of the starshine beyond in the streets with a growing echo. Coming closer. Angry voices accompanied by the clatter of hard-leather boot heels and the jangle of arms.

"Forget the horses!" he snarled at McAfferty.

"On foot?" Asa demanded in a harsh whisper. "All the way to Workman's?"

"You figger us to make it out of town in our own saddles? When those horses are out in front on that street?"

For a moment in the dim, silvery light, McAfferty stared this way and that—his mind working feverishly. Then shook his head. "We'll have to steal a couple of horses on our way out."

"We better," Bass swore as they started away, pressing themselves into the shadows along the adobe wall. "We gotta make it to Workman's place afore the soldiers do . . . or our hash is fried."

The bear of a shadow loomed out of the night as if it were a tattered shred of the black sky itself.

Bringing up his knife, Bass braced himself on his good leg, prepared to cut his way through more enemies—

"Bass!"

Confused, Scratch turned to glance at McAfferty a flicker of a moment, whispering, "Who is it knows my name?"

"Kinkead!"

"Damn," he sighed in relief as the shadow inched closer, taking shape as the big American stepped into the starshine. "Matthew."

"It really is you, Asa McAfferty," the shadowy shape said as it came to a halt right before them.

"Pray—what finds you here, Mr. Kinkead?"

"You don't have the time to listen to my story," Kinkead explained, seizing them both by the shoulder and shoving them back toward the shadows at the side of that narrow street, the very same shadows where he had just emerged.

Scratch looked in one direction, then another. "Where?"

"Out of town, now!" Matthew ordered. "On four legs!"

"I'll kill for that horse of yours!" Bass husked. "I won't make it on my two—"

"He's game," McAfferty explained. "Took it in the leg."

Kinkead turned on Bass. "You walk on your own?"

"How far?" Titus asked, his face pinched in pain.

"The corner," Matthew said, pointing. "Here," and he swung an arm around Scratch's shoulder, nearly hoisting him off the ground as he set off in a trot, Bass's feet all but dangling on the crusty snow.

Leading them around a corner at the end of the long row of low-roofed adobe houses, Kinkead lunged for the reins of one of the three horses he had tied to a tall wooden post buried in the ground. "Take your pick of them two—but leg up quick, fellas."

Bass watched Matthew swing up into the saddle and settle before he lumbered against the post and untied the first animal. Quickly lashing his clothing behind the Spanish saddle, he stuffed his left foot into the stirrup and dragged the wounded leg over the cantle before adjusting the tails of his capote.

Wagging his big head, Kinkead chuckled. "You're bare-assed naked under that capote, ain'cha?"

Scratch came alongside as they wheeled about and put heels to their horses. "Never rode with a naked man afore?"

Down the street, voices grew louder.

"Don't make no never-mind to me." And Kinkead grinned. "Long as you got your business done afore them *soldados* showed up. Vamoose!"

All three put their animals into a rolling gallop, threading themselves through the dark tapestry of that sleepy village. Behind them the shouts of soldiers quickly faded as they raced on, submerged in a maze of shadows where disembodied dogs barked and every few houses a candle fluttered into life behind a frost-coated, rawhide-covered window where frightened faces briefly appeared.

On the far side of Bass, McAfferty asked, "We going to your place?"

"Hell, no!" Matthew grumbled. "Gonna keep you two troublemakers far away as I can from Rosa and me!"

"Maybeso you ought'n turn back now," Scratch said as they shot past the last houses and reined toward the low ridge where the night lay its deepest.

"Hep!" was Matthew's reply as he kicked his horse into a harder gallop. "Me leave you niggers on your own now? Just when you've gone and stirred up more fun than this sleepy village seen in years?"

Kinkead ended up leading them along the patchy shadows of the broken butte until the village disappeared from sight behind them. Only then did he rein his horse up a narrow switchback trail the Mexican shepherds used to guide their flocks of sheep to the top of the mesa. On that flat above the distant village, Matthew headed cross-country, making a beeline for Workman's canyon beneath the cold, starry sky. Already the North Star was slipping into the west.

"Who's there?" the sleepy voice called from the stone house when Kinkead sang out their arrival.

"It's Kinkead, Willy! Got a couple troublemakers with me."

Workman noisily dragged back the door on its earthen perch and stood there before them of a sudden like a thin strip of coal cotton in the night, his rifle laid across his elbow. "What'd they do?"

"Said they killed a couple of soldiers."

Bass looked up from his right leg. "More'n two—"

"Shit!" the whiskey maker grumbled.

"We only come to get our plunder," McAfferty explained as he leaped down, handing Kinkead his reins, and started to turn away. "We'll be gone afore any more of them greasers catch up to us."

Workman stepped into the starshine, stopping Asa in his tracks. "Where you gonna go that the *soldados* won't chase you?"

"The mountains," Bass declared, dragging his bad leg off the saddle and landing with a grunt.

"It's the middle of winter!" Workman snorted.

"Maybeso we'll ride to Santy Fee," Asa said, starting to push past the whiskey maker.

Kinkead himself reached out and grabbed McAfferty's arm, stopping him. "And wait for the soldiers to figger out you gone south?"

"There's a place where they can lay in," Workman declared quietly. "Fella by the name of Vaca."

"Ol' Vaca?" Kinkead repeated. Then he turned on Bass. "Has him a rancho at the mouth of the Peñablanca. South of Santy Fee, not far down the Rio Grande, fellas."

Workman nodded. "Heard from the tongue of Ewing Young hisself that Vaca been hiding furs for gringos at his place last few winters."

Scratch stepped up close to the whiskey maker. "The name's Vaca?"

With a nod Workman said, "Luis Maria Cabeza de Vaca. But among us Americans he's knowed as Ol' Vaca."

"Head for his place," Kinkead demanded firmly. "And stay there till you figger out how to keep your necks outta the hangman's noose."

"Them soldiers had it coming!" Bass snarled, the cold sinking to the bone in that wounded leg. "Ramirez busted in on me, looking for trouble—"

"Likely so," Matthew interrupted. "Ever since we stole their thunder with the governor's wife—but Mex is Mex and gringo is gringo down here, Scratch . . . and now them *soldados* got 'em a license not just to arrest you for your beaver—but they got a reason to kill you where you stand."

Bass looked over at McAfferty. Asa nodded.

So Scratch said, "Let's get what little the two of us own packed up and on the animals."

"What all plews you wanna leave with me," Workman offered, "I'll keep 'em till I can sell 'em off and hold the money for you."

"You get the money to us at Vaca's?" McAfferty inquired.

"Just tell me so, and I'll bring it to you there."

"Maybeso to keep the soldiers off your trail, Willy," Bass said, "send Johnny Rowland down with the money what we get for our plews."

Wagging his head, Kinkead replied, "Johnny's gone, Scratch. How long for, I ain't got no idea."

Scratch asked, "Rowland—gone? Where?"

"Threw in with Antoine Robidoux's bunch, last fall. Not long after he talked a squaw from out to the pueblo into riding with him."

"So Johnny's got him 'nother woman now?"

Matthew nodded. "Seems a likely enough gal. Someone help ease him over his Maria."

"Good for him," Workman agreed.

"Where they going?" McAfferty inquired.

"Winty country," Matthew explained as the four of them started for the cavern. "Fixing to get some trapping in afore winter comes."

"That country gets its share of snow early enough," Asa declared. "Maybeso it ain't so smart of Robidoux to winter 'em up there."

"A might safer'n greaser country is for the two of you," Workman scoffed.

"All right—we'll send you word how to get the money to us, Willy," Bass said as he limped behind them, all four men hurrying down the narrow path that led to the cavern where they had stowed their goods.

By the time Titus had dressed, and he and McAfferty had their packs separated and had hauled what they could take out of the torch-lit cavern, Workman and Kinkead had the horses and Hannah ready to go. Between the four of them it took but a matter of minutes to get what few possibles and supplies they were taking with them lashed onto the pack frames. Then Bass turned to the whiskey maker.

"Willy—you do what you can with them plews of ours, but don't sell 'em cheap."

"I'll get best dollar I can."

They shook, and Titus gripped both of his hands around Workman's, saying, "I know you will."

As McAfferty stepped up and took the trader's hand, Scratch turned to Kinkead. "Don't know the next time I'll see you, Matthew."

He smiled broadly, those big teeth of his glittering in the night like a string of mother-of-pearl buttons. "Just you count on seeing me again, Scratch. Don't worry about the when. Could be next month. Could be next year. Hell, I might not lay eyes on you for winters yet to come."

Damn! But this tug at his heart always caused his eyes to smart. "Take care of Rosa for me," he asked. "She's a fine woman, Matthew. And she's got her a good man too."

Kinkead threw his arms around Bass, nearly squeezing the juices out of the smaller man before he stepped back and said, "You two watch over each other, won't you?"

"We will," McAfferty vowed as he held out his hand. "Way I figger it— we both saved each other's hash now."

Titus painfully pulled himself into the saddle. "Seems the score's even atween us, Asa."

"That don't matter a tinker's dam if you niggers don't live to get out of Mexico," Workman growled. "Best get!"

"Time to get high behind," Bass agreed, shifting some weight off the wounded leg.

McAfferty whirled about and swung into the saddle, adjusting his moccasins in the stirrups, tucking the tail of his capote around his leggings.

"I swear I'll see you boys again," Bass promised as he nudged his horse into motion, yanking on Hannah's lead rope.

"Just make sure you don't show your faces around Taos till folks down here forget just how ugly you two niggers really are," Kinkead chided them. "Give it least a winter or two."

"Tell Rosa to keep you fed and happy in the sack, Matthew!" Bass said, turning in the saddle to hurl his voice back at Kinkead as they loped away. His words echoed off the canyon walls, "And keep your eye on the skyline. One day soon you'll see this child back on your doorstep!"

It was Christmas the day they reached Santa Fe. The plaza and surrounding streets were jammed with worshipers headed for mass: horses and donkeys, carts and wagons and carriages, all squeezing past one another as the two Americans slipped off the hills and onto the muddy, rutted, snow-covered road, disappearing among the throngs merging to celebrate the Savior's birth long, long ago.

Swept along with the pious and the noisy, Bass and McAfferty stayed among the crowds as those masses pushed for the town square. Once there, they could thread their way back out on the far side of the village with little chance of standing out in the throng. Safer that, what with all the soldiers coming and going.

Maybe the *soldados* posted here hadn't been alerted to the killings in Taos. But maybe they had.

As the streaming masses began to converge on the outskirts of town, Bass and McAfferty were swept on through the clutter of hovels where Santa Fe's poorest inhabitants lived. Tiny pole-and-wattle huts, these were really shelters no more than a single room where a large family eked out their daily existence. While the walls of some were constructed with crude mud bricks, so too were the low roofs. Because they were nothing more than dirt and straw spread across a network of branches and limbs, when the rains came, or the soaking of wet winter snows, those roofs invariably leaked, often collapsing on the sleeping inhabitants below.

If there happened to be any windows in the walls of those adobe huts the two Americans passed by this morning, they weren't covered with glass. That extravagance was found only on the richest of homes standing closer to the town plaza. Here where the poorest lived, the tiny windows, most no larger than portholes, were covered instead with rawhide scraped to a translucent thinness, or even sheets of transparent mica quarried from the nearby hills.

In the shadow of every house stood the squat outdoor ovens fashioned from adobe as well, each one shaped very much like bone-china coffee cups turned upside down on the icy ground. During the day these beehive-shaped ovens contained the fires tended by a woman for her baking; at night they and their warm coals provided shelter for each family's dogs.

Among the songs and joyous shouts, the two trappers were swept along beneath bright strips of cloth fluttering from banners held high, the Mexicans joining the brays and bleats of nervous animals, curses from the poor owners of the crude *carretas,* and cries from Indian servants guiding the carriages of their wealthy owners through the crowds along the hard-packed streets— faceless Americans lost in the cacophony of this sacred day, pushed ever onward toward the central square and the huge, towering cathedral. Along each side of the narrow avenues stood those carts and stalls of vendors crying out to the passing crowds, their loud and shrill voices hawking trinkets or cloth, coffee or sweets, perhaps some shiny bauble to offer a loved one, or a candle to light for the Virgin Madonna on this special day.

In the air drifted the close smell of animal and man, fresh dung and old sweat, in addition to a mingling of savory spices simmering in a hundred different kettles hung over fires burning along each avenue. Cedar and piñon added their thready smoke to the cold, frosty air as the huge bells began to peal and the crowd shouted anew, surging forward in a hurry through the rutted streets of icy corduroy. All were eager to reach the cathedral and find themselves a place to sit, if only a place to stand, before the priests began their sacred high mass on this most holy day.

Here the wealthy rancho owners and their families rubbed shoulders with the hacienda peons and the slaves who worked their fields. Many of the tribes in the region raided neighboring bands, stealing children from one another, then selling these prizes to slave traders, who would bring them to the Mexican villages where the captives would be sold at auction. Young boys grew up working in the fields or tending the owner's animals. There was an even higher demand for young girls to work the many household chores it took to keep their master's rancho operating. The Navajo were the most numerous and, therefore, made the most wealth at this trade in human misery, while the destitute Paiute were driven to venture to the Mexican towns, where, having no captives of their own and possessing nothing else to trade, they reluctantly sold their children into slavery.

Suddenly the Nativity procession came to an abrupt halt as a parade of small children streamed in from a side street, raising their beautiful voices in a song of the blessed birth, some of them bearing streamers over their heads, the rest carrying tall tallow candles, flames fluttering on the morning air as they marched in formation past the braying burros and whinnying mules, the crowd clapping and joining in that joyous, youthful song. At the end of their line came groups of the oldest youngsters, who carried on their shoulders long platforms bearing crude papier-mâché effigies of the magi, lowly shepherds, the sacred Madonna and Joseph, and of course the infant Christ swaddled and lying in his simple corncrib.

Immediately behind these children appeared the holy fathers: a half-dozen black-robed priests, swinging the smudge of their sacred incense and surrounded by their young acolytes. As the holy men passed by, some of those in the crowd fell to their knees and cried out for heavenly mercy and temporal blessings; others turned their faces and palms heavenward, making sacred vows, while most merely bowed their heads in silence while the padres moved on past, the oldest of the altar boys struggling beneath the huge wooden cross he dragged along.

As soon as that replica of the dying Christ nailed to the crossed timbers went by, the somber devout rose from their knees, joyous smiles returning to their faces, and songs began to spill from their tongues, many clapping in ecstasy as they resumed their celebration of this holiest of Christian holidays.

Here in this last push toward the plaza many of the revelers who were wrapped in thick multicolored Navajo blankets or kept themselves warm beneath striped serapes were huffing mightily on their last corn-shuck cigarillo rolled from a mild native tobacco wrapped in a small sliver of husk, this vice enjoyed by man and woman alike: a few last puffs taken before they would join the hundreds in climbing the steps to enter the cathedral's huge double doors.

Past the bustle of carriages and carts rumbling noisily to a halt in the midst of that teeming throng of those on foot who streamed toward the morning mass, the two lone Americans eventually reached the far side of the plaza. Here they were forced to squeeze their horses against one side of the narrow street as they swam against the surging tide of bodies and carts, horses and burros, all those pilgrims intent upon reaching the town square. Then of a sudden the crowds thinned and trickled off, just about the moment the cathedral bells pealed one last time.

Joyous voices, the clamor of celebration, the bleats and whinnies and brays, all faded quickly behind them as the two trappers hurried down the trampled street toward the southern side of the sprawling village. Here and there they encountered a rumbling cart or a carriage chock-full of a family of anxious churchgoers realizing they were already late, racing past the Americans without so much as a greeting or a second look. Back in the shadows of the side streets mangy hounds and ribby, mixed-breed dogs roamed in pairs and packs, sniffing among piles of refuse. Some of the braver animals ventured out to bark or yip among their horses' legs, yelping in surprise and pain when Hannah tumbled an unwary cur with her hoof.

Beneath the low-tracking sunlight of this midwinter day the whitewashed walls of the wealthy residents soon gave way to the earth-toned sepia of the poorer adobe homes, the appearance of it all quite striking against the expanse of those hills rising beyond the outskirts of town. There at the far reaches of Santa Fe among the growing stench of the open-air sewers, Bass and McAfferty hurried on by the well-marked bordellos and watering holes where a few bleary-eyed inhabitants stumbled from the doorways to stand in the morning sun, staring up at the two Americans. Half-dressed soldiers and still-drunk vaqueros emerged to shade their eyes as they gazed at the pair. Some of the dusky-skinned, buxom women pulled cigarillos from their lips and pushed unruly sprigs of black hair back from their faces to call out invitations to the trappers as the pair plodded on by. It struck Bass how a whole section of this capital city was devoted to whiskey and women, revelry and sin.

Just the sort of deadly mix that had put the two of them on the run.

With all the celebration of this holy day they had slipped on through the inhabitants of Santa Fe to reach the southern road that would take them to the hacienda of wealthy rancho owner Luis Maria Cabeza de Vaca.

"If we don't find no one around out to his place down on the Peña-blanca," McAfferty said at last as they nudged the horses into a lope, putting the mud-walled village behind them, "I figger they've all come here for church."

"We'll just lay low out to Vaca's place," Scratch agreed, "till the old man can come back to hide us."

TWENTY-ONE

Ol' Vaca was dead.

Killed the day before Christmas.

Only a matter of hours before Bass and McAfferty showed up at his hacienda, Luis Maria Cabeza de Vaca had been shot resisting a detail of Governor Manuel Armijo's soldiers sent from Santa Fe to confiscate the beaver pelts and other property of Americans suspected of being hidden at Vaca's rancho.

Near noon on that sacred holiday as the two gringos rode down from the low hills toward the mouth of the Peñablanca, instead of looking down from the heights on the splendor of the Vaca-family empire, they gazed at the deserted, still-smoldering ruin of half the buildings. As soon as they reined into the smoky yard, more than a dozen armed men appeared from all sides, every one of them smeared with cinders, their faces and clothing streaked with ebony and dried blood.

Among them were Vaca's three sons, as well as a nephew who knew a little English—enough to explain that the governor's *soldados* had come on the evening of the sacred holiday with a writ to search the grounds and buildings, orders to seize all Americans' property and confiscate any goods being trafficked with the gringos.

"My family has been on this land for generations," the nephew explained. "This is no way to treat my family!"

True to his personal code of honor, the old man had stood before the overwhelming array of soldiers without a weapon and refused the captain permission to search the grounds. Which prompted the officer to rein up to the old man and brutally slash him across the face with his quirt, splitting Vaca's cheek open and knocking him down. Yet he struggled back to his feet and immediately attempted to yank the impudent soldier out of the saddle.

"The captain—he pull his pistol and shoot my uncle," the nephew disclosed.

Before the smoke from that single pistol shot could clear, a general melee broke out as family members and ranch hands turned and raced for their weapons while the soldiers began their rampage. In the end it was Vaca's old wife who ventured out of the hacienda waving a large white handkerchief in the stiff, cold wind, surrendering so that no more of her family would die, so that she could go to the body of her husband where he lay mortally wounded in the trampled yard, bleeding to death near the foot of their porch. A patch of dirty crimson still stained the crusty snow where Vaca fell.

After rounding up all the family and their employees, placing them all under guard in the middle of the yard, the soldiers rummaged through the house and outbuildings before they moved on to the barn and the barracks where the ranch workers slept. Only then did a young Paiute house servant turn back to look at the hacienda and emit a horrified scream. The house was on fire.

At first the captain had refused to allow the ranch hands to fight the flames, claiming that such a catastrophe was no work of his men. But after nearly half of the graceful old building had been consumed, he relented and allowed Vaca's men to put up a valiant but hopeless effort against the flames.

Instead of ordering his men to help the family, the captain had his soldiers continue their search: eventually managing to find over two hundred pounds of beaver pelts hidden beneath a trapdoor in the barn floor. Beyond that there was nothing conclusive to indicate that Vaca had been dealing with the Americans. Besides, the angry captain had been informed there would be gringos to arrest.

His men found no Americans.

"The governor and his *soldados,*" explained the nephew, "they hate the Americanos. They want us to hate them too. My uncle, he not hate. What he had he give to all who come to his door, to all guests. And now he lay in his grave."

Three dark mounds stood out against the sunlit snow in the family cemetery on a low knoll behind the hacienda. Three new wooden crosses marked the last resting place of Cabeza de Vaca, along with two of his workers. This last resting place of the old man's hospitality to American trappers.

Bass waited with the horses as McAfferty walked through the crude iron fence and knelt at the foot of that freshly turned sod so stark against the gleaming snow beneath a cloudless sky.

" *'Thou art my hiding place; thou shalt preserve me from trouble; thou shalt compass me about with songs of deliverance,'* " Asa grumbled as he returned and took up his reins. "There ain't nothing for us here now, Mr. Bass."

As McAfferty kicked his horse in the ribs and turned away, Bass reached down and shook hands with the old man's sons, then told the nephew, "Your uncle died a brave man. Near every one of them soldiers I run onto—they been cowards. But a brave man like your uncle, he's gone now to a place where there ain't a single yellow-backed polecat coward . . . a place beyond the sky where other men of honor have welcomed him."

The two of them swept around to the south before turning north by northeast for the foothills of the mountains. This would be far harder going than the road offered a wayfarer traveling north to Taos along the Rio Grande road. But they were wanted men, and it was clear there were soldiers out, prowling.

Just as clear that this was not a good season for an American in northern Mexico.

Four days later, after traveling during the cold of night and hiding out each day, Bass and McAfferty found a well-concealed *rito,* one of those narrow canyons through which a stream flowed out of the mountains toward the Rio Grande itself. After leaving their horses concealed from roving eyes, they moved out at moonrise on foot, reaching Workman's place close to midnight.

"Bill Williams been out to see me," the whiskey trader announced after he had hurried them into the back room of his stone house and they had explained why they weren't hiding out at Ol' Vaca's place.

"Bill already heard what happen't to us?" McAfferty asked.

Nodding, Workman continued, "He brought me a dozen traps for you boys. Soon as he heard the story of what you done over at the Barcelos place, he come right on out here to see what he could do to help. I told him we just shooed you off to Santa Fe—but that I had some of your furs here. That's when he said you told him you was needing some traps to replace them what you had to leave behind on the Heely."

"Damn straight—I told him we was pretty short on traps," Bass replied.

Workman hauled a huge sack out of a dark corner. As he swung it across the earth floor, it clattered, coming to a rest. "Juniata steel, boys. Best traps a feller can buy him in Mexico."

Titus asked, "We square with Bill?"

"He took what he needed in trade from your plews," Workman answered. Then his eyes got anxious. "You ain't fixing on staying here, are you?"

Scratch could see the apprehension glazing the man's eyes. He said, "Naw, we just come for what was left here when we lit out afore."

Workman's shoulders sagged, limp with relief. "Ain't safe around here for you."

"Ain't safe down in Santy Fee neither," McAfferty added.

"Tomorrow night we'll be back to gather up what's ours and be gone," Bass said. "Afore we do, you take what's fair for all you done by us."

The whiskey maker waved a hand in the dark room. "You boys don't owe me a thing."

"It's only right," Scratch protested. "For all you done—"

"Mr. Bass is right," Asa added. "Likely them *soldados* will be back to see you."

They were out of there before the eastern sky grayed. And back at dark the next night to load up what they had left behind more than a week before. With every hour Bass himself grew all the more anxious, all the more certain in McAfferty's belief that the soldiers would be back. After seeing Vaca's place, and those three fresh scars on the earth—it was almost enough to make him a praying man: begging God to spare William Workman and all the rest who had put their necks in a gallows noose simply to help out a few Americans come to Mexico.

But every bit as much as a man might pray, Scratch realized a man also had to keep his powder dry and his weapons close at hand. And never be caught praying down on his knees with his eyes closed. Suicide, sure and certain.

"Maybeso one day I'll come back this way," Asa told Workman as they swung into their saddles.

"Give it some time, like Kinkead said," the whiskey trader reminded them. Then he turned of a sudden and held up his hand to Titus Bass.

"Near forgot to tell you, Scratch. Wanted to wish you a happy birthday."

"H-happy birthday?"

Workman nodded. "Figger it's well past midnight already. That makes it New Year's Day, eighteen and thirty. How many rings that give you now?"

"Thirty-six," he replied, astonished. "Already a new year."

"You boys watch your hair," Workman said as he took a step back and slapped Bass's horse on the rump.

"You watch your'n, Billy Workman!" Scratch cried as they reined away.

At the top of the prairie McAfferty came alongside him as they loped beneath the North Star.

"That's twice now since we threw in together what I didn't think we'd make the new year, Mr. Bass."

"Maybeso you're a hard-user on your partners, Asa."

"Me?"

"You was the one what rode us off down to Apache country."

McAfferty snorted. "And you was the one took us off down to whore country! *'For true and righteous are His judgments: for He hath judged the great whore, which did corrupt the earth with her fornication!' "*

When Titus turned to gaze at Asa, he found the white-head's eyes glimmering with mirth. "Awright, you slick-tongued son of a bitch. I s'pose we are even. You got us in that fix down on the Heely, and I got us out."

"Then I pulled us out of the next mess you plopped us down in," McAfferty concluded.

"Way I see it," Scratch declared, "we're square, Asa McAfferty. No matter what happens atween us partners now, we're square."

Scratch figured they couldn't have anywhere near as much trouble from there on out as the two of them had their first few months after throwing in together. Leastways, that's what he told himself as they loped out of the valley of the Rio Grande, slogged their way over the pass, and finally plunged down to the foot of the Front Range, where they struggled on north.

At times they happened across a likely-looking stream flowing down from those emerald foothills and set up camp for a few days to work the banks hard, doing their best to strip the place clean of what beaver they could bring to bait. More times than he would care to count that winter and on into the early spring, they were forced to hole up and hunker down as a storm blustered over them, delaying their journey north. Nonetheless, those days imprisoned in camp gave them a chance to make needed repairs to traps, tune the locks in their rifles and pistols, sharpen knives, and reinforce saddles and tack.

Those hours also gave Asa an opportunity to discourse on a variety of celestial and theological subjects, his long, meandering monologues taking him from the rightful place of the devil and evil among mankind, all the way to his assertions that the end of the world had already been foretold and its date was therefore cast in stone. No matter how good mankind might believe it would ever become, man was by nature still an evil creature and one day would be brought to task for his errant ways.

"Even you, Asa McAfferty?" Bass asked skeptically.

The white-head had looked up from the oiled strop where he was dragging a knife blade back and forth. The sharp edge lay still as he studied Scratch. After a long moment of reflection, he answered gravely, "Especially me."

As his partner went back to sliding the honed blade up and down the strop, Bass echoed, "You?"

"The harshest penalty come that day of judgment for this wicked world will be meted out to those of us who have sought how best to serve the Lord our God . . . and failed Him in the end," McAfferty explained. " *'And I saw the dead, small and great, stand before God; and the books were opened: and another book was opened, which is the book of life: and the dead were judged out of those things which were written in the books, according to their works.' "*

Scratch stared into the fire for a long time and eventually asked, "Ever thort to just turn away from all your Bible-spouting ways?"

"There ain't but a handful of men I've met in me life what'd understand what I'm about to say, Mr. Bass—but I figger you're one of the few," Asa began with measured confidence. "See, comes a time in his life a man does what he knows to be right . . . even when he knows no one else thinks he's right. That might be my saving grace. My only prayer of spending eternity in the sky."

Oh, how Scratch had wanted McAfferty to explain all that, cursing himself for not being near smart enough to figure out the riddles and parables the man used to explain things. But in the end Titus was reluctant to admit his ignorance of spiritual matters. In the end he let it lay, and did not ask.

As winter grew old, they crossed the South Platte, then struck its northern branch. Along it the pair traveled west toward the interior basin, then struck out for the Wind River. North to the Bighorn, eventually reaching the south bank of the Yellowstone itself.

By and large the ice was growing spongy that day late in March, so they were forced to push downstream until they found a patch of more open water. There they stripped out of all their clothing but moccasins, tied all of it right onto the top of their packs, and led the reluctant animals into the icy river. Yelling their encouragement to one another and to the animals, their teeth chattering like bone dice in horn cups, the trappers swam across the mighty Roche Jaune, gripping bridles or saddle horns with trembling hands.

On the far side Bass and McAfferty emerged from the water shivering so hard they could hardly stand, their half-frozen fingers fighting to loosen wet knots, finally freeing the oiled hides where they had safely wrapped their clothing. Back inside their warm buckskins, an outer pair of buffalo-hide moccasins, and their thick blanket capotes pulled over buffalo-fur vests, they made camp for the night on the spot—then pressed on the next morning.

North by northwest they pointed their noses now, their faces battered by a wild mix of brutal spring rains, freezing sleet, and some soggy, late-season snows until more than a dozen days after putting the Yellowstone at their backs they struck a narrow, winding river where the redbud and willow were just beginning to bloom beneath a clearing sky.

"By my reckoning, this here gotta be the Mussellshell," McAfferty asserted as they dropped to the ground in that lush bottomland.

Bass studied the stream up, then down, making note of the surrounding landforms. "You heard tell this was good beaver country, eh?"

"Said to be prime beaver," Asa replied; then he raised his rifle and gestured at the jagged line of peaks lying along the western horizon. "That yonder's the edge of Blackfoot country."

They slept off and on throughout the lengthening days, grabbing a short nap here and there in the morning and afternoons, catching a few hours at night. This was a dangerous land where one of them had to arise in the dark hours after the moon had set and take half their animals out to graze in plain sight of camp. The other horses they kept tied close at hand just to be ready, in the event they had to run to save their scalps.

While a trapper's normal routine would have him going out early in the morning and again late in the afternoon, neither of these wary veterans ventured from their secluded camps during the daylight hours. Instead, Bass and McAfferty went to their traps only in the darkness before dawn, and in the blackness after twilight had faded from the sky.

As they slowly worked their way up the Mussellshell toward the mountains, then crossed over the low divide and began to trap down the Judith River, the pair cautiously chose their camps: finding a spot with enough tall willow to hide their horses and their plunder, enough of the blooming cottonwood branches overhead to disperse the smoke rising from their tiny fires. A cold and horrid winter had given way to a wet and miserable spring, fraught with daily thunderstorms that soaked man and animal alike and made a man hanker for the coming warmth of summer days and the prospect of rendezvous.

As the weeks tumbled behind them, their animals labored under the growing weight of heavier and heavier packs of beaver. And though they occasionally came across sign of war parties moving this way and that up the Mussellshell or down through the Judith Basin, neither Bass nor McAfferty saw a single warrior. By late spring it was almost enough to make a man grow complacent, if not downright lazy.

With as warm and sunny as it had become that afternoon, Titus determined to move out of their new camp before slap-dark had descended upon the valley. At sunset he took up the big Mexican butcher knife they used in camp and stuffed it into the back of his belt. His rifle in one hand, his trap sack in the other, he nudged Asa with a toe.

"Goin' out—set me some traps."

McAfferty squinted into the afternoon light, then rubbed both eyes with his knuckles. "Ain'cha waiting till dark?"

He snorted. "We ain't see'd a feather."

"But we seen lots of sign up here this close't the Missouri."

"You're like a mother hen," Titus replied as he turned away. "It's only bait sticks I'm cutting. Ain't no Bug's Boys gonna catch me out."

Still wet from that afternoon's thundershower, the tall grass and leafy brush soon soaked through his leggings and moccasins, beading on the long flaps of his thick wool capote. Constantly moving his eyes across the surrounding hills, looking for anything that shouldn't be there, Scratch searched for a likely spot to cut his bait- and float-sticks. Plenty of green willow up and down the Judith—but where would he find a place concealed enough to work?

At the edge of the river he spotted the narrow sandbar that ran in a jagged strip from the bank toward the edge of the water, a damp piece of ground some thirty yards long. Up to his left the sandbar jutted against a sharp cutbank better than eight, maybe ten, feet high. And off to his right the cutbank fell away to nothing but a gentle slope as the grassy bank descended to the river's edge.

Damn good place to cut his willow, peel it, and prepare his traps—all of it out of sight from the surrounding hills and meadows. A pretty spot, too, here as the light was beginning to fade and turn the rustling leaves to a deeper hue.

After clambering through the thick copse of willow and buckbrush, Titus dropped his heavy trap sack onto the edge of the sandbar and propped his rifle against it. Directly behind him hung a wide canopy of willow suspended over the edge of the cutbank. It was there he pulled the tomahawk from his belt and began to hack at the base of some of the thicker branches, tossing them into a pile near the trap sack. After he had nearly two dozen cut, Scratch turned back and squatted on the sandbar to begin peeling the first limb, slowly fashioning it into a bait-stick, sharpening its thicker end so that he could drive it into the bank just above a set he would make come morning. At the other end of the stick he used his knife and fingers to peel back layers until he had the limb fanned out for some three or four inches down the wand. The better to hold more of the "beaver milk" that would lure a curious flat-tail to drop one of its feet within the jaws of his trap.

Downstream . . . there among the willow along that gently sloping, grassy bank . . . maybe it was only the wind sighing.

But he waited. Glanced over at his rifle, and waited a moment more. Yeah, probably only the breeze rustling those branches up there.

He tossed the finished stick aside and picked up another, starting to hack off the small limbs and nubs with that big butcher knife. Peeling, stripping, peeling some more.

Of a sudden the hair stood on the back of his neck as the breeze shifted into his face and he frantically sorted out the meaning of that rank smell. Whatever it was, he scratched up a memory strong enough to trigger revulsion, then some growing fear. He kept clawing for the answer as he turned slightly, his right hand beginning to tremble—and that scared the hell out of him. Just to look down at the butcher knife and see it quaking.

Perhaps it was an Indian pony—this rank odor of dampness. Maybeso it might even be a damned Blackfoot he smelled on that hint of wind coming into his face, bristling the guard hairs on the back of his neck, stirring him to remember. Something like the fetid, putrid stench of bear oil smeared on a warrior's skin, or the bear grease rubbed into his braids . . . a smell so suddenly recognizable as the red nigger rushed close enough to grapple with you—

With their snorts of surprise and curiosity, he watched them both lumber his way out of the willow. But the moment he fell back to his haunches and struggled to drag his legs back under him, the two grizzly cubs skidded to a halt, whirled ungainly, and bumped into one another, their eyes frightened of this big creature they had just discovered. And then they began to whimper.

A sure call for their mother.

So fast did the next few heartbeats thump within his chest—enough time for the sow to burst through the thick willow brush behind her cubs. Time enough for her to stick her nose into the breeze and size up the threat posed to her offspring. Time only for him to start scooting backward.

She shakily rose on her back legs, opening her massive jaws and rolling back her muzzle to expose those yellowed fangs dripping with foamy slobber.

Glancing at the rifle that lay between them, Bass got only to his knees in that instant the sow dropped to all four and heaved his way with a lurch. Shoving the butcher knife into his left hand with that half-peeled willow branch he was already holding, he yanked out his pistol and raked back the goosenecked hammer, getting it up in front of him just in time to blot out her snout as she opened that gaping maw and began to roar.

Wau-augh!

He felt the pistol buck in his hand as she was yanked up short—immediately swiping the arm and that tiny weapon aside as smartly as she would swat a troublesome mosquito, the pistol's smoky bark buried beneath the terrible battle cry of a mother wronged and duty bound to protect her young. She brought that paw up to rub at the side of her jaw where the ball smashed through her face. Then gazed down at her enemy and grumbled something great and fearful at the back of her throat the moment she rocked back down onto all four and lumbered into motion.

In that final moment before she swatted him, and the pistol went wheeling into the willow, he remembered how the thick tufts of green grass exploded into the air as she sank each paw into the ground, how the glittering sand spurted from each foot in a golden cascading spray as she exploded toward him.

One powerful paw crashed over the rifle and the heavy trap sack as she scrambled past the cubs and closed on her prey—the open sack clattering across the wet earth, the rifle cartwheeling end over end toward the water lapping against the rain-dampened sandbar.

Wau-au-au-au-gh-gh-gh!

With her huge maw open and dripping with that terrifying roar, the sow bellowed the grizzly's battle cry as she pounced upon Bass with such a powerful rage that she bowled both of them over, spilling them across the wet sand and into the tall grass like the la   rawhide balls small Indian boys batted back and forth across the ground in their exuberant, youthful games.

He felt the sudden, hot tenderness at his back, rolling groggily onto an elbow, knowing she had caught him with a paw, raking him with one or more of her four-inch claws as she burst past him—

Wau-au-au . . . gh-gh-gh!

Already she was catapulting onto her hind legs, digging in with her forepaws, wrenching up sand and grass as she righted herself and twisted about in her turn. Angrier perhaps that she had not crushed the puny creature in that first grand charge. Just the way she had had to deal with any male she encountered ever since that day in early spring when she had emerged from her den with those two young cubs given birth and suckled during the last of winter's rage suffered on this north country.

Waughgh!

Leaping across those last ten feet, the sow cut off the light, cut off all air as she dropped out of the sky onto the trapper scrambling like a crab to get out of her path. He landed on his back as everything went black, went suffocating.

Scratch cried out as she reared back suddenly and smacked him with a monstrous paw, as if he were no more than a bothersome badger she was trying to dig out from beneath a rotted log. The fire around his lungs was so great, it felt as if his ribs had been torn loose from his chest as he was hurtled to the side on the sandbar.

Waugh!

Again she bellowed as he blinked grains of sand from his eyes, dragging his cheek off the ground, finding her resting on all fours a few yards away, turned to look at her cubs. Calling to them noisily with those jaws, that curving muzzle drawn back to expose the rows of monstrous yellowed teeth.

The moment the two cubs started his way, Bass shoved onto a hip, his chest refusing him a deep breath, his back burning, hot one instant, icy cold the next as the wind slashed across it. If he could run now, he might stand a chance of getting to the rifle a heartbeat before she got to him. Just spin around as he cocked the hammer, fire as she settled upon him again—

Then he knew it was too late already. That flicker of time's candle to consider what to do and how to do it had already cost him his chance.

Just take her with his own bare hands.

When she spotted him rising to his knees, coming shakily to his feet, she wheeled fully on him. Then twisted her head to locate her cubs the moment before they bounced against her.

Enraged, her hump hair stiffened. The sow batted the first aside, backhanded the second, sending them both sprawling away toward the cutbank, yelping and whimpering as they tumbled to a stop, licking at their bruises. Then she slowly turned on the trapper, wobbly on his two legs.

He tried to blink the sandy grit from his eyes, clear the dry shreds of cobweb from his head as she flexed her back, shifted her feet, planting them squarely as she rose on those huge haunches. Then she too stood on hind legs.

And windmilled at the air with those long, deadly instruments, her claws bared, glinting in the last rays of the sun.

Just take her with his own bare hands.

And for the first time he realized his hands were not empty.

In the terror of her first strike, he must have gripped on to what he had been holding with the might of a trap's jaws. In his left hand remained that chunk of willow limb a little thicker than his own thumb, already sharpened at the end.

And in his gritty right hand was the bone handle attached to that curved, ten-inch blade of Mexican steel.

Tottering on her hind legs, the sow lumbered forward, closing those last few yards, towering over the puny human by more than a foot in shaggy, silver-tipped height. Sawing her arms back and forth, she pounced the last two steps and blacked out the sky once more as her awful roar deafened all sound from his ears.

His back burned anew as she clutched him into her with one great paw, burying his face in her chest. Lunging with all he had in that weakened left shoulder, Titus sank the sharpened end of the branch into her thick hide, sensing the point pierce that heavy layer to plunge on into the muscle, shoved on past bone. He felt her jerk as the willow spear went home, driven deep within her lights.

Knowing in that next instant it was not enough to kill the she-brute.

Again she raked at him, and again. Her shaggy forearms only brushing, bruising, battering his shoulder blades and the small of his back as she struggled to rake him with her claws—but she held him too close to get at him. Too close, right there against her: smothered, trapped against the beast that was about to finish him off.

Gagging, Bass could smell nothing but the rank odor of her damp hide, the milk going sour at her two shriveled dugs.

Knowing by this time of the season she was likely giving up nursing the two cubs, teaching them instead to feast on plants and small animals, ants and that meat of whatever big game presented itself to them.

Meat. Four-legged or two. Including a hapless trapper.

As he felt her crush his chest with a fiery pressure, the sow straightened to full height, dragging his feet off the ground, shaking him helplessly against her great stinking mass. He dangled in her grip, his legs flopping like one of his sister's sock dolls.

How he needed a breath of air. Just one breath more. Sensing his supper rise against his tonsils, Bass gasped, sickened by the dank sour-milk odor of her as he drew back the butcher knife and plunged it into her chest.

Too low!

But instead of drawing it out, with both hands clamped around the wet, sticky, warm handle, he sawed the blade to the side savagely. Hearing her grunt with each new plunge of the blade within her gut.

Feeling the rumble of each of her battle cries, feeling each of her painful groans as they reverberated within her chest and rattled against his cheek, he even sensed her cries shake the handle of that weapon he gripped with white knuckles. Then he himself echoed the sow's dull roar that shuddered beneath his eye pressed deeply against her stinking fur.

The bear hooked a claw around his hip and raked back. He felt the sudden cold as the legging gave way and the breechclout with it—his hide laid bare to the bone across the top of his hip.

He heard a shrill cry coming to him in the midst of that muffled, dark hole of her massive being where she had herself wrapped around him—just as surely as if she had swallowed him whole. And he realized that inhuman cry was his.

Then, as the cry faded, Scratch heard a new, strange sound.

One thunderous thump echoed through her body, and he listened to her whimper like her cubs when she had batted them aside in fury. Pulling back one mighty arm from the grip she had on him, Bass could suddenly see shafts of rosy alpenglow, slivers of trees and brush suspended against the sky overhead. And smell glorious air.

He shoved back against the other paw for leverage and yanked the knife free of her. Swinging it up in a short arc, Bass buried the long blade right below her jawline. She nearly shook him free, nearly tore his grip from that bloody handle as she shivered and whipped her head from side to side to rid herself of the torment.

Scratch attempted to saw the knife to the side but encountered bone. Instead he yanked the weapon free once more, rocked back, and plunged it in. Back out and in again. Out once more, just enough to give himself some leverage against that grizzly foreleg that gripped and raked and pummeled him—then back in with all the strength he could muster. Sensing his will seep out of him with each new thrust. Turning, twisting, screwing the blade brutally an instant before he jerked it back out.

Waugh-gh-gh-gh!

With her roar garbled by her own blood, Bass felt the beast falling, pitching forward with him beneath her. Helpless, he twisted and screwed at the knife's handle as his face was buried again. Sealing out all light, suffocating him. Shutting off the rest of the world.

She had swallowed him whole.

The grizzly had won, and now she was devouring his soul. Not just what wreck was left of his body. But feasting on his very spirit. Like an evil specter come lunging out of a ragged tear between his world and its own—lunging through to devour him and drag his soul back to its world of eternal despair.

Better to be dead than seized and hauled back through that crack in the sky by this evil spirit.

Suddenly he felt his leg being pulled, yanked. The wounded, bloody hip yelped in pain as his ankle was twisted brutally.

Certain it must be the cubs, feasting on his flesh now that their mama had killed him. Believing these last few seconds of his life would be even more torture than those last painful moments of their battle—for now he realized he had lost to this demonic creature. Now he knew the cubs were going to gnaw on his bones, and the sow would ultimately drag his soul back to where her evil seed was whelped.

Of a sudden he felt the cold air slap his face, sneak in to tickle his bare flesh where the long, curved claws had raked the buckskin shirt to ribbons at his back. How cruel the breeze was to brush over the riven muscle across his hip. So cruel to tease him with its cool, fresh breath here the moment before he would breathe his last, the moment before his heart would stop and he would be no more than wounded soul.

Knowing he had lost and was now a captive of that evil beast come through the sky to his world seeking new prey.

She was picking him up, seizing his head, peeling his upper body out of the sand, ready to hurtle with him back across the grass and the sandbar and through the willow, back to where she had emerged right out of the twilight, right out of the air itself. . . . He blinked at the sand tormenting his eyes— how he wanted to stare this beast in the face, look it in the eye as she seized dominion over his soul.

One last look—

"Mr. Bass!"

Swimming right above him, the great creature's face spewed its fetid breath down across his cheeks. Hot breath—unlike the cool touch of the evening breeze.

"Mr. Bass!"

A dream this was. Feeling himself shaken by the creature, believing it was all part of the great evil to see McAfferty's face swimming above his.

"*Arrrghgh!*" Scratch groaned, flailing his arms helplessly at the beast.

His arms were quickly pinned and the face came right over his once more. Shaking his shoulders. "Mr. Bass—it's Asa! Asa!"

Again he tried to fight the evil of its lie.

"For the love of God, Mr. Bass . . . the bear is dead! We killed it. I killed it. God knows *you* killed it too."

Somehow he managed to sputter the word, "A-asa?"

"Yes. It's Asa, Mr. Bass. Praises be to heaven for your deliverance!"

Whether it truly had been heaven's intervention as Asa believed, or it had been the two rifle balls McAfferty deftly fired into the base of the sow's head at close range, along with those savage blows the white-hair delivered with Bass's own tomahawk found beside that pile of unpeeled willow limbs . . . there were times in those next few days when Scratch wasn't all that sure he was grateful for that divine deliverance.

As much pain as the simple act of living on brought him, it might well have been better to go under then and there to that sow grizzly.

Had it not been for his fear of losing his mortal soul to something monstrously evil, something he knew he could never fathom—simple man that he was. Were it not for his fear of a life everlasting wherein a man whimpered helplessly before the great unknown . . . he might well have given up and crossed over that last divide in those next few hours.

"Damn, but this ain't good," McAfferty muttered again and again as he hovered over him on that sandbar, down on his knees inspecting Scratch's wounds up and down. "This . . . this ain't good. A bear . . . chewed up like this . . . it ain't no good, Mr. Bass."

He had passed out with the pain when Asa had attempted to free his other leg from under the grizzly's carcass. Then he came to again, groaning in pain to find McAfferty pulling off his capote to lay over him.

"Damn them evil abominations gathered round us!" Asa growled.

Titus closed his eyes and listened for a moment as McAfferty trotted away up the sandbar, moving off from the cutbank in a hurry; then all was quiet.

It was full dark by the time the white-head nudged him awake as gently as he could, snagging Bass under the armpits and raising him off the sand, painfully dragging Scratch a matter of yards to the crude travois he had hurriedly constructed back at camp from some strips of rope and rawhide and a buffalo robe. Despite the curly softness of the thick hair, Bass felt the hard pinch of the hemp rope beneath his ripped and torn flesh at his back, across his hip, behind one ear as Asa laid him out on the crosshatch web and pulled a blanket over him.

Without a word Asa went thin-lipped with determination, then turned aside as Bass's eyes fluttered closed and he passed out again. How merciful unconsciousness can be at times, giving a man relief when he has reached a point where he can no longer bear up under the pain. How blessedly merciful.

In those next few days he tolerated the brutal bathing of his crusty, grit-coated wounds, as well as surviving the constant chatter from the partner who had saved his life this second time. Now he was beholden to McAfferty. No longer were they square. Bass listened to what he could of the man's preaching, to his praying over him, to his rambling fire-and-brimstone cant.

" *'And I will lay sinews upon you, and will bring up flesh upon you, and cover you with skin, and put breath into you, and ye shall LIVE!'* "

And in the midst of those terrible days Scratch heard Asa try to explain to them both what that run-in with the sow meant in terms far too theological for a simple man like him to understand, much more metaphysical than anything he had ever heard Asa McAfferty preach before.

"You done right with that she-bitch of a grizzly."

He kept his eyes closed. "Right?"

"Leave'd your knife in 'er."

"Damn! You're hurtin' me—"

"Gotta keep some of these here wounds open," McAfferty interrupted unapologetically, "or they'll grow shut with the p'isen inside."

"What p'isen?"

" 'Nough evil already around us for a man to worry over that you don't wanna have evil shut up inside ever' one of your wounds, Mr. Bass."

"Asa."

"Yeah?"

"I . . . I took the knife out."

"Knife was in 'er when I pulled you free," Asa grumbled as he continued his ministrations with that water he heated at the edge of the fire. "That's all that counts. Leave the knife in the bear: it'll bleed 'em out inside."

"Leave the knife in," Scratch repeated, his puffy lips so swollen and dry from fever that they had cracked. "Leave knife in."

Bass remembered how day after day it seemed the man talked of nothing much more than the same topic. Instructing his wounded partner on the two places where you could place a lead ball certain to kill a grizzly.

"There be jest two places where a nigger can put his ball into a devil beast such as that to know his lead'll do the trick certain. One be just under the ear. T'other—why that be just back and down of the front leg, Mr. Bass. Where the evil heart beats in that beast. Hide so damned thick, can't allays count on the ball going in nowhere else to any account. I killed that she-bitch with two balls to the head, just under her ears. And I finished her off with your tomahawk. Nearly got her head cut clean off afore she fell over with you still wrapped in her arm."

In addition, the white-head muttered in and out and roundabout, speaking of that Ree medicine man who wore a grizzly's head for his own powerful headdress, wore a cluster of grizzly claws around his neck, even performed his incantations with his two hands stuffed inside a pair of dried and shriveled grizzly paws, which he swiped at the air to invoke the bear's spirit when he came to demand McAfferty's Bible. Came to steal Asa's personal medicine.

"Leastways—that's how I knowed that son of a bitch was a hand servant of the devil his own self," McAfferty growled. "He come to me to make his grizzly medicine on me—and when I didn't just hand over me Bible to him . . . he made more evil medicine on me, called the grizzly spirit to come fetch me."

From time to time Bass awoke to find McAfferty talking still, talking to no one at all—Scratch supposed—for Asa was standing, slowly moving this way around the fire, then turning to walk in the other direction. The way the white-head hunched himself over at times, arms held out from his body, fingers clawed before him, growling like a bear, then muttering or shouting in fury. Moving again, sputtering his fireside sermons on and on through the dark of night or the light of those late-spring days as Bass slept, gathering strength.

"A evil omen, this," McAfferty mumbled one of those starless nights as the rain smacked the broad leaves overhead.

So thick was the cottonwood canopy that little of the mist reached them here in this copse of trees. Like hailstones striking rawhide, Bass believed he could hear each and every drop hit the leaves.

"We been trouble for each other, Mr. Bass," he explained another time as he helped Scratch eat, pulling the broiled meat apart with his fingers and laying small fibers of the elk tenderloin on Titus's tongue.

"Trouble?"

"The bear—it's only the latest sign, don't you see?"

Scratch chewed on the meat, sensing his strength slowly returning after enduring days of nothing but broth and bone soup. "I figger ary a man gonna run onto Injuns, Asa."

"Them Apache stalked us like demons. They wasn't human."

"Then it was demons I killed aside the Heely, McAfferty," he argued. "And I kill't me a lot of 'em to save your hide. To save us."

McAfferty measured him with an appraising look, then stared back down at the meat he was tearing apart with his fingers. "Those greaser soldiers too—"

"They was looking to get some gal forked around 'em," Bass snorted. "Weren't no demons there."

"Taos used to be a good place," he reminded. "I went there times afore and it was a good place, Mr. Bass."

"You ever have you a spree and look for a woman, there in Taos?"

"No. I never laid with no whore. *'Come out of her, my people, that ye be not partakers of her sins, and that ye receive not of her plagues.'* "

For a moment he felt stung by Asa's condemnation. But then—every man here in the mountains was entitled to live in his own way. Long as no man passed judgment on him, Titus Bass would abide by that man.

Then Scratch said, "I'm a man what wants to lay with a woman, Asa. I need that. And it's all right that you don't—"

" *'But her end is bitter as wormwood, sharp as a two-edged sword. Her feet go down to death; her steps take hold on hell.'* "

"Don't you see I love the feel, the smell . . . I love the taste of a woman."

"Maybe we're come of two different worlds, Mr. Bass," he finally declared.

There. It was said. No sense in asking the white-head what he meant by that. Pretty plain to see Asa's thinking, to grasp just what he had come to across the last few days as Bass lay in and out of this world. Hell, it was easy enough for a man all on his own to talk himself into most anything. All the easier for that preacher to see the bear as something more than a bear.

Finally he took the small piece of meat from McAfferty and began to slowly pull slivers off for himself. "Mayhaps you're right. So you figger to lay all our troubles at my door?"

"Never in my life have I suffered such tribulations as I have with you, Mr. Bass," he admitted quietly, almost apologetic for speaking it. "But don't get me wrong: the trapping's been good with you. I admire any man what'll go where you gone with me to trap beaver."

"We made us a pair," Bass agreed, knowing the tear in this fabric would never be rewoven. "But you're of a mind to go your own way."

"Ain't you ready your own self? Ready to go your own way 'thout me?"

He couldn't admit that he wasn't ready.

Yet Titus knew he wasn't the sort who could go days and weeks and much less months without some human contact. Be it a partner, or an outfit of free trappers, even a wandering band of Indians who spoke a language he hardly understood. How precious was just the sight of a human face, the sound of a human voice, the possibility of some human touch.

But instead Scratch said, "I reckoned on it a time or two in the last year."

"Been paired up almost that long, ain't we?"

"Almost a year. Ronnyvoo's coming."

McAfferty nodded. "Soon as you're able to travel, we'll mosey south. Trap along the way if we find a likely place. Soon as you're strong enough, Mr. Bass."

He didn't figure there was a lick of sense in beating a dead mule. How'd you figure to change a man's mind when it was his heart already made up? Why waste his breath when Asa McAfferty believed Titus Bass was the cause of all his tribulations? When Asa refused to even consider that it was his belief in evil and spirits and the Ree medicine man that brought him to tear apart the best partnership in these mountains?

Was there any sense in trying to talk to McAfferty about it come a month from now? Perhaps when he had more strength to argue with the white-head. Maybeso days and weeks from now, someplace on down the trail. Somewhere closer to rendezvous. Someplace away from this river valley where he had made the mistake of bumping into the sow grizzly and her cubs.

Somewhere much, much farther away from this low-hanging, evil patch of torn and sundered sky.

TWENTY-TWO

Spring was all but done anyway. And with it the good trapping too.

Time for a man to be making tracks for rendezvous.

Time for him to be sorting through just what he would do when company trappers and free men gathered in the valley of the Wind River. Soon he'd have to decide if he would throw in with Mad Jack Hatcher's boys . . . or if he would set off on his own hook now. Alone against the mountains.

Maybeso this was the season to set his own direction. Just as he had six years before: leaving behind St. Louis and the east and all that he had been. Proving to himself that he could reach the high mountains on his own.

But even then Bass remembered—just as he was beginning to believe he had beaten the odds stacked against him, he was suddenly forced to stare failure in the eye . . . about the time the three of them had shown up. To his reckoning, events never had allowed him the chance to succeed, or let him fail all on his own. Back then Silas, Billy, and Bud had come along to save his hash.

And ever since then it seemed that every time he had chosen to steer his own course—why, his fat had tumbled right back into the fire. Damn the fates if it hadn't.

Only God knew how Titus Bass had tried to make it alone

after his first three partners had disappeared down the river, getting themselves rubbed out in the bargain.

For all his trouble trying to set his own course, he went and got himself scalped.

It took Jack Hatcher's bunch to yank his fat from the fire that time.

Then shortly after deciding to pull off from those fellas, he and McAfferty had come a gnat's hair from going under down in Apache country, close as he ever wanted to come again in his living life. Only bright spot in that whole dank memory had been the fact that he had saved McAfferty's life along with his own in reaching that river in time to end their thirst, in time to prepare for the Apache.

But no sooner did they make it back to the Mexican villages than Asa had to rescue him in that knocking shop. Later to save his life a second time with that she-grizz.

Scratch wondered if his wanting to stay together with McAfferty might only come from his longing to right the scales. To square himself with the man who had not just evened things by rescuing him at the whorehouse . . . but had gone on to pull him back from death's door on that sandbar beside the Mussellshell River. Maybe, just maybe, Scratch thought, he might be resisting McAfferty's notion of splitting up only because that would make it near impossible for him ever to clear his accounts with the white-head.

If he was anything, Titus Bass realized he wasn't the sort of man who could stand going through the rest of his days knowing that he owed someone for saving his life a second time.

It was something that nettled him as they began their journey south from the Judith, up near the Missouri itself, then continued to eat at him as they made their way on down the valley of the Mussellshell, picking their way between mountain ranges. After crossing the Yellowstone, Bass and McAfferty reined to the southeast, skirting the foot of some tall snow-covered peaks then steered a course that took them through a wide cleft in two lower ranges. Near there they struck the Bighorn, following it south until the Bighorn became the Wind River.

At the hot springs they tarried for two nights among the remnants of countless Shoshone and Crow campsites. Here where warrior bands had visited far back into the time of any old man's memory, the two had the chance to sit and soak in the scalding waters so comforting that they made Scratch limp as a newborn babe before he would crawl out, crabbing over to a cold trickle of glacial snow-melt that had tumbled all the way down to the valley from the Owl Creek Mountains. There he splashed cold handfuls of the frigid water against his superheated flesh, then scampered back, shivering every step, to settle once again into the steaming pools. Back and forth he dragged his slowly healing carcass, sensing the stinking, sulphur-laden water draw at those poisons that could near eat up a man's soul. Like one of his mam's drawing poultices she would plaster upon an ugly, gaping wound, Bass felt those hours he lay in the springs renew not only his flesh, but his spirit as well.

By late in the afternoon of that second day, Titus called for McAfferty to bring his knife along to the pools. Once more the heated water had softened the tough sinew Asa had used to sew up his ragged wounds—and now he was ready.

"Come cut your stitches out," he asked of the white-head.

"Lemme have a good look at 'em first."

"They're heal't."

McAfferty finally pulled his knife from its scabbard and plunged it beneath the scalding water after he had inspected the thick ropes of swollen welt. "You heal fast, Mr. Bass. *'This poor man cried, and the Lord heard him, and saved him out of all his troubles.'* "

Titus bent over and turned his bare back and hip toward his partner. "I'm ready. Cut 'em out of me."

"My sewing wasn't purty," Asa muttered as he pricked the end of the first short length of animal tendon and began to tug it from the tight new skin become a rosy pink with the heat.

"But your sewing likely saved my life."

Between the long edges of every jagged laceration, McAfferty had stitched tiny fluffs of downy-soft beaver felt as he'd crudely closed the wounds by the fire's light. But now nothing was left of that beaver felt—all of it absorbed by Scratch's body until all that remained were those thick purplish-red welts roping their way across his shoulder, down his back, over his hip.

Titus Bass would carry that mark of the bear for the rest of his natural life.

As tight as it was, in time that new skin would stretch and loosen, and he would move that shoulder, move that hip without so much as a protest from it. But Scratch knew he would never . . . could never . . . forget coming face-to-face with a force so powerful it could rip the sky asunder, reach through, and devour his very soul.

No more than two days later they reached the valley where the Popo Agie drained into the Wind River. Those wide and verdant meadows were dotted with several camps of Indian lodges, small herds of grazing horses, and a scattering of blanket-and-canvas shelters lying stark against the green banks of both rivers.

"Har, boys!" Scratch cried, feeling an immediate and very tangible joy rise in him like sap in autumn maples.

A handful of white men came out of the shady trees to squint up at the two newcomers. One of them asked, "Where you in from?"

Bass replied, "The Mussellshell and the Judith."

Another stranger inquired, "You must be free men?"

"We are that," McAfferty answered this time.

So Titus asked, "You know of Jack Hatcher?"

A third man nodded and moved forward a step as he pointed on up the valley. "Seen him and his outfit, come in already. Don't know if they're still here. But they was camped on past Bridger's bunch."

"D-don't know if they're still here?" Bass repeated, disappointment welling in him like a boil. "They pull out early?"

"Naw," replied the first man. "Just that ronnyvoo's 'bout done for this year. Ain't no more beaver for Sublette to wrassle from us. You boys are the last to wander in from the hills."

Bass gulped and straightened in the saddle, licking his lips. "Trader still got him any whiskey?"

"Might'n have him a little left," the second trapper explained as two of his group turned away and headed back to the shade where swarms of flies droned. "He brought the hull durn shiterree out from St. Lou in wagons this year. Can you cotton to that?"

The first man cackled. "Ain't never been a wagon roll all the way out here! And if that don't beat all—Sublette brung him two Dearborns along too!"

"Carriages?" Bass squeaked in a high voice, disbelieving. "Dearborns and wagons—here in this wilderness? Shit," Scratch grumbled as he turned to flick a raised eyebrow at McAfferty. "What's all this big open coming to? Next thing there'll be white women and town halls out here!"

"So you say Sublette still got his tents open?" Asa inquired, clearly anxious. "Need me some trade goods."

"Seemed he had some of near ever'thing left yestiddy," the trapper answered. "You looking for supplies—lead, powder, coffee?"

With a shrug Asa explained, "Want me some goods for the Injun trade: Chinee vermilion, ribbon and calico, maybeso a passel of beads and tacks and hawk's bells—the likes of that."

Bass gazed at the white-head in consternation. "Now, where you figger to use all that?"

"Injun country, Mr. Bass," he answered cryptically, then turned his head to look again at the stranger below them. "You said Sublette's got his tents on up the valley?"

The man pointed. "Just other side of the bend in the river. That Hatcher feller's camped not far past the trader hisself."

"Much 'bliged," Asa said, tapping heels against his horse.

They hadn't gone more than a hundred yards when Scratch caught up with McAfferty at a lope. "Damn if you don't seem in the hurry. Who lit the fire under you?"

"I can't go 'thout them trade goods, Mr. Bass," Asa explained, anxiety already graying his face.

He could see how something was chewing away at McAfferty. "Why are them trade goods so all-fired important?"

"I know now the Lord's given me a sign. Showed me the road to go. *'For all the land which thou seest, to thee will I give it, and to thy seed for ever.'*"

"What land?" he asked. "And what sign was give you?"

"Up north there, that's the country give me by the hand of God," McAfferty explained. "The sign come to me on the Judith—after you was near kill't by the bear."

"That can't be the land been given you!" Bass replied in disbelief. "There's Injuns there."

Asa nodded. "*'And he that overcometh, and keepeth my works unto the end, to him will I give power over the nations.'*"

"I don't understand," Scratch admitted. "That surely can't be where you been told to go, Asa."

"North. I been told north."

"B-but that's Blackfoot country."

McAfferty nodded solemnly, his eyes never touching Bass. "I will trust in the Lord that there will be *many* Blackfoot where I aim to go."

Titus swallowed on that hard lump stuck in his throat, beginning to sense that this friend of his had found himself a sure and quick way to snuff out his own candle. "With your trade goods—you're fixing to head north to trade with them Blackfoot?"

At last Asa turned to look at Scratch. "I'm no trader, Mr. Bass. But the geegaws and the foofaraw give me something to set before the heathen chiefs when I get there to talk."

"You . . . you really figger you're gonna ride right in to have yourself a palaver with them Blackfoot? Them red killers?"

"*'And I looked, and, behold, a whirlwind came out of the north, and a great cloud, and a fire infolding itself, and a brightness was about it,'*" McAfferty declared, his blue eyes relit with that ice-cold fire.

"What whirlwind gonna come out of the north?"

"The Blackfoot, Mr. Bass," Asa said, then turned away to search the riverbank ahead. "The heathen Blackfoot."

For a moment longer Scratch studied the man's face, how it was illuminated by a most unholy light. Then he figured he was only spooking himself. Why, if he came to believe half of what Asa McAfferty spouted in his Bible talk, then he figured he was soft-brained his own self.

When he turned to look at the small herd immediately ahead of them, Titus suddenly squinted in the bright afternoon sun, not certain he could trust his eyes. "I ain't believing what I'm seeing, Asa!"

"Believe it!" he whooped with laughter.

"Cows!"

"Five of 'em, Mr. Bass!" And McAfferty wagged his head. "One even looks to be a milker too!"

Sure enough, this summer William Sublette brought four head of beef cattle and a milch cow to accompany his ten big freight wagons each topped with huge canvas-covered bows and that pair of fancy Dearborn carriages.

"Jumping Jehoshaphat," Scratch mumbled sourly. "Man can't hardly get away from settlement doings, can he?"

"It's only ronnyvoo!" McAfferty cheered with a smile. "Them cows and wagons and such gonna be turning right back for St. Louie soon enough."

"S'pose you're right," Bass replied eventually as they approached the grazing cows. "Ain't none of them settlement doings gonna last out here longer'n ronnyvoo."

The Sublette camp was mammoth this year, and bustling like a hive. There was no mistaking the many newcomers to the mountains from those hivernants who had endured at least one winter in the wilderness. Men moved about like ants on a prairie hill at midday. Trappers both free and company came and went on horseback and foot. Others clustered beneath the shade of the trade canopies or sprawled out near the last of the nearby whiskey kegs. Why, Bass had never seen so many humans gathered in one place since he'd put St. Louis behind.

Wagging his head, Scratch declared, "It purely bumfuggles my mind to try to figger how all these here fellers gonna find enough beaver in these mountains to make their trappin' worth their while."

"I don't reckon all these niggers gonna make a living at all," McAfferty replied as they reached the fringe of a small herd of horses and moved on past. "A goodly number of 'em likely to go under, that's a fact. Other'ns gonna skedaddle back east with Sublette come next summer's ronnyvoo."

"After they see'd the elephant, eh?"

"Damn right," Asa agreed. "Not every man gonna keep his hide or hair out in this country. *'For the Lord my God has set my foot down in the wilderness and abideth with me.'* "

"Jack! Lookee here!"

Scratch jerked about to stare at the trees up ahead where the voice had called out. If that didn't look like Elbridge Gray!

Hatcher peeled himself away from the base of a cottonwood tree where he had been leaning. Clambering to his feet, Jack roared, "Titus Bass? And Asa McAfferty too! Ye lily-livered polecats! We figgered ye both for wolf-bait by now!"

"Just 'cause we're a li'l late for whiskey?" he bellowed, standing in the stirrups as he drew closer to Hatcher and those five men who gathered about him. "Jack Hatcher—don't you dare take on airs now!"

"Take on airs?" Hatcher cried, thumping his chest. "Why, I ought'n kick yer bony arse—"

"Kick my arse, will you?" Scratch cried in glee. "Don't you know I'm here to give you the thumping you been needing ever since't last ronnyvoo!"

"Thump me now, Titus Bass? Why, I'll have ye know I can outride, outshoot, and outthump ary a man in this hull valley! Mad Jack Hatcher be the nigger what can outlie, outdrink, and outpuke all the rest of ye poor sons put together! We'll wrassle if'n ye think ye're man enough, Titus goddamned Bass!"

Reining up sharply, Scratch immediately flung his leg across the saddle and dropped to the ground, bursting into motion as his feet hit the grass—sprinting low and headlong for Hatcher. They collided with a mighty gust of air from them both as the two spilled onto the ground, a writhing, snaky mass of arms and legs, flying fists and buckskin fringe, spewing and grunting as they rolled over and over atop one another.

"Leave the poor man be, Scratch!" Caleb Wood lunged up to their side laughing as the pair tussled and romped in the grass, thumping one another with their fists and giggling like two schoolboys let out to recess.

"L-leave off me yer own self, Caleb!" Hatcher grumbled as he shoved Bass back, rocked onto his knees, and started brushing dirt and flecks of grass from his bare, sweaty flesh. "I gotta give a old friend a proper greeting!"

"Proper greeting?" McAfferty called. "Why, you ain't never made me wrassle with you, Jack."

Hatcher brushed some of his long, dark hair back out of his eyes and swiped at a bead of sweat sliding down the bridge of his nose when he peered up at the white-head as if measuring his words before he set them free.

"Asa McAfferty," Jack said evenly in that way a man might when he had decided it best to leave certain feelings unspoken. "Didn't figger either of ye for coming in alive this summer." Then he turned back to Bass, looping an arm over Scratch's shoulder. "Damn, but it's good to lay eyes on ye both again."

"I'll be et for the devil's tater if it ain't good to see you boys again too!" Titus cried, thumping a fist into Hatcher's taut belly.

"You'll camp with us?" Solomon Fish pleaded as the rest came up in turn to give Bass a hearty embrace.

"Ain't no other place I'd rather spread my robes," Scratch declared, basking in the glow of these friends.

Rufus Graham looked up at McAfferty. "You getting down off that horse, Asa? Or maybeso you don't figger to camp with your partner here."

For a fleeting moment Titus glanced at McAfferty. He explained, "Asa and me—well, we reckon to go our own ways for the fall hunt."

"I'll be go to hell!" Caleb exclaimed.

Hatcher himself said, "That news s'prises me."

"Don't s'prise me none," Elbridge grumped. "Asa allays been one to go off on his own. Ain'cha, McAfferty?"

Instead of answering, Asa rocked out of the saddle and came to the ground, busying himself with throwing up a stirrup and loosening the cinch.

Hatcher studied Scratch's face a moment, as if he might divine some clue thereupon. Eventually Jack said, "Asa ain't never reckoned on pulling away on his own this quick, boys." He grinned disarmingly as he turned to McAfferty. "Something really must trouble ye 'bout riding with Titus Bass."

Only then did Asa slowly step around the horse. "Any man be proud to ride with Mr. Bass."

"Awright," Hatcher said with a little disgust at not learning what he wanted to know. "Which one of ye niggers is gonna dust off the truth and spit it right out—"

"The two of us," Titus interrupted, "we had us a couple bad scrapes, Jack." He glanced over at McAfferty, seeing the appreciation shine in the white-head's eyes. "Nothing more'n some Injuns tracking us down on the Heely. Then a few Mex soldiers jumped us in a whorehouse when we rode back in to Taos."

"Any soldiers we know?" Graham inquired with a grin.

"That sergeant what they made a lieutenant."

Hatcher asked, "Ye get in yer licks afore ye was run out of town, fellas?"

"I kill't him," McAfferty admitted flatly.

Caleb whistled low, and Rufus asked, "Ramirez?"

"That's the truth," Scratch added. "Him and a bunch of 'em . . . well, I don't figger I can head back down to Taos for a few winters."

"Lordee!" Caleb hooted gustily. "That Mex nigger had it coming!"

"Sounds to me like ye boys got tales to weave and stories to tell round our campfire tonight!" Jack howled. Then he whirled on McAfferty. "So ye gonna throw yer bed robes down with this bunch of bad mothers' sons?"

Asa looked over at Bass for a heartbeat, then gazed at Hatcher. "Yep, Jack. I'll camp with my partner, Mr. Bass—right on through till it's time for us to go our own trails for the fall hunt."

"He says the Lord's steering him for the north country," Bass explained to Hatcher, Wood, and Graham a few days later. "Keeps talking 'bout the Three Forks."

"Shit," Jack said, wagging his head. "It ain't like McAfferty don't know that's smack-dab in Blackfoot country."

"Why would a man up and decide to go there on his own?" Graham asked.

"Sounds to me like a sure way to lose his hair," Caleb grumbled. "So purty, long, and white—the nigger won't have it for long he goes up there."

"There's a hunnert ways for a man to die in Blackfoot country," Rufus added grimly.

"I don't figger he's worried a nit 'bout Blackfoots," Bass declared. "Fact is, he wants to run onto 'em."

Hatcher shook his head, bewildered. "Man's crazy what goes riding off to the Three Forks and he ain't worried 'bout Blackfoot raising his hair."

Nodding slightly, Scratch stated, "Could be you're not far off the mark there, Jack."

"Trapping's real good up there," Rufus admitted. "But a man'd have to be soft-brained to want that beaver so bad that he'll risk his hide to get it when there's plenty 'nough beaver other places."

"With what I can make out from all he's said to me—it ain't for trapping that he's headed to Blackfoot country, fellas," Bass said, watching how his declaration brought the others up short with a morbid curiosity.

Jack demanded, "What the hell for, then, if it ain't for the beaver?"

"I can't say right now," he admitted. "I don't know. But I'm sure it's got something to do with that Ree medicine man and the bear what jumped me and them evil hoo-doos been following McAfferty last few years."

With a snort Hatcher said, "I thort Asa had him his Bible to keep off all them evil spirits!"

Dragging the coffeepot toward him to refill his cup that morning, Scratch replied, "You may damn well just put your finger on it, Jack. Asa McAfferty might be coming to think the power of his Bible ain't near as strong as the evil spirits in these here mountains. Maybeso—not near as strong as that ol' medicine man's evil powers."

Hatcher asked, "Evil for evil, is it?"

"When good ain't strong enough to protect him," Bass sighed, "I figure a man will just twist the evil around any way he can."

On his way west with those wagons, carriages, and cattle, William Sublette's eighty-one new hands had to kill and eat no more than eight of his small beef herd before they reached buffalo country, supplying them with the meat that would see them on through to the Wind River Rendezvous. Those fourscore greenhorns were immediately set upon by the hordes of veterans hungry for news from the States as the trader opened his mail pouches and cut through the twine tying up bundles of old newspapers. Then Sublette got down to cracking open his kegs of grain alcohol, sugared Monongahela rum, along with heavy bales of blankets, boxes of beads, tacks, and ribbon, as well as hundredweight barrels of sugar and coffee.

It had been enough to make a man's eyes bug right out of his head, Hatcher told Scratch. Why, with each of those ten high-walled, canvas-topped wagons weighed down with more than eighteen hundred pounds of supplies apiece, all of it valued at some thirty thousand dollars—trader Billy had reached that sixth annual rendezvous with more staples and geegaws to hanker after than any man had ever seen in the mountains!

And there had even been enough left among the "necessaries" for Titus Bass to outfit himself for what was to be the first winter on his own.

A pair of black-striped Indian trade blankets—one red and the other green—went for twenty-five dollars in fur. Coffee and sugar, some salt and a little flour, along with a carefully calculated amount of St. Louis shot-tower bar lead and more of the black coarse-grained English powder.

"Most everything's been picked over," apologized a bulb-nosed, weasel-eyed clerk with a warm smile as he placed the items Bass was selecting in a large square wicker basket. "You been waiting to come trade off them furs of yours?"

"Nawww. I happed to come in late for ronnyvoo this year."

"Sounds like you rode in from far off."

"North," he explained as he brought up a handful of the long-spiked brass-headed tacks he could use for repairs, or for decoration on knife scabbard or riflestock. "Been up near the Englishers' land."

"That's a ways for a man to travel for supplies," the clerk marveled, flashing that genuine smile.

"Ain't so far," Scratch explained. "Not when there ain't but one place for a man to outfit hisself for the coming year. And that be right here."

The clerk pulled back on his leather braces self-importantly. "This here's my second trip west with Mr. Sublette."

Bass looked up from the trays before him, laying a half-dozen hanks of large Crow beads in the clerk's basket. "Sublette gonna be back next ronnyvoo?"

"Most certainly," the man replied. "Just because the old company sold out to a new one, Mr. Sublette still has the contract to supply their summer fair. He says as long as he can make a profit for himself and his investors, he'll be buying up goods each winter and starting out west from St. Louis each spring—just as soon as the prairie's dry enough for the wagons."

"Wagons," Scratch repeated with a snarl, glancing up at those two nearby carriages that came and went almost steadily with company men and free trappers taking themselves rides in the fancy conveyances, roaring with laughter and giddy with the silliness of such vehicles making it all the way to the Rocky—by God—Mountains! "Prefer a good mule my own self."

"Mr. Sublette says he can get more in a wagon for his money," the clerk admitted.

"I'll bet he can," Scratch replied, and fingered some soft sateen ribbon. "And he's gotta make him his profit, or the new company will have to go off and find it 'nother trader."

Despite the fact that this summer's trade fair was undeniably the largest held to date—taking in more than 170 packs of beaver, the most ever—it was plain to see that Jedediah Smith, David Jackson, and William Sublette were beginning to question the future profits they might wrench from the mountain trade. Or maybe it was nothing more than the toll taken by all those seasons in the Rockies, those years gone from kin left behind in the East, every winter-count giving a man far too much time to dwell on old friends rubbed out and no longer around.

When Sublette handed mail to his two partners, Davy learned that he had lost another member of his family to pneumonia. And 'Diah opened a letter from his brother, reading that their mother had died.

Maybe the partners' decision to sell out was nothing more than those two of them believing they had had enough of the uncompromising wilderness and the unforgiving winters. Perhaps the time had come to invest their fortunes in more civilized ventures. Besides, Sublette had arrived at rendezvous with news that John Jacob Astor's American Fur Company no longer appeared to be content to stay on the Missouri. And not only were Astor's men eager to entice small bands of free trappers to the new fort they were raising at the mouth of the Yellowstone—but word was that American Fur had even dispatched a full-fledged brigade into the Central Rockies so they could give the upstarts a run for their money.

Maybe the time had come for the three of them to find a smarter way to make their fortunes than this annual gamble that was the Rocky Mountain fur trade. So while Billy reaffirmed his desire to continue supplying the summer rendezvous during that first week of August in the valley of the Wind River, 'Diah and Davy decided that they just might invest their hard-won earnings in the lucrative Santa Fe trade down in the southwest.

Over the past two days with most of the bartering done for the year and the old company accounts being settled, the firm of Smith, Jackson, and Sublette formally dissolved their partnership, and for a promissory note in the amount of more than fifteen thousand dollars they sold out to five new partners. Now Billy Sublette would be supplying his brother, Milton, along with Tom Fitzpatrick, Henry Fraeb, Jean Baptiste Gervais, and Jim Bridger himself—all long-time veterans of the mountain trade.

And with their new partnership, the five gave birth to the Rocky Mountain Fur Company.

Gabe, Milt, and Broken Hand would take more than two hundred men north along the Bighorn, cross the Yellowstone and plunge into the heart of Blackfoot country—performing a grand and daring sweep that would take them all the way to the Great Falls of the Missouri before circling south toward the Three Forks, then trapping their way to the east along the Yellowstone with plans to winter at the mouth of the Powder. Just let Bug's Boys dare try tackling a brigade that size.

Those Blackfoot be damned!

At the same time, Ol' Frapp and Jervy laid plans to lead their brigade west from rendezvous for the continental divide, striking the Snake, which they would follow west to its forks before the great cold began to close in and they made for their winter camp in Willow Valley.

And come the spring that enterprising brigade would venture even farther to the west now that Jedediah Smith was no longer a booshway, no longer able to object to his partners and force his employees to refrain from trapping in that land beyond the spine of the continent, a region jointly held by treaty with the English of the Hudson's Bay Company. Come spring more than a hundred Americans of the newly born Rocky Mountain Fur Company intended once again to lay claim to that beaver-rich region.

The English be damned.

Let there be no mistake! The Rocky Mountain Fur Company had come to the mountains!

Every one of those hot summer days at rendezvous hundreds upon hundreds of dollars had been spent upon supplies, foofaraw, and the trader's grain alcohol—a lot of it bartered for women, bet on games of chance with cards or dice, and wagered on horse races, wrestling matches, shooting contests, and footraces for those hearty or daring enough to venture out into the late-July heat.

"They had a feller get so drunk he kill't one of his friends," Caleb exclaimed one afternoon, coming back with Bass from watering their horses.

"Funniest damned thing," Scratch added, wagging his head and smiling with those teeth the color of pin acorns, "they had the feller what did the killing tied up to a tree till he sobered."

"And was he ever bellering!" Wood declared.

Snorting with a gust of laughter, Titus continued, "But they had the dead feller he killed laid out on the ground right where he was shot, flat on his belly. And the four of 'em what tied the killer up . . . why—they was using that dead nigger for a card table while they was all playing eucher!"

Caleb slapped Bass on the shoulder, laughing. "With that poor, dead nigger going stiff on 'em!"

His eyes narrowing in disgust, Asa McAfferty grumbled, "Don't s'prise me one whit. So much alcohol. This many niggers. Why, a man gets tight enough on all that demon rum in Sublette's kegs . . . purely amazing to me more men don't get theirselves killed."

Hatcher watched the white-head shuffle off. "Asa—maybe ye ought'n go get ye a drink of Sublette's milk!"

"Milk?" he roared in disbelief the instant he wheeled about on his heel.

"That damn milch cow!" Elbridge Gray explained. "I had me a pint cup of it this afternoon—warm it was, fresh from the udder like I 'membered it back to Ohio."

Scratch couldn't fathom it himself. "Milk? You gone and drunk yourself milk here in the Rocky Mountains?"

"I done it too," Solomon boasted. "Sublette's been selling it ever' morning and evening: two dollar a pint cup."

"Jumping Jehoshaphat!" Bass grumbled, and shook his head. "First off he brings wagons and fine folks' carriages and beef cows out to ronnyvoo in these here tall hills . . . and now Sublette sells milk to trappers? What is the Rocky Mountains coming to?"

"Sublette and his other two partners are turning back for St. Louie in the morning," Rufus explained. "You want you a drink of milk, Titus Bass—you better make it tonight!"

"Shit! I'd ruther let you fellers suck down all of Sublette's milk so I can go tell Bug's Boys that Jack Hatcher's bunch is coming north: a bunch more likely to nurse on their mamas' breasts as they are to hanker after a fight with them Blackfoot!"

Late on the morning of August 4, Smith, Jackson, and Sublette did indeed set off at the head of that column of ten wagons, a pair of carriages, and some fifty men, heading south by east for the North Platte and the settlements, hauling a small fortune in beaver pelts. Both brigades of the Rocky Mountain Fur Company rolled out to bid them farewell, as well as most of the free men of the mountains—all of them eager to see the booshways off in proper style.

Unlike General Ashley, these three were men who had first come to the mountains as nothing more than hire-ons. They had worked hard, played their cards smart, and stepped forward when called upon to do the difficult. All three had seen more than their share of friends cut down by enemy warriors. All three had suffered the cold, endured the heat and thirst, put up with the hunger and the fatigue like any man.

So it was that three grand and rousing huzzahs were raised for the three booshways at the moment they set off for the States. Cheers and whistles, accompanied by a final shaking of hands and backslapping all around. Here was a trio who would do to ride the river with. Here were three men who had come from humble beginnings to rise all the way to the top of the mountain trade itself.

Here were men who would be missed in those seasons yet to come.

At least Sublette would return come summer, Bass mulled as he turned back to camp with the others. And those five partners of the newly formed Rocky Mountain Fur Company weren't the sort to quake with fear at the prospect of Blackfoot or tremble at the threat of John Jacob Astor. Sure, there were places in the Rockies where the beaver had been thinned out. But down in the marrow of him, Scratch knew there still had to be a passel of holes back in the mountains where a man could find virgin streams overrun by the flat-tails.

All a man had to do was ride a little farther, work a little harder, climb a little higher, and he would discover those untouched valleys.

Especially if he rode alone.

"Yestiddy—over in the company camp—I come upon a feller named Green reading to some other niggers," Rufus declared that night as the Wind River Valley quieted just past dark.

"Reading?" Hatcher repeated.

"I gone over and sat for a while myself," Graham continued. "Listened to a story he was reading for them others."

"He had a book he was reading from?" Bass inquired, his interest suddenly pricked.

Rufus nodded, spreading out his hands across his lap to show the tome's size. "A big damn book."

"What sort of story was it?" Titus asked, his interest piqued.

"That feller Green said it was Shakes . . . Shakes . . . ah, shit! I can't remember—"

McAfferty interrupted, "Shakespeare?"

"That's it!" Rufus cheered with a snap of his fingers. "Shakespeare. Some story of a king."

"Richard?" Asa inquired.

"Naw," Graham replied.

McAfferty brushed the long white hair off his shoulder. "Must've been Macbeth."

Rufus shook his head in amazement. "That's it! Macbeth! Green was reading that story to a bunch of 'em. Why, he even had him a Bible laying by his side. Told me he read to any fellers what would listen ever' day—winter or summer, on the trail or not. Said that big ol' Shakespeare book of his had more'n one story in it, and his Bible was crammed full of tales to read round a campfire."

"The Lord's truth that is," McAfferty agreed. " 'Praise ye the Lord. Praise God in His sanctuary: praise Him in the firmament of His power!' "

"So, McAfferty?" Hatcher asked. "Ye ever read any of that Shake-speare?"

Asa said, "Some I have. Not much. But enough to know that when I set off time to read, I'll read the stories in my Bible. God's own word."

"You ever read that Macbeth story?" Titus inquired.

"Not much of it," McAfferty admitted. "Only far enough to know that one man hankered to be king enough to think he just might murder the real king. Now, the Bible has a story about the first Asa."

"The first Asa?" Solomon echoed.

"He was a king back in Bible day," McAfferty said. " 'Abijah slept with his fathers, and they buried him in the city of David: and Asa his son reigned in his stead. In his days the land was quiet ten years. And Asa did that which was good and right in the eyes of the Lord his God: for he took away the altars of the *strange gods, and the high places, and brake down the images, and cut down the groves.'"*

Jack asked, "So if you was named after an old king, why didn't ye finish yer reading that Macbeth story Rufus told us about?"

"I give up on that tale when Shakespeare kept on writing about witches and their evil spells," Asa confessed.

Scratch shifted, anxious to hear more. "Witches? Real witches in that Shakespeare story?"

"Evil creatures," Asa confirmed with a shudder as he looked up at the night sky. "Abominations and she-bitches what call forth familiar spirits and demons from the other side, Mr. Bass. *'A man also or woman that hath a familiar spirit, or that is a wizard, shall surely be put to death: they shall stone them with stones: their blood shall be upon them.'"*

"She-bitches," Titus repeated the word, thinking of the bear. "Like that sow what tore through my hide?"

McAfferty looked him in the eye long, his brow furrowing. "Perhaps. A man never knows what form evil will take when it tempts him. Maybeso a grizzly. Or a Injun warrior. Mayhaps a whore what gets a man hot to poke her. The fornicating slut—"

"Whooeee!" Solomon hooted from the far side of the fire.

"Hurraw for she-bitches, witches, and whores!" Hatcher whooped, slapping the tops of both thighs exuberantly.

Visibly perturbed at their lighthearted response to his dire warning, McAfferty turned back to Titus. "The devil puts all sorts of temptations down before a man. If he turns away from one, the devil will come up with another. Sooner or later the devil will find a temptation every man will fall to, Mr. Bass."

"Now, tell me what all temptations you gone and fall to, Asa." Hatcher demanded.

He thought a moment, then answered, "Damn near all of them. Whiskey, pride, avarice . . . and the lure of a false woman. *'O God, thou knowest my foolishness; and my sins are not hid from Thee!'* I committed near all of them, Mr. Hatcher. Oh—and I've been one to stub my toe and stumble on the temptation of following the lead of other men . . . instead of letting the Lord guide my steps."

Damn, if Asa McAfferty didn't have a surefire way of putting an end to conversation around the dancing flames of their campfire, dashing cold water the way he did on their last night together.

"Sure ye don't wanna throw in with us come morning, Scratch?" Hatcher asked later in the inky darkness as he crouched to slide beneath his blankets. "We're fixing on riding south to the Bayou for fall hunt."

"Like I told you the first time—you make me proud when you ask me to throw in with you fellas again," Bass explained in a whisper as the others shifted and settled in their robes to drift off to sleep all around them. "But I've come to figger this is my calling, Jack. I ain't never truly been on my own hook afore."

"Ye learn't yourself just how dangerous it was too."

"Hell if I ain't learned what danger is," he echoed. Then a moment later he said, "But there comes a time when I figger a man should grab for what he dreams. And if he goes under for it—then I don't reckon he's really failed, Jack."

"How ye figger that?"

"Way I see it," Titus explained, "only feller what truly fails is a man what has him a dream . . . but don't have the guts to go make a grab for it."

For a long time after that Hatcher remained quiet, so long that Bass figured Jack had fallen asleep. So it surprised him when the brigade leader finally spoke in a hushed whisper again, just as Titus was drifting off.

"I figger you and McAfferty got that same sort of itch in ye both."

"What sort of itch is that?" he asked sleepily.

"Ye're riding off to look for something I figger you'll come upon soon enough," Jack explained in the dark. "And Asa—he's chasing after something he ain't never gonna find."

"But that don't sound like we really got the same kind of itch to scratch."

For a moment Hatcher was quiet; then he explained, "S'pose you're right, Scratch. One sort of itch just drives a man on. Like yers. And Asa's . . . why, his be the sort of itch what just drives a man crazy."

At its best, this was squaws' work. The sort of work fit only for a farmer, for a man who loved grubbing in the soil, caking the moist, rain-softened earth under his nails. The sort of man back east who didn't mind at all sweating even though this autumn air was cold and those clouds gathering overhead presaged another storm.

A trapper wasn't cut out for grubbing in the ground the way his father had forced him to back in Kentucky—pulling out stumps and laying aside row after row of deep, damp furrows where Thaddeus Bass came along to drop his seed each spring. A trapper come to the mountains was simply above this sweaty, dirty groundhog and badger clawing sort of demeaning chore.

But for the life of him Titus Bass hadn't figured out any other way for a man to dig himself a cache.

Gulping another long drink from the kettle he kept nearby, Scratch dragged a dirty hand across his mouth, then spit, finding he had turned the dirt on the back of his hand to a nasty mud, rubbing it onto his lips. Grabbing the tail of his long blanket capote, he swiped his face clear of sweat and dirt and that muddy paste. Then he sighed and leaped down into the narrow hole, dragging the short-handled, iron-toothed shovel behind him as he squatted, went to his knees, and crawled forward into the short neck of his cache.

Emerging on the other side after some three feet of tunnel, Titus crabbed a few feet to the far wall and flung the shovel against the earth. Down here where the autumn breeze couldn't reach his flesh, he was sweating again in minutes. Out there the air chilled his skin. Down here it was the sort of work he detested more than just about anything. Why, he was the sort of man made for sitting high atop lofty places, able to look out upon hundreds of miles of untouched country. Down here in this hole he found his breathing growing short, his heart thumping anxiously, his very soul yearning to burst free of this earth-bound grave he had dug himself.

Even the fluttering light thrown off by that big wax candle he had set into a notch he'd scraped in the wall of the cache wasn't enough to ease the dank otherworldly feel of this hole. As if by wriggling through the narrow neck, he had instead pushed himself through to another existence.

Gasping with his exertion, Bass turned around and went to the narrow neck. There he reached back to seize the edge of the elk hide and started dragging it out through the neck behind him—bringing with it a load of dirt he had just scratched from the walls. Once he sensed the cool air on his sweaty back, Titus rose, easing his shoulders through the narrow hole until he stood halfway in the ground, and halfway out.

Heaving himself from the hole, he lay down on the ground beside it and leaned in to grab the corner of the elk hide again, folding it over the small pile of dirt. Side by side by side he laid the skin over the dirt until he could drag it from the hole without spilling the earth. After swilling down the last drink at the bottom of the iron kettle, Bass grabbed the kettle's bail in one hand, and the edge of the elk hide in the other, and carried them off toward the nearby creek.

At the bank he knelt to dip the kettle into the cool water. With that set aside, he stood and moved downstream a few yards with the elk hide bundle clutched in both arms, then stepped right off the grassy bank into the middle of the stream. Once there, he let the hide fall open—spilling another load of dirt from his digging into the creek, hiding every last clump of that damp earth from any roving, suspicious eyes who might happen upon this spot in the days to come.

It had been this way for two days now: digging, eating, digging some more, sleeping, digging again, always the digging.

Having come south from making his fall hunt on the Mussellshell, Bass found a likely spot for his cache back against a thickly wooded hillside that jutted out into some bottomland deposited aeons before by the junction of two small creeks that flowed toward the north bank of the Yellowstone. That following morning Titus had begun what turned out to be some of the hardest work he had ever done. At sundown the first day he had completed the narrow neck of the cache and pitched into the grueling labor of widening the hole as he inched deeper into the ground, until he reached some four feet below the surface. As soon as the light had begun to sink in the west, he went to his packs and pulled out one of the tall candles he had purchased back in Taos from Bill Williams.

While the feeble light hadn't been much, it nonetheless allowed him to keep scratching at the walls of his ever-widening cache until it was slap-dark outside and his belly was no longer just whimpering in hunger—it had begun to holler for fodder.

He was up in the gray of predawn that morning and had been at it with only one stop at midday for a meal of some dried meat and a short nap. Awaking to a gentle, cold mist of a rain, Bass went back to work despite the chill on his bare skin each time he emerged from the hole. By midafternoon the rain passed on over and the sky cleared for a time. Then another cluster of gray-black clouds appeared on the western horizon, tossing their heads angrily as they rumbled his way down the Yellowstone Valley.

He pressed on despite the threat of more rain. Just as he persevered now as the breeze came up, its heaving breath rank with the promise of another storm.

This was, after all, why he had come here now to dig his cache. The earth was much softer in these damp days of early autumn than it would be when winter froze the ground and made digging in it all but impossible. If a man was going to have himself a winter cache, he damn well better get that hole dug well before the first snow fell on this north country.

Back in camp he dropped the elk hide beside the hole, then set the sloshing kettle nearby. With a deep sigh he knelt, slid into the dark tunnel where the candle's light flickered. And remembered back to that final day of rendezvous, to that first day he would finally set off on his own.

Had he ever been ready to make tracks for this land north of the Yellowstone!

Half-froze for the trail by the time he packed what he owned on the backs of the two horses and his dear Hannah. Their camp was but one of many bustling with activity in that valley of the Wind River last August as the two large Rocky Mountain Fur Company brigades made ready to put out on the trail. In addition, Hatcher and his men were striking camp, preparing to head west toward the Snake River country.

"Davy Jackson ain't gonna be there to call Jackson's Hole his own this year!" Caleb Wood had declared enthusiastically.

Solomon added, "We thought we'd see how that country looks for beaver afore we point south for to winter down in the Bayou."

Then Bass remembered how he went alone in the first faint light of that last morning to find McAfferty at work loading the horses.

"Looks to be you're not waiting for Bridger's bunch afore you ride north," Bass exclaimed with no real surprise as Asa threw on a packsaddle pad made from the hide of a mountain goat. Nearby sat the canvas-wrapped bundles the white-head would lash atop his pack animals.

"What's sense in waiting for that gaggle?" and he tried to smile before turning back to his work. " *'Arise, walk through the land in the length of it and in the breadth of it; for I will give it unto thee.' "*

"Should've knowed better'n trying to talk you into hanging close to Bridger's men. Just like me, you're of a mind to go off on your own."

"I am of that mind, but we are different in many ways," McAfferty replied. " *'Again, when the wicked man turneth away from his wickedness that he hath committed, and doeth that which is lawful and right, he shall save his soul alive.' "*

For a few minutes he helped Asa tie up a pair of bundles onto a pack-saddle without either saying a word. Finally Titus asked, "No matter that you're riding for Blackfoot country?"

His blue eyes touched Bass's, and he said, "Where I'm bound in Black-foot country, Bridger's men won't be showing their faces, Mr. Bass."

"It don't make no sense to me, no sense at all."

" *'For he remembered that they were but flesh; a wind that passeth away, and cometh not again,'* thus sayeth the Lord that I should not be scared." McAfferty stopped tying a knot to attempt explaining something so clearly confusing. "Mr. Bass, *'Man that is born of a woman is of a few days, and full of trouble. He cometh forth like a flower, and is cut down.' "*

Scratch felt the hair prickle at his neck. It sounded to him as if Asa were saying he wanted to die in a bad way. "So you ain't afraid, are you?"

"No, *'I go the way of all the earth,' "* McAfferty answered.

"I'm gonna miss the good times we had, Asa," he admitted quietly. "And I'll likely think back on all them scrapes we had us too. I thank you for saving my hide, more'n once you saved me."

"There comes a time for all of us to go our own way," the white-head said. "There comes a time when we see our end and no longer are afraid, Mr. Bass."

"You're not afraid of dying neither?"

" *'And in those days shall men seek death, and shall not find it; and shall desire to die, and death shall flee from them.'* I'm not afraid of the Blackfoot. They become my people, here in my latter days," McAfferty replied. " *'And thou shalt come from thy place out of the north parts, thou, and many people with thee, all of them riding upon horses, a great company, and a mighty army.' "*

Wagging his head in exasperation, Bass stammered, "I'm t-trying to understand what it is pulling you up there, Asa. Up north to Blackfoot country. All this talk about your final days, and not being afraid to die—"

"The ways of the Lord are mysterious ways. We are not meant to question, or understand. A man is only meant to follow the hand of the Lord."

"Will I see you come ronnyvoo in Willow Valley?" Scratch asked as Hatcher and his men came up to stand near McAfferty's horses.

"If it's God's will and I got my hair—I'll be in Willow Valley next summer," Asa said, taking up the long rawhide rein to his horse. "If it's God's will, Mr. Bass."

The white-head swung up into the saddle, then held down his hand to each of those who stepped up in turn to shake with him. In the end he put his hand out to Scratch.

Bass shook, saying, "I truly hope you find what you're looking for up there in Blackfoot country, Asa."

With a smile he replied, "I don't think there's a way I could fail to find what I'm going up there for. If God allows, I'll see you next summer so I trust you'll fare well till then."

Letting go his grip on Scratch's hand, McAfferty took up the long lead to the first packhorse, clucked his tongue, and gave heels to his saddle mount, reining away from the cottonwood grove, the other animals clattering behind him. Stepping out into dawn's dim light themselves, they watched the white-head lope away for a few minutes until he slowly faded out of sight, gone downriver, riding for the far hills.

"Man's in a hurry to be gone from here, 'pears to me," Rufus exclaimed.

As they all turned back to their campsite, Hatcher said, "He's damn well got him somewhere to be, fellas. That's for certain."

"Wish I was the sort what could figger folks out," Bass admitted, still staring after McAfferty even though he could no longer see the distant figures. "Sometimes what I know a man is keeping from me gets in my craw and eats at me for not knowing."

Later that morning Jack came to a halt where Bass was finishing his work lashing the last bundle atop his pack animals. "Ye're still bound for the Judith?" he asked.

"Good trapping, that country," Scratch had answered as he tied off the last knot, knowing the saddest of moments had arrived. "If I keep my head and don't let no roaming Blackfoots know I'm about—I'll hang on to my hair."

Hatcher had stepped up, opening his arms wide, seizing Titus within his bony embrace. "You'll damn well watch over what ye got left for hair, won'cha?"

He heard a sob thicken the sound of Jack's words. It made his own heart rise in his throat as he squeezed Hatcher fiercely, fiercely. "I'm prideful of my purty hair, Mad Jack. It's gonna be long and gray afore you'll ever think of seeing it hanging from any warrior's lodgepole."

One by one he had hugged the others, slapped them each on the back and promised to buy them a drink come whiskey time in Willow Valley, come the summer of thirty-one. But for now the rest were headed west, and he felt the Judith pulling him north once more. As if that country might become as much his as he had come to love the Bayou Salade.

Jack stepped close and held up his hand after Bass was in the saddle. For a long moment Hatcher was silent before he finally spoke. "Yers is a damned ugly scalp anyway, Titus Bass. Not a warrior wuth anything a'tall gonna wanna take yer poor scalp."

"You flea-bit, broke-down, crow-bait of a buzzard." Bass shook heartily one last time, then flung Hatcher's hand down with a wide smile and waved to them all. "You ain't got no room to talk about just who's got the worst case of the uglies! You boys watch your backtrail now! I'll see you come summer!"

A painful memory, recalling how he rode off for the north, how he had turned in the saddle that one last time to look behind him, finding the six of them still standing. How they had all raised their arms and some had waved hats . . . it again brought that dry clutch high in his chest here beside the Yellowstone, two moons later.

But he had a cache to finish before he could push on for the Judith. To find a certain sandbar. And there to make medicine.

The sort of medicine a man could make only when he was truly alone. Truly on his own at long, long last.

TWENTY-THREE

How good were those last hot days of summer to think back upon now that winter had clamped its jaws tight upon this land. Those days that he rode out the long hours from well before sunrise until twilight squeezed down until nothing but starshine fell from the sky. Even the cool rainy days of autumn when he had turned back from the Mussellshell to dig his cache near the Yellowstone would have felt far better than this marrow-numbing cold.

Up ahead beneath the aching winter blue of the clear sky, he recognized that bulk of those hills as they tumbled down toward the valley of the Judith.

"Looks like we found it, girl!" he flung his voice back to Hannah, eager to share his mounting anxiousness with another. "Maybeso we'll make camp up yonder for the night."

For days now it had felt as if it were the thing to do: locate the place where he and Asa had camped late last spring as they'd worked their way north to the Missouri River—the site where for days McAfferty had ministered to his wounds, sewn up the worst of them on his hip and back with those short strips of buffalo sinew and downy tufts of beaver felt, then through day and night nursed Scratch back to health with bone broth and broiled bits of meat.

It hurt to think about his old friend, pained him to wonder

just what it was that lured a man into Blackfoot country all on his own—to go where certain death waited, go where few other white men would ever tread. A tangible ache throbbed in his chest each time he tried to figure out what made McAfferty ride off into a sure and certain death carrying nothing more than his Bible and his rock-hard faith that all his steps were guided by his God.

Most times Scratch could put his mind on other things, the way a man would pick up a checker piece and move it to another square. But there were times in the black of night, or the coming gray of morning, or in the day-long swaying rock of the saddle, that he found it wasn't so damned easy to shift his thoughts away from a mortal fear for McAfferty's life, if not his very soul.

Not so much afraid that the Blackfoot would butcher Asa as he was afraid of something he could not describe, could not put his hand out and touch. To fear a man of flesh and blood who came at you with his gun or club or knife was one thing. But Bass was coming to fear this journey of McAfferty's had everything to do with what Scratch himself could not understand.

Titus Bass had never really been afraid of what he could look in the eye—whether it be man or beast. It was what Scratch could not see that scared the bejesus out of him now.

After hollowing out that hole on the north side of the Yellowstone not far from that huge, flat-topped sandstone monolith that stood on the river's south bank, he went out that third morning and cut some willow branches, a mile downstream where they might not be missed and arouse suspicion. Then he chopped up some five-foot lengths of cottonwood deadfall and dragged them down into the hole, where he laid them out side by side to form a solid floor. On them his supplies would rest up and out of the dirt and mud in the event any water seeped into his cache. After a first layer of willow was stood against the walls and across the cottonwood floor, Bass started down with the plews that he would not need to pack around until he was headed south for rendezvous next summer.

When he had all those autumn pelts and a little extra plunder secured in the cache, Scratch backed out through the neck of the hole and shoved in a last half-dozen leafy willow branches to finish off the lining of that shaft. Up on the ground once more, he jammed a cross-hatch network of willow limbs across the narrow neck of the cavern until it could support the replacement of the sod he had carefully removed in four large pieces when he had begun his excavation two days before.

The final act was then to start his supper fire right on the top of that entrance to the cache, hoping to obliterate as much evidence as he could. As the sun came up the next morning and he prepared to ride north for the Judith to trap on into the early winter, Scratch took note of two nearby landmarks one last time: the position of the two big cottonwoods and that outcropping of red sandstone rock, in addition to how many paces his treasure lay from the downed tree, how many paces up from the bank of the narrow creek.

Early next spring when his winter in Crow country was drawing to a close, he would come back here to dig up his autumn's take and those few supplies he felt he could do without. But for now he had put the Yellowstone at his back and turned his nose north for the Judith, setting his course for that ground where the sow grizzly had forever changed everything between two men.

He brought the horse, Hannah, and the packhorses to a halt and sighed in the silence of this place.

Collars of old snow clung back in the shady places there in the copse of trees rising on the west bank of the river.

"It was good enough for us back then, girl," he said quietly as he swung off his horse and rubbed his thighs quickly, "so it ought'n do for us now."

As much as he wanted to walk down to the riverbank then and there, Bass resisted and instead busied himself with pulling the loads from the backs of the animals, removing saddles and blankets and pads from them all, leading them one by one toward a small clearing where the cool autumn nights were beginning to brown the last of the tall grass. He secured the forelegs of the last of the three with twisted rawhide hobbles, rubbed each animal down with tufts of sage, then turned back to see to his camp. After resetting the firestones he and Asa had used there last spring, Scratch went in search of firewood, forced to look for more than a half mile in any direction before he found enough to last him through the coming two nights. It was plain that McAfferty had cleared the nearby ground of every last scrap of deadfall that would burn as he kept his vigil over the mauled and mutilated Titus Bass.

Then beside the fire pit he plopped down a hindquarter of the antelope he had shot that morning. With enough firewood laid in, and his bedding spread out, the time had come to fetch some water from the riverbank. Snatching up the bail of his small cast-iron kettle, Scratch took a deep breath and started for the willows that lined the Judith a few yards off through the tall brush blanketing the meadow.

On the far side of the river the beaver had been at work for years without count. Those industrious creatures had backed up part of the river into some low bottomland, where they had constructed at least half a hundred mud-and-branch lodges. He spotted some two dozen of the flat-tails still swimming about in the shallow waters or at work on the trunks of nearby trees. And there, off to his left, was the narrow strip of sandbar lying beneath the sharp cutbank, at least what remained of it after the spring floods had uprooted huge sections of the river bottom and carved away large slabs of the bank, relocating them downstream.

Scratch wasn't sure at first, but that spot some twenty yards to his left had a familiar feel about it—what with the gentle curve of the river, the overhanging vegetation, that small copse of trees on the far bank.

He and McAfferty had been gone from here about the time the snow-melt was gorging all the streams and creeks and tiny rivulets that fed the Judith, swelling the river in its wide channel—well beyond the level of the sandbar. And with the way this land dried out at the end of each summer, that strip of ground at the bottom of the cutbank was once again exposed here in these chilly days as winter sank ever southward from the arctic.

Halfway there he grew pretty sure. After another half-dozen steps he was certain. Although the Judith had deposited some sand and native silt, along with some limbs and roots and assorted river trash around the re-mains—that big a carcass could only be but one of two creatures. Either a buffalo, or a grizzly.

And this skull plainly wasn't huge and wide, nor did it bear a healthy set of horns.

No. That was the skull of a grizzly.

His veins ran cold of a sudden. And his belly crimped the way it did when he had gone the better part of a day without feeding. His mouth went dry and pasty, almost the way it had with his ordeal down in the desert of Apache country.

Predators had come and picked the bones all but clean before, perhaps since, the spring floods. A mountain man would call it high meat. A revolting victual Asa said the Mandans loved to eat on the high Missouri—meat gone bad . . . so decomposed it had liquefied enough that the Indians could spoon it out of the rotting carcasses of buffalo floating down the flood-swollen Missouri. When there was no end to rich, tender red meat a man could find on the hoof, why would anyone consider that putrid, stinking, worm-infested slime a delicacy?

In revulsion Titus swallowed his gorge back down and took two steps closer to the skeleton. Then a final step that brought him right to its side, awash in memory. Snatches of recall, tattered shreds of recollections: where he had been when he had fired his pistol, when he had rammed the stake into her chest, where he likely landed when she pounced on him and blotted out the sky; and . . . could he remember anything at all of where he'd been when McAfferty pulled him out from beneath the dead sow?

Just beyond the bones. There.

Bass stepped over, stopped. Trembling slightly.

It was almost like standing there and looking down on . . . on his own grave.

Had it not been for Asa, he would have died right there.

For a moment he fought the sting of tears and looked up and down the riverbank until he realized he could not stifle the sob.

Bass sank to his knees in the hard, frozen sand beside the grizzly carcass. Put out his hand. And laid it on the huge shoulder blade.

"You and me both, we was in the wrong place at the wrong time," he said quietly. "If it been just the two of us—you'd won that day. If it'd been just me . . ."

Then he suddenly thought of the two cubs, orphaned the moment their mother had lunged out of the willows after them, having scented danger in the smell of a man who had blundered into the midst of their play. Bears had 'em a mighty, mighty strong nose.

And he knew in the marrow of him he could have been a quarter of a mile away, even a half mile or more . . . and it would have made no difference. He and that bear had been destined to bump up against one another on this very ground.

Scooting around on his knees, he leaned forward, and there beside the bear's skull Scratch smoothed out a circle of sand some two feet across. At the edge of that crude circle he stuck some small twigs he broke off a chunk of driftwood to mark the four directions of the wind. The he pulled his tomahawk from his belt and used the back of the blade to break loose the sun-bleached skull from the top of the spine, setting it in the middle of his circle.

Squatting at the edge of this crude altar and crossing his legs, Bass dragged up his belt pouch and pulled out a twist of Billy Sublette's trade tobacco, laying it atop the skull. Using his skinning knife, he cut a little of the dry leaf from the twist and chopped it up fine enough to stuff down a pipe bowl. Setting the pouch, twist, and knife aside, Bass pulled his much-used clay pipe from its pocket in his shooting pouch, and stuffed it with those shreds of tobacco.

He dragged his dirty fingers beneath each eye and smeared away the hot tears, then stuffed his hand back into his shooting pouch to pull out his strike-a-light tin. From it he took a piece of black char cloth, a small chunk of flint, and the large curl of fire steel. Holding the flint and char in his left hand, he hit the stone with sharp downward strikes, sending sparks into the charred cotton where the embers smoldered until he brought them to his lips, blowing on them gently. Over these tiny glowing dots of heat he laid a small shred of dried tinder and blew some more until the tinder caught. Laying the glowing tinder over the top of the bowl, he sucked steadily until the coals licked through the dry tobacco, and his pipe was lit.

First a puff to each of the four directions, then one to the cold, cloudless blue sky overhead, and some final smoke he blew into the sacred circle he had smoothed before him.

That done, he stared off at the nearby bluffs and the distant hills, feeling the sinking track of the sun as he smoked, and thought, and felt what this ground had to tell him. What it yet had to teach him.

When he finally looked back down into that circle, Scratch put out his left hand and laid the fingers atop the bear's skull.

"Give me the power of this animal," he asked in a quiet voice, feeling more humble than ever before in his life.

"Because it died here, I could live," Titus went on in a sob-choked whisper. "Make the rest of my days as strong as they can be because you give me a second chance here."

Then he puffed some more on the pipe, drawing in each breath deep, like a prayer in itself, feeling the smoke course deep into his lungs where he held it before he exhaled. And when the tobacco had all been consumed, he turned the bowl over and knocked out the ashes on the top of the skull. With his fingers he smeared the black and gray into the stark white bone, forming a large, dark circle.

That circle, and the circle of this sand altar, both were symbolic of the circle he realized was his own story. People, places, events—they were all to be experienced by him for a reason in the constant turn in the seasons of his life. He had been drawn here, compelled to venture this close to Blackfoot country for a good reason he now sensed he could understand.

While he could not fathom what lured Asa McAfferty to go where he had gone, something told Scratch that the white-head's journey was of a purpose . . . and Titus felt at peace with that. While McAfferty believed he was directed to go here and there by God, Bass believed people moved in and out of one another's lives for reasons they might not know at those very moments.

Come a day soon, perhaps, Bass figured he would understand why he and Asa had had their time together, why they had shared those terrible tribulations and bloody battles, why they had both come to know it was time to part from one another. Maybe one day he would understand about McAfferty—but not until he understood more about the workings of the mysterious, the ways of the spirit world.

So here at last, here beside this sand altar and the remains of the huge creature that had almost killed him, Titus Bass discovered an inner serenity despite his not knowing.

One day he might well sort out the mysteries of life. But for now, he was at peace with it.

He'd follow the sonsabitches all winter if he had to.

One thing was for certain: their village couldn't be all that far away.

And . . . they were cocky bastards too. They didn't even give a red piss that they were leaving a good trail for him to follow.

After all, they were on horseback. And they had left him afoot.

Alone, and on foot here as winter deepened its bone-numbing cold, and the horizon far to the west threatened to snow in another day or so.

Whoever they were, the red niggers had stolen in to make off with Hannah and the horses a few hours back. In those last seconds Bass heard them whooping as they swept down on the animals, as he was thrashing his way out of his blankets and robes, grabbing his weapons, and sprinting toward the patch of grass where he had picketed the critters.

Beneath the silvery light of that half-moon he made out four riders, then a fifth as they loped away, driving his three animals ahead of them—still whooping, all flushed with their success.

"Five of 'em, against one stupid, bonehead nigger!" he had grumbled while he watched the dark shadows bob as they faded across the snow, ultimately swallowed by that black of the distant hills themselves.

"Goddamned Blackfoot!"

His heart pounded. And he damn near felt close to tears, ready to bawl in frustration and rage. That hot adrenaline squirting into his veins was no longer enough to keep him warm as he stood there in the snow up past his ankles, the wind cutting at him as it weaved through the trees where he had made his last camp before he would reach the cache sometime around midday tomorrow.

"Hannah!" he suddenly shouted into the darkness, despairing he would lose her.

Only when he could no longer hear the hoofbeats on the hard, frozen ground did he finally think to breathe again. Staring at the half-moon still hanging about three hands over the western ridge, his eyes slowly descended onto the widening vee of trampled snow as the thieves' trail emerged from the distance.

Just like some roving bunch of Blackfoot. Cocky bastards that they were.

But he swore he'd have 'em—their scalps and their balls too—if it took all winter. If it took all goddamned winter.

Turning on his heel, Scratch lunged back to camp on cold, wood legs. There he knelt at the coals of last night's fire and laid a few dry limbs upon the ashes. Bending low, he pulled the coyote-fur cap from his head and blew on the dim spots of crimson among the gray. They soon leaped to life, capturing the limbs, licking hungrily along the dry branches.

He rocked back on his haunches and grabbed the old coffee kettle, shaking it. Still enough left in it to reheat, so he set the kettle right against the rekindled flames. Rubbing his hands over the fire, he realized he had but two choices. He could stay here where he would be guaranteed of warmth and commiserate with himself over the loss of his animals, willing to wait until he figured out how to come up with some more animals—which meant he was willing to let the red niggers get away with what was his.

Or he could start moving now: here in the dark, hiding his plunder and furs from roaming eyes, then set off on that trail the thieves left behind.

The gall of it burned in his belly like a twelve-hour coal. They loped off, knowing they had put him afoot, and thinking that he wasn't about to follow them since he was at a decided disadvantage—either because he was one against a half dozen, or because he was on foot and they were covering ground much faster on horseback.

Dammit! He may well be one against that handful of red thieves, but it didn't make no never-mind to him that he was on foot against horsemen.

Bass decided they wouldn't figure a lone white man to be coming after them . . . so that arrogance just might work in his favor.

From the looks of the moon hanging above those southwestern ridges, he calculated that he might have as much as two more hours before it was light enough to take off after them.

Not that he couldn't go now, racing off into the snow-covered night. But he was damned suspicious one of the thieves, maybe even two of them, might turn back in the dark, hiding somewhere along the trail left by the others, watching for any possible pursuit from the lone trapper.

Better was it for him to wait until there was sufficient light to see far enough ahead along the thieves' backtrail.

Besides, he had him plenty to do until the gray of predawn came sliding over the bluffs to hail its first greeting to the Yellowstone valley.

After warming his hands over the flames a moment more, Titus snatched up his small camp ax and turned toward the tall willow clustered along the riverbank. Wouldn't be long before he'd have a sweat worked up, cutting enough branches to hide his plunder and plews.

More than two weeks ago he had turned south from the Judith basin as the weather grew unbearably miserable. No longer was winter merely dallying with the northern plains. Deep cold left in the wake of a hellish storm descended so quickly upon this country that it left a man no doubt that autumn was long done with. Bass had pushed his luck about as far as any savvy man might, lingering that far north along the Missouri River country, trapping past the time when lesser men might have turned tail and run.

But, damn—weren't the plews fine!

Big, fat beaver, the sort what wore pelts so large the mountain man called them blankets. And thick? Jumpin' Jehoshaphat—but they were seal fat and sleek! It was damn near the finest trapping Titus Bass had ever done in the weeks he tarried past the falling of the leaves, the freezing of the smaller creeks and streams, lingering past the first icy glazing to the surface of the Judith and even the mighty Upper Missouri itself.

Battling his way south, back up the Judith until it reached the foothills, he struggled on through the narrow breach between two mountain ranges, eventually crossing the low divide to drop into the valley of the Mussellshell. Scratch plodded south by east only as long as the animals' strength held up each day, slowly making for his cache on the north bank of the Yellowstone.

When he could tell they were close to being all but done in, Titus would be forced to find them someplace to camp where a small patch of grass had been blown clear. If he wasn't that lucky, Bass would spend the last hour of light each afternoon chopping cottonwood he would peel before throwing the limbs onto his fire. Though it wasn't the best of fodder for the animals—it had to be better than some of the withered, wind-dried grasses the stock had been forced to eat as the seasons quickly turned against man and beast in this icy land.

This was to have been his last camp before reaching the cache. One last sleep before he would spend a day or so reopening the hole, laying in his high Missouri pelts with what he had already stashed away of the catch from earlier in the autumn. In addition, he had planned to stow away what he knew he wouldn't need until late in the winter—like the extra weight of his traps, both American and Mexican made—when the streams and creeks and rivers began to open. And before he resealed the cache, he figured he should pull out a little of this and a little of that from his Taos and rendezvous goods: gifts of foofaraw and geegaws for the Crow.

This one last camp before . . .

After he had slogged back to his plunder with that first armload of brush, Scratch took a few minutes to pull his hands from his blanket mittens and warm them over the fire before turning to the business of dragging the bundles back into the willow near a small stand of cottonwood saplings. Retying each pack, Titus made sure every square inch was covered by the oiled Russian sheeting. Then he dragged up the first of the brush he had cut, working carefully to stuff the limbs down into the ropes on the top and all four sides.

A second trip added more brush to his cover. A third, fourth, and finally a fifth time he trudged down to the riverbank to chop more limbs. By the time the sky to the east turned as red as that afterbirth expelled by a buffalo cow dropping a calf, he stood back and was satisfied he had concealed what he owned.

Now he had to go after the rest of what little he had in this world.

Stuffing his hands back into the mittens after rubbing his flesh over the fire, Bass laid his two buffalo robes one on top of the other. After folding his two blankets, he placed them inside the robes before turning in the edges of the furry hides. With a bundle more than two feet thick, Scratch took the last long braid of rawhide rope and lashed it all together into a pack some four feet long and nearly as wide.

Rising from the cold, blue snow just beginning to turn a pale pink presaging the sun's arrival, he hurriedly chopped down three of the strongest cottonwood saplings and trimmed them of branches and knots. Crossing one of the long, thin saplings over another, he tied the two together with some short sections of hemp rope. After cutting the third sapling into two pieces, he tied both sections across the wide vee formed by the others. Then, with his last piece of rope, Titus lashed his bedding and a small packet of dried meat to his improvised travois.

By then it was light enough to plainly see the trail left by the raiders. Time to move out.

Stepping into the vee just ahead of his bundle, Bass shoved the barrel of his rifle through two of the bedding ropes. He jabbed his pistol under another rope, then turned and adjusted the knife and tomahawk at his back, shifted the shooting pouch over his shoulder.

Then he stepped forward, bent down, and pulled the two saplings off the ground.

Surprised to find it wasn't so heavy after all. And if he had left enough room at the base of the travois below that bottom crosspiece, the drag should ride well enough over the sagebrush and rocky ground, keeping his robes out of the ankle-deep powder.

Squinting into the west as the light began to balloon around him, he thought of Hannah.

Remembered how she had run off that day the Arapaho had jumped them. How she had come back later. How the mule had saved him, saved them both.

"I'm coming for you, girl," he vowed in a cold, dry whisper.

Ain't no red niggers gonna get you from me 'less I die trying to get you back.

The intense cold of that early dawn nearly froze the hot mist in his eyes as he set out on the trail, realizing just how warm a man could be when he nursed on revenge.

Stopping only long enough to blow and catch his wind or get a drink of water that first day, Bass didn't eat until evening. After chewing on some dried strips of venison, he bent over the bank and cracked the thick scum of ice forming along the Yellowstone. He drank long and deep, knowing how vital it was to quench his thirst several times a day in this high, dry, cold land.

Every bit as important, if not more so, as it was to take in water during the heat of late summer—just as crucial as such a thing could be in Apache country. Water might mean the difference between his keeping up with the raiders or never even standing a chance of catching them . . . the difference between life and death, alone as he was in this winter wilderness.

He stood again, his weary bones protesting, pushing his face on into the brutal slash of that drying west wind.

A while after the sun went down ahead of him, the wind died, no longer tormenting the valley, nor rawhiding his leathery face. Throughout the day's march he had stopped here and there long enough to swipe one mitten or the other over his face, scouring the frost from his eyebrows and lashes, scrubbing the icicles from his mustache and beard where they collected as his heaving gusts of breath froze in a coating over his face. All day hauling his little travois onward in the path of the falling sun.

Then, as twilight deepened the hues of that snow covering the nearby hills to shades of rose and lavender, he lunged to a stop, weary, exhausted, thirsty so quickly again . . . his heart rising to his throat in frustration and fear as he peered down the raiders' trail.

The hoofprints turned sharply to the left, following the gentle slope of the bank toward the river. The trampled snow he had been following disappeared through a wide notch in the brush and cottonwood.

It would make a fine spot for an ambush. The sort of place where one or two of the warriors would lie back after the others had gone on, waiting there in hiding for the white man—if they suspected they were followed.

But the more he stared at that wide breach in the brush along the bank, at that gentle descent the slope made as it fell away to the shallow ford, as he studied the skeletal trees up and down the river, listening . . . Scratch grew all the more certain these warriors were so cocky they didn't even give a good goddamn if they were followed by one lone trapper.

So maybe he should let the sonsabitches know he was coming.

"Hannah!"

He listened to the voice echo back at him from the low hills lying south of the river. The deepening cold swallowed that plaintive sound quickly as a mist began to form at the river's surface.

Then Bass whispered, "I'll find you yet, Hannah. I swear it, by God."

At the river's edge he stared across the Yellowstone. A thickening ice had rimed itself along both banks in a scum more than two feet wide. He bent and chopped himself a wide hole, then leaned out and drank. The drops froze on his face as he stood to swipe off that thin crusting with a mitten.

And, Lord, how that hurt too—merely rubbing his nose and cheeks with the stiffened wool of his mitten!

Hannah was somewhere on the other side now. And the thieves were on the south bank of the Yellowstone with her and the horses. How far ahead, he had no way of knowing. But if he hesitated here, one thing was certain: he never would get the mule back. He never would catch up to the raiders. He never would see the startled looks on their faces as he rained his retribution down upon them.

Just the way Asa McAfferty's avenging angels would rain fire and brimstone down upon the unholy come their Judgment Day.

If he camped here, he might as well give up.

But if he crossed now, and pushed on into and through this night . . . he might just stand a chance of catching them somewhere west of the ford, catching them sometime tomorrow. Because red niggers as cocky as this bunch would most assuredly figure on stopping close to dark, making their beds around a warm fire, and sleeping out the night in warmth.

Bass listened to the river lap against the bank beneath that thickening rime of ice near his feet. And realized it was the only way.

He dropped the travois and turned around to the bundle of robes and blankets. Stripping off his mittens, he stuffed them under a top section of rope where he could grab them quickly, without fumbling. A man's hands would have to be warm enough to grip a thin piece of char, hold a chunk of flint at the right angle, to sweep down with that gentle curve of the fire-steel without trembling if he was going to get himself a fire started on the far bank.

Next came the thick fur-lined buffalo moccasins he stuffed under the ropes, as well as an inner pair of fur-lined elk-hide moccasins. Bass decided to leave on the soft, smoke-tanned elk-hide moccasins he wore right against his flesh: he might well need that thin layer of protection against the river-bottom rocks, the grip they could give him as he raced across this ford of the Yellowstone.

Now came the leggings, one shivering leg at a time. After he had removed his shooting pouch and powder horn and laid them both alongside his rifle, he pulled the thick blanket capote from his arms and laid it atop the bedding bundle. Next he dragged the rifle from the ropes and set the weapon down within the coat, wrapping the leggings around the muzzle, clear back to the lock. By the time he pulled off the breechclout and his belt, his legs were shaking with the bite of intense cold.

Scratch clenched his chattering teeth together and yanked the long buckskin war shirt over his head, off his arms, and slapped it down on the rifle. Rolling it into a long tube that covered the lock and buttstock, he had one last item of clothing to remove.

His frozen fingers trembled as they fought the buttons loose from their holes on his faded red wool longhandles. Yanking it down off his arms, on down off his chest and belly, Bass tugged the dirty, smoke-stained cloth over each moccasin and stood again to drape it across the rifle and his buckskin clothing. He swaddled the sides of the coat over it all, rolled up his bundle, and wedged this long wool-wrapped packet under two sections of rawhide rope.

Pausing only long enough to take a deep breath, Titus whirled and seized the cottonwood saplings of his travois, rising from the snow with them. At the riverbank he hesitated a moment, gazing at the ice and the slow-moving water . . . his eyes eventually moving across the wide black ribbon to the far bank where the raiders' trail disappeared into the brush. . . . Then he finally looked at the sky to the west.

Snow before morning.

If it stormed hard enough . . . and he hadn't caught them by sunup, his chances ran somewhere between slim and none that he would have a trail clear enough to follow.

Titus stepped into that wide crack he had hacked through the layer of ice skimming the riverbank.

His breath immediately seized in his chest—so sudden and tight were the frozen bands around his ribs that Scratch doubted he would ever breathe again.

Already his feet and calves ached with the deep cold, just standing there. . . .

"It ain't nothing you haven't felt afore," he convinced himself as he stepped deeper into the water, the cold quickly climbing up his legs, sensing the travois poles begin to float their load on the river's surface behind him.

Before he plunged any deeper, Titus realized he would have to step out of the vee and float his travois the rest of the way as he plodded across on foot. The slow water swirled sluggishly at midthigh, gushing up against his shrinking scrotum and manhood as he high-stepped out of the travois, pushed it ahead of him, and plunged on into the river—measuring each step carefully as his toes felt their way along the river bottom in the growing darkness, each foot securing a hold before he moved another half-yard.

All too quickly the water rose past his hips, over his waist, to midchest and finally to his armpits as he pushed on—not even a third of the way across yet. So deep already that he grew worried this wasn't a shallow ford at all. But the raiders had to know.

So he pressed on, struggling with his travois every now and then as the river's surface tugged at it, shoving it sideways from him. Nearly halfway across, the water rose above his shoulders, lapped at his ragged beard.

Damn, if it really weren't warmer here under the water!

Then he realized that would mean the air itself was colder than the Yellowstone.

Bass knew his life depended upon how quickly he could move across the second half of the river, onto the bank, and into his clothes.

By the time he was no more than calf-deep in the Yellowstone and no more than a few feet from the river's edge, Bass felt his muscles beginning to fail his willful heeding. Slow, sluggish, moving no faster than the oozing flow of pine sap.

Reaching that ice scum frozen against the south bank, he flung his wooden arms aside and dropped the cottonwood saplings, his fingers still cramped into frozen, unresponsive claws. Slowly, painfully, he turned in that cold air, his legs half-submerged in the Yellowstone, ordering his body back toward the bundle, toward the clothing protected by that capote.

As much as he cursed his fingers, he still couldn't get them to respond. So in one last, desperate move, Scratch used his teeth to drag the first mitten free of the rawhide rope, and stuffed the unwilling hand inside its warmth.

Then, realizing his strength was quickly failing, he yanked the second mitten free and plunged his right hand inside.

With clawlike fists he started to rub the scratchy wool up and down each bare arm quickly, over the flesh on his chest and belly, down across his thighs, knees, and calves—right to the river's surface as he lumbered back slowly, almost stumbling and going down twice on his frozen feet. One at a time, it seemed, his fingers began to respond to his commands, moving within their woolen cocoon until he could ball up a fist and release it.

Pulling one hand from its mitten, Scratch seized the top of the travois and dragged it up the frozen bank until the bedding bundle no longer bobbed atop the water's surface. With both hands back in their mittens, he valiantly struggled to pull the long bundle of his capote from beneath the lashing. Clumsily yanking back on the flaps of the coat, he pulled it out from beneath the rifle and his other clothing. How glorious it felt to stuff his arms into that warmth! Even with his hands trembling terribly, he somehow got the wide finger-woven sash knotted at his waist.

Maybe he would make it after all.

Hannah was counting on him. He knew that. If she couldn't get freed from her captors, then he knew she was counting on him to come after her. Driven by the same deep bond that had compelled her to come back for him after the Arapaho had driven her off, scalped him, and left the white man for dead.

He owed her for that, and for the other times she had been there to warn him of danger, times when she pulled his hash out of one fix or another.

Shaking like a quaky leaf in a September gale, Bass snatched up his shooting pouch and looped it over his shoulders before he lunged thick-legged up the gentle slope of the bank, his soggy moccasins slipping on the icy crust as the leather began to freeze. Collapsing into the snow beside a large branch of deadfall cottonwood, Titus hurriedly brushed aside what he could of the ice at the base of a low drift, then began snapping off the smaller limbs and twigs. As soon as he had a pile formed at his knees, Scratch dragged his pouch into his lap, fought up the flap.

Stuffing his right mitten between his teeth, he yanked it from his hand and began to dig through the pouch for his tinderbox. From the container made of German silver back in Kentucky, he took a small chunk of blackened char. Against it he laid a piece of flint, then pulled out his fire-steel.

As soon as a tiny spark ignited the char, he pulled a small nest of tinder from the box and laid it upon the cloth and blew until the dried tinder burst into flame. Oh, to feel that welcome warmth on his face!

Placing the fiery tinder atop some of the twigs, he gradually laid more of the tiny branches over the struggling flames—adding one piece at a time as each new twig caught fire.

Finally he laid on some of the branches as thick as his wrist. Feeling confident enough that the flames wouldn't snuff themselves out, Bass stood shakily, dragging his frozen knees and calves out of the snow. Snugging the flaps of his capote around him, he stood dangerously close to the flames, sensing how quickly the sudden, surprising warmth seeped into the flesh of his lower body. Through the layers of his coat, he vigorously rubbed his thighs again, then moved away only long enough to grab his longhandles and leggings.

How warm and dry the faded underwear felt against his near-frozen flesh!

Pulling each one of the buckskin tubes on over the wet moccasins, Scratch tied each legging to the belt he had buckled around his waist. Reluctantly he pulled the capote from his arms and hurriedly replaced it with his war shirt. And with the coat knotted around him once again, Bass sat back against the small bundle of his bedding, sucked on his bare fingers to warm them a moment, then struggled with the soggy knots of his moccasins. One at a time the stark, white, nearly frozen flesh of his feet was exposed—but only for a moment as he dragged on the pair sewn so the elk hair lay inside against his skin. Over them he tied the heavy, thick moccasins with their curly buffalo hair turned inside.

As soon as he laid on the last of that dried cottonwood, Bass realized he was going to need more wood to build up the fire before he had rewarmed enough to set off into the coming night all but done with sucking the last of the light from the valley.

Looking downriver, then up—he decided to go in search of wood to his right. He took only one step when he stopped suddenly, staring at the footprint before he dropped to one knee to inspect it more closely in the firelight. Now he knew. There could be no doubt. Not with the way the outer seam of the moccasin ran back from the big to the little toe at a sharp angle. This was Crow.

He had seen a winter's worth of those prints to know a Crow moccasin from a Cheyenne, a Ute from a Blackfoot or Shoshone. Two years back he had learned from Bird in Ground to recognize how Crow squaws cut and sewed up their moccasins.

"Damn them cocky Sparrowhawks," he grumbled as he rose and plodded away into the snow.

Dragging back more deadfall, Scratch snapped off all the limbs and branches he could break with his hands, the sole of his feet, or hack loose with the small ax. In minutes he had the sort of fire that would warm a half-dozen men.

And as he gazed off to the west and that band of indigo blue shrinking to black, Scratch was sure they were warming themselves around a fire right then too.

"You niggers go right on and sleep real snug," he said quietly to the night. "Titus Bass is coming."

The half-moon was just climbing over the tops of the bare cottonwood downriver when he felt he had restoked his own inner flames enough to push on into the darkness. With the snow beginning to brilliantly reflect the feeble starshine and the light of that rising moon, Scratch felt certain he could follow the trail of trampled snow heading west up the Yellowstone.

Stepping into the travois, he secured his rifle back under two ropes, then turned and hoisted the drag. Leaning against the saplings, he plunged into the darkness, into the wilderness, into the unknown.

"What's one goddamned white nigger gonna do?" he groused under his breath as he struggled along, dragging the travois behind him across the sagebrush and rocky ground.

"Bet that's what them Sparrowhawk bastards is asking themselves!"

They ain't worried one whit about me.

And that made Titus smile.

Jehoshaphat, but did they have a surprise coming!

The sky behind him had just begun to faint up the last time he had turned his head and looked over his shoulder to the east. The cold, frozen mist clung beside the riverbanks, thick among the brush and bare-bone cottonwood. Damned cold here, but this was where they cut their trail through the snow. A mist so thick and dark all night long that it made him think of cotton bolls dipped in tanner's black. But finally, far behind him to the east, it appeared the sky was finally relinquishing its first hint of the dawn to come.

He had to keep pushing, Bass reminded himself. Couldn't slow up now. Come first light—they'd be up and on the move again. Maybe not right at sunup, but soon after. They weren't worried about hurrying out of their blankets, not cocky as this bunch was.

Turning his nose back upriver, he leaned into the vee and lunged forward, driven to keep moving here past the point of exhaustion, though his feet felt like chunks of ice and every stirring of the breeze tormented his frostbitten face. Time and again he rubbed his nose, the tops of his cheeks, with a mitten, trying his best to somehow keep the flesh warm enough that it would not die, turn black, and sluff off. He had seen enough men who carried such disfiguring scars: ears and noses and cheeks.

Tugging the fur of the coyote-skin cap down lower on his forehead, Bass suddenly stopped and sniffed the breeze again.

How the quickening wind made his raw flesh cry out in agony . . . but suddenly that breeze also carried on it the smell of something new to his nose.

He'd be boiled for the devil's tater if that didn't smell like . . . like firesmoke.

Damn—if that didn't take the circle!

Scratch peered through the dim light of dawn coming, straining his eyes into the thick, murky, frozen fog clinging along the riverbank. Now, they might be camped up ahead before the Yellowstone took a gentle sweep to the north, or they might be camped just beyond, where they would likely have taken shelter behind that low rise.

He sniffed again and again until he felt sure of making a savvy guess. The fragrance of firesmoke was so faint that it couldn't be coming from very close. That fire, and those who were gathered beside it, had to be around that river bend, just on the far side of that low hill jutting toward the north and forcing the river to flow around it.

With a sudden surge of energy he threw himself forward into the cold and the darkness, drinking in that hint of a fire, that faintest shred of hope that he was nearing the end of his pursuit.

Where once he had been bone weary and benumbed at his night-long chase, now Bass congratulated himself on deciding to push on while his quarry slept confident that no man would be following them through the long winter night.

Out of the trees he stepped, staring at the low hill he would have to climb now to follow the trail. There was no room left for man or horse to walk between the vertical bluff and the Yellowstone itself. Left without a choice, he continued in the wake of those hoofprints.

Stopping near the crest of the rise as the scent of his enemy grew stronger in his nostrils, Scratch sensed more of the firesmoke greeting him on that breeze rising from the river valley.

Quietly he let the travois fall to the trampled snow, stepped out of the vee, and cautiously approached the top of the hill. Just shy of the crest he went to his belly and pushed himself up between some stunted cedar.

Smoke struck him in the face, strong as anything he had ever smelled.

And there below him in the rising, dispersing mist were the dancing flames of that fire.

Around it stood four figures more shadow than substance. Then a fifth emerged from the brush readjusting his breechclout. He immediately snatched up a blanket and pulled it over his shoulders.

For a moment more Bass watched them talking around that fire, some of them gesturing; then finally two of the Crow turned away and began rolling up buffalo robes while another pair started kicking snow into their fire pit, snuffing the flames and sending up an eruption of thick smoke. He was watching that column rise into the graying sky when a familiar sound suddenly reached him where he lay on the crest of the hill.

Hannah's plaintive, brassy bawl.

Off to the side he watched the fifth warrior attempting to approach the mule secured to a tree trunk. As the man inched closer, she began to swing her rump toward him, preparing to kick—but he deftly leaped away. Five times he attempted to maneuver in like that without success; then the warrior lunged to the side and swept up a chunk of deadfall about as long as his arm. With this held overhead he dashed toward the mule.

Leaping onto his knees, Bass let out a pained howl just as Hannah *scree-awww*ed again. Loud enough that she drowned out her master's call from the hilltop.

It felt as if he had been smacked between the eyes the moment that piece of wood cracked against her head.

He felt his stomach lurch, empty and cold as he watched the mule stumble sideways. The Indian with the club quickly stepped in and yanked her lead rope loose from where he had tied it against a low-hanging branch.

Strutting in victory, the warrior pulled the stunned mule toward the other ponies and horses as the faint trickle of laughter drifted up the side of the hill and reached his ears with a cruel clarity.

Before he could rise from his knees to get to his feet, the stunned trapper watched the five Indians leap atop their horses, turn about, and head out. Riding off toward the west once more. Into the shadows of predawn.

Far enough out of reach that it made him ache to his core.

He had managed to stumble here too late to save her.

TWENTY-FOUR

Bass dived into the brush the instant he spotted the blackened tops of those buffalo-hide lodges, dropping his travois.

Here—just past midday—a thick pall of firesmoke clung to the bone-bare branches of the leafless cottonwood, clotted in a dirty halo about the graceful whorl of poles that rose above every lodge. The air barely moved, not so much as a sigh of wind in the valley of the Yellowstone now.

Cursing himself for not spotting the low-hanging smoke earlier, Scratch knelt there in the brush, his heart hammering against his ribs. What with the way the low, heavy clouds had moved in right after sunrise, and the way the air barely stirred all morning, a man didn't have a chance of spying that camp smoke rising from every fire pit, no chance of smelling the village before he bumped right into it.

Titus glanced across that ten yards separating him from the travois . . . and his rifle. Then back at the village. If they saw him, they saw him. He'd damn well need that gun if they did anyhow. Bass quickly crabbed out to the bundle, crouching behind it to reach up so he could grip the buttstock, pulling the rifle free of the two ropes.

Then in a crouch he scurried back to his hiding place in the brush.

Sure enough, the raiders' trail had brought him right to the village. He swallowed at the scratchy knot in his throat, his mind galloping, digging away at his options the way he'd scratch at a troublesome mosquito bite that refused relief for anything longer than a moment. Then Titus decided that he had left himself no other choice.

After all, what had he stumbled all these miles through the snow for? Why had he crossed the Yellowstone and damn well froze himself to death? If not to confront the horse thieves, then why had he trudged on through the night so he could catch up to the raiders while they rested?

Through those trees lying between him and the village drifted the tatters of laughter and trilling tongues, cheers and war whoops. Dogs joined in and children shouted too—then he heard Hannah's bawl.

And remembered the way it had torn him apart that morning just before dawn as he'd watched the Crow warrior smack his mule across the head with that piece of firewood.

With that remembering Bass knew why he had endured the miles and hours, the icy snow and the river crossing. He had come to reclaim what was his.

Licking at the ooze of blood seeping from the wide crack in his lower lip, Scratch slowly swiped the mitten down his face, feeling the agonized torment the harsh wool sanded through his windburned, frostbitten flesh. He stood and pulled that mitten from his right hand under his left armpit, stuffing his fingers into his shooting pouch so he could scoop out a half-dozen .54-caliber lead balls. Plopping them into his mouth, he tongued them over so they would lie between his cheek and gum, then squared the pouch where it hung beneath his right elbow.

After looking to the priming powder on both the rifle and the pistol he stuffed back into his sash, Titus laid the long weapon across the crook of his left arm and stepped out of the brush, striding purposefully along the ground trampled not only by the pony raiders returning to this village, but by a growing number of converging trails.

At that moment it began to snow lightly—huge, ash-curl flakes swirling down on the still, frozen air. The heavy fragrance of firesmoke slapped him in the face, reminding him that he was one, walking into a village to confront the many who had done him wrong.

Licking at the oozy lower lip, the wound yelped in pain as he entered the thick belt of cottonwood and brush behind which the tops of the lodges disappeared. A few more steps and he realized the village actually sat across a narrow river that dumped itself into the Yellowstone.

For no more than the measure of a few heartbeats he stopped among the leafless willow and studied the lodges on the western bank. Then looked at the river itself, and the ford leading down to it. After drawing back the rifle hammer to full-cock, Bass dragged the pistol from his sash . . . and moved out of the brush, down the trampled, muddy snow to the ford.

Straight into the icy water that swirled around his ankles, then up his calves to splay the bottom of his capote out upon the river surface as he reached midstream. A woman coming down to the bank upriver to his left stopped, watched for a moment, then turned about and lunged up the trampled snow, shouting. Her shrill cry sent a trio of magpies bursting from the low branches hanging over the far side of the crossing.

Knots of children suddenly emerged from the open places between the lodges, hurrying for a glimpse of him as he reached the west bank. A half-dozen horsemen whooped up out of the thickening snow, halting with a cascade of icy clods, brandishing their weapons and shouting at him.

Camp guards.

Stopping, he glared at them, each one in turn, letting them see that he was not afraid of their boasts, letting them see that though his rifle was not pointed up the low rise right at them, it was nonetheless ready to fire in their direction. He brought the pistol arm up and rested the long barrel of the heavy rifle across the left wrist. And pushed on up the rise toward the outlying lodges as more of the curious gathered to watch his approach.

Around to his left poured three horsemen, piercing the thick grove of cottonwood, perhaps seeking to sweep behind him.

Bass turned, his knees slightly bent, whirling and bringing up the rifle's muzzle. One of the riders signaled the other two, and they all three halted; then the one sent the pair across the river.

"*No*, you stupid red nigger!" Scratch growled at the horseman. Then he quickly stuffed the pistol back into his belt and raised that left hand, holding up one finger. Quickly he brought that finger down to jab at his own chest. "There's only one of me!"

Yanking the pistol back out of his sash, Scratch continued to the top of the low rise as children, women, and dogs began to part before him, opening a wide gauntlet for the stranger. Faces emerged out of the crowd, heads poking around others, children staring out between the legs of adults, dogs slinking behind him to sniff warily at his heels until he wheeled and swung the heavy iron muzzle of the rifle at one of the curs—catching the animal in the ribs, bowling it over, driving the dog off yelping and whimpering with its tail between its legs.

"Ti-tess!"

Sounded something like his name.

Bass whirled again on the crowd and started moving once more—the hair prickling on the back of his neck. As he pushed ahead through the widening gauntlet, his eyes searched the faces, spotting a man forcing his way through the pack to stand in the open some twenty feet away between the two columns.

"Ti-tess!"

"Bird in Ground?" He quickly looked over the man wrapped in a heavy wool blanket. "That really you?"

"Me, Ti-tess!" the man-woman shouted, and came hurrying across the snow as fast as his blanket would allow.

The blanket opened as Bird in Ground reached the trapper, revealing the beautiful dress the man-woman wore, heavily decorated with elk milk teeth. The Crow threw his arms around Scratch, embracing and pounding the startled white man on the back.

"I'll be damned," Bass muttered.

"Yes, damned," the Indian repeated in his best imitation of his mentor's speech.

"I recall some of these here faces . . ." and his voice trailed off. Then he set the rifle butt on the ground and signed while he spoke in what little Crow he remembered from winters gone before. "This is *your* camp?"

The man-woman nodded. "Some of these people remember your visit so many winters ago."

Quickly gazing at the cluster of faces watching the two of them expectantly, Bass drew his shoulders back. "My friend: in your camp . . . there are five thieves."

"Thieves?" Bird in Ground repeated.

He signed for "horse," remembering the Crow didn't have a word for "mule." "Pony thieves. Five of your men took my three horses. Two nights ago. I followed them here."

"Yes," and the man-woman turned, pulling the blanket around his shoulders. He pointed off through the camp. "They came in a short time ago. Shouting, happy—proud of their new horses."

"I want my horses back," Bass signed and said in his stuttering Crow. "Then . . . I want those five—here."

"You came to take their scalps?" Bird in Ground asked, his eyes narrowing.

"I get my horses back," he explained, "I won't want their lives. Just want some of their blood."

"You will fight all five—as one finger would fight the whole other hand?"

"If I have to," Bass answered. "But one especially: the man I watched beat one of my animals."

"Where was this?" a voice demanded above the murmurs of the crowd.

Scratch turned, peering over Bird in Ground's shoulder at the tall, regal warrior approaching them from afar. Already the crowd had parted for this impressive figure the moment he had emerged from his lodge, which sat at the center of the great camp circle. Quickly Bass glanced at the tall tripod standing near the doorway as the villagers stepped back in deference to this hand-some and powerful man.

Turning back to Bird in Ground, Titus asked, "You lived with Big Hair's band—"

"These are the same people," the man explained as the tall warrior approached. "We were Big Hair's band."

"What became of your chief?"

"Big Hair was killed in a fight with the Blackfoot," the man-woman explained just as the tall warrior came to a halt and his expressive eyes measured the white man. Bird in Ground continued, "The new chief of our people . . . is Arapooesh."

"Ara . . . Arapooesh," Bass repeated, then took off his mitten and held out his hand.

For a moment the chief looked down at it, then seized Bass's wrist in his hand, and they shook, gripping one another's forearms. The tall man had a warm and genuinely disarming smile.

"Ti-tuzz Bazz," Bird in Ground explained the white man's name.

After repeating the foreign sounds for himself, Arapooesh pointed at the fur cap pulled so far down over Bass's head it reached clear to the eyebrows, hung below his ears on both sides. He said something so rapidly to Bird in Ground that Scratch was able to follow none of it.

"Arapooesh asked if you had a long trip. If you stayed warm."

"Yes, I stayed warm," Bass replied, wondering how much of that answer was the truth. "Tell your chief why I am here."

Bird in Ground asked, "The horse thieves?"

"Thieves?" Arapooesh echoed.

"Yes," the Crow man-woman told the chief. "The white man followed the men who stole his horses. Their trail led him to our camp."

"The horse thieves came here?"

Bird in Ground nodded, his eyes narrowing. "I know the ones, Arapooesh. I saw them return this morning after they were gone many days. They brought two ponies and the white man's strange horse with them."

"Strange horse?" Arapooesh asked.

"Half-a-horse," the Crow man-woman attempted to explain.

"Ahh, I have seen some of those," and then the chief studied Bass a moment more. "Are you a friend of Bird in Ground?"

And the Crow man quickly responded, "Yes, he is a friend of mine."

"No," Arapooesh snapped, his eyes coming back to Scratch. "I asked the white man."

"I am Bird in Ground's friend."

"Are you a friend of the Crow?" asked the chief.

For a moment he thought, then said, "I am the friend of all Crow who do not steal from me. I am friend of all Crow who have honor."

The chief seemed to measure the heft of those words, then replied, "My people like horses very much. Sometimes we find horses, we take them for our own—"

"I have never done a thing to hurt the Crow," Bass interrupted angrily.

"This is a good man, Arapooesh," Bird in Ground explained. "He listens to our people talk and tries to understand. He even tries to understand about a woman who was born in this man's body."

As Arapooesh regarded Bass, he scratched his smooth, plucked chin and finally said, "Tell me, Bird in Ground . . . tell me the names of the men who stole the white man's horses."

Clearing his throat, plainly nervous, the man-woman toed the snow before him and eventually spoke the names of the five he believed were the raiders.

Arapooesh's eyes narrowed with concern. "You are certain?"

"These are the five I saw come to camp this morning with the two ponies and the half horse."

"But," Arapooesh said, wagging his head, "these are not . . ."

"They stole from the white man. They stole from the man who is my friend. Stole from one who has done no wrong to our people."

As he drank in a deep breath, his chest swelling in contemplation, the chief finally turned away to raise his voice over the crowd. "I call for these five to come here so that I may talk to them: Red Leggings, Comes Inside the Door, Crow Shouting, Sees the Star, and . . . and Pretty On Top."

As several voices in the crowd took up the cry, echoing those five names and shouting the chief's command through the village, the rest in the great throng started to murmur and whisper. Just when Bass was coming to believe that the five would not dare show their faces, the crowd parted in a rush of noisy excitement. Through that widening gap stepped the five.

Titus blinked his eyes, recognizing the tall, thick curl heavily greased and pinned atop one of the thieves' heads. He was Hannah's tormentor.

Suddenly seething all the way to the soles of his feet, Scratch started to lunge forward—then stopped abruptly. Shocked: for the first time looking closely at the five, into the faces of those horse thieves, into the eyes of these . . . boys.

He whipped around on Bird in Ground, flushing with sudden rage. "W-what is this!" he sputtered in English, then asked in that foreign tongue. "These are boys!"

"Boys," the chief repeated in Crow as the five came to a stop near Arapooesh, eyeing the white man suspiciously. "Yes, they are boys."

"We are men now," disputed the one with the tall greased curl on his head.

Bird in Ground sneered. "You are men because you stole three horses from one white man?"

"Three was all he had," said another of the youngsters, then laughed with the rest.

"So you did take this man's horses?" Arapooesh asked, silencing them.

Perhaps believing that he had good reason to boast, the one with the curl said, "We went out to steal horses, Arapooesh. We stole some and brought them back to our camp."

"But you stole a lone man's horses!" Bird in Ground protested.

The curled one snorted, "I will not be talked to like this by a creature who has a manhood between his legs but does not want to be a man!"

As swiftly as a camp robber swoops down to raid the meat-drying racks, Bird in Ground lunged forward and smacked his flat hand across the youth's face. "Pretty On Top!" he shrieked. "I am a person of honor . . . one who is strong enough to kill you with my bare hands!"

Arapooesh stepped between Bird in Ground and the youngster as Pretty On Top started for the man-woman. "There will be no fighting between my people today."

"No woman talks to a warrior like this—"

"You are not a warrior!"

Again the youngster leaped for Bird in Ground, his hands thrashing like claws ripping the air.

But Arapooesh restrained him. "What he says is true, Pretty On Top. You are not a warrior."

Wounding crossed his face: Pretty On Top slowly brought the fingers of one hand up to touch the bright-red mark on his cheek where he had been slapped. But it was plain that his feelings suffered more pain than had his flesh. "How will you ever call me a warrior, or how will any man ever ask me to come along on a scalp raid . . . if you won't even consider me a man when I steal a white man's horses."

"The white man," Arapooesh started to explain, "he is not our enemy."

"Ever since the first white men came to our country," Pretty On Top argued, "our people have stolen their horses."

Sees the Star agreed, his head bobbing. "The Crow have never killed a white man."

"You will never steal from this man!" Bird in Ground demanded.

Pretty On Top snorted with laughter. "Is this white man your . . . *husband*?"

Some of the young people in the crowd sniggered behind their hands.

Bird in Ground's cheeks flushed with anger. "Little boys like you will never understand the ways of a real man," he declared, putting his face up close to the youth's, "because you will never grow up to become a man."

This time the tall adolescent swung his arm back, ready to slap the older man, when his wrist was suddenly caught in the trapper's mitten.

"That's right. You're no man yet," Bass grunted in Crow as he pushed the strong youth's arm down, "because a man would never strike a friend."

Pretty On Top seized the wrist of the hand the white man had clamped on him, and for a moment they glared into one another's eyes. "You are no friend of mine!" And he tried to fling Bass's arm aside.

Instead, Scratch slowly released his grip. "I am a friend of the Crow. I am a friend to all men of honor and bravery." He turned to look into the face of Arapooesh, saying, "Until the Crow blacken their faces against me, I will be a friend to your people. Your friends are my friends. Your enemies . . . they are my enemies too."

"My people, we are not many," the chief exclaimed as he laid his hand on the big youth's shoulder. "We cannot afford to turn away any man who says he is our friend, any man who says he will stand against our enemies with us."

Some of the women in the crowd trilled their tongues in approval, and several of the old men raised their voices in triumph.

"It was good you came to us this winter," Bird in Ground said.

With a smile Scratch replied, "I did not intend to visit your camp this soon."

With his strong hand Arapooesh turned to Pretty On Top so that he stared the tall youth directly in the eye. "We have this problem of the white man's horses."

"They are our horses now!" the youth barked in protest.

Bird in Ground lunged up to shout, "You stole from a friend of ours!"

"You've never stolen a horse in your life!" Red Leggings snapped as he came to stand beside Pretty On Top.

Arapooesh laid his other hand on Red Legging's shoulder. Now he clamped his hands down hard and said to them, "We do not steal from those who are our friends."

The five youths started to sputter in protest, but the chief dug his fingers into the shoulders of the two until their knees began to buckle and they howled in pain.

"But we went out to risk our lives!" Pretty On Top wailed. "We wanted to show our people we were brave enough to go on a pony raid of our own!"

And Comes Inside the Door agreed, "If the older warriors weren't going to ask us along on the raids they were leading, then Pretty On Top said we would have our own raid to show our bravery!"

"And you all were very, very brave," Arapooesh declared. "No man or woman in this camp will question your courage. From this day all will know that you five are brave enough to start on the path that will make you warriors. And . . . all of our people will know that you five are wise, that you are men of honor who will do what is right."

For a moment the youths looked at one another; then Pretty On Top asked, "You are ordering us to return the white man's horses?"

"You tell me," the chief said. "What would a true warrior do? One who did not care about his own wealth, but only about the wealth of his people?"

"But a warrior grows rich by going to war!" Crow Shouting protested.

"And one day you will go to war," Arapooesh replied. "So tell me: what would an honorable man do?"

Pretty On Top hung his head a moment. And when he spoke, the words came out as if they had a bitter taste on his tongue. "He would return the horses to the white man."

In a loud voice the chief asked, "Is that the answer for all of you?"

The other four muttered their agreement.

Clapping his hands on the two shoulders of the youngsters standing before him, Arapooesh roared with approval. "You three, go bring me the white man's animals."

Crow Shouting, Sees the Star, and Comes Inside the Door immediately turned away and pushed their way through the crowd.

As they left, the chief announced in his booming voice, "Today the heart of our people has been strengthened! Whenever a man does an honorable act, all our people are made stronger for it! And when a man does something that reflects well upon our people, we will reward his good works!"

Wildly cheering, the throng responded, singing and whooping.

Arapooesh continued. "As chief of our people, I will honor these five young men who have shown their bravery in going out to prove their courage. And I will celebrate these five because they have today shown us they are indeed men who do what is right for our people—they are men of honor!"

Again the crowd raised its collective voice of approval.

"Bird in Ground, I want you to take these five young men who exemplify Crow courage and honor to the place where my own ponies graze among our herds. Let them choose from among those animals that belong to me—all but my war pony and the horse that my wife loves so dearly."

The throng laughed while Bird in Ground said, "If you gave away your wife's horse, Arapooesh . . . you would have to find you a new place to sleep tonight!"

"These young men can choose from my ponies," Arapooesh repeated with a smile.

"Th-this is a great thing!" Pretty On Top gushed, his eyes wide with wonder. "You took back from us the white man's three horses . . . and now you replace them with three of your own!"

"No!" the chief said, shaking his head. "Not three. I said each of you will select a pony for himself. For five young men of courage and honor, I will award you each a pony!"

"F-five ponies?" Red Leggings stammered.

"This is a marvelous thing," Bird in Ground declared to Pretty On Top and Red Leggings. "This shows you how a man of honor can become a great man, how a man of honor can become a leader of our people!"

Several of the old men came up suddenly, whooping their songs of celebration just as the three youths led the trapper's horses and mule into the middle of the camp circle.

"It is good that you are here this winter!" Bird in Ground exclaimed as he turned to Bass, having to shout his words above the noisy celebration.

Scratch watched the three frightened animals approach, their nostrils flaring, eyes wide as they were led through the crowd. He said, "This will be a good winter, here among friends."

"Your guns will help make us strong come spring when the Blackfoot raid from the north again."

But the trapper wagged his head and explained, "By spring I must be far from here."

"The beaver are not good in Absaroka?" the chief said as he moved close.

"I have far to travel to the place where all the white men gather next summer," he tried to explain.

"This is the place my people choose to live," Arapooesh said. "I have never understood why you white men have to come and go, come and go great distances."

With a smile Bass explained, "Whenever I leave Absaroka, it reminds me how good your country is. So it is really not a bad thing to go and come back when I find out how poor everywhere else is."

The chief clamped his hand on the taller man's shoulder as the three youths brought up the animals and stopped before Arapooesh. He asked of Titus, "These are your horses?"

"Yes."

"Then we have settled this matter to your satisfaction?"

Stepping aside, Bass nuzzled Hannah between her eyes, rubbed his mitten along her neck, then turned back to the chief.

"Arapooesh," he said, "there is something that still troubles me."

His brow furrowing, the chief said, "Tell me so we can put this matter behind us."

Scratch thought a moment on how to express it, then said, "Your war pony, you care very much for it?"

"I care for it the way I would care for a true friend," the chief answered.

Scratch nodded. "Then you would not want to see someone strike your horse between the eyes with a tree branch?"

Arapooesh flinched but did not answer immediately. Instead, his eyes moved from Bass, to the mule the white man was petting, then shifted to stare at Pretty On Top. Without taking his harsh gaze from the youth, the chief asked, "Did you see your horse friend hit by a Crow?"

"Yes."

Continuing to glare at Pretty On Top, the chief asked, "Is that person here?"

"Yes, he is here."

Licking his lips thoughtfully, Arapooesh said, "A man of honor, a true warrior of his people—he would ask you how he could make restitution for hurting such a friend of yours. Do you find any fault with my words . . . Pretty On Top?"

"No," the youth answered in a voice almost too quiet to hear as the crowd fell hushed. When he took his eyes off the ground, he looked at the trapper. "How can I make this up to you for hurting this half horse?"

Titus wasn't sure just how a man could ever truly make amends for injuring something so important as another man's friend, be it a trapping partner, or . . . his mule. Wasn't Hannah a true partner? Hadn't she proved herself to be every bit as faithful, loyal, and steadfast to him as any person had ever been? Wasn't she even more of a friend to him than many people had been throughout the years?

"I do not know," he eventually admitted, wagging his head as he looked into the face of Pretty On Top. Then—something struck him of a sudden. "Perhaps for this young warrior to tell me he knows that my animals are my truest friends . . . and that I would do anything to see that my friends are not hurt."

Contrite, the youth dropped his eyes. "I am truly sorry."

"I—I am sorry too," chimed in Red Leggings.

Arapooesh turned to the trapper. "No, this cannot be enough to pay you for the cruelty to your animal—for the hurt to your friend."

But Bass surprised them, saying, "Yes—their apology is enough, Arapooesh." He watched the shock strike all the faces around him. Some of the bystanders even clamped hands over their mouths in amazement.

Arapooesh asked, "Is this true what you are saying?"

"Pretty On Top . . . I think he has grown many years this morning. He is older beyond his winters now for it. I believe he is already a true Crow warrior: a man of honor and courage. So I will consider this matter settled, Arapooesh . . . if Pretty On Top will tell me . . . that he will be a true friend to me."

Many of the old, wrinkled, scarred, and weathered warriors in the crowd yelped and cried out with shrill songs of celebration, raising their thin, reedy voices to the snowy sky overhead.

"Pretty On Top?" the chief turned to ask. "You have heard the white man—"

"I will be honored to be this white man's friend," the youth interrupted in a flurry, his lips quivering, betraying the emotions he fought to hide.

Pretty On Top stepped away from Arapooesh, stopping in front of the trapper and his mule where the youngster placed his right fist over his heart while he held his left arm out to the white man.

Bass immediately laid his right fist over his heart and held out his left arm. They gripped fiercely and looked one another in the eye.

"You are my friend, Pretty On Top?"

"I am your friend," the youth replied. "Until I die, your friends are my friends."

Bass nodded, feeling the mist in his eyes. "And your enemies . . . they are my enemies."

As the throng burst into cheers, Arapooesh stepped up and slapped them both on the back. "We will celebrate tonight! A feast! A feast! For a true friend has returned to visit!"

Turning to Bass, the chief leaned close to say in the white man's ear, "It makes my heart happy to hear that you will spend your winter among us . . . the better for me to come to know this stranger who has proved to be a man of dignity and honor himself . . . a man who is strong enough, brave enough, that he dares to be both merciful and generous too."

He squinted into the light of that early-summer sun.

Dragging the wide-brimmed hat off his head, Scratch tugged on a wide corner of the black silk bandanna he had tied around his neck, swiping his face with it. Suddenly recalling how so simple a touch had caused his flesh so much agony last winter.

Up ahead at the far side of the valley, he studied that thin line of dust rising against the distant hills. And wondered if they might be Indians. A war party of Bannock. Maybeso a small band of Snake on their way to rendezvous too.

Turning to glance over his shoulder in worry, Bass found he hadn't limned himself against the pale sky, placing him and the animals right along the horizon so that he stuck out in plain view. No, he always did his best to ride somewhere on down the slope some so that he would not be spotted by any distant pair of roving eyes. He always crossed a ridge or divide through some saddle or swale low enough so that he couldn't be spied right against the sky.

He was thirsty. His mouth gone pasty. Through the long morning the animals had dampened the leather harness, soaking it with their sweat.

Instead of slapping the hat back down on his head, he laid it atop the large saucer-shaped horn at the front of the Spanish saddle and grabbed for the bottom of the buckskin war shirt. He tugged it up, over his head, and off both arms, then turned and lashed it to the back of the saddle there with his capote. At this season it was still cold enough early in the morning on this high desert west of the southern pass that a man started out his day shivering, later went to sweating as the sun climbed high, then ended his day shivering all over again as he started his fire, ready to climb into his sleeping robes.

The cloth shirt he had bought from Bill Williams more than a year ago had faded with so many washings along the banks of streams, vigorously rubbing the material with sand scooped from the creekbed, beating it against the rocks. No more damned nits, he had vowed. Never again.

Which made him remember how he and McAfferty had stripped off all their clothing at one campsite south along the Heely in Apache country, plopping their cloth and leather garments down upon a series of huge anthills, where they sat out the day completely naked but for their hats and moccasins, content to watch the huge red creatures swarm over the tiny lice that had burrowed into every seam of their clothing.

He had vowed he'd never again travel with any man who was infested with graybacks. After all, it was only a matter of time before the lice from one host migrated on over to Titus Bass. No more damned nits.

Those distant horsemen beneath the thin cloud of dust on the horizon were traveling from north to south. As he sat there studying their ragged line of movement, Scratch could see that they were riding for the same spot off to the southwest where he himself was headed. He squinted into the high, bright light. Just across that low range of hills to the west of him, down there the Big Sandy dumped itself into the Green, and those emerald-tinged waters contin-ued their tumble south to the Colorado.

Glancing back up at the sun as if to curse its blinding glare, he pulled his hat back over the faded blue bandanna of silk, then rocked his horse into motion, tugging on the long lead rope that played back to Hannah's neck. In turn she tugged on the lead rope running back to the packhorse. What with those unexpected travelers, it was better for him to cross this upper dogleg of the valley and scoot west a bit more before he plunged on south. Keep as much distance as he could between him and those riders. Maybe he would try catching up come later in the afternoon, drawing close enough to them by the time the strangers went into camp that he could slip up on them and from a safe distance see if they might be foe or friend.

For a child out here on his lonesome, the chances were far greater that he would run onto a foe than he would bump into a friend.

Friend.

How good the word sounded. And how it made his already heavy heart ache with more longing.

Friends to rendezvous with, tell tall stories to, companions to regale with his windies and whoppers and outright bald-face balderdash. Friends who didn't mind when he grew thick-tongued and stumble-lipped as he drank deep to the bottom of his cups and finally threw up or passed out. One good, gut-busting revel a year—every man was due at least that. Jehoshaphat, but to lay eyes on friends he hadn't seen for a full year?

That was cause enough to celebrate, to drink until he got sick and blacked out then and there in the dirt, among the sage and the saddles and the sand thorns.

Titus hadn't seen Jack and Caleb and all the others since last summer after Sublette headed east and those two big company brigades set off for their fall hunt.

Why, he hadn't seen a white face since late last autumn when he had bumped into that big outfit run by Bridger and Fitzpatrick up in Crow country. They had already punched their way into and back through Blackfoot territory, and were headed east to winter up over toward the Powder River, when Scratch spotted the smokes of all their fires and cautiously rode off the hills to investigate. It was good to see Bridger again, along with some of the others too, and they had themselves a good evening of it, sharing stories and swapping lies the way they did.

The young booshway had explained how his bunch had even run across Asa up there north of the Three Forks country.

"We was partners."

"Didn't know you ever rode with him," Bridger had admitted.

"For a time we did. He say what he was doing up there all by hisself? How he was getting along?"

Fitzpatrick had wagged his head. "Had him a few pelts on them packhorses of his—but it didn't seem to me he was up there to trap, that for certain. Man like him gotta be crazed to figger he can last out the Blackfeet much longer up that way all on his lonesome."

"Maybe he's eager to get his hair raised," Bridger added.

Bass had stared at the fire, thinking back on things gone wrong between two men, and said, "I don't figger I'll ever see that white-head nigger again."

Brushing one flat palm across the other quickly, Bridger said morosely, "That's a nigger what's good as dead awready, Scratch."

Aw, Asa, he thought now as he dropped down into the bottom below the narrow saddle, feeling the grass brush the bottoms of his moccasins. Why, Asa? Why?

He halted at midday just on the other side of that low saddle, loosened cinches, and let the three critters graze in the lush spring growth as he chewed at some of the meat he had cooked over last night's fire before moving on to sleep a few miles from where he had supped. Just out of caution, in new country, a man ate one place, made a cold camp, and slept out the night in another. As he ate, he watched that distant line of dust rise against the glorious summer blue painted across the canvas above the western hills.

Close enough now to calculate there couldn't be more than twenty riders, maybe two dozen at most.

Not likely to be a small band of Snake traipsing south for the white man's rendezvous in Willow Valley. Might so be some damned Bannock. He knew they was the sort to skedaddle if the odds wasn't real long in their favor, the sort what laid into any white men if the red niggers could raise some horses and plunder, maybe even some scalps if their medicine was right that day. Goddamn them Bannocks.

Not good Injuns like them Crow.

They was the sort to take a man in, make him welcome, put him up in one lodge or the other till the chief's two sisters sewed together a buffalo-hide shelter something on the order of a white man's lean-to. A half-domed affair with a big flap that covered the wide entrance, which he could tie up during the day or lash down for protection from the cold at night, or when a new snowstorm came slashing through the valley. He'd barely gotten used to the dwelling last winter when it came time for the village to move a few miles upstream away from the Yellowstone. The camp had begun to stink something awful from all the gut-piles, rotting meat, and human offal piling up back in the trees. Maybe as much as a half-dozen times Arapooesh's band would move each winter, finding themselves another place that offered open water, plenty of firewood and grass for their pony herds, along with some protection against the possibility of attack.

As winter deepened, it seemed the Crow grew more relaxed—less concerned about their most fearsome enemy. Too damned cold now, the snow drifted too deep for the Blackfoot to try anything as foolish as a major assault on a village in the heart of Absaroka—home of the Crow.

It hadn't been long before Scratch had felt a part of them too. Much more a part of them than he had years back when he had come to the Bighorn country with Silas, Billy, and Bud. Perhaps he had felt set apart from the tribe because the three of them had not tried in the least to fit in with their winter hosts. Just as they had refused to do with the Ute. Instead, the trio of white men had stayed apart, taking all that they needed from the Crow and doing little to repay in kind all that had been given them with such generous hospitality. Whether it was food, or a woman offered to warm their robes, or some shelter from the raging winter blizzards—Silas and the others had considered themselves above their hosts, remaining as aloof as those company brigades traveling through one tribe's territory or another.

But for a lone man eager to learn all the more about these attractive pale-brown people, the past winter in Absaroka with Bird in Ground and Pretty On Top was all that he had hoped it would be. And from that first night's feasting and celebration, it seemed that old Arapooesh took to the white man, right off.

"Rotten . . . Belly?" he had repeated the words spoken to him by Bird in Ground.

The man-woman rubbed his stomach with a flat hand, bending over slightly and groaning as if he were sick. "Rotten Belly, yes."

"That's Arapooesh's name?"

Indeed, it was how the venerable chief was known among the two divisions who roamed Absaroka. Recently he had brought his wife and family back to live with her band of the Apsaalooke after spending many years among his River Band. And with the regrettable death of Big Hair, his wife's people turned to the respected warrior and tribal counselor to lead them into the coming winters.

After recouping his strength in the Crow village for several days, Bass had journeyed east to retrieve the trade goods and supplies he had abandoned when he'd set out on the trail of the horse thieves—just one day shy of reaching his cache. After taking two days to bury the last of his pelts in that black hole, he loaded up the rest of what he needed for the winter on Hannah's back and turned about for Rotten Belly's camp. He made it back just as a howling blizzard raked the land. That first night back he slept in Bird in Ground's lodge, inviting the chief and some of the old warriors, along with Pretty On Top and other youngsters, to a giveaway dinner.

Oh, the way those Crow eyes sparkled as he passed around small gifts of coffee and sugar, some powder and brass tacks, fingerings and bracelets, hanks of ribbon and beads! The men clucked and laughed—for it had been a long, long time since any of them had seen such riches as these!

"Do you see, Pretty On Top?" Bird in Ground playfully chided the young man. "See what a man receives in return when he gives away his friendship to a stranger?"

Later on as that winter grew old, as the wind keened and twisted through the Yellowstone Valley, the chief gathered his friends and advisers in his lodge for a red-stick feast. From the pot for this traditional Crow celebration, the invited guests all plucked tender pieces of elk. Afterward they scraped the greasy marrow from bones they pulled from the coals and cracked upon the rocks ringing the fire pit. Then they smoked and related their coups.

When it came time for Bass to count his own exploits sitting there at Rotten Belly's left hand, he enthralled them into the deep hours with his tales, stripping off his shirt and showing them those scars earned at the hands of the Blackfoot, being hunted down by the Apache far to the southwest of Absaroka, fighting the Mexican soldiers and fierce Comanche raiders in that land of warm waters, as well as his two struggles with the grizzly—letting them see the scars of his few seasons among the mountains, how the wilderness had marked his whipcord-lean white body.

After the sixteen men nodded and murmured in approbation that he still lived, Arapooesh had refilled his pipe and sent it around the circle another time. And when it reached the chief at the end of its circuit, Rotten Belly solemnly proposed to give a name to the man who had come to his people earlier that winter—on foot and wearing the fur of a coyote wrapped around his head so that only the white man's eyes and cheeks showed above his beard and mustache, those frosted whiskers similar in color to the gray pelt of that coyote Scratch had worn for winters beyond count already.

"So I give my white friend a name I will call him from this night onward," Arapooesh declared. *"Pote Ani.* Because when he came to us, this man seemed to have the head of a coyote on his shoulders. But more than that, my new friend has the cunning of the coyote that allows him to survive both the wolf and the winter. Because the coyote is an animal faithful to its own, steadfast to its friends . . . because this white man is loyal to my people—I pledge I will always remain loyal to him."

The rest of those gathered in the lodge had cheered with approval, slapping their thighs, banging their tin cups on the rocks ringing the fire.

Then Arapooesh had continued. "So, my friends—it is with a full and happy heart that I take this white man as my brother. From this night he will be known among our people as *Pote Ani.* And he will be my brother."

It never failed to bring a smile to his heart, warming him, every time he thought about his dear friend, Rotten Belly. Remembering how the chief and Bird in Ground and even young Pretty On Top had come to mean so much to him through those winter moons. The sort of men who formed a bulwark against the storms in a man's life.

Like Jack Hatcher, Caleb Wood, and the others.

Men red and white, men for all the seasons of his life.

As the ice on the Yellowstone had begun to crack and shatter, opening the river early that spring, he had taken his leave as Rotten Belly's band started upriver to the south, while he pointed his nose down the valley to the east. Just past the big rock, he had crossed to the north bank of the Yellowstone and located the patch of ground where he had dug his cache last autumn, the frozen earth lying beneath a snowdrift he had to shovel aside.

As he pried back the thick sod lid to the cache's neck, Scratch had suddenly remembered what he hadn't during that winter in Absaroka—he had turned thirty-seven!

Although there had been times during his winter with the Crow that he had wondered on Christmas and remembered Taos during the Nativity festival, thinking too how his own birthday came only a week after that celebration . . . Bass hadn't given all that much thought to adding another ring to his years.

It had simply been too wonderful a winter in the land of the Crow: new friends, plenty of protection from the wind and the cold among a people who from time to time provided their guest with one woman or another to relieve the trapper's pent-up hungers.

"Who's been sending me these women who come to my lodge?" he had asked Bird in Ground one cold day as they were out gathering deadfall for their fires.

The strange man of the Apsaalooke stood and looked squarely at Bass. "Since you do not want me for your wife, I decided that you must satisfy your appetites with the women of our tribe."

"Believe me when I say, if I ever wanted to settle down with a man-woman among your people for the rest of my winters, I would choose you, Bird in Ground."

"I am afraid I will never have a husband," the Crow sighed. "Look around. There aren't any others now who are like me—touched by this same spirit medicine. Perhaps I can find some way to show the power of my medicine, to prove to other young men of our tribe that I would make them a good wife."

"It is not hard for any man to see that you would make a good wife."

The man-woman smiled in that gentle way of his. "I realize you will never be my husband. But you will always stay one of those strong in my heart."

"And you will always stay one of those strong in my heart too."

Had to be Bannock under that distant dust cloud. Damn. They sure weren't good folks like the Crow.

Bannock.

Certain that's what they were, Bass tarried a while longer after finishing his cold meat before retightening cinches and pushing on into the afternoon. He'd do all he could to give the Bannock war party a wide berth.

Not long after the saffron orb had slinked from the summer sky, Scratch noticed how that smudge of dust to the south had faded. The riders must have put in for camp up there a ways in the valley of Black's Fork. And from there he calculated it wasn't more than nine, ten days at the most before he'd finally reach the inner-mountain valley where Sublette promised to meet the company brigades for July.

Before long he grew wary, figuring he had dogged the war party's back-trail close enough and found himself a place where he tied off the animals, letting them graze while he set off on foot along the east side of the valley. Watching to the southwest as the shadows lengthened, sticking his nose in the wind for firesmoke, keeping his eyes moving from horizon to horizon. That bunch might have hunters out, after all. Making meat for supper. It wouldn't pay to have a run-in with one or two of the bastards, then find himself tracked by the rest as they tried to run him down.

Goddamned Bannocks. Who the hell did they think they was, anyway? He'd been run down by the best of 'em—riding day and night with the Apache breathing down on his ass. No way these here Bannocks ever come close to measuring up to Apache.

He stopped there in the shadows of the man-sized willow that bordered the coulee and sniffed again. Woodsmoke.

His mouth went dry.

That weren't no summer thunderstorm grass fire. No, that was a smell altogether different. This was woodsmoke. Even had the smell of broiling meat braided around the edges of that stronger scent.

And that made his dry mouth water.

Then Bass remembered that he was slipping up on some thieving red bastards, scolding himself that he'd better forget his feed bag for now.

After checking the priming in both the rifle and pistol for the fifth or sixth time, Titus angled down the side of the coulee toward the river valley, hanging with the cover offered him by the thick, leafy brush.

Less than a half hour later, he stopped suddenly—his nose greeted by horse sweat wafted on that cooling breeze nuzzling its way down the river-bank. Another twenty yards and . . . he heard them.

Parting the willow with the rifle's muzzle, Titus spotted the horses. Son of a bitch if that wasn't a white man's tack on that piebald! Not no braided buffalo-hair hackamore.

And that roan! Hell if he hadn't seen it before!

One of the horses on the far side of the bunch whinnied low as a figure stepped out of the tree shadows and headed for the piebald. Scratch's heart stopped then and there in his chest—

"Rufus Graham!"

The figure wheeled at the call of his name, yanking on the pistol he had stuffed into the wide, colorful sash at his waist.

"Don't shoot me, Rufus!"

As Bass rose to his feet there in the thick willow, he watched the horses part, listened to the ground reverberate with running feet. At the far side of the clearing where a wary Rufus Graham stood frozen, there suddenly appeared the other five.

Titus didn't know when their ugly, hairy faces had ever looked prettier!

"Eegod, boys!" Jack Hatcher yelped as he stepped closer, a wide slash of a grin splitting the lower half of his bearded face. "If it ain't Titus Bass his own self . . . riz right up from the dead!"

TWENTY-FIVE

The six of them had near pounded him to black-and-blue there in that little clearing as the horses snorted around them.

"Lookee here, boys!" Hatcher roared as he grabbed hold of the front of Bass's shirt—cocking his head this way, then that, looking at Scratch from different angles. "If this nigger ain't graying up like a ol' barn owl!"

"Ain't he now!" Solomon agreed, yanking the wide-brimmed hat off Scratch's head. He held up that narrow braid of hair hanging there in front of Bass's left ear.

Titus nabbed it away from Fish, his eyes crossing as he focused on it. "Gray?"

"See what I tol't you!" Elbridge roared. "Hell, Jack—Titus Bass rode with Asa McAfferty too long awready!"

Caleb asked, "You mean he's getting white-headed like that ol' preacher?"

"My hair ain't white!" he protested.

Jack rocked back on his heels, grinning like a house cat put out to the barn where all the mice are at play. "Sure are getting ol't, Scratch. Maybeso ye ain't had nothing scare yer hair to white . . . but this here's certain sign ye're getting ol't!"

Bass lunged for him suddenly, sweeping low beneath

Hatcher's right arm to hoist the surprised man onto his shoulders as he straightened, raising Jack right off the ground and flipping him right on across his back so that Hatcher flopped into the waist-high grass. The other five roared, holding their bellies as they guffawed at the stunned Hatcher, some pounding their knees, bent over in a laughing fit.

"Tell me now just how ol't I am, Jack Hatcher!" Scratch bellowed like a wounded bull, standing over the man sprawled on the ground, balling his fists on his hips, just daring Hatcher to get back to his feet again.

"Ol't enough ye ought'n know better!" and Jack swung out with his leg, catching Bass at the ankles, sweeping Scratch's feet cleanly off the ground, toppling him right beside Hatcher. "Damn, if it ain't good to see ye!" Jack bawled, slugging a fist into Scratch's shoulder.

"We had you figgered for gone under!" Rufus declared as he dropped to his knee nearby.

Isaac lunged up, saying, "You see'd hair or hide of McAfferty?"

"Naw," Scratch answered as he slowly got to his feet, dusting off his leggings. "Heard of him—from Bridger's bunch. Said they saw him last fall."

"Up to Three Forks?" Solomon asked.

"On north of there a good ways Asa run onto 'em."

Hatcher whistled low. "That's hair-liftin' country, ever there was one."

"Told us he was going there," Caleb explained.

"I don't figger him to make it to Willow Valley," Isaac said.

"Hard for a man to come through a hull winter and spring that far into Blackfoot country," Hatcher stated. "Damn, but I'm glad to see *you* again, Scratch."

He looked round at those six faces. "It's damned good to lay these ol' eyes on you boys too."

"Bet you've got some lies to tell, don'cha?" Elbridge asked.

"Me?" he replied with mock indignation. "Ever'thing I'm gonna tell you fellers tonight at the fire gonna be the God's truth."

"You hear that, Jack?" Caleb roared.

"Let's see: I wrassled with ol' Ephraim . . . aw, hell—I awready told you boys about that," Scratch grumped. "And I damn near got killed by some greaser soldiers—"

"You and McAfferty done tol't us about that too," Rufus interrupted.

So Hatcher lazily looped an arm over Bass's shoulder. "Just what the hell you done with yourself since we saw you last summer over on the Wind River?"

After fetching up his animals and turning them out to graze with those of Hatcher's bunch, Scratch told them about his journey far north to the Judith, where he returned to the site of his bear mauling, regaling them with the story of his long walk to track the Crow horse thieves, finishing with his spring trapping on some tributaries of the Bighorn, his stop to soak aching bones at the tar springs before pushing on to the Wind River, climbing over South Pass to make his way to the Sandy—where he first spotted their dust cloud.

"You ain't a very cautious bunch," Bass told them, wagging his head with mock criticism.

"Just what the hell ye mean?" Hatcher growled. "We knowed we didn't have to be careful when it was only a bone-headed horse's ass named Titus Bass following us!"

"You owe me a drink for smearing my name in such a way, Jack Hatcher," he grumbled, and held his cup up for more coffee as Rufus brought the pot around the fire. "And I don't mean none of your bad coffee neither."

"Gladly, Titus Bass! We'll all have us more'n one round of Billy Sublette's whiskey when we reach Willow Valley!"

But they wouldn't drink any whiskey that year. And the mountain men sure as hell wouldn't have their rendezvous hurraw in the Willow Valley either.*

As it turned out, after crossing to the west bank of the Green the next morning and setting out for the day, they ran onto a small group of free trappers heading east.

"Where you bound?" their leader asked as Bass and Hatcher's bunch hailed the strangers, and both groups came to a noisy halt.

"For ronnyvoo in Willow Valley!" Jack cried exuberantly. "Ain'cha going?"

"Not to be no ronnyvoo in the Willow," their leader replied. "We was coming south from the lower Snake country where we trapped this past spring."

"Near Sweet Lake, we was," interrupted another of the strangers.

The first man continued, "When we come across some of Bridger's men, he sent out to pass the word."

"Pass what word?" Caleb demanded.

"Rocky Mountain Fur wants all free men to meet 'em on the Green, up near what they call Horse Creek."

"Horse Creek, no shit?" Hatcher echoed.

Pointing his arm north, the leader explained, "A ways yonder, up the Green."

---

* Near present-day Cove, Utah. Although one of the contemporary sources intimates that Jim Bridger, Milt Sublette, and Henry Fraeb met with their combined brigades in what is today called Cache Valley, what the mountain men of the era called Willow Valley, the majority of fur-trade historians appear to agree that the preponderance of the remaining contemporary sources show conclusively that the Rocky Mountain Fur Company outfits actually united on the Green River that July of 1831.

And with that, Scratch shuddered. "Heard that's damned cold country come winter."

"Heard that myself," the leader replied, looking over the rest of Hatcher's free men. "You care to throw in with us for the trip to ronnyvoo?"

Quickly Jack turned to the rest, seeing them nod. He looked back to the stranger. "Name's Hatcher," and he held out his hand as he continued. "I figger we might as well all ride up the Green together."

As each of the free trapper bands reached the growing encampment nestled down in the fertile, grassy bottoms along the Green near the mouth of Horse Creek, one or another of the company booshways made a point to come over to explain this change of site.

"Fitz didn't get off for St. Lou early as we'd planned for him to," Bridger declared to the group who rode in with Hatcher. "What with Willow Valley being a far piece to the west, me and the partners figgered to move ronnyvoo some to the east so Fitz and Billy Sublette could reach us quicker when they come out from St. Lou."

Titus asked, "What's ronnyvoo got to do with Fitzpatrick making it back to St. Louie?"

Bridger cleared his throat. "When we bought out Smith, Jackson, and Sublette last year, we promised 'em we'd have a man back to St. Lou arranging for supplies afore March each spring, when a mule train's got to make its start west. Just like it was when Sublette hisself went back. Trouble was, we didn't get Fitz away from the mouth of the Powder this spring as soon as we wanted to."

Bass felt concern taking root within him. "Jim, you don't figger there won't be no trader this year, do you?"

The younger booshway shook his head and smiled. "Fitz ain't the sort to cache hisself, boys. He'll make it back just fine. 'Sides—Smith, Jackson, and Sublette are savvy fellers: they know we're all needing supplies to make out the next year."

"That's right," Titus worked to convince himself. "Sublette and the rest gotta know every man out here needs provisions, year in, year out."

Jack bellowed like a bull with its bangers caught on cat-claw brush, "We'll damn well go under we don't get powder and lead—"

"Whiskey and tobacco!" Rufus whimpered.

Bass agreed and echoed, "Whiskey and tobacco, some coffee and sugar too. Why, hell—how's a man to winter up 'thout the trader's supplies less'n he's got a band of friendlies to hunker in with, or he points his nose south for the greaser diggings?"

Bridger nodded, shoving his floppy felt hat back onto his head. "I know how you feel, boys. Just 'member: we all suffer the same in this. Seems we just have to wait together and keep our eyes peeled for Broken Hand."

They did keep their eyes locked on the eastern horizon for Tom Fitzpatrick, William Sublette, and those wagons every man was sure the trader was bound to bring back for a second trip to the mountains. Day, after day, after day they kept up their vigil . . . while July grew old and August loomed close.

Even the unflappably gruff Henry Fraeb finally grew concerned enough to seek out the services of an aging shaman traveling with a small band of Crow who had come in to trade with the white men.

"Frapp said he told the ol' boy he'd give him some tobacco and coffee if he'd do his medicine and figger out what happened to Fitz. He's figgering Broken Hand went under—never made it back to St. Louie," Scratch explained to the others late one afternoon when he returned to the spot where he was camped with Hatcher's men.

"That medicine man come up with a answer for us?" Isaac asked.

Bass nodded as he settled at the fire. "The ol' goat was at it for more'n a day. Just a while back he come to Frapp and told 'em all that Fitz ain't dead—"

"That's some plumb fine news!" Caleb hooted, stomping a foot.

Jack shushed the sudden clatter and noise, "But if he ain't dead, where's he? And where's the whiskey?"

"That old Crow says Fitzpatrick ain't gone under, but he's on the wrong trail."

"On the wrong trail!" Rufus squeaked.

"Hell—we ain't gonna get no whiskey now!" Elbridge groaned as he slapped his forehead and turned away with utter disgust.

Hatcher flapped his hands again for quiet. "What's that mean: wrong trail?"

"Ain't no one knows," Scratch answered with a shrug. "So Frapp's going out in the morning to look for Fitz."

Biting on his lower lip, Solomon advised, "There ain't a snowball's chance in hell Frapp gonna find Fitz out there to the east."

"Not in time for us to have a ronnyvoo!" Graham complained.

"Shuddup, goddammit!" Hatcher demanded again. "To hell with ronnyvoo!"

Caleb leaped to his feet, hulking over Hatcher, bristling like a spit-on hen. "To hell with ronnyvoo?"

Jack glared up at his friend. "Damn right. We got bigger problems, boys." He waited a minute as Wood turned back to the group and the others settled around the fire to hear what their leader had to say. "For a man to miss ronnyvoo one's thing . . . but for a man to figger him out a way to get through the winter in Injun country 'thout supplies—that's the real fly in this nigger's ointment."

"Jack's right," Bass replied. "Like I said when we come in and Bridger told us the trader wasn't here yet—man's got to make one of two choices."

As Hatcher looked them over, the rest stared into the fire as afternoon's shadows grew longer. "So what's it gonna be, fellers?"

Elbridge drew himself up and jutted out his proud chin. "Taos. There we'll find Workman's lightning and Mex gals."

"What 'bout them soldiers?" Graham worried.

"That is a problem," Hatcher agreed thoughtfully.

Scratch grumbled, "Damn, but me and Asa really boogered things good down there, didn't we?"

"Weren't none of yer fault," Jack scolded. "Any one of us done the same if we was jumped by a greaser soldier."

" 'Specially when you was jumped same time you was crawling the hump of some Mex whore!" Rufus roared.

"Maybeso we can slip into Workman's place one night," Solomon suggested, holding his hands up for quiet. "Ask him about the lay of the land with the governor's men."

"If things don't look good," Bass continued, "you can skedaddle back north."

"We?" Jack chimed in. "You mean ye ain't gonna come to Taos with us for the winter?"

Scratch shook his head and snorted. "Ain't gonna be healthy for this child down there for a couple winters yet."

"So if we care to slip on down to Taos for the winter and supply-up," Hatcher commented as he turned on Bass, "what ye gonna do for yer own self?"

For long moments he stared at the fire, poking a long stick into the flames. When he brought out the fiery end of that dry limb and peered at it, Scratch said, "I got friends back in Crow country. I'll winter up there."

"You'll be awright 'thout no supplies?"

"Hell, yes," Titus answered. "Might run low on ball and powder afore next summer . . . but I'll get by. 'Sides, fellers—just think what Sublette's gonna have to pay us next summer for beaver!"

"Whoooeee!" Caleb cheered.

Isaac said, "And ain't there gonna be a heap of it too come next year?"

"When you was over visiting Bridger," Jack inquired, turning to Bass, "you hear any word from the company booshways on where they'll join up for next ronnyvoo?"

"Heard talk about Pierre's Hole," Bass replied. "But I don't figger they've decided hard on it."

That ended up being the best any of those few hundred men gathered on the Green could do—company trapper or free man: nothing more than talk about and dream on next summer, next rendezvous, next time they'd see Billy Sublette's trade caravan coming in. But with the way a man planned for, anticipated, and downright lusted after each annual gathering for a whole year . . . it was all he could do to calmly accept that there would be another autumn, another winter, and another spring of wading knee-deep in icy mountain streams before he would trade some of his furs in for whiskey, for enough foofaraw to get him laid with a bright-eyed squaw gal.

It was purely painful there in the valley of the upper Green after Henry Fraeb pulled out to look for partner Fitzpatrick as each new day of August came and went.

When Tom Fitzpatrick did not show up in St. Louis by the agreed-upon date, the partners of Smith, Jackson, and Sublette proceeded with their initial plans of entering the Santa Fe trade. By the time the eastbound Fitzpatrick reached the settlement of Independence, he learned that the three partners had already come through with a caravan bound not for the mountains, but for Mexico. There was little other choice but to gallop after the wagon train. Somewhere in that hot, waterless country of what is today southwestern Kansas, he caught up to the three partners. They told Fitzpatrick he would have to join them all the way to Taos, where they would outfit him with supplies for the Rocky Mountain Fur Company.

By then the caravan had entered the most dangerous and deadly water scrape on the Santa Fe Trail. Far out ahead of the wagons, searching for water in any of the few sandy, dry river bottoms, Jedediah Smith was confronted by some Comanche buffalo hunters. Although his life oozed out on the end of a deadly fourteen-foot buffalo lance, his body was never found.

Even with Smith missing, Jackson and Sublette proceeded on to Taos, where they disbanded their partnership after turning over some six thousand dollars in supplies to Fitzpatrick. While Jackson headed west to California and his own fortunes, Sublette turned back for St. Louis to begin gathering finances and goods for his 1832 trading venture to the mountains.

Leaving Tom Fitzpatrick to load up what little he had been given on the backs of the mules he purchased in Taos, he hired some extra hands eager to go north into the Rockies, and made for the mountains—already more than a month late and with little hope of finding the company brigades and the free men still gathered, still awaiting his arrival.

Without any coffee and not so much as a twist of tobacco. And whiskey? Only in a man's dreams was there any whiskey! It was shaping up to be another long, dry year.

What few bands of friendly Flathead and Shoshone showed up didn't hang around long. With summer growing old, it would soon be a time for making winter meat.

Bass and the rest watched the lodgeskins come down, seeing the women tie the poles together into travois, watched the dust trails disappear against the horizon. Then the first of the free men began to pack up their plews and set off.

"Bridger offered any of us to throw in and travel with the company brigades to their fall hunt," Solomon declared late one morning as he returned to Hatcher's camp.

"What the hell we do that for?" Caleb demanded.

Fish shrugged. "He says Frapp's gonna find Fitzpatrick. And when he does, Fitz is gonna have supplies for Rocky Mountain Fur. Only way any free man's gonna get supplies is he's gonna have to be hanging close to a company brigade."

"The hell with 'em," Rufus griped.

Elbridge asked, "We'll go to Taos, right, Jack?"

"We're gonna drown that goddamned Sublette in beaver next summer," Hatcher declared.

"Pierre's Hole gonna be ass-deep in beaver, that's certain!" Bass exclaimed.

That evening Jack suggested his bunch pull out come morning. He cupped a hand at his ear and grinned in the fire's light. "I hear them beaver calling to me from the Bayou."

Isaac giggled and squeaked in a high voice, "Jack? Jack Hatcher? Why don't you come catch me in your trap, Jack Hatcher?"

The rest guffawed and went back to tearing hunks off their antelope steaks using only their fingers and knives, wiping grease on their long hair to give it the same sheen a warrior gave his long braids with bear oil.

A sudden gust of wind slashed through their camp that twilight just then, scattering tiny coals like a swarm of fireflies dipping and swirling through camp until they snuffed themselves out.

In that surprising silence Scratch quietly said, "You fellas don't s'pose . . . that Asa's gone under, do you?"

Jack cleared his throat, tonguing the chunk of meat to the side of his mouth. "He ain't showed up a'tall, has he?"

Bass looked around at the others, eager perhaps to find something in their faces to hang his faint hope upon. "Maybe he went on down to Willow Valley, boys—and didn't get no word about ronnyvoo getting moved over here on the Green."

Caleb shook his head, absently replying, "I don't figger Asa McAfferty for the kind to sit there in Willow Valley all by hisself for long. Most likely he's gone and got hisself—"

But Wood was suddenly interrupted by a stern glare from Hatcher. Nothing was spoken—only that gaze of disapproval.

Wood coughed, then corrected himself, "What I mean to say is . . . maybe he's gone off on his own like he allays does. Somewheres."

Bass wiped his bloody knife across the front of his right legging, long ago grown black beneath rubbings of old grease. With a thickened voice he said, "S'pose you're right, Caleb. Asa's allays been a contrary cuss."

"Asa's set to do what's on his mind and his mind alone," Jack agreed.

"Man decides to go to Blackfoot country," Bass continued, attempting to console himself, "them what he leaves behind shouldn't go counting on seeing that nigger again. 'Less they're plain, ignernt-headed fools."

"He knowed what he was doing," Caleb explained apologetically. "Wasn't no way you was gonna keep him from where he was bound to go."

Solomon declared, "When Asa said God was telling him to go to Blackfoot country, I knowed there was no use in me wasting my breath telling him not to."

"We all know of fellers what don't come in to ronnyvoo each year," Jack said sadly. "But I'm damned happy to see your face here with us again, Titus Bass."

He looked up through his swimming eyes, a knot of sour sentiment clogging his throat, making it hard for him to speak. Eventually, he said, "I figger that's what Asa's done: picked him his way to die."

"About the most important thing a man can do in his life," Hatcher agreed.

" 'Cept for choosing how he's gonna *live* his life," Scratch replied, "I s'pose choosing the way he's gonna die runs close."

Elbridge exclaimed, "You said yourself, Scratch—that Asa knowed there was Bridger's brigade he could hang close to if'n he'd wanted to be sure he was safer."

Wagging his head, Bass disagreed. "That wasn't Asa's way. He damned well wouldn't have stayed anywhere near no company men. Naw, Asa had him something real serious stuck in his craw what made him go up there all brassy and bold, marching into Blackfoot country all on his lonesome."

"So if McAfferty chose him this way to die," Isaac commented, "then it's for the rest of us to drink us a toast to him, and go on with our own living."

"But we ain't got no whiskey to toast him!" Rufus bellowed.

"Then we'll drain our cups for him come next summer in Pierre's Hole!" Caleb reminded them.

"Yep," Bass agreed hauntingly. "We'll just have to wait another year till we meet again in Pierre's Hole . . . till we can drink to Asa's ghost."

Looking back on things now as another winter hinted it was about to squeeze its grip down upon this land, Scratch realized how a man could get things wrinkled but good on him. How the perfectly good rope of his life could begin at times to unravel into wild strands. But a man always had a choice to go on, or go back.

And Titus Bass had never been one to go back.

As much as there were some folks who had come into his life, taught him something, then were gone . . . he most missed those few who had refused to ask more than they gave back to life: folks like Ebenezer Zane and his boatmen, Ol' Gut Washburn, Mad Jack Hatcher, and even Asa McAfferty in his own way—although Scratch was certain he still had to sort out the why and wherefore of the white-head.

And included with the rest of those who gave back to life in equal measure was the Crow man-woman named Bird in Ground.

But Bird in Ground was dead.

Perhaps even worse to accept was that it had happened early in the fall, when Titus had been trapping over east on the Tongue. No more would he have Bird in Ground to tutor him. No more would Scratch have the man's smile and his patience and his hearty laugh. No more would he have that good friend.

Bird in Ground had taught him just how important it was to laugh at what scared him most. No fear could ever be near as great after a man laughed at it. How the Indian had taught him that special quality of laughter in the face of a terrible, immobilizing fear.

What sort of man was it who openly set himself apart from other men— declaring that he would be a warrior unlike any other warriors, that he was a man-woman who would do some man things, and some woman things too? How much courage had that taken?

"Bird in Ground was killed in battle," Arapooesh explained as soon as Scratch had arrived at the tribe's first winter camp established on the lower Bighorn.

He had choked on the news, unable to speak for minutes as a few of the other tribal elders and some of the young warriors gathered to welcome back *Pote Ani* to Absaroka with no more than a muted celebration.

Rotten Belly continued. "Two moons ago. He elected to go on a scalp raid against the Blackfoot with some of our strongest warriors. Bird in Ground had gone into battle before. He was not a stranger to fighting. He was not always a woman. On that raid no one feared for him, especially with the strongest of men going on that journey north."

"North?"

Arapooesh pointed, nodding. "They intended to go far beyond the Three Forks country. Sure to find Blackfoot there. Bird in Ground said it was time for him to ride against the enemy, time to make his man side strong once more."

"Yes," Scratch replied. "He told me he always raided against the enemy once a year or so."

"For this journey he asked a young man to go with him, someone to hold and care for his war pony," Arapooesh explained. "He asked Pretty On Top to go to war with him."

Bass's eyes slowly shifted to the youngster standing nearby, silent as a winter night. "You went on the raid with our friend, Bird in Ground?"

"He made me proud," Pretty On Top answered, his sad eyes misting over. "No man ever before asked me to go with him on a raid against our most terrible enemy."

Swallowing hard against the sour ball collecting in the back of his throat, Scratch said, "To ask you to go with him, he must have been very proud of you."

Titus watched Pretty On Top struggle to keep from spilling his emotions, just the way the Crow elders taught this same detached stoicism to every young man hoping one day to become a warrior. Scratch said, "You became a good friend not only to Bird in Ground," Titus declared, "but to me."

The youth bit at his quivering lower lip.

Suddenly something cold in Bass's gut reminded him . . . and just as quickly he was sure he knew to the day when Bird in Ground was killed. It made the hair bristle at the back of his neck, made it prickle down his arms— merely to be in the presence of something he did not understand, to be standing right here sensing the undeniable presence of something far, far bigger than any of them.

Earlier that autumn Scratch had been trapping the Tongue, when late of an afternoon he had gone cold. As much as he had tried, he could not shake the trembling. So extreme was it that he finally gave up trying to set his traps in that narrow river valley, and shuffled back to camp. There he had laid more wood on the fire, set the coffee over the coals to reheat, then squatted close to the flames with a blanket clutched around his shoulders. Although the fire grew hotter, it failed to warm him.

Shuddering with an icy emptiness, Scratch had snatched up a buffalo robe and wrapped it around himself head to knee, its furry warmth turned inside. When the coffee began to steam, he poured himself a cup and drank it down despite how it scalded his tongue. But as warm as it was momentarily, even the coffee could not drive away that deep inner chill.

Its icy fingers seemed to penetrate right to the very marrow of him.

Finally, after more than three hours of shaking like an aspen leaf in an autumn gale, Scratch sensed the chill suddenly departing. Instead of the icy fear and the confusion clinging to his very core, he felt a warming sense of tranquillity come over him. No longer was he so frightened of this uncanny cold.

"H-how was he killed?"

Pretty On Top gazed up at the trapper evenly, saying, "One of our men was wounded and fell from his pony during the battle. With some men on horseback, others fighting on the ground, there was so much confusion and noise—no one really noticed the man fall at first, not until the enemy began to withdraw with their wounded and what ponies we hadn't taken from them."

Rotten Belly continued, "That's when our men noticed that one of our warriors had fallen behind the Blackfoot lines."

"This was Bird in Ground? The one who fell among the Blackfoot?"

"No," and Pretty On Top shook his head. "It was one of my uncles. But while others stopped a moment to decide what to do, Bird in Ground rushed forward without waiting . . . without fear. He killed two of the enemy who came back to kill my uncle, then picked the man off the ground and started back to our side with him."

"That's when the enemy started shooting at Bird in Ground," Arapooesh explained. "All of the Blackfoot trained their weapons on him."

The youngster took up the story. "We watched the arrows fall around Bird in Ground, as if nothing could touch his body while he stumbled forward under the weight of my uncle. But then . . . one of the enemy reloaded his medicine iron—like the long one you carry—and pointed it at Bird in Ground. As the weapon roared, we saw him start to stumble, but he caught himself and hung on to the wounded man as he kept on coming for our side."

"Just to see Bird in Ground's valor—that's when more of our warriors were rallied again!" Rotten Belly exclaimed proudly. "Many of us rushed forward, racing right past him and the man he was carrying to safety, charging the Blackfoot."

"They drove the enemy back for good at that moment," Pretty On Top said. "But Bird in Ground slowly came to a stop on his wobbly legs. I ran to him, reaching him just before he fell, as he laid the wounded man out. I got there when he collapsed, unable to stand—sitting there singing his prayer song. When I looked at his back, I saw the small hole. But there was much more blood on the front of his shirt. 'See to your uncle,' he told me. 'He can live from his wounds but I . . . I cannot.' "

When the youngster fell silent, struggling to hold in the strong emotion, Arapooesh filled the void. "As our men returned from driving the Blackfoot off, they were celebrating, happy, bringing the enemy's ponies with them. But all fell silent when they arrived to see Bird in Ground sitting there, bleeding to death and not calling for anything to dull his pain, wanting no one to take from him this courageous death he had earned."

Now Pretty On Top nodded, rubbing the back of his hand beneath his nose, and said, "He sat there talking to us for a long time. While the sun traveled from there, to there. Talking most of the while as if there were no pain. Then, after a long time of quiet from him, he told me, 'Remember my death, Pretty On Top. Remember that in the end we all choose how we live. But very few of us get to choose how we die. Remember that I did not choose to be a man-woman of the Crow . . . that medicine was thrust upon me when I had no choice. But I did bear up my strong medicine with dignity all of my days. And now I choose to die fighting my people's enemy. Remember my death.' "

When the young man turned away, averting his misty eyes, the chief continued. "That's when Bird in Ground slowly fell over to the side and closed his eyes. After all that time and pain, he simply laid over and closed his eyes . . . as if he were going to sleep."

"I will never forget that look on his face," Pretty On Top declared. "He was content. He died at peace with his medicine. At peace with the way he chose to die—as a man of honor. As a very, very brave warrior."

After a long time Scratch was able to speak. He pointed to one of the brown buffalo-hide cones. "Is that his lodge?"

"Yes," Rotten Belly answered. "Among our people the lodge is something a woman possesses. Not a man. But Bird in Ground's medicine told him different, because he was a man-woman. We have not let anyone tear it apart or take it down in mourning. I don't know what I will choose to do when we have to move from this camp—"

"May I sleep in it?" Titus suddenly interrupted.

For a long moment Arapooesh looked into the white man's face. "Yes," he finally answered. "I think that would be a good thing, *Pote Ani.*"

Pretty On Top agreed. Quietly he said, "I know Bird in Ground would say it is a good thing too—this, what you do to stay close to the spirit of your friend."

She lay warm against him within the scratchy warmth of the wool blankets, both of them nestled under the weight of two buffalo robes. His own skin still smelled of hers and their coupling in the firefly darkness of the lodge where Bird in Ground once lived.

This woman who had been with him for several weeks now was younger than some who had come to be a bed warmer for him on the long winter nights spent among the Crow. This woman who had lost two infants to sickness and told him she could never carry another in her belly because something was torn inside her. No children, and now no husband. He had gone off to hunt one day early last fall, gone to bring in some game for their lodge . . . and never come back.

She too battled the beast of loneliness.

Here in the deep hours of the long winter night, Bass smelled the firesmoke in her tangled hair and thought back on the faces and hair, the breasts and bellies, hips and legs, of all those who had gone before her. And with those memories Scratch wasn't at all surprised to find he still sensed the same sort of seeping emptiness he had always felt, something akin to that first flush of contentment that washed over him right after the moment of coupling began to seep out of him like milk oozing from a crack in one of his mam's earthenware crocks.

Maybe, Titus told himself, he should be at peace with what he had shared with each of them in turn. Maybe that was enough.

Suddenly there in the darkness beneath that patch of dark sky hung above him at the smoke hole, Scratch found himself looking back on Amy as his very first stumble, falling headlong into the world of women. Oh, how he had been swept up with what his own body was experiencing while his hands raced over virginal Amy's warm flesh, those soft breasts and rounded hips, the downy fur of her down below—all of it arousing him frantically: while his head didn't have any idea what to do next, it was his body that took command of him that night at the swimming hole.

In the end Titus had to run away from her, from the prison she and those farmer's fields would make for him.

By the time he found Mincemeat in that Ohio River tippling house as he was closing in on his seventeenth birthday, he came to appreciate all that a woman could do for a man when she herself knew and practiced more of all those mysteries of how a woman and a man pleasured one another.

But unlike that Kentucky farmer's daughter he had escaped, Mincemeat ran away from him, leaving him a raw and open wound for the longest time.

When he had chanced upon the carnal warmth of Marissa in the loft of her father's barn, Bass was beguiled at just how one woman could heal all those places left so tender and painful by the woman come before her. So good was what Marissa gave him of her body that Able Guthrie's daughter almost did make young Titus forget the hurt, forget that he had vowed to make his way to St. Louis, forget that he swore he would never settle down in one place to work the land like his pap.

Lo, that second time he forced himself to flee from the prison he was sure his affection for Marissa would make for him, chaining him down to what he feared most.

In those brawling back ways and along the waterfront shanties of St. Louis, young Bass discovered no settlers' daughters to threaten his freedom—only a procession of faceless whores who took no more than he was ready to give . . . until the night he ventured back to a tiny crib with a coffee-skinned quadroon just come up the river from New Orleans. In the candlelight of that tiny hovel, he found her skin to have the same sheen and color of damp mud along the banks where the Mississippi lapped.

Each time he visited the mulatto, Titus reluctantly promised himself that he couldn't love a whore who lay with other men. But when he wasn't with her, he was forced to admit that he couldn't stop thinking about her, nor that pleasure she brought him. How good she made him feel about himself.

Yet in the end she too had deserted him—leaving for a man wealthy enough to buy her pleasures all for himself, just as a person would put something away on a shelf for no one else to enjoy. All Titus had left were the memories of the quadroon, and the blue silk bandanna she had tied around his neck.

During those dark and drunken days that followed, Bass had brooded only long enough to decide that it all proved beyond a doubt that he would never be anything more than a bone-headed idiot when it came to the fair sex.

The women who wanted him surely wanted him only for security—something that scared him enough that he fled.

But what of those women *he* wanted so desperately? Why, they just up and disappeared on him—without so much as a fare-thee-well or an explanation of why they abandoned him. Each time it happened, his not knowing why served only to crust another thin layer of scar over his heart, like the layers of an onion, every new crust protecting the others below it.

That's probably why the Indian women had come like a breath of mountain breeze on a still, airless day. Fawn had asked so little from him that winter he had spent with the Ute in Park Kyack. And Pretty Water had wanted only to nurse him back to health that long autumn he had healed among the Shoshone at the foot of the Wind River Mountains. Even the procession of robe-warmers who had come to him in turn across each of the three winters he had spent among the Crow in Absaroka had demanded nothing more than to feel his body pressed against theirs in the darkness of their lodges.

Maybe it was better that he think of them as meaning nothing more to him than those whores like Conchita down in Taos: women who walked into his life and stayed for but a moment only to take away a little of that constant agony of his loneliness. They had come for nothing more than stolen moments, flickers of time a person snatched here and there the way he had snatched at fireflies as a boy.

Truth was, as a young man, that's all he had really cared for: a woman of the moment to soothe an immediate need until he got itchy moccasins and moved on. A woman to stay only until he had rubbed his horns and the fever of the rut was gone.

So why was it not the same this winter? Why was he no longer able to curl up with a warm brown body, take his pleasure and give the woman hers, then sleep the rest of the night away without remorse? Why the hell had he begun to feel as if something was missing?

Hell, he had all he wanted to eat, and a warm shelter out of the wind. He had him a good mule and horses and a darn fine rifle and traps. And when it came to friends, why—Scratch figured no man could go any finer than the men Titus Bass called friend, both white and red. Besides, he didn't answer to no booshway, and he sure didn't bow and scrape to no gussied-up, apron-stringed eastern gal with her should-do-this and shouldn't-do-that!

So why the hell was he lying here in the dark next to this warm, pretty, naked woman . . . and grappling with something a man of his spare talents had no damned business grappling with?

There had never been any doubt that he was the sort who stumbled through anything dealing with women, stubbing his toe and stumbling, yet somehow managing on in his own bumbling way—somehow just getting by when it came to the fairer sex. After all, right from day one back at that swimming hole in Boone County, Kentucky, when he had crawled atop his first woman, Titus Bass had been in way over his head. And the best he ever figured he could do was tread water till . . .

Till . . . maybeso he found himself a full-time night-woman who would keep his lodge warm and his pots boiling when he came back from seeing to his traps every evening. A woman who would listen when he wanted her to listen to what he had to say, a woman who would talk when he wanted to hear that gentle sound of a female's voice—so appealing after so many seasons of nothing but deep, bass-toned, bullock voices there at his ear. The sort of gal who'd be there knowing when he wanted to scream and when he wanted to cry. The sort of woman what'd know the difference.

Were these feelings troubling him this winter after so many winters gone before it . . . simply because he had turned thirty-eight?

Did a man start thinking of so weighty a matter as that of finding a full-time night-woman for himself when he had added a certain tally of rings and his hair had started to gray? Could that be the reason he was dwelling on why he hadn't already found himself one good woman, wondering when he'd stop making the rounds of one roll in the robes after another? Was this brooding late at night on such things just one more sign of his getting on in his years?

In the late winter darkness, his skin slightly moist where it lay right against hers, he strained to remember the faces of those gone before this one. Most names he could recall—but strained to conjure up the eyes and nose and mouth of Amy . . . Abigail Thresher . . . Marissa Guthrie . . . even the quadroon and those women who had taken him into their lodges and allowed him between their legs season after season after season.

If he tried hard enough, staring long enough at that place where the poles were bound one to the other, he figured he just might come up with a composite of their faces—putting them all together in some murky memory puddle the way rain made earth colors run. The best eyes and nose, the warmest lips and the rounded breasts . . . all of them thrown in and stirred up in his remembrance the way his mam would stir up her stew of so many ingredients.

Unable to remember any one of them alone any longer now, Scratch had to satisfy himself that he could recall just enough to put them together into a watery, filmy, half-focused face, all mouth and breasts, hips and legs.

But because he failed to draw up a clear image of any one of them from the past, lately Scratch had become certain he would never be worthy of having just one for the rest of his days. He had no right to want just one woman to last him all the seasons yet to come in his life. If he could not pay homage to all that the many had given him from the past, then Titus figured he was certain he had no right to hope for finding that one woman who would stand at his side through those seasons yet unborn.

Perhaps, he decided, he had been blessed enough . . . so maybe it was enough to accept what he did of each new day, thanking that which was larger than all of them, there at the end of each day granted him. With all that he had been given already, to want a full-time night-woman for the last of his years was simply more than he had the right to ask.

And so Titus consoled himself that dark morning as he had been consoling himself for many nights this winter now grown old. Doing his best to push the loneliness back, to push away the emptiness that cried out within him, its voice become louder and louder while spring loomed on the far horizon.

Oh, how he hungered for white faces as he floated adrift in this sea of copperskins. Like a dry man not knowing when he would next have a drink of water—Scratch thirsted for white voices and white laughter and the soul-healing potion of strong, saddle-varnish liquor.

If he did not have a woman come to fill those empty places in his soul, at least he knew there would always be friends and voices, laughter and whiskey, to soothe those raw and oozing places in his life.

Perhaps he would have enough of all the rest . . . so that one day he would eventually forget this deepest, most secret need of all.

TWENTY-SIX

More and more with every turn of the seasons, Titus Bass came to know that no matter how long or hard the winters of his life, spring was always sure to come.

Sure enough, a little earlier than normal last autumn, Hannah and his horses had furred up just like the creatures of the wild. And they kept their heavy coats longer into the spring too. Although the skies domed a brilliant blue overhead as the air began to warm, large fields of snow lasted long on the north-facing slopes. The thaw came late to the Yellowstone country that eighth spring of his come out of St. Louis.

By the time he made ready to leave Arapooesh's band, Titus Bass was packing two more large bundles of beaver hung from the elk-horn packsaddle on Hannah's back. He had kept himself busy through the long months of short days.

When she brayed at him in protest at the load, he said, "Don't know if that means you're ready for the trail, or you're squawking at me for packing you after you ain't had much of nothing on your back all winter."

He stepped up to her muzzle and grasped it between both hands and cocked her head so she could gaze at him with one eye. "Now, you know I ain't no damned Ned. Ain't never been one what plants his nose under a robe all winter—no matter how warm the womens might be. Never has Titus Bass been a child to lay around camp all through a robe season."

She rolled that near eye and brayed at him again. "I s'pose that means you and me both 'bout ready for the trail, ol' girl. But first we best pay our respects."

As Scratch slowly approached Rotten Belly leading his three animals, the chief emerged from his door, stretched lazily, then stepped around to the side of the lodge where the morning sun would warm him with its full glory. He sat, leaned back in his warmest buffalo robe, and closed his eyes. And didn't even open them as the trapper came to a stop at his elbow.

"I hear the sound of heavy horses," the chief said without looking up.

"We are ready to go, my friend."

"You were happy this winter?"

Scratch thought a moment, glancing over at the lodge where he had spent many a night with the widow. "I had all I needed—yes, Arapooesh."

"So you'll come back our way soon?"

"I want to hunt the waters north of the Yellowstone next fall," Bass replied. "Yes, I think it will be a good thing to come find your camp when the winter winds begin to blow."

With a long sigh the chief finally looked up into the bright morning light and shaded his eyes with a flat hand. "You will stay safe, won't you, *Pote Ani?*"

"I will."

"Because I cannot talk you out of riding west from Absaroka, you must promise me that you will stay safe so that my eyes can look upon my old friend again come next winter."

Kneeling beside the chief, Bass pulled off his mitten and laid the hand on Rotten Belly's arm under that buffalo robe. The chief looked up at him, and Titus said, "I'll be back soon. You know how short the seasons are up this far north, when winter lasts so long."

Arapooesh knifed his hand through the flap in his robe and laid it on Bass's arm, saying, "My prayers go west with you. When you leave Absaroka in that direction, there is so much danger that can find a man alone."

Standing, Scratch said with a smile, "I'm not looking to die just yet. I'll watch behind me."

Closing his eyes again, Rotten Belly said, "See you in the winter."

"See you then, my friend."

It took better than four days to ride down the Yellowstone to his cache, what with all the drifted snow and the boggy bottom ground, having to double back here and there. But eventually he dug at the icy, frozen snow that lay crusted over the earthen circle that plugged the neck of his small underground vault. For the next two days he busied himself with pulling out each bundle of beaver in turn, dusting every individual plew with Hannah's currycomb, then closely inspecting each hide for sign of vermin that might burrow into the beaver felt and destroy the value of a hide. Once the plews were ready for their long spring journey toward rendezvous, Bass tied them back into bundles, then pushed the buffalo-hide shelter down into the cache. Positioning it high upon some freshly cut willow saplings, Bass left it at the center of the floor and backed out of the hole. Reweaving a network of narrow limbs, he finished his labors by muscling the round earthen lid back over the hole.

That night he built a fire atop his cache and the next morning scattered the ashes before he took up Hannah's lead rope and rose into the saddle. Turning toward the Yellowstone, Bass headed west until he reached the crossing used for years without count by the massive herds blanketing these northern plains.

"Man knows what to look for, he can always find a buffalo crossing," he said to Hannah, having taken to talking to her more and more with every day of his enforced separation from other humankind. "Don't you know a man can't hardly go wrong if he lays his nose along a buffalo trail."

On the opposite bank of the river he pointed their noses west. Creek by creek, beaver stream by beaver stream, he trapped as he went those days of early spring, shivering through the wintry cold of each night, savoring the brief hours of sunny warmth as the earth's rising heat formed puffy clouds across the deep spring blue like the snowflash feathers of ducks upended and fishing in a spring pond.

At times he came across sign of hunters out from one band or another of the River or Mountain Crow, but Scratch never saw another person in those first few weeks as he took his time marching for that cleft through the mountains west of the big bend of the Yellowstone, a crossing he had made years before with Silas Cooper. Bass turned in the saddle and gazed back at the large packs of beaver both Hannah and the packhorse carried. Hard to believe what he had done in the past year: he hadn't trapped this many pelts since the seasons he had traveled with those three who had taken him under their wings his first seasons in the mountains. But that learning had cost him—first in what share Silas split off for himself, and then to lose all the rest of his plews when the trio floated off downriver with his fur.

"Likely gone to the bottom of the goddamned Yellowstone," he grumbled.

Likely where their three carcasses are right now, he brooded. All them plews and all that work—

Then he scolded himself. "No sense in thinking on what was and can't do nothing about now."

Titus turned around, putting his face into the cold slash of wind and tucked the long flaps of the capote back around his legs. As Scratch rocked gently in the Spanish saddle, his horse steadily carried him higher up the winding switchbacks that took him in and out of patches of timber and across broad, open, grassy meadows where he flushed up small herds of elk, spooking the creatures back into the shadows where they warily watched the three strange animals slowly climb out of sight as the sun sank lower against the far curve of the earth.

Across that last saddle before he reached the pass, Scratch discovered so much snow still crusted in the open places that it stretched all the way to the far line of mountain and sky. He reined up, cautious. For a few moments he calculated how much light he still had himself in the day, then turned and looked behind at the beckoning timber where he could get out of the constant, cutting wind.

Better to try sloughing his way across that deep snowfield come morning when the animals were fresh and they had more hours of daylight to work the ground. Besides, the cold temperatures would refreeze the top layer of the snow and make it far better going right after dawn than it would be now after the high sun had mushed the icy crust.

"C'mon, girl," he crooned to Hannah as he reined the horse around sharply and clucked to the mule to follow.

That night he lay awake by the dying fire listening to the wind moaning above him in the pines, remembering how the wind called to him at times as if in warning. Stirred by something he couldn't reach out and touch, Bass kicked free of his robes and went over to Hannah. He led her closer to the saddle horse and tied the mule's long lead rope in a loose loop around the horse's neck. Then he played out the long rawhide rope knotted around the horse's neck and trudged back to his bedding. There he wrapped the end of the rope beneath his capote belt and stuffed himself back between the robes.

Closing his eyes once more, Bass laid the long flintlock between his knees, tucking the pistol against his chest as he made a warm place for his cheek against the dark, curly hump fur.

The robber jays awoke him the next morning, cackling at him and the animals from the branches overhead, their shrill protests making him start with surprise. Blinking into the new light just then warming the eastern plains below him, Titus threw back the robes and blankets, then glanced up the slopes toward the snowy saddle where the first rosy rays of light angled up from beyond the east, striking the snowfields and turning them a pale, blood-tinged pink.

He'd slept longer than he had wanted—angry at himself because he had planned to be at the edge of the frozen pass just as soon as it was light enough to make their crossing.

Promising himself some coffee on the far side, Scratch tied up his bedding, then stepped out into the open, where he dampened the ground. After pulling up some thick branches of the gray sage, he went to the animals. He dragged off the dirty, greasy, trail-sweated chunks of canvas he laid over their backs on those coldest of nights, the better to help those creatures preserve some of their own body heat. One by one, he rubbed them down with those clusters of sage, warming himself in the process with the exertion. Then in turn the three were padded, saddled, cinched, and loaded with his few possessions and the fruits of his labor.

Behind them the sun was just beginning to raise its bleary red eye in the east as he reached the edge of the extensive snowfield.

"We'll be across afore midday," he reminded the animals, tapping his heels into the horse's ribs.

One hoof at a time, one short, slow step—Scratch carefully calculated his crossing of the crusty, frozen snow. He kept his eyes moving from the surface right below him to the rosy appearance of the snow some twenty, maybe as much as thirty, feet ahead of him, studying the way the ice had shrunk around the edges of a boulder, the way the crust lay in frozen, scalloped patterns where the wind constantly chiseled across it day and night. Warming each day beneath the sun, then refreezing beneath the spatter of starlight right overhead.

For a moment he gazed at the shocking blue of the heavens domed above them, and sighed. "Up this high, up here where that sky is so clear . . . where the sky is so damned close—if a man listens just right, Hannah—why, he might well hear angels sing."

Closer to heaven was he here, and therefore much closer to that other existence Asa McAfferty spoke of in such hushed tones. Being this high—with nothing between him and the full, aching stretch of sky right beyond his fingertips—if a man himself wasn't wary and careful, he just might slip right on through that crack to the far side of life and death and all that lay in between.

Was it a land of the unknown crossed only by those who slipped in and out of that crack in the sky . . . or by those who had themselves come eye to eye with one such spirit from that realm of the unknown? Just as Asa had with that Ree.

Thinking on those hoo-doos gave Titus such a chill that he pulled the capote's flaps tighter around his chest and turtled his neck down a bit farther.

Step by step, one yard at a time, and he'd be off this wide-open snowfield and on the far side of the pass. Out here under the wide sky where the spirits might look down upon him creeping along, his animals like a trio of beetles burrowing their way across the bottom of a buffalo chip—might those spirits look down upon him and pluck him right up?

Scaring himself, Bass stared up at the blue, his chin quivering with the cold, shivering with the fright.

"You ain't ever gonna get me 'thout a fight," he suddenly bellowed at the cloudless sky.

Though it hurt his throat to yell that loud, he went on, "Might be some men what ride off to look for you . . . like Asa done—coming to stare death and dying in the eye. Like Asa had such a hankering to die hisself."

Below him at the far western edge of the snowfield four magpies suddenly took flight from the tops of the distant trees as his voice boomed in an echo over their perch.

"But not me! I ain't going nowhere easy as Asa McAfferty done! You're gonna have to come for me. You're gonna have to come ready to fight."

He shuddered less with the wind by the time he reined up on the western side of the snowfield, turning the horse around and halting to gaze back at that open expanse of saddle he had just crossed there beneath the blue, there where a man had nowhere to hide, nowhere to run.

"Hoo-doos won't dare come for a man what aims to fight," Scratch boasted as he nudged his horse into motion once more. "Long as I ain't so tired I can't fight . . ."

Descending the steep western side of the pass, Scratch spent the rest of that day and the next locating a patch of ground he would use as his first camp for what he planned would be an extended stay in this country just east of the Three Forks. Years ago the trapping there had been almost as good as it had been along the Mussellshell and Judith. A dangerous land where only the wary survived, however. But by the time he ran across a site that offered good cover, grass, wood, and water, Bass hadn't crossed any trails nor come across any sign that would tell him the Blackfoot routinely made this valley part of their travels.

Except for that single fire, that lone point of light he had spotted down in the bottom of this valley years before, when he and the trio had come here to trap. Someone had built themselves a fire big enough to warm a passel of men.

Someone.

That next morning he awoke in the dark to find a cold early-spring fog cloaking the river bottom. Overhead no more than a matter of feet hung a foreboding layer of low clouds threatening to drizzle at any moment—it and the fog were both as cold and gray as ash flake in a long-dead fire. Stirring out of the robes and blankets, Bass stomped feeling back into his feet, then crabbed over to his packs to dig out the buffalo-hide moccasins. He planned to wear them to and from every trap site, taking them off before he entered the water to make his sets, then pulling them on once he was ready to turn back for camp.

Looking again to the priming in both pistol and rifle, he stuffed the camp ax and a tomahawk into the back of his belt, where his skinning knife hung in its rawhide scabbard. Throwing the heavy buffalo-hide sack bearing a dozen American and Mexican traps over his shoulder and clutching his long bait-sticks under his arm, Bass lunged forward through the frosty grass as the dark canopy limned a thin line of sunny blue behind the jagged eastern skyline above his valley camp.

At the water's edge he dropped the sticks and sack, then leaned the rifle against a clump of willow. Throwing his mittens down beside the traps, he pulled off his capote and yanked up his shooting pouch. Overlapping the wide strap, Titus poked a long leather whang through a series of holes so that he could fasten it with a knot. That done to severely shorten the strap, Bass could count on keeping his pouch and horn tucked high above the surface of the creek, pulled right under his armpit now as he waded into the freezing water.

By the time he had seven traps set at the foot of slides and other likely spots where the lush new grass had been trampled by tiny paws, or saplings had been felled by the toothy rodents, Scratch was finding he wasn't near so cold. With the sun's impending arrival, the air had begun to warm slightly. How good a fire would feel against his skin, how good some hot coffee would feel in his empty belly when he made it back to camp—

He looked up, froze. Listening. Something twitching inside him. Like a warning.

Staring at the far bank, Scratch watched the shudder and dance of the fog as it thinned, just then beginning to burn off. Like a gauzy tangle of lace laid against a bride's dark hair, the mist clung in tatters against the dark, leafy brush. Somewhere on that far bank a bird chattered.

And he finally breathed again.

"Sometimes it gets too damned quiet," he sighed.

Bending again to work at the shelf he had been scraping away with the camp ax a few inches below the water's surface, Titus watched the way the light glittered across the slowly moving surface of the water. A magpie suddenly broke into flight overhead, freezing him immediately. The noisy rush of those black wings faded; then all was quiet once more.

"Got yourself spooked," he whispered. "Only natural—this close to Blackfoot country again."

As he carefully pulled the trap off the bank and slowly lowered it into the water, pan set and ready for business, Bass thought on McAfferty.

Had Asa ever found what he was looking for? But, then, what was it the white-head wanted most? he wondered. It wasn't money, really. So was it power? Something many men desired.

Scratch wasn't sure, but there at the end he had come to believe McAfferty had acted as if he was trying to find himself a sure way to die. Was it death that the white-head wanted most—the death that so far had eluded the man, frustrating him, because Asa believed he wasn't worthy of living?

No—Titus knew it had to be something else that Asa had gone to do in Blackfoot country. Something besides getting himself killed by a band of Blood or Piegan or Gros Ventre. Just riding into that country to find some warriors to cut him down and hack off his hair wasn't the neat, tidy end to McAfferty's story, Bass decided.

He struggled to make sense of why some folks did what they did with their lives. Then decided such metaphysical matters were simply beyond his reach.

Stepping upstream a few yards, Scratch hoisted himself out of the water where he wouldn't leave his smell near the last trap-set. Standing, he allowed his leggings to drip on the warm ground just now starting to steam, the mists rising into the cold air as the sun peeked over the mountain skyline.

With that first, frightening yip—he whirled on his heel, staring at the far bank. Down into the water leaped three screaming horsemen. A fourth reined up on the opposite bank, his pony shuffling in a sidestep as its rider twisted on its back, brought down his straightened arms in pointing the arrow at the white man.

Bass was moving in a crouch as the arrow hissed behind him.

From the corner of his eye he saw the painted bowman nocking another arrow against his string.

Behind him the horsemen clattered across the creek, their ponies severely slowed by the water that swirled up to their bellies as their powerful legs churned against the current. Wild cock's-combs of brilliant spray spewed into fans of cascading, iridescent waterfalls around the legs of each warrior. For but an instant a lone beam of early sunlight glinted off that single knife blade embedded in a long wooden staff swung at the end of one of the brown arms.

Their cries boiling upon his heels, Scratch whirled as he heard one of the ponies lunge onto the bank behind him.

Yanking the pistol from his belt, he dragged back the hammer, straightened his left arm, and pulled the trigger.

Damp powder in the pan . . .

Swooping up on his pony, the Indian drew back with his tomahawk as Titus yanked his weapon from the small of his back where he had it stuffed in his belt. Only time enough to grip the handle in both hands as the pony hurtled past, the warrior swinging down as Bass bent at the knees, springing forward, planting the wide blade in the man's belly as the Blackfoot's weapon knocked the fur cap right off the trapper's head.

Hot blood splattered Scratch's face as the dying warrior raced on past, pitching off the far side of his pony with a loud grunt.

For no more than a heartbeat he glanced at the bush where he had dropped his coat and mittens, where he had stood his rifle before entering the stream. Then the rising falsetto in that voice yanked him around like a child's string toy—twisting so quickly in his waterlogged moccasins on that frosted grass that Scratch stumbled to his knees an instant before a tomahawk cartwheeled past him, careening noisily through the thick brush behind him.

Pulling the skinning knife from his belt, he watched the closest one yank up a war club where it had hung by a thong at the saddle's horn in front of the warrior. Over his head the Indian swung this terrible weapon studded with a half-dozen six-inch-long deer-antler tines embedded in a round knot of carved wood to which a handle was attached with rawhide and brass tacks like a medieval mace, closing in on his prey.

Titus lunged aside as the tines slashed the air beside his cheek. Landing on his elbow, he rolled up onto his knees, cocking his arm back far enough before he flung the knife at that third horseman racing for him with an arrow strung in his bow.

The warrior's bow pitched forward as he suddenly clutched at the knife that caught him high in the chest below one outstretched arm. His pony hurtled past in a blur.

Just beyond the spot where Bass's rifle stood, the Blackfoot with the antler-studded club was already yanking back on his rein, nearly bringing his pony to its knees as he savagely wrenched its head to the side. Bass glanced at the rifle, instantly calculating its distance from him, how fast the warrior would reach him, how much time it would take for a tired old trapper to reach the weapon . . . then set himself in a crouch as the horseman kicked speed back into his mount, racing into the open with that club held high overhead, his mouth o-o-ing with some primal death cry as he lunged toward his pale-skinned enemy.

Starting to leap to the right, Bass feinted and instantly whirled to the left at the last moment instead, causing the warrior to swing his club off balance. It was all the man could do to stay on his pony's back as he galloped by.

Now he had both time and distance to his advantage.

Rising immediately to burst into a sprint, Scratch raced headlong for the rifle as he heard the cries of not one, but both, of the last two horsemen. He dared not look over his shoulder, afraid to find the bowman from the far bank suddenly within arm's length.

Onto his soggy knees he skidded, snatching at the rifle as he slid against the brush, yanking back the hammer to full-cock. Setting the rearmost of the two triggers, he started his turn. Wheeling about with the weapon, Bass rose on one knee and rammed the buttstock back into his shoulder, jamming his bare finger into the front of the trigger guard.

Finding that enraged horseman setting his pony in motion again after a knee-grinding turn, kicking the pony savagely as he cried out in rage, swinging his fearsome weapon into the coming light of day . . . Bass held.

Held.

Held a little longer as he let the front blade rise while the Blackfoot lunged closer. Both warrior and pony wide-eyed, the man's mouth a large black hole, that horse's nostrils shooting jets of steam into the cold of the early-spring morning.

Held—

With a roar the rifle erupted.

The ball struck the Blackfoot with such force that it jerked the man back to the rear flanks of the pony, where he sat for a moment as if unfazed; then with the next bounce the body pitched on backward in a graceful somersault to land on its belly. Unmoving, as still as winter grass.

When Titus yanked at the knot on the pouch strap, the shooting bag dropped to his hip as he watched the bowman's horse leap onto the bank no more than twenty yards away. Digging a hand into the bottom of the bag, he pulled out three balls, stuffing them into his mouth before he jammed the powder-horn stopper between his teeth and pulled it free.

With the horn's narrow end against the muzzle, he poured some powder down the barrel as the warrior neared, swinging up his bow at the end of his outstretched arm.

Pressing his lips against the rifle's muzzle, Bass spat a single ball down the barrel at the same moment he yanked the ramrod from its brass thimbles along the underside of the forestock.

No time to prime the son of a bitch.

Without any conscious thought, acting only on animal instinct, Scratch reversed the rifle, gripping both hands around the end of the barrel, starting its swing into the air as the bowman leaned off his pony, smacking that short elk-horn bow against the white man's temple at the very moment Titus planted the rifle butt in the horseman's belly.

Stunned into seeing hot, red stars, Scratch pitched to his knees—part of him yelling out to the rest . . . ordering him to move, to get off his knees, to forget the nausea and the shower of lights and get himself out of danger.

Stumbling up onto one knee, he wobbled to the side and fell over, his head in as much pain as the day he had been scalped by the Arapaho. Feeling as heavy as his trapsack, Titus feared he wouldn't get his head off the ground before the warrior got to his feet.

Less than twenty feet away the Blackfoot rolled to a stop against a clump of brush, lunged over onto his knees where he shook his head, then seemed to draw a sudden bead on the white man still stretched upon the frosty ground.

The moment the warrior started forward, the Indian drew a huge double-bladed knife from a long beaver-tailed scabbard at his hip.

Like a puff of winter breathsmoke suddenly gone with a gust of wind, Bass squeezed his eyes shut, then dragged them open reluctantly. Leaning onto his left knee and arm, he struggled to rise, reaching at the back of his belt for the camp ax.

Then remembered it was at water's edge by his trap sack.

Tomahawk gone. And the knife scabbard empty.

He rose to his full height, wobbled shakily there on the balls of his feet, wondering how much longer his dizzy head would let him focus on the charging warrior, setting himself for the coming impact . . . his eyes transfixed on that huge, double-edged dagger clutched in the Blackfoot's hand.

In that last moment Titus glanced at the painted face, the lower half completely black from just below the eyes—that horizontal line disappearing back at both ears, this greasy black smeared over the chin and down the jawline in a ragged semicircle that arced from the bottom of one ear to the bottom of the other. . . . Then Titus tried hard to fix his wavering, watery eyes on the dagger as his knees buckled, going soft as freshly boiled Kentucky sour mash.

Likely what saved him.

So surprising the warrior that the Blackfoot stumbled, lunging forward with his left arm straightened before him—seizing the white man's capote in that hand as Bass collapsed backward, yanking the Indian over him in an ungainly somersault.

By the time Titus had rolled onto his hip and rocked up to his feet, the warrior had braced himself on the ground and lashed out with a leg, whipping it against Bass's ankles—knocking them out from under him. As Titus spilled onto his back, he watched the Blackfoot blotting out a piece of the sky as soon as the Indian leaped for him.

With both hands Scratch locked a grip around the brown wrist that clutched the handle of that huge dagger, its dark wood decorated with the tiny heads of more than a hundred brass nails. Which meant the warrior was free to squeeze down on the white man's throat with his left hand.

For those next few heartbeats that Bass figured might be his last, he stared up at the contorted face just inches away—the eyes squinted and glaring into his there above that shelf of black war paint. As the warrior grunted, struggling to force the wide double-edged blade into his enemy with one hand, straining to crush the white man's windpipe with the other—Titus smelled the dried meat on the Indian's hot, stinking breath.

As much as he tried to breathe, he couldn't drag any air past that claw closed around his throat. How his lungs began to burn while the black of night slowly seeped down across his eyes. Not much left of the strength needed to hold off that knife.

He had moments left, only heartbeats before he became nothing more than a scalp on some goddamned Blackfoot's war club or bridle and a coup story told around a fire. Wouldn't that take the circle? When this red son of a bitch yanked off his fur cap and the bandanna, going to scalp him—finding he'd already lost some hair!

"The last joke's on you," he growled, none of those words understandable from that pinched, raspy throat.

But as he said them, he shifted his left hand to dig at the brown fingers—prying. With the other he squeezed down on the wrist, twisting. So painfully slow, the hand that held that dagger began to turn the more Bass twisted and pried. He watched the Blackfoot's eyes shift suddenly, staring down at his own hand now.

That pain in his throat . . .

Not knowing how many more breaths he could sacrifice before he had no fight left, Scratch suddenly released the enemy's fingers and seized a handful of the hair at the back of the Blackfoot's head in his left hand, pulling with all he had to the side. When the warrior yanked away, Bass was there to drive his forehead up savagely into the warrior's blackened chin.

With that sharp pain the Indian yanked to the side, away from Bass's grip, trying to free his hair—just as the dagger twisted up in an agonizingly slow half circle, the tip of the blade now pointed toward that chin where a jagged slash of the black war paint had smeared off on the trapper's forehead.

He saw the black curtain oozing down over his mind, over his failing strength, over all that he remembered and knew that he ever was . . . then yanked once more on the enemy's hair—savagely jerking the head straight back.

At the very instant the warrior resisted, tugging his head forward against the white man's painful pull, Scratch had the sharp point of the dagger positioned right below the chin . . . when it dropped violently.

Not only did Bass feel the wide blade pierce the cartilage and soft tissue on its path upward through the back of the throat, on past the hard palate, and into the bottom of the man's brain—but he heard its noisy journey of death as it cracked through hard tissue. Blood and gore gushed down over that handle decorated with those tiny brass nails.

Above that border of black pain the warrior's eyes suddenly rolled back to whites as his throat gurgled and his body went limp, pitching to the side, the double-edged blade penetrating the base of the Indian's brain, severing motor control.

Scratch's throat whimpered with that first breath of air he dragged in, so painfully did it rush down his windpipe—like shards of shattered mirror glass the moment he rolled onto his side, away from the Blackfoot, coughing so violently he was sure he would expel pieces of his lung. He gasped in agony as he lumbered onto his hands and knees, watching the warrior's legs thrash spastically for a moment, then go still as the man's bowels voided in death.

How it hurt to drag in anything larger than a tiny breath as his heart thundered in his ears like the beating of a war drum, the vapor hanging gauzy in front of his face as he looked about that small clearing. Four of them. So much blood beginning to slicken the frosty ground. Dead men come to kill him.

Scratch felt the first heave of his empty stomach, sensed the initial burn of gall at the back of his throat—then his belly revolted as he rocked forward on hands and knees, spilling the putrid yellow bile on the trampled, frozen grass. Again, and again, and again he heaved up what little his stomach held, until there was nothing left but the spastic, wrenching seizures of each dry wretch.

Did the killing ever get easier for a man?

And if it ever did, at what cost?

Wiping his mouth with the back of his right hand, he tasted the Blackfoot's blood that had splattered over him as that knife plunged up through the throat and into the man's brain. It made him gag anew.

On the frosty broken shafts of grass he frantically wiped his hands, smearing the frozen moisture across his face—wiping, wiping, wiping at the blood smearing his flesh while hot, stinging tears pooled in his eyes.

Then he finally crouched to the side, and with that half-frozen, bloodstained hand Bass yanked the crimson-coated knife from the enemy's head . . . raised it toward the sky . . . and slashed a jagged line down from heaven above toward this earth below where men walked out their numbered days.

"Bass!" he croaked with searing pain in his throat.

"Bass!"

And when the strident echo flung its answer upon him from the hills, that lone man hurled it back at the spirits of this great wilderness which must never forget his name.

"BASS!"

His left eye had sparkled for the first time later that spring while Scratch sat in a hot pool he chanced across near the Land of Smoking Waters on his slow tramp toward the southern pass, easing toward rendezvous.

And now it lit up a second time as he sat in that hot, tarry pool of thick black goo here in the Bighorn basin.

So many fiery, shooting stars burst in a brilliant fan of shimmering color from that lone left eye that when he shut the right, he found himself all but blinded.

At first Titus believed it was somehow nothing more than those wavering veils of steam rising off the hot pools of thick, stinking, sulphurous ooze that collected in these low places widely known among the beaver hunters who crisscrossed the mountain west. But even when he stood with his naked, sticky body and trudged a few yards away from that steamy vent to the cooling relief of a nearby stream, where he plopped down onto his rump, submerged right up to his chest—the eye still sparkled with the fire only a Rocky Mountain night could rain upon the earth.

So he sat there until his hide grew cold as winter meat.

Rising, Titus lunged back to the tar pool, where he eased his bare flesh down into the hot, thick ooze with a long sigh. Taking one last check on the horizons, Bass closed his eyes and let the heat soak to his marrow. He hadn't been this warm since . . . since sometime last fall. Indian summer. Some seven, maybe eight suns since he had run onto those white faces and white voices he ached so to see now.

Here in this aching silence where only the spring breeze or the flap of a bird's wing or the distant passing of a fluff of cloud brought any sound to his ears, Bass grinned—remembering how last fall up on the Bighorn he had crossed trails with that large brigade of some two dozen Rocky Mountain Fur trappers on their way south for winter encampment and he was making for Absaroka. They made camp together that cold night so old friends could share stories of the land, the price of beaver, word on this tribe or that, and any shred of news that might make the prospect of a lonely winter a bit more bearable.

Seems that Tom Fitzpatrick and his supplies had finally made it north from Taos all the way to the Platte, where Henry Fraeb finally ran onto him in all his desperate searching. Throughout those early days of autumn, Broken Hand and his hired men had their work cut out for them: with winter coming they could accomplish nothing save for traipsing around Blackfoot and Yellowstone country, running down the various brigades so the overdue Fitzpatrick could reoutfit them from those much-needed goods brought up from the Jackson and Sublette train when it reached Taos from the States.

"We was all just starting to settle in over to the mouth of the Powder—just like we done last winter, Scratch," Jim Bridger had explained beside that one night's fire they had shared in their trail crossing. "Cutting cottonwood for horse fodder, laying in grass, and building our huts for the time the wind blows mean."

"That there's pretty mild country for winter doin's," Bass had commented. "Man can make meat, and the snow don't get all that deep."

"But we got drove out!" Henry Fraeb bellowed from the far side of the fire.

"Frapp means to say the goddamned American Fur men showed up in our own blessed backyard like ticks sucking blood from a bull!" Milt Sublette exclaimed angrily.

"Am-american Fur?" Bass repeated with worry. "Wasn't it just a couple year back Hugh Glass was preaching to every nigger at ronnyvoo about a fort American Fur was building at the mouth of the Yellowstone? Saying we all ought'n take our furs there 'stead of trading at ronnyvoo?"

"Mackenzie," Bridger snarled, nodding. "That's the bastard building the post."

Then Sublette added, "He's took to calling himself 'King of the Missouri'!"

"Now the son of a bitch sent out two fellers named Vanderburgh and

Dripps to run down our brigades," Tom Fitzpatrick spoke up for the first time as he whittled on a green bough. "Them two had 'em a bunch of green hands along—don't bet any of 'em ever laid a trap under water!"

"Shit! Ain't a one of 'em knows fat cow from poor bull!" Bridger roared with laughter. "So them two booshways said right to our faces they was gonna camp where we was camped, and go where we was to go—all so they could learn the best of the beaver trade in the mountains afore they snatched it right out from under us!"

"Was they serious?" Scratch had asked.

"We could tell they wasn't just flapping their jaws!" Sublette grumbled. "They was American Fur—so that means John Jacob Astor . . . which means all the money in the world throwed up against us poor boys."

"Sons of a bitch," Fraeb grumbled in his thick German accent.

Fitzpatrick declared, "Then and there we figgered to hold us a council and see which way our stick would float."

Bridger nodded. "All five of us decided we wasn't the sort to hang around and watch Vanderburgh and Dripps camped across the river all winter, then have 'em dog our shadows come spring green-up."

"So the next night—right at slap-dark—we slipped out and got skedaddling away from them bastards," Sublette explained.

Bass shook his head sadly. "May come a time when American Fur's money is the only money in the mountains," he growled.

"Astor's always been the sort what runs off all competition wherever he sets hisself down," Sublette agreed.

"So if you're running from this here Vanderburg and Dripps now," Scratch began, "where is it you're fixing to winter up?"

Bridger answered, "The five of us decided to get over to the west side of the mountains. Cross the southern pass, jump the Green, and on to the Snake afore the last of the passes close."

"Seems there'd be Nepercy and some Flathead over yonder," Sublette explained. "Those Injuns a little friendlier than the folks up there in Blackfoot country."

"Where you bound for this winter?" Fitzpatrick asked.

"Crow land," he had said. "Rotten Belly's band. Not till the creeks is froze."

Early the following morning a few of the young, green hands who had come up from Taos with Fitzpatrick had thought to have themselves a bit of fun ribbing Bass and Fraeb about being too old to muster the mountains.

"Lookit them ol' gray-heads, will you?" one had roared as Scratch had tightened the last of the ropes on Hannah's packs.

"Lucky Ol' Frapp's got us along to take keer of him when times get lean or we run onto some Injuns!" a second cried, eliciting more wild laughter that Fraeb and Bass did their best to ignore.

But the third made the mistake of saying, "Lookee there! What 'bout that other'n we run onto yestiddy? Looks to be this man's fixing to ride off on his own like some crazy ol' coot what wouldn't know no better."

Titus had slowly turned on the three young tormentors. "You young pups figger me for old?"

At which the trio of greenhorns had busted out with so much guffawing that he was sure they liked to bust a belly seam.

"Listen to this ol' bastard!"

"Not so old I can't pin your ears up a'hint your ass, son," he growled, slowly pulling his pistol from his belt to stuff it under one of the pack ropes.

"Watch out, now!" one of the trio cried in laughter.

"We better not move too fast for 'im!"

The third shouted, "What the hell's one ol' man gonna do against the three of us?"

And that hired hand got to laughing so hard that he fell right over and rolled on the cold ground. Titus figured he had taken about all he was going to take—even if these were Bridger's men.

Lunging for the one laughing uncontrollably and rolling on the ground beside the fire, Scratch seized the young man at the collar and by the belt, and with that strength most often stoked by the fires of anger, he hurled the greenhorn off the ground and flung him into the other two. With arms and legs flailing, the young man went crashing into the first greenhorn, but the second and larger of the pair managed to sidestep and immediately rushed for Bass, both thick arms swinging with wild, windmill haymakers.

Scratch ducked to the side, tripping the young man as he rushed by, sending him sprawling onto his belly. Whirling about, Bass landed on the man's back, knocking off his hat and yanking back on the greasy hair with his left hand at the same time he was pulling his knife from its scabbard with his right. He pressed the blade against the taut, outstretched neck just hard enough that a little blood began to bead along the razor-sharp metal.

"Scratch . . . Scratch," Bridger cooed the moment he reached the scene.

"Get this crazy ol' man off me, Bridger!"

A few yards away the other two tormentors were bellowing and bawling like newborn calves until Fraeb told them to shut up.

Calmly, Scratch said, "I figger to show this brassy young'un how a old man whips a ignernt greenhorn, Jim."

Bridger replied, "Shame of it is, Bass—we need ever' man we got. Now that American Fur's come to the mountains—"

"Even this'un what don't know his own asshole from a badger den?"

"Maybeso we can teach this'un something afore he gets his hair raised," Sublette said as he came up, doing his best to stifle a laugh.

"Cut 'im, I say," Fraeb grumped. "The young nigger's got it coming, boys. He was rawhiding me and Bass here."

And Scratch added, "Said we was too old for the mountains—"

"You ain't! You ain't too old!" the greenhorn whimpered there beneath the veteran mountain man.

"Damn well knocked all three down, did you?" Bridger asked as he stroked his beard.

"I did, Jim. But I was fixing to kill only one of 'em."

Bridger walked over slowly, thoughtfully cupping his chin in one hand as he stared down at the greenhorn. "Being old back east where you come from is one thing, mister."

"Y-yes," the man whined plaintively with wide, frightened eyes as Bass tugged back on his hair again, exposing more of the young man's white flesh and maintaining the blade's pressure against the neck.

Then the booshway knelt at the young man's head. "Don't look to be you got far to go till you kill 'im quick, Bass," Bridger said, peering at the knife first this way, then that. "Where you got it now, you'll cut right through his windpipe slick as crap through a goose if I know how sharp you keep your knives."

"It's sharp, Jim. Damned sharp."

By now the greenhorn sobbed. "P-please, Bridger."

The booshway gazed down at the newcomer to the mountains. "Are you paying attention to what this here cast-iron mountain nigger's teaching you?"

"I'm t-trying!"

"Like I said—being a old man back east is one thing, son," Jim said as he stood slowly and rubbed his knees. "But any old man you run onto out here got him the hair of the bear in him. There's a damned good reason he's got old out here in these mountains while a lot of li'l young shits like you gone under and got themselves rubbed out."

Sublette said, "You ever again run onto a man old as Titus Bass here—you best figger that son of a bitch has managed to live all those years out west cause he's tough enough to take all what the mountains can throw at him."

For a moment the greenhorn's eyes rolled back toward Scratch. "Yes, sir, Mr. Titus Bass, sir."

Scratch wobbled the knife blade back and forth a little more against the flesh of the neck. "You got something to say to me, son?"

"I-I . . . I'm sorry I talked bad 'bout you being old—"

With such swiftness that it startled the youth, Bass pulled the knife away, releasing the youngster's hair so suddenly that his chin smacked the ground. Scratch stood, taking his knee from the middle of the young man's back.

Slowly rolling onto his hip and rising onto his knees, the greenhorn rubbed his neck with his hand, then held that hand out before him to stare at the blood on his palm.

"You damn well could've killed me!"

"I was fixin' on it—but you pulled your own hash from the fire."

Looking up at Bridger, the youngster gasped, "Awright. I figger I didn't have no room to be talking like that to this fella—"

"Like I told you: one thing you're gonna learn out here," Bridger explained as he pulled on his woolen mittens, "if you don't know who you're talking to, or you don't know what the devil you're talking about . . . you bloody well better keep your goddamned mouth shut and your ears open."

"Otherwise," Milt Sublette added, "your scalp might soon be hanging on some red nigger's lodgepole."

With a snort Henry Fraeb growled, "Or better yet—your hair be hanging from some ol' man's belt!"

Spring had mellowed as Bass wandered south, hankering to have himself another look at Park Kyack. Maybeso to run onto that band of Ute after all these years. See if Fawn had found herself a man.

Lord, but that was a good woman what deserved a decent man to see after her.

But he hadn't found the Ute, hadn't run across any bands of Shoshone either when he turned around and headed back north toward that country where the Crow roamed. Horse thieves that they were, in the end they had always done right by him.

Climbing across the foothills of the Wind River range late that spring, he had fashioned a hat out of the fur of a kit beaver caught in one of his traps down on the Popo Agie. Nowhere big enough to warrant a man's trading it at the coming rendezvous planned for Pierre's Hole, Scratch dug out the sinew he kept among his possibles and made himself a respectable replacement for the rubbed and worn coyote-skin cap that had seen him through many a winter.

By the time he found himself at the southern end of the Wind Rivers, turning west to make for the far side of the Tetons, Titus had attracted a trio of troublesome coyotes who followed him whenever he left camp to see to his traps. For days now he'd been feeding them with beaver carcasses and the bones of the game he brought down. Then a few days back he awoke to find his packhorse down, eyes open wide, barely breathing. A dark, gummy blood had gushed from its anus. He knelt at the pony's head, rubbing an ear. As much as he had wanted to mourn what its loss would mean, Titus knew there was nothing he could do to save the animal.

Eventually he stood, pulling the pistol from his belt. "You're likely et up inside with something terrible."

The only thing for him to do was finish the job nature herself had begun.

What with all he fed them, the coyotes faithfully stayed with him. In fact, the trio had dogged his backtrail so relentlessly Titus thought it strange that they weren't loping around his camp this morning, making a nuisance of themselves as he went about packing for the day's journey.

Maybeso he ought to put another three or four suns behind him before he looked for a likely stream to trap. Seemed like summer was here and he had miles to go before he would reach Pierre's Hole. Best to put some more country behind him.

Sensing time slipping away from him like riverbottom sands, Scratch hurried to lash a pair of packs behind his saddle so they rested on the horse's flanks, then turned to hang all the rest from Hannah's elk-antler packsaddle. From the look she gave him, the mule didn't much like the idea of carrying most everything on her back.

The early sun was already climbing off that red smear of horizon far to the east. Damn, but he was burning daylight.

No sooner had Bass gathered up Hannah's lead rope and crawled into the saddle than the mule set up a noisy bawl. She yanked the rope from his hand so swiftly Bass almost lost his rifle. And by the time he had swung out of the saddle and laid the long weapon on the ground, the mule was wildly pitching about in a ragged circle—dipping her nose almost to the ground as she threw her hind legs into the air, *hee-rawww*ing loud enough to wake the dead, or at least scare away every winged thing for miles around.

When he dodged out of her way, then immediately dived in to grab hold of her bridle, Hannah swung her big head in his direction, batting him out of her way as she passed on over the trapper—one of her small hooves landing squarely on his left foot.

"God-*damn*!" he screeched as he collapsed in pain, making almost as much noise as the mule while she bucked and jumped about the small meadow.

Sweeping up his rifle to use as a crutch, Bass hobbled out of her way, muttering unearthly curses on all those dim-witted brutes created to trouble man. Collapsing at the side of the clearing, it took only minutes for him to cut the moccasin off the foot, finding it already bruised and swelling while the mule went right on acting as if she were possessed of the devil.

He clambered clumsily to his feet, stumbling and hopping over toward the animal as she flung the loads on her back this way and that. If he didn't know better, Titus guessed she was trying to get herself out from under all those heavy packs he had just fixed atop her. Seizing a hitch rope, he hung on with one hand as the other frantically grappled at the first knot. Up and down she jolted him along with her loosening burdens until he suddenly freed the last knot and everything exploded off the mule. Including him.

In the midst of the scattered bundles of possibles and plews he sat up, dusting himself off.

"There, now, you cussed animule. Let's just simmer down some," he coaxed gently as she slowed her wild jig, eyeing him constantly.

Bass got to his feet, standing on that good leg with the rifle propped under an arm as he hobbled over to the mule.

"You're ol' bag of bones, you are, gal. And you could sure put a man in a fine fix up here."

After stroking her muzzle, he patted his way down her side to find the ugly gash opened up along her spine. As if someone had worked a knife back and forth to get that jagged slash in her hide. And that's when it struck him.

Wheeling about on that one good foot, he stumbled back to the packs, went to his knees, and dug at that small bundle of his possibles until he found it.

"Damned sure," he grumbled, angry at himself for not packing any better in his haste to be on their way that morning—too much in a hurry to see that certain possessions were kept from shifting, from working themselves loose.

Like the Blackfoot dagger he had taken off that red nigger weeks ago. Plain enough to see how it had been jostled enough that it spilled from its beaver-tail scabbard, then cut right through the waterproof sheeting, then on through the mountain-goat saddle pad until its point began to jab along Hannah's backbone. And as soon as she started to buck against the pain, her wild thrashing only made the laceration worse as the blade slashed back and forth to make for an ugly wound.

After pushing some moistened tobacco leaf into the wound and covering it with a patch of beaver fur, Scratch sensed a weary loneliness come over him. The new sun was only then beginning to climb high enough off the hills that its warming rays had just started to descend down the border of thick green timber ringing this tiny meadow.

Maybe there would be time enough to put the miles behind him for the day after he had rested here a bit longer. He could chance to let some of that pain ooze out of Hannah's wound, to rest his swollen foot . . . to close his eyes and dream on things that had been, to dream on what was to be.

Before him danced images of those Crow women moving in and out of Bird in Ground's lodge that cold winter day not long after Bass had arrived. Although the entire village was packed and ready to move on, a large crowd gathered around this solitary lodge still standing. Emerging from the doorway a handful of old women brought out the dead man's possessions and gave them away, one by one by one until most all of Rotten Belly's people had received a little something that had once belonged to the warrior who had lived many years with his powerful man-woman medicine.

And once the lodge was stripped of all that could be given away, an old, bent woman took up a burning brand from a nearby fire, and as others keened and wailed, she set the lodge hides aflame. Slowly turning aside, the people went to their horses and travois, setting off to the south for a new winter campsite.

While a black, greasy spiral rose from what had once been his friend's home.

Friends. And home.

Where he found friends, Titus Bass had always found a home.

White faces swam before him now as those copperskins of the Crow faded from view. Come rendezvous he would reunite with old friends, make him some new ones . . . and drink that annual toast to the missing few who failed to come in.

Recalling in that early-morning reverie how he had vowed to hoist a drink to Asa McAfferty's memory—

Through a sudden narrow crack that opened in his reverie, Scratch listened as the magpie took flight over him, cawing noisily in alarm.

He did not move, peering through squinted eyes, listening to every sound, testing every smell the breeze brought to him.

Nearby Hannah lifted her muzzle into the air.

Were it a Injun—she'd be raising a ruckus.

Could it really be a white man she'd winded?

The old man squinted and barely made out the felt hat sitting motionless now behind some low brush across the clearing.

Damn—but he hadn't seen a white face in longer'n he ever cared to go again.

Sudden hope fluttered in his chest like the rush of a thousand pairs of wings—raising his own spirit as high as that seamless blue belt stretched far above him, higher than his spirit had been in a long . . . long time.

A white man.

He figured there were answers come to the most private of prayers.

"I heard you, nigger!" Titus hollered. "Might'n come out now!"

Reluctantly, the felt hat rose, with the hairy face of a young man appearing beneath its wide brim, frightened eyes about as big as the quilled rosettes on Scratch's leather shirt.

Titus looked up and down the intruder's frame. The bearded stranger already wore his hair hung long over his collar. Maybeso this feller'd been out here some time already.

But he was still wearing store-bought woolen clothes—mussed and dirty to be sure, torn and ripped in places. And it was plain to see that his leather belt was notched up tight around a waist surely much skinnier than it had once been.

And suddenly Titus Bass remembered that he too had been this young of a time long ago, come to these far and terrible mountains when he had been so damned ignorant that he wouldn't have lasted 'less someone took him under a wing.

His eyes misting with the heartfelt swell of inexplicable joy, Scratch's voice croaked when now he used it.

"C'mon over here. Lemme take a look at you."

ABOUT THE AUTHOR

TERRY C. JOHNSTON was born in 1947 on the plains of Kansas and has lived a varied life as a roustabout, history teacher, printer, paramedic, dog catcher, and car salesman, all the while immersing himself in the history of the early West. His first novel, *Carry the Wind,* won the Medicine Pipe Bearer's Award from the Western Writers of America, and his subsequent books, among them *Cry of the Hawk, Winter Rain, BorderLords,* and the Son of the Plains trilogy, have appeared on bestseller lists throughout the country. Terry C. Johnston lives and writes in Big Sky country near Billings, Montana.